Meanwhile, in Another Part of the Forest

A culture is no better than its woods.
  – W.H. Auden, "Bucolics"

There isn't a part of the forest that doesn't have its particular meaning; not a clearing, not a thicket that doesn't have its mirror in the
maze of the human mind.
  – Honoré de Balzac, *Le Curé de village*

I am for the woods against the world,
But are the woods for me?
  – Edmund Blunden, "The Kiss"

There *are* strange creatures in this forest. But are they *all* wild?
  – L. Frank Baum, *The Wizard of Oz*

All the beasts of the forest are mine.
  – *The Book of Common Prayer*, 50:10

Contents

Introduction

I. *Mapping the forest*

> *Damn braces. Bless relaxes.*
> – William Blake

In the middle of the third century BC, the Cyrene poet Callimachus undertook the task of cataloguing the half-million volumes housed in the famous Library of Alexandria. The task was prodigious, not only because of the number of books to be inspected, dusted, and shelved, but because it entailed the conception of a literary order which was supposed somehow to reflect the vaster order of the universe. In attributing a certain book to a certain shelf—Homer to "Poetry" or Herodotus to "History", for example—Callimachus had first to determine that all writing could be divided into a specific number of categories or, as he called them, *pinakes*, "tables"; and then he had to decide to which category each of the thousands of unlabelled books belonged. Callimachus divided the colossal library into eight "tables" which were to contain every possible fact, conjecture, thought, imagination ever scrawled on a sheet of papyrus; future librarians would multiply this modest number to infinity. Jorge Luis Borges recalled that in the numeric system of the Institut Bibliographique in Brussels, number 231 corresponded to God.

Any reader who has ever derived pleasure from a book holds little confidence in these cataloguing methods. Subject indexes, literary genres, schools of thought and style, literatures classified by nationality or race, chronological compendiums and thematic anthologies (like the one you now hold in your hand) suggest to the reader merely one of a multitude of points of view, none comprehensive, none even grazing the breadth and depth of a mysterious piece of writing. Books refuse to sit quietly on shelves: *Gulliver's Travels* jumps from "Chronicles" to "Social Satire" to "Children's Literature", and will not be faithful to any one of these labels. Our reading, much like our sexuality, is multifaceted and fluid. "I am large," wrote Walt Whitman, "I contain multitudes."

The notion of "gay literature" is guilty on two counts: first, because it implies a narrow literary category based on the sexuality of either its authors or its characters; second, because it implies a narrow sexual category that has somehow found its definition in a literary form. And yet the notion of "gay literature", albeit recent, doubtlessly exists in the public mind. Certain bookstores have "gay literature" shelves, certain publishers publish "gay literature" books, and there are magazines and papers that regularly bring out stories and poems under the rubric of "gay literature".

What then is this "gay literature"?

In general, what is understood by "gay literature" is literature concerned with gay subjects. This can swing from obscure hints about "the love that dare not speak its name", in Lord Alfred Douglas's self-silencing phrase, apparent in some nineteenth-century writing, to explicit chronicles of gay life in our time, by authors who may or may not be gay. Sometimes books dealing with non-gay subjects by gay writers (E. M. Forster's *A Passage to India*, Edward Albee's *Who's Afraid of Virginia Woolf*, for instance) are put on the same "gay literature" shelf as books with an explicitly gay content—Marguerite Yourcenar's *Alexis* or Manuel Puig's *Kiss of the Spider Woman*—as if the critic, editor, or bookseller were deliberately attempting to catalogue the person, not the person's work. Certain writers refuse to have their work labelled "gay" (David Leavitt, Timothy Findley) and refer to it as "books by a writer who happens to be gay". As usual with this kind of labelling, the exceptions to any proposed definition make the process finally useless, so that every time the label is applied it must be redefined.

Claude J. Summers, in his collection of essays *Gay Fictions*, defines his subject as "the fictional representation of male homosexuals by gay male and lesbian writers". This leaves out a fair number of works by non-gay writers which are thus excluded simply by reason of their authors' sexuality. A writer's sexual preferences probably colour the text, but a reader does not require careful study of the *National Enquirer* to be able to read literature. Being told that D. H. Lawrence was attracted to older women may or may not inform the reading of *Lady Chatterley's Lover*, but is in no way essential for reading that too-famous novel. A study of Melville's life might shed light on homo-erotic elements in *Moby-Dick*, but is such a study essential in order to discover those same elements? And is a short story by William Faulkner on a gay subject readable only if we have proof of his experience in this field? Doesn't the word "fiction" imply the creation of an imagined rather than a physically experienced world? And if knowledge of the author's inclinations is essential to the understanding of a text, wouldn't reading anonymous literature (and so much erotic literature is anonymous) be ultimately impossible?

II. *Paths through the forest*

The fairy way of writing
which depends only upon the force of imagination.
   – John Dryden, *King Arthur*

It has been said that "every writer creates his own precursors". The same is true for genres or types. Edgar Allan Poe invented the detective story, and in doing so allowed us to include in the definition tales as old as the Bible. The label "gay literature" is a recent creation, probably no older than the founding of the gay magazine *Christopher Street* in 1975, but it now includes much earlier work. An anthology of English-language gay poetry would feature many names from the traditional canon, from Shakespeare to Lord Byron; examples of English-language gay fiction are not as venerably old, perhaps because poetry lends itself more readily to an ambiguous reading and (as is the case in many spurious explanations of Shakespeare's homo-erotic sonnets) to a bigoted interpretation, while prose can be less easily subverted for the sake of social decorum. Thomas Hardy suggested that a writer could "get away with things in verse that would have a hundred Mrs. Grundys on your back if said in prose".

A chronological list of gay fiction in English might begin with obscure novels such as Bayard Taylor's *Joseph and His Friend* (1871) or Theodore Winthrop's *Cecil Dreme* (1876), or with better-known works such as Oscar Wilde's "The Portrait of Mr W. H."(a short story written *circa* 1890); it might continue with Henry James's almost too subtle depiction of a gay infatuation, "The Pupil" (1891), E.M. Forster's posthumously published *Maurice* (finished in 1914), D. H.

Lawrence's "The Prussian Officer" (also 1914), and Ronald Firbank's *Concerning the Eccentricities of Cardinal Pirelli* (1926), up to Gore Vidal's *The City and the Pillar*, one of the earliest mainstream fictional accounts of gay life, published in 1948—the year that also saw the publication of two other gay classics: Truman Capote's *Other Voices, Other Rooms* and Tennessee Williams's collection *One Arm and Other Stories*. Similar lists could be made in the literature of other languages.

By 1950, two main trends in English-language gay literature had been established: one apologetically addressing a "straight" audience, trying to justify and atone for the fact of being gay; the other unabashedly celebrating another, equally vital sexuality, and speaking mainly to an enlightened reader. *The City and the Pillar*, which follows both trends to some degree, is the first novel to make use of an important device (suggested perhaps by André Gide's *Si le grain ne meurt* of 1926) evident in almost all the gay fiction that follows it: the autobiographical voice. Edmund White, himself the author of one of the most influential gay autobiographical fictions in North America, *A Boy's Own Story* (1982), has remarked that "since no one is brought up to be gay, the moment he recognizes the difference he must account for it." Non-gays learn about their sexual mores (mostly from conservative, sexist sources) in hundreds of different places: home, school, workplace, television, film, print. Gays are, by and large, deprived of any such geography. They grow up feeling invisible, and must go through the apprenticeship of adolescence almost invariably alone. Gay fiction—especially autobiographical gay fiction—therefore serves as a guide that both reflects and allows comparison with the reader's own experience.

Much of this factual prose is illuminating and encouraging (something much needed in the age of AIDS), and allows the reader to admit the fact of being gay as part of everyday life. Camille Paglia has commented that gays, unlike other minority groups, do not reproduce themselves, and therefore, like artists everywhere, "their only continuity is through culture, which they have been instrumental in building." Authors such as Christopher Isherwood (*A Single Man*), David Leavitt (*The Lost Language of Cranes* and *Equal Affections*), and Armistead Maupin (in his soap-opera saga *Tales of the City*) make this "continuity through culture" explicit: they place their gay characters in the midst of a multifaceted society, so that their reality is not "other" but "another", part of a historical cultural whole, with no reigning central entity determining what is normal according to his own image.

Because of the instructional use to which gay literature can be put, gay stories that bow to prejudice, implicitly accepting the patriarchal verdict about the wages of sin, commit literary terrorism and deserve to be housed on the same shelf as moralistic Victorian fables. A number of good writers fall into this category: Dennis Cooper, for instance, whose fiction depicts necro-homoerotic longings and explores the aesthetics of sickness and decay, with death as the inevitable end; and at times the timorous Gide, who believed that homosexuality was "an error of biology" and whose heroes are so terribly ridden by Catholic angst.

Because it needs to instruct, because it needs to bear witness, because it needs to affirm the right to exist of a group that the power-holding majority of society wishes to ignore or eliminate, gay literature has been, up to now, staunchly realistic. Lagging behind the rights demanded and partly achieved by other oppressed groups, gay men are depicted in a literature that is still largely at an informative or documentary stage. Women's literature can produce fantasies such as Margaret Atwood's *The Handmaid's Tale* or Jeanette Winterson's *The Passion*; black literature can invent ghost stories such as Toni Morrison's *Beloved*; with one or two little-known exceptions, gay literature has no fantastic stories, no imaginary worlds. Instead, its strength lies in the subversive possibilities of its language.

Appropriating everyday language, undermining the bureaucratic use of common words, using the guerrilla tactics of the surrealists to fill the commonplace with a sense of danger—these are the things gay literature, like any literature of the oppressed, can do best. Jean Genet, the French poet, playwright, and novelist who died in 1985, created, better than any other gay writer in any language, a literary voice to explore the gay experience. Genet understood that no concession should be made to the oppressor. In a hypocritical society that condemns gay sexuality but condones the exploitation of women, arrests pickpockets but rewards robber barons, hangs murderers but decorates torturers, Genet became a male prostitute and a thief, and then proceeded to describe the outcast's vision of our world. This vision was so unsettling that when Jean Cocteau showed Paul Valéry the manuscript of Genet's *Our Lady of the Flowers*, Valéry's response was "Burn it." In English, Oscar Wilde, Joe Orton, William Burroughs—

all forced or voluntary outsiders of society—set social language against its overlords. (Unfortunately, a number of these writers did not write short stories and therefore are not represented in this volume.)

Perhaps the literature of all segregated groups goes through similar stages: apologetic, self-descriptive and instructive, political and testimonial, iconoclastic and outrageous. If that is the case, then the next stage, which can I think be recognized in certain novels by Patrick Gale, introduces characters who *happen to be gay* but whose circumstances are defined well beyond their sexuality, which is once again seen as part of a complex and omnivorous world.

III. *Marking the trees*

Years hence, perhaps, may dawn an age,
More fortunate, alas! than we,
Which without hardness will be sage,
And gay without frivolity.
  – Matthew Arnold, "Stanzas from the Grande Chartreuse"

Naked except for a fur-trimmed gauze négligée and waddling about in bare feet, Cary Grant announced to an enquiring May Robson that he was thus attired because he had gone "gay". With this pronouncement in the 1939 film *Bringing Up Baby*, the word "gay" meaning "male homosexual" publicly entered the English language of North America.

It was not an auspicious beginning. Cary Grant's usage reflected a stereotype: that being "gay" somehow involves dressing up in women's clothing, wishing to be the other sex, and consequently becoming an involuntary parody of a woman. No doubt some gay men dress up in drag, but all transvestites are not homosexual, and all homosexuals are certainly not transvestites. Society, for the majority of Cary Grant's audience, appeared to be an immutable reality in which men and women fulfilled certain specific roles, dressed in specific ways, and reacted in specific manners, and the questioning of the necessity of these roles and styles was seen as deviant—and therefore wrong. Today, some of these perceptions have changed but the changes have been mostly superficial. Beneath the apparently tolerant manners of Cary Grant's new audiences, the same traditional standards continue to rule and the same old discomfort continues to be felt.

The historical origins of this meaning of the word "gay" are somewhat dubious. "*Gai savoir*" meant "poetry" in thirteenth-century Provençal, and, as some troubadour poems were explicitly homosexual, it is possible that the word came to designate this particular aspect of their repertoire. Other inquisitive etymologists have traced its origins to Old English, where one of the meanings of the word "*gal* " was "lustful", as in modern German "*geil*". Whatever the sources, by the early twentieth century "gay" was commonly used in English homosexual subculture as a password or code. Nowadays, "gay" or "*gai*" is the usual term for "male homosexual" in French, Dutch, Danish, Japanese, Swedish, and Catalan.

"Gay" is reserved for male homosexualities. Female homosexualities—lesbianism, to use the term still ignored in the 1971 edition of the *Oxford English Dictionary*—have a vocabulary and career of their own. In spite of the prejudice that views all unconventional sexualities as part of the same herd of sinners, and in spite of the common political force that results from being the object of such a prejudice, male and female homosexualities differ in their public image, their vocabularies, and their histories. Lesbianism, for instance, is empowered by its association with feminism—gay males have no such support from any equivalent male group—and lesbian acts are ignored in certain heterosexual codes of law; Britain's notorious anti-homosexual laws of the past century were meant exclusively for males, as Queen Victoria (tradition has it) refused to believe "that women did such things". In most countries, female couples are considered "respectable" while male couples are unthinkable except as an abomination, perhaps because, in the heterosexual male imagination which dominates most societies, two women living together do so only because they haven't been able to acquire a man, and are either to be pitied because of this shortcoming, or to be praised for undertaking on their own tasks which are normally a man's responsibility. Similarly, lesbian images are accepted—in fact, encouraged—in heterosexual male pornography, the fantasy being that these women are making love among themselves in expectation of the male to come. The heterosexual male code of honour is thereby safe.

A person not complying with these pre-set codes seemingly threatens the received identity of the individuals who uphold these codes in their society. In order to dismiss the transgressor with greater ease, it is best to caricature him (as the success of things such as *La Cage aux Folles* seems to prove), thereby creating the myth of the Good Homosexual. The Good Homosexual, as in Harvey Fierstein's *Torchsong Trilogy*, is the man who deep down inside wants to be like his mother—have a husband, have a child, putter around the house—and is prevented from doing these things by a quirk of nature. Underlying the myth of the Good Homosexual is the conviction (upheld by the American Psychological Association until 1973) that a homosexual is a heterosexual gone wrong: that with an extra gene or so, a little more testosterone, a dash of tea and sympathy, the homosexual will become cured, become normal. And if this cannot be achieved (because in some cases the malady is too far advanced), then the best thing for the creature to do is assume the other, lesser role designed by society in its binary plan: that of an ersatz woman. I remember a psychological test set for my all-boys class by a school counsellor concerned with "particular friendships". A previous class had warned us that, if we drew a female figure, the counsellor would assume that our fantasy was to be a woman; if we drew a male figure, that we were attracted to a man. In either case we would be lectured on the terrors of deviancy. Deviants, the counsellor had told the other class, always ended up murdered by sailors on the dockside. When my turn came, I drew the figure of a monkey.

IV. The forest in history

> *... and warming his hands to the fire exclaimed,*
> *"Now where would we be without faggots?"*
> – Sir Walter Scott, *Kenilworth*

Homosexuality was not always socially condemned. In other societies human sexuality was known to cover a larger spectrum. In Greece and Rome, no moral distinction was made between homosexual and heterosexual love; in Japan, gay relationships were formally accepted among the samurai; in China, the emperor himself was known to have male lovers. Among the native people of Guatemala, gays are not seen as outsiders; "Our people," said the native leader Rigoberta Menchú, "don't differentiate between people who are homosexual and people who aren't; that only happens when we go out of our society. What's good about our way of life is that everything is considered a part of nature."

In European society, hostility against gays did not become widespread until the mid-twelfth century. "The causes of this change," wrote Yale historian James Boswell, "cannot be adequately explained, but they were probably closely related to the increase in intolerance of minority groups apparent in ecclesiastical and secular institutions throughout the thirteenth and fourteenth centuries." And yet, in spite of this hostility, until the nineteenth century the homosexual was not perceived as someone distinct, someone with a personality different from that of the heterosexual, someone who could be persecuted not only for a specific act *contra natura* but merely for existing. Until then, noted Michel Foucault in his *History of Sexuality*, "the sodomite had been a temporary aberration; the homosexual was now a species."

With the invention of the species "homosexual", intolerance created its quarry. Once a prejudice is set up, it traps within its boundaries a heterogenous group of individuals whose single common denominator is determined by the prejudice itself. The colour of one's skin, one's varying degrees of alliance to a certain faith, a certain aspect of one's sexual preferences, can and do become the obverse of an object of desire—an object of hatred. No logic governs these choices: prejudice can couple an Indonesian lawyer and a Rastafarian poet as "coloured people", and exclude a Japanese businessman as "an honorary white"; revile an Ethiopian Jew and an American Hassid, yet pay homage to Solomon and David as pillars of the Christian tradition; condemn a gay adolescent and poor Oscar Wilde, but applaud Liberace and ignore the homosexuality of Leonardo da Vinci and Alexander the Great.

Thus, the group created by prejudice comes into existence not by the choice of the individuals forming it, but by the reaction of those outside it. The infinitely varying shapes and shades of sexual desire are not the pivot of everyone's life, yet gay people find themselves defined through that single characteristic—their physical attraction to others of the same sex—notwithstanding that those who attract them run the entire gamut of the human male—tall, short, thin, fat, serious, silly, rough, dainty, intelligent, slow-witted, bearded, hairless, rightwing, left-wing, young, old—with nothing in common except a penis. Once limited and defined by this grouping, the quarry can be taunted, excluded from certain areas of society, deprived of certain rights, sometimes arrested, beaten, killed. In England, the promotion of homosexuality is illegal; in Argentina, gays are routinely blackmailed; in the U.S. and Canada, their inclusion in the armed forces is contested; in Cuba, they are imprisoned; in Saudi Arabia, they are put to death. In Germany, homosexuals who were victimized by the Nazis are still denied restitution, on the grounds that they were persecuted for their criminal, not political, activities.

A group, a category, a label may be formed and transformed throughout history, but direct experience of this isn't necessary for a writer to express that experience in artistic terms—to compose a poem, to write a novel. Many stories touching on a gay theme stem from writers forced to exist within the gay ghetto. But many others have been written by men and women who have not been condemned to such enclosures. As works of fiction, they are indistinguishable from one another, as our anthology attempts to show.

V. *Variations in the landscape*

Such and so various are the tastes of men.
  – Mark Akenside, *The Pleasures of the Imagination*

The fourth book of the *Odyssey* tells of Proteus, King of Egypt, known as "the Ancient one of the Sea", able to tell the future and to change shape at will. According to one version of the story, he was the first man, imagined by the gods as a creature of endless possibilities. Like the apparent shapes of that ancient king, our desire need not be limited. Heterosexuality and homosexuality were no doubt two of those Protean forms, but they are neither exclusive nor impermeable. Like our literary tastes, our sexual affinities need only declare allegiance and define themselves under duress. In the moment of pleasure, we are as indefinable as the moment itself. Perhaps that generous sense of pleasure will ultimately prevail.

Our social organizations, however, still demand labels, require catalogues, and these unavoidably become hierarchies and class systems in which some assume power and others are excluded. Every library has its shadow: the endless shelves of books unchosen, unread, rejected, forgotten, forbidden. And yet the exclusion of *any* subject from literature, whether by design of the reader or of the writer, is an inadmissible form of censorship that degrades everyone's humanity. The groups ostracized by prejudice may be, and usually are, cut off, but not for ever. Injustice, as we should have learned by now, has a curious effect on people's voices. It lends them potency and clarity and resourcefulness and originality, which are all good things to have if one is to create a literature.

VI. *A word about the title*

> *Whom do you flee, madman?*
> *Even gods have lived in the woods.*
> – Virgil, *Eclogue II*, 60

In the days when I was an avid reader of comic books, the line that thrilled me most, because it promised to reveal something that had been taking place at the same time as the more obvious bits of the plot, was *"Meanwhile, in another part of the forest..."*—usually inked in capital letters in the top left-hand corner of the box. To me (who, like any devoted reader, wished for an infinite story) this line promised something close to that infinity: the possibility of knowing what had happened on that other fork of the road, the one not yet taken, the one less in evidence, the mysterious and equally important path that led to another part of the adventurous forest. It is in that same spirit that Craig Stephenson and I offer this book to the inquisitive reader.

Alberto Manguel

Arthur Snatchfold

E. M. Forster

"I hate the idea of causes," said E.M. Forster in 1938, speaking in public just before the beginning of the Second World War. "And if I had to choose between betraying my country and betraying my friend, I hope I should have the guts to betray my country." His advice to patriots was also his literary credo: "Do good, and possibly good may come from it. Be soft even if you stand to get squashed. Beware of the long run. Seek understanding dispassionately, and not in accordance with a theory."

Forster never claimed for his characters any wisdom gained through suffering. Being a victim grants experience—of racial prejudice in A Passage to India, *of xenophobia in* Where Angels Fear to Tread, *of misogyny in* Howards End, *of homophobia in* Maurice—*but does not automatically make one a better person. Forster, whose keen eye for the horrors and follies of social conventions allowed him to describe so vividly English society at home and abroad, never accepted for himself the status of mere victim. Even though, for fear of criminal persecution in England, he was forced to leave unpublished his writings dealing openly with homosexuality—the novel* Maurice, *the stories in* The Life to Come—*he fought strenuously against censorship, campaigning in 1928 against the banning of Radclyffe Hall's lesbian novel,* The Well of Loneliness, *and standing in 1960 as witness for the defence in the trial of the publishers of D. H. Lawrence's* Lady Chatterley's Lover. *"Arthur Snatchfold", set in the midst of the social hypocrisies Forster so relentlessly denounced, is the story of a victim—but also of a secret and unexpected hero.*

I

Conway (Sir Richard Conway) woke early, and went to the window to have a look at the Trevor Donaldsons' garden. Too green. A flight of mossy steps led up from the drive to a turfed amphitheatre. This contained a number of trees of the lead-pencil persuasion, and a number of flower-beds, profuse with herbaceous promises which would certainly not be fulfilled that weekend. The summer was heavy-leaved and at a moment between flowerings, and the gardener, though evidently expensive, had been caught bending. Bounding the amphitheatre was a high yew hedge, an imposing background had there been any foreground, and behind the hedge a heavy wood shut the sky out. Of course what was wanted was colour. Delphinium, salvia, red-hot-poker, zinnias, tobacco-plant, anything. Leaning out of the baronial casement, Conway considered this, while he waited for his tea. He was not an artist, nor a philosopher, but he liked exercising his mind when he had nothing else to do, as on this Sunday morning, this country morning, with so much ahead to be eaten, and so little to be said.

The visit, like the view, threatened monotony. Dinner had been dull. His own spruce grey head, gleaming in the mirrors, really seemed the brightest object about. Trevor Donaldson's head was mangy, Mrs. Donaldson's combed up into bastions of iron. He did not get unduly fussed at the prospect of boredom. He was a man of experience with plenty of resources and plenty of armour, and he was a decent human being too. The Donaldsons were his inferiors—they had not travelled or read or gone in for sport or love, they were merely his business allies, linked to him by a common interest in aluminium. Still, he must try to make things nice, since they had been so good as to invite him down. "But it's not so easy to make things nice for us business people," he reflected, as he listened to the chonk of a blackbird, the clink of a milk-can, and the distant self-communings of an electric pump. "We're not stupid or uncultivated, we can use our minds when required, we can go to concerts when we're not too tired, we've invested—even Trevor Donaldson has—in the sense of humour. But I'm afraid we don't get much pleasure out of it all. No. Pleasure's been left out of our packet." Business occupied him increasingly since his wife's death. He brought an active mind to bear on it, and was quickly becoming rich.

He looked at the dull costly garden. It improved. A man had come into it from the back of the yew hedge. He had on a canary-coloured shirt, and the effect was exactly right. The whole scene blazed. *That* was what the place wanted—not a flower-bed, but a man, who advanced with a confident tread down the amphitheatre, and as he came nearer Conway saw that besides being proper to the colour scheme he was a very proper youth. His shoulders were broad, his face sensuous and open, his eyes, screwed up against the light, promised good temper. One arm shot out at an angle, the other supported a milk-can. "Good morning, nice morning," he called, and he sounded happy.

"Good morning, nice morning," he called back. The man continued at a steady pace, turned left and disappeared in the direction of the servants' entrance, where an outburst of laughter welcomed him.

Conway hoped he might return by the same route, and waited. "That is a nice-looking fellow, I do like the way he holds himself, and probably no nonsense about him," he thought. But the vision had departed, the sunlight stopped, the garden turned stodgy and green again, and the maid came in with his tea. She said, "I'm sorry to be late, we were waiting for the milk, sir." The man had not called him sir, and the omission flattered him. "Good morning, sir" would have been the more natural salutation to an elderly stranger, a wealthy customer's guest. But the vigorous voice had shouted "Good morning, nice morning," as if they were equals.

Where had he gone off to now, he and his voice? To finish his round, welcomed at house after house, and then for a bathe perhaps, his shirt golden on the grass beside him. Ruddy brown to the waist he would show now.... What was his name? Was he a local? Sir Richard put these questions to himself as he dressed, but not vehemently. He was not a sentimentalist, there was no danger of him being shattered for the day. He would have liked to meet the vision again, and spend the whole of Sunday with it, giving it a slap-up lunch at the hotel, hiring a car, which they would drive alternately, treating it to the pictures in the neighbouring town, and returning with it, after one drink too much, through dusky lanes. But that was sheer nonsense, even if the vision had been agreeable to the programme. He was staying with the Trevor Donaldsons; and he must not repay their hospitality by moping. Dressed in a cheerful grey, he ran downstairs to the breakfast-room. Mrs. Donaldson was already there, and she asked him how his daughters were getting on at their school.

Then his host followed, rubbing his hands together, and saying "Aha, aha!" and when they had eaten they went into the other garden, the one which sloped towards the water, and started talking business. They had not intended to do this, but there was also of their company a Mr. Clifford Clarke, and when Trevor Donaldson, Clifford Clarke and Richard Conway got together it was impossible that aluminium should escape. Their voices deepened, their heads nodded or shook as they recalled vast sums that had been lost through unsound investments or misapplied advice. Conway found himself the most intelligent of the three, the quickest at taking a point, the strongest at following an argument. The moments passed, the blackbird chonk-chonked unheeded, unnoticed was the failure of the gardener to produce anything but tightly furled geraniums, unnoticed the ladies on the lawn, who wanted to get some golf. At last the hostess called, "Trevor! Is this a holiday or isn't it?" and they stopped, feeling rather ashamed. The cars came round, and soon they were five miles away, on the course, taking their turn in a queue of fellow merry-makers. Conway was good at golf, and got what excitement he could from it, but as soon as the ball flew off he was aware of a slight sinking feeling. This occupied them till lunch. After coffee they walked down to the water, and played with the dogs—Mrs. Donaldson bred Sealyhams. Several neighbours came to tea, and now the animation rested with Donaldson, for he fancied himself as a country magnate, and wanted to show how well he was settling into the part. There was a good deal of talk about local conditions, women's institutes, education through discipline, and poaching. Conway found all this quite nonsensical and unreal. People who are not feudal should not play at feudalism, and all magistrates (this he said aloud) ought to be trained and ought to be paid. Since he was well-bred, he said it in a form which did not give offence. Thus the day wore away, and they filled in the interval before dinner by driving to see a ruined monastery. What on earth had they got to do with a monastery? Nothing at all. Nothing at all. He caught sight of Clifford Clarke looking mournfully at a rose-window, and he got the feeling that they were all of them looking for something which was not there, that there was an empty chair at the table, a card missing from the bridge-pack, a ball lost in the gorse, a stitch dropped in the shirt; that the chief guest had not come. On their way out they passed through the village, on their way back past a cinema, which was giving a Wild West stunt. They returned through darkling lanes. They did not say, "Thank you! What a delightful day!" That would be saved up for tomorrow morning, and for the final gratitude of departure. Every word would be needed then. "I *have* enjoyed myself, I *have*, absolutely marvellous!" the women would chant, and the men would grunt, as if moved beyond words, and the host and hostess would cry, "Oh but come again, then, come again." Into the void the little unmemorable visit would fall, like a leaf it would fall upon similar leaves, but Conway wondered whether it hadn't been, so to speak, specially negative, out of the way unflowering, whether a champion, one bare arm at an angle, hadn't carried away to the servants' quarters some refreshment which was badly needed in the smoking-room.

"Well, perhaps we shall see, we may yet find out," he thought, as he went up to bed, carrying with him his raincoat.

For he was not one to give in and grumble. He believed in pleasure; he had a free mind and an active body, and he knew that pleasure cannot be won without courage and coolness. The Donaldsons were all very well, but they were not the whole of his life. His daughters were all very well, but the same held good of them. The female sex was all very well and he was addicted to it, but permitted himself an occasional deviation. He set his alarm watch for an hour slightly earlier than the hour at which he had woken in the morning, and he put it under his pillow, and he fell asleep looking quite young.

Seven o'clock tinkled. He glanced into the passage, then put on his raincoat and thick slippers, and went to the window.

It was a silent sunless morning, and seemed earlier than it actually was. The green of the garden and of the trees was filmed with grey, as if it wanted wiping. Presently the electric pump started. He looked at his watch again, slipped down the stairs, out of the house, across the amphitheatre and through the yew hedge. He did not run, in case he was seen and had to explain. He moved at the maximum pace possible for a gentleman, known to be an original, who fancies an early stroll in his pyjamas. "I thought I'd have a look at your formal garden, there wouldn't have been time after breakfast" would have been the line. He had of course looked at it the day before, also at the wood. The wood lay before him now, and the sun was just tipping into it. There were two paths through the bracken, a broad and a narrow. He waited until he heard the milk-can approaching down the narrow path. Then he moved quickly, and they met, well out of sight of the Donaldsonian demesne.

"Hullo!" he called in his easy out-of-doors voice; he had several voices, and knew by instinct which was wanted.

"Hullo! Somebody's out early!"

"You're early yourself."

"Me? Whor'd the milk be if I worn't?" the milkman grinned, throwing his head back and coming to a standstill. Seen at close quarters he was coarse, very much of the people and of the thick-fingered earth; a hundred years ago his type was trodden into the mud, now it burst and flowered and didn't care a damn.

"You're the morning delivery, eh?"

"Looks like it." He evidently proposed to be facetious—the clumsy fun which can be so delightful when it falls from the proper lips. "I'm not the evening delivery anyway, and I'm not the butcher nor the grocer, nor'm I the coals."

"Live around here?"

"Maybe. Maybe I don't. Maybe I flop about in them planes."

"You live around here, I bet."

"What if I do?"

"If you do you do. And if I don't I don't."

This fatuous retort was a success, and was greeted with doubled-up laughter. "If you don't you don't! Ho, you're a funny one! There's a thing to say! If you don't you don't! Walking about in yer night things, too, you'll ketch a cold you will, that'll be the end of you! Stopping back in the 'otel, I suppose?"

"No. Donaldson's. You saw me there yesterday."

"Oh, Donaldson's, that's it. You was the old granfa' at the upstairs window."

"Old granfa' indeed ... I'll granfa' you," and he tweaked at the impudent nose. It dodged, it seemed used to this sort of thing. There was probably nothing the lad wouldn't consent to if properly handled, partly out of mischief, partly to oblige. "Oh, by the way..." and he felt the shirt as if interested in the quality of its material. "What was I going to say?" and he gave the zip at the throat a downward pull. Much slid into view. "Oh, I know—when's this round of yours over?"

" 'Bout eleven. Why?"

"Why not?"

" 'Bout eleven *at night*. Ha ha. Got yer there. Eleven at night. What you want to arst all them questions for? We're strangers, aren't we?"

"How old are you?"

"Ninety, same as yourself."

"What's your address?"

"There you go on! Hi! I like that. Arstin questions after I tell you No."

"Got a girl? Ever heard of a pint? Ever heard of two?"

"Go on. Get out." But he suffered his forearm to be worked between massaging fingers, and he set down his milk-can. He was amused. He was charmed. He was hooked, and a touch would land him.

"You look like a boy who looks all right," the elder man breathed.

"Oh, stop it…. All right, I'll go with you."

Conway was entranced. Thus, exactly thus, should the smaller pleasures of life be approached. They understood one another with a precision impossible for lovers. He laid his face on the warm skin over the clavicle, hands nudged him behind, and presently the sensation for which he had planned so cleverly was over. It was part of the past. It had fallen like a flower upon similar flowers.

He heard "You all right?" It was over there too, part of a different past. They were lying deeper in the wood, where the fern was highest. He did not reply, for it was pleasant to lie stretched thus and to gaze up through bracken fronds at the distant treetops and the pale blue sky, and feel the exquisite pleasure fade.

"That was what you wanted, wasn't it?" Propped on his elbows the young man looked down anxiously. All his roughness and pertness had gone, and he only wanted to know whether he had been a success.

"Yes…. Lovely."

"Lovely? You say lovely?" he beamed, prodding gently with his stomach.

"Nice boy, nice shirt, nice everything."

"That a fact?"

Conway guessed that he was vain, the better sort often are, and laid on the flattery thick to please him, praised his comeliness, his thrusting thrashing strength; there was plenty to praise. He liked to do this and to see the broad face grinning and feel the heavy body on him. There was no cynicism in the flattery, he was genuinely admiring and gratified.

"So you enjoyed that?"

"Who wouldn't?"

"Pity you didn't tell me yesterday."

"I didn't know how to."

"I'd a met you down where I have my swim. You could 'elped me strip, you'd like that. Still, we mustn't grumble." He gave Conway a hand and pulled him up, and brushed and tidied the raincoat like an old friend. "We could get seven years for this, couldn't we?"

"Not seven years, still we'd get something nasty. Madness, isn't it? What can it matter to anyone else if you and I don't mind?"

"Oh, I suppose they've to occupy themselves with somethink or other," and he took up the milk-can to go on.

"Half a minute, boy—do take this and get yourself some trifle with it." He produced a note which he had brought on the chance.

"I didn't do it fer that."

"I know you didn't."

"Naow, we was each as bad as the other.... Naow ... keep yer money."

"I'd be pleased if you would take it. I expect I'm better off than you and it might come in useful. To take out your girl, say, or towards your next new suit. However, please yourself, of course."

"Can you honestly afford it?"

"Honestly."

"Well, I'll find a way to spend it, no doubt. People don't always behave as nice as you, you know?"

Conway could have returned the compliment. The affair had been trivial and crude, and yet they both had behaved perfectly. They would never meet again, and they did not exchange names. After a hearty handshake, the young man swung away down the path, the sunlight and the shadow rushing over his back. He did not turn round, but his arm, jerking sideways to balance him, waved an acceptable farewell. The green flowed over his brightness, the path bent, he disappeared. Back he went to his own life, and through the quiet of the morning his laugh could be heard as he whooped at the maids.

Conway waited for a few moments, as arranged, and then he went back too. His luck held. He met no one, either in the amphitheatre garden or on the stairs, and after he had been in his room for a minute the maid arrived with his early tea. "I'm sorry the milk was late again, sir," she said. He enjoyed it, bathed and shaved and dressed himself for town. It was the figure of a superior city-man which was reflected in the mirror as he tripped downstairs. The car came round after breakfast to take him to the station, and he was completely sincere when he told the Trevor Donaldsons that he had had an out-of-the-way pleasant weekend. They believed him, and their faces grew brighter. "Come again then, come by all means again," they cried as he slid off. In the train he read the papers rather less than usual and smiled to himself rather more. It was so pleasant to have been completely right over a stranger, even down to little details like the texture of the skin. It flattered his vanity. It increased his sense of power.

II

He did not see Trevor Donaldson again for some weeks. Then they met in London at his club, for a business talk and a spot of lunch. Circumstances which they could not control had rendered them less friendly. Owing to regrouping in the financial world, their interests were now opposed, and if one of them stood to make money out of aluminium the other stood to lose. So the talk had been cautious. Donaldson, the weaker man, felt tired and worried after it. He had not, to his knowledge, made a mistake, but he might have slipped unwittingly, and be poorer, and have to give up his county state. He looked at his host with hostility and wished he could harm him. Sir Richard was aware of this, but felt no hostility in return. For one thing, he was going to win, for another, hating never interested him. This was probably the last occasion on which they would foregather socially; but he exercised his usual charm. He wanted, too, to find out during lunch how far Donaldson was aware of his own danger. Clifford Clarke (who was allied with him) had failed to do this.

After adjourning to the cloakroom and washing their hands at adjacent basins, they sat opposite each other at a little table. Down the long room sat other pairs of elderly men, eating, drinking, talking quietly, instructing the waiters. Inquiries were exchanged about Mrs. Donaldson and the young Miss Conways, and there were some humorous references to golf. Then Donaldson said, with a change in his voice: "Golf's all you say, and the great advantage of it in these days is that you get it practically anywhere. I used to think our course was good, for a little country course, but it is far below the average. This is somewhat of a disappointment to us both, since we settled down there specially for the golf. The fact is, the country is not at all what it seems when first you go there."

"So I've always heard."

"My wife likes it, of course, she has her Sealyhams, she has her flowers, she has her local charities—though in these days one's not supposed to speak of 'charity'. I don't know why. I should have thought it was a good word, charity. She runs the Women's Institute, so far as it consents to be run, but Conway, Conway, you'd never believe how offhand the village women are in these days. They don't elect Mrs. Donaldson president yearly as a matter of course. She takes turn and turn with cottagers."

"Oh, that's the spirit of the age, of course. One's always running into it in some form or other. For instance, I don't get nearly the deference I did from my clerks."

"But better work from them, no doubt," said Donaldson gloomily.

"No. But probably they're better men."

"Well, perhaps the ladies at the Women's Institute are becoming better women. But my wife doubts it. Of course our village is particularly unfortunate, owing to that deplorable hotel. It has had such a bad influence. We had an extraordinary case before us on the Bench recently, connected with it."

"That hotel did look too flash—it would attract the wrong crowd."

"I've also had bother bother bother with the Rural District Council over the removal of tins, and another bother—a really maddening one—over a right of way through the church meadows. That almost made me lose my patience. And I really sometimes wonder whether I've been sensible in digging myself in in the country, and trying to make myself useful in local affairs. There is no gratitude. There is no warmth of welcome."

"I quite believe it, Donaldson, and I know I'd never have a country place myself, even if the scenery is as pleasant as yours is, and even if I could afford it. I make do with a service flat in town, and I retain a small furnished cottage for my girls' holidays, and when they leave school I shall partly take them and partly send them abroad. I don't believe in undiluted England, nice as are sometimes the English. Shall we go up and have coffee?"

He ran up the staircase briskly, for he had found out what he wanted to know: Donaldson was feeling poor. He stuck him in a low leathern armchair, and had a look at him as he closed his eyes. That was it: he felt he couldn't afford his "little place", and was running it down, so that no one should be surprised when he gave it up. Meanwhile, there was one point in the conversation it amused him to take up now that business was finished with: the reference to that "extraordinary case" connected with the local hotel.

Donaldson opened his eyes when asked, and they had gone prawn-like. "Oh, that was a case, it was a really really," he said. "I knew such things existed, of course, but I assumed in my innocence they were confined to Piccadilly. However, it has all been traced back to the hotel, the proprietress has had a thorough fright, and I don't think there will be any trouble in the future. Indecency between males."

"Oh, good Lord!" said Sir Richard coolly. "Black or white?"

"White, please, it's an awful nuisance, but I can't take black coffee now, although I greatly prefer it. You see, some of the hotel guests—there was a bar, and some of the villagers used to go in there after cricket because they thought it smarter than that charming old thatched pub by the church—you remember that old thatched pub. Villagers are terrific snobs, that's one of the disappointing discoveries one makes. The bar got a bad reputation of a certain type, especially at week-ends, someone complained to the police, a watch was set, and the result was this quite extraordinary case.... Really, really, I wouldn't have believed it. A *little* milk, please, Conway, if I may, just a little; I'm not allowed to take my coffee black."

"So sorry. Have a liqueur."

"No, no thanks, I'm not allowed that even, especially after lunch."

"Come on, do—I will if you will. Waiter, can we have two double cognacs?"

"He hasn't heard you. Don't bother."

Conway had not wanted the waiter to hear him, he had wanted an excuse to be out of the room and have a minute alone. He was suddenly worried in case that milkman had got into a scrape. He had scarcely thought about him since—he had a very full life, and it included an intrigue with a cultivated woman, which was gradually ripening—but nobody could have been more decent and honest, or more physically attractive in a particular way. It had been a charming little adventure, and a remarkably lively one. And their parting had been perfect. Wretched if the lad had come to grief! Enough to make one cry. He offered up a sort of prayer, ordered the cognacs, and rejoined Donaldson with his usual briskness. He put on the Renaissance armour that suited him so well, and "How did the hotel case end?" he asked.

"We committed him for trial."

"Oh! As bad as that?"

"Well, we thought so. Actually a gang of about half a dozen were involved, but we only caught one of them. His mother, if you please, is president of the Women's Institute, and hasn't had the decency to resign! I tell you, Conway, these people aren't the same flesh and blood as oneself. One pretends they are, but they aren't. And what with this disillusionment, and what with the right of way, I've a good mind to clear out next year, and leave the so-called country to stew in its own juice. It's utterly corrupt. This man made an awfully bad impression on the Bench and we didn't feel that six months, which is the maximum we were allowed to impose, was adequate to the offence. And it was all so revoltingly commercial—his only motive was money."

Conway felt relieved; it couldn't be his own friend, for anyone less grasping....

"And another unpleasant feature—at least for me—is that he had the habit of taking his clients into my grounds."

"How most vexatious for you!"

"It suited his convenience, and of what else should he think? I have a little wood—you didn't see it—which stretches up to the hotel, so he could easily bring people in. A path my wife was particularly fond of—a mass of bluebells in springtime—it was there they were caught. You may well imagine this has helped to put me off the place."

"Who caught them?" he asked, holding his glass up to the light; their cognacs had arrived.

"Our local bobby. For we do possess that extraordinary rarity, a policeman who keeps his eyes open. He sometimes commits errors of judgement—he did on this occasion—but he's certainly observant, and as he was coming down one of the other paths, a public one, he saw a bright yellow shirt through the bracken—upsa! Take care!"

"Upsa!" were some drops of brandy, which Conway had spilt. Alas, alas, there could be no doubt about it. He felt deeply distressed, and rather guilty. The young man must have decided after their successful encounter to use the wood as a rendezvous. It was a cruel stupid world, and he was countenancing it more than he should. Wretched, wretched, to think of that good-tempered, harmless chap being bruised and ruined ... the whole thing so unnecessary—

betrayed by the shirt he was so proud of.... Conway was not often moved, but this time he felt much regret and compassion.

"Well, he recognized that shirt at once. He had particular reasons for keeping a watch on its wearer. And he got him, he got him. But he lost the other man. He didn't charge them straight away, as he ought to have done. I think he was genuinely startled and could scarcely believe his eyes. For one thing, it was so early in the morning—barely seven o'clock."

"A strange hour!" said Conway, and put his glass down, and folded his hands on his knee.

"He caught sight of them as they were getting up after committing the indecency, also he saw money pass, but instead of rushing in there and then he made an elaborate and totally unnecessary plan for interrupting the youth on the further side of my house, and of course he could have got him any time, any time. A stupid error of judgement. A great pity. He never arrested him until 7.45."

"Was there then sufficient evidence for an arrest?"

"There was abundant evidence of a medical character, if you follow me—what a case, oh, what a case!—also there was the money on him, which clinched his guilt."

"Mayn't the money have been in connection with his round?"

"No. It was a note, and he only had small change in connection with his round. We established that from his employer. But however did you guess he was on a round?"

"You told me," said Conway, who never became flustered when he made a slip. "You mentioned that he had a milk round and that the mother was connected with some local organization which Mrs. Donaldson takes an interest in."

"Yes, yes, the Women's Institute. Well, having fixed all that up, our policeman then went on to the hotel, but it was far too late by that time, some of the guests were breakfasting, others had left, he couldn't go round cross-questioning everyone, and no one corresponded to the description of the person whom he saw being hauled up out of the fern."

"What was the description?"

"An old man in pyjamas and a mackintosh—our Chairman was awfully anxious to get hold of him—oh, you remember our Chairman, Ernest Dray, you met him at my little place. He's determined to stamp this sort of thing out, once and for all. Hullo, it's past three, I must be getting back to my grindstone. Many thanks for lunch. I don't know why I've discoursed on this somewhat unsavoury topic. I'd have done better to consult you about the right of way."

"You must another time. I did look up the subject once."

"How about a spot of lunch with me this day week?" said Donaldson, remembering their business feud, and becoming uneasily jolly.

"This day week? Now can I? No, I can't. I've promised this day week to go and see my little girls. Not that they're little any longer. Time flies, doesn't it? We're none of us younger."

"Sad but true," said Donaldson, heaving himself out of the deep leather chair. Similar chairs, empty or filled with similar men, receded down the room, and far away a small fire smoked under a heavy mantelpiece. "But aren't you going to drink your cognac? It's excellent cognac."

"I suddenly took against it—I do indulge in caprices." Getting up, he felt faint, the blood rushed to his head and he thought he was going to fall. "Tell me," he said, taking his enemy's arm and conducting him to the door, "this old man in the mackintosh—how was it the fellow you caught never put you on his track?"

"He tried to."

"Oh, did he?"

"Yes indeed, and he was all the more anxious to do so, because we made it clear that he would be let off if he helped us to make the major arrest. But all he could say was what we knew already—that it was someone from the hotel."

"Oh, he said that, did he? From the hotel."

"Said it again and again. Scarcely said anything else, indeed almost went into a sort of fit. There he stood with his head thrown back and his eyes shut, barking at us. "Th'otel. Keep to th'otel. I tell you he come from th'otel." We advised him not to get so excited, whereupon he became insolent, which did him no good with Ernest Dray, as you may well imagine, and called the Bench a row of interfering bastards. He was instantly removed from the court and as he went he shouted back at us—you'll never credit this—that if he and the old grandfather didn't mind it why should anyone else. We talked the case over carefully and came to the conclusion it must go to Assizes."

"What was his name?"

"But we don't know, I tell you, we never caught him."

"I mean the name of the one you did catch, the village boy."

"Arthur Snatchfold."

They had reached the top of the club staircase. Conway saw the reflection of his face once more in a mirror, and it was the face of an old man. He pushed Trevor Donaldson off abruptly, and went back to sit down by his liqueur-glass. He was safe, safe, he could go forward with his career as planned. But waves of shame came over him. Oh for prayer!—but whom had he to pray to, and what about? He saw that little things can turn into great ones, and he did not want greatness. He was not up to it. For a moment he considered giving himself up and standing his trial, however what possible good would that do? He would ruin himself and his daughters, he would delight his enemies, and he would not save his saviour. He recalled his clever manoeuvres for a little fun, and the good-humoured response, the mischievous face, the obliging body. It had all seemed so trivial. Taking a notebook from his pocket, he wrote down the name of his lover, yes, his lover who was going to prison to save him, in order that he might not forget it. Arthur Snatchfold. He had only heard the name once, and he would never hear it again.

The Outing

James Baldwin

The medieval cabalists imagined that Adam was never alone in the Garden, that before the creation of Eve he was accompanied by a feminine figure (most scholars argue that she was also a demon) with whom Adam had the world's first conversations. Without that Other, the cabalists argued, Adam would have had no consciousness of his existence; for that reason, no creature was created single in God's world.

Freud, many centuries later, disregarded the cabalistic argument and maintained that a baby was a single creature, primarily narcissistic and autoerotic. Modern research now suggests that Freud got it wrong: a baby is in fact predisposed to relationships, to reaching out from the very beginning, like Adam in the Garden, to somebody else. We may like to imagine ourselves independent creatures, invulnerable to the hooks of the outside world, but our essential humanity—as James Baldwin makes clear in "The Outing"—resides in our vulnerability. "We all exist, after all, and crucially, in the eye of the beholder," Baldwin observed in an essay on homosexuality published in 1985, some twenty years after writing "The Outing". "We all react to and, to whatever extent, become what that eye sees. This judgement begins with the eyes of one's parents (the crucial, the definitive, the all-but-everlasting judgement), and so we move, in the vast and claustrophobic gallery of Others, on up or down the line, to the eye of one's enemy or one's friend or one's lover."

Each summer the church gave an outing. It usually took place on the Fourth of July, that being the day when most of the church-members were free from work; it began quite early in the morning and lasted all day. The saints referred to it as the "whosoever will" outing, by which they meant that, though it was given by the Mount of Olives Pentecostal Assembly for the benefit of its members, all men were free to join them, Gentile, Jew or Greek or sinner. The Jews and the Greeks, to say nothing of the Gentiles—on whom, for their livelihood, most of the saints depended—showed themselves, year after year, indifferent to the invitation; but sinners of the more expected hue were seldom lacking. This year they were to take a boat trip up the Hudson as far as Bear Mountain where they would spend the day and return as the moon rose over the wide river. Since on other outings they had merely taken a subway ride as far as Pelham Bay or Van Cortlandt Park, this year's outing was more than ever a special occasion and even the deacon's two oldest boys, Johnnie and Roy, and their friend, David Jackson, were reluctantly thrilled. These three tended to consider themselves sophisticates, no longer, like the old folks, at the mercy of the love or the wrath of God.

The entire church was going and for weeks in advance talked of nothing else. And for weeks in the future the outing would provide interesting conversation. They did not consider this frivolous. The outing, Father James declared from his pulpit a week before the event, was for the purpose of giving the children of God a day of relaxation; to breathe a purer air and to worship God joyfully beneath the roof of heaven; and there was nothing frivolous about *that*. And, rather to the alarm of the captain, they planned to hold church services aboard the ship. Last year Sister McCandless had held an impromptu service in the unbelieving subway car; she played the tambourine and sang and exhorted sinners and passed through the train distributing tracts. Not everyone had found this admirable, to some it seemed that Sister McCandless was being a little ostentatious. "I praise my Redeemer wherever I go," she retorted defiantly. "Holy Ghost don't leave *me* when I leave the church. I got a every day religion."

Sylvia's birthday was on the third, and David and Johnnie and Roy had been saving money for her birthday present. Between them they had five dollars but they could not decide what to give her. Roy's suggestion that they give her underthings was rudely shouted down: did he want Sylvia's mother to kill the girl? They were all frightened of the great, rawboned, outspoken Sister Daniels and for Sylvia's sake went to great pains to preserve what remained of her good humor. Finally, at the suggestion of David's older sister, Lorraine, they bought a small, gold-plated pin cut in the shape of a butterfly. Roy thought that it was cheap and grumbled angrily at their combined bad taste ("Wait till it starts turning her clothes green!" he cried) but David did not think it was so bad; Johnnie thought it pretty enough and he was sure that Sylvia would like it anyway; ("When's *your* birthday?" he asked David). It was agreed that David should present it to her on the day of the outing in the presence of them all. ("Man, I'm the oldest cat here," David said, "you know that girl's crazy about me"). This was the summer in which they all abruptly began to grow older, their bodies becoming troublesome and awkward and even dangerous and their voices not to be trusted. David perpetually boasted of the increase of down on his chin and professed to have hair on his chest—"and somewhere else, too," he added slyly, whereat they all laughed. "You ain't the only one," Roy said. "No," Johnnie said, "I'm almost as old as you are." "Almost ain't got it," David said. "Now ain't this a hell of a conversation for church boys?" Roy wanted to know.

The morning of the outing they were all up early; their father sang in the kitchen and their mother, herself betraying an excitement nearly youthful, scrubbed and dressed the younger children and laid the plates for breakfast. In the bedroom which they shared Roy looked wistfully out of the window and turned to Johnnie.

"Got a good mind to stay home," he said. "Probably have more fun." He made a furious gesture toward the kitchen. "Why doesn't *he* stay home?"

Johnnie, who was looking forward to the day with David and who had not the remotest desire to stay home for any reason and who knew, moreover, that Gabriel was not going to leave Roy alone in the city, not even if the heavens fell, said lightly, squirming into clean underwear: "Oh, he'll probably be busy with the old folks. We can stay out of his way."

Roy sighed and began to dress. "Be glad when I'm a man," he said.

Lorraine and David and Mrs. Jackson were already on the boat when they arrived. They were among the last; most of the church, Father James, Brother Elisha, Sister McCandless, Sister Daniels and Sylvia were seated near the rail of the boat in a little semi-circle, conversing in strident tones. Father James and Sister McCandless were remarking the increase of laxity among God's people and debating whether or not the church should run a series of revival meetings. Sylvia sat there, saying nothing, smiling painfully now and then at young Brother Elisha, who spoke loudly of the need for a revival and who continually attempted to include Sylvia in the conversation. Elsewhere on the boat similar conversations were going on. The saints of God were together and very conscious this morning of their being together and of their sainthood; and were determined that the less enlightened world should know who they were and remark upon it. To this end there were a great many cries of "Praise the Lord!" in greeting and the formal holy kiss. The children, bored with the familiar spectacle, had already drawn apart and amused themselves by loud cries and games that were no less exhibitionistic than that being played by their parents. Johnnie's nine year old sister, Lois, since she professed salvation, could not very well behave as the other children did; yet no degree of salvation could have equipped her to enter into the conversation of the grown-ups; and she was very violently disliked among the adolescents and could not join them either. She wandered about, therefore, unwillingly forlorn, contenting herself to some extent by a great display of virtue in her encounters with the unsaved children and smiling brightly at the grown-ups. She came to Brother Elisha's side. "Praise the Lord," he cried, stroking her head and continuing his conversation.

Lorraine and Mrs. Jackson met Johnnie's mother for the first time as she breathlessly came on board, dressed in the airy and unreal blue which Johnnie would forever associate with his furthest memories of her. Johnnie's baby brother, her youngest, happiest child, clung round her neck; she made him stand, staring in wonder at the strange, endless deck, while she was introduced. His mother, on all social occasions, seemed fearfully distracted, as though she awaited, at any moment, some crushing and irrevocable disaster. This disaster might be the sudden awareness of a run in her stocking or private knowledge that the trump of judgment was due, within five minutes, to sound: but, whatever it was, it lent her a certain agitated charm and people, struggling to guess what it might be that so claimed her inward attention, never failed, in the process, to be won over. She talked with Lorraine and Mrs. Jackson for a few moments, the child tugging at her skirts, Johnnie watching her with a smile; and at last, the child becoming always more restive, said that she must go—into what merciless arena one dared not imagine—but hoped, with a despairing smile which clearly indicated the improbability of such happiness, that she would be able to see them later. They watched her as she walked slowly to the other end of the boat, sometimes pausing in conversation, always (as though it were a duty) smiling a little and now and then considering Lois where she stood at Brother Elisha's knee.

"She's very friendly," Mrs. Jackson said. "She looks like you, Johnnie."

David laughed. "Now why you want to say a thing like that, Ma? That woman ain't never done nothing to you."

Johnnie grinned, embarrassed, and pretended to menace David with his fists.

"Don't you listen to that old, ugly boy," Lorraine said. "He just trying to make you feel bad. Your mother's real good-looking. Tell her I said so."

This embarrassed him even more, but he made a mock bow and said, "Thank you, Sister." And to David: "Maybe now you'll learn to keep your mouth shut."

"Who'll learn to keep whose mouth shut? What kind of talk is that?"

He turned and faced his father, who stood smiling on them as from a height.

"Mrs. Jackson, this is my father," said Roy quickly. "And this is Miss Jackson. You know David."

Lorraine and Mrs. Jackson looked up at the deacon with polite and identical smiles.

"How do you do?" Lorraine said. And from Mrs. Jackson: "I'm very pleased to meet you."

"Praise the Lord," their father said. He smiled. "Don't you let Johnnie talk fresh to you."

"Oh, no, we were just kidding around," David said. There was a short, ugly silence. The deacon said: "It looks like a good day for the outing, praise the Lord. You kids have a good time. Is this your first time with us, Mrs. Jackson?"

"Yes," said Mrs. Jackson. "David came home and told me about it and it's been so long since I've been in the country I just decided I'd take me a day off. And Lorraine's not been feeling too strong, I thought the fresh air would do her some good." She smiled a little painfully as she spoke. Lorraine looked amused.

"Yes, it will, nothing like God's fresh air to help the feeble." At this description of herself as feeble Lorraine looked ready to fall into the Hudson and coughed nastily into her handkerchief. David, impelled by his own perverse demon, looked at Johnnie quickly and murmured, "That's the truth, deacon." The deacon looked at him and smiled and turned to Mrs. Jackson. "We been hoping that your son might join our church someday. Roy brings him out to service every Sunday. Do you like the services, son?" This last was addressed in a hearty voice to David; who, recovering from his amazement at hearing Roy mentioned as his especial pal (for he was Johnnie's friend, it was to be with Johnnie that he came to church!) smiled and said, "Yes sir, I like them alright," and looked at Roy, who considered his father with an expression at once contemptuous, ironic and resigned and at Johnnie, whose face was a mask of rage. He looked sharply at the deacon again; but he, with his arm around Roy, was still talking.

"This boy came to the Lord just about a month ago," he said proudly. "The Lord saved him just like that. Believe me, Sister Jackson, ain't no better fortress for nobody, young or old, than the arms of Jesus. My son'll tell you so, ain't it, Roy?"

They considered Roy with a stiff, cordial curiosity. He muttered murderously, "Yes sir."

"Johnnie tells me you're a preacher," Mrs. Jackson said at last. "I'll come out and hear you sometime with David."

"Don't come out to hear me," he said. "You come out and listen to the Word of God. We're all just vessels in His hand. Do you know the Lord, sister?"

"I try to do His will," Mrs. Jackson said.

He smiled kindly. "We must all grow in grace." He looked at Lorraine. "I'll be expecting to see you too, young lady."

"Yes, we'll be out," Lorraine said. They shook hands. "It's very nice to have met you," she said.

"Goodbye." He looked at David. "Now you be good. I want to see you saved soon." He released Roy and started to walk away. "You kids enjoy yourselves. Johnnie, don't you get into no mischief, you hear me?"

He affected not to have heard; he put his hands in his pants' pockets and pulled out some change and pretended to count it. His hand was clammy and it shook. When his father repeated his admonition, part of the change spilled to the deck and he bent to pick it up. He wanted at once to shout to his father the most dreadful curses that he knew and he wanted to weep. He was aware that they were all intrigued by the tableau presented by his father and himself, that they were all vaguely cognizant of an unnamed and deadly tension. From his knees on the deck he called back (putting into his voice as much asperity, as much fury and hatred as he dared):

"Don't worry about me, Daddy. Roy'll see to it that I behave."

There was a silence after he said this; and he rose to his feet and saw that they were all watching him. David looked pitying and shocked, Roy's head was bowed and he looked apologetic. His father called:

"Excuse yourself, Johnnie, and come here."

"Excuse me," he said, and walked over to his father. He looked up into his father's face with an anger which surprised and even frightened him. But he did not drop his eyes, knowing that his father saw there (and he wanted him to see it) how much he hated him.

"What did you say?" his father asked.

"I said you don't have to worry about me. I don't think I'll get into any mischief." And his voice surprised him, it was more deliberately cold and angry than he had intended and there was a sardonic stress on the word "mischief." He knew that his father would then and there have knocked him down if they had not been in the presence of saints and strangers.

"You be careful how you speak to me. Don't you get grown too fast. We get home, I'll pull down those long pants and we'll see who's the man, you hear me?"

Yes we will, he thought and said nothing. He looked with a deliberate casualness about the deck. Then they felt the lurch of the boat as it began to move from the pier. There was an excited raising of voices and "I'll see you later," his father said and turned away.

He stood still, trying to compose himself to return to Mrs. Jackson and Lorraine. But as he turned with his hands in his pants' pockets he saw that David and Roy were coming toward him and he stopped and waited for them.

"It's a bitch," Roy said.

David looked at him, shocked. "That's no language for a saved boy." He put his arm around Johnnie's shoulder. "We're off to Bear Mountain," he cried, "*up* the glorious Hudson"—and he made a brutal gesture with his thumb.

"Now suppose Sylvia saw you do that," said Roy, "what would you say, huh?"

"We needn't worry about her," Johnnie said. "She'll be sitting with the old folks all day long."

"Oh, we'll figure out a way to take care of *them*," said David. He turned to Roy. "Now you the saved one, why don't you talk to Sister Daniels and distract her attention while we talk to the girl?

You the baby, anyhow, girl don't want to talk to you."

"I ain't got enough salvation to talk to that hag," Roy said. "I got a Daddy-made salvation. I'm saved when I'm with Daddy." They laughed and Roy added, "And I ain't no baby, either, I got everything my Daddy got."

"And a lot your Daddy don't dream of," David said.

Oh, thought Johnnie, with a sudden, vicious, chilling anger, *he doesn't have to dream about it!*

"Now let's act like we Christians," David said. "If we was real smart now, we'd go over to where she's sitting with all those people and act like we wanted to hear about God. Get on the good side of her mother."

"And suppose *he* comes back?" asked Johnnie.

Gabriel was sitting at the other end of the boat, talking with his wife. "Maybe he'll stay there," David said; there was a note of apology in his voice.

They approached the saints.

"Praise the Lord," they said sedately.

"Well, praise Him," Father James said. "How are you young men today?" He grabbed Roy by the shoulder. "Are you coming along in the Lord?"

"Yes, sir," Roy muttered, "I'm trying." He smiled into Father James's face.

"It's a wonderful thing," Brother Elisha said, "to give up to the Lord in your youth." He looked up at Johnnie and David. "Why don't you boys surrender? Ain't nothing in the world for you, I'll tell you that. He says, 'Remember thy Creator in the days of thy youth when the evil days come not.'"

"Amen," said Sister Daniels. "We're living in the last days, children. Don't think because you're young you got plenty of time. God takes the young as well as the old. You got to hold yourself in readiness all the time lest when He comes He catch you unprepared. Yes sir. Now's the time."

"You boys going to come to service today, ain't you?" asked Sister McCandless. "We're going to have service on the ship, you know." She looked at Father James. "Reckon we'll start as soon as we get a little further up the river, won't we, Father?"

"Yes," Father James said, "we're going to praise God right in the middle of the majestic Hudson." He leaned back and released Roy as he spoke. "Want to see you children there. I want to hear you make a *noise* for the Lord."

"I ain't never seen none of these young men Shout," said Sister Daniels, regarding them with distrust. She looked at David and Johnnie. "Don't believe I've ever even heard you testify."

"We're not saved yet, sister," David told her gently.

"That's alright," Sister Daniels said. "You *could* get up and praise the Lord for your life, health and strength. Praise Him for what you got, He'll give you something more."

"That's the truth," said Brother Elisha. He smiled at Sylvia. "I'm a witness, bless the Lord."

"They going to make a noise yet," said Sister McCandless. "Lord's going to touch everyone of these young men one day and bring them on their knees to the altar. You mark my words, you'll see." And she smiled at them.

"You just stay around the house of God long enough," Father James said. "One of these days the Spirit'll jump on you. I won't never forget the day It jumped on me."

"That *is* the truth," Sister McCandless cried, "so glad It jumped on me one day, hallelujah!"

"Amen," Sister Daniels cried, "amen."

"Looks like we're having a little service right now," Brother Elisha said smiling. Father James laughed heartily and cried, "Well, praise Him anyhow."

"I believe next week the church is going to start a series of revival meetings," Brother Elisha said. "I want to see you boys at every one of them, you hear?" He laughed as he spoke and added as David seemed about to protest, "No, no, brother, don't want no excuses. You *be* there. Get you boys to the altar, then maybe you'll pay more attention in Sunday School."

At this they all laughed and Sylvia said in her mild voice, looking mockingly at Roy, "Maybe we'll even see Brother Roy Shout." Roy grinned.

"Like to see you do some Shouting too," her mother grumbled. "You got to get closer to the Lord." Sylvia smiled and bit her lip; she cast a glance at David.

"Now everybody ain't got the same kind of spirit," Brother Elisha said, coming to Sylvia's aid. "Can't *all* make as much noise as you make," he said, laughing gently, "we all ain't got your energy."

Sister Daniels smiled and frowned at this reference to her size and passion and said, "Don't care, brother, when the Lord moves inside you, you bound to do something. I've seen that girl Shout all night and come back the next night and Shout some more. I don't believe in no dead religion, no sir. The saints of God need a revival."

"Well, we'll work on Sister Sylvia," said Brother Elisha.

Directly before and behind them stretched nothing but the river, they had long ago lost sight of the point of their departure. They steamed beside the Palisades, which rose rough and gigantic from the dirty, broad and blue-green Hudson. Johnnie and David and Roy wandered downstairs to the bottom deck, standing by the rail and leaning over to watch the white, writhing spray which followed the boat. From the river there floated up to their faces a soft, cool breeze. They were quiet for a long time, standing together, watching the river and the mountains and hearing vaguely the hum of activity behind them on the boat. The sky was high and blue, with here and there a spittle-like, changing cloud; the sun was orange and beat with anger on their uncovered heads.

And David muttered finally, "Be funny if they were right."

"If who was right?" asked Roy.

"Elisha and them—"

"There's only one way to find out," said Johnnie.

"Yes," said Roy, "and I ain't homesick for heaven yet."

"You always got to be so smart," David said.

"Oh," said Roy, "you just sore because Sylvia's still up there with Brother Elisha."

"You think they going to be married?" Johnnie asked.

"Don't talk like a fool," David said.

"Well it's a cinch you ain't never going to get to talk to her till you get saved," Johnnie said. He had meant to say "we." He looked at David and smiled.

"Might be worth it," David said.

"*What* might be worth it?" Roy asked, grinning.

"Now be nice," David said. He flushed, the dark blood rising beneath the dark skin. "How you expect me to get saved if you going to talk that way? You supposed to be an example."

"Don't look at me, boy," Roy said.

"I want you to talk to Johnnie," Gabriel said to his wife.

"What about?"

"That boy's pride is running away with him. Ask him to tell you what he said to me this morning soon as he got in front of his friends. He's your son, alright."

"What did he say?"

He looked darkly across the river. "You ask him to tell you about it tonight. I wanted to knock him down."

She had watched the scene and knew this. She looked at her husband briefly, feeling a sudden, outraged anger, barely conscious; sighed and turned to look at her youngest child where he sat involved in a complicated and strenuous and apparently joyless game which utilized a red ball, jacks, blocks and a broken shovel.

"I'll talk to him," she said at last. "He'll be alright." She wondered what on earth she would say to him; and what he would say to her. She looked covertly about the boat, but he was nowhere to be seen.

"That proud demon's just eating him up," he said bitterly. He watched the river hurtle past. "Be the best thing in the world if the Lord would take his soul." He had meant to say "save" his soul.

Now it was noon and all over the boat there was the activity of lunch. Paper bags and huge baskets were opened. There was then revealed splendor: cold pork chops, cold chicken, bananas, apples, oranges, pears, and soda-pop, candy and cold lemonade. All over the boat the chosen of God relaxed; they sat in groups and talked and laughed; some of the more worldly gossiped and some of the more courageous young people dared to walk off together. Beneath them the strong, indifferent river raged within the channel and the screaming spray pursued them. In the engine room children watched the motion of the ship's gears as they rose and fell and chanted. The tremendous bolts of steel seemed almost human, imbued with a relentless force that was not human. There was something monstrous about this machine which bore such enormous weight and cargo.

Sister Daniels threw a paper bag over the side and wiped her mouth with her large handkerchief. "Sylvia, you be careful how you speak to these unsaved boys," she said.

"Yes, I am, Mama."

"Don't like the way that little Jackson boy looks at you. That child's got a demon. You be careful."

"Yes, Mama."

"You got plenty of time to be thinking about boys. Now's the time for you to be thinking about the Lord."

"Yes'm."

"You *mind* now," her mother said.

"Mama, I want to go home!" Lois cried. She crawled into her mother's arms, weeping.

"Why, what's the matter, honey?" She rocked her daughter gently. "Tell Mama what's the matter? Have you got a pain?"

"I want to go home, I want to go home." Lois sobbed.

"A very fine preacher, a man of God and a friend of mine will run the service for us," said Father James.

"Maybe you've heard about him—a Reverend Peters? A real man of God, amen."

"I thought," Gabriel said, smiling, "that perhaps I could bring the message some Sunday night. The Lord called me a long time ago. I used to have my own church down home."

"You don't want to run too fast, Deacon Grimes," Father James said. "You just take your time. You been coming along right well on Young Ministers' Nights." He paused and looked at Gabriel. "Yes, indeed."

"I just thought," Gabriel said humbly, "that I could be used to more advantage in the house of God."

Father James quoted the text which tells us how preferable it is to be a gate-keeper in the house of God than to dwell in the tent of the wicked; and started to add the dictum from Saint Paul about obedience to those above one in the Lord but decided (watching Gabriel's face) that it was not necessary yet.

"You just keep praying," he said kindly. "You get a little closer to God. He'll work wonders. You'll see." He bent closer to his deacon. "And try to get just a little closer to the *people*."

Roy wandered off with a gawky and dazzled girl named Elizabeth. Johnnie and David wandered restlessly up and down the boat alone. They mounted to the topmost deck and leaned over the railing in the deserted stern. Up here the air was sharp and clean. They faced the water, their arms around each other.

"Your old man was kind of rough this morning," David said carefully, watching the mountains pass.

"Yes," Johnnie said. He looked at David's face against the sky. He shivered suddenly in the sharp, cold air and buried his face in David's shoulder. David looked down at him and tightened his hold.

"Who do you love?" he whispered. "Who's your boy?"

"You," he muttered fiercely, "I love you."

"Roy!" Elizabeth giggled, *"Roy Grimes.* If you *ever* say a thing like that *again."*

Now the service was beginning. From all corners of the boat there was the movement of the saints of God. They gathered together their various possessions and moved their chairs from top and bottom decks to the large main hall. It was early afternoon, not quite two o'clock. The sun was high and fell everywhere with a copper light. In the city the heat would have been insupportable; and here, as the saints filed into the huge, high room, once used as a ballroom, to judge from the faded and antique appointments, the air slowly began to be oppressive. The room was the color of black mahogany and coming in from the bright deck, one groped suddenly in darkness; and took one's sense of direction from the elegant grand piano which stood in the front of the room on a little platform.

They sat in small rows with one wide aisle between them, forming, almost unconsciously, a hierarchy. Father James sat in the front next to Sister McCandless. Opposite them sat Gabriel and Deacon Jones and, immediately behind them, Sister Daniels and her daughter. Brother Elisha walked in swiftly, just as they were beginning to be settled. He strode to the piano and knelt down for a second before rising to take his place. There was a quiet stir, the saints adjusted themselves, waiting while Brother Elisha tentatively ran his fingers over the keys. Gabriel looked about impatiently for Roy and Johnnie, who, engaged no doubt in sinful conversation with David, were not yet in service. He looked back to where Mrs. Jackson sat with Lorraine, uncomfortable smiles on their faces, and glanced at his wife, who met his questioning regard quietly, the expression on her face not changing.

Brother Elisha struck the keys and the congregation joined in the song, "Nothing Shall Move Me from the Love of God", with tambourine and heavy hands and stomping feet. The walls and the floor of the ancient hall trembled and the candelabra wavered in the high ceiling. Outside the river rushed past under the heavy shadow of the Palisades and the copper sun beat down. A few of the strangers who had come along on the outing appeared at the doors and stood watching with an uneasy amusement. The saints sang on, raising their strong voices in praises to Jehovah, and seemed unaware of those unsaved who watched and who, some day, the power of the Lord might cause to tremble.

The song ended as Father James rose and faced the congregation, a broad smile on his face. They watched him expectantly, with love. He stood silent for a moment, smiling down upon them. Then he said, and his voice was loud and filled with triumph:

"Well, let us all say, Amen!"

And they cried out obediently, "Well, Amen!"

"Let us all say, praise Him!"

"Praise Him!"

"Let us all say, hallelujah!"

"Hallelujah!"

"Well, glory!" cried Father James. The Holy Ghost touched him and he cried again, "Well, bless Him! Bless His holy name!"

They laughed and shouted after him, their joy so great that they laughed as children and some of them cried as children do; in the fullness and assurance of salvation, in the knowledge that the Lord was in their midst and that each heart, swollen to anguish, yearned only to be filled with His glory. Then, in that moment, each of them might have mounted with wings like eagles far past the sordid persistence of the flesh, the depthless iniquity of the heart, the doom of hours and days and weeks; to be received by the Bridegroom where He waited on high in glory; where all tears were wiped away and death had no power; where the wicked ceased from troubling and the weary soul found rest.

"Saints, let's praise Him," Father James said. "Today, right in the middle of God's great river, under God's great roof, beloved, let us raise our voices in thanksgiving that God has seen fit to save us, amen!"

"Amen! Hallelujah!"

"—and to keep us saved, amen, to keep us, oh glory to God, from the snares of Satan, from the temptation and the lust and the evil of this world!"

"Talk about it!"

"*Preach!*"

"Ain't nothing strange, amen, about worshipping God *wherever* you might be, ain't that right? Church, when you get this mighty salvation you just can't keep it in, hallelujah! you got to talk about it—"

"Amen!"

"You got to live it, amen. When the Holy Ghost touches you, you *move*, bless God!"

"Well, it's so!"

"Want to hear some testimonies today, amen! I want to hear some *singing* today, bless God! Want to see some *Shouting*, bless God, hallelujah!"

"Talk about it!"

"And I don't want to see none of the saints hold back. If the Lord saved you, amen, He give you a witness *every*where you go. Yes! My soul is a witness, bless our God!"

"Glory!"

"If you ain't saved, amen, get up and praise Him anyhow. Give God the glory for sparing your sinful life, *praise* Him for the sunshine and the rain, praise Him for all the works of His hands. Saints, I want to hear some praises today, you hear me? I want you to make this old boat *rock*, hallelujah! I want to *feel* your salvation. Are you saved?"

"Amen!"

"Are you sanctified?"

"Glory!"

"Baptized in fire?"

"Yes! So glad!"

"*Testify!*"

Now the hall was filled with a rushing wind on which forever rides the Lord, death or healing indifferently in His hands. Under this fury the saints bowed low, crying out "holy!" and tears fell. On the open deck sinners stood and watched, beyond them the fiery sun and the deep river, the black-brown-green, unchanging cliffs. That sun, which covered earth and water now, would one day refuse to shine, the river would cease its rushing and its numberless dead would rise; the cliffs would shiver, crack, fall and where they had been would then be nothing but the unleashed wrath of God.

"Who'll be the first to tell it?" Father James cried. "Stand up and talk about it!"

Brother Elisha screamed, "Have mercy, Jesus!" and rose from the piano stool, his powerful frame possessed. And the Holy Ghost touched him and he cried again, bending nearly double, while his feet beat ageless, dreadful signals on the floor, while his arms moved in the air like wings and his face, distorted, no longer his own face not the face of a young man, but timeless, anguished, grim with ecstasy, turned blindly toward heaven. *Yes, Lord,* they cried, *yes!*

"Dearly beloved ..."

"Talk about it!"

"Tell it!"

"I want to thank and praise the Lord, amen ..."

"Amen!"

"... for being here, I want to thank Him for my life, health, and strength...."

"Amen!"

"Well, glory!"

"... I want to thank Him, hallelujah, for saving my soul one day...."

"Oh!"

"Glory!"

"... for causing the light, bless God, to shine in my heart one day when I was still a child, amen, I want to thank Him for bringing me to salvation in the days of my *youth*, hallelujah, when I have all my faculties, amen, before Satan had a chance to destroy my body in the world!"

"Talk about it!"

"He saved me, dear ones, from the world and the things of the world. Saved me, amen, from cardplaying ..."

"Glory!"

"... saved me from drinking, bless God, saved me from the streets, from the movies and all the filth that is in the world!"

"I *know* it's so!"

"He saved me, beloved, and sanctified me and filled me with the blessed Holy Ghost, *hallelujah!* Give me a new song, amen, which I didn't know before and set my feet on the King's highway. Pray for me beloved, that I will stand in these last and evil days."

"Bless your name, Jesus!"

During his testimony Johnnie and Roy and David had stood quietly beside the door, not daring to enter while he spoke. The moment he sat down they moved quickly, together, to the front of the high hall and knelt down beside their seats to pray. The aspect of each of them underwent always, in this company a striking, even an exciting change; as though their youth, barely begun, were already put away; and the animal, so vividly restless and undiscovered, so tense with power, ready to spring had been already stalked and trapped and offered, a perpetual blood-sacrifice, on the altar of the Lord. Yet their bodies continued to change and grow, preparing them, mysteriously and with ferocious speed, for manhood. No matter how careful their movements, these movements suggested, with a distinctness dreadful for the redeemed to see, the pagan lusting beneath the blood-washed robes. In them was perpetually and perfectly poised the power of revelation against the power of nature; and the saints, considering them with a baleful kind of love, struggled to bring their souls to safety in order, as it were, to steal a march on the flesh while the flesh still slept. A kind of storm, infernal, blew over the congregation as they passed; someone cried, "Bless them, Lord!" and immediately, honey-colored Sister Russell, while they knelt in prayer, rose to her feet to testify.

From the moment that they closed their eyes and covered their faces they were isolated from the joy that moved everything beside them. Yet this same isolation served only to make the glory of the saints more real, the pulse of conviction, however faint, beat in and the glory of God then held an undertone of abject terror. Roy was the first to rise, sitting very straight in his seat and allowing his face to reveal nothing; just as Sister Russell ended her testimony and sat down, sobbing, her head thrown back and both hands raised to heaven. Immediately Sister Daniels raised her strong, harsh voice and hit her tambourine, singing. Brother Elisha turned on the piano stool and hit the keys. Johnnie and David rose from their knees and as they rose the congregation rose, clapping their hands singing. The three boys did not sing; they stood together, carefully ignoring one another, their feet steady on the slightly tilting floor but their bodies moving back and forth as the music grew more savage. And someone cried aloud, a timeless sound of wailing; fire splashed the open deck and filled the doors and bathed the sinners standing there; fire filled the great hall and splashed the faces of the saints and a wind, unearthly, moved about their heads. Their hands were arched before them, moving, and their eyes were raised to heaven. Sweat stained the deacon's collar and soaked the tight headbands of the women. Was it true then? and had there indeed been born one day in Bethlehem a Saviour who was Christ the Lord? who had died for them—for *them!*—the spat-upon and beaten with rods, who had worn a crown of thorns and seen His blood run down like rain; and who had lain in the grave three days and vanquished death and hell and risen again in glory— *was it for them?*

Lord, I want to go, show me the way!

For unto us a child is born, unto us a son is given—and His name shall be called Wonderful, the mighty God, the everlasting Father, the Prince of Peace. Yes, and He was coming back one day, the King of glory; He would crack the face of heaven and descend to judge the nations and gather up His people and take them to their rest.

Take me by my hand and lead me on!

Somewhere in the back a woman cried out and began the Shout. They looked carefully about, still not looking at one another, and saw, as from a great distance and through intolerable heat, such heat as might have been faced by the Hebrew children when cast bound into the fiery furnace, that one of the saints was dancing under the arm of the Lord. She danced out into the aisle, beautiful with a beauty unbearable, graceful with grace that poured from heaven. Her face was lifted up, her eyes were closed and the feet which moved so surely now were not her own. One by one the power of God moved others and—as it had been written—the Holy Ghost descended from heaven with a Shout. Sylvia raised her hands, the tears poured down her face, and in a moment, she too moved out into the aisle, Shouting. Is it true then? the saints rejoiced, Roy beat the tambourine. David, grave and shaken, clapped his hands and his body moved insistently in the rhythm of the dancers. Johnnie stood beside him, hot and faint and repeating yet again his struggle, summoning in panic all his forces, to save him from this frenzy. And yet daily he recognized that he was black with sin, that the secrets of his heart were a stench in God's nostrils. *Though your sins be as scarlet they shall be white as snow. Come, let us reason together, saith the Lord.*

Now there was a violent discord on the piano and Brother Elisha leapt to his feet, dancing. Johnnie watched the spinning body and listened, in terror and anguish, to the bestial sobs. Of the men it was only Elisha who danced and the women moved toward him and he moved toward the women. Johnnie felt blow over him an icy wind, all his muscles tightened, as though they furiously resisted some imminent bloody act, as the body of Isaac must have revolted when he saw his father's knife, and, sick and nearly sobbing, he closed his eyes. It was Satan, surely, who stood so foully at his shoulder; and what, but the blood of Jesus, should ever set him free? He thought of the many times he had stood in the congregation of the righteous—and yet he was not saved. He remained among the vast army of the doomed, whose lives—as he had been told, as he now, with such heart-sickness, began to discover for himself—were swamped with wretchedness and whose end was wrath and weeping. Then, for he felt himself falling, he opened his eyes and watched the rejoicing of the saints. His eyes found his father where he stood clapping his hands, glittering with sweat and overwhelming. Then Lois began to shout. For the first time he looked at Roy; their eyes met in brief, wry wonder and Roy imperceptibly shrugged. He watched his mother standing over Lois, her own face obscurely troubled. The light from the door was on her face, the entire room was filled with this strange light. There was no sound now except the sound of Roy's tambourine and the heavy rhythm of the saints; the sound of heavy feet and hands and the sound of weeping. Perhaps centuries past the children of Israel led by Miriam had made just such a noise as they came out of the wilderness. *For unto us is born this day a Savior who is Christ the Lord.*

Yet, in the copper sunlight Johnnie felt suddenly, not the presence of the Lord, but the presence of David; which seemed to reach out to him, hand reaching out to hand in the fury of flood-time, to drag him to the bottom of the water or to carry him safe to shore. From the corner of his eye he watched his friend, who held him with such power; and felt, for that moment, such a depth of love, such nameless and terrible joy and pain, that he might have fallen, in the face of that company, weeping at David's feet.

Once at Bear Mountain they faced the very great problem of carrying Sylvia sufficiently far from her mother's sight to present her with her birthday present. This problem, difficult enough, was made even more difficult by the continual presence of Brother Elisha; who, inspired by the afternoon's service and by Sylvia's renewal of her faith, remained by her side to bear witness to the goodness and power of the Lord. Sylvia listened with her habitual rapt and painful smile. Her mother, on the one side and Brother Elisha on the other, seemed almost to be taking turns in advising her on her conduct as a saint of

God. They began to despair, as the sun moved visibly westward, of ever giving her the gold-plated butterfly which rested uncomfortably in David's waistcoat pocket.

Of course, as Johnnie once suggested, there was really no reason they could not go up to her, surrounded as she was, and give her the jewel and get it over with—the more particularly as David evinced a desire to explore the wonders of Bear Mountain until this mission should have been fulfilled. Sister Daniels could scarcely object to an innocuous memento from three young men, all of whom attended church devoutly and one of whom professed salvation. But this was far from satisfactory for David, who did not wish to hear Sylvia's "thank-you's" in the constricting presence of the saints. Therefore they waited, wandering about the sloping park, lingering near the lake and the skating rink and watching Sylvia.

"God, why don't they go off somewhere and sleep? or pray?" cried David finally. He glared at the nearby rise where Sylvia and her mother sat talking with Brother Elisha. The sun was in their faces and struck from Sylvia's hair as she restlessly moved her head, small blue-black sparks.

Johnnie swallowed his jealousy at seeing how Sylvia filled his comrade's mind; he said, half-angrily, "I still don't see why we don't just go over and give it to her."

Roy looked at him. "Boy, you sound like you ain't got good sense," he said.

Johnnie, frowning, fell into silence. He glanced sidewise at David's puckered face (his eyes were still on Sylvia) and abruptly turned and started walking off.

"Where you going, boy?" David called.

"I'll be back," he said. And he prayed that David would follow him.

But David was determined to catch Sylvia alone and remained where he was with Roy. "Well, make it snappy," he said; and sprawled, full length, on the grass.

As soon as he was alone his pace slackened; he leaned his forehead against the bark of a tree, shaking and burning as in the teeth of a fever. The bark of the tree was rough and cold and though it offered no other comfort he stood there quietly for a long time, seeing beyond him—but it brought no peace—the high clear sky where the sun in fading glory traveled; and the deep earth covered with vivid banners, grass, flower, thorn and vine, thrusting upward forever the brutal trees. At his back he heard the voices of the children and the saints. He knew that he must return, that he must be on hand should David at last outwit Sister Daniels and present her daughter with the golden butterfly. But he did not want to go back, now he realized that he had no interest in the birthday present, no interest whatever in Sylvia— that he had had no interest all along. He shifted his stance, he turned from the tree as he turned his mind from the abyss which suddenly yawned, that abyss, depthless and terrifying, which he had encountered already in dreams. And he slowly began to walk, away from the saints and the voices of the children, his hands in his pockets, struggling to ignore the question which now screamed and screamed in his mind's bright haunted house.

It happened quite simply. Eventually Sister Daniels felt the need to visit the ladies' room, which was a long ways off. Brother Elisha remained where he was while Roy and David, like two beasts crouching in the underbrush, watched him and waited their opportunity. Then he also rose and wandered off to get cold lemonade for Sylvia. She sat quietly alone on the green rise, her hands clasped around her knees, dreaming.

They walked over to her, in terror that Sister Daniels would suddenly reappear. Sylvia smiled as she saw them coming and waved to them merrily. Roy grinned and threw himself on his belly on the ground beside her. David remained standing, fumbling in his waistcoat pocket.

"We got something for you," Roy said.

David produced the butterfly. "Happy birthday, Sylvia," he said. He stretched out his hand, the butterfly glinted oddly in the sun, and he realized with surprise that his hand was shaking. She grinned widely, in amazement and delight, and took the pin from him.

"It's from Johnnie, too," he said. "I—we—hope you like it—"

She held the small gold pin in her palm and stared down at it; her face was hidden. After a moment she murmured, "I'm so surprised." She looked up, her eyes shining, almost wet. "Oh, it's wonderful," she said. "I never expected anything. I don't know what to say. It's marvelous, it's wonderful." She pinned the butterfly carefully to her light blue dress. She coughed slightly. "Thank you," she said.

"Your mother won't mind, will she?" Roy asked. "I mean—" he

stammered awkwardly under Sylvia's sudden gaze—"we didn't know, we didn't want to get you in any trouble—"

"No," David said. He had not moved; he stood watching Sylvia. Sylvia looked away from Roy and up at David, his eyes met hers and she smiled. He smiled back, suddenly robbed of speech. She looked away again over the path her mother had taken and frowned slightly. "No," she said, "no, she won't mind."

Then there was silence. David shifted uncomfortably from one foot to the other. Roy lay contentedly face down on the grass. The breeze from the river, which lay below them and out of sight, grew subtly more insistent for they had passed the heat of the day; and the sun, moving always westward, fired and polished the tips of trees. Sylvia sighed and shifted on the ground.

"Why isn't Johnnie here?" she suddenly asked.

"He went off somewhere," Roy said. "He said he'd be right back." He looked at Sylvia and smiled. She was looking at David.

"You must want to grow real tall," she said mockingly. "Why don't you sit down?"

David grinned and sat down cross-legged next to Sylvia. "Well, the ladies like 'em tall." He lay on his back and stared up at the sky. "It's a fine day," he said.

She said, "Yes," and looked down at him; he had closed his eyes and was bathing his face in the slowly waning sun. Abruptly, she asked him:

"Why don't you get saved? You around the church all the time and you not saved yet? Why don't you?"

He opened his eyes in amazement. Never before had Sylvia mentioned salvation to him, except as a kind of joke. One of the things he most liked about her was the fact that she never preached to him. Now he smiled uncertainly and stared at her.

"I'm not joking," she said sharply. "I'm perfectly serious. Roy's saved—at least he *says* so—" and she smiled darkly, in the fashion of the old folks, at Roy—"and anyway, you ought to be thinking about your soul."

"Well, I don't know," David said. "I *think* about it. It's—well, I don't know if I can—well, live it—"

"All you got to do is make up your mind. If you really want to be saved, He'll save you. Yes, and He'll keep you too." She did not sound at all hysterical or transfigured. She spoke very quietly and with great earnestness and frowned as she spoke. David, taken off guard, said nothing. He looked embarrassed and pained and surprised. "Well, I don't know," he finally repeated.

"Do you ever pray?" she asked. "I mean, *really* pray?"

David laughed, beginning to recover himself. "It's not fair," he said, "you oughtn't to catch me all unprepared like that. Now I don't know what to say." But as he looked at her earnest face he sobered. "Well, I try to be decent. I don't bother nobody." He picked up a grass blade and stared at it. "I don't know," he said at last. "I do my best."

"*Do* you?" she asked.

He laughed again, defeated. "Girl," he said, "you *are* a killer."

She laughed too. "You black-eyed demon," she said, "if I don't see you at revival services I'll never speak to you again." He looked up quickly, in some surprise, and she said, still smiling, "Don't look at me like that. I mean it."

"All right, sister," he said. Then: "If I come out can I walk you home?"

"I got my mother to walk me home—"

"Well, let your mother walk home with Brother Elisha," he said, grinning, "Let the old folks stay together."

"Loose him, Satan!" she cried, laughing, "loose the boy!"

"The brother needs prayer," Roy said.

"Amen," said Sylvia. She looked down again at David. "I want to see you at church. Don't you forget it."

"All right," he said. "I'll be there."

The boat whistles blew at six o'clock, punctuating their holiday; blew, fretful and insistent, through the abruptly dispirited park and skaters left the skating rink; boats were rowed in furiously from the lake. Children were called from the swings and the seesaw and the merry-go-round and forced to leave behind the ball which had been lost in the forest and the torn kite which dangled from the top of a tree. ("Hush now," said their parents, "we'll get you another one—come along." *"Tomorrow?"*—"Come along, honey, it's time to go!") The old folks rose from the benches, from the grass, gathered together the empty lunch-basket, the half-read newspaper, the Bible which was carried everywhere; and they started down the hillside, an army in disorder. David walked with Sylvia and Sister Daniels and Brother Elisha, listening to their conversation (good Lord, thought Johnnie, don't they ever mention anything but sin?) and carrying Sylvia's lunch-basket. He seemed interested in what they were saying; every now and then he looked at Sylvia and grinned and she grinned back. Once, as Sylvia stumbled, he put his hand on her elbow to steady her and held her arm perhaps a moment too long. Brother Elisha, on the far side of Sister Daniels, noticed this and a frown passed over his face. He kept talking, staring now and then hard at Sylvia and trying, with a certain almost humorous helplessness, to discover what was in her mind. Sister Daniels talked of nothing but the service on the boat and of the forthcoming revival. She scarcely seemed to notice David's presence, though once she spoke to him, making some remark about the need, on his part, of much prayer. Gabriel carried the sleeping baby in his arms, striding beside his wife and Lois—who stumbled perpetually and held tightly to her mother's hand. Roy was somewhere in the back, joking with Elizabeth. At a turn in the road the boat and the dock appeared below them, a dead gray-white in the sun.

Johnnie walked down the slope alone, watching David and Sylvia ahead of him. When he had come back, both Roy and David had disappeared and Sylvia sat again in the company of her mother and Brother Elisha; and if he had not seen the gold butterfly on her dress he would have been aware of no change. She thanked him for his share in it and told him that Roy and David were at the skating rink.

But when at last he found them they were far in the middle of the lake in a rowboat. He was afraid of water, he could not row. He stood on the bank and watched them. After a long while they saw him and waved and started to bring the boat in so that he could join them. But the day was ruined for him; by the time they brought the boat in, the hour, for which they had hired it, was over; David went in search of his mother for more money but when he came back it was time to leave. Then he walked with Sylvia.

All during the trip home David seemed preoccupied. When he finally sought out Johnnie he found him sitting by himself on the top deck, shivering a little in the night air. He sat down beside him. After a moment Johnnie moved and put his head on David's shoulder. David put his arms around him. But now where there had been peace there was only panic and where there had been safety, danger, like a flower, opened.

The Cinderella Waltz

Ann Beattie

The dictionary defines "family" as "a group of kindred people". Upon this generous notion, Western society used to impose the restriction of two parents of different sexes and their dependent children, with the male parent in full charge. Other societies have admitted more fluid formations. In Polynesia, children flock around an adult, usually a woman, who becomes the mother of the group. Among the Mormons, the patriarch rules over a family of not one but several women. Among the Onas of Patagonia, the grandparents raise the children and share the authority with the parents. Our society has come to recognize the single-parent family and is beginning to entertain the idea of two parents of the same sex. Whether these variations would have satisfied Gide, who condemned all families with the exclamation "Families, I hate you!", we don't know. It may be that, no matter what the arrangement, we are destined to form groups only to make one another's lives miserable.

"The Cinderella Waltz" explores two family variations—a single mother, and a gay father and his mate—but the story's core lies not in the sexual identities of its characters but rather in the complex relationships created by that creature we call "family". The American writer David Leavitt's advice to the reader seems useful here: "The sexuality of the characters is less important than the situation that they're in, which may be caused by their sexuality but is ultimately more interesting than that fact in itself."

Milo and Bradley are creatures of habit. For as long as I've known him, Milo has worn his moth-eaten blue scarf with the knot hanging so low on his chest that the scarf is useless. Bradley is addicted to coffee and carries a Thermos with him. Milo complains about the cold, and Bradley is always a little edgy. They come out from the city every

Saturday—this is not habit but loyalty—to pick up Louise. Louise is even more unpredictable than most nine-year-olds; sometimes she waits for them on the front step, sometimes she hasn't even gotten out of bed when they arrive. One time she hid in a closet and wouldn't leave with them.

Today Louise has put together a shopping bag full of things she wants to take with her. She is taking my whisk and my blue pottery bowl, to make Sunday breakfast for Milo and Bradley; Beckett's *Happy Days*, which she has carried around for weeks, and which she looks through, smiling—but I'm not sure she's reading it; and a coleus growing out of a conch shell. Also, she has stuffed into one side of the bag the fancy Victorian-style nightgown her grandmother gave her for Christmas, and into the other she has tucked her octascope. Milo keeps a couple of dresses, a nightgown, a toothbrush, and extra sneakers and boots at his apartment for her. He got tired of rounding up her stuff to pack for her to take home, so he has brought some things for her that can be left. It annoys him that she still packs bags, because then he has to go around making sure that she has found everything before she goes home. She seems to know how to manipulate him, and after the weekend is over she calls tearfully to say that she has left this or that, which means that he must get his car out of the garage and drive all the way out to the house to bring it to her. One time, he refused to take the hour-long drive, because she had only left a copy of Tolkien's *The Two Towers*. The following weekend was the time she hid in the closet.

"I'll water your plant if you leave it here," I say now.

"I can take it," she says.

"I didn't say you couldn't take it. I just thought it might be easier to leave it, because if the shell tips over the plant might get ruined."

"O.K.," she says. "Don't water it today, though. Water it Sunday afternoon."

I reach for the shopping bag.

"I'll put it back on my window sill," she says. She lifts the plant out and carries it as if it's made of Steuben glass. Bradley bought it for her last month, driving back to the city, when they stopped at a lawn sale. She and Bradley are both very choosy, and he likes that. He drinks French-roast coffee; she will debate with herself almost endlessly over whether to buy a coleus that is primarily pink or lavender or striped.

"Has Milo made any plans for this weekend?" I ask.

"He's having a couple of people over tonight, and I'm going to help them make crêpes for dinner. If they buy more bottles of that wine with the yellow flowers on the label, Bradley is going to soak the labels off for me."

"That's nice of him," I say. "He never minds taking a lot of time with things."

"He doesn't like to cook, though. Milo and I are going to cook. Bradley sets the table and fixes flowers in a bowl. He thinks it's frustrating to cook."

"Well," I say, "with cooking you have to have a good sense of timing. You have to coordinate everything. Bradley likes to work carefully and not be rushed."

I wonder how much she knows. Last week she told me about a conversation she'd had with her friend Sarah. Sarah was trying to persuade Louise to stay around on the weekends, but Louise said she always went to her father's. Then Sarah tried to get her to take her along, and Louise said she couldn't. "You could take her if you wanted to," I said later, "Check with Milo and see if that isn't right. I don't think he'd mind having a friend of yours occasionally."

She shrugged. "Bradley doesn't like a lot of people around," she said.

"Bradley likes you, and if she's your friend I don't think he'd mind."

She looked at me with an expression I didn't recognize; perhaps she thought I was a little dumb, or perhaps she was just curious to see if I would go on. I didn't know how to go on. Like an adult, she gave a little shrug and changed the subject.

At ten o'clock Milo pulls into the driveway and honks his horn, which makes a noise like a bleating sheep. He knows the noise the horn makes is funny, and he means to amuse us. There was a time just after the divorce when he and Bradley would come here and get out of the car and stand around silently, waiting for her. She knew that she had to watch for them, because Milo wouldn't come to the door. We were both bitter then, but I got over it. I still don't think Milo would have come into the house again, though, if Bradley hadn't thought it was a good idea. The third time Milo came to pick her up after he'd left home, I went out to invite them in, but Milo said nothing. He was standing there with his arms at his sides like a wooden soldier, and his eyes were as dead to me as if they'd been painted on. It was Bradley whom I reasoned with. "Louise is over at Sarah's right now, and it'll make her feel more comfortable if we're all together when she comes in," I said to him, and Bradley turned to Milo and said, "Hey, that's right. Why don't we go in for a quick cup of coffee?" I looked into the back seat of the car and saw his red Thermos there; Louise had told me about it. Bradley meant that they should come in and sit down. He was giving me even more than I'd asked for.

It would be an understatement to say that I disliked Bradley at first. I was actually afraid of him, afraid even after I saw him, though he was slender, and more nervous than I, and spoke quietly. The second time I saw him, I persuaded myself that he was just a stereotype, but someone who certainly seemed harmless enough. By the third time, I had enough courage to suggest that they come into the house. It was embarrassing for all of us, sitting around the table—the same table where Milo and I had eaten our meals for the years we were married. Before he left, Milo had shouted at me that the house was a farce, that my playing the happy suburban housewife was a farce, that it was unconscionable of me to let things drag on, that I would probably kiss him and say, "How was your day, sweetheart?" and that he should bring home flowers and the evening paper. "Maybe I would!" I screamed back. "Maybe it would be nice to do that, even if we were pretending, instead of your coming home drunk and not caring what had happened to me or to Louise all day." He was holding on to the edge of the kitchen table, the way you'd hold on to the horse's reins in a runaway carriage. "I care about Louise," he said finally. That was the most horrible moment. Until then, until he said it that way, I had thought that he was going through something horrible—certainly something was terribly wrong—but that, in his way, he loved me after all. "*You don't love me?*" I had whispered at once. It took us both aback. It was an innocent and pathetic question, and it made him come and put his arms around me in the last hug he ever gave me. "I'm sorry for you," he said, "and I'm sorry for marrying you and causing this, but you know who I love, I told you who I love." "But you were kidding," I said. "You didn't mean it. You were kidding."

When Bradley sat at the table that first day, I tried to be polite and not look at him much. I had gotten it through my head that Milo was crazy, and I guess I was expecting Bradley to be a horrible parody—

Craig Russell doing Marilyn Monroe. Bradley did not spoon sugar into Milo's coffee. He did not even sit near him. In fact, he pulled his chair a little away from us, and in spite of his uneasiness he found more things to start conversations about than Milo and I did. He told me about the ad agency where he worked; he is a designer there. He asked if he could go out on the porch to see the brook—Milo had told him about the stream in the back of our place that was as thin as a pencil but still gave us our own watercress. He went out on the porch and stayed there for at least five minutes, giving us a chance to talk. We didn't say one word until he came back. Louise came home from Sarah's house just as Bradley sat down at the table again, and she gave him a hug as well as us. I could see that she really liked him. I was amazed that I liked him, too. Bradley had won and I had lost, but he was as gentle and low-key as if none of it mattered. Later in the week, I called him and asked him to tell me if any free-lance jobs opened in his advertising agency. (I do a little free-lance artwork, whenever I can arrange it.) The week after that, he called and told me about another agency, where they were looking for outside artists. Our calls to each other are always brief and for a purpose, but lately they're not just calls about business. Before Bradley left to scout some picture locations in Mexico, he called to say that Milo had told him that when the two of us were there years ago I had seen one of those big circular bronze Aztec calendars and I had always regretted not bringing it back. He wanted to know if I would like him to buy a calendar if he saw one like the one Milo had told him about.

Today, Milo is getting out of his car, his blue scarf flapping against his chest. Louise, looking out the window, asks the same thing I am wondering: "Where's Bradley?"

Milo comes in and shakes my hand, gives Louise a one-armed hug.

"Bradley thinks he's coming down with a cold," Milo says. "The dinner is still on, Louise. We'll do the dinner. We have to stop at Gristede's when we get back to town, unless your mother happens to have a tin of anchovies and two sticks of unsalted butter."

"Let's go to Gristede's," Louise says. "I like to go there."

"Let me look in the kitchen," I say. The butter is salted, but Milo says that will do, and he takes three sticks instead of two. I have a brainstorm and cut the cellophane on a leftover Christmas present from my aunt—a wicker plate that holds nuts and foil-wrapped triangles of cheese—and, sure enough: one tin of anchovies.

"We can go to the museum instead," Milo says to Louise. "Wonderful."

But then, going to the door, carrying her bag, he changes his mind. "We can go to America Hurrah, and if we see something beautiful we can buy it," he says.

They go off in high spirits. Louise comes up to his waist, almost, and I notice again that they have the same walk. Both of them stride forward with great purpose. Last week, Bradley told me that Milo had bought a weathervane in the shape of a horse, made around 1800, at America Hurrah, and stood it in the bedroom, and then was enraged when Bradley draped his socks over it to dry. Bradley is still learning what a perfectionist Milo is, and how little sense of humor he has. When we were first married, I used one of our pottery casserole dishes to put my jewelry in, and he nagged me until I took it out and put the dish back in the kitchen cabinet. I remember his saying that the dish looked silly on my dresser because it was obvious what it was and people would think we left our dishes lying around. It was one of the things that Milo wouldn't tolerate, because it was improper.

When Milo brings Louise back on Saturday night they are not in a good mood. The dinner was all right, Milo says, and Griffin and Amy and Mark were amazed at what a good hostess Louise had been, but Bradley hadn't been able to eat.

"Is he still coming down with a cold?" I ask. I was still a little shy about asking questions about Bradley.

Milo shrugs. "Louise made him take megadoses of vitamin C all weekend."

Louise says, "Bradley said that taking too much vitamin C was bad for your kidneys, though."

"It's a rotten climate," Milo says, sitting on the living-room sofa, scarf and coat still on. "The combination of cold and air pollution...."

Louise and I look at each other, and then back at Milo. For weeks now, he has been talking about moving to San Francisco, if he can find work there. (Milo is an architect.) This talk bores me, and it makes Louise nervous. I've asked him not to talk to her about it unless he's actually going to move, but he doesn't seem to be able to stop himself.

"O.K.," Milo says, looking at us both. "I'm not going to say anything about San Francisco."

"*California* is polluted," I say. I am unable to stop myself, either.

Milo heaves himself up from the sofa, ready for the drive back to New York. It is the same way he used to get off the sofa that last year he lived here. He would get up, dress for work, and not even go into the kitchen for breakfast—just sit, sometimes in his coat as he was sitting just now, and at the last minute he would push himself up and go out to the driveway, usually without a goodbye, and get in the car and drive off either very fast or very slowly. I liked it better when he made the tires spin in the gravel when he took off.

He stops at the doorway now, and turns to face me. "Did I take all your butter?" he says.

"No," I say. "There's another stick." I point into the kitchen.

"I could have guessed that's where it would be," he says, and smiles at me.

When Milo comes the next weekend, Bradley is still not with him. The night before, as I was putting Louise to bed, she said that she had a feeling he wouldn't be coming.

"I had that feeling a couple of days ago," I said. "Usually Bradley calls once during the week."

"He must still be sick," Louise said. She looked at me anxiously. "Do you think he is?"

"A cold isn't going to kill him," I said. "If he has a cold, he'll be O.K."

Her expression changed; she thought I was talking down to her. She lay back in bed. The last year Milo was with us, I used to tuck her in and tell her that everything was all right. What that meant was that there had not been a fight. Milo had sat listening to music on the phonograph, with a book or the newspaper in front of his face. He didn't pay very much attention to Louise, and he ignored me entirely. Instead of saying a prayer with her, the way I usually did, I would say to her that everything was all right. Then I would go downstairs and hope that Milo would say the same thing to me. What he finally did say one night was "You might as well find out from me as some other way."

"Hey, are you an old bag lady again this weekend?" Milo says now, stooping to kiss Louise's forehead.

"Because you take some things with you doesn't mean you're a bag lady," she says primly.

"Well," Milo says, "you start doing something innocently, and before you know it it can take you over."

He looks angry, and acts as though it's difficult for him to make conversation, even when the conversation is full of sarcasm and double-entendres.

"What do you say we get going?" he says to Louise.

In the shopping bag she is taking is her doll, which she has not played with for more than a year. I found it by accident when I went to tuck in a loaf of banana bread that I had baked. When I saw Baby Betsy, deep in the bag, I decided against putting the bread in.

"O.K.," Louise says to Milo. "Where's Bradley?"

"Sick," he says.

"Is he too sick to have me visit?"

"Good heavens, no. He'll be happier to see you than to see me."

"I'm rooting some of my coleus to give him," she says. "Maybe I'll give it to him like it is, in water, and he can plant it when it roots."

When she leaves the room, I go over to Milo. "Be nice to her," I say quietly.

"I'm nice to her," he says. "Why does everybody have to act like I'm going to grow fangs every time I turn around?"

"You were quite cutting when you came in."

"I was being self-deprecating." He sighs. "I don't really know why I come here and act this way," he says.

"What's the matter, Milo?"

But now he lets me know he's bored with the conversation. He walks over to the table and picks up a *Newsweek* and flips through it. Louise comes back with the coleus in a water glass.

"You know what you could do," I say. "Wet a napkin and put it around that cutting and then wrap it in foil, and put it in water when you get there. That way, you wouldn't have to hold a glass of water all the way to New York."

She shrugs. "This is O.K.," she says.

"Why don't you take your mother's suggestion," Milo says. "The water will slosh out of the glass."

"Not if you don't drive fast."

"It doesn't have anything to do with my driving fast. If we go over a bump in the road, you're going to get all wet."

"Then I can put on one of my dresses at your apartment."

"Am I being unreasonable?" Milo says to me.

"I started it," I say. "Let her take it in the glass."

"Would you, as a favor, do what your mother says?" he says to Louise.

Louise looks at the coleus, and at me.

"Hold the glass over the seat instead of your lap, and you won't get wet," I say.

"Your first idea was the best," Milo says.

Louise gives him an exasperated look and puts the glass down on the floor, pulls on her poncho, picks up the glass again and says a sullen goodbye to me, and goes out the front door.

"Why is this my fault?" Milo says. "Have I done anything terrible? I—"

"Do something to cheer yourself up," I say, patting him on the back.

He looks as exasperated with me as Louise was with him. He nods his head yes, and goes out the door.

"Was everything all right this weekend?" I ask Louise.

"Milo was in a bad mood, and Bradley wasn't even there on Saturday," Louise says. "He came back today and took us to the Village for breakfast."

"What did you have?"

"I had sausage wrapped in little pancakes and fruit salad and a rum bun."

"Where was Bradley on Saturday?"

She shrugs. "I didn't ask him."

She almost always surprises me by being more grownup that I give her credit for. Does she suspect, as I do, that Bradley has found another lover?

"Milo was in a bad mood when you two left here Saturday," I say.

"I told him if he didn't want me to come next weekend, just to tell me." She looks perturbed, and I suddenly realize that she can sound exactly like Milo sometimes.

"You shouldn't have said that to him, Louise," I say. "You know he wants you. He's just worried about Bradley."

"So?" she says. "I'm probably going to flunk math."

"No, you're not, honey. You got a C-plus on the last assignment."

"It still doesn't make my grade average out to a C."

"You'll get a C. It's all right to get a C."

She doesn't believe me.

"Don't be a perfectionist, like Milo," I tell her. "Even if you got a D, you wouldn't fail."

Louise is brushing her hair—thin, shoulder-length, auburn hair. She is already so pretty and so smart in everything except math that I wonder what will become of her. When I was her age, I was plain and serious and I wanted to be a tree surgeon. I went with my father to the park and held a stethoscope—a real one—to the trunks of trees, listening to their silence. Children seem older now.

"What do you think's the matter with Bradley?" Louise says. She sounds worried.

"Maybe the two of them are unhappy with each other right now."

She misses my point. "Bradley's sad, and Milo's sad that he's unhappy."

I drop Louise off at Sarah's house for supper. Sarah's mother, Martine Cooper, looks like Shelley Winters, and I have never seen her without a glass of Galliano on ice in her hand. She has a strong candy smell. Her husband has left her, and she professes not to care. She has emptied her living room of furniture and put up ballet bars on the walls, and dances in a purple leotard to records by Cher and Mac Davis. I prefer to have Sarah come to our house, but her mother is adamant that everything must be, as she puts it, "fifty-fifty." When Sarah visited us a week ago and loved the chocolate pie I had made, I sent two pieces home with her. Tonight, when I left Sarah's house, her mother gave me a bowl of Jell-O fruit salad.

The phone is ringing when I come in the door. It is Bradley.

"Bradley," I say at once, "whatever's wrong, at least you don't have a neighbor who just gave you a bowl of maraschino cherries in green Jell-O with a Reddi-Whip flower squirted on top."

"Jesus," he says. "You don't need me to depress you, do you?"

"What's wrong?" I say.

He sighs into the phone. "Guess what?" he says.

"What?"

"I've lost my job."

It wasn't at all what I was expecting to hear. I was ready to hear that he was leaving Milo, and I had even thought that that would serve Milo right. Part of me still wanted him punished for what he did. I was so out of my mind when Milo left me that I used to go over and drink Galliano with Martine Cooper. I even thought seriously about forming a ballet group with her. I would go to her house in the afternoon, and she would hold a tambourine in the air and I would hold my leg rigid and try to kick it.

"That's awful," I say to Bradley. "What happened?"

"They said it was nothing personal—they were laying off three people. Two other people are going to get the ax at the agency within the next six months. I was the first to go, and it was nothing personal. From twenty thousand bucks a year to nothing, and nothing personal, either."

"But your work is so good. Won't you be able to find something again?"

"Could I ask you a favor?" he says. "I'm calling from a phone booth. I'm not in the city. Could I come talk to you?"

"Sure," I say.

It seems perfectly logical that he should come alone to talk—perfectly logical until I actually see him coming up the walk. I can't entirely believe it. A year after my husband has left me, I am sitting with his lover—a man, a person I like quite well—and trying to cheer him up because he is out of work. ("Honey," my father would say, "listen to Daddy's heart with the stethoscope, or you can turn it toward you and listen to your own heart. You won't hear anything listening to a tree." Was my persistence willfulness, or belief in magic? Is it possible that I hugged Bradley at the door because I'm secretly glad he's down and out, the way I used to be? Or do I really want to make things better for him?)

He comes into the kitchen and thanks me for the coffee I am making, drapes his coat over the chair he always sits in.

"What am I going to do?" he ask.

"You shouldn't get so upset, Bradley," I say. "You know you're good. You won't have trouble finding another job."

"That's only half of it," he says. "Milo thinks I did this deliberately. He told me I was quitting on him. He's very angry at me. He fights with me, and then he gets mad that I don't enjoy eating dinner. My stomach's upset, and I can't eat anything."

"Maybe some juice would be better than coffee."

"If I didn't drink coffee, I'd collapse," he says.

I pour coffee into a mug for him, coffee into a mug for me.

"This is probably very awkward for you," he says. "That I come here and say all this about Milo."

"What does he mean about your quitting on him?"

"He said ... he actually accused me of doing badly deliberately, so they'd fire me. I was so afraid to tell him the truth when I was fired that I pretended to be sick. Then I really *was* sick. He's never been angry at me this way. Is this always the way he acts? Does he get a notion in his head for no reason and then pick at a person because of it?"

I try to remember. "We didn't argue much," I say. "When he didn't want to live here, he made me look ridiculous for complaining when I knew something was wrong. He expects perfection, but what that means is that you do things his way."

"I *was*. I never wanted to sit around the apartment, the way he says I did. I even brought work home with me. He made me feel so bad all week that I went to a friend's apartment for the day on Saturday. Then he said I had walked out on the problem. He's a little paranoid. I was listening to the radio, and Carole King was singing 'It's Too Late,' and he came into the study and looked very upset, as though I had planned for the song to come on. I couldn't believe it."

"Whew," I say, shaking my head. "I don't envy you. You have to stand up to him. I didn't do that. I pretended the problem would go away."

"And now the problem sits across from you drinking coffee, and you're being nice to him."

"I know it. I was just thinking we look like two characters in some soap opera my friend Martine Cooper would watch."

He pushes his coffee cup away from him with a grimace.

"But anyway, I like you now," I say. "And you're exceptionally nice to Louise."

"I took her father," he says.

"Bradley—I hope you don't take offense, but it makes me nervous to talk about that."

"I don't take offense. But how can you be having coffee with me?"

"You invited yourself over so you could ask that?"

"Please," he says, holding up both hands. Then he runs his hands through his hair. "Don't make me feel illogical. He does that to me, you know. He doesn't understand it when everything doesn't fall right into line. If I like fixing up the place, keeping some flowers around, therefore I can't like being a working person, too, therefore I deliberately sabotage myself in my job." Bradley sips his coffee.

"I wish I could do something for him," he says in a different voice. This is not what I expected, either. We have sounded like two wise adults, and then suddenly he has changed and sounds very tender. I realize the situation is still the same. It is two of them on one side and me on the other, even though Bradley is in my kitchen.

"Come and pick up Louise with me, Bradley," I say. "When you see Martine Cooper, you'll cheer up about your situation."

He looks up from his coffee. "You're forgetting what I'd look like to Martine Cooper," he says.

Milo is going to California. He has been offered a job with a new San Francisco architectural firm. I am not the first to know. His sister, Deanna, knows before I do, and mentions it when we're talking on the phone. "It's middle-age crisis," Deanna says sniffily. "Not that I need to tell you." Deanna would drop dead if she knew the way things are. She is scandalized every time a new display is put up in Bloomingdale's window. ("Those mannequins had eyes like an Egyptian princess, and *rags*. I swear to you, they had mops and brooms and ragged gauze dresses on, with whores' shoes—stiletto heels that prostitutes wear.")

I hang up from Deanna's call and tell Louise I'm going to drive to the gas station for cigarettes. I go there to call New York on their pay phone.

"Well, I only just knew," Milo says. "I found out for sure yesterday, and last night Deanna called and so I told her. It's not like I'm leaving tonight."

He sounds elated, in spite of being upset I called. He's happy in the way he used to be on Christmas morning. I remember him once running into the living room in his underwear and tearing open the gifts we'd been sent by relatives. He was looking for the eight-slice toaster he was sure we'd get. We'd been given two-slice, four-slice, and six-slice toasters, but then we got no more. "Come out, my eight-slice beauty!" Milo crooned, and out came an electric clock, a blender, and an expensive electric pan.

"When are you leaving?" I ask him.

"I'm going out to look for a place to live next week."

"Are you going to tell Louise yourself this weekend?"

"Of course," he says.

"And what are you going to do about seeing Louise?"

"Why do you act as if I don't like Louise?" he says. "I will occasionally come back East, and I will arrange for her to fly to San Francisco on her vacations."

"It's going to break her heart."

"No it isn't. Why do you want to make me feel bad?"

"She's had so many things to adjust to. You don't have to go to San Francisco right now, Milo."

"It happens, if you care, that my own job is in jeopardy. This is a real chance for me, with a young firm. They really want me. But anyway, all we need in this happy group is to have you bringing in a couple of hundred dollars a month with your graphic work and me destitute and Bradley so devastated by being fired that of course he can't even look for work."

"I'll bet he is looking for a job," I say.

"Yes. He read the want ads today and then fixed a crab quiche."

"Maybe that's the way you like things, Milo, and people respond to you. You forbade me to work when we had a baby. Do you say anything encouraging to him about finding a job, or do you just take it out on him that he was fired?"

There is a pause, and then he almost seems to lose his mind with impatience.

"I can hardly *believe*, when I am trying to find a logical solution to all our problems, that I am being subjected, by telephone, to an unflattering psychological analysis by my ex-wife." He says this all in a rush.

"All right, Milo. But don't you think that if you're leaving so soon you ought to call her, instead of waiting until Saturday?"

Milo sighs very deeply. "I have more sense than to have important conversations on the telephone," he says.

Milo calls on Friday and asks Louise whether it wouldn't be nice if both of us came in and spent the night Saturday and if we all went to brunch together Sunday. Louise is excited. I never go into town with her.

Louise and I pack a suitcase and put it in the car Saturday morning. A cutting of ivy for Bradley has taken root, and she has put it in a little green plastic pot for him. It's heartbreaking, and I hope that Milo notices and has a tough time dealing with it. I am relieved I'm going to be there when he tells her, and sad that I have to hear it at all.

In the city, I give the car to the garage attendant, who does not remember me. Milo and I lived in the apartment when we were first married, and moved when Louise was two years old. When we moved, Milo kept the apartment and sublet it—a sign that things were not going well, if I had been one to heed such a warning. What he said was that if we were ever rich enough we could have the house in Connecticut *and* the apartment in New York. When Milo moved out of the house, he went right back to the apartment. This will be the first time I have visited there in years.

Louise strides in front of me, throwing her coat over the brass coatrack in the entranceway—almost too casual about being there. She's the hostess at Milo's, the way I am at our house.

He has painted the walls white. There are floor-length white curtains in the living room, where my silly flowered curtains used to hang. The walls are bare, the floor has been sanded, a stereo as huge as a computer stands against one wall of the living room, and there are four speakers.

"Look around," Milo says. "Show your mother around, Louise."

I am trying to remember if I have ever told Louise that I used to live in this apartment. I must have told her, at some point, but I can't remember it.

"Hello," Bradley says, coming out of the bedroom.

"Hi, Bradley," I say. "Have you got a drink?"

Bradley looks sad. "He's got champagne," he says, and looks nervously at Milo.

"No one *has* to drink champagne," Milo says. "There's the usual assortment of liquor."

"Yes," Bradley says. "What would you like?"

"Some bourbon, please."

"Bourbon." Bradley turns to go into the kitchen. He looks different; his hair is different—more wavy—and he is dressed as though it were summer, in straight-legged white pants and black leather thongs.

"I want Perrier water with strawberry juice," Louise says, tagging along after Bradley. I have never heard her ask for such a thing before. At home, she drinks too many Cokes. I am always trying to get her to drink fruit juice.

Bradley comes back with two drinks and hands me one. "Did you want anything?" he says to Milo.

"I'm going to open the champagne in a moment," Milo says. "How have you been this week, sweetheart?"

"O.K.," Louise says. She is holding a pale-pink, bubbly drink. She sips it like a cocktail.

Bradley looks very bad. He has circles under his eyes, and he is ill at ease. A red light begins to blink on the phone-answering device next to where Bradley sits on the sofa, and Milo gets out of his chair to pick up the phone.

"Do you really want to talk on the phone right now?" Bradley asks Milo quietly.

Milo looks at him. "No, not particularly," he says, sitting down again. After a moment, the red light goes out.

"I'm going to mist your bowl garden," Louise says to Bradley, and slides off the sofa and goes to the bedroom. "Hey, a little toadstool is growing in here!" she calls back. "Did you put it there, Bradley?"

"It grew from the soil mixture, I guess," Bradley calls back. "I don't know how it got there."

"Have you heard anything about a job?" I ask Bradley.

"I haven't been looking, really," he says. "You know."

Milo frowns at him. "Your choice, Bradley," he says "I didn't ask you to follow me to California. You can stay here."

"No," Bradley says. "You've hardly made me feel welcome."

"Should we have some champagne—all four of us—and you can get back to your bourbons later?" Milo says cheerfully.

We don't answer him, but he gets up anyway and goes to the kitchen. "Where have you hidden the tulip-shaped glasses, Bradley?" he calls out after a while.

"They should be in the cabinet on the far left," Bradley says.

"You're going with him?" I say to Bradley. "To San Francisco?"

He shrugs, and won't look at me. "I'm not quite sure I'm wanted," he says quietly.

The cork pops in the kitchen. I look at Bradley, but he won't look up. His new hairdo makes him look older. I remember when Milo left me I went to the hairdresser the same week and had bangs cut. The next week, I went to a therapist who told me it was not good trying to hide from myself. The week after that, I did dance exercises with Martine Cooper, and the week after that the therapist told me not to dance if I wasn't interested in dancing.

"I'm not going to act like this is a funeral," Milo says, coming in with the glasses. "Louise, come in here and have champagne! We have something to have a toast about."

Louise comes into the living room suspiciously. She is so used to being refused even a sip of wine from my glass or her father's that she no longer even asks. "How come I'm in on this?" she asks.

"We're going to drink a toast to me," Milo says.

Three of the four glasses are clustered on the table in front of the sofa. Milo's glass is raised. Louise looks at me, to see what I'm going to say. Milo raises his glass even higher. Bradley reaches for a glass. Louise picks up a glass. I lean forward and take the last one.

"This is a toast to me," Milo says, "because I am going to be going to San Francisco."

It was not a very good or informative toast. Bradley and I sip from our glasses. Louise puts her glass down hard and bursts into tears, knocking the glass over. The champagne spills onto the cover of a big art book about the Unicorn Tapestries. She runs into the bedroom and slams the door.

Milo looks furious. "Everybody lets me know just what my insufficiencies are, don't they?" he says. "Nobody minds expressing himself. We have it all right out in the open."

"He's criticizing me," Bradley murmurs, his head still bowed. "It's because I was offered a job here in the city and I didn't automatically refuse it."

I turn to Milo. "Go say something to Louise, Milo," I say. "Do you think that's what somebody who isn't brokenhearted sounds like?"

He glares at me and stomps into the bedroom, and I can hear him talking to Louise reassuringly. "It doesn't mean you'll *never* see me," he says. "You can fly there, I'll come here. It's not going to be that different."

"You lied!" Louise screams. "You said we were going to brunch."

"We are. We are. I can't very well take us to brunch before Sunday, can I?"

"You didn't say you were going to San Francisco. What *is* San Francisco, anyway?"

"I just said so. I bought us a bottle of champagne. You can come out as soon as I get settled. You're going to like it there."

Louise is sobbing. She has told him the truth and she knows it's futile to go on.

By the next morning, Louise acts the way I acted—as if everything were just the same. She looks calm, but her face is small and pale. She looks very young. We walk into the restaurant and sit at the table Milo has reserved. Bradley pulls out a chair for me, and Milo pulls out a chair for Louise, locking his finger with hers for a second, raising her arm above her head, as if she were about to take a twirl.

She looks very nice, really. She has a ribbon in her hair. It is cold, and she should have worn a hat, but she wanted to wear the ribbon. Milo has good taste: the dress she is wearing, which he bought for her, is a hazy purple plaid, and it sets off her hair.

"Come with me. Don't be sad," Milo suddenly says to Louise, pulling her by the hand. "Come with me for a minute. Come across the street to the park for just a second, and we'll have some space to dance, and your mother and Bradley can have a nice quiet drink."

She gets up from the table and, looking long-suffering, backs into her coat, which he is holding for her, and the two of them go out. The waitress comes to the table, and Bradley orders three Bloody Marys and a Coke, and eggs Benedict for everyone. He asks the waitress to wait awhile before she brings the food. I have hardly slept at all, and having a drink is not going to clear my head. I have to think of things to say to Louise later, on the ride home.

"He takes so many *chances*," I say. "He pushes things so far with people. I don't want her to turn against him."

"No," he says.

"Why are you going, Bradley? You've seen the way he acts. You know that when you get out there he'll pull something on you. Take the job and stay here."

Bradley is fiddling with the edge of his napkin. I study him. I don't know who his friends are, how old he is, where he grew up, whether he believes in God, or what he usually drinks. I'm shocked that I know so little, and I reach out and touch him. He looks up.

"Don't go," I say quietly.

The waitress puts the glasses down quickly and leaves, embarrassed because she thinks she's interrupted a tender moment. Bradley pats my hand on his arm. Then he says the thing that has always been between us, the thing too painful for me to envision or think about.

"I love him," Bradley whispers.

We sit quietly until Milo and Louise come into the restaurant, swinging hands. She is pretending to be a young child, almost a baby, and I wonder for an instant if Milo and Bradley and I haven't been playing house, too—pretending to be adults.

"Daddy's going to give me a first-class ticket," Louise says. "When I go to California we're going to ride in a glass elevator to the top of the Fairman Hotel."

"The Fairmont," Milo says, smiling at her.

Before Louise was born, Milo used to put his ear to my stomach, and say that if the baby turned out to be a girl he would put her into glass slippers instead of bootees. Now he is the prince once again. I see them in a glass elevator, not long from now, going up and up, with the people below getting smaller and smaller, until they disappear.

Contact

John Lonie

"Men's rooms"—locker rooms, communal showers, public washrooms in the bus terminal, the gym, the college library—are exclusive settings in which male desire for another man can suddenly emerge. For both gay and straight men, these places are uniquely defined by a varied yet common masculinity. For John Lonie (as for Joe Orton, John Rechy, Jean Genet) the washroom itself—the "john", the "glory hole", the notorious French "vespasienne"—is a liminal place in which men play out ancient ceremonies of encounter. The ubiquitous washroom graffiti (which initiate the events in "Contact") attest to a tidal bore of male fantasies more or less below consciousness during the daily rituals of the male toilette.

The critic Camille Paglia describes these fantasies as part and parcel of the masculine impulse. For gay men "to have anonymous sex in a dark alleyway is to pay homage to the dream of male freedom. The unknown stranger is a wandering pagan god. The altar, as in prehistory, is anywhere you kneel. Similarly, straight men who visit prostitutes are valiantly striving to keep sex free from emotion, duty, family—in other words, from society, religion, and procreative Mother Nature."

"Everyone wanks," says the fresh graffiti on the back of the door. And below, in what looks like the same hand, is a drawing of a huge hand-held ejaculating cock with, by way of a postscript, "If this is what you like doing to young spunks, try Michael Travers at the Palms Caravan Park." Graffiti becomes message.

I'm in the bleached and shabby Spanish-Mission style change sheds at one of the unfashionable beaches on the Sunshine Coast, a place which attracts people who can't afford or who disdain the glitter and brashness of the Gold Coast or Noosa. And these door-messages bring me to life, not so much at the thought of the "young spunk" as at the pleasant knowledge that up here, I am not alone. Not having seen anyone in the past few days other than the odd cute papa walking his children along the surf beach, I muse on the identity of the author or authors.

Then the thought crosses my mind that this Michael Travers could be advertising on his own behalf. If it be him, there are hundreds of candidates, all looking so alike, you'd be hard-pressed to tell one from another. They're as if factory-made and, up here in pre-migrant Oz, come in two basic colours; light blond and dark blond. The only parts of them grown-up are their huge feet and their dicks and they go around in buzzing swarms of sexual tension, ever-ready to pounce on deviant behaviour by any member. Would one of them be so self-possessed and brave as to break ranks? Hardly.

Then there is The Cute Papa. Down the hill from my family's house is a block of fibro flats, each with a verandah. Every day, in the one nearest to us, I've watched the Cute Papa playing with his two baby children, clad only in shorts and with legs and feet of such perfection as to attract a Michelangelo. Does he realize how beautiful he is? His wife does. She gazes at him with adoration through the large open window from the kitchen. I've seen them both walking along the beach. Her eyes hardly ever leave him. Him? Is he the author?

This fantasy becomes very distracting now for whereas before, I've observed the Cute Papa as one looks at a beautiful painting, now I feel the cutting stab of loneliness which, along with desire, I've repressed these past six days. Six days I can manage. On the seventh, there is no rest. This, Paul, I say to myself as warning, brings on the madness. Leave.

Seconds later, I'm in the water, one eye each on two nieces as they splash about in the small but still powerful waves at the edge of the surf while one hand grabs a little nephew who is a stranger to fear. If I wasn't holding on to him, he'd be happily swept away. He's German, this one. Sharks, says the Oz niece to scare her German cousin. *Der Haifisch kommt*, she calls over to Hans, translating the words to her little brother and the threat. But Hans doesn't scare. Where? he asks me, excited by the prospect of a face-to-face meeting. This attracts more of his cousins, four little Australians who, despite the language barrier, have grabbed every chance to terrify their German cousins with tales of sharks, snakes, spiders and crocodiles. Little do they realize this is just grist to the mill for little Hans who relishes the bit in the Grimm tale about Aschenputtl when the step-sisters have to cut off their big toe and heel to fit their feet into the golden slipper.

It's such an irony that up here on holidays, the children are made my reason-of-being. I'm a modern version of the family aunt. Every family has one, says Charlotte Vale in *Now Voyager*. Once a comfort to aged parents, now, in these less charitable days, I fear we're just a plain never-ending unmarried worry to our mothers and fathers. Unlike selfish Mrs. Vale, they want to get us off their hands.

It's out of concern for me that my mother has invented this new reason for my existence. To spend time with my nieces and nephews. It's good for me and the children. My siblings and their spouses have taken this up with enthusiasm. It's all bull of course, because, sick of their children, they are now free to sit up on the beach, smoke fags and gossip while I look after their offspring. And that's exactly what they're doing right now, smoking, gossiping and having "views". None of my family is short of a "view". Except possibly my younger brother who lives in Germany. He lies a little away from the group and behind the camouflage of his sunglasses, eyes off women younger and prettier than his plump and homely Prussian wife Hannelore. They're here to see if Hannelore would like living in Australia. She is under-whelmed at the moment. Everyone goes about barefoot. It's all a bit Third World for Ajax-clean Hannelore from smart Dahlem in Berlin.

You're great with the kids, says my young sister's American hus-band, who is keen to add to the family brood now the house is built. After a year here, he's become a passionate Australian even if he does get little things wrong now and then. Yesterday in the fruit shop Byron asked for a kilometre instead of a kilogram of mangoes and then fell into sweet confusion when the children all laughed at him. He tries so hard, he who at first hated the heat and wearing no clothes, so there's hope yet for Hannelore.

Then Hannelore says it too—*Du bist doch fantastisch mit den Kindern, Paul.* It's true, I am good with the children. I love them all and, oddly, quite like them all too, even if the two eldest nieces think me entirely wet. Hans, who is Hannelore's four-year-old son, has firmly claimed me. Mother says we're as thick as thieves. How right she is. I enjoy being Uncle/*Onkel*. In reality, I'm one of them, proof of that being that my room is the children's dormitory, except I'm still in it. My father still wants to know where I'm going, who I'm seeing. Mother gives me chocolates like some little reward for being good.

Parents never stop being parents but it's easier when the child is child-less.

So we play, all of us, a mad bi-lingual mix with me as the Big Kid, a role reinforced by being the translator when grunts, squeals, shoves, fists and laughter fail to bridge the language barrier. It's one up, all up, so by early evening, everyone is so tired, it's almost one in, all in. Each evening, I've been reading the Grimm's Tales, alternately in English and German, but I'm so stuffed sometimes, I forget which until the offended nationality, jealous of its language rights, protests.

It's a moment like this with the children which chips away the last vestiges of my quaint 70's belief that human nature is not fixed at birth.

That night, the children have turned my room into a fort and capture me. My heart's not in it. I am too conscious of my mask. Before, I didn't care. This is part of the reason for holidaying with family. I don't have to negotiate my job, lovers or the city but it's the lovers whose presence I now miss with a sudden ache. Being homosexual has removed me from all that surrounds me up here at my family's holiday house. They all know, of course, but "it" is never mentioned. Once, I would never have put up with being an "it", then, in those golden days when I holidayed only with my own tribe and whenever I saw my family, I lectured them on the burning issues of the day. I too had "views".

I escape torture and further incarceration by reading yet another Grimm story although, because it's a new one, the old Accord of different languages on alternate nights is deemed over and World Wars One and Two break out again. As in the history books, the Huns bite the dust, although predictably, not without causing horrendous damage, mainly because little Hans has whacked his older Oz cousin Peter on the nose and blood is well and truly spilt. All to no avail. I continue in English as a sop to the wounded Peter. It's the one about the poor fisherman who hauls in a halibut with magic powers. The fisherman's greedy wife forces him to ask the fish for ever more and more until, after he's turned her into the Pope, she asks to become Almighty God himself. The fish turns her back into a harping *hausfrau*, sitting in her pig-pen hovel. Be satisfied with your lot, children, I say as I escape.

My exit from the house is thwarted by my mother telling me to play Scrabble with them. I feel like a walk, I say. Nonsense, she says and sets up a chair. Now play seriously, she admonishes me, because I keep putting out words like "was" and "but" and "and". There's no point in doing something unless you put your heart and soul into it, she adds. I'm trying, Mother, I reply. God how I'm trying but you keep getting in my way, I add to myself.

Finally, I walk along the beach. It's about 10 o'clock. Out at sea, the lights flash on the shipping buoys and then, around the point, comes a large container ship, all lit up like a passenger liner. The boats come in quite close to the shore as they make their way up and down to the port. At night, you can hear the throb of their engines across the water. I stand and watch it sail by, so near it tantalizes me with thoughts of where it's come from and where after here, it goes. The world, my world.

It's dark tonight. There's no moon but the change sheds are open and lit. I dawdle about by the pool. An old lady swims freestyle so slowly that she must sink but doesn't. She's the only one about. I go into the sheds, heart pounding. It's an age since I've done this and I'm reminded of why I used to do it myself—excitement, pure and simple. A single light bulb shines weakly. No one in the shower room. Further along to the toilets and I can see no-one there and I relax some as expectation and fantasy fade. I push open the door and go inside to review the messages.

The one about Michael Travers is gone. The dick is still there with its "Everyone wanks" motto. But up the top, maybe in the same hand, is a new message. "Any sex here over the holidays?" "Yes," I scrawl under the message, annoyed that I've missed him. Him, I keep thinking of the author as "him". I wonder if I might give "him" a name. But if it is Michael Travers he already has an identity. I'm hoping it's not so I decide to keep thinking about "him". The space where the Michael Travers message had been seems terribly blank now. I'm disappointed in a way except it is proof that this door is still in print. I wonder if, thinking he'd been advertising long enough, he removed the message himself. Or what if his father had seen it and rubbed it out and then gone home and rubbed Michael Travers out. Or what ... I stop this silliness and add to my "yes" on the wall, "Tuesday night, after 10." Then I look at it and think I am headed for purgatory. Fancy me writing messages on toilet walls. It's ludicrous and I laugh. But oh, I am consumed by curiosity and by need of my own kind, even a glance, a smile. Recognition.

Back home, my room is covered with sleeping children and I resent their presence greatly. They smell of children, a mixture of milk and sweat and shit. This is driving me spare. I can't sleep so I read but not very successfully as the night with its heat and humidity calls. Sweaty weather.

Next morning, one up, all up. Aren't you taking the kids down to the beach? my eldest brother asks with an injured tone as I head out the door solo. No, I snap and leave. It's very early and I walk around the headland and along the beach which stretches white and unbroken almost all the way up to Noosa 30 or 40 kilometres away. I haven't been here for years. There used to be an old shipwreck on this beach which in our childhood was still quite substantial. You could climb up the stern quite safely and at low tide, see the rusty propeller sticking out of the sand.

But now, I see it's reduced to some rusted ribbing sticking out of the sand, not, as a fisherman tells me, wholly because of Mother-Sea. Mostly because of souvenir hunters over the past few years. How dare they. We loved that wreck, my cousin and I. We'd sit on the stern and talk till the waves nearly washed us off. And we'd spin marvellous fantasies of what we'd do when we grew up. I look at this wreckage of a wreck and think sourly, bits of my past are sitting in some suburban living room, pathetic relic of a holiday in Queensland. I feel more and more pessimistic about "people" and in so doing, become more and more my parents' son.

Further along the beach, past where until the 70's, civilization ended but which now has houses, I walk up into the sand dunes and into the bosky softness of the banksias and casuarinas which, miracle of miracles, still stand guard against the encroachments of the Pacific and the depredations of the greedy. There is one old banksia in particular—I think it is the one—and I sit on its lower trunk. The sun's light dapples the ground and in the familiar mix of the slightly rank smell of the cool sand and the spiciness of the decaying casuarina needles on the ground, I smell memory.

My cousin and I, he nearly 16, a year older than me, would get up at 4.30 in the morning, just before the midsummer sun peeked over the Pacific horizon. We wore nothing but our Speedos with T-shirts to ward off the morning chill and we carried an air rifle to shoot cane toads because we hated them. They had been responsible for poisoning one of our dogs, so had to be exterminated. But we'd soon get sick of potting these unpottable monsters and go down to the top of the dunes to watch the sun come up. Then Alex would take a small jar of Vaseline from the rifle bag, grease up his erection and fuck me. I remember the delight of the dawn, the sun just warm enough to tingle the skin, the chill of the soft sand under my back, the magpies and currawongs singing and Alex lifting my legs and entering me slowly. He never looked at me. He'd always look ahead, out to the sea. I'd look at him all the time.

The first time, I was amazed. I was lying on the sand looking up at the sky. Without a word, he knelt in front of me, peeled my Speedoes from me which exposed my own excitement, lifted my legs and was in. I must have felt very calm and relaxed with him that first time because it didn't hurt—on the contrary. But the second time, it did and it was a little while before it became easy and just like that first time, which dazed me with its intensity. It never worried me that Alex didn't ever look at me. It never crossed my mind that it was odd. He always sensed where I was for we always came together. I recognized him as being in charge and he was.

Afterwards, he'd stay where he was, his eyes closed, his hands holding my feet against his shoulders, me lying before him so light and tranquil that I might have floated away except I was earth bound by his cock inside me. Mostly, we'd start again for that is the age of the permanent erection. Then, down to the water and we'd body-surf together in the waves before running home. By then, everyone would be up and mother would be preparing breakfast. She called us her morning glow-worms because, she said, we glowed after our early morning frolics in the water.

It went on for just over three years, mostly during our holidays, May, August then Christmas, sometimes Easter. I didn't see much of Alex back home because we went to different schools. Alex boarded at Geelong because his parents were diplomats although on his freedom weekends—as he called them—he came to us. Then we'd do it a lot, hidden in the bush down in the Yarra Bend National Park not far from home. Once, in mid-flight, we saw what could have been a tiger snake a few metres away, its head raised slightly, staring at us in shocked amazement like some reptilian schoolmaster. We laughed so much, we both lost our erections. With Alex, I felt fearless.

The beginning of 1969. Alex was just 18 and he was to go back down to Melbourne for his matriculation results. The day he was to leave, we went out before dawn. For over a year now, we'd ignored the cane toads and the air rifle was quietly rusting in a cupboard. We walked along the beach and back, hardly a word between us. We went to our spot and he fucked me twice. After the second time, I remember looking up at him and glorying in how handsome he was, such long dark eye-lashes, dark hair and olive skin—my brothers and sister and I were all fair and looked just like every other teenager in our narrow world. But Alex didn't. I realized just how much I worshipped him. And then he so surprised me by saying something. I must have looked puzzled because he looked down at me and smiled. He'd said my name and he said it again as he nuzzled his face against my feet which were resting on his shoulders. Then he kissed my left foot before gently letting my legs down and helping me up. He gazed at me, lifting his hand to stroke my cheek. At that moment, he looked right into me, and had he said, run away with me to sea or fly with me to the moon, death alone would have stopped me. Then, he sighed and something changed in his eyes, I can't remember exactly except that the intense contact was gone. Suddenly he tweaked my nose and raced off to the water, calling on me to follow. I remember I had an almost uncontrollable urge to burst into tears for I must have sensed what had happened.

Married with a young family, at the Victorian Bar, a successful barrister, I've hardly seen him since. And now, as I savour the memory, I don't want to move. I close my eyes and there's an unspoken wish to return to childhood, my childhood, to this spot 20 years back, for while I couldn't have realized it at the time, in those few years, I was content as I've never been since.

You are very distant? says Hannelore as she irons the bedsheets. She's the only one who notices I'm not my sunny self. No, I reply, just a bit flat. Ach, she says sagely in German, here with your family and you are lonely. She's quite right and I recoil at the touch of her words. The only thing keeping me from hoping on the sparkling new ICE-Train down to Brisbane and a plane south is curiosity about tonight's rendezvous at 10 pm.

I wonder what brings me here, what on earth joins me to my mother and father. Parents and children are only accidentally related, says hunchbacked Rhoda to her accidental brother Hurtle in *The Vivisector*. If we are all reincarnated, then my parents as well as being the genetic means for this incarnation, are also possibly my trial and I am theirs. If so, I'm doing much better than they are.

Such a long face, my mother says to me. Help me wipe up. So I do. She talks about a poorly lemon-scented gum in her garden. Mother's trees. We have a lot of land here and over the years Mother has planted trees from all over tropical Australia. From using them as childhood playthings to student cynicism about her motive for planting them—merely to improve the worth of the property—Mother's trees are now genuinely absorbing for me. They are one thing we actually can share. I say I'll help her lop some of the diseased branches.

Hans is at me to go to the rock pools to watch the crabs scuttle away as he stomps Germanically into their homes. Hans can only be a little poofter-basher in training and if I were truly mindful of my tribe's well-being, I should let him fall in and drown. But he fascinates me more than any of the others for the very reason we are attracted by the archetypal Young Australian Male which even though he's German and four, little Hans, in behaviour, resembles alarmingly. A friend of mine refers to them derisively as Yams.

They are good-looking of course with the beauty of youth but it is their energetic maleness which is fascinating, although for us, that is a bit like the lethal fascination the snake has for the hapless frog. Social class is at work too and even if I do scoff at the English Grands like those characters of E.M. Forster's fantasies, aristos who can find fulfilment only with the under-gamekeeper, I too have fantasized about being scooped up by some smudgy mechanic and loved senseless. The Cute Papa will do very nicely. But there's not the remotest chance I would allow it. It's sad, I think sometimes, that with growing older, one becomes wise to the idiocy of falling for the sort of beauty which, you find out all too quickly, does indeed have the intelligence of a yam. So, I mightn't be the snake but I certainly am no frog. I observe Hans and his ilk for the most part, quite dispassionately.

Off we go, the girls their own gaggle and me with the boys. The rocks are slippery. This deters the girls who collect shells on the sand. The older boys climb the cliff-face. I have Hans who is not deterred by slippery rocks although he does show unusual wisdom in holding firmly onto my hand. We could both go, I think.

Hans is thoroughly absorbed by the tiny fish and the crabs until, suddenly, let's kill them, he shouts, with Teutonic relish. This after I've been telling him about the wonders of life, of conservation, of loving all creatures. But all that's as water off a duck's back to this little von Moltke. What counts is I'm bigger than he is and I say I'll give him a clout on the ear if he so much as raises his little finger against a sandfly. Good old violence. Oddly, a whack on the ear doesn't sound at all impressive in German but it works all the same.

A gangly teenager, 15 or 16, lolls about in the large rock pool. He's all arms and legs. I notice him because he is by himself. That is rare up here. You belong to a swarm or you're dead. It was like that when I was his age except we were self-contained, my brothers and cousins and our house was away from the town. We were called then "the Victorians" by the locals because in those days, we were the only ones.

The gangly boy gets out of the rock pool and sits on the sand nearby where his towel and belongings are. He lights a cigarette which he smokes self-consciously and then I notice he's holding the silly thing between his middle and third fingers. He sees me looking at him and he grins and I say g'day. He nods his head, still grinning and says hallo—not the ubiquitous "hi" but "hallo". If he were a member of a swarm, he'd scowl in self-defence and start chewing his fingernails. I'm very tempted to say, are you Michael Travers? Then Hans falls into the rock pool and yells blue murder that he's all wet. The little bugger is only attention-getting but, *in loco parentis*, I scoop him out and take him home to change. Why Hannelore didn't put his swimmers on, I don't know. The gangly teenager watches me as I go. See ya, he says and coolly draws on his fag, as if he were in a 30's film doing cigarette-acting.

Who's that? Hans demands. Who? I ask. Him, he says unexpectedly in English, pointing at the gangly teenager. One of the boys who went away with the Pied Piper from Hamelin, I spin and go on to tell him the horrors they went through before they came to Australia where they're now living happily ever after. Hans is utterly absorbed by my explanation and forgets to whinge that he's wet. He repeats the bare bones to Hannelore when we get home, the really horrible bits of course, and she casts a baleful look in my direction.

I sit on the balcony. I'm convinced now that Him has to be that lad and that he probably is Michael Travers. Just my luck and if he's there tonight, what on earth am I going to do? I won't go, I say to myself, quite certain of course that nothing on Earth will keep me away from satisfying, at least my curiosity. But what will I do? Knock him off? Give him a good time? Something to remember and look for again? A role model? Didn't I, doesn't every gay boy, dream of being found by an attractive man and taken off to paradise?

Yet I'm no missionary. Slaking his desire, I may feed his soul. But what about me? I feel at the moment only the sort of desire that makes one quite undiscriminating. More madness. Maybe I'll get my brother to drive me over to Nambour to the ICE-Train and I can be back home by tonight.

Night. Story time is over quickly because if it isn't, I'll bloody smother you—in English and German. At 9.45 I go for a walk. In the distance along the beach, I see figures at the pool and my heart tightens as I think, ah, right, it's all a poofter-bashers' ploy and I'm about to walk right into their trap. The snake has me in its grip however and I trot along the beach, pretending to be a late-night jogger.

The figures around the pool are the old lady from before and an even older-looking gentleman, both so wizened, they look just like frill-necked lizards. They're leaving as I come up to the pool. Nice evening, I say in shaky voice. Yairs, they both say as they toddle away. Very nice. 9.58 and I'll explode. No one about so I quickly go in through the portals and into the mens' change rooms, heart almost stopping. It's exciting and I'm loving every second of the anticipation.

No one. Empty. Nothing. I push open the door. "Please, can only do daytime," says the message under my "meet you at ten." God save me. It is that wretched teenager. Any wimp can sneak out at night. What's wrong with him! So could the Cute Papa. I'm furious. The only way to calm down is to take off all my clothes and swim back and forth in the pool. I do at least a kilometre.

It's always like this, I grumble. If it were my friend and ex, Wolfgang, the place would be awash with men. No matter where we went, some chap would pop out of the woodwork. Of all the unlikely places, Leningrad once, a soldier in the Red Army, though not, it has to be said, in uniform which disappointed Wolf greatly. Words failed me at the time as they did when, after I'd left Germany for home and he'd followed me out here, we were on our way to Adelaide in the car and pulled into a motel in the middle of a desert and sure enough, as soon as Wolf got out of the car, out popped an attractively moustached face. But now he has the bug and I am grateful each day the bug doesn't have him because I love him. He's away in the snow in Enzed with his boyfriend, pretending he's 20 and back in Kitzbuehel.

My single bed surrounded by a sea of sleeping children, I sleep on the unfairness of life soothed only by the scent from mother's eucalypts which the night breeze wafts in through the open window.

"Please, can only do daytime." It's not just a message for a possible rendezvous, it's the tribal calling card, and even if our affections in lonely places like this are mediated by cock—and what's wrong with that—we have the affection of one of our own, however fleeting. And if you are 16 or 66, it will please you and make you feel less alone. Am I indeed to be a missionary or is it social worker? Whoever Him is, there's Life out there and I am its representative here and now. Grab a sample. Oh loneliness, we know all about loneliness, about sitting with your family and not being able to tell the truth.

The sun is hardly up. "2 pm today," I write on the door and leave. Children, parents, brothers and sisters and the whole caboodle snooze then. So does the whole town for at long last, Whitey accepts he lives in the tropics and not in Europe.

After breakfast, having decided the *eucalyptus citriadora* is not long for the world, Mother asks me to help her plant another, which we do. Nothing is said as we dig the hole, prepare it and put the sapling in. I enjoy the ritual and so does she. There, isn't that nice, she says happily and I realize it is not just the tree-planting she means. It's also my being there in both spirit as well as body. It's simple really. I give her happiness and pleasure by helping her plant the tree, simply by being there. I realize she knows when I am not there and it must trouble her because her concern is for me to be happy. You'll be terribly lonely, she said to me years ago when I told her. We walk among her trees and she says, the trees keep me company, you know.

It's two o'clock in the change room and I change into my swimmers. The gangly lad from the rock pool, bold as brass, strides in. He grins. I laugh. Not here, he says and beckons me to follow. Madness. I follow.

Over the hill and into the bush until he stops in a quiet secluded spot. How old are you? I ask. Nineteen, he says. Bull, I say. Seventeen, he corrects and I still think he's lying. He drops his shorts and steps out of them, his erection springing up and flapping against his tummy. Fool, I say to myself. I've built up to this rendezvous, I've walked all this way with him, what else is he going to expect. The madness has brought you to this idiocy. Hang on honey, I say and put a paternal hand to his face. I am about to say you're too young for me and I'm too old for you when I feel him trembling under my touch and he puts his hand up to my hand and presses it against his cheek. My heart melts. He's scared, so scared he's shaking, and I realize that it is he who's taken the huge risk, not me. I fold him in to me and hold him and he hangs on tightly, so tightly.

His erection hasn't gone away and then he shudders and grabs me hard as I feel him come against my thigh. I hold him tight and press my face to his, stroking the back of his neck and head. Then I feel dampness on my cheek and he's crying softly. It's okay, I say quietly, hoping he feels safe with me, cry all you want. And he does.

For ages, we stand there, him hanging on tight. I can hear his heart beat and the sound of the blood coursing through his veins, this stranger. I should be looking after him, not that little thug Hans or any of my nieces and nephews. They've got their parents. This one, he's my tribe, that's for sure. Who looks after him? Who looks after any of us at that time?

I use my handkerchief and dry his eyes which are bloodshot. I kiss him on the cheek and motion to him to sit down. I cover his nakedness with my towel. He takes out his cigarettes and offers me one and I accept, even though I don't smoke. He lights us up and I have him lean against me as I lean against the soft trunk of a large paperbark. I can smell the pungent sweetness of its flowers.

Here on holidays, he lives in an inland coal town, up north on the Tropic of Capricorn. He's doing matric, is nearly 18 and now I believe him. To me, anyone under 25 looks 16. He hopes to go to university in Brisbane next year. I tell him how brave he is, taking such a chance. So are you, he says, we're illegal up here, you know. Not "it's" illegal but "we're" illegal. He is so lonely, so very lonely, you can taste the need on his skin.

Multiply him by thousands and what other way is there than the change rooms or a public toilet whose doors become a *samizdat*? And when as strangers we collide in that fleeting moment, the immensity of feeling between us creates such a closeness that we go on searching for it, desperate just once more to taste the sweetness it brings. It surely is the kindness of strangers.

I tell him my name. What's yours? I ask, knowing the answer full well. But so much for that because, David, he replies, David Franken.

Michel

Marco Denevi

Homosexuality is a very recent subject in Argentinian fiction. Up to 1968, when Manuel Puig published, to great scandal, Betrayed by Rita Hayworth, *there were no gay characters of any importance in Argentinian fiction. There is a scene in a 1926 novel by Roberto Arlt—*El Juguete Rabioso (The Furious Toy)—*in which the protagonist, who has taken a room in a cheap hotel, is told by the manager that he must share the room with a certain young man. As it turns out, the young man pays the manager to let him know when interesting single men arrive at the hotel and then attempts to seduce them in the hope of becoming "someone's little woman". The protagonist wards him off in disgust. The young man is depicted as a ridiculously effeminate and miserable creature, perverted (he wears women's dirty underwear) and unsatisfied with his sex. Arlt is echoing the well-known stereotype: a homosexual is a man who aspires to be a woman, and a male should define himself through a horror of anything feminine. It isn't surprising that, well into the thirties, the toughs of the Buenos Aires underworld danced the tango only among themselves, because dancing with a woman was considered unmanly.*

*Argentinian society is notoriously homophobic. In spite of occasional months of abeyance, police persecution has been—and continues to be, even now—exceptionally vicious, and blackmail of gays is common procedure. The detective story, in which Marco Denevi excels—*Rose at Ten *and* Secret Ceremony *are masterpieces of the genre—serves in "Michel" to map, inexorably, the tragedy of misdirected desire.*

Hey, come on, of course my name is not Michel. My name is Gonzalo Maritti. I'll never know why the old lady—her name was Rosina Maritti, Italian—gave me that Spanish name, Gonzalo. But at Le Matelot all the waiters had to have French names. One of the funny ideas of the boss, Gaston, whose real name was Hector. It was Freddy who chose Michel, because I, to tell you the truth, don't know a fucking word in French. I had been working at Le Matelot for a week. It was my first job, you know, because while the old lady was alive she supported me so that I could go to school. I didn't really go to school, but I wanted to keep the old lady happy, so I would tell her I did. So when the old lady died I found myself out on the street. Freddy, who knows everyone from God upwards, found me the job at the bar. He was a friend of Gaston and Gaston, as soon as he saw me, looked at Freddy and said yes, I'd be okay.

No kidding, I'd be okay. Eighteen years old and so handsome it made you blink twice. Now you see me sort of worn out, but just imagine me then. Two days later I was the most popular of the waiters. Gaston first sent me to the tables, but then saw the looks I was getting and stood me behind the bar. You should have seen the fruits at the bar. They would shake my hand, try to chat me up, ask me for a match every five minutes. But I stayed on my perch. Polite, sure, but on my perch. Because, after all, who were those, the whole fucking lot? Snotty kids like myself. That was the worst about Le Matelot. It was full of kids. And what was I going to do with kids, you tell me. I was expecting something else, you understand. Something like Freddy, when Freddy was loaded and say three years younger. But Freddy was now broke and he had suddenly turned into a little old man, with one foot in the grave, because of his illness, you know.

That night the guy appeared, the whole lot of fruits at the bar stopped cackling, imagine that, and nailed him on the spot with their eyes. Then they started elbowing each other and puffing their feathers. Or as Gaston would say, took out their powder-puffs. Look *who* was making fun of the fruits! But the guy wasn't looking at any of them. He looked at me, you know, from the very first moment.

The guy was sort of forty years old, shaped like a body-builder, blond, bronzed. He looked like Buster Crabbe, to give you an idea. You don't know who he is. It doesn't matter. He was a guy who played Tarzan when you weren't yet born. I had a Buster Crabbe photo in my room—Freddy had bought it for me—dressed in a tigerskin loincloth, patting a lion, and smiling like a toothpaste ad. A guy like that, yes, I thought. I would even have done it like for free. Well maybe not completely free. But it would be enough if he just took me to dinner or bought me a tie. But to tell you the truth, what I'd really have liked was if he'd made me his bodyguard or his private secretary. During the day, everything above-board. And at night ... you understand. Or that he adopt me as his son. Can you imagine? Who would know? And I'd be okay in the bucks department.

I swooped down on him like an eagle. Watch my tactics. I put both hands on the edge of the counter, lean forward toward the customer, and in a low voice, serious, you know, but polite, I ask him: "Can I get you something, sir?" Because there are assholes who say "What you having?" But where do they think they are? In a donut shop? I instead would ask: "Can I get you something, sir?" Notice the difference? I get *you* something. I to *you*. Because that's why I'm here, to serve you, and you are here to order. You ask and I obey. A customer with class can appreciate these things. They notice them just like that and they thank you for them. He answered: "A J&B." Terrific, I thought. He's not one of those misers who ask for orange juice or local booze.

He had a butch voice and a face that, seen from close by, was unbelievable, I swear. And the clothes! Italian tie, poplin shirt, a light-grey three-piece made in heaven. I used to be crazy about clothes, and figured out how much the lot was worth.

I was still learning toward him. "Ice? Water? Perrier?"

"On the rocks."

"Yes, sir."

And all the while I stared into his eyes, green eyes, so green they sent a shiver down your back, know what I mean, and he also was staring. Both very serious, you understand. No cutesy smiles. But that kind of serious ... I don't know how to explain ... that kind of serious like two guys passing some secret information they don't want others to know about.

I was about to get the whisky when I saw him put a cigarette to his mouth. In a flash I lit it with my solid gold Dupont. Freddy had given me the Dupont. It always worked and in the darkness of the place it shone like a jewel. He thanked me with a nod and kept looking. There was something already, just a little, but already something between the two of us.

Now came a bit of just being the waiter. I went up to the shelves, got the bottle of J&B, the glass, the pail of ice, the measuring cup, asked Gaston for the bill, all this without looking at him, almost always turning my back on him, but everything very fast, you know, to see if he'd still watch, to show him that I knew that he was a classy customer and that you mustn't make classy customers wait.

I came back and poured out the J&B in front of him, something I didn't do for everyone, even if they ask for the real stuff, and said: "One? Two?"

"Two, please."

I put in the two ice cubes, marked the bill, and now to the third part of my tactics. You stand very close to the customer, very straight, not looking at him, and you watch the tables or the people in the street. But if the guy pulls out another cigarette you run to light it. So the guy realizes that even if you're looking somewhere else you're really watching him, and if you're not looking at him straight in the eye it's so as not to get on his tits and let him drink in peace, but that you are there, near enough, ready to satisfy his every wish. You know, a classy customer appreciates these things.

The nuisance was the fruits at the bar, all ruffled up as they were, wanting to spoil my game. They were trying to draw the guy's attention and they found nothing better than calling me at the top of their voices:

"Michel, another glass of water."

"Michel, another daiquiri."

"Michel, a light."

And Michel this and Michel that. Well, anyway, at least he'd know my name. He could see that the customers were friendly with me and that even if they tried to be a bit too friendly I was able to handle it without going too far, you understand. That if I wasn't an easy pick-up, I wasn't an untouchable, either.

The guy, from time to time, looked around the place. The fruits, thinking that he wanted to make connections, would get all frantic. But he would look at me again or look into his glass, and smoke. I noticed everything without having to pin my eyes on him, and was having a laugh all to myself. The kids also realized what was happening, because they have experience, you know. But no one said anything to me. That's a sacred law in this world, you know. Had I been on the other side of the bar, then yes, one would have come up to me and said: "Congratulations, darling. It seems you hooked yourself a beauty."

But I was just a waiter, and they would not give in. And out of spite, just to break my balls, they kept asking for this and asking for that. Break *my* balls. Poor darlings.

Just as one of the fruits at the bar, I don't remember which one, was making me change his glass, I saw that Jorge, better known as Jorgelina, a fag who was into drugs and threw wild parties at his house, or so they say because I never went to one, had poured half a glass of rum and coke on Buster Crabbe's sleeve just to get to talk to him.

I left the guy who wanted his glass changed and ran to the other end of the bar, where Buster Crabbe was sitting. Just to show him that for me, he was more important than that whole bunch of fags put together.

Jorge, with that voice of his, like a pregnant chicken, said: "Oh I'm so sorry, so sorry," and pulled out a handkerchief and tried to mop the sleeve. Buster Crabbe, without even looking at what the other was doing, answered: "It's okay," and went on drinking his whisky.

When I came up to him, it seemed to me that he was smiling with his eyes, you know, like saying to me: "But can you imagine, how far a fruit like this will go?" I stood there very formal, you know, not wanting to make Jorgelina angry, after all she leaves me three big ones every night, and said: "Allow me, sir."

And I also pulled out my handkerchief, the only one of the lot Freddy had given me, Irish linen, real class.

He stopped me: "Don't bother, thanks." But you see, not aggressively. You know, I say aggressively, and my head fills up with things I remember. *Aggressively*. That was Freddy's favourite word. For Freddy you were or you were not aggressive, somebody loved aggressively or made fun of you aggressively. I understand what he meant. For example, Buster Crabbe said "Don't bother." And he said it seriously, but not aggressively. On the contrary. Look, it was like he was being serious just to show me that there, among the bunch of kids, the only one of his own kind was me, but that he didn't or couldn't show it in front of everyone, so he would show it just a little, in a way that no one would know, so that only I, so intelligent, would know. And to tell you the truth, I liked that. And I decided to carry on with his little game.

So that when, after the "don't bother" he asked me for another drink I said very seriously and without looking at him: "Yes, sir." And I went off to get the J&B.

I heard Jorge's clucking: "Am I forgiven?" And the butch voice of Buster Crabbe: "Yes, if you buzz off."

Incredible! That guy was incredible! I was dying to laugh, really. I wanted to turn around and see the look on the fruit's face. But when I got to the bar and managed to turn around, Jorge had disappeared and Buster Crabbe was smoking another cigarette and I had lost my chance to light it and, maybe, start a conversation.

He stayed there all night. From time to time he would check out the kids at the bar or the couples on the dance floor, but with a self-sufficient look, you know, like a guy who knows what he's doing. Not like those greaseballs who sometimes appeared at Le Matelot by chance, and when they realized where they were, they'd pull a face that you knew they wanted to start bashing up the fruits. Not him, you see? He watched them as if it were a show, just for the fun of it. But at about two o'clock he began to look bored. Of course: he wanted the whole bunch of fruits to fuck off and leave him alone with me, so that we could talk in peace and quiet. Because an English gentleman like that wasn't going to open up in front of that birdcage. But one thing was certain: he kept looking at me, more and more. This is what he'd do: he would stare me in the eye, then look away, then stare again, then look away again, and it went on like that for hours. Just like Freddy, when Freddy met me at La Farola. I was sure he was getting ready for the big move.

I too wanted everyone to leave. But they wouldn't. When two would leave, three would come in, and the bar would be again full of people. I thought it was about time to make him understand that I knew what he wanted and that I was with him all the way, because I was afraid that this guy would get fed up with sitting and waiting, and take off. So I started smiling. But listen: I've got my tactics. Freddy always said that I was the only one he knew who could smile without stretching his lips. He said I was a ventriloquist with smiles. Buster Crabbe understood as quickly as that; I knew, because his eyes began to sparkle.

I helped him to his third drink without asking Gaston.

"This one's on the house, sir."

I poured the whisky for him and put in the two ice cubes, and it seemed to me that knowing that he wanted it on the rocks, to help him to it without asking, was like knowing all his tastes, like being his private secretary, his right arm. It was great.

And just as I was about to go and place myself, as I said before, just a few steps away from him, he said in a low voice: "Thanks, Michel."

It sent shivers all down my spine. You see? He had called me Michel. A guy who had come to Le Matelot for the first time, a fancy guy, an English gentleman, and with those great looks. No problem, Buster Crabbe was mine.

But then, so that no one should catch on what was happening, I started to look like serious. Well, to tell you the truth, a little because I didn't want anybody to notice, and also because, when one of those guys tries to pick me up, I don't know why, I just get angry and nervous. The same happened with Freddy. You should have seen what Freddy looked like when I met him. I was barely fifteen. Well, who remembers Freddy now? The thing is that if you had come into Le Matelot that night and seen me, you would have thought that I was mad as hell.

At last, at almost half past four, he was the only one at the bar and there was just one couple left necking on the dance-floor.

Then I saw, even though I was pretending to look somewhere else, that he was calling me with his hand. I ran up to him. Again I put both hands on the bar, leaned forward toward him, like the first time—remember I told you what my tactics were—but now I looked at him in the eyes and smiled at him with my whole face. In the early morning I always look more handsome. I looked pale, with dark blue lines under my eyes, and everybody said I was the spitting image of James Dean. On many nights, around that time, one of the customers, pissed as hell, would ask, in a hoarse voice: "Michel, Michel, how much do you charge?"

But all he said was: "Last one," and pointed at the glass.

I served him his fourth J&B. The bill was twelve hundred pesos. I just stood next to him, in front of him, not trying to hide anything, as if waiting, as if giving him rope. He looked at me and smiled, a little pissed, I thought. When they're pissed even the straightest guy kicks his shoes off. Then, in a low voice, I don't know why, because Gaston was at the other end of the bar adding up his figures, and the couple was necking about thirty feet away, but maybe to make the conversation more intimate, or maybe because he wanted the whole thing to be mysterious, he asked: "Is your name really Michel?" He asked it outright, the bastard. And suddenly I thought: a cop. Again I pretended to look sad, but what I was was angry and frightened.

"No sir. They make you change your name here."

"And what is your real name?"

"Gonzalo."

He lowered his eyes and sent me a Colgate smile. "Nice name. I like it better than Michel."

"I do too, sir."

That's true. Michel sounds like a fruit. Michel is okay for a hairdresser or for a dressmaker, but not for me. Gonzalo is a nice butch name, Spanish but butch.

He drank down the whisky as if he were dying of thirst, as if it were Pepsi. I, still thinking he was a cop, looked toward the street, but just in case I looked angry.

"Have you been working here long?"

"One week."

"And do you like this job?"

Nice trap. Who did he think I was? Like born yesterday?

"No, sir. I don't really like it."

"And why do you do it then?"

"Beggars can't be choosers. I couldn't get anything better."

"How old are you?"

"Eighteen, almost nineteen."

"And your parents don't mind?"

We spoke as if we were at confession. I know it looked as if we were making some strange deal. Gaston, from the other end, had realized that something was happening, as he told me afterwards. But if you couldn't hear us, you would have thought that I was like squealing to the cops, because I was answering so aggressively. See, Freddy's word. It's stuck, since the old days, and I still use it. Well, as I was saying, I was answering aggressively. But he kept asking ever so nicely.

"I have no parents, sir. I have no one. I'm alone in the world." I said it all at once. If he was with the police, that would be useful. To be an orphan, to be eighteen, to be alone in the world....

He sat there a while in silence. A long while, so long, that I at last dared to look at him. His eyes were shining. What eyes, dear God! As if he had been sniffing coke. He was even better-looking than Buster Crabbe.

To hide those eyes, the eyes of a tiger, he looked down again. "Where do you live?"

"Canning and Las Heras."

"Alone?"

For the cops, living alone is a point against you, But maybe he was asking to see whether I had a place for us to go. In any case, with Mrs. Zulma, I couldn't take the risk. So, I thought, the best thing is to tell him the truth.

"No. I have a place in a rooming house. I used to live there with my mother. But now that my mother died...."

"Long ago?"

"Ten days."

"Oh, I'm sorry."

Sure he was sorry. He was just pretending, good manners and all that, but inside, I thought, he's dancing on one leg.

I, just in case he was a cop, even though he didn't really look like a cop, kept on explaining. "Before we had two rooms, Mum and I. But now with one it's enough."

"I understand."

"I had to tighten my belt."

"I understand. Of course."

He was silent for a while, looking at his glass and turning it in his hands. There was no whisky left in it. Only half a melted ice cube. I was waiting. I knew, because of Freddy, that a guy who's young, good-looking, and broke is the best bait.

"Michel."

"Yes, sir?"

He was still silent, looking at the glass. He preferred Gonzalo but he still called me Michel. He didn't dare stop pretending. He was even shyer than Freddy. Or maybe more of a gentleman. And I was looking at him desperately, wanting to say to him: But yes, my love, I understand and I'm here, I'm all yours. I'll be your bodyguard, I thought. I'll be your adopted son. To call you Dad in front of everyone and even kiss you, without anyone saying anything, and at night be his lover and still call him Dad. That was always my dream. But Freddy didn't want to be called Dad.

Finally he said it. "Michel, what time do you leave?"

"We close at five. Quarter past I'm out."

He had begun the final run. I swear my heart was beating, because of all the emotion and also because I was frightened he might be a cop. A gay cop would have been okay. A cop, someone in the army, maybe an airline pilot, thinking of me for some fun. Another of my fantasies.

Suddenly he nailed me on the spot with his eyes. I understood why.

Because if he had asked me while he was looking down it would have seemed as if he were begging for something, something he was ashamed of, but he had to make me believe that he wasn't asking for anything dirty, and that he wasn't offending me, wasn't frightening me, you understand?

"Michel, I'll wait for you outside in my car. It's parked at the corner of Libertador. It's a black Thunderbird."

A cop doesn't have a black Thunderbird. Even if he is into all sorts of funny business. A cop doesn't spend all night drinking whisky. What for? To know if Le Matelot is what everybody knows, even the lollipop ladies, even Mrs. Zulma? To lay a trap for me? Me? And who was I? Was I Al Capone to spend all that effort on me? No. All this song and dance was not stuff for a cop. This was more along Freddy's line, someone more careful than Freddy.

So quietly, just like that, I said: "I'll be there at a quarter past five."

That way, if he had felt embarrassed, I'd show him there was no need.

He paid, left me an enormous tip which I pocketed without a word, and he left without saying goodbye. You see, I liked the fact that he didn't say goodbye. It was a way of saying, I'll be waiting.

Gaston asked: "So, who was that guy?"

"What guy?"

"The guy who just left."

I looked toward the door as if I didn't quite remember. "Sort of blond …?"

"Yeah, that one."

"I think he was a cop."

"Why?"

"He was asking things."

"What things?"

"If I had seen a fat gay guy around here, white hair, someone called Rudi."

"Not here."

"That's what I said."

"And he didn't tell you why he was looking for him?"

"You crazy? Why would he tell me?"

"So why do you think he's a cop?"

"I don't know. I just thought so."

"No, he's no cop."

Quarter past five I was at the corner of Libertador, next to the black Thunderbird, red seats, a dream. I felt like really cool. I had looked at myself in the cloakroom mirror and, let me tell you, seeing myself in a mirror made me feel good. Because with a face like that I had a right to everything. To pick up Buster Crabbe the very first night at Le Matelot, I, the waiter, and not the fruits at the bar with their Rolexes on their wrists and their Peugeots at the door. The right to get Buster Crabbe to buy me suits, shirts, ties, let me drive his Thunderbird, and maybe one day take me with him to Europe, and there in Europe, who knows, I might pick someone up with even more bucks.

First we just talked any old shit. That the car's brakes were not working well, that it cost him an arm and a leg to keep it, and that he wanted to change it for a domestic make. I remember that the same thing happened with Freddy. You know why? Because at first they feel a little over-excited, a little too uneasy. You know, it's all a bit too quick, so just talking like that, talking about just anything, like two friends, like two straight guys, the situation becomes easier. Or maybe, who knows, they are so happy they can't believe it, and they try to go into it slowly just to get accustomed, not to get too nervous, or to convince themselves they're not dreaming, as they must have dreamt so many times of some young guy who finally gets away with some skirt, and here they had me, in the car, next to them, ready for anything, I, with my face and my body.

But three minutes later, without looking at me, staring out of the window in front of him, he asked: "And before working in the bar, what did you do?"

"I went to school."

"And what did you live on?"

I didn't have to lie. "My mother earned enough for both of us."

"What did you study?"

This is where I had to make up something.

"Technical school."

"Probably the last year, I imagine."

"The last year. And that's when I had to leave."

"What would you have liked to be?"

"An engineer."

"A good profession."

Look, you have to let them ask you everything, about your family, about the dog, about the neighbour's parrot. Because a friend already knows all that and doesn't need to ask you anything. But they, just think of it, they don't know you at all. So you have to give them a speed course because if you don't, they have to go to bed with you like cold and they don't like that, they don't trust it, they think they're just going to bed with some fucking sailor, and little English gentlemen like Freddy don't enjoy that.

"Couldn't you find another job? Because look I'm sorry to say so, but Le Matelot is a terrible place."

It made me a little angry, this putting on airs. So I said to him: "So what were you doing there?" I said it so aggressively that I felt sorry and changed my tune: "I mean, is that the first time you've been there?"

"First and last."

"And how did you find it?"

"By chance. I don't live in Buenos Aires. I live away most of the year."

"In Europe?"

"No, in the country."

I let out a little laugh, loud enough for him to hear me.

"What are you laughing at?"

"Nothing. You know what I thought you were? A cop."

He also laughed, but louder. "What made you think I was a cop?"

"I don't know. The things you asked."

"Did they bother you?"

"No."

"Have you had trouble with the police?"

"No. What trouble?"

"But you're afraid of them."

"No, never. Why should I be afraid? But Le Matelot has a bad reputation, so even if I'm clean I can get hit on the rebound."

We had reached that little square at the end of Avenida Alvear. He stopped the car. He turned around, his full body, and looked at me in the eye. I sat sideways, against the door, and also looked at him. The moment has come, I thought.

"Do you usually accept invitations from customers at the bar?"

You can imagine, I didn't like that. But I knew that Buster Crabbe was really like Freddy. Freddy went to the same places, liked the same things, did the same stuff as the other gays, but didn't want to be mistaken for one of them. You've got to see the difference, he used to say. The difference of what? The difference between a fruit like Jorge who says it to you in the face as soon as she sees you, and these here, who instead talk to you first about the brakes of the car not working. But okay, just humour them. Anyway, I like them like that. Something else I'll tell you: Freddy used to go to all sorts of gay bars, was always surrounded by young kids and fruits, and then he'd be all worried because everyone would say he was gay. I'll never understand that.

I answered, without seeming offended: "This is the first time."

"And why did you accept this time?"

"Because I know the difference."

Freddy would have liked the flattery. But he didn't seem to. He was more complicated than Freddy.

"But you thought I was a cop."

"All the braver, then, for accepting."

Dig that one, I thought. He couldn't help smiling. "So this sort of place didn't corrupt you?"

I was beginning to understand. He liked first nights. But I played dumb: "Corrupt how?"

"I don't know. I imagine that at Le Matelot there must be drug addicts, car thieves, hustlers …"

I was waiting for the word. And he said it: "… homosexuals."

I had on my best innocent face. "I don't think so. They all seem like guys from good families."

"But you yourself said that Le Matelot had a bad reputation."

I'd been an asshole. I tried to fix it up. "Yes, like all the bars around here. People talk, but…."

"Not all the bars have a bad reputation."

"But you saw, there were lots of straight couples."

"I mean the ones at the bar."

"If those are homosexuals, then I don't know. I only know them as customers at the bar. And all they do there is have a drink and talk."

"Talk to you."

"So who talks to me? All they say is, give me a whisky, give me a light, give me the bill, and that's all."

"That's all?"

I was starting to get angry. I looked at him: "What else?"

"Ask you to go out with them."

"Never."

"So I'm the first. Of course you've been working there for barely a week. They're probably waiting to know you better."

The bastard was making fun of me, and how. I was getting really mad. "Yes, sir. The first. The first even if I had been working there for ten years."

He also seemed angry: "And to what do I owe the honour of having been accepted?"

I got aggressive: "I told you. Because I know how to distinguish. And I thought you also knew how to distinguish. But I was wrong, so I'm sorry." I thought: here he gets really mad. But no, he laughed.

"Don't get angry. I'm not asking these questions with any bad intention. But don't you think it's a little strange to go out with a man the first time you see him?"

I crouched in my seat, looked out in front of me, spoke as if I had a knot in my throat. "Very, very strange, yeah. Except if you're alone in the world and have no parents, no friends, no one. The only people you know are these nicely brought-up kinds who treat you as if you were their servant. So it's not so strange if you catch on to the first rope somebody throws out. Some sort of feeling, some affection. Something to make you feel a person, not just a waiter."

I turned around and looked at him in the eye, ready to go for it. I know how to make tears come to my eyes. "But if I was wrong about you, or you were wrong about me, I can get out here, and walk back home." I thought: either he beats me up or he kisses me.

He didn't do either. He looked at me for a long while, with a really strange face, like studying me. This one is really weirder than Freddy, I thought. Then he patted my leg, he patted it a little more than necessary (he must have been testing the quality, I thought), and said: "Okay."

Nothing more: "Okay."

He started the car again, took Cerrito, two blocks further, and stopped the car. He pointed to a door. "I've got a flat there, where I stay when I come to Buenos Aires. Come up with me." And, as he thought I had made some sort of gesture (I hadn't moved), he looked at me: "Come on. Don't be afraid." Again the Colgate smile: "I'm not what you think."

Freddy's very same words. I answered, as I had to Freddy: "I know, sir."

Again he sat there for a while studying me (I thought he was thinking: maybe I'm landed with this goof). Then he said: "I've got to talk to you."

The same as Freddy, Freddy, when he took me that first night to his place, had to talk to me. And as soon as we got in he started taking his clothes off.

He opened the door of the car. I got out by the other door. There was no one in the street. We entered the building. No one saw us go in. We crossed a hall almost as big as Le Matelot, all carpeted. At the far end were elevators. We got into one, also carpeted and full of mirrors. I looked up and saw myself so handsome that I understood that Buster Crabbe had been putting up a fight up to the very last minute because he knew that with me he was lost. We got to a certain floor, he opened the door of an apartment, turned on the light, and I was just looking around when he started hugging me.

"Gonzalo," he said with half a voice, and I thought that he was panting. "Gonzalo."

I also began to hug him, but slowly, to make him want me more.

"Gonzalo," he said, and he held my face with one hand. "I've got something to say to you."

"It's not necessary," I said. "I know." And I kissed him on the mouth.

Look, it was all so quick and unexpected that I don't really remember. I know that with both his hands he shook my arms from his body. I saw that his face looked terrible. And immediately he began to beat me up.

You know, I can't stand anybody laying a finger on me. Not even the old lady ever hit me. Least of all one of these guys. So when he began hitting me, a sort of madness came over me. I don't know what I did. All I know is that I saw him lying on the floor, the eyes open, and the blond hair full of blood. I felt his chest. He was dead.

Imagine, I was so frightened I could have shat in my pants. I ran from the apartment. At six I was back home.

For a while I couldn't sleep. I thought that nobody had seen me with the guy, so that when they discovered the body, the cops, even if they looked far and wide, would not be able to incriminate me. And if they found out about his visit to Le Matelot, well, so what? I didn't know him, I had served him some drinks till half past four, then he had left and I hadn't seen him again, and I would also tell them the story I had told Gaston, of the little fat white-haired fruit, a certain Rudi, and Gaston would be my witness, and the police would think it was some sort of a gay crime. I was also thinking, why had he beaten me up? Where had I gone wrong? I thought first that he was maybe one of these loonies who first lead you on and then beat you up, or first beat you up and then get you into bed. At last I fell asleep and slept till two in the afternoon.

At two o'clock Mrs. Zulma came in. "Come on, get up," she shouted. "What time will you have lunch?"

Look, I'll tell it to you all in one go, because at first I was half asleep and didn't understand what she was asking and didn't answer, and then, when I began to realize, I got so desperate I almost went crazy.

"Listen, didn't a man go to see you, last night, at the bar? Tall blond, very good-looking? Because last night, as soon as you left, he came round here and asked for you. I told him you weren't there, that you had gone out. He wanted to know more, but I, just imagine, didn't know who he was so I wouldn't tell him anything, because I thought, God knows who this one is and probably that good-for-nothing got into some trouble. But when he showed me the envelope with a letter and I recognized your poor mother's handwriting I thought things were different. Yes, I never said anything to you because Rosina asked me not to say anything. But now I will. The day before she died Rosina gave me a sealed envelope with a letter inside, to put in the mailbox after she died. But Rosina, I said to her, you're not going to die. I told her that to make her feel better, because I knew she wasn't going to last more than twenty-four hours. And she also knew it, poor soul. Well, that's how it was. Two or three days after we buried her I put the envelope in the mailbox. It was addressed to a certain Gonzalo of this-and-that, a lot of very distinguished surnames, and the address was an estate in Córdoba. Rosina had asked me not to say anything to you, because if the letter didn't achieve any results you didn't need to know, but obviously it did, and that's why I'm telling you. So when the man showed me the envelope I realized that he was the Gonzalo from Córdoba, and told him everything. He was here for like an hour, asking about Rosina and about you, especially about you. He wanted to know what you were like, what you did, what you didn't do. I told him that you used to go to school, but that now, after Rosina's death, you had had to start to work, as a waiter, and in a place I really didn't like. He told me he'd go there, to meet you. Didn't he go? Maybe he thought better of it and meant to meet you here. And I think he did well, because that bar, my boy, let me tell you.... So get up and get dressed, because he'll probably be here any moment now and you shouldn't keep him waiting. Because you can see he's a gentleman, and the car he has, so luxurious. I bet he hasn't come all the way from Córdoba just to give you his condolences. I don't know a thing, but for some reason Rosina gave you his name. Poor Rosina, always so proud. She probably never told him, but when she knew you were going to be alone in the world she sent him the letter. Get up and get dressed, this is probably your big day."

Then the bell rang.

"What did I tell you? I bet it's him."

It was the police. They had reached me through the letter the old lady had sent him and which they found in his pocket. They didn't suspect anything. They were just coming to ask a few questions, that's all. But I immediately confessed.

Hands

Sherwood Anderson

Perhaps the small-town chronicle is an American invention. If so, no name is more clearly associated with this "genre" than that of Sherwood Anderson, author of Winesburg, Ohio *(1919). From* Winesburg *springs a whole geography of small American towns: Sinclair Lewis's Gopher Prairie, Thornton Wilder's Grover's Corners, even Grace Metalious's Peyton Place—microcosms that reflect the vaster purgatory of America. Anderson believed the small town to be emblematic of his society's great evils: the denial of instinct, the imposition of common standards, the repression of individual longings. Salvation, he felt, was to be found in the senses, in the experience of nature, and, above all, in sex. In* Perhaps Women, *an essay written in 1931 (long before Margaret Thatcher could prove him wrong), he suggested that salvation lay in female leadership.*

It is in the senses, in the feeling of touch specifically, that Wing Biddlebaum, the hero of "Hands", seeks his salvation. In the preface to Winesburg, Ohio *(in which "Hands" was first published), Anderson attempted to explain how a personal belief could be, and usually was, destroyed by a small town's need to preserve its adamantine cohesion. "The moment one of the people took one of the truths to himself, called it his truth, and tried to live his life by it, he became a grotesque and the truth he embraced became a falsehood." The small town, Anderson seems to say, holds no room for individual truths.*

Upon the half decayed veranda of a small frame house that stood near the edge of a ravine near the town of Winesburg, Ohio, a fat little old man walked nervously up and down. Across a long field that had been seeded for clover but that had produced only a dense crop of yellow mustard weeds, he could see the public highway along which went a wagon filled with berry pickers returning from the fields. The berry pickers, youths and maidens, laughed and shouted boisterously.

A boy clad in a blue shirt leaped from the wagon and attempted to drag after him one of the maidens, who screamed and protested shrilly. The feet of the boy in the road kicked up a cloud of dust that floated across the face of the departing sun. Over the long field came a thin girlish voice. "Oh, you Wing Biddlebaum, comb your hair, it's falling into your eyes," commanded the voice to the man, who was bald and whose nervous little hands fiddled about the bare white forehead as though arranging a mass of tangled locks.

Wing Biddlebaum, forever frightened and beset by a ghostly band of doubts, did not think of himself as in any way a part of the life of the town where he had lived for twenty years. Among all the people of Winesburg but one had come close to him. With George Willard, son of Tom Willard, the proprietor of the New Willard House, he had formed something like a friendship. George Willard was the reporter on the *Winesburg Eagle* and sometimes in the evenings he walked out along the highway to Wing Biddlebaum's house. Now as the old man walked up and down on the veranda, his hands moving nervously about, he was hoping that George Willard would come and spend the evening with him. After the wagon containing the berry pickers had passed, he went across the field through the tall mustard weeds and climbing a rail fence peered anxiously along the road to the town. For a moment he stood thus, rubbing his hands together and looking up and down the road, and then, fear overcoming him, ran back to walk again upon the porch on his own house.

In the presence of George Willard, Wing Biddlebaum, who for twenty years had been the town mystery, lost something of his timidity, and his shadowy personality, submerged in a sea of doubts, came forth to look at the world. With the young reporter at his side, he ventured in the light of day into Main Street or strode up and down on the rickety front porch of his own house, talking excitedly. The voice that had been low and trembling became shrill and loud. The bent figure straightened. With a kind of wriggle, like a fish returned to the brook by the fisherman, Biddlebaum the silent began to talk, striving to put into words the ideas that had been accumulated by his mind during long years of silence.

Wing Biddlebaum talked much with his hands. The slender expressive fingers, forever active, forever striving to conceal themselves in his pockets or behind his back, came forth and became the piston rods of his machinery of expression.

The story of Wing Biddlebaum is a story of hands. Their restless activity, like unto the beating of the wings of an imprisoned bird, had given him his name. Some obscure poet of the town had thought of it. The hands alarmed their owner. He wanted to keep them hidden away and looked with amazement at the quiet inexpressive hands of other men who worked beside him in the fields, or passed, driving sleepy teams on country roads.

When he talked to George Willard, Wing Biddlebaum closed his fists and beat with them upon a table or on the walls of his house. The action made him more comfortable. If the desire to talk came to him when the two were walking in the fields, he sought out a stump or the top board of a fence and with his hands pounding busily talked with renewed ease.

The story of Wing Biddlebaum's hands is worth a book in itself. Sympathetically set forth it would tap many strange, beautiful qualities in obscure men. It is a job for a poet. In Winesburg the hands had attracted attention merely because of their activity. With them Wing Biddlebaum had picked as high as a hundred and forty quarts of strawberries in a day. They became his distinguishing feature, the source of his fame. Also they made more grotesque an already grotesque and elusive individuality. Winesburg was proud of the hands of Wing Biddlebaum in the same spirit in which it was proud of Banker White's new stone house and Wesley Moyer's bay stallion, Tony Tip, that had won the two-fifteen trot at the fall races in Cleveland.

As for George Willard, he had many times wanted to ask about the hands. At times an almost overwhelming curiosity had taken hold of him. He felt that there must be a reason for their strange activity and their inclination to keep hidden away and only a growing respect for Wing Biddlebaum kept him from blurting out the questions that were often in his mind.

Once he had been on the point of asking. The two were walking in the fields on a summer afternoon and had stopped to sit upon a grassy bank. All afternoon Wing Biddlebaum had talked as one inspired. By a fence he had stopped and beating like a giant woodpecker upon the top board had shouted at George Willard, condemning his tendency to be too much influenced by the people about him. "You are destroying yourself," he cried. "You have the inclination to be alone and to dream and you are afraid of dreams. You want to be like others in town here. You hear them talk and you try to imitate them."

On the grassy bank Wing Biddlebaum had tried again to drive his point home. His voice became soft and reminiscent, and with a sigh of contentment he launched into a long rambling talk, speaking as one lost in a dream.

Out of the dream Wing Biddlebaum made a picture for George Willard. In the picture men lived again in a kind of pastoral golden age. Across a green open country came clean-limbed young men, some afoot, some mounted upon horses. In crowds the young men came to gather about the feet of an old man who sat beneath a tree in a tiny garden and who talked to them.

Wing Biddlebaum became wholly inspired. For once he forgot the hands. Slowly they stole forth and lay upon George Willard's shoulders. Something new and bold came into the voice that talked. "You must try to forget all you have learned," said the old man. "You must begin to dream. From this time on you must shut your ears to the roaring of the voices."

Pausing in his speech, Wing Biddlebaum looked long and earnestly at George Willard. His eyes glowed. Again he raised the hands to caress the boy and then a look of horror swept over his face.

With a convulsive movement of his body, Wing Biddlebaum sprang to his feet and thrust his hands deep into his trousers pockets. Tears came to his eyes. "I must be getting along home. I can talk no more with you," he said nervously.

Without looking back, the old man had hurried down the hillside and across a meadow, leaving George Willard perplexed and frightened upon the grassy slope. With a shiver of dread the boy arose and went along the road toward town. "I'll not ask him about his hands," he thought, touched by the memory of the terror he had seen in the man's eyes. "There's something wrong, but I don't want to know what it is. His hands have something to do with his fear of me and of everyone."

And George Willard was right. Let us look briefly into the story of the hands. Perhaps our talking of them will arouse the poet who will tell the hidden wonder story of the influence for which the hands were but fluttering pennants of promise.

In his youth Wing Biddlebaum had been a school teacher in a town in Pennsylvania. He was not then known as Wing Biddlebaum, but went by the less euphonic name of Adolph Myers. As Adolph Myers he was much loved by the boys of his school.

Adolph Myers was meant by nature to be a teacher of youth. He was one of those rare, little-understood men who rule by a power so gentle that it passes as a lovable weakness. In their feeling for the boys under their charge such men are not unlike the finer sort of women in their love of men.

And yet that is but crudely stated. It needs the poet there. With the boys of his school, Adolph Myers had walked in the evening or had sat talking until dusk upon the schoolhouse steps lost in a kind of dream. Here and there went his hands, caressing the shoulders of the boys, playing about the tousled heads. As he talked his voice became soft and musical. There was a caress in that also. In a way the voice and the hands, the stroking of the shoulders and the touching of the hair were a part of the schoolmaster's effort to carry a dream into the young minds. By the caress that was in his fingers he expressed himself. He was one of those men in whom the force that creates life is diffused, not centralized. Under the caress of his hands doubt and disbelief went out of the minds of the boys and they began also to dream.

And then the tragedy. A half-witted boy of the school became enamored of the young master. In his bed at night he imagined unspeakable things and in the morning went forth to tell his dreams as facts. Strange, hideous accusations fell from his loose-hung lips. Through the Pennsylvania town went a shiver. Hidden, shadowy doubts that had been in men's minds concerning Adolph Myers were galvanized into beliefs.

The tragedy did not linger. Trembling lads were jerked out of bed and questioned. "He put his arms about me," said one. "His fingers were always playing in my hair," said another.

One afternoon a man of the town, Henry Bradford, who kept a saloon, came to the schoolhouse door. Calling Adolph Myers into the school yard he began to beat him with his fists. As his hard knuckles beat down into the frightened face of the schoolmaster, his wrath became more and more terrible. Screaming with dismay, the children ran here and there like disturbed insects. "I'll teach you to put your hands on my boy, you beast," roared the saloon keeper, who, tired of beating the master, had begun to kick him about the yard.

Adolph Myers was driven from the Pennsylvania town in the night. With lanterns in their hands a dozen men came to the door of the house where he lived alone and commanded that he dress and come forth. It was raining and one of the men had a rope in his hands. They had intended to hang the schoolmaster, but something in his figure, so small, white, and pitiful, touched their hearts and they let him escape. As he ran away into the darkness they repented of their weakness and ran after him, swearing and throwing sticks and great balls of soft mud at the figure that screamed and ran faster and faster into the darkness.

For twenty years Adolph Myers had lived alone in Winesburg. He was but forty but looked sixty-five. The name of Biddlebaum he got from a box of goods seen at a freight station as he hurried through an eastern Ohio town. He had an aunt in Winesburg, a black-toothed old woman who raised chickens, and with her he lived until she died. He had been ill for a year after the experience in Pennsylvania, and after his recovery worked as a day laborer in the fields, going timidly about and striving to conceal his hands. Although he did not understand what had happened he felt that the hands must be to blame. Again and again the fathers of the boys had talked of the hands. "Keep your hands to yourself," the saloon keeper had roared, dancing with fury in the schoolhouse yard.

Upon the veranda of his house by the ravine, Wing Biddlebaum continued to walk up and down until the sun had disappeared and the road beyond the field was lost in the gray shadows. Going into his house he cut slices of bread and spread honey upon them. When the rumble of the evening train that took away the express cars loaded with the day's harvest of berries had passed and restored the silence of the summer night, he went again to walk upon the veranda. In the darkness he could not see the hands and they became quiet. Although he still hungered for the presence of the boy, who was the medium through which he expressed his love of man, the hunger became again a part of his loneliness and his waiting. Lighting a lamp, Wing Biddlebaum washed the few dishes soiled by his simple meal and, setting up a folding cot by the screen door that led to the porch, prepared to undress for the night. A few stray white bread crumbs lay on the cleanly washed floor by the table; putting the lamp upon a low stool he began to pick up the crumbs, carrying them to his mouth one by one with unbelievable rapidity. In the dense blotch of light beneath the table, the kneeling figure looked like a priest engaged in some service of his church. The nervous expressive fingers, flashing in and out of the light, might well have been mistaken for the fingers of the devotee going swiftly through decade after decade of his rosary.

Clancy in the Tower of Babel

John Cheever

Jorge Luis Borges noted that the peculiar logic of hatred allows us to accuse someone "of never having been to China" and "in the temples of that country, of having insulted the gods". The Nazis found Heine's poem Die Lorelei *to be "too German to be Jewish" and issued a decree pronouncing it anonymous. At the end of the Second World War, a tree associated with General Pétain was sentenced and executed for collaborating with the enemy. Hatred and its corollary, prejudice, construct in our imagination something more powerful than that to which our eyes bear witness—something that in fact replaces the details of what we see. It is impossible to hate in details: to hate well, we require generalities. "We can scarcely hate," wrote William Hazlitt, "any one that we know."*

John Cheever's fiction deals in details. His characters (such as Clancy, the New York elevator man) may try to see the world in a generalizing way, but the details distract them, lead them into what Clancy calls "half blindness". The inextinguishable and astounding variety of the human animal contradicts any labels that someone such as Clancy tries to impose on his surroundings. The world, to Cheever's characters, is ultimately irreducible. Cheever himself said many times that he refused to be reduced to epithets. He didn't want to be known as a New Yorker writer, as a writer of social satire, as a writer inspired by alcohol, certainly not as a homosexual writer. He wanted—and in this he succeeded wonderfully—to be known simply as a writer of the human condition.

James and Nora Clancy came from farms near the little town of Newcastle. Newcastle is near Limerick. They had been poor in Ireland and they were not much better off in the new country, but they were cleanly and decent people. Their home farms had been orderly places, long inhabited by the same families, and the Clancys enjoyed the grace of a tradition. Their simple country ways were so deeply ingrained that twenty years in the New World had had little effect on them. Nora went to market with a straw basket under her arm, like a woman going out to a kitchen garden, and Clancy's pleasant face reflected a simple life. They had only one child, a son named John, and they had been able to pass on to him their peaceable and contented views. They were people who centered their lives in half a city block, got down on their knees on the floor to say "Hail Mary, full of grace," and took turns in the bathtub in the kitchen on Saturday night.

When Clancy was still a strong man in his forties, he fell down some stairs in the factory and broke his hip. He was out of work for nearly a year, and while he got compensation for this time, it was not as much as his wages had been and he and his family suffered the pain of indebtedness and need. When Clancy recovered, he was left with a limp and it took him a long time to find another job. He went to church every day, and in the end it was the intercession of a priest that got work for him, running an elevator in one of the big apartment houses on the East Side. Clancy's good manners and his clean and pleasant face pleased the tenants, and with his salary and the tips they gave him he made enough to pay his debts and support his wife and son.

The apartment house was not far from the slum tenement where James and Nora had lived since their marriage, but financially and morally it was another creation, and Clancy at first looked at the tenants as if they were made out of sugar. The ladies wore coats and jewels that cost more than Clancy would make in a lifetime of hard work, and when he came home in the evenings, he would, like a returned traveler, tell Nora what he had seen. The poodles, the cocktail parties, the children and their nursemaids interested him, and he told Nora that it was like the Tower of Babel.

It took Clancy a while to memorize the floor numbers to which his tenants belonged, to pair the husbands and wives, to join the children to their parents, and the servants (who rode on the back elevators) to these families, but he managed at last and was pleased to have everything straight. Among his traits was a passionate sense of loyalty, and he often spoke of the Building as if it were a school or a guild, the product of a community of sentiment and aspiration. "Oh, I wouldn't do anything to harm the Building," he often said. His manner was respectful but he was not humorless, and when 11-A sent his tailcoat out to the dry cleaner's, Clancy put it on and paraded up and down the back hall. Most of the tenants were regarded by Clancy with an indiscriminate benevolence, but there were a few exceptions. There was a drunken wife-beater. He was a bulky, duck-footed lunkhead, in Clancy's eyes, and he did not belong in the Building. Then there was a pretty girl in 11-B who went out in the evenings with a man who was a weak character—Clancy could tell because he had a cleft chin. Clancy warned the girl, but she did not act on his advice. But the tenant about whom he felt most concerned was Mr. Rowantree.

Mr. Rowantree, who was a bachelor, lived in 4-A. He had been in Europe when Clancy first went to work, and he had not returned to New York until winter. When Mr. Rowantree appeared, he seemed to Clancy to be a well-favored man with graying hair who was tired from his long voyage. Clancy waited for him to re-establish himself in the city, for friends and relatives to start telephoning and writing, and for Mr. Rowantree to begin the give-and-take of parties in which most of the tenants were involved.

Clancy had discovered by then that his passengers were not made of sugar. All of them were secured to the world intricately by friends and lovers, dogs and songbirds, debts, inheritances, trusts, and jobs, and he waited for Mr. Rowantree to put out his lines. Nothing happened. Mr. Rowantree went to work at ten in the morning and returned home at six; no visitors appeared. A month passed in which he did not have a single guest. He sometimes went out in the evening, but he always returned alone, and for all Clancy knew he might have continued his friendless state in the movies around the corner. The man's lack of friends amazed and then began to aggravate and trouble Clancy. One night when he was on the evening shift and Mr. Rowantree came down alone, Clancy stopped the car between floors.

"Are you going out for dinner, Mr. Rowantree?" he asked.

"Yes," the man said.

"Well, when you're eating in this neighborhood, Mr. Rowantree," Clancy said, "you'll find that Bill's Clam Bar is the only restaurant worth speaking of. I've been living around here for twenty years and I've seen them come and go. The others have fancy lighting and fancy prices, but you won't get anything to eat that's worth sticking to your ribs excepting at Bill's Clam Bar."

"Thank you, Clancy," Mr. Rowantree said. "I'll keep that in mind."

"Now, Mr. Rowantree," Clancy said, "I don't want to sound inquisitive, but would you mind telling me what kind of a business you're in?"

"I have a store on Third Avenue," Mr. Rowantree said. "Come over and see it someday."

"I'd like to do that," Clancy said. "But now, Mr. Rowantree, I should think you'd want to have dinner with your friends and not be alone all the time." Clancy knew that he was interfering with the man's privacy, but he was led on by the thought that this soul might need help. "A good-looking man like you must have friends," he said, "and I'd think you'd have your supper with them."

"I'm going to have supper with a friend, Clancy," Mr. Rowantree said.

This reply made Clancy feel easier, and he put the man out of his mind for a while. The Building gave him the day off on St. Patrick's, so that he could march in the parade, and when the parade had disbanded and he was walking home, he decided to look for the store. Mr. Rowantree had told him which block it was in. It was easy to find. Clancy was pleased to see that it was a big store. There were two doors to go in by, separated by a large glass window. Clancy looked through the window to see if Mr. Rowantree was busy with a customer, but there was no one there. Before he went in, he looked at the things in the window. He was disappointed to see that it was not a clothing store or a delicatessen. It looked more like a museum. There were glasses and candlesticks, chairs and tables, all of them old. He opened the door. A bell attached to the door rang and Clancy looked up to see the old-fashioned bell on its string. Mr. Rowantree came out from behind a screen and greeted him cordially.

Clancy did not like the place. He felt that Mr. Rowantree was wasting his time. It troubled him to think of the energy in a man's day being spent in this place. A narrow trail, past tables and desks, urns and statues, led into the store and then branched off in several directions. Clancy had never seen so much junk. Since he couldn't imagine it all being manufactured in any one country, he guessed that it had been brought there from the four corners of the world. It seemed to Clancy a misuse of time to have gathered all of these things into a dark store on Third Avenue. But it was more than the confusion and the waste that troubled him; it was the feeling that he was surrounded by the symbols of frustration and that all the china youths and maidens in their attitudes of love were the company of bitterness. It may have been because he had spent his happy life in bare rooms that he associated goodness with ugliness.

He was careful not to say anything that would offend Mr. Rowantree. "Do you have any clerks to help you?" he asked.

"Oh, yes," Mr. Rowantree said. "Miss James is here most of the time. We're partners."

That was it, Clancy thought. Miss James. That was where he went in the evenings. But why, then, wouldn't Miss James marry him? Was it because he was already married? Perhaps he had suffered some terrible misfortune, like having his wife go crazy or having his children taken away from him.

"Have you a snapshot of Miss James?" Clancy asked.

"No," Mr. Rowantree said.

"Well, I'm glad to have seen your store and thank you very much," Clancy said. The trip had been worth his while, because he took away from the dark store a clear image of Miss James. It was a good name, an Irish name, and now in the evenings when Mr. Rowantree went out, Clancy would ask him how Miss James was.

Clancy's son, John, was a senior in high school. He was captain of the basketball team and a figure in school government, and that spring he entered an essay he had written on democracy in a contest sponsored by a manufacturer in Chicago. There were millions of entries, but John won honorable mention, which entitled him to a trip to Chicago in an airplane and a week's visit there with all expenses paid. The boy was naturally excited by this bonanza and so was his mother, but Clancy was the one who seemed to have won the prize. He told all the tenants in the Building about it and asked them what kind of city Chicago was and if traveling in airplanes was safe. He would get up in the middle of the night and go into John's room to look at the wonderful boy while he slept. The boy's head was crammed with knowledge, Clancy thought. His heart was kind and strong. It was sinful, Clancy knew, to confuse the immortality of the Holy Spirit and earthly love, but when he realized that John was his flesh and blood, that the young man's face was *his* face improved with mobility and thought, and that when he, Clancy, was dead, some habit or taste of his would live on in the young man, he felt that there was no pain in death.

John's plane left for Chicago late one Saturday afternoon. He walked to confession and then walked over to the Building to say goodbye to his father. Clancy kept the boy in the lobby as long as he could and introduced him to the tenants who came through. Then it was time for the boy to go. The doorman took the elevator, and Clancy walked John up to the corner. It was a clear, sunny afternoon in Lent. There wasn't a cloud in the sky. The boy had on his best suit and he looked like a million dollars. They shook hands at the corner, and Clancy limped back to the Building. Traffic was slow on the elevator, and he stood at the front door, watching the people on the sidewalk. Most of them were dressed in their best clothes and they were off to enjoy themselves. Clancy's best wishes followed them all. At the far end of the street he saw Mr. Rowantree's head and shoulders and saw that he was with a young man. Clancy waited and opened the door for them.

"Hello, Clancy," Mr. Rowantree said. "I'd like to have you meet my friend Bobbie. He's going to live here now."

Clancy grunted. The young man was not a young man. His hair was cut short and he wore a canary-yellow sweater and a padded coat but he was as old as Mr. Rowantree, he was nearly as old as Clancy. All the qualities and airs of youth, which a good man puts aside gladly when the time comes, had been preserved obscenely in him. He had dope in his eyes to make them shine and he smelled of perfume, and Mr. Rowantree took his arm to help him through the door, as if he were a pretty girl. As soon as Clancy saw what he had to deal with, he took a stand. He stayed at the door. Mr. Rowantree and his friend went through the lobby and got into the elevator. They reached out and rang the bell.

"I'm not taking you up in my car!" Clancy shouted down the lobby.

"Come here, Clancy," Mr. Rowantree said.

"I'm not taking that up in my car," Clancy said.

"I'll have you fired for this," Mr. Rowantree said.

"That's no skin off my nose," Clancy said. "I'm not taking you up in my car."

"Come here, Clancy," Mr. Rowantree said. Clancy didn't answer. Mr. Rowantree put his finger on the bell and held it there. Clancy didn't move. He heard Mr. Rowantree and his friend talking. A moment later, he heard them climb the stairs. All the solicitude he had felt for Mr. Rowantree, the times he had imagined him walking in the Park with Miss James, seemed like money lost in a terrible fraud. He was hurt and bitter. The idea of Bobbie's being in the building was a painful one for him to take, and he felt as if it contested his own simple view of life. He was curt with everyone for the rest of the day. He even spoke sharply to the children. When he went to the basement to take off his uniform. Mr. Coolidge, the superintendent, called him into his office.

"Rowantree's been trying to get you fired for the last hour, Jim," he said. "He said you wouldn't take him up in your car. I'm not going to fire you, because you're a good, steady man, but I'm warning you now. He knows a lot of rich and influential people, and if you don't mind your own business, it won't be hard for him to get you kicked out." Mr. Coolidge was surrounded by all the treasures he had extricated from the rubbish baskets in the back halls—broken lamps, broken vases, a perambulator with three wheels.

"But he—" Clancy began.

"It's none of your business, Jim," Mr. Coolidge said. "He's been very quiet since he come back from Europe. You're a good, steady man, Clancy, and I don't want to fire you, but you got to remember that you aren't the boss around here."

The next day was Palm Sunday, and, by the grace of God, Clancy did not see Mr. Rowantree. On Monday, Clancy joined his bitterness at having to live in Sodom to the deep and general grief he always felt at the commencement of those events that would end on Golgotha. It was a gloomy day. Clouds and darkness were over the city. Now and then it rained. Clancy took Mr. Rowantree down at ten. He didn't say anything, but he gave the man a scornful look. The ladies began going off for lunch around noon. Mr. Rowantree's friend Bobbie went out then.

About half past two, one of the ladies came back from lunch, smelling of gin. She did a funny thing. When she got into the elevator, she stood with her face to the wall of the car, so that Clancy couldn't see it. He was not a man to look into somebody's face if they wanted to hide it, and this made him angry. He stopped the car. "Turn around," he said. "Turn around. I'm ashamed of you, a woman with three grown children, standing with your face to the wall like a crybaby."

She turned around. She was crying about something. Clancy put the car into motion again. "You ought to fast," he mumbled. "You ought to go without cigarettes or meat during Lent. It would give you something to think about." She left the car, and he answered a ring from the first floor. It was Mr. Rowantree. He took him up. Then he took Mrs. DePaul up to 9. She was a nice woman, and he told her about John's trip to Chicago. One the way down, he smelled gas.

For a man who has lived his life in a tenement, gas is the odor of winter, sickness, need, and death. Clancy went up to Mr. Rowantree's floor. That was it. He had the master key and he opened the door and stepped into that hellish breath. It was dark. He could hear the petcocks hissing in the kitchen. He put a rug against the door to keep it open and threw up a window in the hall. He stuck his head out for some air. Then, in terror of being blown into hell himself, and swearing and praying and half closing his eyes as if the poisonous air might blind him, he started for the kitchen and gave himself a cruel bang against the doorframe that made him cold all over with pain. He stumbled into the kitchen and opened the doors and windows. Mr. Rowantree was on his knees with his head in the oven. He sat up. He was crying. "Bobbie's gone, Clancy," he said. "Bobbie's gone."

Clancy's stomach turned over, his gorge opened and filled up with bitter spit. "Dear Jesus!" he shouted. "Dear Jesus!" He stumbled out of the apartment. He was shaking all over. He took the car down and shouted for the doorman and told him what had happened.

The doorman took the elevator, and Clancy went into the locker room and sat down. He didn't know how long he had been there when the doorman came in and said that he smelled more gas. Clancy went up to Mr. Rowantree's apartment again. The door was shut. He opened it and stood in the hall and heard the petcocks. "Take your God-damned fool head out of that oven, Mr. Rowantree!" he shouted. He went into the kitchen and turned off the gas. Mr. Rowantree was sitting on the floor. "I won't do it again, Clancy," he said. "I promise, I promise."

Clancy went down and got Mr. Coolidge, and they went into the basement together and turned off Mr. Rowantree's gas. He went up again. The door was shut. When he opened it, he heard the hissing of the gas. He yanked the man's head out of the oven. "You're wasting your time, Mr. Rowantree!" he shouted. "We've turned off your gas! You're wasting your time!" Mr. Rowantree scrambled to his feet and ran out of the kitchen. Clancy heard him running through the apartment, slamming doors. He followed him and found him in the bathroom, shaking pills out of a bottle into his mouth. Clancy knocked the pill bottle out of his hand and knocked the man down. Then he called the precinct station on Mr. Rowantree's phone. He waited there until a policeman, a doctor, and a priest came.

Clancy walked home at five. The sky was black. It was raining soot and ashes. Sodom, he thought, the city undeserving of clemency, the unredeemable place, and, raising his eyes to watch the rain and the ashes fall through the air, he felt a great despair for his kind. They had lost the warrants for mercy, there was no movement in the city around him but toward self-destruction and sin. He longed for the simple life of Ireland and the City of God, but he felt that he had been contaminated by the stink of gas.

He told Nora what had happened, and she tried to comfort him. There was no letter or card from John. In the evening, Mr. Coolidge telephoned. He said it was about Mr. Rowantree.

"Is he in the insame asylum?" Clancy asked.

"No," Mr. Coolidge said. "His friend came back and they went out together. But he's been threatening to get you fired again. As soon as he felt all right again, he said he was going to get you fired. I don't want to fire you, but you got to be careful, you got to be careful." This was the twist that Clancy couldn't follow, and he felt sick. He asked Mr. Coolidge to get a man from the union to take his place for a day or so, and he went to bed.

Clancy stayed in bed the next morning. He got worse. He was cold. Nora lighted a fire in the range, but he shivered as if his heart and his bones were frozen. He doubled his knees up to his chest and snagged the blankets around him, but he couldn't keep warm. Nora finally called the doctor, a man from Limerick. It was after ten before he got there. He said that Clancy should go to the hospital. The doctor left to make the arrangements, and Nora got Clancy's best clothes together and helped him into them. There was still a price tag on his long underwear and there were pins in his shorts. In the end, nobody saw the new underwear and the clean shirt. At the hospital, they drew a curtain around his bed and handed the finery out to Nora. Then he stretched out in bed, and Nora gave him a kiss and went away.

He groaned, he moaned for a while, but he had a fever and this put him to sleep. He did not know or care where he was for the next few days. He slept most of the time. When John came back from Chicago, the boy's company and the story of his trip picked Clancy's spirits up a little. Nora visited him every day, and one day, a couple of weeks after Clancy entered the hospital, she brought Frank Quinn, the doorman, with her. Frank gave Clancy a narrow manila envelope, and when Clancy opened it, asking crossly what it was, he saw that it was full of currency.

"That's from the tenants, Clancy," Frank said.

"Now, why did they do this?" Clancy said. He was smitten. His eyes watered and he couldn't count the money. "Why did they do this?" he asked weakly. "Why did they go to this trouble? I'm nothing but an elevator man."

"It's nearly two hundred dollars," Frank said.

"Who took up the collection?" Clancy said. "Was it you, Frank?"

"It was one of the tenants," Frank said.

"It was Mrs. DePaul," Clancy said. "I'll bet it was that Mrs. DePaul."

"One of the tenants," Frank said.

"It was you, Frank," Clancy said warmly. "You was the one who took up the collection."

"It was Mr. Rowantree," Frank said sadly. He bent his head.

"You're not going to give the money back, Jim?" Nora asked.

"I'm not a God-damned fool!" Clancy shouted. "When I pick up a dollar off the street, I'm not the man to go running down to the lost-and-found department with it!"

"Nobody else could have gotten so much, Jim," Frank said. "He went from floor to floor. They say he was crying."

Clancy had a vision. He saw the church from the open lid of his coffin, before the altar. The sacristan had lighted only a few of the Vaseline-colored lamps, for the only mourners were those few people, all of them poor and old, who had come from Limerick with Clancy on the boat. He heard the priest's youthful voice mingling with the thin music of the bells. Then in the back of the church he saw Mr. Rowantree and Bobbie. They were crying and crying. They were crying harder than Nora. He could see their shoulders rise and fall, and hear their sighs.

"Does he think I'm dying, Frank?" Clancy asked.

"Yes, Jim. He does."

"He thinks I'm dying," Clancy said angrily. "He's got one of them soft heads. Well, I ain't dying. I ain't taking any of his grief. I'm getting out of here." He climbed out of bed. Nora and Frank tried unsuccessfully to push him back. Frank ran out to get a nurse. The nurse pointed a finger at Clancy and commanded him to get back into bed, but he had put on his pants and was tying his shoelaces. She went out and got another nurse, and the two young women tried to hold him down, but he shook them off easily. The first nurse went to get a doctor. The doctor who returned with her was a young man, much smaller than Clancy. He said that Clancy could go home. Frank and Nora took him back in a taxi, and as soon as he got into the tenement, he telephoned Mr. Coolidge and said that he was coming back to work in the morning. He felt a lot better, surrounded by the smells and lights of his own place. Nora cooked him a nice supper and he ate it in the kitchen.

After supper, he sat by the window in his shirtsleeves. He thought about going back to work, about the man with the cleft chin, the wife-beater, Mr. Rowantree and Bobbie. Why should a man fall in love with a monster? Why should a man try to kill himself? Why should a man try to get a man fired and then collect money for him with tears in his eyes, and then perhaps, a week later, try to get him fired again? He would not return the money, he would not thank Mr. Rowantree, but he wondered what kind of judgment he should pass on the pervert. He began to pick the words he would say to Mr. Rowantree when they met. "It's my suggestion, Mr. Rowantree," he would say, "that the next time you want to kill yourself, you get a rope or a gun. It's my suggestion, Mr. Rowantree," he would say, "that you go to a good doctor and get your head examined."

The spring wind, the south wind that in the city smells of drains, was blowing. Clancy's window looked onto an expanse of clotheslines and ailanthus trees, yards that were used as dumps, and the naked backs of tenements, with their lighted and unlighted windows. The symmetry, the reality of the scene heartened Clancy, as if it conformed to something good in himself. Men with common minds like his had built these houses. Nora brought him a glass of beer and sat near the window. He put an arm around her waist. She was in her slip, because of the heat. Her hair was held down with pins. She appeared to Clancy to be one of the glorious beauties of his day, but a stranger, he guessed, might notice the tear in her slip and that her body was bent and heavy. A picture of John hung on the wall. Clancy was struck with the strength and intelligence of his son's face, but he guessed that a stranger might notice the boy's glasses and his bad complexion. And then, thinking of Nora and John and that this half blindness was all that he knew himself of mortal love, he decided not to say anything to Mr. Rowantree. They would pass in silence.

When I Was Thirteen

Denton Welch

Born in Shanghai of missionary parents, and educated in England after spending his childhood in China, Denton Welch thought of himself as destined for a life in the arts. A bicycle accident suffered when he was twenty left him an invalid in constant pain. Confined to his chair, he began writing short fiction that was largely autobiographical: wistful accounts of beauty denied and frustrated longings.

His fictional world is profoundly erotic: his geography is sensual, his memories are of delicious tastes and smells and sounds, his descriptions of the male body suggest touch. And yet desire is never spelled out; rather, as in certain landscape paintings, it is implied in the style itself. The young adolescent in "When I Was Thirteen" wanders through a mysterious but gratifying world in which his desires remain nameless because nothing demands that they be separated from the essential act of living. Then prejudice appears, and the world is shattered by a brutal irruption of words without meaning, terrifying as madness.

The adult world defines itself through labels; perhaps for that reason, Welch's stories deal mainly with adolescents poised on the brink of instruction, at a time when many things are pleasing because they still lack names. In Youth Is Pleasure *is the title of one of his best books. Denton Welch died in 1948, aged 33.*

When I was thirteen, I went to Switzerland for the Christmas holidays in the charge of an elder brother, who was at that time still up at Oxford.

In the hotel we found another undergraduate whom my brother knew. His name was Archer. They were not at the same college, but they had met and evidently had not agreed with each other. At first my brother would say nothing about Archer; then one day, in answer to a question of mine, he said: "He's not very much liked, although he's a very good swimmer." As he spoke, my brother held his lips in a very firm, almost pursed, line which was most damaging to Archer.

After this I began to look at Archer with more interest. He had broad shoulders but was not tall. He had a look of strength and solidity which I admired and envied. He had rather a nice pug face with insignificant nose and broad cheeks. Sometimes, when he was animated, a tassel of fair, almost colorless, hair would fall across his forehead, half covering one eye. He had a thick beautiful neck, rather meaty barbarian hands, and a skin as smooth and evenly colored as a pink fondant.

His whole body appeared to be suffused with this gentle pink color. He never wore proper skiing clothes of waterproof material like the rest of us. Usually he came out in nothing but a pair of gray flannels and a white cotton shirt with all the buttons left undone. When the sun grew very hot, he would even discard this thin shirt, and ski up and down the slopes behind the hotel in nothing but his trousers. I had often seen him fall down in this half-naked state and get buried in snow. The next moment he would jerk himself to his feet again, laughing and swearing.

After my brother's curt nod to him on our first evening at the hotel, we had hardly exchanged any remarks. We sometimes passed on the way to the basement to get our skis in the morning, and often we found ourselves sitting near one another on the glassed-in terrace; but some Oxford snobbery I knew nothing of, or some more profound reason, always made my brother throw off waves of hostility. Archer never showed any signs of wishing to approach. He was content to look at me sometimes with a mild inoffensive curiosity, but he seemed to ignore my brother completely. This pleased me more than I would have admitted at that time. I was so used to being passed over myself by all my brother's friends that it was pleasant when someone who knew him seemed to take a sort of interest, however slight and amused, in me.

My brother was often away from the hotel for days and nights together, going for expeditions with guides and other friends. He would never take me because he said I was too young and had not enough stamina. He said that I would fall down a crevasse or get my nose frostbitten, or hang up the party by lagging behind.

In consequence I was often alone at the hotel; but I did not mind this; I enjoyed it. I was slightly afraid of my brother and found life very much easier and less exacting when he was not there. I think other people in the hotel thought that I looked lonely. Strangers would often come up and talk to me and smile, and once a nice absurd Belgian woman, dressed from head to foot in a babyish suit of fluffy orange knitted wool, held out a bright five-franc piece to me and told me to go and buy chocolate caramels with it. I think she must have taken me for a much younger child.

On one of these afternoons when I had come in from the Nursery Slopes and was sitting alone over my tea on the sun terrace, I noticed that Archer was sitting in the corner huddled over a book, munching greedily and absentmindedly.

I, too, was reading a book, while I ate delicious rum-babas and little tarts filled with worm-castles of chestnut purée topped with caps of whipped cream. I have called the meal tea, but what I was drinking was not tea but chocolate. When I poured out, I held the pot high in the air, so that my cup, when filled, should be covered in a rich froth of bubbles.

The book I was reading was Tolstoy's *Resurrection*. Although I did not quite understand some parts of it, it gave me intense pleasure to read it while I ate the rich cakes and drank the frothy chocolate. I thought it a noble and terrible story, but I was worried and mystified by the words "illegitimate child" which had occurred several times lately. What sort of child could this be? Clearly a child that brought trouble and difficulty. Could it have some terrible disease, or was it a special sort of imbecile? I looked up from my book, still wondering what about this phrase "illegitimate child," and saw that Archer had turned in his creaking wicker chair and was gazing blankly in my direction. The orchestra was playing "The Birth of the Blues" in a rather remarkable Swiss arrangement, and it was clear that Archer had been distracted from his book by the music, only to be lulled into a daydream, as he gazed into space.

Suddenly his eyes lost their blank look and focused on my face. "Your brother off up to the Jungfrau Joch again, or somewhere?" he called out.

I nodded my head, saying nothing, becoming slightly confused.

Archer grinned. He seemed to find me amusing.

"What are you reading?" he asked.

"This," I said, taking my book over to him. I did not want to call out either the word "Resurrection" or "Tolstoy." But Archer did not make fun of me for reading a "classic," as most of my brother's friends would have done. He only said: "I should think it's rather good. Mine's frightful; it's called *The Story of my Life*, by Queen Marie of Roumania." He held the book up and I saw an extraordinary photograph of a lady who looked like a snake-charmer in full regalia. The headdress seemed to be made of white satin, embroidered with beads, stretched over cardboard. There were tassels and trailing things hanging down everywhere.

I laughed at the amusing picture and Archer went on: "I always read books like this when I can get them. Last week I had Lady Oxford's autobiography, and before that I found a perfectly wonderful book called *Flaming Sex*. It was by a French woman who married an English knight and then went back to France to shoot a French doctor. She didn't kill him, of course, but she was sent to prison, where she had a very interesting time with the nuns who looked after her in the hospital. I also lately found an old book by a Crown Princess of Saxony who ended up picnicking on a haystack with a simple Italian gentleman in a straw hat. I love these 'real life' stories, don't you?"

I again nodded my head, not altogether daring to venture on a spoken answer. I wondered whether to go back to my own table or whether to pluck up courage and ask Archer what an "illegitimate child" was. He solved the problem by saying "Sit down" rather abruptly.

I subsided next to him with "Tolstoy" on my knee. I waited for a moment and then plunged.

"What exactly does 'illegitimate child' mean?" I asked rather breathlessly.

"Outside the law—when two people have a child although they're not married."

"Oh." I went bright pink. I thought Archer must be wrong. I still believed that it was quite impossible to have a child unless one was married. The very fact of being married produced the child. I had a vague idea that some particularly reckless people attempted, without being married, to have children in places called "night-clubs," but they were always unsuccessful, and this made them drink, and plunge into the most hectic gaiety.

I did not tell Archer that I thought he had made a mistake, for I did not want to hurt his feelings. I went on sitting at his table and, although he turned his eyes back to his book and went on reading, I knew that he was friendly.

After some time he looked up again and said: "Would you like to come out with me tomorrow? We could take our lunch, go up the mountain and then ski down in the afternoon."

I was delighted at the suggestion, but also a little alarmed at my own shortcomings. I thought it my duty to explain that I was not a very good skier, only a moderate one, and that I could only do stem turns. I hated the thought of being a drag on Archer.

"I expect you're much better than I am. I'm always falling down or crashing into something," he answered.

It was all arranged. We were to meet early, soon after six, as Archer wanted to go to the highest station on the mountain railway and then climb on skis to a nearby peak which had a small resthouse of logs.

I went to bed very excited, thankful that my brother was away on a long expedition. I lay under my enormous feather-bed eiderdown, felt the freezing mountain air on my face, and saw the stars sparkling through the open window.

I got up very early in the morning and put on my most sober ski socks and woollen shirt, for I felt that Archer disliked any suspicion of bright colors or dressing-up. I made my appearance as workmanlike as possible, and then went down to breakfast.

I ate several crackly rolls, which I spread very quickly with dewy slivers of butter and gobbets of rich black cherry jam; then I drank my last cup of coffee and went to wax my skis. As I passed through the hall I picked up my picnic lunch in its neat grease-proof paper packet.

The nails in my boots slid and then caught on the snow, trodden hard down to the basement door. I found my skis in their rack, took them down and then heated the iron and the wax. I loved spreading the hot black wax smoothly on the white wood. Soon they were both done beautifully.

I will go like a bird, I thought.

I looked up and saw Archer standing in the doorway.

"I hope you haven't put too much on, else you'll be sitting on your arse all day," he said gaily.

How fresh and pink he looked! I was excited.

He started to wax his own skis. When they were finished, we went outside and strapped them on. Archer carried a rucksack and he told me to put my lunch and my spare sweater into it.

We started off down the gentle slopes to the station. The sun was shining prickingly. The lovely snow had rainbow colors in it. I was so happy I swung my sticks with their steel points and basket ends. I even tried to show off, and jumped a little terrace which I knew well. Nevertheless it nearly brought me down. I just regained my balance in time. I would have hated at that moment to have fallen down in front of Archer.

When we got to the station we found a compartment to ourselves. It was still early. Gently we were pulled up the mountain, past the water station stop and the other three halts.

We got out at the very top where the railway ended. A huge unused snowplow stood by the side of the track, with its vicious shark's nose pointed at me. We ran to the van to get out our skis. Archer found mine as well as his own and slung both pairs across his shoulders. He looked like a very tough Jesus carrying two crosses, I thought.

We stood by the old snowplow and clipped on our skis; then we began to climb laboriously up the ridge to the wooden resthouse. We hardly talked at all, for we needed all our breath, and also I was still shy of Archer. Sometimes he helped me, telling me where to place my skis, and, if I slipped backwards, hauling on the rope which he had half-playfully tied round my waist.

In spite of growing tired, I enjoyed the grim plodding. It gave me a sense of work and purpose. When Archer looked round to smile at me, his pink face was slippery with sweat. His white shirt above the small rucksack was plastered to his shoulder blades. On my own face I could feel the drops of sweat just being held back by my eyebrows. I would wipe my hand across my upper lip and break all the tiny beads that had formed there.

Every now and then Archer would stop. We would put our skis sideways on the track and rest, leaning forward on our sticks. The sun struck down on our necks with a steady seeping heat and the light striking up from the snow was as bright as the fiery dazzle of a mirror. From the ridge we could see down into two valleys; and standing all round us were the other peaks, black rock and white snow, tangling and mixing until the mountains looked like vast teeth which had begun to decay.

I was so tired when we reached the long gentle incline to the resthouse that I was afraid of falling down. The rope was still round my waist, and so the slightest lagging would have been perceptible to

Archer. I think he must have slackened his pace for my benefit, for I somehow managed to reach the iron seats in front of the hut. I sank down, with my skis still on. I half-shut my eyes. From walking so long with my feet turned out, my ankles felt almost broken.

The next thing I knew was that Archer had disappeared into the resthouse. He came out carrying a steaming cup.

"You must drink this," he said, holding out black coffee which I hated. He unwrapped four lumps of sugar and dropped them in the cup.

"I don't like it black," I said.

"Never mind," he said sharply, "drink it."

Rather surprised, I began to drink the syrupy coffee. "The sugar and the strong coffee will be good for you," said Archer. He went back into the resthouse and brought out a glass of what looked like hot water with a piece of lemon floating in it. The mountain of sugar at the bottom was melting into thin Arabian Nights wreaths and spirals, smoke-rings of syrup.

"What else has it got in it?" I asked, with an attempt at worldliness.

"Rum!" said Archer.

We sat there on the terrace and unwrapped our picnic lunches. We both had two rolls, one with tongue in it, and one with ham, a hard-boiled egg, sweet biscuits, and a bar of delicious bitter chocolate. Tangerine oranges were our dessert.

We began to take huge bites out of our rolls. We could not talk for some time. The food brought out a thousand times more clearly the beauty of the mountain peaks and sun. My tiredness made me thrillingly conscious of delight and satisfaction. I wanted to sit there with Archer for a long time.

At the end of the meal Archer gave me a piece of his own bar of chocolate, and then began to skin pigs of tangerine very skillfully and hand them to me on his outstretched palm, as one offers a lump of a sugar to a horse. I thought for one moment of bending down my head and licking the pigs up in imitation of a horse; then I saw how mad it would look.

We threw the brilliant tangerine peel into the snow, which immediately seemed to dim and darken its color.

Archer felt in his hip pocket and brought out black, cheap Swiss cigarettes, wrapped in leaf. They were out of a slot machine. He put one between my lips and lighted it. I felt extremely conscious of the thing jutting out from my lips. I wondered if I would betray my ignorance by not breathing the smoke in and out correctly. I turned my head a little away from Archer and experimented. It seemed easy if one did not breathe too deeply. It was wonderful to be really smoking with Archer. He treated me just like a man.

"Come on, let's get cracking," he said, "or, if anything happens, we'll be out all night."

I scrambled to my feet at once and snapped the clips of the skis round my boot heels. Archer was in high spirits from the rum. He ran on his skis along the flat ridge in front of the resthouse and then fell down.

"Serves me right," he said. He shook the snow off and we started properly. In five minutes we had swooped down the ridge we had climbed so painfully all morning. The snow was perfect; new and dry with no crust. We followed a new way which Archer had discovered. The ground was uneven with dips and curves. Often we were out of sight with each other. When we came to the icy path through a wood, my courage failed me.

"Stem like hell and don't get out of control," Archer yelled back at me. I pointed my skis together, praying that they would not cross. I leant on my sticks, digging their metal points into the compressed snow. Twice I fell, though not badly.

"Well done, well done!" shouted Archer, as I shot past him and out of the wood into a thick snowdrift. He hauled me out of the snow and stood me on my feet, beating me all over to get off the snow, then we began the descent of a field called the "Bumps." Little hillocks, if maneuvered successfully, gave one that thrilling sinking and rising feeling experienced on a scenic railway at a fun fair.

Archer went before me, dipping and rising, shouting and yelling in his exuberance. I followed more sedately. We both fell several times, but not in that unpleasant, bouncing way which brings you to your feet again almost at once.

Archer was roaring now and trying to yodel in an absurd, rich contralto.

I had never enjoyed myself quite so much before. I thought him the most wonderful companion, not a bit intimidating, in spite of being rather a hero.

When at last we swooped down to the village street, it was nearly evening. Early orange lights were shining in the shop windows. We planked our skis down on the hard, iced road, trying not to slip.

I looked in at the *patisserie, confiserie* window, where all the electric bulbs had fluffy pink shades like powder-puffs. Archer saw my look.

"Let's go in," he said. He ordered me hot chocolate with whipped cream, and *croissant* rolls. Afterwards we both went up to the little counter and chose cakes. I had one shaped like a little log. It was made of soft chocolate, and had green moss trimmings made in pistachio nut. When Archer went to pay the bill he bought me some chocolate caramels, in a little bird's-eye maple box, and a bar labeled "*Chocolat Polychrome.*" Each finger was a different-colored cream: mauve, pink, green, yellow, orange, brown, white, even blue.

We went out into the village street and began to climb up the path to the hotel. About halfway up Archer stopped outside a little wooden chalet and said: "This is where I hang out."

"But you're staying at the hotel," I said incredulously.

"Oh yes, I have all my meals there, but I sleep here. It's a sort of little annex when there aren't any rooms left in the hotel. It's only got two rooms; I've paid just a bit more and got it all to myself. Someone comes every morning and makes the bed and stokes the boiler and the stove. Come in and see it."

I followed Archer up the outside wooden staircase and stood with him on the little landing outside the two rooms. The place seemed wonderfully warm and dry. The walls were unpainted wood; there were double windows. There was a gentle creaking in all the joints of the wood when one moved. Archer pushed open one of the doors and ushered me in. I saw in one corner a huge white porcelain stove, the sort I had only before seen in pictures. Some of Archer's skiing gloves and socks were drying round it on a ledge. Against another wall were two beds, like wooden troughs built into the wall. The balloon-like quilts bulged up above the wood.

"I hardly use the other room," said Archer. "I just throw my muck into it and leave my trunks there." He opened the connecting door and I saw a smaller room with dirty clothes strewn on the floor; white shirts, hard evening collars, some very short pants, and many pairs of thick gray socks. The room smelled mildly of Archer's old sweat. I didn't mind at all.

Archer shut the door and said: "I'm going to run the bath."

"Have you a bathroom too—all your own?" I exclaimed envi-
ously. "Every time anyone has a bath at the hotel, he has to pay two
francs fifty to the fraulein before she unlocks the door. I've only had
two proper baths since I've been here. I don't think it matters though.
It seems almost impossible to get really dirty in Switzerland, and you
can always wash all over in your bedroom basin."

"Why don't you have a bath here after me? The water's lovely and
hot, although there's not much of it. If you went back first and got
your evening clothes, you could change straight into them."

I looked at Archer a little uncertainly. I longed to soak in hot water
after my wonderful but grueling day.

"Could I really bathe here?" I asked.

"If you don't mind using my water. I'll promise not to pee in it. I'm
not really filthy, you know."

Archer laughed and chuckled, because he saw me turning red at
his coarseness. He lit another of his peasant cigarettes and began to
unlace his boots. He got me to pull them off. I knelt down, bowed my
head and pulled. When the ski boot suddenly flew off, my nose
dipped forward and I smelled Archer's foot in its woolly, hairy, humid
casing of sock.

"Would you just rub my foot and leg?" Archer said urgently, a
look of pain suddenly shooting across his face. "I've got cramp. It
often comes on at the end of the day."

He shot his leg out rigidly and told me where to rub and massage.
I felt each of his curled toes separately and the hard tendons in his leg.
His calf was like a firm sponge ball. His thigh, swelling out, amazed
me. I likened it in my mind to the trumpet of some musical instrument. I went on rubbing methodically. I was able to feel his pain melting away.

When the tense look had quite left his face, he said, "Thanks," and
stood up. He unbuttoned his trousers, let them fall to the ground, and
pulled his shirt up. Speaking to me with his head imprisoned in it, he
said: "You go and get your clothes and I'll begin bathing."

I left him and hurried up to the hotel, carrying my skis on my
shoulder. I ran up to my room and pulled my evening clothes out of
the wardrobe. The dinner jacket and trousers had belonged to my
brother six years before, when he was my age. I was secretly ashamed
of this fact, and had taken my brother's name from the inside of the
breast pocket and had written my own in elaborate lettering.

I took my comb, face flannel and soap, and getting out my toboggan slid back to Archer's chalet in a few minutes. I let myself in and heard Archer splashing. The little hall was full of steam and I saw Archer's shoulders and arms like a pink smudge through the open bathroom door.

"Come and scrub my back," he yelled; "it gives me a lovely feeling." He thrust a large stiff nailbrush into my hands and told me to scrub as hard as I could.

I ran it up and down his back until I'd made harsh red tramlines. Delicious tremors seemed to be passing through Archer.

"Ah! go on!" said Archer in a dream, like a purring cat. "When I'm rich I'll have a special back-scratcher slave." I went on industriously scrubbing his back till I was afraid I would rub the skin off. I liked to give him pleasure.

At last he stood up all dripping and said: "Now it's your turn."

I undressed and got into Archer's opaque, soapy water. I lay back and wallowed. Archer poured some very smelly salts on to my stomach. One crystal stuck in my navel and tickled and grated against me.

"This whiff ought to cover up all remaining traces of me!" Archer laughed.

"What's the smell supposed to be?" I asked, brushing the crystals off my stomach into the water, and playing with the one that lodged so snugly in my navel.

"Russian pine," said Archer, shutting his eyes ecstatically and making inbreathing dreamy noises. He rubbed himself roughly with the towel and made his hair stand up on end.

I wanted to soak in the bath for hours, but it was already getting late, and so I had to hurry.

Archer saw what difficulty I had in tying my tie. He came up to me and said: "Let me do it." I turned round relieved, but slightly ashamed of being incompetent.

I kept very still, and he tied it tightly and rapidly with his ham-like hands. He gave the bows a little expert jerk and pat. His eyes had a very concentrated, almost crossed look and I felt him breathing down on my face. All down the front our bodies touched featherily; little points of warmth came together. The hard-boiled shirts were like slightly warmed dinner plates.

When I had brushed my hair, we left the chalet and began to walk up the path to the hotel. The beaten snow was so slippery, now that

we were shod only in patent-leather slippers, that we kept sliding
backwards. I threw out my arms, laughing, and shouting to Archer to
rescue me; then, when he grabbed me and started to haul me to him,
he too would begin to slip. It was a still, Prussian-blue night with
rather weak stars. Our laughter seemed to ring across the valley, to hit
the mountains and then to travel on and on and on.

We reached the hotel a little the worse for wear. The soles of my
patent-leather shoes had become soaked, and there was snow on my
trousers. Through bending forward, the studs in Archer's shirt had
burst undone, and the slab of hair hung over one of his eyes. We went
into the cloak-room to readjust ourselves before entering the dining-
room.

"Come and sit at my table," Archer said; then he added: "No,
we'll sit at yours; there are two places there already."

We sat down and began to eat Roman *gnocchi*. (The proprietor of
the hotel was Italian-Swiss.) I did not like mine very much and was
glad when I could go on to *oeufs au beurre noir*. Now that my brother
was away I could pick and choose in this way, leaving out the meat
course, if I chose to, without causing any comment.

Archer drank Pilsner and suggested that I should too. Not wanting
to disagree with him, I nodded my head, although I hated the pale,
yellow, bitter water.

After the meal Archer ordered me *crème de menthe* with my coffee; I had seen a nearby lady drinking this pretty liquid and asked him
about it. To be ordered a liqueur in all seriousness was a thrilling
moment for me. I sipped the fumy peppermint, which left such an
artificial heat in my throat and chest, and thought that apart from my
mother who was dead, I had never liked anyone so much as I liked
Archer. He didn't try to interfere with me at all. He just took me as I
was and yet seemed to like me.

Archer was now smoking a proper cigar, not the leaf-rolled cigarettes we had had at lunchtime. He offered me one too, but I had the
sense to realize that he did not mean me to take one and smoke it
there before the eyes of all the hotel. I knew also that it would have
made me sick, for my father had given me a cigar when I was eleven,
in an attempt to put me off smoking forever.

I always associated cigars with middle-aged men, and I watched
Archer interestedly, thinking how funny the stiff fat thing looked
sticking out of his young mouth.

We were sitting on the uncurtained sun-terrace, looking out on to the snow in the night; the moon was just beginning to rise. It made the snow glitter suddenly, like fish-scales. Behind us people were dancing in the salon and adjoining rooms. The music came to us in angry snatches, some notes distorted, others quite obliterated. Archer did not seem to want to dance. He seemed content to sit with me in silence.

Near me on a what-not stand stood a high-heeled slipper made of china. I took it down and slipped my hand into it. How hideously ugly the china pom-poms were down the front! The painted centipede climbing up the red heel wore a knowing, human expression. I moved my fingers in the china shoe, pretending they were toes.

"I love monstrosities too," said Archer, as I put the shoe back inside the fern in its crinkly paper-covered pot.

Later we wandered to the buffet bar and stood there drinking many glasses of the *limonade* which was made with white wine. I took the tinkly pieces of ice into my mouth and sucked them, trying to cool myself a little. Blood seemed to rise in my face; my head buzzed.

Suddenly I felt full of *limonade* and lager. I left Archer to go to the cloak-room, but he followed and stood beside me in the next china niche, while the water flushed and gushed importantly in the polished copper tubes, and an interesting, curious smell came from the wire basket which held some strange disinfectant crystals. Archer stood so quietly and guardingly beside me there that I had to say: "Do I look queer?"

"No, you don't look queer; you look nice," he said simply.

A rush of surprise and pleasure made me hotter still. We clanked over the tiles and left the cloak-room.

In the hall, I remembered that I had left all my skiing clothes at the chalet.

"I shall need them in the morning," I said to Archer.

"Let's go down there now, then I can make cocoa on my spirit-lamp, and you can bring the clothes back with you."

We set out in the moonlight; Archer soon took my arm, for he saw that I was drunk, and the path was more slippery than ever. Archer sang "Silent Night" in German, and I began to cry. I could not stop myself. It was such a delight to cry in the moonlight with Archer singing my favorite song; and my brother far away up the mountain.

Suddenly we both sat down on our behinds with a thump. There was a jarring pain at the bottom of my spine but I began to laugh wildly; so did Archer. We lay there laughing, the snow melting under us and soaking through the seats of our trousers and the shoulders of our jackets.

Archer pulled me to my feet and dusted me down with hard slaps. My teeth grated together each time he slapped me. He saw that I was becoming more and more drunk in the freezing air. He propelled me along to the chalet, more or less frog-marching me in an expert fashion. I was quite content to leave myself in his hands.

When he got me upstairs, he put me into one of the bunks and told me to rest. The feathers ballooned out round me. I sank down deliciously. I felt as if I were floating down some magic staircase forever.

Archer got his little meta-stove out and made coffee—not cocoa as he had said. He brought me over a strong cup and held it to my lips. I drank it unthinkingly and not tasting it, doing it only because he told me to.

When he took the cup away, my head fell back on the pillow, and I felt myself sinking and floating away again. I was on skis this time, but they were liquid skis, made of melted glass, and the snow was glass too, but a sort of glass that was springy, like gelatine, and flowing like water.

I felt a change in the light and knew that Archer was bending over me. Very quietly he took off my shoes, undid my tie, loosened the collar and unbuttoned my braces in front. I remember thinking, before I finally fell asleep, how clever he was to know about undoing the braces; they had begun to feel so tight pulling down on my shoulders and dragging the trousers up between my legs. Archer covered me with several blankets and another quilt.

When I woke in the morning, Archer was already up. He had made me some tea and had put it on the stove to keep warm. He brought it over to me and I sat up. I felt ill, rather sick. I remembered what a glorious day yesterday had been, and thought how extraordinary it was that I had not slept in my own bed at the hotel, but in Archer's room, in my clothes.

I looked at him shamefacedly. "What happened last night? I felt peculiar," I said.

"The lager and the lemonade, and the *crème de menthe* made you a bit tight, I'm afraid," Archer said, laughing. "Do you feel better now? We'll go up to the hotel and have breakfast soon."

I got up and washed and changed into my skiing clothes. I still felt rather sick. I made my evening clothes into a neat bundle and tied them on to my toboggan. I had the sweets Archer had given me in my pocket.

We went up to the hotel, dragging the toboggan behind us.

And there on the doorstep we met my brother with one of the guides. They had had to return early, because someone in the party had broken a ski.

He was in a temper. He looked at us and then said to me: "What have you been doing?"

I was at a loss to know what to answer. The very sight of him had so troubled me that this added difficulty of explaining my actions was too much for me.

I looked at him miserably and mouthed something about going in to have breakfast.

My brother turned to Archer fiercely, but said nothing.

Archer explained: "Your brother's just been down to my place. We went skiing together yesterday and he left some clothes at the chalet."

"It's very early," was all my brother said; then he swept me on into the hotel before him, without another word to the guide or to Archer.

He went with me up to my room and saw that the bed had not been slept in.

I said clumsily: "The maid must have been in and done my room early." I could not bear to explain to him about my wonderful day, or why I had slept at the chalet.

My brother was so furious that he took no more notice of my weak explanations and lies.

When I suddenly said in desperation, "I feel sick," he seized me, took me to the basin, forced his fingers down my throat and struck me on the back till a yellow cascade of vomit gushed out of my mouth. My eyes were filled with stinging water; I was trembling. I ran the water in the basin madly, to wash away this sign of shame.

Gradually I grew a little more composed. I felt better, after being sick, and my brother had stopped swearing at me. I filled the basin with freezing water and dipped my face into it. The icy feel seemed to bite round my eye-sockets and make the flesh round my nose firm again. I waited, holding my breath for as long as possible.

Suddenly my head was pushed down and held. I felt my brother's hard fingers digging into my neck. He was hitting me now with a slipper, beating my buttocks and my back with slashing strokes, hitting a different place each time, as he had been taught when a prefect at school, so that the flesh should not be numbed from a previous blow.

I felt that I was going to choke. I could not breathe under the water, and realized that I would die. I was seized with such a panic that I wrenched myself free and darted round the room, with him after me. Water dripped on the bed, the carpet, the chest of drawers. Splashes of it spat against the mirror in the wardrobe door. My brother aimed vicious blows at me until he had driven me into a corner. There he beat against my uplifted arms, yelling in a hoarse, mad, religious voice: "Bastard, Devil, Harlot, Bugger!"

As I cowered under his blows, I remember thinking that my brother had suddenly become a lunatic and was talking gibberish in his madness, for, of the words he was using, I had not heard any before, except "Devil."

Reprise

Edmund White

"Since no one is brought up to be gay, the moment he recognizes the difference he must account for it. Such accounts are a kind of primitive gay fiction, the oral narrations told and retold as pillow talk or in pubs or on the psychoanalytic couch." So begins Edmund White's foreword to his remarkable anthology of gay short fiction. White's own literature includes what is perhaps the classic account of growing up gay in America, A Boy's Own Story. Like the spontaneous oral narrations he refers to (but deliberately crafted), semi-autobiographical gay fiction also becomes, for the gay male coming to terms with his sexuality, a learning device, a new kind of exemplary literature. For someone who finds in the society around him no mirrors or models, only stereotypes and caricatures, these fictions are testimonials. They allow him to say, "At last, this reflects my experience, this maybe is who I am."

Gay or straight, our early sexual experiences can be read like first chapters in a novel, be it comic or tragic. Who we were then and what happened to us in those astonishing moments are illuminated and coloured by what we have since become. "When the generation is gone," wrote Robert Louis Stevenson when he was still a young man, "when the play is over, when the thirty years' panorama has been withdrawn in tatters from the stage of the world, we may ask what has become of these great, weighty, and undying loves, and the sweethearts who despised mortal conditions in a fine credulity."

A novel I'd written, which had flopped in America, was about to come out in France, and I was racing around vainly trying to assure its success in translation. French critics seldom give nasty reviews to books, but they often ignore a novel altogether, especially one by a foreign writer, even one who like me lives in Paris.

In the midst of these professional duties I suddenly received a phone call. A stifled baritone voice with a Midwestern accent asked if I was "Eddie." No one had called me that since my childhood. "It's Jim Grady. Your mother gave me your number."

I hadn't seen him in almost forty years, not since I was fourteen and he twenty, but I could still taste the Luckies and Budweiser on his lips, feel his powerful arms closing around me, remember the deliberate way he'd folded his trousers on the crease rather than throwing them on the floor in romantic haste as I'd done.

I met Jim through our parents. My mother was dating his father, an arrangement she'd been falling back on intermittently for years although she mildly despised him. She went out with him when there was no one better around. She was in her fifties, fat, highly sexed, hard-working, by turns bitter and wildly optimistic (now I'm all those things, so I feel no hesitation in describing her in those terms, especially since she was to change for the better in old age). My father and she had divorced seven years earlier, and she'd gone to work partly out of necessity but partly to make something of herself. Her Texas relations expected great things from her and their ambitions had shaped hers.

Before the divorce she'd studied psychology, and now she worked in the public schools of suburban Chicago, traveling from one to another, systematically testing all the slow learners, problem cases, and "exceptional" children ("exceptional" meant either unusually intelligent or retarded). She put great stock in making an attractive, even stunning appearance at those smelly cinder-block schools and rose early in the morning to apply her makeup, struggle into her girdle, and don dresses or suits that followed the fashions better than the contours of her stubby body.

In the gray, frozen dawns of Chicago winters she would drive her new Buick to remote schools, where the assistant principal would install her in an empty classroom and bring her one child after another. Shy, dirty, suspicious kids would eye her warily, wag their legs together in a lackluster parody of sex, fall into dumb trances, or microscopically assay the hard, black riches they'd mined from their nostrils, but nothing could dim my mother's glittering determination to be cheerful.

She never merely went through the motions or let a more appropriate depression muffle her performance. She always had the highly colored, fatuously alert look of someone who is listening to compliments.

Perhaps she looked that way because she was continuously reciting her own praises to herself as a sort of protective matra. Most people, I suspect, are given a part in which the dialogue keeps running out, a supporting role for which the lazy playwright has scribbled in "Improvise background chatter" or "Crowd noises off." But my mother's lines had been fully scored for her (no matter that she'd written them herself), and she couldn't rehearse them often enough. Every night she came home, kicked off her very high heels, wriggled out of her orthopedically strong girdle, shrinking and filling out and sighing "Whooee!"—something her Ranger, Texas, mother would exclaim after feeding the chickens or rustling up some grub in the summer heat.

Then my mother would pour herself a stiff bourbon and water, first of the many highballs she'd need to fuel her through the evening. "I saw fifteen patients today: twelve Stanford-Binets, one Wexford, one House-Tree-Person. I even gave a Rorschach to a beautiful little epileptic with high potential." On my mother's lips "beautiful" meant not a pretty face but a case of grimly classic textbook orthodoxy. "The children loved me. Several of them were afraid of me—I guess they'd never seen such a pretty, stylish lady all smiling and perfumed and bangled. But I put them right at ease. I know how to handle those backward children, they're just putty in my hands."

She thought for a moment, regarding her hands, then became animated. "The assistant principal was so grateful to me for my fine work. I guess she'd never had such an efficient, skilled state psychologist visit her poor little school before. She accompanied me to my automobile, and boy, you should have seen her eyes light up when she realized I was driving a fine Buick." Mother slung her stocking feet over the arm of the upholstered chair. "She grabbed my hand and looked me right in the eye and said, 'Who *are* you?'" This was part of the litany I always hated because it was obviously a lie. "'Why, whatever do you mean?' I asked her. 'You're no ordinary psychologist,' she said. 'I can see by your fine automobile and your beautiful clothes and your fine mind and lovely manners that you are a real lady.'" It was the phrase "fine automobile" that tipped me off, since only Southerners like my mother said that. Chicagoans said "nice car." Anyway I'd never heard any Midwesterner praise another in such a gratifying way; only in my mother's scenarios were such heady scenes a regular feature.

As the night wore on and my sister and I would sit down to do our homework on the cleared dining room table, as the winter pipes would knock hypnotically and the lingering smell of fried meat would get into our hair and heavy clothes, our mother would pour herself a fourth highball and put on her glasses to grade the tests she'd administered that day or to write up her reports in her round hand, but she'd interrupt her work and ours to say, "Funny, that woman simply couldn't get over how a fine lady like me could be battling the Skokie slush to come out to see those pitiful children." The note of pity was introduced only after the fourth drink, and it was, I imagine, something she felt less for her patients than for herself as the telephone stubbornly refused to ring.

At that time in my mother's life she had few friends. Going out with other unmarried women struck her as a disgrace and defeat. She was convinced couples looked down on her as a divorcée, and those single men who might want to date a chubby, penniless, middle-aged woman with two brats hanging around her neck were, as she'd say, scarce as hen's teeth.

That's where Mr. Grady came in. He was forty-five going on sixty, overweight, and utterly passive. He too liked his drinks, although in his case they were Manhattans; he fished the maraschino cherries out with his fingers. He didn't have false teeth, but there was something weak and sunken around his mouth as he mumbled his chemically bright cherries. His hairless hands were liver-spotted, and the nails were flaky, bluish, and unusually flat, which my mother, drawing on her fragmentary medical knowledge, called "spatulate," although I forget which malady this symptom was supposed to indicate. His wife had left him for another man, much richer, but she considerately sent Mr. Grady cash presents from time to time. He needed them: he lived reasonably well and he didn't earn much. He worked on the city desk of a major Chicago daily, but he'd been there for nearly twenty years, and in that era, before the Newspaper Guild grew strong, American journalists were badly paid unless they were flashy, opinionated columnists. Mr. Grady wrote nothing and had few opinions. He occasionally assigned stories to reporters, but most of the time he filled out columns that ran short with curious scraps of information. These items were called, for some reason, "boilerplate" and were composed weeks, even months in advance. For all I knew they were bought ready-made from some Central Bureau of Timeless Information.

Although Mr. Grady seldom said anything interesting and was much given to dithering over the practical details of his daily life, his work furnished him with the odd bit of startling knowledge.

"Did you realize that Gandhi ate meat just once in his life and nearly died of it?" he'd announce. "Did you know there is more electric wire in the Radio City Music Hall organ than in the entire city of Plattsburgh?"

He was capable of going inert, like a worm that poses as a stick to escape a bird's detection (I have my own stock of boilerplate). When mother would hector him for not demanding a raise or for not acting like a man, his face would sink into his jowls, his chin into his chest, his chest into his belly, and the whole would settle lifelessly onto his elephantine legs. His eyes behind their thick glasses would refuse all contact. In that state he could remain nearly indefinitely until at last my mother's irritation would blow over and she would make a move to head off for Miller's Steak House, a family restaurant with a menu of sizzling T-bones, butter and rolls, French-fried onions, and hot fudge sundaes, which would contribute to Mr. Grady's early death by cardiac arrest.

In September 1954 the Kabuki Theater came from Tokyo to Chicago for the first time, and my mother and Mr. Grady bought tickets for themselves and me and Mr. Grady's son Jim, whom we had never met (my sister didn't want to go—she thought it sounded "weird," and the prospect of meeting an eligible young man upset her).

The minute I saw Jim Grady I became sick with desire—sick because I knew from my mother's psychology textbooks, which I'd secretly consulted, just how pathological my longings were. I had looked up "homosexuality" and read through the frightening, damning diagnosis and prognosis so many times with an erection that finally, through Pavlovian conditioning, fear instantly triggered excitement, guilt automatically entailed salivating love or lust or both.

Jim was tall and tan and blond with hair clipped soldier-short and a powerful upper lip that wouldn't stay shaved and always showed a reddish gold stubble. His small, complicated eyes rapidly changed expression, veering from manly impenetrability to teenage shiftiness. He trudged rather than walked, as though he were shod with horseshoes instead of trim Oxford lace-ups. He wore a bow tie, which I usually associated with chipper incompetence, but in Jim's case seemed more like a tourniquet hastily tied around his large, mobile

Adam's apple in a makeshift attempt to choke off its pulsing male-ness. If his Adam's apple was craggy, his nose was small and thin and well made, his bleached-out eyebrows so blond they shaded off into his tanned forehead, his ears small and neat and red and peeling on top and on the downy lobes.

He seemed eerily unaware of himself—the reason, no doubt, he left his mouth open whenever he wasn't saying "Yes, ma'am" or "No, ma'am" to my mother's routine questions, although once he smiled at her with the seductive leer of a lunatic, as though he were imitating someone else. He had allergies or a cold that had descended into his larynx and made his monosyllables sound becomingly stifled—or maybe he always talked that way. He could have been a West Point cadet, so virile and impersonal did his tall body appear, except for that open mouth, those squirming eyes, his fits of borrowed charm.

Someone had dressed him up in a hairy alpaca suit jacket and a cheap white shirt that was so small on him that his red hands hung down out of the cuffs like hams glazed with honey, for the backs of his hands were brushed with gold hair. The shirt, which would have been dingy on anyone less tan, was so thin that his dark chest could be seen breathing through it like a doubt concealed by a wavering smile. He wasn't wearing a T-shirt, which in those days was unusual, even provocative.

Mr. Grady was seated at one end, my mother next to him, then Jim, then me. My mother took off her coat and hat and combed her hair in a feathery, peripheral way designed to leave the deep structure of her permanent intact. "You certainly got a good tan this summer," she said.

"Thank you, ma'am."

His father, heavily seated, said tonelessly, without lifting his face from his chin or his chin from his chest, "He was working outside all summer on construction, earning money for his first year in med school."

"Oh, really!" my mother exclaimed, suddenly fascinated, since she had a deep reverence for doctors. I too felt a new respect for him as I imagined the white surgical mask covering his full upper lip; "I want you on your hands and knees," I could hear him telling me, "now bend forward, cross your arms on the table, turn your face to one side, and lay your cheek on the back of your forearm. Arch your back, spread your knees still wider." He was pulling on rubber gloves and from my strange, sideways angle I could see him dipping his sheathed finger into the cold lubricant....

"Have you chosen a specialty already?" my mother asked as the auditorium lights dimmed.

"Gynecology," Jim said—and I clamped my knees together with a start.

Then the samisens squealed, kotos thunked dully, and drums kept breaking rank to race forward faster and faster until they fell into silence. A pink spotlight picked out a heavily armored and mascaraed warrior frozen in midflight on the runway, but only the scattered Japanese members of the audience knew to applaud him. The program placed a Roman numeral IV beside the actor's name, which lent him a regal importance. Soon Number Four was stomping the stage and declaiming something in an angry gargle, but we hadn't paid for the earphones that would have given us the crucial simultaneous translation since my mother said she always preferred the gestalt to the mere details. "On the Rorschach I always score a very high W," she had coyly told the uncomprehending and uninterested Mr. Grady earlier over supper. I knew from her frequent elucidations that a high W meant she saw each inkblot as a whole rather than as separate parts, and that this grasp of the gestalt revealed her global intelligence, which she regarded as an attribute of capital importance.

A mincing, tittering maiden with a homely, powdered white face and an impractical hobble skirt (only later did I read that the performer was a man and the fifth member of his improbable dynasty) suddenly metamorphosed into a sinister white fox. With suicidal daring I pressed my leg against Jim's. First I put my shoe against his, sole planted squarely against sole, Then, have staked out this beachhead, I slowly cantilevered my calf muscles against his, at first just lightly grazing him. I even withdrew for a moment, proof of how completely careless and unintended my movements were, before I sat forward, resting my elbows on my knees in total absorption, leaning attentively into the exotic squealing and cavorting on stage—an intensification of attention that of course forced me to press my slender calf against his massive one, my knobby knee against his square, majestic one.

As two lovers rejoiced or despaired (one couldn't be sure which) and tacky paper blossoms showered them, Jim's leg held fast against mine. He didn't move it away. I stole a glance at his profile, but it told me nothing. I pulsed slightly against his leg but still didn't move away.

I rubbed my palms together and felt the calluses that months of harp practice had built up on my fingertips.

If I kept up my assaults, would he suddenly and indignantly withdraw—even, later, make a remark to his father, who would feel obliged to tip off my mother about her son the fairy? I'd already been denounced at the country club where I'd worked as a caddie the previous summer. While waiting on the benches in the stifling hot caddie house for golfers to arrive, I'd pressed my leg in just this way against that of an older caddie named Mikey, someone who until then had liked shooting the shit with me. Now he stood up and said, "What the hell are you, anyway, some sort of fuckin' Liberace?" He'd tried to pull away several times, but I'd ignored his hints.

This time I'd wait for reciprocal signals. I wouldn't let my desire fool me into seeing mutual longing where only mine existed. I was dreading the intermission because I didn't know if I could disguise my tented crotch or the blush bloom that was slowly drifting up my neck and across my face.

I flexed my calf muscle against Jim's and he flexed back. We were football players locked into a tight huddle or two wrestlers each struggling to gain the advantage over the other (an advantage I was only too eager to concede). We were about to pass over the line from accident into intention. Soon he'd be as incriminated as I. Or did he think this dumb show was just a joke, indicative of other intentions, anything but sexual?

I flexed my calf muscles twice and he signaled back twice; we were establishing a Morse code that was undeniable. On stage, warriors were engaged in choreographed combat, frequently freezing in midlunge, and I wondered where we would live, how I would escape my mother, when I could kiss those full lips for the first time.

A smile, antic with a pleasure so new I scarcely dared to trust it, played across my lips. Alone with my thoughts but surrounded by his body, I could imagine a whole long life with him.

When the intermission came at last, our parents beat a hasty retreat to the bar next door, but neither Jim nor I budged. We had no need of highballs or a Manhattan; we already had them and were already in New York or someplace equally magical. As the auditorium emptied out, Jim looked at me matter-of-factly, his Adam's apple rising and falling, and he said, "How are we ever going to get a moment alone?"

"Do you have a television set?" I asked (they were still fairly rare).

"Of course not. Dad never has a damn cent; he throws his money away with both hands."

"Why don't you come over to our place on Saturday to watch the Perry Como show, then drink a few too many beers and say you're too tight to drive home and ask to stay over. The only extra bed is in my room."

"Okay," he said in that stifled voice. He seemed as startled by my efficient deviousness as I was by his compliance. When our much livelier parents returned and the lights went back down, I wedged a hand between our legs and covertly stroked his flexed calf, but he didn't reciprocate and I gave up. We sat there, knee to knee, in a stalemate of lust. I'd been erect so long my penis began to ache, and I could feel a pre-come stain seeping through my khakis. I turned bitter at the prospect of waiting three whole days till Saturday. I wanted to pull him into the men's room right now.

Once at home, my mother asked me what I thought of Jim, and I said he seemed nice but dumb. When I was alone in bed and able at last to strum my way to release (I thought of myself as the Man with the Blue Guitar), I hit a high note (my chin), higher than I'd ever shot before, and I licked myself clean and floated down into the featherbed luxury of knowing that big tanned body would soon be wrapped around me.

Our apartment was across the street from the beach and I loved to jump the Lake Michigan waves. Now I'm astonished I enjoyed doing anything that athletic, but then I thought of it less as sport than as opera, for just as in listening to 78 records I breasted one soaring outburst after another by Lauritz Melchior or Kirsten Flagstad, so was I thrilled by the repeated crises staged by the lake in September—a menacing crescendo that melted anticlimactically away into a creamy glissando, a minor interval that swelled into a major chord, all of it as abstract, excited, and endless as Wagner's *Ring*, which I'd never bothered to dope out motif by leit-motif, since I too preferred an ecstatic gestalt to tediously detailed knowledge. We were careless in my family, careless and addicted to excitement.

Jim Grady called my mother and invited himself over on Saturday evening to watch the Perry Como show on television. He told her he was an absolute fanatic about Como, that he considered Como's least glance or tremolo incomparably cool, and that he especially admired his long-sleeved golfer's sweaters with the low-slung yoke necks, three buttons at the waist, coarse spongy weave, and bright colors. My mother told me about these odd enthusiasms; she was puzzled by them because she thought that fashion concerned women alone and that even over women its tyranny extended only to clothes, certainly not to ways of moving, smiling, or singing. "I wouldn't want to imitate anyone else," she said with her little mirthless laugh of self-congratulation and a disbelieving shake of her head. "I like being me just fine, thank you very much."

"He's not the first young person to swoon over a pop star," I informed her out of my infinite world-weariness.

"Men don't swoon over men, dear," Mother reminded me, peering at me over the tops of her glasses. Now that I unscramble the signals she was emitting, I see how contradictory they were. She said she admired the sensitivity of a great dancer such as Nijinsky, and she'd even given me his biography to make sure I knew the exact perverse composition of that sensitivity: "What a tragic life. Of course he ended up psychotic with paranoid delusions, martyr complex, and degenerative ataxia." She'd assure me, with snapping eyes and carnivorous smile, that she liked men to be men and a boy to be all boy (as who did not), although the hearty heartlessness of making such a declaration to her willowy, cake-baking, harp-playing son thoroughly eluded her. Nor would she have tolerated a real boy's beer brawls, bloody noses, or stormy fugues. She wanted an obedient little gentleman who would sit placidly in a dark suit when he wasn't helping his mother until, at the appropriate moment and with no advance fuss, he would marry a plain Christian girl whose unique vocation would be the perpetual adoration of her *belle-mère*.

At last, after our dispirited Saturday night supper, Jim Grady arrived, just in time for a slice of my devil's food cake and the Perry Como show. My sister skulked off to her room to polish her hockey stick and read through fan-magazine articles on Mercedes McCambridge and Barbara Stanwyck. Jim belted back the six-pack he'd brought along and drew our attention with repulsive connoisseurship to every cool Como mannerism. I now realize that maybe Como was the first singer who'd figured out that the TV lens represented twenty million horny women dateless on Saturday night; he looked searchingly into its glass eye and warbled with the calm certainty of his seductive charm.

As a homosexual, I understood the desire to possess an admired man, but I was almost disgusted by Jim's ambition to imitate him. My mother saw men as nearly faceless extras who surrounded the diva, a woman; I regarded men as the stars; but both she and I were opposed to all forms of masculine self-fabrication, she because she considered it unbecomingly narcissistic, I because it seemed a sacrilegious parody of the innate superiority of a few godlike men. Perhaps I was just jealous that Jim was paying more attention to Como than to me.

Emboldened by beer, Jim called my mother by her first name, which I'm sure she found flattering, since it was suggested he saw her as a woman rather than as a parent. She drank one of her many highballs with him, sitting beside him on the couch, and for an instant I coldly appraised my own mother as a potential rival, but she lost interest in him when he dared to shush her during a bit of the singer's studied patter. In those days before the veneration of pop culture, unimaginative highbrows such as my mother and I swooned over opera, foreign films of any sort, and "problem plays" such as *The Immoralist* and *Tea and Sympathy*, but in spite of ourselves we were guiltily drawn to television with a mindless, vegetablelike tropism best named by the vogue word of the period, apathy. We thought it beneath us to study mere entertainment.

Jim was so masculine in the way he held a Lucky cupped between his thumb and middle finger and kept another unlit behind his ear, he was so inexpressive, so devoid of all gesture, that when he stood up to go, shook his head like a wet dog, and said, "Damn! I've had one too many for the road," he was utterly convincing. My mother said, "Do you want me to drive you home?" Jim laughed insultingly and said, "I think you're feeling no pain yourself. I'd better stay over, Delilah, if you have an extra bed."

My mother was much more reluctant to put Jim up than I'd anticipated. "I don't know, I could put my girdle back on...." Had she picked up the faint sex signal winking back and forth between Jim and her son? Or was she afraid he might sneak into her bedroom after lights out? Perhaps she worried how it might look to Mr. Grady: drunk son spends night in lakeside apartment—and such a son, the human species at its peak of physical fitness, mouth open, eyes shifting, Adam's apple working.

At last we were alone, and operatically I shed my clothes in a puddle at my feet, but Jim, undressing methodically, whispered, "You should hang your clothes up or your mother might think we were up to some sort of monkey business." Hot tears sprang to my eyes, but they dried as I looked at the long torso being revealed, with its small, turned waist and the wispy hairs around the tiny brown nipples like champagne grapes left to wither on a vine gone pale. His legs were pale because he'd worn jeans on the construction site, but he must have worn them low. For an instant he sat down to pull off his heavy white socks, and his shoulder muscles played under the overhead light with all the demonic action of a Swiss music box, the big kind with its works under glass.

He lay back with a heavy-lidded, cool expression I suspected was patterned on Como's, but I didn't care, I was even pleased he wanted to impress me as I scaled his body, felt his great warm arms around me, tasted the Luckies and Bud on his lips, saw the sharp focus in his eyes fade into a blur. "Hey," he whispered, and he smiled at me as his hands cupped my twenty-six-inch waist and my hot penis planted its flag on the stony land of his perfect body. "Hey," he said, hitching me higher and deeper into his presence.

Soon after that I came down with mononucleosis, the much-discussed "kissing disease" of the time, although I'd kissed almost no one but Jim. I was tired and depressed. I dragged myself with difficulty from couch to bed, but at the same time I was so lonely and frustrated that I looked down from the window at every man or boy walking past and willed him to look up, see me, join me, but the will was weak.

Jim called one afternoon, and we figured out he could come by the next evening when my mother was going somewhere with my sister. I warned him he could catch mono if he kissed me, but I was proud that after all he did kiss me long and deep. Until now the people I'd had sex with were boys at camp who pretended to hypnotize each other or married men who cruised the Howard Street Elevated toilets and drove me down to the beach in station wagons filled with their children's toys. Jim was the first man who took off his clothes, held me in his arms, looked me the eye, and said, "Hey." He who seemed otherwise so stiff and ill at ease became fluent in bed.

I was bursting with my secret, all the more so because mononucleosis had reduced my world to the size of our apartment and the books I was almost too weak to hold (that afternoon it had been Oscar Wilde's *Lady Windermere's Fan*). In the evening my mother was washing dishes and I was drying, but I kept sitting down to rest. She said, " Mr. Grady and I are thinking of getting married." The words just popped out of my mouth: "Then it will have to be a double wedding." My brilliant repartee provoked not a laugh but an inquisition, which had many consequences for me over the years, both good and bad. The whole story of my homosexual adventures came out, my father was informed, I was sent off to boarding school and a psychiatrist—my entire life changed.

My mother called up Jim Grady and boozily denounced him as a pervert and child molester, although I'd assured her I'd been the one to seduce him. I did not see him again until almost forty years later in Paris. My mother, who'd become tiny, wise, and sober with age, had had several decades to get used to the idea of my homosexuality (and my sister's, as it turned out). She had run into Jim Grady twice in the last three years and warned me he'd become maniacally stingy to the point he'd wriggle out of a drinks date if he thought he'd have to pay.

And yet when he rang me up from London, where he was attending a medical conference, he didn't object when I proposed to book him into the pricey hotel next door to me on the Ile St. Louis.

He called from his hotel room, and I rushed over. He was nearly sixty years old, with thin gray hair, glasses with clear frames he'd mended with black electrician's tape, ancient Corfam shoes, an open mouth, a stifled voice. We shook hands, but a moment later he pulled me into his arms. He said he knew, from a magazine interview I'd given, that this time I was infected with a virus far more dangerous than mononucleosis, but he kissed me long and deep, and a moment later we were undressed.

Over the next four days I had time to learn all about his life. He hadn't become a gynecologist after all but a sports doctor for a Catholic boys' school, and he spent his days bandaging the bruised and broken bodies of teenage athletes. His best friend was a fat priest nicknamed "The Whale," and they frequently got drunk with one of Jim's soldier friends who'd married a real honey, a little Chinese gal. Jim owned his house. He'd always lived alone and seemed never to have had a lover. His father had died from an early heart attack, but Jim felt nothing but scorn for him and his spendthrift ways. Jim himself had a tricky heart, and he was trying to give a shape to his life. He was about to retire.

It was true he'd become a miser. He bought his acrylic shirts and socks in packs of ten. His glasses came from Public Welfare. At home he went to bed at sunset to save on electricity. We spent hours looking for prints that cost less than five dollars as presents for The Whale, the army buddy, and the Chinese gal. We were condemned to eating at the Maubert Self, a cafeteria, or nibbling on cheese and apples we'd bought at the basement supermarket next to the Métro St. Paul. He explained his economies to me in detail. Proudly he told me that he was a millionaire several times over and that he was leaving his fortune to the Catholic church, although he was an atheist.

I took him with me to my literary parties and introduced him as my cousin. He sat stolidly by like an old faithful dog as people said brilliant, cutting things in French, a language he did not know. He sent every hostess who received us a thank-you letter, which in America was once so common it's still known as a "bread-and-butter note" although in France it was always sufficiently rare as to be called a "*lettre de château*." The same women who'd ignored him when he sat at their tables were retrospectively impressed by his New World courtliness.

On his trip to Paris I slept with him just that first time in his hotel room; as we kissed, he removed his smudged, taped welfare glasses and revealed his darting young blue eyes. He undressed my sagging body and embraced my thirty-six-inch waist and bared his own body, considerably slimmer but just as much a ruin with its warts and wattles and long white hair. And yet, when he hitched me into his embrace and said, "Hey," I felt fourteen again. "You were a moron to tell your mom everything about us," he said. "You made us lose a lot of time." And if we had spent a life together, I wondered, would we each be a bit less deformed now?"

As his hands stroked my arms and belly and buttocks, everything the years had worn down or undone, I could hear an accelerating drum and see, floating just above the rented bed, our young, feverish bodies rejoicing or lamenting, one couldn't be sure which. The time he'd come over when I had mono, my hot body had ached and shivered beside his. Now each time I touched him I could hear music, as though a jolt had started the clockwork after so many years. We watched the toothed cylinder turn under the glass and strum the long silver notes.

Punchlines

W. P. Kinsella

One rainy afternoon, Robert Louis Stevenson's nephew, Lloyd Osborne, asked the writer to invent for him an adventure story full of pirates and bloody deeds. He imposed only one condition: that there be no women in it. Stevenson complied and in the fall of 1883 Treasure Island was published. To the young Lloyd Osborne, as to so many other male readers, a world that was exclusively male must have seemed wonderfully safe from any erotic temptations.

Like the world of adventure stories "for boys", the traditionally male world of sports has become carefully purified of any erotic connotations. Men touching men, male bodies on male bodies, uniforms that exaggerate or outline the male form, the wielding of bats and sticks, the sweaty intimacy of locker rooms—the iconography, in fact, of gay pornography—all of this is strenuously proclaimed to be fiercely heterosexual. Gay athletes are regarded as oxymorons, and events such as the Gay Games are seen as profoundly disturbing because they challenge a key heterosexual symbol. W.P. Kinsella, who has made baseball one of his particular fictional realms, plays in "Punchlines" with the dissembling nature of this symbolic universe, and the men who embody its contradictions. Kinsella's favourite quotation comes from the American writer Donald Barthelme: "The aim of literature is to create a strange object covered in fur which breaks your heart."

Pascoe and Martinez came to visit me at Vancouver General Hospital the day after I picked up forty-one stitches from running through the glass wall next to the front door of my girlfriend's apartment building.

Pascoe is black, but beside Martinez he looks gray. Martinez is new to the team; his home is in the Dominican Republic; he comes from the famous town where they have a factory that turns out iron-armed shortstops who gobble up ground balls like they were PacMan. Martinez speaks only about ten words of English, so he's happy to have anybody pay any attention to him. He has worried brown eyes and is so black his round cheeks and wide forehead give off a glare in bright sunlight. Martinez doesn't know he's getting himself in the manager's bad books, making himself an outcast by hanging around with me. Pascoe does.

My name is Barry McMartin. Reporters describe me as the Vancouver Canadians' designated flake. The team bad boy. A troublemaker. Most of my teammates don't like me very much, in fact most are a little afraid of me. Some of them think I'm on drugs. There's more than the usual hassle about athletes and drugs in these post–Len Bias days. But I've never done drugs. I have some common sense, even if most people tend to think the amount I have is minimal.

At the hospital, Pascoe stuck his head around the doorjamb and when he saw me he said, "How the hell did you get all the way to Triple A on one fucking brain cell?"

I smiled, though it hurt like hell. Nine of those stitches were in my hairline. Martinez grinned his greeting, showing off his white eyes and teeth. He said something in Spanish, ending by clapping his hands once and doing a little dance step. I assume he was wishing me well.

"How long will you be out of action this time?" Pascoe asked. He is our first baseman. This is his third year in Triple A, and he's not likely to go any higher. He is six foot seven and shaves his head to resemble Otis Sistrunk, the football player; he looks mean as a boil, but one of the reasons he's never had a shot at the Bigs is that he lacks the killer instinct. He plays an average first base, but for such a big man he has only warning-track power as a hitter.

"Management put me on the fifteen-day disabled list. I'll be ready to go in less than that. The doctors said I was real lucky. 'You are very lucky you're not dead,' is what the doctor in emergency said to me as he was sewing up my cuts. 'A couple of guys get killed every month by doing what you did tonight. You must have a guardian angel; it's a miracle you didn't permanently disable yourself. You'll be back playing baseball inside of two weeks.'"

I pulled up my hospital gown and showed the guys the rest of my stitches. The cuts made a primitive mark of Zorro on my chest. None were deep, not even close to a tendon or a vital artery. What did scare me almost to death at the time was that a shard of glass clipped off the tip of my right earlobe and I bled like a stuck pig. When I recovered my senses, I was lying in a pool of blood and broken glass in the entrance-way to Judy's apartment building. I thought I was a goner for sure.

"Well, what are we gonna do to cheer our friend up, Marty?" Pas-coe says, with a smile that goes halfway to his ears.

"*Sí,*" says Martinez.

"Tell me a joke," I say.

"We know he can't play baseball, lady. We want to use him for second base," says Pascoe, and we both break up, while Martinez watches us, mystified. My laughter lasts only a few seconds before pain from my stitches brings me up short.

One night last season, soon after I became Pascoe's roommate, we stayed up all night telling jokes. We were sitting in a twenty-four-hour café called the Knight & Day, and we just kept drinking coffee and telling stories until the sun came up. We both agreed that we'd told every joke, clean or dirty, that we both knew. And as we got to know each other better we decided that instead of retelling a whole story we'd just shout out the punchline. We both knew the joke so we could both laugh. To give an example, there's a long shaggy-dog story about a white man trying to prove himself to the Indian tribe he's living with. The Indians give him a list of acts to perform that will establish his courage. When he comes back to camp looking happy but torn to rat shit, one of the Indians says to him, "You were supposed to *kill* the bear and *make love* to the woman." So now instead of retelling that story we just shout out the punchline and both of us, and anyone else who knows the story, have a good laugh. But it stymies some of the other players and doesn't go over well when we're out on dates.

"The trouble was the pilot was gay," I say, and this time Martinez laughs along.

Martinez is so congenial we are genuinely trying to teach him English. Not like some of the Spanish-speaking players. We've been known to take them to restaurants and have them say to the waitress, thinking that they're ordering a hamburger, "I'd like to eat your pussy, please."

"What did management have to say?" Pascoe asks, changing the subject. There is genuine concern on his face.

"When you get to my balls try to act as if nothing unusual is happening," I reply. That's a punchline from a joke about Sonny Crocker going undercover, dressed as a woman. "Hey, the nurses here are terrific, there was this one last night pulled the screen close around my bed...."

"I'm serious," says Pascoe.

"So am I."

"Goddamnit, Barr. How much trouble are you in?"

"Well, Skip didn't come down. As you know, Skip hates my guts. Skip wanted to fire my ass. Or so says Osterman. But I'm too valuable for them to do that. Milwaukee's going to call me up inside of a month—see if they don't. So it was Old Springs came down himself."

Springs is what we call Osterman, the general manager of the baseball team. He is one of these dynamic guys who walks like he's got springs in his shoes, and he's read all these inspirational books like *How to Fuck Your Friends, Rip Off Your Neighbors, and Make a Million by Age 30.* He's always talking to us ballplayers about long-term investments, five-year plans, and networking.

"You're an asshole, McMartin," he said to me. "You're a fuck-up, you're an asshole, you're a jerk. You're also a criminal. If it wasn't for baseball, your ass would be in jail in some town out in the Oklahoma desert, or you'd be in a psych hospital, which is where I think you belong. Skip said he'd personally kill you if he visited you himself. So he sent me. For some reason he figures I have more self-control. Skip says to tell you he wishes you'd cut your troublemaking throat when you fell through that window, or whatever you did."

"Yeah, well, you tell Skip his wife's not bad in bed. But she's not nearly as good as your wife."

I was sorry as soon as the words were out. I knew I'd gone too far, again. I don't really want these guys to hate me. I just want to make it clear that I don't take shit from *anybody*.

"You really are pure filth, McMartin," Springs growls. " The front office personnel voted unanimously not to send you flowers or wish you a speedy recovery. Unfortunately, in Milwaukee they don't know what an asshole you are; they think you might be able to hit thirty home runs for them next year. They'd let fucking Charles Manson bat cleanup if they thought he'd hit thirty homers. But just let me remind you, the minimum wage in Oklahoma is about three-fifty an hour, and out of a baseball uniform you're not even worth that."

"Try to imagine how little I care," I said.

"We're going to tell the press you were being chased out of the apartment by an angry husband," said Springs. "It will fit your image and make you look less like a fool. But let me tell you, Milwaukee is fed up with your antics, too. This is absolutely the last time."

"Did management suspend you, or what?" asks Pascoe.

"Naw, I told you. I'm their fair-haired boy. I'm on the D.L. for fifteen days. I'll be out of this hospital tomorrow morning. So while you guys fuck off to Portland and Phoenix and get your asses whipped eight out of nine without your favorite cleanup hitter, I'll be sitting in Champagne Charlie's pounding a Bud and drooling over the strippers."

"I should have that kind of luck," says Pascoe. "I don't know, Barry, you got to stop acting so ... so external, man," he added, shaking his head sadly.

I should treat Pascoe better. He's a decent guy. I don't know why he hangs around with me. Lately everything I touch seems to turn to shit. Pascoe's really a good friend. When I first arrived he showed me around Vancouver, which bars and clubs to visit, which to stay away from.

"Stay away from the King's Castle," he said to me as we walked down Granville Street one evening, heading toward Champagne Charlie's strip joint. "It's the biggest gay bar in Vancouver. Stay away from the Royal Bar, too. Bikers and Indians; half the people in the bar have shivs in their boots—and those are the women." There were flamingo neon bars above the entrance to the King's Castle and a dozen young men were standing in groups or lounging individually against the walls near the entrance, all caught in the pinkish glow of the neon.

"Fucking queers," I said as we passed, not caring if I was heard.

"Behave yourself," said Pascoe.

The first real *incident* happened the second week of the season. I have to admit I am naturally a loud person. I tend to shout when I speak; I walk with a bit of a swagger; I keep my head up and my eyes open. I've never minded being stared at. I like it that girls often turn and stare after me on the street.

The incident: there is a play in baseball called a suicide squeeze. A manager will call for it with a runner on third, and none or one out. As the pitcher goes into the stretch, the runner breaks from third; it is the hitter's duty to get the ball on the ground anywhere in the ballpark, though they usually try to bunt it between the pitcher and third or first. The idea is that by the time the ball is fielded, the base runner will have scored, the fielder's only play being to first. If, however, the hitter misses the pitch, the base runner is dead, hence the term suicide squeeze.

We were playing Phoenix in Vancouver, at Nat Bailey Stadium, a ballpark that, like the City of Vancouver, is clean and green; the only stadium in the Pacific Coast League that can compare to it is the one at the University of Hawaii, where the Islanders play part of their schedule. I tripled to lead off the second inning. Pascoe was batting fifth and he popped up weakly to the shortstop. The manager put on the suicide squeeze. The pitcher checked me, stretched, and delivered. I broke. The batter, a substitute fielder named Denny something, bunted, but he hit the ball way too hard. It was *whap! snap!* and the ball was in the pitcher's glove. He fired to the catcher, who was blocking the plate, and I was dead by fifteen feet. But I'd gotten up a real head of steam. I weigh 217 and stand six foot two, and I played a lot of football in high school back in Oklahoma. I hit the guy with a cross block that could have gotten me a job in the NFL. He was a skinny little weasel who looked like he was raised somewhere where kids don't get fed very often. I knocked him about five feet in the air, and he landed like he'd been shot in flight. The son of a bitch held on to the ball, though. The guy who bunted was at second before someone remembered to call time. They pried the ball out of the catcher's fingers and loaded him on a stretcher.

I'd knocked him toward our dugout and had to almost step over him to get to the bench. What I saw scared me. His neck was twisted at an awkward angle and he was bleeding from the mouth.

The umpire threw me out of the game for unsportsmanlike conduct. The league president viewed the films and suspended me for five games. The catcher had a concussion, a dislocated shoulder, and three cracked ribs. He's still on the D.L. as far as I know.

The next time I played against Phoenix, I got hit by a pitch the first time up. I charged the mound, the benches cleared, but before I even got to the pitcher, Pascoe landed me on my back and took me right out of the play. Suddenly, there were three or four guys wrestling on top of us.

"Behave yourself," Pascoe hissed into my ear, as he held me pinioned to the ground, while players milled around us. Those have become Pascoe's favorite words as the summer has deepened, and I keep finding new ways to get into trouble.

Pascoe was happy when I started dating July. Word even got back to Skip, and he said a couple of civil words to me for the first time since I coldcocked the Phoenix catcher. Judy was a friend of a girl Pascoe dated a couple of times. She was a tiny brunette, a year younger than me, with dancing brown eyes, a student at the University of British Columbia, studying sociology.

"You're just shy," she said to me on our second date.

"Ha!" cried Pascoe. He and his girlfriend were sitting across from us in a Denny's.

"It's true," said Judy. "People who talk and laugh loudly in order to have attention directed to them are really very shy."

"You are, aren't you? Shy, I mean," Judy said later that evening in bed at her apartment. Our lovemaking had been all right, but nothing spectacular.

"I suppose," I said. "But I'd never admit it."

"You just did, " said Judy, leaning over to kiss me.

The next thing that got me in bad with management was far worse than just coldcocking a catcher with a football block. Pascoe, Martinez, and I had been out making the rounds after a Saturday night game. I had several beers, but not enough that I should have been out of control. We closed up Champagne Charlie's, decided to walk home instead of taking a taxi. When we crossed the Granville Street Bridge, the pre-dawn air was sweet and foggy. We were near Broadway and Granville, swinging along arm in arm, when the police cruiser pulled up alongside us.

The passenger window of the police car rolled down and an officer no older than Pascoe or me said, "Excuse me, gentlemen, but I'd like to see some identification."

Pascoe was reaching for his wallet when I said, "What the fuck are you hassling us for? We're minding our own business."

The officer ignored me, but opened the door and stepped out, accepting the piece of ID Pascoe handed him.

Martinez, coming from a country where the police do not always exhibit self-control, stayed behind us, looking worried.

The officer returned Pascoe's ID. "And you, sir?" he said to Martinez.

"Leave him alone," I said. "He doesn't speak English."

"I'm not addressing you," the officer said to me.

"Fuck off," I yelled. "Leave him alone." I stepped in front of Martinez.

"Behave yourself," said Pascoe, and grabbed my arm. But I shoved him away, and before he could recover his balance, I shoved the officer back against the car. As the driver was getting out I leapt on the hood of the police car.

What happened next is a blur. I remember screaming curses at the police, dancing madly on the hood of the police car, feeling the hood dimple under my weight, dodging the grasping hands of the police and Pascoe.

I remember hearing Pascoe's voice crying out, "Oh, man, he's just crazy, don't shoot him." Then there was a hand on my ankle and I toppled sideways to the pavement. My mouth was full of blood and someone was sitting on me and my arms were being pulled behind my back and the handcuffs fastened.

I missed the Sunday afternoon game because management let me sit in jail until my court appearance Monday morning. The police had charged Martinez with creating a disturbance, but when the translator explained what had happened the prosecutor dropped the charge. I faced a half-dozen charges, beginning with assaulting a police officer.

The judge looked down at me where I stood, unshaven, my shirt torn and bloodstained, the left side of my face scraped raw from where I landed on the pavement. He remanded me for fourteen days for psychiatric evaluation.

"I'm not fucking crazy," I said to no one in particular.

The Vancouver Canadians' lawyer got on the phone to Milwaukee, and the Milwaukee Brewers' high-powered lawyers got in on the act. Before the end of the day, they struck a deal. If I agreed to spend an hour every afternoon with a private psychiatrist, the team would guarantee my good behavior, and my sentencing would be put off until the end of the baseball season.

Management had me by the balls. "You fuck up again and you're gone, kid," Skip said to me. "It doesn't matter how talented you are, you're not worth the aggravation."

I saw the shrink every afternoon for the whole home stand, weekends included. I took all these weird tests. Questions like "Are you a

messenger of God?" and "Has your pet died recently?" I wore a
jacket and tie to every session and talked a lot about what a nice girlfriend I had and how much I respected my parents.

"Well, Barry," the doctor said to me after about ten sessions, "you
don't appear to have any serious problems, but I do wish you'd make
an effort to be more cooperative. I am here to help you, after all."

"I thought I was being cooperative," I said innocently.

"In one sense you have been, but only partially. I find that you are
mildly depressive, that you're anxious, under a lot of stress. Stress is
natural in your profession, but I sense that there is something else
bothering you, and I wish you'd level with me. To use an analogy, it is
said that with a psychiatrist one tends to bare the body, scars and all,
tear open the chest so to speak, and expose your innermost feelings.
However, to date, you have scarcely taken off your overcoat."

"Look, I'm okay, honest. I had too much to drink, I got out of
control. It won't happen again."

"Suit yourself," said the doctor.

My life leveled out for almost a month. We went on a road trip. I continued to hit well; I watched the American League standings, studied
Milwaukee's box score in each day's newspaper, watched them fade
out of the pennant race. I wondered how much longer it would be
before I got my call to the Bigs. Once in Tacoma, Pascoe had to keep
me from punching the lights out of a taxi driver who said something
insulting about ballplayers, but other than that incident I stayed cool.
I phoned Judy almost every night. I found myself doing with her what
Pascoe so often did with me; I analyzed the game, dissected my at-bats
pitch by pitch. I knew what I was saying wasn't very interesting for
her, but it was a release for me, and not only did Judy not seem to
mind, she gave the impression she enjoyed it.

I can't understand why I continue to fuck up. Judy brought two
friends to a Sunday afternoon game. It was a perfect blue day and the
stands at Nat Bailey Stadium are close enough to the field that I could
look over at Judy and smile while I stood in the on-deck circle swinging a weighted bat. Her friends were a couple, Christine, a bouncy
blonde with ringlets and a sexy way of licking her lips, and her husband, a wimpy guy who wore a jacket and tie and looked like he was
shorter than Christine.

Although I had three hits and two RBIs, I wasn't in a good mood after the game. We went to one of these California-style restaurants with white walls and pink tablecloths, where everything is served in a sauce, and they look at you like you just shit on the floor if you ask for French fries. To top it off, I didn't like Trevor, and he didn't like me. I pounded about three Bud and then I drank a whole pitcher of this wine-cooler slop that tastes like Kool-Aid.

What really threw the shit into the fan was when the three of them decided the four of us would go to a movie, something called *Kiss of the Spider Woman*, about a couple of queers locked up in a prison in Argentina or someplace. Trevor gave us a little lecture about the *eloquent statement* the director was trying to make.

"There's no fucking way I'm going to a movie like that," I said, standing up to make my point.

"Barry, don't you dare make a scene," said Judy.

"No need to be boisterous about it," said Trevor. "You've simply been outvoted. We'd be happy to let you choose but I don't think *The Texas Chainsaw Massacre* is showing in Vancouver at the moment."

I didn't say anything. I just grabbed the tablecloth and pushed everything across the table into Trevor's lap, then turned and stomped out.

I was surprised when Judy caught up with me a half block down the street.

"You were only half to blame for that scene," she said. "I'm always willing to go halfway," she added, taking my arm.

"I'd rather you went all the way," I said.

But things didn't go well back at her apartment.

"For goodness' sake, Barry, relax," Judy said. "You're still mad. Nobody can make love when they're mad."

But I was thrashing about the room; I'd pulled on most of my clothes by the time I got to the door. Ignoring the elevator, I ran down the stairs, realizing about halfway that I'd abandoned my shoes in Judy's apartment.

I crossed the lobby running full out, and it felt to me as if I was on one prolonged suicide squeeze, the catcher twenty feet tall, made of bricks, waiting with the ball, grinning. I didn't even slow down as I hit the wall of glass next to the door.

In spite of my bragging about spending my time in the strip joints while the team was on its road trip, I actually stayed out of downtown the whole time. Last night I met this chick at a club over on Broadway, near the University of British Columbia. She was with a date, but she knew who I was and made it pretty plain she liked me. I made a late date for after the game tonight. I'm supposed to meet her at some white wine and fern restaurant in the financial district downtown, in the same building as the American embassy. Vicki is her name. She's tall with red-gold hair and freckles on her shoulders. Last night she was wearing a white sundress that showed off her tan.

"Bazoos that never quit," I said to Pascoe. "You should see her, man." I made a lapping motion with my tongue.

The game ended early. I took right up where I left off before the accident; I hit two dingers, a single, and stole a base. After each home run, I toured the bases slowly, my head erect, trying to look as arrogant as possible; I have a lot to prove to Skip, to management, to the self-righteous bastards I play with.

Sometimes I can't help but think about a note that was shoved through one of the vent slats in my locker at Nat Bailey Stadium. It was written on a paper towel from the washroom, printed in a childish scrawl. "Management pays Pascoe 300 a month to be you're freind," it said. For an instant my stomach dipped and I thought I might vomit. I quickly crumpled the towel and stuffed it in my back pocket. I glanced around to see if I could catch anybody watching me. No luck. I'd never ask Pascoe. What if it was true? I hate to admit it, but that note got to me. I think about it more than I ever should.

"Let's the three of us stop by Champagne Charlie's," I said to Pascoe and Martinez in the locker room. "We can pound a few Bud and eyeball the strippers. There's a new one since you guys have been out of town. You should see the fucking contortions she goes through. Someone there said she licks her own pussy during the midnight show."

"I thought you had this red-hot date," said Pascoe.

"Fuck her," I said. "Let her wait. They like you better if you treat them like shit."

We headed off, three abreast, just like old times. Me in the center, Pascoe to my left, Martinez linked to my right arm.

"Just like a fucking airplane," I said, walking fast, watching pedestrians part or move aside to let us pass.

"Punchline!" I shouted, as we loped along. "So I stood up, tried to kick my ass, missed, fell off the roof, and broke my leg."

Pascoe laughed. Martinez grinned foolishly.

"The nun had a straight razor in her bra," said Pascoe, the bluish streetlights reflecting off his teeth.

"Fucking, right on," I said.

We swaggered into Champagne Charlie's, got seats at the counter, right in front of the stage, ordered a round of Bud, and settled in.

"This Canadian beer tastes like gopher piss," I said, drawing a few ugly stares from the other customers. But we knocked back three each anyway.

The stripper was named La Velvet and was very tall and black. She took a liking to Pascoe, winked and crinkled her nose at him as she did the preliminary shedding of clothes. When she was naked except for red high-heeled shoes, she dragged her ass around the stage like a cat in heat. Then, facing us, with her hands flat on the floor at her sides, she edged toward us, braced her heels on the carpet at the edge of the stage, spreading her legs wide until her pussy was about a foot from Pascoe's face.

"Way to go, baby," I yelled. "Hey, Marty, how'd you like to eat that for breakfast? And lunch? And dinner?"

Martinez grinned amiably, pretending to understand.

I stood up and clapped in rhythm to her gyrating body.

"Behave yourself," hissed Pascoe.

"Way to go, baby. Wrap those long legs around his neck. Show me a guy who won't go down on his lady, and I will."

The bouncer came over and tapped me on the shoulder.

"Sit down," he said.

I was holding a bottle of Bud in my right hand. For half a second I considered smashing it across his face. He was obviously an ex-fighter, with a nose several times broken and heavy scar tissue across his eyebrows. Then I felt Pascoe's huge hand on my arm.

"Sit down, Barry," he growled. "Why do you always have to act like an asshole, man? Why do you have to be bigger and tougher and raunchier and more rough-and-ready than everybody else?"

I sat down. La Velvet was gathering up her robe and heading down some stairs at the back of the stage. I noticed that her nails were painted a deep, dark red, the color of a ripe cherry.

"Sorry, I just get carried away," I said lamely.

Pascoe glared at me.

"You spoiled my chances, man. Why do you have to act like a fucking animal?"

I didn't have any answer for him. I suppose I could blame it on the summer, the pressure of playing pro ball, being a long way from home for the first time.

La Velvet, wrapped in a scarlet robe that matched her high heels, appeared from a door on Martinez's side of the counter. As she walked behind us she leaned close to Pascoe and said in a throaty voice, "My last show's at midnight. You plannin' to be here?"

"Somebody'd have to kill me to keep me away," said Pascoe, grinning like a maniac.

"Don't you have a date?" he said to me as soon as La Velvet was gone.

"Yeah," I replied.

"You don't seem very excited about it anymore."

"Why don't you guys walk over to the restaurant with me? Just to keep me company."

"Naw, I want to sit here and dream about that midnight show and what's comin' after it," said Pascoe.

"You want to come for a walk, Marty?" I said.

Martinez stared at me, smiling, uncomprehending.

"Walk. Hike. El tromp-tromp. How the hell do you say *walk* in Spanish?"

Martinez continued to look confused. He glanced from me to Pascoe, as if seeking advice.

"Walk with me!" I howled, standing up, my beer bottle clutched in my hand. Out of the corner of my eye I could see the bouncer start in our direction.

"Behave yourself," said Pascoe urgently, standing up, too. "We'll come with you, just stop acting like a jerk," To the bouncer he said, "We're just leaving. Two drinks and my buddy here thinks he's Tarzan."

"Pound that Bud," I called out as Pascoe pulled me toward the exit. People were staring at us as we made our way across the nightclub and up the stairs to the street.

The movies were just out and Granville Street was teeming as we walked along three abreast, arms linked. I forged ahead, the point of the wedge, the pilot. Pascoe relived that night's game, every at-bat, every play he was involved in.

"Man, if I'd just laid back and waited for the slider," he was saying. He struck me out with an off-speed slider because I was guessing fast ball—"

"Punchline!" I shouted. "If you can get up and go to work, the leasht I can do ith pack you a lunch."

I guffawed loudly. Martinez grinned, jiggling along beside me. Pascoe, however, continued to analyze the game.

As we rolled along, we passed the shadowy entrance to the King's Castle. One door was open, but it was too dark to see inside. A fan expelled the odors of warm beer and cigarette smoke onto the sidewalk. There were several men in the entranceway. Two of them stood near the doorway, touching, talking earnestly into each other's faces. Pascoe talked on, looking neither right nor left. A tawny-skinned young man in tight Levis, his white shirt open, tied in a knot across his belly, leaned insolently against a wall.

"Fucking queers," I yelled, pushing on faster.

"Behave yourself," snapped Pascoe.

Beyond the King's Castle I breathed easier. As we were passing, my eyes had flashed across those of the tawny-skinned boy and I had felt that he knew. As I know. That it is not a matter of will I or won't I, but only of how long before I do.

"Punchline!" I wailed. "Trouble was, the pilot was gay."

"Ha, ha," cried Martinez, thinking he understood.

An Intimate Death

Marie-Claire Blais

The English novelist Adam Mars-Jones said that it is almost impossible to write about AIDS because AIDS is its own narrative, determines its own plot. Metaphors tend to trivialize or distract from its tragedy; chronicles don't do justice to the agony. AIDS seems, in our time, a subject beyond literature. And yet, how can writers address the subject of gay lives without addressing the subject of gay deaths? How can writers leave such a subject in the precincts of silence?

AIDS enters literature unnamed in Susan Sontag's 1983 story "The Way We Live Now". Sontag wrote about the new, insidious disease through allusion, through the absence of direct address, through the uneasy conversations of a group of friends (she of all people would of course refuse the recourse of metaphor, having condemned its overuse in two books of essays). Marie-Claire Blais also uses absence in "An Intimate Death", though here the absence is only that of the unmentioned, unmentionable disease: the dead man, the man who has recently died, is present through his friends' memories in blazing and living detail. Catholic funeral rites speak of "body present, spirit absent". In Blais's elegiac prose the reverse is true. The body is not there, has no movement, no tongue. But the spirit—and the reminder is essential in this time when disappearances are so sudden—is overwhelmingly present, and fills the page, without room for paragraph breaks, from the first to the final word.

His books are still there, untouched, just as he arranged them on the shelves of his study, the books he read, the books he wrote, his papers, his notes are still spread over his worktable, because surely he still has lots of time to finish a novel, an essay, the pictures, the drawings he loved, are also untouched on the orange wall he'd just painted, one of those pictures that remind you of Gauguin, with brown bodies in the sun, is an allegory of the sensual, paradisiacal life a person can lead on an island where it's always sunny and hot, he'd hung the picture on the orange wall above the table at which he reads and writes all day, but when evening comes and his work is done you can hear him laughing with his friends, although it's a sober laugh even when he smokes the euphoriant cigarettes he offers to everyone in that hot, nocturnal, intoxicating air, because there's barely enough wind at night, a breath of cool on the back of the neck, there's nothing but intoxication on this terrace, in this garden and at night we can hear him wandering lazily through the streets of the town, yes him, the intellectual who used to be so reserved, so discreet he seemed almost haughty, letting himself go in the blissful listlessness of the island, gradually he succumbs to his voluptuous temptations because surely he still has lots of time ahead of him, later, when he doesn't have to teach at that hidebound university back there, he'll come and live here among his books and his friends, and suddenly, how did it happen, one April morning, they made up a hospital bed in his room, under the towering trees that cover the roof of the tropical house with their branches, their tangled leaves, and he's thinking under this nest of lianas and stifling vegetation, lying on his hospital bed of intense pain while air comes to him in a mask and nourishment percolates drop by drop through tubes attached to his weakened flesh, he is thinking, those trees should have been cut long ago, they're so bushy, huge, they block the light, and their laughter can be heard from the garden, or the terrace, Vic and Frank and now they're here in this room leaning over him, washing him, changing him, turning him in his bed, for a few weeks already they've been here at his bedside, at first they offered him a hash cigarette, slipping it between his lips, then he refused, didn't he once tell them discreetly during a meal that he'd lost his taste for spicy food, those flavours that used to burn his throat, from now on, in the evening air, it's time for that indispensable morphine, and isn't it true they had to get rid of the young male nurse who was stealing the drugs prescribed for terminal patients at the hospital, and what would become of that kid from the black ghetto? His papers are spread over the table, the writing on them having become illegible, with hunched, tortured letters, and now he sees the misty silhouettes of Vic and Frank who are folding him in their arms because they have to change him, wash him like a baby, yesterday, indescribable consolation, they put some toys in his bed, then they took them away from him again because any object could hurt him, even a plush teddy bear, weren't his arms and legs covered with bruises, things have changed since the time they could still give him refreshing baths, now they have to turn him in his bed, he hardly weighs anything, and always those hunched, tortured letters among the notes on the worktable, under the picture that was hung on the wall painted orange last year, he's strong enough to say in a tone of deprived, repressed rage, he wants them to listen this time when he says, yes, his voice rattling, in a kind of incoherent sigh, when will it all be over, anyway, when will it all be over? Because there's other proof that his time has come, he thinks, and that is the hibiscus Peter brought yesterday, the one with the yellow flowers just blooming, which stopped suddenly, the buds glossy in the light wouldn't open, there's the sign, he thinks vaguely, the sign of departure, the trees are too high, too bushy, no ray of sun can get through any more, it's a yellow, tepid light at this hour of the morning, what did he say, Frank and Vic could barely hear him, a little water, yes, for the past few hours the water couldn't get past his burning lips any more, they'd sat him up with great tenderness, helped him support his head against the pillow, but it was no use, the cool water no longer soothed him, all he could do was repeat, when will it all be over, my friends, when will it all be over? He loved parties so much, too bad he's not here this evening with his friends, his colleagues, a few distant relatives as well, celebrating in this sumptuous historical house where Frank and Vic have organized a banquet in his honour, the man who loved parties so much is somewhere else, there in the Gulf of Mexico where his ashes are cooling, they rented a boat, says David, and the green waves rocked them, never saw so many ashes, says David, and the boat skimmed over the green water, carrying all of them along with the man who wouldn't return from the voyage, yes, but that night during the banquet the hibiscus began to bloom once more even though the air was glacial for this warm season, the hibiscus was blooming again spreading its wide, yellow corollas, and it was Peter, wasn't it, standing near the plant in shy silence, who noticed it first, the hibiscus is blooming and the man who couldn't drink or eat any more, never mind do what they asked and roll onto his side to relieve the pain a little, he too had seen that vigorous plant, the hibiscus Peter had brought him and at that moment he'd felt the breathing grow slow in his chest, Peter and the plant were the incarnation of that living beauty he would never attain again, even by stretching out his hand, that emaciated hand opening in the void, lots of time ahead of him, later on he'd come to rest and write in his island house, he'll write still more books, be an editor and poet by turns, he'll discover authors and make them known in foreign lands, and suddenly, one morning in March a male nurse pushes his wheelchair through the Miami airport and indeed it's him, the sportsman, the athlete who only yesterday was diving in the ocean waves, it is indeed him, so feeble today he can't walk any more, it is indeed him they're pushing in the wheelchair from one airport to another, under the pitying and fearful eyes of a crowd full of latent hostility, because this man passing has a contagious disease, and the contagion is formidable, it's a contagion of fear that nourishes prejudice, racism, hate he thinks while the crowd parts to let him through and he shivers with cold in this oppressive heat, touching his face and feeling the premature wrinkles under his trembling fingers, the sky is blue and hot, Vic and Frank are waiting for him there, feebly listless he'd let himself be dressed that morning in his blue sweater and grey corduroy slacks, fully aware that the young black male nurse was gradually stripping him of the morphine he'd need later on, who knows, maybe in a few days, but feebly listless, he'd let himself be dressed for the journey, but what did those people in the crowd see, under his sweater, his slacks, the sores, the black stigmata, because no part of his body had been spared, he was suffering as much inside as out, his breath was short and constricted, his pink colouring had faded in a few weeks, and when would it all be over, anyway, when would it all be over, that secret fire that wind of putrefaction blowing over him? And in this historical house on the island they were celebrating glass in hand, celebrating the man who used to be strong and beautiful, vigorous and tender, the lover of life when life was no longer there, they were celebrating the man who would never come back from the Gulf of Mexico and in the plane that was taking him back to the island the male nurse had raised him in his seat so he could see the ocean and there was a glint of joy in his blue eyes and the glint quickly disappeared as his gaze with its stricken intelligence became fixed on the green water, he saw the island lost amid thick vegetation, his island, and that evening Frank and Peter admitted they'd hardly recognized him when they saw him at the airport with the male nurse pushing the wheelchair, and in Frank's car they'd toured the island, saw once more its houses, the gardens he'd never see again and he'd said, I feel better

already, they'd toured the alleys and the streets of this town full of
odours surrounded by ocean, and they remembered how he'd spoken
then about his eyes, yes, his eyes were still good, his sight wasn't
affected, he could still read and work, and his books, his papers with
the illegible, hunched, tortured letters were still there in the house
under the trees, and they held a banquet in his honour but he wasn't
there any more, among his relatives, his friends, he couldn't feel the
night wind pass over the back of his neck, couldn't see the starry sky,
at the end, said David, he wasn't aware of much, fortunately, he no
longer knew what was happening to him, like a baby being changed
and swabbed, such a proud man but he wasn't aware and we've got to
be thankful for that small mercy, he was sinking all alone into a shadowy despair, laughing and crying, and yet he said, my God, when will
it all be over, anyway, and his blue, intelligent gaze wandered all
around him, around his abandoned and damaged body, the glint in
his eyes suddenly paralyzed in the dawn light, and they each had a
copy of that recent photo of him where the dazzling glint of his blue
eyes had blazed for the last time in the faded pallor of his face, on that
day too he was wearing the grey corduroy slacks, the blue wool
sweater and looked as if he were resting nonchalantly in a red canvas
chair, holding his head in his left hand, he must have felt good that
day, they said to themselves while contemplating the shy grace of his
smile, and the sick man's head, so very frail, bending towards the left
hand which supported the frail head as if it were about to fall, yes,
that's right, said David, and they all stared at this farewell snapshot,
discovering in it the premature wrinkles on his forehead, the melancholy of his smile, wasn't there a kind of laziness in his pose that day,
David was saying, a sweet nonchalance like in the good old days
when he used to smoke his intoxicating cigarettes beside his friends,
remember that night back when he used to go bar hopping after dark
and he met Lee, Lee, the Japanese boy in the striped pullover roller-
skating past the sidewalk bars that night with a luminous green band
around his close-cropped head glowing like a dragonfly in the night,
others said, there's a kind of abandon in his smile and in that movement of the hand, and such grace too, such extreme nonchalance, he
used to work a lot, but taking it easy, he also really liked doing nothing, just dreaming through the sensual sluggishness of those apparently endless summer days.... Behind him in the photograph there's
the landscape of water and sand that belonged to him so many times,

behind the man nonchalantly seated, relaxed, ready to laugh his sober laugh in the red canvas chair, he used to welcome his friends while resting in that chair in the garden, writers who'd come from every corner of the world and then they set up the hospital bed in the bedroom and he'd noticed how the trees were so high and bushy against the sky, no, the air couldn't get in any more and the sunlight, and the hibiscus Peter had placed near his bed, the hibiscus with its yellow flowers had suddenly stopped blooming as if it had been draped in a shroud of frost or deprived of the sun's glare, overwhelmed by the same contemptible, servile suffering he'd felt, even that night when he'd told his friends he didn't like spicy food any more, the lightness of his smile had faded, the cool water would no longer pass his burning lips, because a putrid fire consumed his heart, his bowels, and that devastated body was barely visible under the trembling damp sheets, even if Vic changed the sheets constantly weren't they always humid, oh! when will it all be over, anyway, when will it all be over? And then at last that glint of fierce anxiety became fixed at dawn in his eyes, the hibiscus stopped blooming finally, and it was all over, and the boats went on gliding over the green water and when the wind became too strong, the young people on their sailboards were cast out by the waves, a cold wind passed furtively over the green water and the hibiscus stopped blooming for two days when the cold wind came and you could feel it cut through you like a knife, and that was the hour a young man died, still overflowing with vitality, his books and his writings still untouched in his study on the worktable where bills in sealed envelopes were also piling up, and they were celebrating him that night, but he wasn't there any more among his relatives, his friends, to feel the breath of wind on the back of his neck and Lee no longer appeared at night on roller skates with a luminous green band around his close-cropped head, they raised their glasses but the man they celebrated wasn't there any more, the man who'd loved parties so much.

The Drapery Man

Bernard MacLaverty

The amorous relationship between an older and a younger man at times possesses the qualities of another kind of relationship: that between a teacher and his disciple. In turn, the teacher-disciple relationship often acquires the features of an erotic bond. The passing of an elder's wisdom and the physical offerings of youth are traditionally the two sides of an exchange, and the matter of moral tales and ribald stories. This exchange has a long tradition. Sanctioned in the Greek academies, permitted with restrictions in the schools of Rome, fiercely condemned in the monastic colleges of the Middle Ages, it never seems to have changed its double nature. Saint Aelred of Rievaulx, for instance, writing in the twelfth century, noted that "friendship" between teacher and disciple is a mirror of one's learning friendship with God, for "God is friendship". Adolescence, according to Aelred, is the time when "a cloud of desire arises from the lower drives of the flesh and the gushing spring of adolescence", and the mind is thus best disposed to receive instruction. And Eros can lend the older man a supreme gift for teaching.

The relationship depicted in Bernard MacLaverty's "The Drapery Man" is part of the history of these exchanges. The young apprentice is also the lover; the older artist is not only the teacher. Their exchange can continue, refined and bettered, even once the sexual attraction is no longer present. And it is in this shifting middle ground of reciprocal attentions and changing roles that the two men and their entire relationship are ultimately defined.

I rise every day and walk the half mile up the hill to Jordan's place with his dog at my heels. I have to take it slowly, for the sake of the dog. It is a small brown and white short-haired terrier which he christened Pangur-Ban. Each evening I take her home with me to prevent

Jordan, as he says, "taking the air on the patio and tramping in shite, then walking it throughout the house." She waddles and her tongue hangs out. Her paws slip on the stone mosaic footpath. The dog is as old in dog years as Jordan.

Today he has asked me to bring tennis balls. I have bought half a dozen packed like eggs in a plastic container which crackles as I walk up the hill.

I used to live with Jordan until things became intolerable. Then he rented a place for me, small but with a good view over the Atlantic. I am on my own when I want to be, which suits me. It suits him as well because a blind man needs to live on his own. He can remember where the furniture is, where he last set something down. The only drawback, Jordan tells me, is that he will probably die on his own, and that frightens him. He is in his seventies, has a bad heart and is expecting the worst.

He is sitting in a director's canvas chair in the middle of the converted barn tilting his head back to the light waiting for me. As soon as he hears the door he shouts, "Here, girl." Pangur-Ban barks twice and runs to him. Even if she doesn't bark he can hear her pads and claws on the stone floor. She wags her tail so much that her whole body seems to move. He scratches her head.

"And my drapery man." I kiss him like we were father and son and lift the dog up on his knee. He caresses the back of my thigh.

He laughs, "This morning when I awoke I had a little stiffness in my joints. One in particular." He laughs. "Isn't that good at my age?"

"I bet it didn't last long," I say, moving away from him.

He is on edge—he wants to start a new painting even though we haven't finished the previous three. I have spent the last few days making canvases to his specifications—one seven feet by fourteen and then a smaller one, six by three.

"Give the big one a wash of turps and burnt sienna—as dilute as possible."

Before he went blind completely he would inspect my colour mixing. He would tell me equal parts viridian and cobalt with just a smear of black and I would mix it for him. He then would bend over the tray, like a jeweller, squinting with his one good eye at the colour. "Yes it's right," or, "More black." It was about this time that he began to wear the glasses with the mudguards at the sides.

Since he has totally lost his sight he uses other things to denote colour. "The blue vase beside the window—the shadowed side of it," or, "The maroon cover of *Marius the Epicurean*." I begin to search the bookshelves.

"Who's it by?"

"Pater." He gives a little sigh. "Walter Pater—an English fuckin hooligan, if ever there was one."

I find it and hold it up to the light. Jordan says, "As a book it's rubbish—but it's the right colour."

Occasionally he uses previous pictures of his own as a reference.

"I want the umber to be exactly what I used in 'Harbinger Three'." And I have to try and remember! Reproductions are only the merest approximation. Colour slides are better but still their colour values are not accurate. Sometimes, when he is being particularly difficult or pernickety, I have to admit to cheating. I will tell him I remember the colour and have got it exactly. He has no way of knowing.

I change into what was a navy blue boiler suit. It is japped and stippled with every colour he has made me use. Because of the heat the only other thing I wear is my underpants. In the old days this used to drive him wild. I squeeze a fat worm of burnt sienna into a roller tray and drown it in turps.

He uses masking tape a lot. That way he can feel with his fingers what he can see in his mind.

"Three verticals of white, the three-quarter inch, spaced like cricket stumps." I peel off the tape when the paint has dried, leaving livid white.

Sometimes he will say, "Let me make a shape," and approach the canvas with a stick of charcoal. He will draw big and simple out of the darkness of his head.

He has an amazing visual memory. To divide up his canvases he will refer me to a book of Flags of the World.

"The three bands should be like the South Vietnamese flag stood on its end," or, "The band at the bottom should be as broad as the blue stripe in the Israeli flag."

The work is as hard as painting a room. He sits listening to the click of the roller and my breathing, fondling the bones of the dog's head. Sometimes her upright ears flick like a cat's when touched.

When the canvas is covered I sit down for a break but he becomes impatient with me.

"Get out what we did yesterday," he says. I turn the outermost canvas from the wall to face him. He drops the dog on the floor and comes over to me, his arms out in front of him. His hands touch the surface and skim lightly over it feeling the layers of paint with the tips of his fingers, the direction of the brush strokes.

"That's the magenta?"

"Yes."

"It's too loosely brushed. I wish you'd sprayed it."

"Why didn't you say?"

"Could you bear to do it again?"

"I suppose so. Jordan, you're a perfectionist."

"Oh fuck." He cups one hand over his eyes. "This is like trying to thread a needle with gloves on."

I begin squeezing out some magenta.

"Why do you go on doing this?"

"Somebody's got to pay the rent—the rents. Two places."

"Jordan—come on. You get the price of a house for one of these things."

"Things! You philistine gobshite."

"I didn't mean it that way."

"It's the way it came out—it was your tone. A middle-class English whine."

"The Irish are racists," I say and storm out of the barn.

He shouts after me, "It wasn't us who fucked up half the world."

It takes me until midday to calm down.

"Jordan! Lunch!" He comes out on to the shaded side of the patio to join me. It is easy to prepare. A bottle of chilled Verde, some bread and pâté. He likes the local pâté and I spread each circle of crusty bread with a thick roof of the stuff. Three small pieces on a plate, easily located, easily eaten. The bread crackles as he bites into it.

"Oh for a piece of bread that doesn't bleed your gums," he says, chewing. "Right now I'd pay a fiver for a slice of Pan loaf. Something soft that'll stick to the roof of your mouth."

I don't answer him and there is a long silence. He feels this for a while, then says, "With regard to this morning. I still have pictures in my head which have to come out but they are limited by the clumsy technique I have to use. Imagine having to paint—not with a brush— but with an English gobshite." This time it sounds funny and he senses my reaction. "In the 'fifties I was attracted to Hard Edge. Now it is all that is left to me. I see the way Beethoven heard. For that reason alone we must continue."

I am his eyes and his right hand. He will occasionally ask me to describe things. If it becomes a chore he will know from the tone of my voice and stop me.

"The Atlantic today is Mediterranean blue." He laughs obediently. "And at this moment I can see two yachts, one a mere arrowhead with a white sail, the other much closer, running behind a blue and white spinnaker." That kind of thing.

He will always have a cutting remark to end with, like, "It pays to increase your word power."

I also read to him. He has become blind so late in life that he is unwilling to learn the new skill of Braille. He likes Beckett—even laughs at him—but I find his prose almost impossible to read aloud and quite, quite meaningless. I come from the kind of house where if my father saw me with a book in my hand he'd say, "Can you not find something better to do?"

Flann O'Brien is also a favourite—especially the pieces from the *Irish Times*—but my English accent is intrusive and my attempts at an Irish one, so Jordan tells me, disastrous. He appreciates my version of a Home Counties voice reading the test match reports which arrive a day late from England. But because they are always a day late his excitement and anticipation is still the same.

"One of my great regrets is that I'll never see this fella Botham play." This from a man who hasn't left Portugal for twenty-five years.

In the winter when cricket reports are scarce occasionally he asks me to read to him from Wisden's Cricketers' Almanack.

"A lizard has just appeared on the wall of your bedroom and is soaking up the sun. Its spine is an S. Why do they never end up straight?"

"We're all bent," says Jordan and gropes for his wine glass. He drains what's left and stands. I lead him back to the barn and he lies down on the divan for a nap. He claims that he can sleep better during the day than at night. I go into the house to wash up the dishes, tidy and make his bed.

I first met him while on holiday in the Algarve about twenty years ago. My mother had been recently widowed and dreaded the thought of spending Christmas in the house. She also dreaded being alone and asked me to accompany her. At the time I was a student of Engineering Drawing and the holidays were sufficiently long to allow me to do this without missing anything. Mother and I had been there about a fortnight and were becoming bored with each other. Both of us admitted to a longing to hear English spoken again. We met Jordan coming out of a bistro. Because he was drunk he was speaking in English, shouting it over his shoulder at those who had annoyed him. Despite the fact that his accent was Irish and that he was well on in drink Mother pounced on him, so avid was she for conversation with someone other than me. She brought him back to our hotel for coffee.

Jordan Fitzgerald was his name. He was then a splendid-looking man in his early fifties, lean and tanned with a beard which was whitening in streaks. Mother simpered before him and asked him what he did.

"I'm a cricketer who paints."

She became, if it was possible, more obsequious when she discovered just how famous an artist he was. She knew nothing of painting—for her, degrees of realism were degrees of excellence and all our house in London could boast of was a number of Victorian prints my father had looted from his own mother's house. Another factor which impressed her was the price his pictures could command. When she eventually got to see some of his work her comment to me afterwards was, "I wouldn't give you tuppence for it."

"Mother, he is one of Ireland's greatest artists and has the accolade of having work in the Tate."

"I don't care where he's worked. I wouldn't hang one of those things on my wall. If your father was alive he could tell him what he was doing wrong."

She thought his interest was in her, handsome in her mid-forties, but I knew by his eyes that I was the focus of his attention.

On the second last night of our holiday we had all been drinking heavily in our hotel and Mother went off to powder her nose.

Jordan leaned forward and said to me in a voice that was hushed and serious, "You are beautiful. Why don't you walk up the hill later?"

I nodded and cautioned him with a look, seeing Mother coming back. He added, "And I'll show you my retchings." We both laughed uncontrollably at this.

"Have I missed a joke?" said Mother.

"I was just telling your handsome boy a story which would offend the ears of a lovely English lady like yourself. I hope you'll forgive me."

She smiled coyly—a smile which said they are just men together.

But I did go to his house later that night. We had sex twice and I stayed with him the next night as well—or at least slipped back into the hotel at five in the morning. Mother remarked on how tired I looked and I proved it by sleeping on the train until Paris.

In the spring Jordan wrote to me one of the shortest letters I have ever received inviting me in almost gruff terms to spend the summer with him. In a PS he said that Mother would also be welcome—in September. I had just finished my course with the highest commendation and felt I deserved the summer off before looking for work. Mother agreed both to my going and to her visit later.

Once I asked him why he had left Ireland.

"It's no place for a homosexual painter who doesn't believe in God," he said, then added after a moment's thought, "Indeed it's no place for a heterosexual painter who's a Catholic." But he cherished aspects of his country. He claimed to be able to quote the label on any bottle of Irish whiskey word for word. I tested him when I arrived back from London after Mother's funeral. I had brought him a bottle of Bushmills and challenged him to make good his boast.

"The label is black like a church window, with a gold rim. It has a vermilion band like a cummerbund across its middle and beneath that is a scatter of gold coins."

"Correct. And the words. You have to quote the words before you can sample it." He held his head in his hands and screwed up his eyes, smiling.

"Special old Irish whiskey. Black Bush. Original grant to distil—sixteen-", he paused slapping the top of his head, "oh-eight. Blended and bottled by the inverted commas Old Bushmills, close inverted commas, Distillery Company Limited, Bushmills, County Antrim. Product of Ireland."

"Correct—you're a genius."

"There's more. At the bottom it says 'registered label'."

He stood and we kissed. He told me how he'd missed me and asked with concern about Mother's cremation.

The nearest I could come to that party trick was to recite the French side of the HP Sauce bottle. "*Cette Sauce de haute qualité ...* etc.*" Jordan made me do it for his friends.

Afterwards he would always announce, "He passed his exams with the highest condemnation."

Sometimes I lie awake at night wondering what I will do when Jordan dies. I have given up my career and my life for him. I remember once reading about Eric Fenby, Delius's amanuensis, and feeling sorry for him. An intelligent man in touch with such talent but devoid of actual genius himself. I have become involved in painting but am useless at it—as useless as Beckett's secretary is at writing, if he has one—as useless as Beckett is, come to think of it.

It has occurred to me that I could, with the right amount of secrecy, continue to produce Jordan Fitzgeralds for a number of years to come, and say to the dealer that they came from stock. But that would necessitate getting him to sign blank canvases. I have never plucked up enough courage to ask him to do such a thing.

I think that Jordan took me on because I would do what I was told—to the letter—exactly. Engineering Drawing is that kind of science. Even then Jordan must have had intimations of his coming blindness. He said a philistine was what he wanted. If I was artistic it would interfere with the translation of his vision on to canvas.

After I had finished my first painting under his direction he went up to it and looked all over its surface from six inches. He nodded with approval.

"I'll call you my drapery man."

"What?"

"An eighteenth-century caper. Portrait painters got a man in to do the time-consuming bits—the lace and the satin stuff. The best of them was Vanaken. Hogarth drew this man's funeral with all the best painters in London behind the coffin weeping and gnashing their teeth."

The sound of the Hoover, even from the distance of the house, wakens him because when I switch it off I hear him calling me. I go across to the barn.

"Are we ready to start again?" he says.

"Okay."

"If you have fully recovered from your high dudgeon."

"I have."

He puts on a querulous voice and says, "Question. What particular altitude is dudgeon inevitably? Answer. High." He laughs and slaps his knees.

"Did you take your pills?" He shakes his head and I have to go all the way back to the house and bring them to him.

When he has swallowed them he says, "I want you to scumble the bottom third with sap green."

"In a straight line?"

"No, tilt it slightly—like the top side of a T-square."

When Mother came down that September I was still living with Jordan, but she thought nothing of it. I had my own room. He had his. Mother always thought sex was something which happened in a bedroom at night when everyone else had retired. I had warned Jordan to be discreet and he only approached me during the early evening when she went for her walk to the cliff top to feel the cool breeze come off the sea.

"It's my favourite time of day," she said.

"Then why do you come here? In England it is that temperature all the time—and even cooler." I was annoyed with her because she had made no mention of going home and it was the first of October. When I finally did broach the subject she said that she was waiting for me to go home with her.

"I am staying here."

"But how will you live? You have to get a job."

"Jordan is now my employer."

"And what do you do, might I ask?"

"I help him. Make up canvases. Clean his brushes. Keep the place in order. Do the shopping. Allow him time to concentrate on painting."

"A houseboy."

"If you like. In pleasant surroundings at a temperature I enjoy. With one of the great artists of the twentieth century."

Before I met Jordan I knew nothing of painting. But he got me interested—gave me books to read, pictures to look at. He would deride his renowned contemporaries—"Patrick's a total wanker," "McGill's line has all the subtlety of a car skid."

All this bewildered me at the time, because I thought them all equally poor. I was more convinced of the worth of the Post-Impressionists. Jordan thought Picasso good enough to envy, and Bonnard. He thought Matisse uneven and as for Manet—he was a disgrace.

When I have finished scumbling with the sap green Jordan says, "Make up a bowl of black and one of turquoise—straight from the tube. A third turps." He takes the container of tennis balls and cracks it open. His fingers hesitate on their furry yellow surface. He removes one and lays his index finger diagonally across it. "Watch the spin," he says and flicks the ball across the barn. It bounces once, breaking back on itself about six inches. Pangur-Ban lurches forward as if to chase it, then decides not to and wags her tail.

"My brother and I used to play cricket, at a time when it was neither profitable nor popular. We had a backyard at home about ten by twelve and we had stumps chalked on one wall. The fielders were buckets—they could catch you out if the ball went in without bouncing. But there were always arguments about when the stumps were hit. We bowled underarm with a tennis ball and solved the arguments by soaking it. Then it left a wet mark on the stumps which could not be denied."

Once a year a furniture van, hired by Jordan's London dealer, arrives and the driver and myself load the paintings on to it. For the last five years it has been the same man. He has no interest in art whatsoever: "They're big this year," he says, or, "He's using a lot of green."

"He's Irish," I say.

"Careful. Easy. He'll go mad if you scrape one of these things." The van-driver speaks to me in whispers, which I find insulting. Somehow his conspiracy makes me no more than a houseboy. I resent this but do not know how to reprimand him. It's not worth it for once a year.

Jordan rarely, if ever, goes out.

"There's no point," he says. "One darkness is the same as another. The only way you can change the landscape for me is to bring in flowers—or pine cones—or fart, for that matter."

The only place he goes is the bank in Albufeira. Once every three months I phone a taxi and take him there. I lead him into the bank by the arm and the manager is waiting to take his other arm. "*Bom dia*, Jordan." They go into an office while I wait at the counter. He has *never* told me how much he is worth—I suppose he has no idea himself.

When I have made up the bowls of colour he asks me to float a tennis ball in each.

"You would do as well to wear rubber gloves," he says. "Now I want you to press the black ball on that mimosa area to the left of the three masking strips—about an inch out. The outline should be fuzzy. Then I want a pyramid of them—just like the medals on the Black Bush bottle."

We ceased to be lovers many years ago but I still feel a sense of responsibility to him. I can't leave him, particularly now that he is blind. Nobody else would put up with him. I find my release and relaxation elsewhere. The beaches here teem with beautiful bodies— the roads are full of young bare-chested boys who drive about on motorbikes which sound like hornets. But it is becoming more difficult year by year. I am forty-three and beginning to thicken. I have breasts like a teenage girl. I'm sure Jordan knows of my affairs but I have never told him.

My annoyance with him reaches peaks and I have walked out on him many times. One of the worst was when I asked him—point-blank—if he had screwed my mother and he said in his own defence, "Not often."

After that I slept on the beach for a week. When I went back he was very kind to me—told me that artists were a race apart. They did things differently because of the albatross of their sensitivity. I think on this occasion he even apologized to me.

The normal and frequent rows we have end with him yelling at me, "Go, go. And good riddance! I am as weak as any other man." But I always come back. It is not for the money that I am staying on—if I know Jordan he will leave me a year's wages and the rest will go to a Cricketing Trust, or Pangur-Ban.

When I have finished dabbing the tennis balls on the surface of the canvas he asks, "How does it look?"

"Fine. Actually it looks really good."

"Ectually," he spits the word out. "I wouldn't have told you to do it if I hadn't *known* it would look good."

"The rubber S shows up negatively in some of them."

"I knew it would."

I lead him to the canvas and kneel him down in front of it.

"I cannot see it but I'm sure it has all the sadness of a thing finished." He feels for the right-angled sides of the corner then signs it with a charcoal stick in his highstepping signature.

He stands with an effort and says, "I'd like you to do my beard." He stretches and sits again in his canvas chair. I lift the sharpest scissors and begin to cut his beard close. He likes it to look like a week's growth.

"Pure white," I say.

"What past tense as applied to the propulsion of motor vehicles is snow as white as?"

I think for a while then guess. "Driven."

He caresses my buttocks and says, "You're coming on."

"Don't do that or I'll cut your lip." He takes his hand away from me.

"Wait," says Jordan. "Get a saucer. Keep the hairs for me."

"What?"

"Let's keep the hairs—they're white. Save them and use them in a painting some time."

"Are you serious, Jordan?"

"Yes I am."

I go and wash a saucer and dry it, then continue clipping his beard on to it.

"I never know with you, whether you're sending me up or not."

"It's a great idea. Hairy paintings. I've used sand in the past—but to … I'd like to put something of myself into just one of these images."

"You *are* joking."

"If I could find the right medium to float them in. Save them anyway—let me think about it."

I put the clippings from the saucer into a polythene bag, tie the neck in a knot and put it on the shelf.

"I want you to read to me tonight. Also I want to get drunk."

I know that this is a command for me to stay with him until whatever hour he chooses and put him safely into his bed. His capacity for drink is prodigious and his aggression proportional to the amount taken. The only thing in my favour is that he is now physically weak and I can master him. He used to throw things at me but that ceased when he finally became blind.

"Very well," I say. It has the makings of a long and difficult night.

The last session—about three weeks ago—he said to me, "I'm getting through it quite well."

"What?"

"My life. There can't be long to go now. The thought of suicide is a great consolation. It has helped me through many a bad night. Do you know who said that?"

"No."

"I didn't think you would. You have a Reader's Digest grasp of the world. Just promise me one thing—don't slot me into one of those wall cupboards in the graveyard."

"But I will. And I'll put one of those nice ceramic photos of you on the door with little roses all round it."

"Burn me and fritter my ashes on the ocean."

Inevitably halfway down the bottle he will begin to cry. The tears will fill his eyes and spill over on to his cheeks and wet his beard. When he stops and blows his nose thoroughly in that navy hanky of his, he will say, "It's amazing that the eyes work so well in that function but in no other way."

If he cries tonight I'll really put the knife in—get even with him for today's nastiness. I'll ask him if he wants his tears kept. If he wants a phial of them put in one of his paintings. If I do say this there will be a God-awful row. He'll wreck the place. The one thing he cannot stand is to have his work ridiculed—even by me.

But no matter how furious the fight, the bitching, the name-calling, I will be back in the morning with Pangur-Ban at my heels. There is now a kind of unspoken acceptance that I am here until he dies.

The Unknown Visitor

Françoise Sagan

*W. H. Auden once wrote that the only thing for which he could not for-
give Oscar Wilde was marrying Constance Lloyd without letting her
know that he was a homosexual. This seemed to Auden "the only really
heartless act of Wilde's life", the betrayal of another human being for
the sake of one's own appearances. Appearances, on which society sets
such value, require these daily deceptions, duplicities, and disguises. We
are all required to wear masks.*

Masks are the subject of Françoise Sagan's fiction. Bonjour
Tristesse, *the book that made her famous at the age of nineteen, con-
cerns, like many of her later novels, the stripping of disguises, the rend-
ing of conventions, the baring of the faces society demands be covered
in the name of good taste. French literature abounds in descriptions of
bourgeois façades crumbling, from Emma Bovary's scandal to the revelations of Duras in* Moderato Cantabile. *None, however, goes about
this demolishing task in the circumventive, ruthless way in which Sagan
brings down, without any apparent violence, the strongest and most
sophisticated of these hypocritical social constructions. Without seeming to tell a story, her dialogues and descriptions hint at intimate
tragedies and outrageous deeds, sometimes vast, as in* Bonjour
Tristesse, *other times small, as in "The Unknown Visitor".*

She took the corner at full speed and pulled up sharply in front of the
house. She always sounded her horn on arrival. She didn't know why,
but every time she arrived home she would give David, her husband,
this warning that she was back. That day, she found herself wondering how and why she had acquired the habit. After all, they had been
married for ten years, they had been living for ten years in this charming cottage outside Reading, and it hardly seemed necessary to
announce herself in this way to the father of her two children, her
husband and ultimate protector.

"Where can he have gone?" she said in the ensuing silence, and she got out of the car and walked with her golfer's stride toward the house, followed by the faithful Linda.

Life had not been kind to Linda Forthman. At the age of thirty-two, after an unhappy divorce, she had remained alone—often courted, but still alone—and it required all Millicent's good nature and enthusiasm to endure, for example, this entire Sunday in her company, playing golf. Though uncomplaining, Linda was infuriatingly apathetic. She looked at men (unmarried men, of course), they looked back at her and things never seemed to go any further. To a woman like Millicent, who was freckled and full of charm and vitality, Linda Forthman's character was an enigma. From time to time, with his usual cynicism, David would offer an explanation: "She's waiting for a chap," he would say. "Like every other girl, she's waiting for some chap she can get her hooks into." Not only was it untrue, it was grossly unfair. In Millicent's view, Linda was simply waiting for someone who would love her, for all her apathy, and take her in hand.

Come to think of it, David was very contemptuous and harsh on the subject of Linda, and indeed of the majority of their friends. She must talk to him about it. For instance, he refused to see the good side of that buffoon Jack Harris, who, even if he was as dumb as an ox, was generosity and kindness itself. David was always saying of him: "Jack's a ladies' man ... without the ladies," at which point he would roar with laughter at his own joke as though it were one of the inimitable witticisms of Shaw or Wilde.

She pushed open the door into the drawing room and paused, flabbergasted, on the threshold. There were overflowing ashtrays and opened bottles all over the place and two dressing gowns lying in a corner in a heap: hers and David's. For one panic-stricken moment she wanted to turn around and leave, and pretend not to have seen. She cursed herself for not having telephoned beforehand to say she was coming back earlier than expected: Sunday night instead of Monday morning. But Linda was there behind her, wide-eyed, a look of dismay on her pale face, and she would have to think up some plausible explanation for the irreparable occurrence that had evidently taken place in her house, Her house...? Their house...? For the past ten years, she had said "our house" and David "the house." For the past ten years, she had talked about potted plants, gardenias, verandas and lawns, and for the past ten years David had said nothing in reply.

"What on earth," said Linda, and her high-pitched voice made Millicent shudder, "what on earth has been going on here? Has David been giving parties in your absence?"

Millicent laughed. She, at least, seemed to be taking it fairly lightly. And indeed it was perfectly possible that David, who had left for Liverpool two days before, had come back unexpectedly, spent the night here and gone out to dine at the nearby country club. Only there were those two dressing gowns, those two gaudy shrouds, those two banners, as it were, of adultery. She was astonished by her own astonishment. After all, David was a very attractive man. He had blue eyes, black hair, fine features and considerable wit. And yet it had never occurred to her, she had never had the slightest presentiment, let alone proof, that he was interested in any other woman. Of that much, without knowing quite why, she was certain. In fact she was absolutely convinced that David had never even looked at another woman.

She pulled herself together, crossed the room, picked up the two incriminating dressing gowns and threw them into the kitchen—hurriedly, but not hurriedly enough to avoid seeing the two used cups on the table and a butter-smeared plate. She shut the door hastily, as though she had witnessed a rape; and, emptying the ashtrays, tidying away the bottles, chatting amiably, she set about trying to distract Linda from her initial curiosity and got her to sit down.

"Such a bore," she said. "Probably the maid didn't come to clean up after last weekend. Do sit down, darling. Shall I make you a cup of tea?"

Linda sat down gloomily, her hand between her knees and her bag dangling from her fingertips.

"If you don't mind," she said, "I'd prefer something stronger than tea. That last round of golf exhausted me...."

Millicent went back to the kitchen, averting her eyes from the cups, grabbed some ice cubes and a bottle of whiskey and set them down in front of Linda. They sat facing each other in the drawing room, that charming drawing room furnished in bamboo and shadowed cretonne, which David had brought back from somewhere or other. The room now looked—if not human—at least presentable once again, and through the French windows the elm trees could be seen swaying in the wind, that same wind that had driven them off the golf course an hour ago.

"David's in Liverpool," said Millicent, and she realized that her voice was peremptory, as if she felt poor Linda was liable to contradict her.

"I know," said Linda amiably, "you told me."

They both stared out of the window, then at their feet, then at one another.

Something was beginning to take hold in Millicent's mind. Like a wolf, or a fox—at any rate, some sort of wild animal—it was gnawing at her. And the pain was getting worse. She gulped down some whiskey to calm herself and caught Linda's eye again. Well, she thought to herself, if it's what I think it is, if it's what any reasonable person might be expected to think it is, at least it isn't Linda. We've been together all weekend and she's just as appalled as I am, in fact even more so, oddly enough. For, to her mind, the idea of David bringing a woman back to their house, whether or not the children were there, the idea of David bringing that woman here and lending her her dressing gown, still seemed absolutely unthinkable. David never looked at other women. In fact David never looked at anyone. And the word "anyone" suddenly resounded in her head like a gong. It was true that he never looked at anyone. Not even at her. David had been born handsome and blind.

Of course it was natural enough, only seemly, really, that after ten years their physical relations should have dwindled to practically nothing. Of course it was only to be expected that after all this time nothing much should remain of the eager, hot-blooded, highly strung young man she had once known, but even so, it was really rather odd that this handsome husband of hers, so blind but so attractive....

"Millicent," said Linda, "what do you make of all this?"

She gestured vaguely around the room, indicating the general disorder.

"What do you expect me to make of it?" said Millicent. "Either Mrs. Briggs, the charwoman, didn't come in last Monday to clean up, or else David spent the weekend here with a call girl."

And she laughed. If anything, she felt rather relieved. Those were the two alternatives; there was no great mystery about it. There was nothing wrong with having a good laugh with a girl friend about being deceived by one's husband and discovering it by chance because it was too windy to play golf.

"But," said Linda (and she, too, was laughing), "but what do you mean, a call girl? David spends his entire time with you and the children and your friends. I can't see how he would have the time for call girls."

"Oh, well," said Millicent, laughing even louder—she really did feel relieved, without knowing why—"perhaps it's Pamela or Esther or Janie.... Search me."

"I don't think any of them would appeal to him," said Linda, almost regretfully, and she made a move as if to get up, to Millicent's alarm.

"Look, Linda," she said, "even if we had caught them in the act, you know very well we wouldn't have made a scene. After all, we've been married for ten years, David and I. Both of us have had the odd fling ... there's nothing to make a fuss about...."

"I know," said Linda, "these things don't matter very much. All the same, I must go, I want to get back to London."

"You don't like David much, do you?"

For a second there was a look of amazement in Linda's eyes, which quickly changed to one of warmth and tenderness.

"Yes, I do, I like him very much. I've known him since I was five years old, he was my brother's best friend at Eton...."

And, having made that pointless and uninteresting statement, she looked intently at Millicent, as though she had just said something of the utmost importance.

"Good," said Millicent. "In that case, I don't see why you can't forgive David for something I myself am prepared to forgive. I know the house is in a mess, but I'd rather stay here than be stuck in that hellish bottleneck all the way back to London!"

Linda picked up the whiskey bottle and poured herself an enormous glassful, or so it looked to Millicent.

"David is very good to you," she said.

"Of course he is," said Millicent unhesitatingly.

And it was true that he had been a considerate husband, courteous, protective and on occasion highly imaginative. He could also, alas, be exceedingly neurotic. But she would keep that to herself. She wasn't going to tell Linda about David lying on the sofa in London with his eyes closed for days on end, refusing to go out. She wasn't going to tell her about David's terrifying nightmares. She wasn't going to tell her about David's manic telephone conversations with some businessman whose name she couldn't even remember. She wasn't going to tell her about David's rages when one of the children failed an exam. Nor would she tell Linda how insufferable David could be about furniture or pictures, nor how forgetful David, the considerate David, sometimes was about his appointments, including those with her. Nor about the state he was sometimes in when he came home. Least of all could she tell Linda about the marks she had seen on his back one day when she caught sight of it in the mirror…. And the mere memory of this was enough to break down her conventional English reticence, and she asked—at least she heard herself ask—"Do you really think it's Esther or Pamela?" Because it was true that he didn't have the time to see other women but those. Women, even women who indulge in illicit affairs, demand a certain amount of time from their lovers. David's adventures, if they existed, could only be crude, frantic, hurried affairs, with prostitutes or specialists. And it was surely impossible to imagine David, proud, fastidious David, as a masochist….

Linda's voice seemed to come from a long way away.

"What makes you think of Pamela or Esther? They're much too demanding…."

"You're right," said Millicent.

She stood up, went over to the mirror on the wall and examined herself in it. She was still beautiful—men had told her so often enough, and sometimes proved they meant it—and her husband was one of the most charming and gifted men in their circle. Why, then, did she seem to see in the mirror a sort of skeleton without flesh or nerves or blood or sinews?

"It seems a pity," she said (she hardly knew what she was saying any longer), "it seems a pity that David hasn't more men friends, as well as women friends. Have you noticed?"

"I've never noticed anything," said Linda, or rather Linda's voice, since dusk had descended and all Millicent could see of her was a silhouette, a sort of mouselike creature perched on the sofa who knew—but what did she know? The woman's name. Why didn't she tell her? Linda was nasty enough or nice enough—how could one tell in such cases?—to murmur a name. Why then, in this July twilight, wrapped in her solitude and her pale suit, did she look as though she was scared out of her wits? One must be rational and down-to-earth about these things. If it was true, she would have to face up to the fact that David was having an affair with some woman, either a friend or a professional. Vulgar recriminations must be avoided at all costs, and, perhaps, later on she might even take a lighthearted revenge with Percy or someone. One must see things in their proper perspective, like a woman of the world. She got to her feet, straightened the cushions with a regal hand and declared:

"Listen, darling, whatever happens, we'll stay here the night. I'll go and see what sort of state the rooms are in upstairs. If by any chance my dear husband has been having an orgy, I'll telephone Mrs. Briggs, who lives down the road, and ask her to give us a hand. Does that suit you?"

"Fine," said Linda from the shadows. "Fine. Anything you say."

And Millicent walked toward the staircase, giving the photograph of their sons an absentminded smile on the way. They were to go to Eton, like David, and who else was it? Oh, yes, Linda's brother. Climbing the stairs, she was surprised to find that she needed to lean on the banisters. Something had deprived her of the use of her legs; it wasn't the golf, nor the thought of possible adultery. Anyone can envisage, indeed must envisage, the possibility of one's partner's infidelity—it wasn't an excuse for creating a scene or putting on an act. Not to Millicent's way of thinking, at any rate. She went into "their" bedroom, the bedroom of "their" house, and noticed without the slightest embarrassment that the bed was unmade, the sheets rumpled, churned up as they had never been, it seemed to her, since her marriage to David. Then she noticed the watch on the bedside table, *her* bedside table. It was a heavy waterproof watch, a man's watch, and she weighed it in her hand for a moment, fascinated and incredulous, until the realization that it must have been left behind by another man finally sank in. She understood everything now. Downstairs, there was Linda, worried sick and getting more and more scared, sitting there in the dark. Millicent went downstairs again, and with a curious, almost pitying expression in her eyes, looked at dear Linda, who also knew.

"Linda, my poor pet," she said, "I'm afraid you were right. There's a pair of salmon-pink shorts in the bedroom I wouldn't be seen dead in."

Dinner for One

Rose Tremain

Saint Francis believed that everything in the universe is related through bonds of blood, that we are brothers and sisters to the dust and to the stars. Fundamentally, our stories are not distinct from one another: everything that happens to another creature is part of our autobiography. We walk among mirrors. Once, when he was still Prince Siddhartha, the Buddha saw an old man, a man devoured by leprosy, and a dead man, and was told that old age, sickness, and death are our common lot. Next, he saw a monk whose desire was neither to live nor to die, and whose face radiated peace. Then Siddhartha had his revelation. In the monk too we are reflected.

Those who propound the ghettos of sexuality, colour, or religion imagine our differences to be essential. They define us by what we don't share, and through these catalogues of absence pretend to classify our universe. It is our commonality that Rose Tremain explores in several of her novels and short stories, with what Victoria Glendinning called a "talent to disturb". The sufferings, the frustrations, even the moments of happiness in married and single life echo in each and every one of us, as both a comment and an explanation. Her tragedies and comedies become exemplary; none of her characters, however isolated, is beyond the reader's experience.

He said: "I'll take you out. We'll go to Partridge's, have something special." She took off her glasses and looked at him doubtfully.

"I don't know, Henry. I don't know that we want to make a fuss about it."

"Well, it's up to you."

"Why is it?"

"Why is it what?"

"Up to me?"

She bewildered him. For years she had bewildered him. "It's your choice, Lal; that's all I meant. It's your choice—whether we go out or not."

She sighed. "I just thought...."

"What?"

"I just thought it might be better simply to treat it like any other day."

"It's not 'any other day'."

"No."

"But it's your decision. You're the one who makes these decisions. So you let me know if you want to go and I'll ring up and book a table."

He walked away from her, sat down in his worn red armchair, fumbled for his glasses, found them and took up *The Times* crossword. She watched him, still holding her glasses in her hand. It's funny, she thought, that whenever we talk to each other, we take our glasses off. We blur each other out. I suppose we're afraid that if we see each other clearly—too clearly—communication between us will cease.

"Six across,..." he murmured from the faded comfort of his chair, "two words, four and three: 'Facts of severing the line'."

"Anagram," she whispered, "I should think."

Henry and Lal weren't what anyone expected. Separate from her, he seemed to belong. He belongs; she doesn't, was what people thought. You could pull old Henry's leg and raise that boisterous laugh of his, but with her you didn't know where you were. Quite ordinary remarks—things that everyone laughed at—seemed to worry her. But she never told you why: she just closed her eyes.

There had been so many friends at the beginning. Henry and Lal had belonged then. "Isn't my wife the belle of the ball?" he used to say. And there were so many balls, once, to be belle of. The changes had stolen gradually into her; the changes had begun after Henry came home from the War, so that people often said: "It was the War that changed her," and even to her face: "It was the War that changed you, Lal, wasn't it?"

But she didn't agree with them. "The War changed everyone," was all she'd say.

"It always seems...."

Henry looked up from the crossword. He was surprised Lal was still in the room. "What, Lal?"

"Such a waste."

"What does?"

"Going out. All that eating."

"We can afford it, darling."

"Oh, it isn't that."

Henry took off his glasses. "Well, I'm damned if I—"

"Look at our stomachs! Look at yours. So crammed with food you couldn't push any more in. And mine, a dreadful bulge."

"Oh, Lal, for heaven's sake."

"It's horrible to eat and eat. What's it for? Just to make us heavier and heavier till we die with all this weight."

"You're not fat, Lal. I'm fat! I'm not ashamed of it."

"Why?"

"Why what?"

"Why aren't you ashamed?"

"Because it's *my* life. I can be any shape I choose."

No, she thought, that's wrong. I am haunted by the wrongness of things.

"Henry," she said, "I hate it—"

"What?"

"I hate it when—"

Larry Partridge was a popular man. "We're so lucky," ran the county's favourite saying, "to have you so near to us!" They didn't mean Larry himself (though they liked his silver-haired politeness), they meant his restaurant which, every night of the week except Tuesdays when it was closed, was packed with them.

"This part of the world was a culinary desert before you came, Larry," they told him, "but now we really are lucky. Partridge's is as good as anything in London and so much more reasonable."

Of course they had been cautious—caution before ecstasy—because, glancing through the windows of the old run-down pub he had bought, they had noted that the old run-down walls were becoming resplendent in indigos and fruit-fool pinks and this had made them nudge each other: "Well, you can tell what *he* is, duckie!"

Now Larry's tightly-clad buttocks circled their contented after-dinner smiles. He extended to each table a limp-handed greeting and waited for the superlatives to flood his ears like warm water. "You're so imaginative with food, Larry!"

"The sauce on the quenelles was out of this world, Larry."
"We've had a superb meal, Larry, really superb."

Larry's parents still lived in Romford. He had moved them from their council flat to a detached house. However, Larry's father still called him Lawrence. Lawrence: to say the name to himself was to remind Larry of his father, was to make him shudder as if the thin shadow of the man—neat in his dark green suit and white shirt, ready for work, working all his life, never giving up his dull and hopeless work till one day he would die at it—passed between him and the sun.

For Larry, Lawrence was dead, buried hideously down in the greasy kitchens of the catering school. Lawrence, born in poverty, reared in repression, was the detritus from which Larry, in all his colourful glory, had sprung. He had sprung in 1964, the year he had met Edwin, and each year since then he had bloomed a little more.

"What can I say about Edwin?" Larry had asked his mother at the time, "except that I love him."

Oh, but they were not prepared for this kind of love, she told him. They had never thought that their own Lawrence, so popular with all the local girls.... No, it had not once entered their minds and she really did think he should have given them some warning, some indication that he wasn't what they thought....

Larry left his parents' flat in Romford and moved into Edwin's flat in Fulham. Edwin found him a job in a local restaurant. Lawrence in Edwin's careful drawing room became Larry, became lover and loved.

All the past, like a dirty old bandage was no longer needed, began to unwind and fall off; Larry was healed.

Edwin's money purchased the pub in 1972. One end of the large building was converted into a flat and the move from Fulham was made. A year later, Partridge's opened, each of its walls a reflection of Edwin's taste, Edwin's imaginative eye.

Larry moved with perfect ease and happiness about his steel kitchen, liking his own little kingdom the better because just outside it was a rich land that he shared with Edwin.

"I do it with love," Larry sometimes said of his cooking. But the great golden weight of his love for Edwin he seldom talked of. It hung inside him, a burdensome treasure that he knew would never leave him.

Visitors to Partridge's never saw Edwin. Larry's nightly ritual of passing from table to table to receive his cupful of praise did not include him. He was glimpsed occasionally; there was talk of him, even questions to Larry.

"But it's all yours," Edwin had said to Larry when the restaurant opened. "My bit's done. Don't involve me any more. Then the success and the glory will really belong to you."

And even the invitations that came—to the lunches and the county cocktail parties—Edwin would never accept. "You're their celebrity, Larry. Why muddle them?"

Edwin was never jealous. "I am quite free of it," he once said to Larry. "I simply do not feel it. Jealousy is the vainest—in all senses— of the emotions. You must learn to rid yourself of that before it works its decay."

But Larry had known no human relationship in which jealousy had not been present—sometimes screamed out, sometimes unspoken, but always there to stain and spoil.

And he knew that his love for Edwin was a jealous, greedy love. He thought to himself: "Edwin is my life. How can I not be jealous of my own life?" Whenever Edwin went away, the weight inside him became a dead weight, immovable, full of pain.

When Edwin returned, he often wanted to run to him, discovering in his body a sudden miraculous lightness.

Daily, Larry watched Edwin for any sign of discontent. Three years younger than Larry his hair was still fair and thick. With an impatient gesture of his hand, he would push back the flopping hair several times in an hour.

Whenever he was angry or agitated, he would push back the hair almost constantly.

Larry dreaded his anger. Its occasional appearance in a man as contained and rational as Edwin was unsightly. Larry couldn't look at him. He would turn away, trembling inside.

But in the hundreds of times he had turned away like this over the years, there was not one time that he had not dreaded to turn round again, afraid suddenly that all the hubbub of Edwin's anger was nothing but an echo and that, unnoticed, Edwin had quietly slipped away and left him.

Edwin did little with his time. He gave to unimportant things the careful attention of his hands. He grew roses. He did occasional pen and ink drawings of old houses, which Larry collected and had framed.

He made an elegant coffee table out of glass and wood. He wrote a little poetry, always laughing at what he had written and throwing it away.

Monday had bought Edwin a studied indolence. "I'm really a rocking-chair man," he once said to Larry. "The little motions I can make are enough."

Certainly, they were enough for Larry. He was quite content for Edwin to be just as he was—as long as he was always there.

Lal said: "I've worked out that anagram." Several moments had passed in silence. Henry had filled in two more clues in *The Times* crossword. Lal had walked to the study window and looked out at the bird table she festooned in winter with strings of nuts and pieces of coconut. The nuts were eaten, the coconut pecked dry: it was springtime.

Henry looked up. "What was that you said, Lal?"

"Two words, four and three, 'Facts of severing the line'."

"I've got that one, haven't I?"

"I don't know. It's 'cast off'—anagram of 'facts of'."

"Let me see, 'cast off'? You're right, Lal. Good for you."

Henry filled it in. Then he looked up at Lal standing by the window. "Made up your mind yet, darling?"

Lal knew that he meant the dinner, knew that she had made up her mind. She didn't want to go out with Henry on that day.

A reward, she thought—a more fitting one for fifty years of marriage—should be to spend that evening alone, without him.

For the clear lines with which she encircled the petty wrongnesses of her life became each time like the lines drawn by aeroplanes in a blue sky: they fuzzed and were dissipated and the spaces where they had been were filled up, so that only a moment later you couldn't see that they had been there. Life went on in the old way.

In the mass of years she kept drawing and redrawing lines, kept believing that things might change one day and she would rediscover something lost.

"I have made up my mind," Lal said. "I think we should go out as you suggested. It would be nice to go to Partridge's, don't you think?"

"Well, I do."

"Only...."

"What?"

"It's a Tuesday. Larry shuts on a Tuesday."

"Damn me! Never mind, we'll make it the Monday. Why not? We can toast the midnight. As they used to say in the army, always better to have the feast before the battle; you might not live to enjoy it afterwards."

Lal turned and stared at Henry. "It has been a battle. The battle's going on...."

"Oh come on, Lal, not one of your frettings."

"We never were really suited, Henry—only at first when we used to want each other all the time. We should have parted when that cooled off. We'd had the best of each other: we'd had all the wonderful things."

"What rubbish you do talk, Lal. As couples go, we've been among the lucky ones. You name the day when we've had arguments. I could count them on the fingers of one hand."

"Not arguments, Henry, but a battle going on inside...."

"The trouble with you, Lal, is you think too much. We're old now. God bless us, so why not give your mind a bit of a rest?"

Lal turned back to the window. "You'll book the table, then, Henry? I do think that if we are going to Partridge's, it would be safer to book."

Spring arrived on the Saturday in the shape of a deep blue sky and a softening of the breeze. Larry never opened the restaurant for lunch. "It simply is not fair on Edwin," he said. Instead, he usually prepared a light lunch for the two of them and they sat by themselves in the restaurant, enjoying its peace.

Edwin always washed up. He did the job so carefully that their few plates and dishes sometimes took him half an hour, a half-hour usually spent by Larry, a cigarette in his curling mouth, in blissful contemplation of his friend. He took as much care over these lunches as he did over his evening menus.

After all, he said to himself, this is our home. Edwin has a right to my time. And to cook for Edwin was pure pleasure. Often, just before sleep, his mind would turn up some little dish that he would make for Edwin as a treat the following day.

Early on the Saturday morning, wandering out onto the patio (laid in intricate patterning of stone and brick by Edwin), Larry felt the warmth of the sun and decided he would lay a table for them outside, make them a cold lunch and serve it with a bottle of hock. He imagined this meal and others like it that they would share during the coming summer, and his imaginings laid on him a hand of such pleasurable gentleness that he didn't want to move.

Indeed was poor suffering Lawrence dead! He was dead without trace and only Larry, head crammed with joy, existed now.

"Larry!"

Edwin called him from an upstairs window. Larry looked up and saw that Edwin, whom he had left sleeping, was dressed.

"I'm going out," Edwin called.

"Where?"

"Just out."

"Oh."

Larry knew that he shouldn't question him. This was what Edwin hated most.

"Will you be back for lunch?" he asked.

"Yes."

He was relieved. They would still have their lunch on the patio and now, if Edwin was going out, he could spend the whole morning in the kitchen, do some preparation for the inevitably busy Saturday evening as well.

Larry waved to Edwin, saw him nod and then disappear from the window. He made himself stay where he was till he heard Edwin's Alfa Romeo roar out of the gate. Then he wandered into the kitchen and tied on his apron.

Larry made an iced tomato and mint soup, a cold curry sauce for a roasted chicken and a watercress salad. He spread a pink cloth with matching napkins on the wooden patio table and set two careful places, each headed by a tall stemmed hock glass. He then went back into the kitchen, checked the contents of his huge fridge and larder against the evening menus for Saturday and Sunday, made a shopping list, took a basket and got into his car.

By the time I get back from shopping, he thought to himself, Edwin will be back; then I can open the hock.

When Lal woke on the Monday morning she experienced that bleakest of sorrows—the realisation that a dream had tricked her with a few seconds' happiness and was now gone.

She had dreamed herself young. She had dreamed a bedroom in

someone's country house and a corridor outside it which creaked under Henry's footsteps as in the dark he fumbled his way towards her room.

She had laughed a secretive laugh full of joy as she lay under the clean linen sheet and waited for him. Their wedding was in a few weeks' time. Then there would be no more creeping down corridors: she would be Mrs. Henry Barkworth and the strong white body under the silk dressing gown that now shuffled towards her, moving slowly, prudently, but running, running like a hare in its desire for her, would lie in a big bed beside her—hers. Yes, Lal remembered, there had been a great feasting of love between her and Henry. Sex had never frightened her as it seemed to frighten some women of her sheltered generation. To touch and be touched became, after Henry's rough taking of her, all. All life, save this, paled and receded into insignificance.

For days together she would not let Henry go to his office, but kept him with her in their wide, comfortable bed.

"We fit so well!" she laughed. "How could anything be more perfect?"

Then came the War. Lal's children were both conceived during Henry's brief periods of leave and born when he was away. When the War was over and he came home, he made love to Lal like a weary stranger. She wept for what they had lost.

Lal sat up, rubbed her eyes with a white hand. It was strange that she could dream a desire she had long since ceased to feel. Life was so stale now.

"We smell bad, Henry and I," she thought bitterly. "We're blemished and fat and no good to anyone. Why do we go on and on?"

The day was interminable. Lal felt bilious, as if the meal they would gobble up at Partridge's was already inside her. She felt like crying. But I've shed so many tears for myself, she thought wearily, why shed more? So the evening crept towards her.

She thought as she dressed for it of the wine Henry would order: a heavy claret that they would both enjoy but which, soon afterwards, would give her indigestion and a headache. Fifty years! We've had fifty years together, so now we celebrate, but the unremarkableness of all that time, the waste of it all....

"Cheer up, darling."

Henry was breezy, tugging on his braces, smelling of aftershave, his bald head gleaming.

"Oh, was I ...?"

"You've been miles away all day, Lal. Something wrong? Not feeling up to it?"

"What? The meal?"

"No! Not just the meal—the occasion!"

"In a way not. We don't need to make any fuss, do we?"

"No, no fuss. But a bottle of fizz at least, don't you think? I asked Larry to put one on ice for us."

"Yes."

Lal dabbed her face with powder. She had decided to wear a black dress—the one concession to her real feelings. Pinned to the dress would be the diamond and sapphire brooch Henry had given her on their wedding day.

There was a small bar just off the dining room in Partridge's; it was too small really for all the diners who congregated there, but was pretty and restful, done up by Edwin in two shades of green. A fine tapestry drape hung down one wall and now Lal leaned back against this, her head almost touching a huntsman's knee behind her.

One of Larry's lady helpers (he had two, both about forty-five and confusingly called Myra and Moira) had brought Henry the champagne he had ordered and he was pouring it excitedly like a thirsty schoolboy might a longed-for Coke.

"This is the stuff, darling!"

Lal smiled and nodded. She often thought that the reason for Henry's pinkness of face and head was that he did simple things with such relish.

"So," he exclaimed, holding up his own glass, "this is it then, Lal! Happy anniversary, darling."

Lal only nodded at Henry, then took a tiny sip of her champagne. "It's a long time," she said, "since we had this."

The restaurant was seldom full on a Monday night. The little bar was completely empty except for Henry and Lal, so that to make some accompaniment to their sipping of the champagne Lal needed to talk.

"Larry's not around, is he? He usually pops into the bar, doesn't he, with his apron on?"

"I expect he's hard at work. We wouldn't want Larry doing anything but concentrating on our dinner, would we?" Henry said jovially.

"I like Larry," she said.

"He's a clever cook."

"I think he's quite shy underneath all that flippety talk and show-ing off his bottom."

"Lal!"

"Well, he does, Henry. He shows it off all the time. Haven't you noticed the way he ties his apron so carefully, so that the bow just bounces up and down on his behind when he walks?"

"No, I haven't noticed."

"I mean, a less shy person wouldn't need the bow, would he?"

"Haven't a clue, Lal."

"Oh, they wouldn't definitely. You can tell that Larry's very dependent."

"On what?"

"Not on what—on Edward or whatever his name is: his friend. He loves that friend and depends on him. Edward's more cultured than Larry is."

Myra (Henry addressed her as Myra but Lal nudged him, fearing it might be Moira) came to take their order. Lal ordered Champignons à la Viennoise, followed by stuffed pork tenderloin with cherry and Madeira sauce; Henry ordered a venison terrine, fol-lowed by Veal Cordon Bleu.

Henry then chose a bottle of fine claret and sat back, one hand on his stomach, the other holding his champagne glass. It's not hard, he thought, to find one's little pleasures—just as long as one isn't poor. He smiled at Lal.

His work done for the evening, Larry took off his apron and hung it up. Only two tables had been occupied—not unusually for a Mon-day evening—and he hoped those few customers would leave early so that he could tidy up and go to bed. He sat down on one of his kitchen stools and took a gulp of the large whisky he had poured him-self. But the whisky did nothing to lessen the pain Larry was feeling. The pain squatted there inside him, an undreamed-of but undeniable parasite.

Even his hands which usually moved so lightly and quickly were slowed by the pain, so that he had kept his few customers waiting for their meal, waiting and growing impatient. I must go out, he thought wearily, and apologize. Not do my little round to hear any praise tonight, but just go out and apologize for the delay, for the gluey quality of the Madeira sauce, for cooking the veal too long....

Larry sighed. He had said nothing to Myra or Moira. For three evenings he had kept going almost as if nothing had happened, so humbled and grieved by the turn his life had taken that he didn't wish to find a word, not one, to express it, but rather held it in—held it so tightly inside him that no one could suspect how changed he was, how absolutely changed.

If I can keep it in, he said to himself, then my body will assimilate it; it will become diluted and one day—perhaps?—it won't be there any more. It will have passed through me—only the vaguest memory—and gone.

"Bill for table four, Mr. Partridge." Myra, carrying four empty wine glasses, came into the kitchen.

Larry got off his stool and, taking his drink, shuffled over to the pine desk Edwin had provided for him at one end of the kitchen. He wrote out and added up the bill for a party of four—young people he had never seen before—and handed it to Myra.

If they're leaving now, Larry thought, then I don't have to go, not to the strangers. I'll wait till they've paid and gone and then I'll go and have a word with the Barkworths.

Larry liked Lal Barkworth. She looked at the world out of fierce brown eyes. Neither the eyes nor the body were still for long: only when something or someone managed to hold her elusive attention did she stop pacing and watching. Larry sensed that she tolerated him—as she seemed not to tolerate most people she met.

But remembering her staring eyes, now he felt afraid of facing her—knowing that she of all people would see at once that something had happened, that his gestures were awkward, his mind slow.

He refilled his whisky glass and sat motionless on the stool, waiting to hear the door close on the party of young people.

When he heard them leave and Myra came back into the kitchen with their money on a saucer, Larry got off the stool and, without looking in the mirror Edwin had hung above his desk to see if his hair was tidy, wandered out into the dining room.

Lal was sitting alone, smoking a cigarette. Forgetting for a moment that he had cooked two dinners, Larry wondered if she had come alone and had sat there all evening in silence. This sudden feeling of pity for her made him forget his pain just for an instant and smile at her. Lal smiled back.

Larry noticed that her brown eyes seemed bereft of some of their sharpness, almost filmed over. So it's all right then, he thought. She's drunk quite a lot; she's not seeing clearly, not into my mind—she won't guess.

"Hello, Larry dear."

"Mrs. Barkworth." Larry held out a limp, hot hand and Lal touched it lightly.

"I expect we're keeping you up," she said.

Larry looked around at the empty restaurant. "Monday night—no one at the feast! Washday doesn't give one an appetite, I daresay."

"We had a good meal."

"Did you? Not one of my best, any of it. We all have our off nights, don't we?"

"Mine was very nice, Larry. I couldn't eat it all, I'm afraid. I never seem to be able to, not when it's something special. I used to eat well when I was young. Will you sit down Larry? Henry's gone to the loo, he won't be long."

"Oh, yes, I see. Well...." Larry felt confused.

He wanted to say: "I thought you'd come alone," then realised that he'd cooked the veal for Henry Barkworth and here on the table of course were two wine glasses, two coffee cups.

He sat, gulping his whisky. Over the rim of his glass he was aware of Lal watching him.

"It isn't the same!" Larry blurted out.

There was a moment's silence; then Lal said: "What isn't?"

"Oh ... you know...." Larry couldn't finish the sentence.

To Lal's amazement, he had begun to weep, making no effort to disguise or cover his crying, his face awash with tears.

"Oh, Larry...."

Larry took another drink from the whisky glass, then stammered: "I haven't told anyone. I thought I could keep it ... inside ... I thought no one would need to know."

"Yes," said Lal, quietly, "yes."

"But...." Larry put a fist up to his eyes now. "I can't. It just isn't possible ... when something like that...."

"Is it something to do with Edward?"

"Edwin. *Edwin.* That's his name. Not Edward. He was never an Edward. Only like himself, like Edwin. And we were so happy. We were just as happy—happier—than some people married. I thought we were. I thought I knew. And I never would have left him, never in my life, so how could he …?"

Larry's voice was choked with his sobbing. Facing him across the table, Lal's body felt freezing cold. She reached out a hand and laid it on his arm. She was glad of the warmth of his arm under her cold hand. "If …" she began.

Larry looked up. "What?"

"If … he had just gone for a while perhaps, for a kind of holiday, a break from routine, well then—"

"No."

"But why then, Larry? Why should he leave you?"

Larry pulled out a purple handkerchief and wiped his eyes. "He…." Larry stopped, sucked at the whisky. "It was on Saturday, I had thought … because of the sunny day, we would have lunch out on the patio. I made us the lunch. Edwin was out. I didn't know where because he didn't tell me. So I made this nice lunch for us and waited for him.

"But when he came back he said he didn't want any lunch and I said: 'Edwin, I made this for you and I opened a bottle of hock and thought we could sit out in the sunshine….'"

"He got into one of his rages. He wanted to get into a rage. He wanted me to do something silly like sulking over the meal so that he could rage at me and leave there and then. He tried to make me the excuse. He said he couldn't bear it the way I always spoiled him and did things for him and then sulked if he didn't like them, but I said: 'Edwin, okay, I do that; I do that because I want you to like things and be happy with me, but that isn't enough! You couldn't leave, not for that.'

"So then he had to admit—he had to admit that wasn't it. He was drunk—got himself drunk on vodkas so that he could tell me. It's someone called Dean, nineteen or something, no more than a kid. Edwin's been sleeping with him. Whenever he goes out, that's where he's gone, to sleep with him. He says he can't be…. He says he's obsessed with him…. He says he can't be without him."

Larry stopped talking. His sobs were only shudders now. Lal kneaded his arm. "Oh, Larry…."

"I'm sorry," he blurted. "I'm sorry to burden you."

"No, Larry, I'm the one who's sorry, so sad, because I knew you had this—this precious kind of love. You see, I can't do any more for anyone now, but I was once very strong because I was loved. I was so strong! I'm too old now. I just turn away. That's all I can do, isn't it, when everything's so ugly—just turn away. But you, Larry, you must fight to get him back, to get your love back. Life is so hideous without love, Larry; it makes you want to die."

"Evening, Larry!"

Henry, jovially wined and full, staggered to the table. "How's tricks, then?" he said.

Lal lay still. The meal lay in her stomach like a stone. Henry lay next to her, sweating a little as he snored.

As quietly as she could, not wanting to wake Henry, Lal got out of bed and crept to the bathroom. She made up one of her indigestion powders and sat on the edge of the bath, watching the powder dissolve.

When she had drunk it down, she belched and a little of the pain left her stomach, as if the stone had been blanketed by snow.

"There won't be another fifty, thank God," she whispered, staring at her empty glass; but even though she smiled at this thought, she found that a tear had slid down her cheek on to her lip. Lal sighed, "Oh, well," she whispered, "at least for once I'm not weeping for myself. I'm weeping for Larry."

The Turkey Season

Alice Munro

Open secrets—stories that are known but not told, alliances that are glimpsed but not named—permeate the small-town Ontario landscapes of Munro's fiction. "Everybody in the community is a stage for all the other people," she has commented. "There's a constant awareness of people watching and listening. And—this may be particularly Canadian—the less you reveal, the more highly thought of you are." What startles the reader of her stories is a paradox concerning this rather cold intransigence: that in her very act of holding back from events, something is revealed which illuminates an unspoken truth.

Henry James, among others, developed the technique of giving the impression of reality through a narrator who appears to have a faulty knowledge of the story. Hesitations, slips of memory, errors of description become part of a subtle fabric that somehow captures, more precisely than a full and confident recording, the story the narrator sets out to tell. Alice Munro is the inheritor of this reluctant tradition. By telling the story of "The Turkey Season" through a recalcitrant narrator, she prompts us to believe in the events portrayed. This also denies us the comfort of an all-powerful, all-knowing voice deciding what things are and should be. When we come to the last words of the story, something true has moved us, and yet—what is it precisely that has been revealed?

When I was fourteen I got a job at the Turkey Barn for the Christmas season. I was still too young to get a job working in a store or as a part-time waitress; I was also too nervous.

I was a turkey gutter. The other people who worked at the Turkey Barn were Lily and Marjorie and Gladys, who were also gutters; Irene and Henry, who were pluckers; Herb Abbott, the foreman, who superintended the whole operation and filled in wherever he was needed. Morgan Elliott was the owner and boss. He and his son, Morgy, did the killing.

Morgy I knew from school. I thought him stupid and despicable and was uneasy about having to consider him in a new and possibly superior guise, as the boss's son. But his father treated him so roughly, yelling and swearing at him, that he seemed no more than the lowest of the workers. The other person related to the boss was Gladys. She was his sister, and in her case there did seem to be some privilege of position. She worked slowly and went home if she was not feeling well, and was not friendly to Lily and Marjorie, although she was, a little, to me. She had come back to live with Morgan and his family after working for many years in Toronto, in a bank. This was not the sort of job she was used to. Lily and Marjorie, talking about her when she wasn't there, said she had had a nervous breakdown. They said Morgan made her work in the Turkey Barn to pay for her keep. They also said, with no worry about the contradiction, that she had taken the job because she was after a man, and that the man was Herb Abbott.

All I could see when I closed my eyes, the first few nights after working there, was turkeys. I saw them hanging upside down, plucked and stiffened, pale and cold, with the heads and necks limp, the eyes and nostrils clotted with dark blood; the remaining bits of feathers—those dark and bloody, too—seemed to form a crown. I saw them not with aversion but with a sense of endless work to be done.

Herb Abbott showed me what to do. You put the turkey down on the table and cut its head off with a cleaver. Then you took the loose skin around the neck and stripped it back to reveal the crop, nestled in the cleft between the gullet and the windpipe.

"Feel the gravel," said Herb encouragingly. He made me close my fingers around the crop. Then he showed me how to work my hand down behind it to cut it out, and the gullet and windpipe as well. He used shears to cut the vertebrae.

"Scrunch, scrunch," he said soothingly. "Now, put your hand in."

I did. It was deathly cold in there, in the turkey's dark insides.

"Watch out for bone splinters."

Working cautiously in the dark, I had to pull the connecting tissues loose.

"Ups-a-daisy." Herb turned the bird over and flexed each leg.

"Knees up, Mother Brown. Now." He took a heavy knife and placed it directly on the knee knuckle joints and cut off the shank.

"Have a look at the worms."

Pearly-white strings, pulled out of the shank, were creeping about on their own.

"That's just the tendons shrinking. Now comes the nice part!"

He slit the bird at its bottom end, letting out a rotten smell.

"Are you educated?"

I did not know what to say.

"What's that smell?"

"Hydrogen sulfide."

"Educated," said Herb, sighing. "All right. Work your fingers around and get the guts loose. Easy. Easy. Keep your fingers together. Keep the palm inwards. Feel the ribs with the back of your hand. Feel the guts fit into your palm. Feel that? Keep going. Break the strings— as many as you can. Keep going. Feel a hard lump? That's the gizzard. Feel a soft lump? That's the heart. O.K.? O.K. Get your fingers around the gizzard. Easy. Start pulling this way. That's right. That's right. Start to pull her out."

It was not easy at all. I wasn't even sure what I had was the gizzard. My hand was full of cold pulp.

"Pull," he said, and I brought out a glistening, liverish mass.

"Got it. There's the lights. You know what they are? Lungs. There's the heart. There's the gizzard. There's the gall. Now, you don't ever want to break that gall inside or it will taste the entire turkey." Tactfully, he scraped out what I had missed, including the testicles, which were like a pair of white grapes.

"Nice pair of earrings," Herb said.

Herb Abbott was a tall, firm, plump man. His hair was dark and thin, combed straight back from a widow's peak, and his eyes seemed to be slightly slanted, so that he looked like a pale Chinese or like pictures of the Devil, except that he was smooth-faced and benign. Whatever he did around the Turkey Barn—gutting, as he was now, or loading the truck, or hanging the carcasses—was done with efficient, economical movements, quickly and buoyantly. "Notice about Herb—he always walks like he had a boat moving underneath him," Marjorie said, and it was true. Herb worked on the lake boats, during the season, as a cook. Then he worked for Morgan until after Christmas. The rest of the time he helped around the poolroom, making hamburgers, sweeping up, stopping fights before they got started. That was where he lived; he had a room above the poolroom on the main street.

In all the operations at the Turkey Barn it seemed to be Herb who had the efficiency and honor of the business continually on his mind; it was he who kept everything under control. Seeing him in the yard talking to Morgan, who was a thick, short man, red in the face, an unpredictable bully, you would be sure that it was Herb who was the boss and Morgan the hired help. But it was not so.

If I had not had Herb to show me, I don't think I could have learned turkey gutting at all. I was clumsy with my hands and had been shamed for it so often that the least show of impatience on the part of the person instructing me could have brought on a dithering paralysis. I could not stand to be watched by anybody but Herb. Particularly, I couldn't stand to be watched by Lily and Marjorie, two middle-aged sisters, who were very fast and thorough and competitive gutters. They sang at their work and talked abusively and intimately to the turkey carcasses.

"Don't you nick me, you old bugger!"

"Aren't you the old crap factory!"

I had never heard women talk like that.

Gladys was not a fast gutter, though she must have been thorough; Herb would have talked to her otherwise. She never sang and certainly never swore. I thought her rather old, though she was not as old as Lily and Marjorie; she must have been over thirty. She seemed offended by everything that went on and had the air of keeping plenty of bitter judgments to herself. I never tried to talk to her, but she spoke to me one day in the cold little washroom off the gutting shed. She was putting pancake makeup on her face. The color of the makeup was so distinct from the color of her skin that it was as if she were slapping orange paint over a whitewashed, bumpy wall.

She asked me if my hair was naturally curly.

I said yes.

"You don't get a permanent?"

"No."

"You're lucky. I have to do mine up every night. The chemicals in my system won't allow me to get a permanent."

There are different ways women have of talking about their looks. Some women make it clear that what they do to keep themselves up is for the sake of sex, for men. Others, like Gladys, make the job out to be a kind of housekeeping, whose very difficulties they pride themselves on. Gladys was genteel. I could see her in the bank, in a navy-blue dress with the kind of detachable white collar you can wash at night. She would be grumpy and correct.

Another time, she spoke to me about her periods, which were profuse and painful. She wanted to know about mine. There was an uneasy, prudish, agitated expression on her face. I was saved by Irene, who was using the toilet and called out, "Do like me, and you'll be rid of all your problems for a while." Irene was only a few years older than I was, but she was recently—tardily—married, and heavily pregnant.

Gladys ignored her, running cold water on her hands. The hands of all of us were red and sore-looking from the work. "I can't use that soap. If I use it, I break out in a rash," Gladys said. "If I bring my own soap in here, I can't afford to have other people using it, because I pay a lot for it—it's a special anti-allergy soap."

I think the idea that Lily and Marjorie promoted—that Gladys was after Herb Abbott—sprang from their belief that single people ought to be teased and embarrassed whenever possible, and from their interest in Herb, which led to the feeling that somebody ought to be after him. They wondered about him. What they wondered was: How can a man want so little? No wife, no family, no house. The details of his daily life, the small preferences, were of interest. Where had he been brought up? (Here and there and all over.) How far had he gone in school? (Far enough.) Where was his girlfriend? (Never tell.) Did he drink coffee or tea if he got the choice? (Coffee.)

When they talked about Gladys's being after him they must have really wanted to talk about sex—what he wanted and what he got. They must have felt a voluptuous curiosity about him, as I did. He aroused this feeling by being circumspect and not making the jokes some men did, and at the same time by not being squeamish or gentlemanly. Some men, showing me the testicles from the turkey, would have acted as if the very existence of testicles were somehow a bad joke on me, something a girl could be taunted about; another sort of man would have been embarrassed and would have thought he had to protect me from embarrassment. A man who didn't seem to feel one way or the other was an oddity—as much to older women, probably, as to me. But what was so welcome to me may have been disturbing to them. They wanted to jolt him. They even wanted Gladys to jolt him, if she could.

There wasn't any idea then—at least in Logan, Ontario, in the late forties—about homosexuality's going beyond very narrow confines. Women, certainly, believed in its rarity and in definite boundaries. There were homosexuals in town, and we knew who they were: an elegant, light-voiced, wavy-haired paperhanger who called himself an interior decorator; the minister's widow's fat, spoiled only son, who went so far as to enter baking contests and had crocheted a tablecloth; a hypochondriacal church organist and music teacher who kept the choir and his pupils in line with screaming tantrums. Once the label was fixed, there was a good deal of tolerance for these people, and their talents for decorating, for crocheting, and for music were appreciated—especially by women. "The poor fellow," they said. "He doesn't do any harm." They really seemed to believe—the women did—that it was the penchant for baking or music that was the determining factor, and that it was this activity that made the man what he was—not any other detours he might take, or wish to take. A desire to play the violin would be taken as more a deviation from manliness than would a wish to shun women. Indeed, the idea was that any manly man would wish to shun women but most of them were caught off guard, and for good.

I don't want to go into the question of whether Herb was homosexual or not, because the definition is of no use to me. I think that probably he was, but maybe he was not. (Even considering what happened later, I think that.) He is not a puzzle so arbitrarily solved.

The other plucker, who worked with Irene, was Henry Streets, a neighbor of ours. There was nothing remarkable about him except that he was eighty-six years old and still, as he said of himself, a devil for work. He had whiskey in his thermos, and drank it from time to time through the day. It was Henry who had said to me, in our kitchen, "You ought to get yourself a job at the Turkey Barn. They need another gutter." Then my father said at once, "Not her, Henry. She's got ten thumbs," and Henry said he was just joking—it was dirty work. But I was already determined to try it—I had a great need to be successful in a job like this. I was almost in the condition of a grownup person who is ashamed of never having learned to read, so much did I feel my ineptness at manual work. Work, to everybody I knew, meant doing things I was no good at doing, and work was what people prided themselves on and measured each other by. (It goes without saying that the things I was good at, like schoolwork, were suspect or held in plain contempt.) So it was a surprise and then a triumph for me not to get fired, and to be able to turn out clean turkeys at a rate that was not disgraceful. I don't know if I really understood how much Herb Abbott was responsible for this, but he would sometimes say, "Good girl," or pat my waist and say, "You're getting to be a good gutter—you'll go a long ways in the world," and when I felt his quick, kind touch through the heavy sweater and bloody smock I wore, I felt my face glow and I wanted to lean back against him as he stood behind me. I wanted to rest my head against his wide, fleshy shoulder. When I went to sleep at night, lying on my side, I would rub my cheek against the pillow and think of that as Herb's shoulder.

I was interested in how he talked to Gladys, how he looked at her or noticed her. This interest was not jealous. I think I wanted something to happen with them. I quivered in curious expectation, as Lily and Marjorie did. We all wanted to see the flicker of sexuality in him, hear it in his voice, not because we thought it would make him seem more like other men but because we knew that with him it would be entirely different. He was kinder and more patient than most women, and as stern and remote, in some ways, as any man. We wanted to see how he could be moved.

If Gladys wanted this, too, she didn't give any signs of it. It is impossible for me to tell with women like her whether they are as thick and deadly as they seem, not wanting anything much but opportunities for irritation and contempt, or if they are all choked up with gloomy fires and useless passions.

Marjorie and Lily talked about marriage. They did not have much good to say about it, in spite of their feeling that it was a state nobody should be allowed to stay out of. Marjorie said that shortly after her marriage she had gone into the woodshed with the intention of swallowing Paris green.

"I'd have done it," she said. "But the man came along in the grocery truck and I had to go out and buy the groceries. This was when we lived on the farm."

Her husband was cruel to her in those days, but later he suffered an accident—he rolled the tractor and was so badly hurt he would be an invalid all his life. They moved to town, and Marjorie was the boss now.

"He starts to sulk the other night and say he don't want his supper. Well, I just picked up his wrist and held it. He was scared I was going to twist his arm. He could see I'd do it. So I say, 'You *what?*' And he says, 'I'll eat it.'"

They talked about their father. He was a man of the old school. He had a noose in the woodshed (not the Paris green woodshed—this would be an earlier one, on another farm), and when they got on his nerves he used to line them up and threaten to hang them. Lily, who was the younger, would shake till she fell down. This same father had arranged to marry Marjorie off to a crony of his when she was just sixteen. That was the husband who had driven her to the Paris green. Their father did it because he wanted to be sure she wouldn't get into trouble.

"Hot blood," Lily said.

I was horrified, and asked, "Why didn't you run away?"

"His word was law," Marjorie said.

They said that was what was the matter with kids nowadays—it was the kids that ruled the roost. A father's word should be law. They brought up their own kids strictly, and none had turned out bad yet. When Marjorie's son wet the bed she threatened to cut off his dingy with the butcher knife. That cured him.

They said ninety per cent of the young girls nowadays drank, and swore, and took it lying down. They did not have daughters, but if they did and caught them at anything like that they would beat them raw. Irene, they said, used to go to the hockey games with her ski pants slit and nothing under them, for convenience in the snowdrifts afterward. Terrible.

I wanted to point out some contradictions. Marjorie and Lily themselves drank and swore, and what was so wonderful about the strong will of a father who would insure you a lifetime of unhappiness? (What I did not see was that Marjorie and Lily were not unhappy altogether—could not be, because of their sense of consequence, their pride and style.) I could be enraged then at the lack of logic in most adults' talk—the way they held to their pronouncements no matter what evidence might be presented to them. How could these women's hands be so gifted, so delicate and clever—for I knew they would be as good at dozens of other jobs as they were at gutting;

they would be good at quilting and darning and painting and papering and kneading dough and setting out seedlings—and their thinking so slapdash, clumsy, infuriating?

Lily said she never let her husband come near her if he had been drinking. Marjorie said since the time she nearly died with a hemorrhage she never let her husband come near her, period. Lily said quickly that it was only when he'd been drinking that he tried anything. I could see that it was a matter of pride not to let your husband come near you, but I couldn't quite believe that "come near" meant "have sex." The idea of Marjorie and Lily being sought out for such purposes seemed grotesque. They had bad teeth, their stomachs sagged, their faces were dull and spotty. I decided to take "come near" literally.

The two weeks before Christmas was a frantic time at the Turkey Barn. I began to go in for an hour before school as well as after school and on weekends. In the morning, when I walked to work, the street lights would still be on and the morning stars shining. There was the Turkey Barn, on the edge of a white field, with a row of big pine trees behind it, and always, no matter how cold and still it was, these trees were lifting their branches and sighing and straining. It seems unlikely that on my way to the Turkey Barn, for an hour of gutting turkeys, I should have experienced such a sense of promise and at the same time of perfect, impenetrable mystery in the universe, but I did. Herb had something to do with that, and so did the cold snap—the series of hard, clear mornings. The truth is, such feelings weren't hard to come by then. I would get them but not know how they were to be connected with anything in real life.

One morning at the Turkey Barn there was a new gutter. This was a boy eighteen or nineteen years old, a stranger named Brian. It seemed he was a relative, or perhaps just a friend, of Herb Abbott's. He was staying with Herb. He had worked on a lake boat last summer. He said he had got sick of it, though, and quit.

What he said was, "Yeah, fuckin' boats, I got sick of that."

Language at the Turkey Barn was coarse and free, but this was one word never heard there. And Brian's use of it seemed not careless but flaunting, mixing insult and provocation. Perhaps it was his general style that made it so. He had amazing good looks: taffy hair, bright-blue eyes, ruddy skin, well-shaped body—the sort of good looks nobody disagrees about for a moment. But a single, relentless notion had got such a hold on him that he could not keep from turning all his assets into parody. His mouth was wet-looking and slightly open most of the time, his eyes were half shut, his expression a hopeful leer, his movements indolent, exaggerated, inviting. Perhaps if he had been put on a stage with a microphone and a guitar and let grunt and howl and wriggle and excite, he would have seemed a true celebrant. Lacking a stage, he was unconvincing. After a while he seemed just like somebody with a bad case of hiccups—his insistent sexuality was that monotonous and meaningless.

If he had toned down a bit, Marjorie and Lily would probably have enjoyed him. They could have kept up a game of telling him to shut his filthy mouth and keep his hands to himself. As it was, they said they were sick of him, and meant it. Once, Marjorie took up her gutting knife. "Keep your distance," she said. "I mean from me and my sister and that kid."

She did not tell him to keep his distance from Gladys, because Gladys wasn't there at the time and Marjorie would probably not have felt like protecting her anyway. But it was Gladys that Brian particularly liked to bother. She would throw down her knife and go into the washroom and stay there ten minutes and come out with a stony face. She didn't say she was sick anymore and go home, the way she used to. Marjorie said Morgan was mad at Gladys for sponging and she couldn't get away with it any longer.

Gladys said to me, "I can't stand that kind of thing. I can't stand people mentioning that kind of thing and that kind of—gestures. It makes me sick to my stomach."

I believed her. She was terribly white. But why, in that case, did she not complain to Morgan? Perhaps relations between them were too uneasy, perhaps she could not bring herself to repeat or describe such things. Why did none of us complain—if not to Morgan, at least to Herb? I never thought of it. Brian seemed just something to put up with, like the freezing cold in the gutting shed and the smell of blood and waste. When Marjorie and Lily did threaten to complain, it was about Brian's laziness.

He was not a good gutter. He said his hands were too big. So Herb took him off gutting, told him to sweep and clean up, make packages of giblets, and help load the truck. This meant that he did not have to be in any one place or doing any one job at a given time, so much of the time he did nothing. He would start sweeping up, leave that and mop the tables, leave that and have a cigarette, lounge against the table bothering us until Herb called him to help load. Herb was very busy now and spent a lot of time making deliveries, so it was possible he did not know the extent of Brian's idleness.

"I don't know why Herb don't fire you," Marjorie said. "I guess the answer is he don't want you hanging around sponging on him, with no place to go."

"I know where to go," said Brian.

"Keep your sloppy mouth shut," said Marjorie. "I pity Herb. Getting saddled."

On the last school day before Christmas we got out early in the afternoon. I went home and changed my clothes and came into work at about three o'clock. Nobody was working. Everybody was in the gutting shed, where Morgan Elliott was swinging a cleaver over the gutting table and yelling. I couldn't make out what the yelling was about, and thought someone must have made a terrible mistake in his work; perhaps it had been me. Then I saw Brian on the other side of the table, looking very sulky and mean, and standing well back. The sexual leer was not altogether gone from his face, but it was flattened out and mixed with a look of impotent bad temper and some fear. That's it, I thought; Brian is getting fired for being so sloppy and lazy. Even when I made out Morgan saying "pervert" and "filthy" and "maniac," I still thought that was what was happening. Marjorie and Lily, and even brassy Irene, were standing around with downcast, rather pious looks, such as children get when somebody is suffering a terrible bawling out at school. Only old Henry seemed able to keep a cautious grin on his face. Gladys was not to be seen. Herb was standing closer to Morgan than anybody else. He was not interfering but was keeping an eye on the cleaver. Morgy was blubbering, though he didn't seem to be in any immediate danger.

Morgan was yelling at Brian to get out. "And out of this town—I mean it—and don't you wait till tomorrow if you still want your arse in one piece! Out!" he shouted, and the cleaver swung dramatically towards the door. Brian started in that direction but, whether he meant to or not, he made a swaggering, taunting motion of the buttocks. This made Morgan break into a roar and run after him, swinging the cleaver in a stagy way. Brian ran, and Morgan ran after him, and Irene screamed and grabbed her stomach. Morgan was too heavy to run any distance and probably could not have thrown the cleaver very far, either. Herb watched from the doorway. Soon Morgan came back and flung the cleaver down on the table.

"All back to work! No more gawking around here! You don't get paid for gawking! What are you getting under way at?" he said, with a hard look at Irene.

'Nothing," Irene said meekly.

"If you're getting under way get out of here."

"I'm not."

"All right, then!"

We got to work. Herb took off his blood-smeared smock and put on his jacket and went off, probably to see that Brian got ready to go on the suppertime bus. He did not say a word. Morgan and his son went out to the yard, and Irene and Harry went back to the adjoining shed, where they did the plucking, working knee-deep in the feathers Brian was supposed to keep swept up.

"Where's Gladys?" I said softly.

"Recuperating," said Marjorie. She, too, spoke in a quieter voice than usual, and "recuperating" was not the sort of word she and Lily normally used. It was a word to be used about Gladys, with a mocking intent.

They didn't want to talk about what had happened, because they were afraid Morgan might come in and catch them at it and fire them. Good workers as they were, they were afraid of that. Besides, they hadn't seen anything. They must have been annoyed that they hadn't. All I ever found out was that Brian had either done something or shown something to Gladys as she came out of the washroom and she had started screaming and having hysterics.

Now she'll likely be laid up with another nervous breakdown, they said. And he'll be on his way out of town. And good riddance, they said, to both of them.

I have a picture of the Turkey Barn crew taken on Christmas Eve. It was taken with a flash camera that was someone's Christmas extravagance. I think it was Irene's. But Herb Abbott must have been the one who took the picture. He was the one who could be trusted to know or to learn immediately how to manage anything new, and flash cameras were fairly new at the time. The picture was taken about ten o'clock on Christmas Eve, after Herb and Morgy had come back from making the last delivery and we had washed off the gutting table and swept and mopped the cement floor. We had taken off our bloody smocks and heavy sweaters and gone into the little room called the lunchroom, where there was a table and a heater. We still wore our working clothes: overalls and shirts. The men wore caps and the women kerchiefs, tied in the wartime style. I am stout and cheerful and comradely in the picture, transformed into someone I don't ever remember being or pretending to be. I look years older than fourteen. Irene is the only one who has taken off her kerchief, freeing her long red hair. She peers out from it with a meek, sluttish, inviting look, which would match her reputation but is not like any look of hers I remember. Yes, it must have been her camera; she is posing for it, with that look, more deliberately than anyone else is. Marjorie and Lily are smiling, true to form, but their smiles are sour and reckless. With their hair hidden, and such figures as they have bundled up, they look like a couple of tough and jovial but testy workmen. Their kerchiefs look misplaced; caps would be better. Henry is in high spirits, glad to be part of the work force, grinning and looking twenty years younger than his age. Then Morgy, with his hangdog look, not trusting the occasion's bounty, and Morgan very flushed and bosslike and satisfied. He has just given each of us our bonus turkey. Each of these turkeys has a leg or a wing missing, or a malformation of some kind, so none of them are salable at the full price. But Morgan has been at pains to tell us that you often get the best meat off the gimpy ones, and he has shown us that he's taking one home himself.

We are holding mugs or large, thick china cups, which contain not the usual tea but rye whiskey. Morgan and Henry have been drinking since suppertime. Marjorie and Lily say they only want a little, and only take it at all because it's Christmas Eve and they are dead on their feet. Irene says she's dead on her feet as well but that doesn't mean she only wants a little. Herb has poured quite generously not just for her but for Lily and Marjorie, too, and they do not object. He has measured mine and Morgy's out at the same time, very stingily, and poured in Coca-Cola. This is the first drink I have ever had, and as a result I will believe for years that rye-and-Coca-Cola is a standard sort of drink and will always ask for it, until I notice that few other people drink it and that it makes me sick. I didn't get sick that Christmas Eve, though; Herb had not given me enough. Except for an odd taste, and my own feeling of consequence, it was like drinking Coca-Cola.

I don't need Herb in the picture to remember what he looked like. That is, if he looked like himself, as he did all the time at the Turkey Barn and the few times I saw him on the street—as he did all the times in my life when I saw him except one.

The time he looked somewhat unlike himself was when Morgan was cursing out Brian and, later, when Brian had run off down the road. What was this different look? I've tried to remember, because I studied it hard at the time. It wasn't much different. His face looked softer and heavier then, and if you had to describe the expression on it you would have to say it was an expression of shame. But what would he be ashamed of? Ashamed of Brian, for the way he had behaved? Surely that would be late in the day; when had Brian ever behaved otherwise? Ashamed of Morgan, for carrying on so ferociously and theatrically? Or of himself, because he was famous for nipping fights and displays of this sort in the bud and hadn't been able to do it here? Would he be ashamed that he hadn't stood up for Brian? Would he have expected himself to do that, to stand up for Brian?

All this was what I wondered at the time. Later, when I knew more, at least about sex, I decided that Brian was Herb's lover, and that Gladys really was trying to get attention from Herb, and that was why Brian had humiliated her—with or without Herb's connivance and consent. Isn't it true that people like Herb—dignified, secretive, honorable people—will often choose somebody like Brian, will waste their helpless love on some vicious, silly person who is not even evil, or a monster, but just some importunate nuisance? I decided that Herb, with all his gentleness and carefulness, was avenging himself on us all—not just on Gladys but on us all—with Brian, and that what he was feeling when I studied his face must have been a savage and gleeful scorn. But embarrassment as well—embarrassment for Brian and for himself and for Gladys, and to some degree for all of us. Shame for all of us—that is what I thought then.

Later still, I backed off this explanation. I got to a stage of backing off from things I couldn't really know. It's enough for me now just to think of Herb's face with that peculiar, stricken look; to think of Brian monkeying in the shade of Herb's dignity; to think of my own mystified concentration on Herb, my need to catch him out, if I could ever get the chance, and then move in and stay close to him. How attractive, how delectable, the prospect of intimacy is, with the very person who will never grant it. I can still feel the pull of a man like that, of his promising and refusing. I would still like to know things. Never mind facts. Never mind theories, either.

When I finished my drink I wanted to say something to Herb. I stood beside him and waited for a moment when he was not listening to or talking with anyone else and when the increasingly rowdy conversation of the others would cover what I had to say.

"I'm sorry your friend had to go away."

"That's all right."

Herb spoke kindly and with amusement, and so shut me off from any further right to look at or speak about his life. He knew what I was up to. He must have known it before, with lots of women. He knew how to deal with it.

Lily had a little more whiskey in her mug and told how she and her best girlfriend (dead now, of liver trouble) had dressed up as men one time and gone into the men's side of the beer parlor, the side where it said "Men Only," because they wanted to see what it was like. They sat in a corner drinking beer and keeping their eyes and ears open, and nobody looked twice or thought a thing about them, but soon a problem arose.

"Where were we going to go? If we went around to the other side and anybody seen us going into the ladies', they would scream bloody murder. And if we went into the men's somebody'd be sure to notice we didn't do it the right way. Meanwhile the beer was going through us like a bugger!"

"What you don't do when you're young!" Marjorie said.

Several people gave me and Morgy advice. They told us to enjoy ourselves while we could. They told us to stay out of trouble. They said they had all been young once. Herb said we were a good crew and had done a good job but he didn't want to get in bad with any of the women's husbands by keeping them there too late. Marjorie and Lily expressed indifference to their husbands, but Irene announced that she loved hers and that it was not true that he had been dragged back from Detroit to marry her, no matter what people said. Henry said it was a good life if you didn't weaken. Morgan said he wished us all the most sincere Merry Christmas.

When we came out of the Turkey Barn it was snowing. Lily said it was like a Christmas card, and so it was, with the snow whirling around the street lights in town and around the colored lights people had put up outside their doorways. Morgan was giving Henry and Irene a ride home in the truck, acknowledging age and pregnancy and Christmas. Morgy took a shortcut through the field, and Herb walked off by himself, head down and hands in his pockets, rolling slightly, as if he were on the deck of a lake boat. Marjorie and Lily linked arms with me as if we were old comrades.

"Let's sing," Lily said. "What'll we sing?"

"'We Three Kings'?" said Marjorie. "'We Three Turkey Gutters'?"

"'I'm Dreaming of a White Christmas.'"

"Why dream? You got it!"

So we sang.

Encounter

Peter Wells

Western society, with characteristic arrogance, assumes that its models are universal. The conquistador Álvar Nuñéz Cabeza de Vaca complained that the natives of New Mexico had no sense of the value of gold, and the Reverend Father Tomasso Dongi pitied the Tehuelche people for being unable to grasp the significance of the Holy Trinity. When the Spaniards discovered homosexuals living ordinarily among the Carib tribes, they set their dogs on them and had them devoured alive. Captain Cook refused to describe the "filthy" customs he found among the inhabitants of the South Seas. Among the Big Namba tribe on Malekula Island, in the New Hebrides, homosexuality was so common that every chief had a number of male lovers as well as wives, and young men were routinely initiated in the arts of love by an older tutor. Among the Maoris of New Zealand, there was for many centuries a ritualistic "feminizing" of certain male children, and transvestism was common.

It took travellers many centuries to discover that not only were other peoples different from themselves, but the very existence of other societies put in question their own assumptions. Robinson Crusoe's Friday is not the white man's inverted reflection, but someone who in his own rights has particular notions and a language and a sense of the world. Sometimes, as in Peter Wells' "Encounter", the confrontation occurs not just between what two cultures consider "different" but also between their sense of what is "normal". What Crusoe, what almost every traveller is reluctant to acknowledge, is the truism Kipling noted:

> *There are nine and sixty ways of constructing tribal lays,*
> *And—every—single—one—of—them—is—right!*

He was walking along Karangahape Road neither slowly nor quickly, with the almost directionless pace of one who has no appointments, no commitments—no one even waiting at the other end, to hear how entirely tedious his day had been, looking for work.

Occasionally he glimpsed the fact that his pursuit of suitable employment—the emphasis was on the word *suitable*—was in itself an end. It provided a structure for his days: he could expand excitingly in an interview and amaze his interlocutor with the range of his past experience: law clerk, stevedore, lighting cameraman, callboy. Yet perhaps it was this very range which finally unnerved the recipient of so much variety. The question almost inevitably arose: how could someone so talented, so accomplished in the English language be so finally unemployable? It was as if there were something a little wrong *architecturally*: like a fantastically ornate Victorian cupola perched precariously on the corrugated-iron roof of a crude concrete *fale*.

That day Henry Lawson looked more Polynesian than Italian. Henry's looks varied greatly according to which racial side sought genetic mastery. When he went out to the pub or nightclub, hair trimmed, clothes neat and chic as possible on a non-existent income, he could pass in dubious lighting as a European of around thirty, possibly of Italian ancestry. This pleased Henry, who had a romantic disposition. Besides, who in New Zealand wanted to claim Polynesian ancestry when it was so often seen as a demerit?

Yet, when Henry grew moody, or blue, or black, his looks underwent a subtle weatherchange: his face became puffy, his clothes less a costume carefully attended to. To any stranger who saw him at these moments—and this was one of them—there was no doubt that he, Henry Lawson, was not an Italian who happened to find himself stranded in this *infinitely tedious village:* he was that discount thing, an Islander on K Road. His Boston-Apostolic genes lay submerged like a frail lost boat on the bottom of the pellucid Pacific.

He was lost, he was lonely. If only he'd bump into one of his many friends, strike a pearl in the net of his vast social acquaintance. Perhaps there was a good-looking man to cruise, leading to an encounter which would dissipate an hour or two—or hopefully several *nights*. He liked to think he was a good lover, or at the very least an entertaining one.

Yet there was no one.

Why was it, Henry asked himself almost hysterically, there were some days when the streets were made of handsome invitations, lingering looks, whereas on others, as today, the world seemed peopled by leftover rejects from a Gormenghast movie, to which one seemed fated, unwillingly, to belong? He let out a grim cackle to himself: he enjoyed the melodramatic bleakness of this thought. With a flourish, he helped himself to his last cigarette. Then caught the bearer of an angry yellow hairdo turning to him, staring at him edgily, as if he, Henry Lawson, almost a Polynesian *princess*, were just another of the resident weirdos who plied their tragic trade along Karangahape boulevard.

The very *idea* of it! He felt like turning round and shrieking at her, with almost Judy Garland–like bravura: "I was *ruined* in my youth!"

So was she, so was she, cried the wind.

As if in confirmation of his inner mood, he saw, presented against a brilliantly backlit cyclorama of cloud, a single figure poised on the very apex of Hopetoun Street bridge. This image of suicide seemed to him almost an hallucination. He gazed at it momentarily then rebuffed the enticement: it was some mere *amateur in existence*, gazing down through the chasms of interweaving motorway.

Too entirely *tedious*.

The only person ahead was a fat Polynesian carrying himself home from work. He had a physique, or, as Henry would say sharply, the *shipwrecked* remains of one. Probably heading for the pub, Henry thought tartly, to drown his sorrows in a glass.

At this thought, like a desire too long suppressed, Henry began to long for the absolution of a good drunk. He remembered the small amount of gin which remained in the bottle back in his room: enough to at least blur the outlines of the present, to allow himself to focus inwards on that sense of self-knowledge—absurd, wronged, ironic—which allowed him to live.

Henry let his eyes rest, theoretically at least, upon the man getting closer to him by the moment. The man's slightly softening form was cloaked in dusty blue overalls which, sexually, casually, were lowered round his hips, as if he were too tired, too exhausted to himself make the connection.

Henry's lovers nearly always turned out to be blue-eyed blonds, as if he were seeking, wordlessly, some lost part of himself. Yet automatically now, cruising on auto-pilot, Henry flirtatiously checked out the Polynesian man's face.

He was possibly forty-five, light brown Polynesian skin yellowed to ricepaper by tiredness and dust. He carried a quietly absorbed air of exhaustion along with him: a man whose physical strength was his one asset. Yet as they drew closer and closer, Henry felt his heart spurt into action.

The features were undeniable, though blurred by age and tiredness: there was no doubt: *it was him.* Henry felt an infinitely powerful electric current of memory start through his body. His eyes clung to the stranger's face. He felt the present and the past activate. And he felt in that one moment of recognition a crumpling of his soul even as he cried out in protest, like the voice of someone far distant, and falling: "I was *ruined* in my youth."

The day was hot as it nearly always was on the island, a pleasant lingering warmth which caressed the coconut trees, sent the waves flopping against the coral reefs: made the flies buzz around the tins of bullybeef cut open in his grandmother's large kitchen. It was Henry's job each day to ring the heavy ship's bell which hung, pendulous as an enormous flower, on the open porch.

This ringing of the bell gave Henry his importance. He was, after all, only ten, yet even as a ten-year-old he was clearly the heir to the master, the favoured grandson. He was the oldest male of the oldest male, gathered back into the grandfather's nest so he could learn the requirements of his chiefly status. Well, now his grandfather was dead. He had, as it were, drifted out to sea in search of his Boston ancestry and never returned. His grandmother, vast, twenty-three stone, commanding as a mobile effigy, was industrious in plying her financially rewarding trade of copra and tomatoes. She ruled her tiny plantation like a replica of the distant queen-empress.

Henry's daily ringing of the bell was, in part, to summon the workers to food. Yet each sharp strong clang sent a further message to the sweat-stained youths and men that it was he, Henry Lawson, son of Josiah, son of Jeremiah, who would one day pay them: it was he, Henry Lawson, who would oversee their lives. And he knew it.

That day, he let the tintinnabulation settle, then die, absorbed in the heat, suffocated by the more persistent drone of surf, cackle of palm tree. He watched the glistening torsos of the men as they moved towards the crude tin shelter which served as a wash-room. His eyes narrowed on one young man in particular, a youth of perfect form and symmetry who glided along slightly apart from the other men, as if enclosed in his own dreamworld which sealed him off from their rough jokes, their sexual jests to which he reacted a little late, as if awakening from another world which moved ceaselessly, colourfully, *persuasively*, in front of him as he moved, hypnotized, along.

Henry felt for this youth a passionate absorption which was so powerful he could only follow behind it, drugged as a sleepwalker, intent, spying and enthralled, needing to fill his eyes every waking moment he could with the vision of Tere, as he moved in his sweet dream behind his plough across the earth.

Henry followed Tere with his eyes as he went into the compound. Each man had a kind of stable-like area to call his own, a cot. Henry picked up his small plastic jet so expensively sent from New Zealand (and the only one among all the children on the island). He moved in counterpoise, seemingly, to Tere's motion, following silently behind him. He walked into Tere's area and stood there, jet in hand, playing it along his palm.

Tere was slumped on his cot, legs apart so Henry saw in the soft dark the lolling shape of his sex which he stared at fixedly, hungrily absorbing its petal-like details, its flowering pendant shape.

A little unnerved by Henry's gaze, Tere shifted his powerful legs to one side and gazed down at Henry. They looked at each other for a moment in silence—during which Henry heard very clearly the rise and fall of Tere's even breathing so that his own breathing fell into accord with it and they breathed together in a frightening duet.

Henry felt an overpowering longing to reach out and touch this *mirage*, to break the union, but at that second one of the other men walked down the narrow passage, and, seeing Henry ahead, called out to him good-naturedly, "Greetings to the Little Capitaine!"

Henry looked at the elderly man with a heavy, serious gaze which made him feel uneasy. He did not like to be stared at so silently by a mere child. But in an instant the mere child had gone.

The impressions were jostled and juxtaposed confusingly. Henry had recently learnt of a strange form of behaviour which fascinated him. The local boys—some his own age, some older—had taken him on raids on neighbouring plantations. During these informal sallies, Tuaivi, the leader, led them silently on a warrior mission whose point was to watch fat Mr. Hastings and fatter Mrs. Kelston wrestling together in the undergrowth, sweating and grunting, both of them, Henry thought, trying to find something which was locked underneath them: yet they were both clamped together so tightly neither could reach it.

Their desperation, the animal cries of Mrs. Kelston and the answering grunts of Mr. Hastings, drew Henry into their vortex. Then Mrs. Kelston's face, drained of blood, sweating, suddenly focused on the ring of watching faces. She let out a cry of fright, of ruptured modesty. Mr. Hastings jerked painfully back, apart. In that moment Henry saw his purple, distended cock, angry as an exclamation mark, glistening and moist. Mrs. Kelston was on her feet, pulling her lavalava up, running away. Mr. Hastings, entangled by his pants, could only bellow. Tuaivi had led the boys away cacophonous with laughter which echoed and re-echoed throughout the village, mocking and hilarious.

They all ran away, fleeing with the knowledge they had just gained, drugged.

Afterwards Henry thought seriously about the purple distended cock and gazed down secretly at his own tiny cockleshell which showed no propensity to stiffen. He touched it softly, roughly pulling it out. The sensation was immediate. He looked down at himself thoughtfully. And above his head, as if the very sky had changed into a silver screen, the heavens became filled with images of Tere, multiplied and remultiplied: and gradually Henry grew languorous.

The following afternoon, when the light was bright and intense as a dream, he followed Tere's shadow into the compound. He had been thinking all night, all morning of what he wanted to do.

Henry held his jet tightly in his hand as he looked at the glistening gilded flesh of Tere as he lay back, spent from labour. He looked silently at the pillowing breast muscles as they planed down towards the large flowering nipples. Above this profusion of taut flesh Tere's face looked down at him, brow furrowed slightly. His eyes had just opened. He had been dreaming about Nane, a girl in the village.

Tere looked a long distance down at the small boy who gazed longingly at him. Without saying a word, Henry reached out his hand and, placing it lightly, uncertainly, even caressingly, he ran his fingertips up Tere's ankle, speckled with mud, to the smooth agate of his calf muscle. Tere let out a small laugh, and his face for a moment became animated. Henry looked intently into Tere's face, with its perfectly symmetrical features, the dark black eyes now gazing down like the sky itself into his own eyes.

Henry slid his hand up further, slowly, looking all the while at Tere. Now Tere's face clouded over. But his hand was almost, now, it was, actually, touching Tere's cock. Tere scissored back. He looked down at Henry, frowning.

"What do you want?" he asked, almost whispering. His voice was thick from sleep.

"I want to feel you."

There was silence for a moment.

"You cannot touch me there."

"*Why?*"

"It is not right."

"*Why?*"

"Mr. Samuels says so."

Henry's small fingers crept closer.

"*Why?*"

"Because the Bible says so."

"*Why?*"

His fingers moved now into a caress.

"Because that is what God has decided."

Henry's answer was to look at him uncomprehendingly and reach his hand out again. This time he went straight for Tere's cock and held on tight. Tere grimaced.

"Go easy! Stop!" he cried out.

One of the men walked by and they fell silent. Tere was now flushing and sweating. To Henry he looked more beautiful than ever, caged, animal.

"I want to feel," Henry said again in a firm voice he had heard his grandmother use. "*I want,*" he said, tersely. And he did.

But as he reached out, Tere effortlessly leant down and swept his hand away. Tere held his hand suspended, so they both looked at it, for one moment, as if it had a separate life, like a crab. It was very hot. The iron roof pinged like a gun. Tere twisted Henry's arm then, painfully. He brought his face close to Henry's.

"Go away and play with your jet. That is what little boys should be doing." He said it not unkindly and immediately released him.

Henry took his arm back with as much dignity as he could muster. He continued looking at Tere intently. He felt a kind of sadness. "You must do as I say," he said very softly.

Tere had to lean forward. Now their faces were very close, Henry could count the number of eyelashes around Tere's eyes, he felt. Tere's warm, pungent breathing fanned softly onto his cheeks.

"You must do as I say," Henry said very clearly, "otherwise I will tell the old Breadfruit"—the men's name for his grandmother—"that you ... forced me."

Henry said the last piece very slowly so that Tere could fully understand it. They both knew of the palagi mission woman who told how she had been forced by a local man and how the man was sent away to prison in New Zealand.

Tere's face went a pale grey as he looked down at his small master. His face receded as he fell into thought. Then his beautiful large eyes slowly moved back to Henry's as Henry said to him in a matter-of-fact voice, as if it had been evident all along, "You must do as I say."

His grandmother had gone to the other side of the island, on one of her tours of ritualistic enactment. Her presence was so powerful that, as soon as she moved around the palms at the bottom of the road, in her sedate old Austin, the whole place seemed to change mood. The workers out on the kumara patch sang to themselves, stopped to have a smoke. Inside the house, Poko, the kitchen woman, a vague relation of his grandmother, would sing old American songs like "Rum and Coca Cola" and listen to the radio from New Zealand.

Henry felt all these changes happening around him uneasily. He knew it placed him in a weak position. Maliciously Poko would flick the end of her broom on his backside, saying to him slightingly the "maggot" must make room for "the meat".

Henry rather dreaded these days because, when he went to ring the bell, the clang no longer seemed to have its old authority. The workers weren't even really working, so how could two sharp tolls signal an end to what had not properly begun? They all looked through him on these days, too, as if he didn't really exist, whereas when his grandmother was around, several of the older men made some attempt to humour him, and call him "the Little Capitaine" in honour of his grandfather.

Now he felt the flick of dust in his face, and he didn't quite like the timbre of the laughter from the men as Poko put down the food for them. He felt almost, at these times, that he himself might end up on the table, dressed and slit open as they all leant forward to take out of his insides the delicate, pink bits.

So he made himself scarce on those days his grandmother went away on business.

This afternoon, the whole plantation was silent. Henry came down from the palm where he was hiding, spying on Tere who alone had kept on working, moving along in straight methodical strips, ploughing. Henry went back towards the house.

First of all he thought everyone had run away, it was so quiet. Then he saw fat Poko polishing the glass in the windows. She had a big white cloth and she was rubbing against the glass, but not industriously: rather she was doing it languorously, in slow, small caresses.

He observed her silently. She did not see him through the window. He moved silently along a little further. She was bent over, leaning towards the glass and he could see a strange thing: there was Mr. Hastings standing behind her, bumping into her rhythmically. Each time Poko cleaned, she bumped forward towards the glass. Henry looked at her face, which was trance-like and sweating, her eyes slightly glazed. She had her mouth open a little and she seemed to be gasping, or was it smiling?

He tiptoed very very quietly across the chill concrete, skirting the noisy mats. Now he was inside the house he could see them side on. He could see Mr. Hastings was joined to the back of Poko, her skirts were thrown up and his trousers were down. They moved together in their strange dance.

"What are you doing?"

They both looked startled for a moment. Then Mr. Hastings' rhythm speeded up urgently, as if they were both caught in an undulation which, once begun, must now continue on to its end or neither would ever rest in peace again. All the while Poko tried to reach him with her duster, trying to shoo him away.

"Pffffftttt! Pfffffssssttt!" she hissed at him angrily.

But Henry stood out of range and silently watched.

The following day Henry waited for Tere to come into the compound. He heard slow footsteps, then Tere stood in front of him. Henry made room for Tere, who sank down silently beside him. Henry quickly, as if there was no time to lose, placed his hands on Tere's cock. He felt its coldness, the way it was pulled up into itself, like a snail unwilling to come out of its shell. He stroked it kindly, then looked up at Tere's face.

Tere lay with his face turned towards him, but his eyes were firmly closed.

Henry ordered him to open his eyes.

Then he squirmed down towards Tere's musky smelling legs. Tere was so inert, so still. He placed his own soft body beside the crisp wiry hairs of Tere's legs. With hand, with palm, with tongue, he now set about coaxing Tere's cock into life so he too could experience the strange dance, the magnetism, he had seen with Poko and Mr. Hastings. But no matter what he did, Tere was gripped so tight that Henry could not make his cock come to life.

It was now the third day of their rendezvous. Henry had begun to feel a little annoyance, a sharp dissatisfaction with his beautifully proportioned lover. He no longer sat up a tree gazing with longing at the ploughboy. The day before they had almost been discovered. Tere had himself caught hold of Henry and held him close, shielding him from one of the old men walking down the passage. Both their hearts crashed in unison and Henry, clamped tight to Tere's chest, almost suffocated under his weight, had felt an exquisite pleasure. But then Tere had lain back again, passive and immobile, a fabulous fountain of flesh which refused to yield its music. Henry had pulled Tere's penis then, painfully, flicking it from side to side with his fingers, like it was some useless toy. It had not been good.

So this day Henry went to Tere feeling full of purpose, power. Tere already lay there, silent, brooding. Henry came closer. Outside he could hear the men laughing. By now it seemed all the men knew and were calling Tere strange names and all their buried dislike of Henry's grandmother was now breaking against Tere in waves. A kind of deep sadness had come over Tere, his beautiful bronzed flesh now seemed yellowed, almost jaundiced. He lay there, still.

Henry began his games.

But today there was no response. There was simply nothing. He persisted. He felt so angry, it was like the day before when his jet refused to go any more. He had picked it up and smashed it against the wall. It hadn't mattered that he was later whipped. The satisfaction of seeing it break was too great. But today, as he felt the clammy, chill flesh of Tere, he had a strangely adult feeling, almost like disgust. Then he heard a strange sound, like a sigh, a moan. In one long movement, Tere turned his face to the wall and began, like a small boy, as if he were Henry's age instead of seven years his senior, to weep.

Henry looked at him silently for a while, amazed.

But Tere's tears did not cease. In fact they increased, and he began sobbing soundlessly, like a girl, like a small boy humiliated, lost.

Henry did not know what to do. "You are useless," he said to Tere finally, looking once again upon his nakedness.

In the end Henry got up and walked away.

And that was the end of it.

Henry's face was now only a few feet away from Tere's in Karanga-hape Road; they were moving closer and closer together and Henry felt a moment of panic that Tere, an aged Tere now, beaten down by work and probably a grandfather already, a son in prison most likely, daughters in the church, might shift his gaze and suddenly recognize him. Henry's sense of humiliation at this possibility was so profound that for that one instant he wanted to cry out to Tere, poor Tere, with his thickened waist, downcast face, to forgive him, to grant him the sweet absolution of accepting that he was only a child, he had hardly known what he was doing.

Then the thought came that Tere would see Henry as he was now, not well-dressed, unemployed, completely unsuited to the world of the palagi around him. Tere might ask after his grandmother, all twenty-three stone of her now as thoroughly vanished as their owner-ship of the estate, now turned into a runway for stinking jets, his grandmother's very grave urinated on nightly by tanked-up tourists uncertain of even where they were on the globe. All these contradic-tory thoughts and feelings—to reach out, to touch, to perhaps make him his lover again for one night, to salve, to heal, to beg forgive-ness—all these feelings flashed through Henry's mind as they moved closer and, oh, infinitely, almost within kissing distance, apart.

At that moment Tere lifted his gaze from the asphalt and his beau-tiful brown eyes, deep as the earth, black as the Pacific night, passed over Henry's face as it would over any stranger's. Perhaps there was for one second an intelligence that this stranger was looking at him so intently: but Tere was tired, and men with strange looks were com-mon on Karangahape boulevard.

At home, in his room, Henry poured himself a stiff gin, filling his glass with water from the tap. He thought about those things he had not considered in over twenty years. In truth he had forgotten Tere completely, his body as it were buried beneath other bodies of more or less beautiful men who were all a form of Tere, although most were more willing, certainly more rapturous. He thought of the lost world of his grandmother, the child he had been, and he began to do something he hardly ever did because he despised it as weakness: he wept.

And as he cried Tere's face came to him silently as it had been on that final day, sweat-sequined, tear-rivered. And as the tears coursed down Henry's cheeks, he had the sudden sensation that they were Tere's tears coming out of his eyes and that, after all—after all that time—they had perhaps truly for the first time come together: they were one.

The Mysteries of the Joy Rio

Tennessee Williams

"*It was his theory, the theory of most immoralists, that the soul becomes intolerably burdened with lies that have to be told to the world in order to be permitted to live in the world, and that unless this burden is relieved by entire honesty with* some one *person, who is trusted and adored, the soul will finally collapse beneath its weight of falsity.*" *This declaration lies at the core of "The Mysteries of the Joy Rio" but could serve as an introduction to the whole of Tennessee Williams' work. In his plays, in his stories, in his poetry, he declared again and again his belief in that one and only beloved who is the goal of life's journey, and whom only a fortunate few ever find.*

Tennessee Williams thought that he himself never had found that destined person. The few lasting relationships he had during his life seemed to him at times meaningless, at times unreal. His successes were overshadowed by a fear of future failure. He felt he was unfaithful to voices from his past—his beloved sister, his dreaded mother—and continued all his life to try to respond to what he believed were their ghosts' demands.

The reality of Williams' fictional world is always tinged with a sense of the fantastic, which appears as the backdrop against which his dramas are played, or as one of his characters on stage. And at times the fantastic takes on the appearance of reality: the hallucinations of desire become present, the nightmares of passion acquire a voice, the phantoms of unfulfilled longings move and embrace. "I don't want realism. I want magic," he says through the voice of Blanche DuBois in A Streetcar Named Desire. "*I don't tell truth, I tell what* ought *to be truth.*"

I

Perhaps because he was a watch repairman, Mr. Gonzales had grown to be rather indifferent to time. A single watch or clock can be a powerful influence on a man, but when a man lives among as many watches and clocks as crowded the tiny, dim shop of Mr. Gonzales, some lagging behind, some skipping ahead, but all ticking monotonously on in their witless fashion, the multitude of them may be likely to deprive them of importance, as a gem loses its value when there are too many just like it which are too easily or cheaply obtainable. At any rate, Mr. Gonzales kept very irregular hours, if he could be said to keep any hours at all, and if he had not been where he was for such a long time, his trade would have suffered badly. But Mr. Gonzales had occupied his tiny shop for more than twenty years, since he had come to the city as a boy of nineteen to work as an apprentice to the original owner of the shop, a very strange and fat man of German descent named Kroger, Emiel Kroger, who had now been dead a long time. Emiel Kroger, being a romantically practical Teuton, had taken time, the commodity he worked with, with intense seriousness. In practically all his behavior he had imitated a perfectly adjusted fat silver watch. Mr. Gonzales, who was then young enough to be known as Pablo, had been his only sustained flirtation with the confusing, quicksilver world that exists outside of regularities. He had met Pablo during a watchmakers' convention in Dallas, Texas, where Pablo, who had illegally come into the country from Mexico a few days before, was drifting hungrily about the streets, and at that time Mr. Gonzales, Pablo, had not grown plump but had a lustrous dark grace which had completely bewitched Mr. Kroger. For as I have noted already, Mr. Kroger was a fat and strange man, subject to the kind of bewitchment that the graceful young Pablo could cast. The spell was so strong that it interrupted the fleeting and furtive practices of a lifetime in Mr. Kroger and induced him to take the boy home with him, to his shop-residence, where Pablo, now grown to the mature and fleshy proportions of Mr. Gonzales, had lived ever since, for three years before the death of his protector and for more than seventeen years after that, as the inheritor of shop-residence, clocks, watches, and everything else that Mr. Kroger had owned except a few pieces of dining-room silver which Emiel Kroger had left as a token bequest to a married sister in Toledo.

Some of these facts are of dubious pertinence to the little history which is to be unfolded. The important one is the fact that Mr. Gonzales had managed to drift enviably apart from the regularities that rule most other lives. Some days he would not open his shop at all and some days he would open it only for an hour or two in the morning, or in the late evening when other shops had closed, and in spite of these caprices he managed to continue to get along fairly well, due to the excellence of his work, when he did it, the fact that he was so well established in his own quiet way, the advantage of his location in a neighborhood where nearly everybody had an old alarm clock which had to be kept in condition to order their lives (this community being one inhabited mostly by people with small-paying jobs), but it was also due in measurable part to the fact that the thrifty Mr. Kroger, when he finally succumbed to a chronic disease of the bowels, had left a tidy sum in government bonds, and this capital, bringing in about a hundred and seventy dollars a month, would have kept Mr. Gonzales going along in a commonplace but comfortable fashion even if he had declined to do anything whatsoever. It was a pity that the late, or rather long-ago, Mr. Kroger, had not understood what a fundamentally peaceable sort of young man he had taken under his wing. Too bad he couldn't have guessed how perfectly everything suited Pablo Gonzales. But youth does not betray its true nature as palpably as the later years do, and Mr. Kroger had taken the animated allure of his young protégé, the flickering lights in his eyes and his quick, nervous movements, his very grace and slimness, as meaning something difficult to keep hold of. And as the old gentleman declined in health, as he did quite steadily during the three years that Pablo lived with him, he was never certain that the incalculably precious bird flown into his nest was not one of sudden passage but rather the kind that prefers to keep a faithful commitment to a single place, the nest-building kind, and not only that, but the very-rare-indeed-kind that gives love back as generously as he takes it. The long-ago Mr. Kroger had paid little attention to his illness, even when it entered the stage of acute pain, so intense was his absorption in what he thought was the tricky business of holding Pablo close to him. If only he had known that for all this time after his decease the boy would still be in the watchshop, how it might have relieved him! But on the other hand, maybe this anxiety, mixed as it was with so much tenderness and sad delight, was actually a blessing, standing as it did between the dying old man and a concern with death.

Pablo had never flown. But the sweet bird of youth had flown from Pablo Gonzales, leaving him rather sad, with a soft yellow face that was just as round as the moon. Clocks and watches he fixed with marvelous delicacy and precision, but he paid no attention to them; he had grown as obliviously accustomed to their many small noises as someone grows to the sound of waves who has always lived by the sea. Although he wasn't aware of it, it was actually light by which he told time, and always in the afternoons when the light had begun to fail (through the narrow window and narrower, dusty skylight at the back of the shop), Mr. Gonzales automatically rose from his stooped position over littered table and gooseneck lamp, took off his close-seeing glasses with magnifying lenses, and took to the street. He did not go far and he always went in the same direction, across town toward the river where there was an old opera house, now converted into a third-rate cinema, which specialized in the showing of cowboy pictures and other films of the sort that have a special appeal to children and male adolescents. The name of this movie house was the Joy Rio, a name peculiar enough but nowhere nearly so peculiar as the place itself.

The old opera house was a miniature of all the great opera houses of the old world, which is to say its interior was faded gilt and incredibly old and abused red damask which extended upwards through at least three tiers and possibly five. The upper stairs, that is, the stairs beyond the first gallery, were roped off and unlighted and the top of the theater was so peculiarly dusky, even with the silver screen flickering far below it, that Mr. Gonzales, used as he was to close work, could not have made it out from below. Once he had been there when the lights came on in the Joy Rio, but the coming on of the lights had so enormously confused and embarrassed him, that looking up was the last thing in the world he felt like doing. He had buried his nose in the collar of his coat and had scuttled out as quickly as a cockroach makes for the nearest shadow when a kitchen light comes on.

I have already suggested that there was something a bit special and obscure about Mr. Gonzales' habitual attendance at the Joy Rio, and that was my intention. For Mr. Gonzales had inherited more than the material possessions of his dead benefactor: he had also come into custody of his old protector's fleeting and furtive practices in dark places, the practices which Emiel Kroger had given up only when Pablo had come into his fading existence. The old man had left Mr. Gonzales the full gift of his shame, and now Mr. Gonzales did the sad, lonely things that Mr. Kroger had done for such a long time before his one lasting love came to him. Mr. Kroger had even practiced those things in the same place in which they were practiced now by Mr.

Gonzales, in the many mysterious recesses of the Joy Rio, and Mr. Gonzales knew about this. He knew about it because Mr. Kroger had told him. Emiel Kroger had confessed his whole life and soul to Pablo Gonzales. It was his theory, the theory of most immoralists, that the soul becomes intolerably burdened with lies that have to be told to the world in order to be permitted to live in the world, and that unless this burden is relieved by entire honesty with *some one* person, who is trusted and adored, the soul will finally collapse beneath its weight of falsity. Much of the final months of the life of Emiel Kroger, increasingly dimmed by morphia, were devoted to these whispered confessions to his adored apprentice, and it was as if he had breathed the guilty soul of his past into the ears and brain and blood of the youth who listened, and not long after the death of Mr. Kroger, Pablo, who had stayed slim until then, had begun to accumulate fat. He never became anywhere nearly so gross as Emiel Kroger had been, but his delicate frame disappeared sadly from view among the irrelevant curves of a sallow plumpness. One by one the perfections which he had owned were folded away as Pablo put on fat as a widow puts on black garments. For a year beauty lingered about him, ghostly, continually fading, and then it went out altogether, and at twenty-five he was already the nondescriptly plump and moonfaced little man that he now was at forty, and if in his waking hours somebody to whom he would have to give a true answer had enquired of him, Pablo Gonzales, how much do you think about the dead Mr. Kroger, he probably would have shrugged and said, *Not much now. It's such a long time ago.* But if the question were asked him while he slept, the guileless heart of the sleeper would have responded, *Always, always!*

II

Now across the great marble stairs, that rose above the first gallery of the Joy Rio to the uncertain number of galleries above it, there had been fastened a greasy and rotting length of old velvet rope at the center of which was hung a sign that said to *Keep Out.* But that rope had not always been there. It had been there about twenty years, but the late Mr. Kroger had known the Joy Rio in the days before the flight of stairs was roped off. In those days the mysterious upper galleries of the Joy Rio had been a sort of fiddler's green where practically every device and fashion of carnality had run riot in a gloom so thick that a chance partner could only be discovered by touch. There were not rows of benches (as there were now on the orchestra level and the one gallery still kept in use), but strings of tiny boxes, extending in semi-circles from one side of the great proscenium to the other. In some of these boxes brokenlegged chairs might be found lying on their sides and shreds of old hangings still clung to the sliding brass loops at the entrances. According to Emiel Kroger, who is our only authority on these mysteries which share his remoteness in time, one lived up there, in the upper reaches of the Joy Rio, an almost sightless existence where the other senses, the senses of smell and touch and hearing, had to develop a preternatural keenness in order to spare one from making awkward mistakes, such as taking hold of the knee of a boy when it was girl's knee one looked for, and where sometimes little scenes of panic occurred when a mistake of gender or of compatibility had been carried to a point where radical correction was called for. There had been many fights, there had even been rape and murder in those ancient boxes, till finally the obscure management of the Joy Rio had been compelled by the pressure of notoriety to shut down that part of the immense old building which had offered its principal enticement, and the Joy Rio, which had flourished until then, had then gone into sharp decline. It had been closed down and then reopened and closed down and reopened again. For several years it had opened and shut like a nervous lady's fan. Those were the years in which Mr. Kroger was dying. After his death the fitful era subsided, and now for about ten years the Joy Rio had been continually active as a third-rate cinema, closed only for one week during a threatened epidemic of poliomyelitis some years past and once for a few days when a small fire had damaged the projection booth. But nothing happened there now of a nature to provoke a disturbance. There were no complaints to the management or the police, and the dark glory of the upper galleries was a legend in such memories as that of the late Emiel Kroger and the present Pablo Gonzales, and one by one, of course, those memories died out and the legend died out with them. Places like the Joy Rio and the legends about them make one more than usually aware of the short bloom and the long fading out of things. The angel of such a place is a fat silver angel of sixty-three years in a shiny dark-blue alpaca jacket, with short, fat fingers that leave a damp mark where they touch, that sweat and tremble as they caress between whispers, an angel of such a kind as would be kicked out of heaven and laughed out of hell and admitted to earth only by grace of its habitual slyness, its gift for making itself a counterfeit being, and the connivance of those that a quarter tip and an old yellow smile can corrupt.

But the reformation of the Joy Rio was somewhat less than absolute. It had reformed only to the point of ostensible virtue, and in the back rows of the first gallery at certain hours in the afternoon and very late at night were things going on of the sort Mr. Gonzales sometimes looked for. At those hours the Joy Rio contained few patrons, and since the seats in the orchestra were in far better condition, those who had come to sit comfortably watching the picture would naturally remain downstairs; the few that elected to sit in the nearly deserted rows of the first gallery did so either because smoking was permitted in that section—or *because*....

There was a danger, of course, there always is a danger with places and things like that, but Mr. Gonzales was a tentative person not given to leaping before he looked. If a patron had entered the first gallery only in order to smoke, you could usually count on his occupying a seat along the aisle. If the patron had bothered to edge his way toward the center of a row of seats irregular as the jawbone of poor Yorick, one could assume as infallibly as one can assume anything in a universe where chance is the one invariable, that he had chosen his seat with something more than a cigarette in mind. Mr. Gonzales did not take many chances. This was a respect in which he paid due homage to the wise old spirit of the late Emiel Kroger, that romantically practical Teuton who used to murmur to Pablo, between sleeping and waking, a sort of incantation that went like this: Sometimes you will find it and other times you won't find it and the times you don't find it are the times when you have got to be careful. Those are the times when you have got to remember that other times you *will* find it, not *this* time but the *next* time, or the time *after* that, and then you've got to be able to go home without it, yes, those times are the times when you have got to be able to go home without it, go home *alone* without it....

Pablo didn't know, then, that he would ever have need of this practical wisdom that his benefactor had drawn from his almost life-long pursuit of a pleasure which was almost as unreal and basically unsatisfactory as an embrace in a dream. Pablo didn't know then that he would inherit so much from the old man who took care of him, and at that time, when Emiel Kroger, in the dimness of morphia and weakness following hemorrhage, had poured into the delicate ear of his apprentice, drop by slow, liquid drop, this distillation of all he had learned in the years before he found Pablo, the boy had felt for this whisper the same horror and pity that he felt for the mortal disease in the flesh of his benefactor, and only gradually, in the long years since the man and his whisper had ceased, had the singsong rigmarole begun to have sense for him, a practical wisdom that such a man as Pablo had turned into, a man such as Mr. Gonzales, could live by safely and quietly and still find pleasure....

III

Mr. Gonzales was careful, and for careful people life has a tendency to take on the character of an almost arid plain with only here and there, at wide intervals, the solitary palm tree and its shadow and the spring alongside it. Mr. Kroger's life had been much the same until he had come across Pablo at the watchmakers' convention in Dallas. But so far in Mr. Gonzales' life there had been no Pablo. In his life there had been only Mr. Kroger and the sort of things that Mr. Kroger had looked for and sometimes found but most times continued patiently to look for in the great expanse of arid country which his lifetime had been before the discovery of Pablo. And since it is not my intention to spin this story out any longer than its content seems to call for, I am not going to attempt to sustain your interest in it with a description of the few palm trees on the uneventful desert through which the successor to Emiel Kroger wandered after the death of the man who had been his life. But I am going to remove you rather precipitately to a summer afternoon which we will call *Now* when Mr. Gonzales learned that he was dying, and not only dying but dying of the same trouble that had put the period under the question mark of Emiel Kroger. The scene, if I can call it that, takes place in a doctor's office. After some hedging on the part of the doctor, the word malignant is uttered. The hand is placed on the shoulder, almost contemptuously comforting, and Mr. Gonzales is assured that surgery is unnecessary because the condition is not susceptible to any help but that of drugs to relax the afflicted organs. And after that the scene is abruptly blacked out....

Now it is a year later. Mr. Gonzales has recovered more or less from the shocking information that he received from his doctor. He has been repairing watches and clocks almost as well as ever, and there has been remarkably little alteration in his way of life. Only a little more frequently is the shop closed. It is apparent, now, that the disease from which he suffers does not intend to destroy him any more suddenly than it destroyed the man before him. It grows slowly, the growth, and in fact it has recently shown signs of what is called a remission. There is no pain, hardly any and hardly ever. The most palpable symptom is loss of appetite and, as a result of that, a steady decrease of weight. Now rather startlingly, after all this time, the graceful approximation of Pablo's delicate structure has come back out of the irrelevant contours which had engulfed it after the long-ago death of Emiel Kroger. The mirrors are not very good in the dim little residence-shop, where he lives in his long wait for death, and when he looks in them, Mr. Gonzales sees the boy that was loved by the man whom he loved. It is almost Pablo. Pablo has almost returned from Mr. Gonzales.

And then one afternoon....

IV

The new usher at the Joy Rio was a boy of seventeen and the little Jewish manager had told him that he must pay particular attention to the roped-off staircase to see to it that nobody slipped upstairs to the forbidden region of the upper galleries, but this boy was in love with a girl named Gladys who came to the Joy Rio every afternoon, now that school was let out for the summer, and loitered around the entrance where George, the usher, was stationed. She wore a thin, almost transparent, white blouse with nothing much underneath it. Her skirt was usually of sheer silken material that followed her heart-shaped loins as raptly as George's hand followed them when he embraced her in the dark ladies' room on the balcony level of the Joy Rio. Sensual delirium possessed him those afternoons when Gladys loitered near him. But the recently changed management of the Joy Rio was not a strict one, and in the summer vigilance was more than commonly relaxed. George stayed near the downstairs entrance, twitching restively in his tight, faded uniform till Gladys drifted in from the afternoon streets on a slow tide of lilac perfume. She would seem not to see him as she sauntered up the aisle he indicated with his flashlight and took a seat in the back of the orchestra section where he could find her easily when the "coast was clear," or if he kept her waiting too long and she was more than usually bored with the film, she would stroll back out to the lobby and inquire in her childish drawl, Where is the Ladies' Room, Please? Sometimes he would curse her fiercely under his breath because she hadn't waited. But he would have to direct her to the staircase, and she would go up there and wait for him, and the knowledge that she was up there waiting would finally overpower his prudence to the point where he would even abandon his station if the little manager, Mr. Katz, had his office door wide open. The ladies' room was otherwise not in use. Its light-switch was broken, or if it was repaired, the bulbs would be mysteriously missing. When ladies other than Gladys enquired about it, George would say gruffly, The ladies' room's out of order. It made an almost perfect retreat for the young lovers. The door left ajar gave warning of footsteps on the grand marble staircase in time for George to come out with his hands in his pockets before whoever was coming could catch him at it. But these interruptions would sometimes infuriate him, especially when a patron would insist on borrowing his flashlight to use the cabinet in the room where Gladys waited with her crumpled silk skirt gathered high about her flanks (leaning against the invisible dried-up washbasin) which were the blazing black heart of the insatiably concave summer.

In the old days Mr. Gonzales used to go to the Joy Rio in the late afternoons but since his illness he had been going earlier because the days tired him earlier, especially the steaming days of August which were now in progress. Mr. Gonzales knew about George and Gladys; he made it his business, of course, to know everything there was to be known about the Joy Rio, which was his earthly heaven, and, of course, George also knew about Mr. Gonzales; he knew why Mr. Gonzales gave him a fifty cent tip every time he inquired his way to the men's room upstairs, each time as if he had never gone upstairs before. Sometimes George muttered something under his breath, but the tributes collected from patrons like Mr. Gonzales had so far ensured his complicity in their venal practices. But then one day in August, on one of the very hottest and blindingly bright afternoons, George was so absorbed in the delights of Gladys that Mr. Gonzales had arrived at the top of the stairs to the balcony before George heard his footsteps. Then he heard them and he clamped a sweating palm over the mouth of Gladys which was full of stammerings of his name and the name of God. He waited, but Mr. Gonzales also waited. Mr. Gonzales was actually waiting at the top of the stairs to recover his breath from the climb, but George, who could see him, now, through the door kept slightly ajar, suspected that he was waiting to catch him coming out of his secret place. A fury burst in the boy. He thrust Gladys violently back against the washbasin and charged out of the room without even bothering to button his fly. He rushed up to the slight figure waiting near the stairs and began to shout a dreadful word at Mr. Gonzales, the word "morphodite." His voice was shrill as a jungle bird's, shouting this word "morphodite." Mr. Gonzales kept backing away from him with the lightness and grace of his youth, he kept stepping backwards from the livid face and threatening fists of the usher, all the time murmuring, No, no, no, no, no. The youth stood between him and the stairs below so it was toward the upper staircase that Mr. Gonzales took flight. All at once, as quickly and lightly as ever Pablo had moved, he darted under the length of the velvet rope with the sign "Keep Out." George's pursuit was interrupted by the manager of the theater, who seized his arm so fiercely that the shoulder seam of the uniform burst apart. This started another disturbance under the cover of which Mr. Gonzales fled farther and farther up the forbidden staircase into regions of deepening shadow. There were several points at which he might safely have stopped but his flight had now gathered an irresistible momentum and his legs moved like pistons bearing him up and up, and then—

At the very top of the staircase he was intercepted. He half turned back when he saw the dim figure waiting above, he almost turned and scrambled back down the grand marble staircase, when the name of his youth was called to him in a tone so commanding that he stopped and waited without daring to look up again.

Pablo, said Mr. Kroger, come up here, Pablo.

Mr. Gonzales obeyed, but now the false power that his terror had given him was drained out of his body and he climbed with effort. At the top of the stairs where Emiel Kroger waited, he would have sunk exhausted to his knees if the old man hadn't sustained him with a firm hand at his elbow.

Mr. Kroger said, This way, Pablo. He led him into the Stygian blackness of one of the little boxes in the once-golden horseshoe of the topmost tier. Now sit down, he commanded.

Pablo was too breathless to say anything except, Yes, and Mr. Kroger leaned over him and unbuttoned his collar for him, unfastened the clasp of his belt, all the while murmuring, There now, there now, Pablo.

The panic disappeared under those soothing old fingers and the breathing slowed down and stopped hurting the chest as if a fox was caught in it, and then at last Mr. Kroger began to lecture the boy as he used to, Pablo, he murmured, don't ever be so afraid of being lonely that you forget to be careful. Don't forget that you will find it sometimes but other times you won't be lucky, and those are the times when you have got to be patient, since patience is what you must have when you don't have luck.

The lecture continued softly, reassuringly, familiar and repetitive as the tick of a bedroom clock in his ear, and if his ancient protector and instructor, Emiel Kroger, had not kept all the while soothing him with the moist, hot touch of his tremulous fingers, the gradual, the very gradual dimming out of things, his fading out of existence, would have terrified Pablo. But the ancient voice and fingers, as if they had never left him, kept on unbuttoning, touching, soothing, repeating the ancient lesson, saying it over and over like a penitent counting prayer beads, Sometimes you will have it and sometimes you won't have it, so don't be anxious about it. You must always be able to go home alone without it. Those are the times when you have got to remember that other times you will have it and it doesn't matter if sometimes you don't have it and have to go home without it, go home alone without it, go home alone without it. The gentle advice went on, and as it went on, Mr. Gonzales drifted away from everything but the wise old voice in his ear, even at last from that, but not till he was entirely comforted by it.

The Sharks

John O'Hara

Christopher Isherwood once pointed out to a young Jewish movie producer that the degree of hatred directed towards Jews was no different from that directed towards gays, and reminded him that in the German concentration camps, Jews wore yellow stars while homosexuals wore pink triangles: "After all," said Isherwood, "Hitler killed six hundred thousand homosexuals." The young man was not impressed. "But Hitler killed six million Jews," he said sternly. "What are you?" asked Isherwood. "In real estate?"

It is a sad fact that we believe we can judge suffering by degrees, so that a single act of injustice (unless we personally experience it) seems less worthy of our indignation than mass persecution or anonymous prejudice. We seem to think that there are some cases in which injustice is permissible and suffering tolerable. It is still possible to argue in the liberal press against the suitability of a gay man as teacher, priest, or soldier, while it has become unthinkable to argue in that same press a similar unsuitability of a black man, a Jew, or a woman.

Homophobia and the ethics of real estate make up the ugly mixture of subjects in John O'Hara's "The Sharks". O'Hara has been called "the best modern case of the writer as social historian", primarily because of his interest in the social details revealed in clinical descriptions and spare dialogue. Conventions, meaningless rituals, degrees of acceptable and unacceptable behaviour appear without comment in his bitter and ironic stories.

Mr. Plastic Rain Cover for His Hat was taking his daily constitutional. "There he goes, Mr. Plastic Rain Cover," said Betty Denning from her position at the window.

"Let him," said her husband.

"But come here and look at him," said Betty Denning.

"I've seen him."

"No, come here. You've only seen him once."

"Oh—" her husband growled, but he got up, took off his reading glasses and went to the window, still holding his newspaper.

"He's looking up here," said Betty Denning.

"Why don't you wave to him?"

"Shall I?" she said. "I wonder what he'd do."

"Well, you can easily find out."

"No, then we'd have him all the time."

"How do you know?"

"He's the type. I wonder which house he has?"

"How do you know he has a house?"

"Because he's on his way back. Yesterday and the day before, he walked toward the west, then fifteen minutes later he walked toward the east and then I didn't see him again. He's going eastward now, which means he's on the way home. That's how I know he has somebody's house. Also, there are no hotels toward the east of us and there are four toward the west."

"Well, you could ask in the village."

"I think I will."

"And then when you have that information safely tucked away? … All you have to do is take the field glasses and see where he leaves the beach. We could easily figure out whose house he has."

"I don't want to stand out in the rain just for that," she said. "And that wouldn't tell me his name."

"Why do you want to know his name? I thought you just wanted to know whose house he has."

"I always like to know people's names when they arouse my curiosity."

"I must say I have damn little curiosity about a man that would wear one of those things. God, they're awful. And the worst of it is, people that wear them never wear good hats."

"You're a sartorial snob," said Betty Denning.

"Indeed I am, and that's hardly news."

"But you don't get anything out of it."

"Of course I do. I get a lot out of it. For instance, a man that wears one of those things isn't likely to be in my circle of friends or any of my friends' circle of friends."

"I know," she said. "I know all that. Therefore you've put your finger on it, why I'm curious about Mr. Plastic Rain Cover."

"How? Or why?"

"Should be obvious," she said. "Who among our circle of friends has rented their house to Mr. Plastic? He's been there now at least three days. Whose house is for rent this summer?"

"Nobody's, up in that direction. All the beach houses are occupied."

"Then who is he visiting?" she said.

"I think you'd better get on the horn and ask around. You could start by calling Fred at the police station."

"Oh, I wouldn't want to do that."

"Fred would know."

"No, I'll ask around more casually when I do the marketing."

"You really don't want to have your mystery spoiled."

"Perhaps," she said.

He began to sing. " 'Perhaps—she's putting on her wraps—perhaps—she's putting on her wraps perhaps.' Now may I finish Mr. Joseph Alsop?"

"Do," she said.

The three-day nor'easter came to an end in the middle of the afternoon, and they went for a swim. "God, the beach is positively filthy," he said.

"You could pick up some driftwood," she said.

"And put it all in a neat pile, and then some kids would come along for a beach picnic and steal it all. I'm through breaking my back for the little bastards."

"It's good exercise if you remember to bend your knees. Uh-oh. We're going to have company. Mr. Plastic Cover."

"I forgot to ask you. Did you find out anything about him?"

"Tell you later."

Mr. Plastic Cover, now not wearing a hat, came toward them. He had on bathing trunks and a Madras jacket. He was walking eastward, and now there could be no doubt that he would stop. "Good afternoon," he said.

"Good afternoon," they said.

"I was admiring your house earlier. That's your house, isn't it?"

"Yes it is," said Betty Denning.

"I was wondering, is it on the market?"

"No, not really," said Betty Denning.

"Not at *all*," said Denning. "We rented it last summer, but to friends."

"But you don't want to sell. Well, I don't blame you. Nice to see the sun out again."

"Very nice," said Denning.

"Well—pleasure talking to you," said Mr. Plastic Cover.

He moved on and when he was out of earshot Denning said, "What'd you find out?"

"He has the Warings' house for the rest of the season, but he's not renting it."

"Who is he?"

"He's supposed to be some relation of Mona Waring's. He seems to have plenty of money. He's from out west and he brought a car with a chauffeur and two of his own servants besides, a cook and a maid."

"You wouldn't think to look at him that he had that kind of money. Aren't the Warings coming down?"

"They were, but now they're going abroad instead. A sudden change of plans."

"A sudden deal with Mr. Hat Cover."

"We don't have to call him Mr. Hat Cover any more. His name is Joshua B. Simmons."

"Well, Joshua's going to be in the hospital with second degree burns if he doesn't stay out of the sun. Did you notice his legs, and his nose and forehead? Wow!"

"I don't think that was the sun. I think that's just Mr. Joshua B. Simmons. He put in a big order for liquor. I found that out. And he buys only the most expensive cuts at the meat market. He gets all the New York and Chicago papers and the air mail edition of the London *Times*. He's having five people down this weekend. And he rented one of the large boxes at the post office, the kind that they usually rent to stores."

"You did quite a job on him. Is he married?"

"I had no trouble at all. The natives were more than willing to talk about him. Naturally they all speak well of him. He's spending money. This is his first summer on Long Island. I haven't answered your question about his marital status because I didn't do so well there. Nobody seems to know. The cook does the marketing by telephone. I guess Mona gave her the names of all the clerks."

"Why would he be interested in buying our house?"

"I think that was just to make conversation."

"More than likely. Well, he's exhausted that topic, and now maybe he won't bother us any more."

"Oh, don't be too hopeful. Tomorrow I'm going to the library and look him up in *Who's Who*. I've become fascinated by him."

Betty Denning was not the only one who was fascinated by Joshua B. Simmons. It soon transpired that he was asking owners of all the most desirable summer houses if their places were for sale, invariably getting no for an answer, and always commenting that he did not blame them. "I don't think he wants to buy," said Betty Denning. "I think it's just a conversational gambit he thought up."

The Warings apparently had made some arrangement for Mr. Simmons to be, in Betty Denning's word, whisked into the golf club and the beach club. It had not been difficult; as soon as his name came up some of the governors recognized it; he was on the board of one of the big Chicago banks and of other imposing corporations. "He was graduated from the University of Chicago," Betty Denning told her husband. "I've never known anyone that graduated from the University of Chicago, have you?"

"Walter Eckersall. Eckie. Great football player before my time, but then he used to officiate. He let me stay in a game once when he could have put me out. There was a Princeton guard named Marlow that was holding me on every play, and I finally smacked him one. Eckie saw me do it and he said to me, 'All right, he had it coming to him, but don't do that again.' And I didn't."

"Was that Tubby Marlow?"

"Yes."

"You didn't hit him hard enough. Anyway, Mr. Joshua B. Simmons is sixty-four years old and not married. Do you want to know what he belongs to?"

"Sure."

"Well, a whole list of clubs in Chicago, and Phi Beta Kappa, and something called Sigma Nu. Unfortunately the *Who's Who* in the village library isn't very up-to-date. In fact, 1940. Nothing about the war, and of course he could have got married since 1940, but I doubt it."

"So do I."

"Do you think the same thing I do?"

"Yes. I think he's a fag."

"You mean his walk?" said Betty Denning.

"Everything about him, not only his walk. I think he's an old queen."

"Well, you're right. I told you he was having five guests last weekend. He did. All men."

"Well, I hope that's not any criterion. I've had five men here during the duck-shooting."

"Huh. That's not what I worry about when you have five men here. Quite the opposite."

"I've never had any women here when you weren't here, and so stop your innuendoes. What about Mr. Simmons and his house party?"

"I'll get to it. Three of the men were young, two of them were about the same age as Simmons."

"Well, that's handy. They could square-dance."

"They would have been better off if they had. Saturday night they all got very tight and went for a moonlight dip without any clothes on. Old Mrs. Howard was kept awake all night and she reported them to Fred. You can imagine her, looking out and seeing six naked men and looking around for six naked women. Fred and one of the other policemen went up to investigate, but by that time they'd all got in cars and gone some place else. But Mr. Simmons has been given his first warning."

"Fred tell you all this?"

"He didn't tell me but he told Jim Carter and Peg relayed it to me. Jim is boiling mad at the Warings, especially Mona."

"Maybe she didn't know about her uncle, or whatever he is."

"Uncle is right. Her mother's brother. No, I can't go along with that. Mona's never liked it here much, and I think she and Billy just took off for Europe and let Uncle Joshua run riot. You can't tell me *Billy* doesn't know about Uncle Joshua."

"No, I guess not. But Billy will overlook anything if he can make a buck out of it, and I imagine Uncle Joshua sends a few bucks his way. He's probably Simmons's New York broker, and if there's thirty-five cents in it, Billy wouldn't care what the old guy did."

"He's having another houseful this weekend, Mr. Simmons."

"I wonder why we haven't seen him on the beach?" said Denning.

"Oh, I've seen him, when you were taking your nap. He prances by, always looks up, but he doesn't see me. Maybe he has his eye on you, dear."

"Maybe. I've always been popular with both sexes. Next time he walks by, wave to him."

"I will not. I don't find the situation very funny. I love this old place, and when an old pansy and his pansy friends start coming here, things aren't the same."

"Things aren't the same anyway, old girl, as you well know. No, it isn't a funny situation. I'm glad our boys are grown up and married."

"Well, Jim and Peg wish theirs were. The thing is that this nasty old man has been inquiring about properties, and the first thing you know we'll have a colony of them. That'll be the end of this place."

"You thought Simmons was just making conversation."

"I was wrong. He made a firm offer to the Ludlows. Forty-five thousand, and they may take him up."

"They wouldn't! Well, maybe they would. They're not getting any younger and their children don't come here any more. Good God, that would bring Simmons that much closer to our house."

"Why don't you and Jim Carter buy the Ludlows', as an investment?"

"I'm afraid that isn't the solution. We might be able to beat him to it on the Ludlow property, but Jim and I can't go on buying every property Simmons bids on."

"What is the solution?"

"There is none. With the best of good will in the world, people like the Ludlows can't afford to let sentiment, nostalgia, interfere."

"You mean that pansy's going to win? He's going to take over and ruin this lovely old place, where we've had such good times? I can't bear it."

"I've often said to you, the Lord doesn't care much about money. Look who He allows to have it."

"That's no comfort, I must say."

"I didn't offer it as comfort, Betty. We're not young ourselves, so let's try to enjoy this summer and next. After that? Well...."

"You wouldn't *sell*?"

"I wouldn't *not* sell if the Simmons types get a toehold."

"Oh, no! Can't we *do* something?"

"Suggest something."

"Let's just kill Mr. Simmons."

"In some ways, the only sensible solution." He squeezed her hand. "You wouldn't even kill a shark."

"What good does it do? Kill the shark, and it only attracts a lot of other sharks."

"Well, we've had a lot of good years here. Between us close to eighty."

"The sixty together were the best. I mean thirty."

On the next Sunday night Mr. Joshua B. Simmons, of Chicago, was murdered. He was stabbed in the chest and neck repeatedly by a young man named Charles W. Randolph. It was all on the radio and in the papers, in time, in fact, for the Monday morning papers.

"Do you know who that is?" said Betty Denning. "That's the boy they call Dipstick Charley, he's always so polite when we get gas. Do you know which one I mean?"

"Sure." Denning was reading the newspaper account of the murder, which differed very little from accounts of similar murders in similar circumstances. The millionaire Chicagoan had taken friends to the station to put them on the Sunday evening train to New York. He had then, according to police, gone to a "cocktail lounge" and there encountered Randolph, whom he invited to his fashionable beach residence for a drink. He made overtures to Randolph, who claimed to have repulsed him, and a scuffle occurred, during which Randolph stabbed him, using a dagger-like letter opener. Randolph then fled in the murdered man's Cadillac sedan and was arrested by state police who suspected him of driving a stolen car. Randolph was brought back to the Simmons beach house, reenacted the crime, and signed a full confession. He was being held without bail in the county prison. There were photographs of Randolph in his army uniform and of Simmons in a business suit, of the dagger-like letter opener and of the beach house and Simmons's Cadillac, and of Randolph in custody between Fred and a state policeman.

Even the tabloids could not keep the story built up for more than the fourth day. "Poor old Mrs. Howard's had a heart attack," said Betty Denning. "She's over at the clinic. Reporters and photographers and you have no idea how many morbid people, mistaking her house for the Warings'."

"They've started to come here."

"What on earth for?"

"The sharks. Do you remember what you said about killing a shark—it only attracts other sharks?"

"Oh, don't remind me."

"It was a very astute remark. While you were doing the marketing I had a caller. He wanted to know if this house was for sale. I said no, and he said he'd been given to understand by a certain friend of his that maybe we might sell. I asked him who the friend was, and he said, 'Well if you must know, it was Josh—Josh Simmons, poor boy.' Poor boy."

"What did you say?"

"I said, 'You get your ass out of here before I kick you out.' He said, 'Oh, you wouldn't do that, would you?' So I showed him I would."

"You kicked him?"

"Of course I kicked him. He won't be back, but others like him will be. You were certainly right about the sharks."

"Oh, dear. Oh, dear," she said.

Ties

Desmond Hogan

Exile is, among other things, a state of mind. The physical wrenching from attachments, the distance in actual miles of land and sea from the place we call our own, is perhaps less ruinous than banishment from the geography of language and feelings and ideas that are essentially our nationality. Exile is a punishment not because one part of the world is in any fundamental way different from another but because of the extraordinary multiplicity of customs of thought. It is these foreign customs that create the strange lands in which we are all strangers.

Exile seems to be an especially Irish occupation. It begins in the dawn of Celtic literature, with the exile of Fergus in Táin Bó Cuailnge, *written in the seventh century; it does not end with the famous exiles of Joyce and Beckett in Paris. In "Ties", Desmond Hogan has given his Irish protagonists several forms of exile, a sort of exile's hell of concentric circles that progress from physical loss to far darker forms of absence. In varying degrees, they suffer exile from the countryside, from their people's lore, from family and business, from Dublin, and ultimately from the objects of their sexual desire. In the end, however, there are those who survive, reconstructing through words worlds lost in time and distance.*

I

The Forty Steps led nowhere. They were grey and wide, shadowed at the sides by creeper and bush. In fact it was officially declared by Patsy Fogarthy that there were forty-four steps. These steps were erected by an English landlord in memorial to some doubtful subject. A greyhound, a wife? If you climbed them you had a view of the recesses of the woods and the places where Patsy Fogarthy practised with his trombone. Besides playing—in a navy uniform—in the brass band Patsy Fogarthy was my father's shop assistant. While the steps were dark grey the counter in my father's shop was dark and fathomless. We lived where the town men's Protestant society had once been and that was where our shop was too. And still is. Despite the fact my father is dead. My father bought the house, built the shop from nothing—after a row with a brother with whom he shared the traditional family grocery-cum-bar business. Patsy Fogarthy was my father's first shop assistant. They navigated waters together. They sold silk ties, demonstrating them carefully to country farmers.

Patsy Fogarthy was from the country, had a tremendous welter of tragedy in his family—which always was a point of distinction—deranged aunts, a paralysed mother. We knew that Patsy's house—cottage—was in the country. We never went there. It was just a picture. And in the cottage in turn in my mind were many pictures—paintings, embroideries by a prolific local artist who took to embroidery when she was told she was destined to die from leukaemia. Even my mother had one of her works. A bowl of flowers on a firescreen. From his inception as part of our household it seems that Patsy had allied himself towards me. In fact he'd been my father's assistant from before I was born. But he dragged me on walks, he described linnets to me, he indicated ragwort, he seated me on wooden benches in the hall outside town opposite a line of sycamores as he puffed into his trombone, as his fat stomach heaved into it. Patsy had not always been fat. That was obvious. He'd been corpulent, not fat. "Look," he said one day on the avenue leading to the Forty Steps—I was seven—"A blackbird about to burst into song."

Patsy had burst into song once. At a St. Patrick's night concert. He sang "Patsy Fagan". Beside a calendar photograph of a woman at the back of our shop he did not sing for me but recited poetry. "The Ballad of Athlone". The taking of the bridge of Athlone by the Williamites in 1691 had dire consequences for this area. It implanted it forevermore with Williamites. It directly caused the Irish defeat at Aughrim. Patsy lived in the shadow of the hills of Aughrim. Poppies were the consequence of battle. There were balloons of defeat in the air. Patsy Fogarthy brought me a gift of mushrooms once from the fields of Aughrim.

Patsy had a bedding of blackberry curls about his cherubic face; he had cherubic lips and smiled often; there was a snowy sparkle in his deep-blue eyes. Once he'd have been exceedingly good-looking. When

I was nine his buttocks slouched obesely. Once he'd have been as the man in the cigarette advertisements. When I was nine on top of the Forty Steps he pulled down his jaded trousers as if to pee, opened up his knickers and exposed his gargantuan balls. Delicately I turned away. The same year he tried to put the same penis in the backside of a drummer in the brass band, or so trembling, thin members of the Legion of Mary vouched. Without a murmur of a court case Patsy was expelled from town. The boy hadn't complained. He'd been caught in the act by a postman who was one of the church's most faithful members in town. Patsy Fogarthy crossed the Irish Sea, leaving a trail of mucus after him.

II

I left Ireland for good and all 11 October, 1977. There'd been many explanations for Patsy's behaviour: an aunt who used to have fits, throwing her arms about like seven snakes; the fact he might really have been of implanted Williamite stock. One way or the other he'd never been quite forgotten, unmentioned for a while, yes, but meanwhile the ecumenical movement had revived thoughts of him.

My mother attended a Protestant service in St. Matthias's church in 1976. As I left home she pressed a white, skeletal piece of paper into my hands. The address of a hospital where Patsy Fogarthy was now incarcerated. The message was this: "Visit him. We are now Christian (we go to Protestant services) and if not forgiven he can have some alms." It was now one could go back that made people accept him a little. He'd sung so well once. He smiled so cheerily. And sure wasn't there the time he gave purple Michaelmas daisies to the dying and octogenarian and well-nigh crippled Mrs. Connaughton (she whose husband left her and went to America in 1927).

I did not bring Patsy Fogarthy purple Michaelmas daisies. In the house I was staying in in Battersea there were marigolds. Brought there regularly by myself. Patsy was nearby in a Catholic hospital in Wandsworth. Old clay was dug up. Had my mother recently been speaking to a relative of his? A casual conversation on the street with a country woman. Anyway this was the task I was given. There was an amber, welcoming light in Battersea. Young deer talked to children in Battersea Park. I crept around Soho like an escaped prisoner. I knew there was something connecting then and now, yes, a piece of paper, connecting the far-off, starched days of childhood to an adulthood which was confused, desperate but determined to make a niche away from family and all friends that had ensued from a middle-class Irish upbringing. I tiptoed up bare wooden stairs at night, scared of waking those who'd given me lodging. I tried to write to my mother and then I remembered the guilty conscience on her face.

Gas works burgeoned into the honey-coloured sky, oblivious of the landscape inside me, the dirty avenue cascading on the Forty Steps.

"Why do you think they built it?"

"To hide something."

"Why did they want to hide something?"

"Because people don't want to know about some things."

"What things?"

Patsy had shrugged, a fawn coat draped on his shoulders that day.

"Patsy, I'll never hide anything."

There'd been many things I'd hidden. A girlfriend's abortion. An image of a little boy inside myself, a blue and white striped T-shirt on him. The mortal end of a relationship with a girl. Desire for my own sex. Loneliness. I'd tried to hide the loneliness, but Dublin, city of my youth, had exposed loneliness like a neon at evening. I'd hidden a whole part of my childhood, the 1950s, but hitting London took them out of the bag. Irish pubs in London, their jukeboxes, united the 1950s with the 1970s with a kiss of a song. "Patsy Fagan". Murky waters wheezed under a mirror in a pub lavatory. A young man in an Italian-style duffle coat, standing erect, eddied into a little boy being tugged along by a small fat man.

"Patsy what is beauty?"

"Beauty is in the eye of the beholder."

"But what is it?"

He looked at me. "Pretending we're father and son now."

I brought Patsy Fogarthy white carnations. It was a sunny afternoon early in November. I'd followed instructions on a piece of paper. Walking into the demesne of the hospital I perceived light playing in a bush. He was not surprised to see me. He was a small, fat, bald man in pyjamas. His face and his baldness were a carnage of reds and purples. Little wriggles of grey hair stood out. He wore maroon and red striped pyjamas. He gorged me with a look. "You're—" I did not

want him to say my name. He took my hand. There was death in the
intimacy. He was in a hospital for the mad. He made a fuss of being
grateful for the flowers. "How's Georgina?" He called my mother by
her first name. "And Bert?" My father was not yet dead. It was as if
he was charging them with something. Patsy Fogarthy, our small-
town Oscar Wilde, reclined in pyjamas on a chair against the shimmering citadels of Wandsworth. A white nun infrequently scurried in
to see to some man in the corridor. "You made a fine young man." "It
was the band I missed most." "Them were the days." In the middle of
snippets of conversation—he sounded not like an Irish bank clerk,
aged though and more graven-voiced—I imagined the tableau of love,
Patsy with a young boy. "It was a great old band. Sure you've been
years out of the place now. What age are ye? Twenty-six. Do you have
a girlfriend? The English girls will be out to grab you now." A plane
noisily slid over Wandsworth. We simultaneously looked at it. An old,
swede-faced man bent over a bedside dresser. "Do ya remember me? I
used to bring you on walks." Of course I said. Of course. "It's not
true what they said about us. Not true. They're all mad. They're all
lunatics. How's Bert?" Suddenly he started shouting at me. "You
never wrote back. You never wrote back to my letters. And all the
ones I sent you." More easy-voiced he was about to return the flowers
until he suddenly avowed. "They'll be all right for Our Lady. They'll
be all right for Our Lady." Our Lady was a white statue, over
bananas and pears, by his bed.

III

It is hot summer in London. Tiger lilies have come to my door. I'd
never known Patsy had written to me. I'd never received his letters of
course. They'd curdled in my mother's hand. All through my adolescence. I imagined them filing in, never to be answered. I was Patsy's
boy. More than the drummer lad. He had betrothed himself to me.
The week after seeing him, after being virtually chased out of the
ward by him, with money I'd saved up in Dublin, I took a week's holiday in Italy. The *trattorias* of Florence in November illumined the
face of a young man who'd been Patsy Fogarthy before I'd been born.
It's now six years on and that face still puzzles me, the face I saw in
Florence, a young man with black hair, and it makes a story that

solves a lot of mystery for me. There's a young man with black hair in a scarlet tie but it's not Patsy. It's a young man my father met in London in 1939, the year he came to study tailoring. Perhaps now it's the summer and the heat and the picture of my father on the wall—a red and yellow striped tie on him—and my illimitable estrangement from family but this city creates a series of ikons this summer. Patsy is one of them. But the sequence begins in the summer of 1939.

Bert ended up on the wide pavements of London in the early summer of 1939. He came from a town in the Western Midlands of Ireland whose wide river had scintillated at the back of town before he left and whose handsome façades radiated with sunshine. There were girls left behind that summer and cricket matches. Bert had decided on the tailoring course after a row with an older brother with whom he'd shared the family grocery-cum-bar business. The family house was one of the most sizeable on the street. Bert had his eyes on another house to buy now. He'd come to London to forge a little bit of independence from family for himself and in so doing he forwent some of the pleasures of the summer. Not only had he left the green cricket fields by the river but he had come to a city that exhaled news bulletins. He was not staying long.

He strolled into a cavern of death for behind the cheery faces of London that summer was death. Bert would do his course in Cheapside and not linger. Badges pressed against military lapels, old dishonours to Ireland. Once Bert had taken a Protestant girl out. They sailed in the bumpers at the October fair together. That was the height of his forgiveness for England. He did not consider playing cricket a leaning to England. Cricket was an Irish game, pure and simple, as could be seen from its popularity in his small, Protestant-built town.

Living was not easy for Bert in London; an Irish landlady—she was from Armagh, a mangy woman—had him. Otherwise the broth of his accent was rebuffed. He stooped a little under English disdain, but his hair was still orange and his face ruddy in fragments. By day Bert travailed; a dusty, dark cubicle. At evenings he walked. It was the midsummer which made him raise his head a little.

Twilight rushing over the tops of the trees at the edge of Hyde Park made him think of his dead parents, Galway people. He was suddenly both proud of and abstracted by his lineage. A hat was vaunted by his red hands on his waist. One evening, as perfumes and colours floated by, he thought of his mother, her tallness, her military posture, the black clothes she had always been stuffed into. In marrying her husband she declared she'd married a bucket. Her face looked a bit like a bucket itself.

Bert had recovered his poise. The width of his shoulders breathed again. His chest was out. It was that evening a young man wearing a scarlet tie stopped and talked to him under a particularly dusky tree by Hyde Park. "You're Irish," the young man had said. "How do you know?" "Those sparkling blue eyes." The young man had worn a kind of perfume himself. "You know," he said—his accent was very posh—"There's going to be a war. You would be better off in Ireland." Bert considered the information. "I'm here on a course." Between that remark and a London hotel there was an island of nothing. Masculine things for Bert had always been brothers pissing, the spray and the smell of their piss, smelly Protestants in the cricket changing rooms. That night Bert—how he became one he did not know—was a body. His youth was in the hands of an Englishman from Devon. The creaminess of his skin and the red curls of his hair had attained a new state for one night, that of an angel at the side of the Gothic steeple at home. There was beauty in Bert's chest. His penis was in the fist of another young man.

Marriage, children, a drapery business in Ireland virtually eliminated it all but they could not quite eliminate the choice colours of sin, red of handkerchiefs in men's pockets in a smoky hotel lounge, red of claret wine, red of blood on sheets where love-making was too violent. In the morning there was a single thread of a red hair on a pillow autographed in pink.

When my father opened his drapery business he ran it by himself for a while but on his marriage he felt the need for an assistant and Patsy was the first person who presented himself for the job. It was Patsy's black hair, his child's lips, his Roman sky-blue eyes that struck a resonance in my father. Patsy came on an autumn day. My father was reminded of a night in London. His partnership with Patsy was a marital one. When I came along it was me over my brothers Patsy chose. He was passing on a night in London. The young man in London? He'd worn a scarlet tie. My father specialized in ties. Patsy wore blue and emerald ones to town dos. He was photographed for the *Connaught Tribune* in a broad, blue, black speckled one. His shy smile hung over the tie. Long years ago my mother knew there was something missing from her marriage to my father—all the earnest hot water jars in the world could not obliterate this knowledge. She was snidely suspicious of Patsy—she too had blackberry hair—and when Patsy's denouement came along it was she who expelled him from the shop, afraid for the part of her husband he had taken, afraid for the parcel of her child's emotions he would abduct now that adolescence was near. But the damage, the violation had been done. Patsy had twined my neck in a scarlet tie one sunny afternoon in the shop, tied it decorously and smudged a patient, fat, wet kiss on my lips.

The Cold Wind and the Warm

Ray Bradbury

When Ray Bradbury's Martian Chronicles *appeared in 1950, Mars became an accessible landscape. Its meticulous geography, its eventful history, the New Earth that its explorers created there while becoming the New Martians, had the absolute truth of perfect fiction. H.G. Wells, perhaps more than others, had discovered that the reality of science-fiction lay in the bothersome details of human life among its future inventions: the discomforts of being invisible, the petty angers and envies among travellers to the moon. To these, Bradbury added descriptions of the fantastic that are everyday and even commonplace, so that the extraordinary on Mars is less the invented machineries and contraptions than, once again, the human beings.*

Once back on Earth, Bradbury reversed the process. Everyday objects became extraordinary, commonplace landscapes turned into dreamscapes, the unexplainable burst into reality through invisible cracks. And amid all this walk ordinary human beings, in awe and wonder. In books like Dandelion Wine *and* The October Country, *the world seems fantastic without the reader knowing exactly why. In stories such as "The Cold Wind and the Warm", ordinary places such as the city of Dublin are described with the vocabulary of Oz or Mars, and the events that take place there, though perfectly normal, become as wonderful and mysterious as the fantasies imagined in Bradbury's science-fiction stories. For Bradbury, even though the future may hold unimaginable nightmares, our present is still capable of miracles such as the one recounted here.*

"Good God in heaven, what's that?"

"What's what?"

"Are you blind, man, look!"

And Garrity, elevator operator, looked out to see what the hall porter was staring at.

And in out of the Dublin morn, sweeping through the front doors of the Royal Hibernian Hotel, along the entryway and to the registry was a tall willowy man of some forty years followed by five short willowy youths of some twenty years, a burst of bird song, their hands flapping all about on the air as they passed, their eyes squinching, batting, and flickering, their mouths pursed, their brows enlightened and then dark, their color flushed and then pale, or was it both?, their voices now flawless piccolo, now flute, now melodious oboe but always tuneful. Carrying six monologues, all sprayed forth upon each other at once, in a veritable cloud of self-commiseration, peeping and twitting the discouragements of travel and the ardors of weather, the *corps de ballet* as it were flew, cascaded, flowed eloquently in a greater bloom of cologne by astonished hall porter and transfixed elevator man. They collided deliciously to a halt at the desk where the manager glanced up to be swarmed over by their music. His eyes made nice round o's with no centers in them.

"What," whispered Garrity, "was that?"

"You may well ask," said the porter.

At which point the elevator lights flashed and the buzzer buzzed. Garrity had to tear his eyes off the summery crowd and heft himself skyward.

"We," said the tall slender man with a touch of gray at the temples, "should like a room, please."

The manager remembered where he was and heard himself say, "Do you have reservations, sir?"

"Dear me, no," said the older man as the others giggled. "We flew in unexpectedly from Taormina," the tall man with the chiseled features and the moist flower mouth continued. "We were getting so awfully bored, after a long summer, and someone said, Let's have a complete change, let's do something wild. What? I said. Well, where's the most improbable place in the world? Let's name it and go there. Somebody said the North Pole, but that was silly. Then I cried, Ireland! Everyone fell down. When the pandemonium ceased we just scrambled for the airport. Now sunshine and Sicilian shorelines are like yesterday's lime sherbet to us, all melted to nothing. And here we are to do ... something *mysterious!*"

"Mysterious?" asked the manager.

"We don't know what it is," said the tall man. "But we shall know it when we see it, or it happens, or perhaps we shall have to make it happen, right, cohorts?"

The cohorts responded with something vaguely like tee-hee.

"Perhaps," said the manager, with good grace, "if you gave me some idea what you're looking for in Ireland, I could point out—"

"Goodness, no," said the tall man. "We shall just plummet forth with our intuitions scarved about our necks, taking the wind as 'twere and see what we shall tune in on. When we solve the mystery and find what we came to find, you will know of our discovery by the ululations and cries of awe and wonder emanating from our small tourist group."

"You can say *that* again," said the hall porter, under his breath.

"Well, comrades, let us sign in."

The leader of the encampment reached for a scratchy hotel pen, found it filthy, and flourished forth his own absolutely pure 14-carat solid gold pen with which in an obscure but rather pretty cerise calligraphy he inscribed the name DAVID followed by SNELL followed by dash and ending with ORKNEY. Beneath, he added "and friends."

The manager watched the pen, fascinated, and once more recalled his position in all this. "But, sir, I haven't said if we have space—"

"Oh, surely you must, for six miserable wanderers in sore need of respite from overfriendly airline stewardesses—one room would do it!"

"One?" said the manager, aghast.

"We wouldn't mind the crowd, would we, chums?" asked the older man, not looking at his friends.

No, they wouldn't mind.

"Well," said the manager, uneasily fumbling at the registry. "We just happen to have two adjoining—"

"*Perfecto!*" cried David Snell-Orkney.

And the registration finished, the manager behind the desk and the visitors from a far place stood regarding each other in a prolonged silence. At last the manager blurted, "Porter! Front! Take these gentlemen's luggage—"

But just then the hall porter ran over to look at the floor.

Where there was no luggage.

"No, no, none." David Snell-Orkney airily waved his hand. "We travel light. We're here only for twenty-four hours, or perhaps only twelve, with a change of underwear stuffed in our overcoats. Then back to Sicily and warm twilights. If you want me to pay in advance—"

"That's won't be necessary," said the manager, handing the keys to the hall porter. "Forty-six and forty-seven, please."

"It's done," said the porter.

And like a collie dog silently nipping the hooves of some woolly long-haired, bleating, dumbly smiling sheep, he herded the lovely bunch toward the elevator which wafted down just at that precise moment.

At the desk, the manager's wife came up, steel-eyed behind him. "Are you mad?" she whispered, wildly. "Why? Why?"

"All my life," said the manager, half to himself, "I have wished to see not one Communist but ten close by, not two Nigerians but twenty in their skins, not three cowboy Americans but a gross fresh from the saddle. So when six hothouse roses come in a bouquet, I could not resist potting them. The Dublin winter is long, Meg; this may be the only lit fuse in the whole year. Stand by for the lovely concussion."

"Fool," she said.

As they watched, the elevator, freighted with hardly more than the fluff from a blown dandelion, whisked up the shaft, away.

It was exactly at high noon that a series of coincidences occurred that tottered and swerved toward the miraculous.

Now the Royal Hibernian Hotel lies half between Trinity College, if you'll excuse the mention, and St. Stephen's Green, which is more like it, and around behind is Grafton Street, where you can buy silver, glass, and linen, or pink hacking coats, boots, and caps to ride off to the goddamned hounds, or better still duck in to Heeber Finn's pub for a proper proportion of drink and talk—an hour of drink to two hours of talk is about the best prescription.

Now the boys most often seen in Finn's are these: Nolan, you know Nolan; Timulty, who could forget Timulty; Mike MaGuire, surely *everyone's* friend; then there's Hannahan, Flaherty, Kilpatrick, and, on occasion, when God seems a bit untidy and Job comes to mind, Father Liam Leary himself, who strides in like Justice and glides forth like Mercy.

Well, that's the lot, and it's high noon, and out of the Hibernian Hotel front who should come now but Snell-Orkney and his canary five.

Which resulted in the first of a dumfounding series of confrontations.

For passing below, sore torn between the sweet shops and Heeber Finn's, was *Timulty* himself.

Timulty, as you recall, when Blight, Famine, Starvation, and other mean Horsemen drive him, works a day here or there at the post office. Now, idling along between dread employments, he smelled a smell as if the gates of Eden had swung wide again and him invited back in after a hundred million years. So Timulty looked up to see what made the wind blow out of the Garden.

And the wind, of course, was in tumult about Snell-Orkney and his uncaged pets.

"I tell you," said Timulty, years later, "I felt my eyes start as if I'd been given a good bash on the skull. A new part ran down the center of my hair."

Timulty, frozen to the spot, watched the Snell-Orkney delegation flow down the steps and around the corner. At which point he decided on sweeter things than candy and rushed the long way to Finn's.

At that instant, rounding the corner, Mr. David Snell-Orkney-plus-five passed a beggar-lady playing a harp in the street. And there, with nothing else to do but dance the time away, was Mike MaGuire himself, flinging his feet about in a self-involved rigadoon to "Lightly o'er the Lea." Dancing, Mike MaGuire heard a sound that was like the passing by of warm weather from the Hebrides. It was not quite a twittering nor a whirr, and it was not unlike a pet shop when the bell tinkles as you step in and a chorus of parakeets and doves start up in coos and light shrieks. But hear he did, above the sound of his own shoes and the pringle of harp. He froze in mid-jig.

As David Snell-Orkney-plus-five swept by all tropic smiled and gave him a wave.

Before he knew what he was doing, Mike waved back, then stopped and seized his wounded hand to his breast. "What the hell am I waving for?" he cried to no one. "I don't know them, *do* I?"

"Ask God for strength!" said the harpist to her harp and flung her fingers down the strings.

Drawn as by some strange new vacuum cleaner that swept all before it, Mike followed the Team down the street.

Which takes care of two senses now, the sense of smell and the use of the ears.

It was at the *next* corner that Nolan, leaving Finn's pub because of an argument with Finn himself, came around the bend fast and ran bang in to David Snell-Orkney. Both swayed and grabbed each other for support.

"Top of the afternoon!" said David Snell-Orkney.

"The Back Side of Something!" replied Nolan, and fell away, gaping to let the circus by. He had a terrible urge to rush back to Finn's. His fight with the owner of the pub was obliterated. He wished now to report upon this fell encounter with a feather duster, a Siamese cat, a spoiled Pekingese, and three others gone ghastly frail from undereating and overwashing.

The six stopped outside the pub looking up at the sign.

Ah, God, thought Nolan. They're going in. What will *come* of it? Who do I warn first? Them? Or Finn?

Then, the door opened. Finn himself looked out. Damn, thought Nolan, that spoils it! Now we won't be allowed to describe this adventure. It will be Finn this, Finn that, and shut up to us all! There was a long moment when Snell-Orkney and his cohorts looked at Finn. Finn's eyes did not fasten on them. He looked above. He looked over. He looked beyond.

But he *had* seen them, this Nolan knew. For now a lovely thing happened.

All the color went out of Finn's face.

Then an even lovelier thing happened.

All the color rushed back into Finn's face.

Why, cried Nolan to himself, he's ... *blushing!*

But still Finn refused to look anywhere save the sky, the lamps, the street, until Snell-Orkney trilled, "Sir, which way to St. Stephen's Green?"

"Jesus," said Finn and turned away. "Who knows *where* they put it, *this* week!" and slammed the door.

The six went on up the street, all smiles and delight, and Nolan was all for heaving himself through the door when a worse thing happened.

Garrity, the elevator operator from the Royal Hibernian Hotel, whipped across the sidewalk from nowhere. His face ablaze with excitement, he ran first into Finn's to spread the word.

By the time Nolan was inside, and Timulty rushing in next, Garrity was all up and down the length of the bar while Finn stood behind it suffering concussions from which he had not as yet recovered.

"It's a shame you missed it!" cried Garrity to all. "I mean it was the next thing to one of them fiction-and-science fillums they show at the Gayety Cinema!"

"How do you mean?" asked Finn, shaken out of his trance.

"*Nothing* they weigh!" Garrity told them. "Lifting them in the elevator was throwing a handful of chaff up a chimney! And you should have *heard*. They're here in Ireland for ..." He lowered his voice and squinched his eyes. "... for *mysterious reasons!*"

"Mysterious!" Everyone leaned in at him.

"They'll put no name to it, but, mark my declaration, they're up to no good! Have you ever seen the like?"

"Not since the great fire at the convent," said Finn. "I—"

But word "convent" seemed one more magic touch. The doors sprang wide at this. Father Leary entered in reverse. That is to say he backed into the pub one hand to his cheek as if the Fates had dealt him a proper blow unbewares.

Reading the look of his spine, the men shoved their noses in their drinks until such time as the father had put a bit of the brew into himself, still staring as if the door were the gates of Hell ajar.

"Beyond," said the father, at last, "not two minutes gone, I saw a sight as would be hard to credit. In all the days of her collecting up the grievances of the world, has Ireland indeed gone mad?"

Finn refilled the priest's glass. "Was you standing in the blast of *The Invaders from the Planet Venus*, Father?"

"Have you seen them, then, Finn?" the father said.

"Yes, and do you guess them bad, your Holiness?"

"It's not so much bad or good as strange and *outré*, Finn, and words like rococo, I should guess, and baroque if you go with my drift?"

"I lie easy in the tide, sir."

"When last seen, where heading?" asked Timulty.

"On the edge of the Green," said the priest. "You don't imagine there'll be a bacchanal in the park now?"

"The weather won't allow, beg your pardon, Father," said Nolan, "but it strikes me, instead of standing with the gab in our mouth we should be out on the spy—"

"You move against my ethics," said the priest.

"A drowning man clutches at anything," said Nolan, "and ethics may drown with him if *that's* what he grabs instead of a lifebelt."

"Off the Mount, Nolan," said the priest, "and enough of the Sermon. What's your point?"

"The point is, Father, we have had no such influx of honorary Sicilians since the mind boggles to remember. For all we know, at this moment, they may be reading aloud to Mrs. Murphy, Miss Clancy, or Mrs. O'Hanlan in the midst of the park. And reading aloud from *what*, I ask you?"

"The Ballad of Reading Gaol?" asked Finn.

"You have rammed the target and sunk the ship," said Nolan, mildly irritated the point had been plucked from him. "How do we know these imps out of bottles are not selling real-estate tracts in a place called Fire Island? Have you *heard* of it, Father?"

"The American gazettes come often to my table, man."

"Well, do you remember the great hurricane of nineteen-and-fifty-six when the waves washed over Fire Island there in New York? An uncle of mine, God save his sanity and sight, was with the Coast Guard there which evacuated the entirety of the population of Fire Island. It was worse than the twice-a-year showing at Fennelly's dress-works, he said. It was more terrible than a Baptist Convention. Ten thousand men came rushing down to the stormy shore carrying bolts of drape material, cages full of parakeets, tomato-and-tangerine-colored sport coats, and lime-colored shoes. It was the most tumultuous scene since Hieronymus Bosch laid down his palette after he painted Hell for all generations to come. You do not easily evacuate ten thousand Venetian-glass boyos with their great blinky cow-eyes and their phonograph symphonic records in their hands and their rings in their ears, without tearing down the middle. My uncle, soon after, took to the heavy drink."

"Tell us *more* about that night," said Kilpatrick, entranced.

"More, hell," said the priest. "Out, I say. Surround the park. Keep your eyes peeled. And meet me back here in an hour."

"That's more like it," cried Kelly. "Let's *really* see what dread thing they're up to!"

The doors banged wide.

On the sidewalk, the priest gave directions. "Kelly, Murphy, you around the north side of the park. Timulty, you to the south. Nolan and Garrity, the east; Moran, MaGuire, and Kilpatrick, the west. Git!"

But somehow or other in all the ruction, Kelly and Murphy wound up

at the Four Shamrocks pub halfway to the Green and fortified themselves for the chase, and Nolan and Moran each met their wives on
the street and had to run the other way, and MaGuire and Kilpatrick,
passing the Elite Cinema and hearing Lawrence Tibbett singing inside,
cadged their way in for a few half-used cigarettes.

So it wound up with just two, Garrity on the east and Timulty on
the south side of the park, looking in at the visitors from another
world.

After half an hour of freezing weather, Garrity stomped up to Timulty and said, "What's *wrong* with the fiends? They're just *standing*
there in the midst of the park. They haven't moved half the afternoon.
And it's cut to the bone is my toes. I'll nip around to the hotel, warm
up, and rush back to stand guard with you, Tim."

"Take your time," called Timulty in a strange sad wandering,
philosophical voice as the other charged away.

Left alone, Timulty walked in and sat for a full hour watching the
six men who, as before, did not move. You might almost have
thought to see Timulty there, with his eyes brooding, and, his mouth
gone into a tragic crease, that he was some Irish neighbor of Kant or
Schopenhauer, or had just read something by a poet or thought of a
song that declined his spirits. And when at last the hour was up and
he had gathered his thoughts like a handful of cold pebbles, he turned
and made his way out of the park. Garrity was there, pounding his
feet and swinging his hands but before he could explode with questions, Timulty pointed in and said, "Go sit. Look. Think. Then *you*
tell *me*."

Everyone at Finn's looked up sheepishly when Timulty made his
entrance. The priest was still off on errands around the city, and after
a few walks about the Green to assuage their consciences, all had
returned, nonplussed, to intelligence headquarters.

"Timulty!" they cried. "Tell us! What? What?"

Timulty took his time walking to the bar and sipping his drink.
Silently, he observed his own image remotely buried beneath the lunar
ice of the barroom mirror. He turned the subject this way. He twisted
it inside out. He put it back wrong-side-to. Then he shut his eyes and
said:

"It strikes me as how—"

Yes, said all silently, about him.

"From a lifetime of travel and thought, it comes to the top of my mind," Timulty went on, "there is a strange resemblance between the likes of them and the likes of us."

There was such a gasp as changed the scintillation, the goings and comings of light in the prisms of the little chandeliers over the bar. When the schools of fish-light had stopped swarming at this exhalation, Nolan cried, "Do you mind putting your hat on so I can knock it off!?"

"Consider," Timulty calmly said. "Are we or are we not great ones for the poem and the song?"

Another kind of gasp went through the crowd. There was a warm burst of approval. "Oh, sure, we're *that!*" "My God, is *that* all you're up to?" "We were afraid—"

"Hold it!" Timulty raised a hand, eyes still closed.

And all shut up.

"If we're not singing the songs, we're writing them, and if not writing, dancing them, and aren't *they* fond admirers of the song and the writing of same and the dancing out the whole? Well, just now, I heard them at a distance reciting poems and singing, to themselves, in the Green."

Timulty had something there. Everyone had to paw everybody and admit it.

"Do you find any *other* resemblances?" asked Finn, heavily, glowering.

"I do," said Timulty, with a judge's manner.

There was a still more fascinated indraw of breath and the crowd drew nearer.

"They do not mind a drink now and then," said Timulty.

"By God, he's right!" cried Murphy.

"Also," intoned Timulty, "they do not marry until very late, if ever at all! And—"

But here the tumult was such he had to wait for it to subside before he could finish:

"And they—ah—have very little to do with women."

After that there was a great clamor, a yelling and shoving about and ordering of drinks and someone invited Timulty outside. But Timulty wouldn't even lift one eyelid, and the brawler was held off and when everyone had a new drink in them and the near-fistfights had drained away, one loud clear voice, Finn's, declared:

"Now would you mind explaining the criminal comparison you have just made in the clean air of my honourable pub?"

Timulty sipped his drink slowly and then at last opened his eyes and looked at Finn steadily, and said, with a clear bell-trumpet tone and wondrous enunciation:

"Where in all of Ireland can a man lie down with a woman?"

He let that sink in.

"Three hundred twenty-nine days a damn year it rains. The rest it's so wet there's no dry piece, no bit of land you would dare trip a woman out flat on for fear of her taking root and coming up in leaves, do you deny that?"

The silence did not deny.

"So when it comes to places to do sinful evils and perform outrageous acts of the flesh, it's to Arabia the poor damn fool Irishman must take himself. It's Arabian dreams we have, of warm nights, dry lands, and a decent place not just to sit down but to lie down on, and not just lie down on but to roister joyfully about on in clinches and clenches of outrageous delight."

"Ah, Jaisus," said Flynn, "you can say *that* again."

"Ah, Jaisus," said everyone, nodding.

"That's number one." Timulty ticked it off on his fingers. "Place is lacking. Then, second, time and circumstances. For say you should sweet talk a fair girl into the field, eh? in her rainboots and slicker and her shawl over her head and her umbrella over that and you making noises like a stuck pig half over the sty gate, which means you've got one hand in her bosom and the other wrestling with her boots, which is as far as you'll damn well get, for who's standing there behind you, and you feel his sweet spearmint breath on your neck?"

"The father from the local parish?" offered Garrity.

"The father from the local parish," said everyone, in despair.

"There's nails number two and three in the cross on which all Ireland's males hang crucified," said Timulty.

"Go on, Timulty, go on."

"Those fellows visiting here from Sicily run in teams. *We* run in teams. Here we are, the gang, in Finn's, are we *not*?"

"Be damned and we are!"

"*They* look sad and are melancholy half the time and then spitting like happy demons the rest, either up or down, never in between, and who does *that* remind you of?"

Everyone looked in the mirror and nodded.

"If we had the choice," said Timulty, "to go home to the dire wife and the dread mother-in-law and the old-maid sister all sour sweats and terrors, or stay here in Finn's for one more song or one more drink or one more story, *which* would all of us men choose?"

Silence.

"Think on that," said Timulty. "Answer the truth. Resemblances. Similarities. The long list of them runs off one hand and up the other arm. And well worth the mulling over before we leap about crying Jaisus and Mary and summoning the Guard."

Silence.

"I," said someone, after a long while, strangely, curiously, "would like ... to see them closer."

"I think you'll get your wish. Hist!"

All froze in a tableau.

And far off they heard a faint and fragile sound. It was like the wondrous morning you wake and lie in bed and know by a special feel that the first fall of snow is in the air, on its way down, tickling the sky, making the silence to stir aside and fall back in on nothing.

"Ah, God," said Finn, at last, "it's the first day of spring...."

And it was that, too. First the dainty snowfall of feet drifting on the cobbles, and then a choir of bird song.

And along the sidewalk and down the street and outside the pub came the sounds that were winter *and* spring. The doors sprang wide. The men reeled back from the impact of the meeting to come. They steeled their nerves. They balled their fists. They geared their teeth in their anxious mouths, and into the pub like children come into a Christmas place and everything a bauble or a toy, a special gift or color, there stood the tall thin older man who looked young and the small thin younger men who had old things in their eyes. The sound of snowfall stopped. The sound of spring birds ceased.

The strange children herded by the strange shepherd found themselves suddenly stranded as if they sensed a pulling away of a tide of people, even though the men at the bar had flinched but the merest hair.

The children of a warm isle regarded the short child-sized and runty full-grown men of this cold land and the full-grown men looked back in mutual assize.

Timulty and the men at the bar breathed long and slow. You could smell the terrible clean smell of the children way over here. There was too much spring in it.

Snell-Orkney and his young-old boy-men breathed swiftly as the heartbeats of birds trapped in a cruel pair of fists. You could smell the dusty, impacted, prolonged, and dark-clothed smell of the little men way over here. There was too much winter in it.

Each might have commented upon the other's choice of scent, but—

At this moment the double doors at the side banged wide and Garrity charged in full-blown, crying the alarm:

"Jesus, I've seen everything! Do you know where they are *now*, and what *doing?*"

Every hand at the bar flew up to shush him.

By the startled look in their eyes, the intruders knew they were being shouted about.

"They're still at St. Stephen's Green!" Garrity, on the move, saw naught that was before him. "I stopped by the hotel to spread the news. Now it's your turn. Those fellows—"

"Those fellows," said David Snell-Orkney, "are here in—" He hesitated.

"Heeber Finn's pub," said Heeber Finn, looking at his shoes.

"Heeber Finn's," said the tall man, nodding his thanks.

"Where," said Garrity, gone miserable, "we will all be having a drink instantly."

He flung himself at the bar.

But the six intruders were moving, also. They made a small parade to either side of Garrity and just by being amiably there made him hunch three inches smaller.

"Good afternoon," said Snell-Orkney.

"It is and it isn't," said Finn, carefully, waiting.

"It seems," said the tall man surrounded by the little boy-men, "there is much talk about what we are doing in Ireland."

"That would be putting the mildest interpretation on it," said Finn.

"Allow me to explain," said the stranger.

"Have you ever," continued Mr. David Snell-Orkney, "heard of the Snow Queen and the Summer King?"

Several jaws trapped wide down.

Someone gasped as if booted in the stomach.

Finn, after a moment in which he considered just where a blow might have landed on him, poured himself a long slow drink with scowling precision. He took a stiff snort of the stuff and with the fire in his mouth, replied, carefully, letting the warm breath out over his tongue:

"Ah ... *what* Queen is that again, *and* the King?"

"Well," said the tall pale man, "there was this Queen who lived in Iceland who had never seen summer, and this King who lived in the Isles of Sun who had never seen winter. The people under the King almost died of heat in the summers, and the people under the Snow Queen almost died of ice in the winters. But the people of both countries were saved from their terrible weathers. The Snow Queen and the Sun King met and fell in love and every summer when the sun killed people in the islands they moved North to the lands of ice and lived temperately. And every winter when the snow killed people in the North, all of the Snow Queen's people moved South and lived in the mild island sun. So there were no longer two nations, two peoples, but *one* race which commuted from land to land with the strange weathers and wild seasons. *The end.*"

There was a round of applause, not from the canary boys, but from the men lined up at the bar who had been spelled. Finn saw his own hands out clapping on the air, and put them down. The others saw their own hands and dropped them;.

But Timulty summed it up, "God, if you only had a brogue! What a teller of tales you would make."

"Many thanks, many thanks," said David Snell-Orkney.

"All of which brings us around to the point of the story," Finn said. "I mean, well, about that Queen and the King and all."

"The point is," said Snell-Orkney, "that we have not see a leaf fall in five years. We hardly know a cloud when we see it. We have not felt snow in ten years, or hardly a drop of rain. Our story is the reverse. We must have rain or we'll perish, right, chums?"

"Oh, yes, right," said all five, in a sweet chirruping.

"We have followed summer around the world for six or seven years. We have lived in Jamaica and Nassau and Port-au-Prince and Calcutta, and Madagascar and Bali and Taormina but finally just today we said we must go north, we must have cold again. We didn't quite know what we were looking for, but we found it in St. Stephen's Green."

"The *mysterious* thing?" Nolan burst out. "I mean—"

"Your friend here will tell you," said the tall man.

"Our friend? You mean—Garrity?"

Everyone looked at Garrity.

"As I was going to say," said Garrity, "when I came in the door. They was in the park standing there ... *watching the leaves turn colors.*"

"Is that *all?*" said Nolan, dismayed.

"It seemed sufficient unto the moment," said Snell-Orkney.

"*Are* the leaves changing color up at St. Stephen's?" asked Kilpatrick.

"Do you know," said Timulty numbly, "it's been twenty years since I *looked.*"

"The most beautiful sight in all the world," said David Snell-Orkney, "lies up in the midst of St. Stephen's this very hour."

"He speaks deep," murmured Nolan.

"The drinks are on me," said David Snell-Orkney.

"He's touched *bottom*," said MaGuire.

"Champagne all around!"

"Don't mind if I do!" said everyone.

And not ten minutes later they were all up at the park, together.

And well now, as Timulty said years after, did you ever see as many damned leaves on a tree as there was on the first tree just inside the gate at St. Stephen's Green? No! cried all. And what, though, about the *second* tree? Well, that had a *billion* leaves on it. And the more they looked the more they saw it was a wonder. And Nolan went around craning his neck so hard he fell over on his back and had to be helped up by two or three others, and there were general exhalations of awe and proclamations of devout inspiration as to the fact that as far as they could remember there had never *been* any goddamn leaves on the trees to begin with, but now they were there! Or if they had been there they had *never* had any color, or if they *had* had color, well, it was so long ago.... Ah, what the hell, shut up, said everyone, and look!

Which is exactly what Nolan and Timulty and Kelly and Kilpatrick and Garrity and Snell-Orkney and his friends did for the rest of the declining afternoon. For a fact, autumn had taken the country, and the bright flags were out by the millions through the park.

Which is exactly where Father Leary found them.

But before he could say anything, three out of the six summer invaders asked him if he would hear their confessions.

And next thing you know with a look of great pain and alarm the father was taking Snell-Orkney & Co. back to see the stained glass at the church and the way the apse was put together by a master architect, and they liked his church so much and said so out loud again and again that he cut way down on their Hail Marys and the rigamaroles that went with.

But the top of the entire day was when one of the young-old boy-men back at the pub asked what would it be? Should he sing "Mother Machree" or "My Buddy"?

Arguments followed, and with polls taken and results announced, he sang *both*.

He had a dear voice, all said, eyes melting bright. A sweet high clear voice.

And as Nolan put it, "He wouldn't make much of a son. But there's a great daughter there somewhere!"

And all said "aye" to that.

And suddenly it was time to leave.

"But great God!" said Finn, "you just arrived!"

"We found what we came for, there's no need to stay," announced the tall sad happy old young man. "It's back to the hothouse with the flowers ... or they wilt overnight. We never stay. We are always flying and jumping and running. We are always on the move."

The airport being fogged-in, there was nothing for it but the birds cage themselves on the Dun Laoghaire boat bound for England, and there was nothing for it but the inhabitants of Finn's should be down at the dock to watch them pull away in the middle of the evening. There they stood, all six, on the top deck, waving their thin hands down, and there stood Timulty and Nolan and Garrity and the rest waving their thick hands up. And as the boat hooted and pulled away the keeper-of-the-birds nodded once, and winged his right hand on the air and all sang forth: "*As I was walking through Dublin City, about the hour of twelve at night, I saw a maid, so fair was she ... combing her hair by candlelight.*"

"Jesus," said Timulty, "do you *hear*?"

"Sopranos, every *one* of them!" cried Nolan.

"Not Irish sopranos, but real *real* sopranos," said Kelly. "Damn, why didn't they *say*? If we'd known, we'd have had a good hour of *that* out of them before the boat."

Timulty nodded and added, listening to the music float over the waters, "Strange. Strange. I hate to see them go. Think. Think. For a hundred years or more people have said we had none. But now they have returned, if but for a little time."

"We had none of *what?*" asked Garrity. "And *what* returned?"

"Why," said Timulty, "the fairies, of course, the fairies that once lived in Ireland, and live here no more, but who came this day and changed our weather, and there they go again, who once stayed all the while."

"Ah, shut up!" cried Kilpatrick. "And listen!"

And listen they did, nine men on the end of a dock as the boat sailed out and the voices sang and the fog came in and they did not move for a long time until the boat was far gone and the voices faded like a scent of papaya on the mist.

By the time they walked back to Finn's it had begun to rain.

Southern Skies

David Malouf

Ancient tribes imagined the Earth to be made up of a number of immortal beings. The Jews imagined it to be the creation of a single god. Proponents of the Gaia theory described the Earth as one huge living creature whose skin is the dust we walk on (Conan Doyle foresaw this definition and had Professor Challenger prove it in "When the World Screamed"). However our planet is imagined, it seems as if we must believe that we are an integral part of its being, and that nothing takes place on Earth which is not reflected in us. Ruskin called this interweaving of our behaviour with that of the planet "the pathetic fallacy", and denounced it as false. "The state of mind which attributes to it [Nature] these characters of a living creature is one in which the reason is unhinged by grief."

And yet it is almost impossible not to recognize at times a kinship of feeling with our Earth. Whether the wind is furious because Lear is angry or perfumed because Cleopatra is in love is hard to say; the truth may be that our emotions are as difficult to define as the physical characteristics of Nature. In what is perhaps David Malouf's finest novel, An Imaginary Life, *the world is described as "a kind of library of forms", "another language whose hieroglyphs" we can "interpret and read". "It flickers all around us: it is water swamps, grass clumps, logs, branches; it is crowded with a thousand changing forms that shrill and sing and rattle and buzz." In the same way, Malouf's "Southern Skies" suggests that our memory best defines past emotions through the recollection of their setting. A place remembered, certain formations of the stars, a change in the weather somehow give a shape or a name to an experienced emotion, as if we require the world around us as a mirror for that which, being inside us, we cannot see.*

From the beginning he was a stumbling-block, the Professor. I had always thought of him as an old man, as one thinks of one's parents as old, but he can't in those days have been more than fifty. Squat, powerful, with a good deal of black hair on his wrists, he was what was called a "ladies man"—though that must have been far in the past and in another country. What he practised now was a formal courtliness, a clicking of heels and kissing of plump fingers that was the extreme form of a set of manners that our parents clung to because it belonged, along with much else, to the Old Country, and which we young people, for the same reason, found it imperative to reject. The Professor had a "position"—he taught mathematics to apprentices on day-release. He was proof that a breakthrough into the new world was not only possible, it was a fact. Our parents having come to a place where their qualifications in medicine or law were unacceptable, had been forced to take work as labourers or factory-hands or to keep dingy shops; but we, their clever sons and daughters, would find our way back to the safe professional classes. For our parents there was deep sorrow in all this, and the Professor offered hope. We were invited to see in him both the embodiment of a noble past and a glimpse of what, with hard work and a little luck or grace, we might claim from the future.

He was always the special guest.

"Here, pass the Professor this slice of Torte," my mother would say, choosing the largest piece and piling it with cream, or, "Here, take the Professor a nice cold Pils, and see you hand it to him proper now and don't spill none on the way": this on one of those community outings we used to go to in the early years, when half a dozen families would gather at Suttons Beach with a crate of beer bottles in straw jackets and a spread of homemade sausage and cabbage rolls. Aged six or seven, in my knitted bathing-briefs, and watching out in my bare feet for bindy-eye, I would set out over the grass to where the great man and my father, easy now in shirtsleeves and braces, would be pursuing one of their interminable arguments. My father had been a lawyer in the Old Country but worked now at the Vulcan Can Factory. He was passionately interested in philosophy, and the Professor was his only companion on those breathless flights that were, along with the music of Beethoven and Mahler, his sole consolation on the raw and desolate shore where he was marooned. Seeing me come wobbling towards them with the Pils—which I had slopped a little— held breast-high before me, all golden in the sun, he would look startled, as if I were a spirit of the place he had failed to allow for. It was the Professor who recognized the nature of my errand. "Ah, how kind," he would say. "Thank you, my dear. And thank the good mama too. Anton, you are a lucky man." And my father, reconciled to the earth again, would smile and lay his hand very gently on the nape of my neck while I blushed and squirmed.

The Professor had no family—or not in Australia. He lived alone in a house he had had built to his own design. It was of pinewood, as in the Old Country, and in defiance of local custom was surrounded by trees—natives. There was also a swimming pool where he exercised twice a day. I went there occasionally with my father, to collect him for an outing, and had sometimes peered at it through a glass door; but we were never formally invited. The bachelor did not entertain. He was always the guest, and what his visits meant to me, as to the children of a dozen other families, was that I must be especially careful of my manners, see that my shoes were properly polished, my nails clean, my hair combed, my tie straight, my socks pulled up, and that when questioned about school or about the games I played I should give my answers clearly, precisely, and without making faces.

So there he was all through my childhood, an intimidating presence, and a heavy reminder of that previous world; where his family owned a castle, and where he had been, my mother insisted, a real scholar.

Time passed and as the few close-knit families of our community moved to distant suburbs and lost contact with one another, we children were released from restriction. It was easy for our parents to give in to new ways now that others were not watching. Younger brothers failed to inherit our confirmation suits with their stiff white collars and cuffs. We no longer went to examinations weighed down with holy medals, or silently invoked, before putting pen to paper, the good offices of the Infant of Prague—whose influence, I decided, did not extend to Brisbane, Queensland. Only the Professor remained as a last link.

"I wish, when the Professor comes," my mother would complain, "that you try to speak better. The vowels! For my sake, darling, but also for your father, because we want to be proud of you," and she would try to detain me as, barefoot, in khaki shorts and an old T-shirt, already thirteen, I wriggled from her embrace. "And put shoes on, or sandals at least, and a nice clean shirt. I don't want that the Professor think we got an Arab for a son. And your Scout belt! And comb your hair a little, my darling—please!"

She kissed me before I could pull away. She was shocked, now that she saw me through the Professor's eyes, at how far I had grown from the little gentleman I might have been, all neatly suited and shod and brushed and polished, if they had never left the Old Country, or if she and my father had been stricter with me in this new one.

The fact is, I had succeeded, almost beyond my own expectations, in making myself indistinguishable from the roughest of my mates at school. My mother must have wondered at times if I could ever be smoothed out and civilized again, with my broad accent, my slang, my feet toughened and splayed from going barefoot. I was spoiled and wilful and ashamed of my parents. My mother knew it, and now, in front of the Professor, it was her turn to be ashamed. To assert my independence, or to show them that I did not care, I was never so loutish, I never slouched or mumbled or scowled so darkly as when the Professor appeared. Even my father, who was too dreamily involved with his own thoughts to notice me on most occasions, was aware of it and shocked. He complained to my mother, who shook her head and cried. I felt magnificently justified, and the next time the Professor made his appearance I swaggered even more outrageously and gave every indication of being an incorrigible tough.

The result was not at all what I had had in mind. Far from being repelled by my roughness the Professor seemed charmed. The more I showed off and embarrassed my parents, the more he encouraged me. My excesses delighted him. He was entranced.

He really was, as we younger people had always thought, a caricature of a man. You could barely look at him without laughing, and we had all become expert, even the girls, at imitating his hunched stance, his accent (which was at once terribly foreign and terribly English) and the way he held his stubby fingers when, at the end of a meal, he dipped sweet biscuits into wine and popped them whole into his mouth. My own imitations were designed to torment my mother.

"Oh you shouldn't!" she would whine, suppressing another explosion of giggles. "You mustn't! Oh stop it now, your father will see— he would be offended. The Professor is a fine man. May you have such a head on your shoulders one day, and such a position."

"Such a head on my shoulders," I mimicked, hunching my back like a stork so that I had no neck, and she would try to cuff me, and miss as I ducked away.

I was fifteen and beginning to spring up out of podgy childhood into clean-limbed, tumultuous adolescence. By staring for long hours into mirrors behind locked doors, by taking stock of myself in shop windows, and from the looks of some of the girls at school, I had discovered that I wasn't at all bad-looking, might even be good-looking, and was already tall and well-made. I had chestnut hair like my mother and my skin didn't freckle in the sun but turned heavy gold. There was a whole year between fifteen and sixteen when I was fascinated by the image of myself I could get back from people simply by playing up to them—it scarcely mattered whom: teachers, girls, visitors to the house like the Professor, passers-by in the street. I was obsessed with myself, and lost no opportunity of putting my powers to the test.

Once or twice in earlier days, when I was playing football on Saturday afternoon, my father and the Professor had appeared on the sidelines, looking in after a walk. Now, as if by accident, the Professor came alone. When I came trotting in to collect my bike, dishevelled, still spattered and streaked from the game, he would be waiting. He just happened, yet again, to be passing, and had a book for me to take home, or a message: he would be calling for my father at eight and could I please remind him, or yes, he would be coming next night to play Solo. He was very formal on these occasions, but I felt his interest; and sometimes, without thinking of anything more than the warm sense of myself it gave me to command his attention, I would walk part of the way home with him, wheeling my bike and chatting about nothing very important: the game, or what I had done with my holiday, or since he was a dedicated star-gazer, the new comet that had appeared. As these meetings increased I got to be more familiar with him. Sometimes, when two or three of the others were there (they had come to recognize him and teased me a little, making faces and jerking their heads as he made his way, hunched and short-sighted, to where we were towelling ourselves at the tap) I would for their benefit show off a little, without at first realizing, in my reckless passion to be admired, that I was exceeding all bounds and that they now included me as well as the Professor in their humorous contempt. I was mortified. To ease myself back into their good opinion I passed him off as a family nuisance, whose attentions I knew were comic but whom I was leading on for my own amusement. This was acceptable enough and I was soon restored to popularity, but felt doubly treacherous. He was, after all, my father's closest friend, and there was as well that larger question of the Old Country. I burned with shame, but was too cowardly to do more than brazen things out.

For all my crudeness and arrogance I had a great desire to act nobly, and in this business of the Professor I had miserably failed. I decided to cut my losses. As soon as he appeared now, and had announced his message, I would mount my bike, sling my football boots over my shoulder and pedal away. My one fear was that he might inquire what the trouble was, but of course he did not. Instead he broke off his visits altogether or passed the field without stopping, and I found myself regretting something I had come to depend on— his familiar figure hunched like a bird on the sidelines, our talks, some fuller sense of my own presence to add at the end of the game to the immediacy of my limbs after violent exercise.

Looking back on those days I see myself as a kind of centaur, half-boy, half-bike, forever wheeling down suburban streets under the poincianas, on my way to football practice or the library or to a meeting of the little group of us, boys and girls, that came together on someone's veranda in the evenings after tea.

I might come across the Professor then on his after-dinner stroll, and as often as not he would be accompanied by my father, who would stop me and demand (partly, I thought, to impress the Professor) where I was off to or where I had been; insisting, with more than his usual force, that I come home right away, with no argument.

On other occasions, pedalling past his house among the trees, I would catch a glimpse of him with his telescope on the roof. He might raise a hand and wave if he recognized me; and sprinting away, crouched low over the handlebars, I would feel, or imagine I felt, that the telescope had been lowered and was following me to the end of the street, losing me for a time, then picking me up again two streets further on as I flashed away under the bunchy leaves.

I spent long hours cycling back and forth between our house and my girlfriend Helen's or to Ross McDowell or Jimmy Larwood's, my friends from school, and the Professor's house was always on the route.

I think of those days now as being all alike, and the nights also: the days warmish, still, endlessly without event, and the nights quivering with expectancy but also uneventful, heavy with the scent of jasmine and honeysuckle and lighted by enormous stars. But what I am describing, of course, is neither a time nor a place but the mood of my own bored, expectant, uneventful adolescence. I was always abroad and waiting for something significant to occur, for life somehow to declare itself and catch me up. I rode my bike in slow circles or figures-of-eight, took it for sprints across the gravel of the park, or simply hung motionless in the saddle, balanced and waiting.

Nothing ever happened. In the dark of front verandas we lounged and swapped stories, heard gossip, told jokes, or played show-poker and smoked. One night each week I went to Helen's and we sat a little scared of one another in her garden-swing, touching in the dark. Helen liked me better, I thought, than I liked her—I had that power over her—and it was this more than anything else that attracted me, though I found it scary as well. For fear of losing me she might have gone to any one of the numbers that in those days marked the stages of sexual progress and could be boasted about, in a way that seemed shameful afterwards, in locker-rooms or round the edge of the pool. I could have taken us both to 6, 8, 10, but what then? The numbers were not infinite.

I rode around watching my shadow flare off gravel; sprinted, hung motionless, took the rush of warm air into my shirt; afraid that when the declaration came, it too, like the numbers, might be less than infinite. I didn't want to discover the limits of the world. Restlessly impelled towards some future that would at last offer me my real self, I nevertheless drew back, happy for the moment, even in my unhappiness, to be half-boy, half-bike, half aimless energy and half a machine that could hurtle off at a moment's notice in any one of a hundred directions. Away from things—but away, most of all, from my self. My own presence had begun to be a source of deep dissatisfaction to me, my vanity, my charm, my falseness, my preoccupation with sex. I was sick of myself and longed for the world to free me by making its own rigorous demands and declaring at last what I must be.

One night, in our warm late winter, I was riding home past the Professor's house when I saw him hunched as usual beside his telescope, but too absorbed on this occasion to be aware of me.

I paused at the end of the drive, wondering what it was that he saw on clear nights like this, that was invisible to me when I leaned my head back and filled my gaze with the sky.

The stars seemed palpably close. In the high September blueness it was as if the odour of jasmine blossoms had gathered there in a single shower of white. You might have been able to catch the essence of it floating down, as sailors, they say, can smell new land whole days before they first catch sight of it.

What I was catching, in fact, was the first breath of change—a change of season. From the heights I fell suddenly into deep depression, one of those sweet-sad glooms of adolescence that are like a bodiless drifting out of yourself into the immensity of things, when you are aware as never again—or never so poignantly—that time is moving swiftly on, that a school year is very nearly over and childhood finished, that you will have to move up a grade at football into a tougher class—shifts that against the vastness of space are minute, insignificant, but at that age solemnly felt.

I was standing astride the bike, staring upwards, when I became aware that my name was being called, and for the second or third time. I turned my bike into the drive with its border of big-leafed saxifrage and came to where the Professor, his hand on the telescope, was leaning out over the roof.

"I have some books for your father," he called. "Just come to the gate and I will get them for you."

The gate was wooden, and the fence, which made me think of a stockade, was of raw slabs eight feet high, stained reddish-brown. He leaned over the low parapet and dropped a set of keys.

"It's the thin one," he told me. "You can leave your bike in the yard." He meant the paved courtyard inside, where I rested it easily against the wall. Beyond, and to the left of the pine-framed house, which was stained the same colour as the fence, was a garden taken up almost entirely by the pool. It was overgrown with dark tropical plants, monstera, hibiscus, banana-palms with their big purplish flowers, glossily pendulous on stalks, and fixed to the pailing-fence like trophies in wads of bark, elk-horn, tree-orchids, showers of delicate maidenhair. It was too cold for swimming, but the pool was filled and covered with a shifting scum of jacaranda leaves that had blown in from the street, where the big trees were stripping to bloom.

I went round the edge of the pool and a light came on, reddish, in one of the inner rooms. A moment later the Professor himself appeared, tapping for attention at a glass door.

"I have the books right here," he said briskly; but when I stood hesitating in the dark beyond the threshold, he shifted his feet and added: "But maybe you would like to come in a moment and have a drink. Coffee. I could make some. Or beer. Or a Coke if you prefer it. I have Coke."

I had never been here alone, and never, even with my father, to this side of the house. When we came to collect the Professor for an outing we had always waited in the tiled hallway while he rushed about with one arm in the sleeve of his overcoat laying out saucers for cats, and it was to the front door, in later years, that I had delivered bowls of gingerbread fish that my mother had made specially because she knew he liked it, or cabbage rolls or herring. I had never been much interested in what lay beyond the hallway, with its fierce New Guinea masks, all tufted hair and boar's tusks, and the Old Country chest that was just like our own. Now, with the books already in my hands, I hesitated and looked past him into the room.

"All right. If it's no trouble."

"No no, no trouble at all!" He grinned, showing his teeth with their extravagant caps. "I am delighted. Really! Just leave the books there. You see they are tied with string, quite easy for you I'm sure, even on the bike. Sit where you like. Anywhere. I'll get the drink."

"Beer then," I said boldly, and my voice cracked, destroying what I had hoped might be the setting of our relationship on a clear, man-to-man basis that would wipe out the follies of the previous year. I coughed, cleared my throat, and said again "Beer, thanks," and sat abruptly on a sofa that was too low and left me prone and sprawling.

He stopped a moment and considered, as if I had surprised him by crossing a second threshold.

"Well then, if it's to be beer, I shall join you. Maybe you are also hungry. I could make a sandwich."

"No, no thank you, they're expecting me. Just the beer."

He went out, his slippers slushing over the tiles, and I shifted immediately to a straight-backed chair opposite and took the opportunity to look around.

There were rugs on the floor, old threadbare Persians, and low down, all round the walls, stacks of the heavy seventy-eights I carried home when my father borrowed them: sonatas by Beethoven, symphonies by Sibelius and Mahler. Made easy by the Professor's absence, I got up and wandered round. On every open surface, the glass table-top, the sideboard, the long mantel of the fireplace, were odd bits and pieces that he must have collected in his travels: lumps of coloured quartz, a desert rose, slabs of clay with fern or fish fossils in them, glass paperweights, snuff-boxes, meerschaum pipes of fantastic shape—one a Saracen's head, another the torso of a woman, like a ship's figurehead with full breasts and golden nipples—bits of Baltic amber, decorated sherds of pottery, black on terracotta, and one unbroken object, a little earthenware lamp that when I examined it more closely turned out to be a phallic grotesque. I had just discovered what it actually was when the Professor stepped into the room. Turning swiftly to a framed photograph on the wall above, I found myself peering into a stretch of the Old Country, a foggy, sepia world that I recognized immediately from similar photographs at home.

"Ah," he said, setting the tray down on an empty chair, "you have discovered my weakness." He switched on another lamp. "I have tried, but I am too sentimental. I cannot part with them."

The photograph, I now observed, was one of three. They were all discoloured with foxing on the passe-partout mounts, and the glass of one was shattered, but so neatly that not a single splinter had shifted in the frame.

The one I was staring at was of half a dozen young men in military uniform. It might have been from the last century, but there was a date in copperplate: 1921. Splendidly booted and sashed and frogged, and hieratically stiff, with casque helmets under their arms, swords tilted at the thigh, white gloves tucked into braided epaulettes, they were a chorus line from a Ruritanian operetta. They were also, as I knew, the heroes of a lost but unforgotten war.

"You recognize me?" the Professor asked.

I looked again. It was difficult. All the young men strained upright with the same martial hauteur, wore the same little clipped moustaches, had the same flat hair parted in the middle and combed in wings over their ears. Figures from the past can be as foreign, as difficult to identify individually, as the members of another race. I took the plunge, set my forefinger against the frame, and turned to the Professor for confirmation. He came to my side and peered.

"No," he said sorrowfully. "But the mistake is entirely understandable. He was my great friend, almost a brother. I am here. This is me. On the left."

He considered himself, the slim assured figure, chin slightly tilted, eyes fixed ahead, looking squarely out of a class whose privileges—inherent in every point of the stance, the uniform, the polished accoutrements—were not to be questioned, and from the ranks of an army that was invincible. The proud caste no longer existed. Neither did the army nor the country it was meant to defend, except in the memory of people like the Professor and my parents and, in a ghostly way, half a century off in another hemisphere, my own.

He shook his head and made a clucking sound. "Well," he said firmly, "it's a long time ago. It is foolish of me to keep such things. We should live for the present. Or like you younger people," bringing the conversation back to me, "for the future."

I found it easier to pass to the other photographs.

In one, the unsmiling officer appeared as an even younger man, caught in an informal, carefully posed moment with a group of ladies. He was clean-shaven and lounging on the grass in a striped blazer; beside him a discarded boater—very English. The ladies, more decorously disposed, wore long dresses with hats and ribbons. Neat little slippers peeped out under their skirts.

"Yes, yes," he muttered, almost impatient now, "that too. Summer holidays—who can remember where? And the other a walking trip."

I looked deep into a high meadow, with broken cloud-drift in the dip below. Three young men in shorts, maybe schoolboys, were climbing on the far side of the wars. There were flowers in the foreground, glowingly out of focus, and it was this picture whose glass was shattered; it was like looking through a brilliant spider's web into a picturebook landscape that was utterly familiar, though I could never have been there. *That is the place*, I thought. *That is the land my parents mean when they say "the Old Country": the country of childhood and first love that they go back to in their sleep and which I have no memory of, though I was born there. Those flowers are the ones, precisely those, that blossom in the songs they sing.* And immediately I was back in my mood of just a few minutes ago, when I had stood out there gazing up at the stars. *What is it,* I asked myself, *that I will remember and want to preserve, when in years to come I think of the Past? What will be important enough?* For what the photographs had led me back to, once again, was myself. It was always the same. No matter how hard I tried to think my way out into other people's lives, into the world beyond me, the feelings I discovered were my own.

"Come. Sit," the Professor said, "and drink your beer. And do eat one of these sandwiches. It's very good rye bread, from the only shop, I go all the way to South Brisbane for it. And Gürken. I seem to remember you like them."

"What do you do up on the roof?" I asked, my mouth full of bread and beer, feeling uneasy again now that we were sitting with nothing to fix on.

"I make observations, you know. The sky, which looks so still, is always in motion, full of drama if you understand how to read it. Like looking into a pond. Hundreds of events happening right under your eyes, except that most of what we see is already finished by the time we see it—ages ago—but important just the same. Such large events. Huge! Bigger even than we can imagine. And beautiful, since they unfold, you know, to a kind of music, to numbers of infinite dimension like the ones you deal with in equations at school, but more complex, and entirely visible."

He was moved as he spoke by an emotion that I could not identify, touched by occasions a million light-years off and still unfolding towards him, in no way personal. The room for a moment lost its tension. I no longer felt myself to be the focus of his interest, or even of my own. I felt liberated, and for the first time the Professor was interesting in his own right, quite apart from the attention he paid me or the importance my parents attached to him.

"Maybe I could come again," I found myself saying. "I'd like to see."

"But of course," he said, "any time. Tonight is not good—there is a little haze, but tomorrow if you like. Or any time."

I nodded. But the moment of easiness had passed. My suggestion, which might have seemed like another move in a game, had brought me back into focus for him and his look was quizzical, defensive. I felt it and was embarrassed, and at the same time saddened. Some truer vision of myself had been in the room for a moment. I had almost grasped it. Now I felt it slipping away as I moved back into my purely physical self.

I put the glass down, not quite empty.

"No thanks, really," I told him when he indicated the half finished bottle on the tray. "I should have been home nearly an hour ago. My mother, you know."

"Ah yes, of course. Well, just call whenever you wish, no need to be formal. Most nights I am observing. It is a very interesting time. Here—let me open the door for you. The books, I see, are a little awkward, but you are so expert on the bicycle I am sure it will be OK."

I followed him round the side of the pool into the courtyard and there was my bike at its easy angle to the wall, my other familiar and streamlined self. I wheeled it out while he held the gate.

Among my parents' oldest friends were a couple who had recently moved to a new house on the other side of the park, and at the end of winter, in the year I turned seventeen, I sometimes rode over on Sundays to help John clear the big overgrown garden. All afternoon we grubbed out citrus trees that had gone wild, hacked down morning-glory that had grown all over the lower part of the yard, and cut the knee-high grass with a sickle to prepare it for mowing. I enjoyed the work. Stripped down to shorts in the strong sunlight, I slashed and tore at the weeds till my hands blistered, and in a trancelike preoccupation with tough green things that clung to the earth with a fierce tenacity, forgot for a time my own turmoil and lack of roots. It was something to *do*.

John, who worked up ahead, was a dentist. He paid me ten shillings a day for the work, and this, along with my pocket-money, would take Helen and me to the pictures on Saturday night, or to a flash meal at one of the city hotels. We worked all afternoon, while the children, who were four and seven, watched and got in the way. Then about five-thirty Mary would call us for tea.

Mary had been at school with my mother and was the same age, though I could never quite believe it; she had children a whole ten years younger than I was, and I had always called her Mary. She wore bright bangles on her arm, liked to dance at parties, never gave me presents like handkerchiefs or socks, and had always treated me, I thought, as a grown-up. When she called us for tea I went to the garden tap, washed my feet, splashed water over my back that was streaked with soil and sweat and stuck all over with little grass clippings, and was about to buckle on my loose sandals when she said from the doorway where she had been watching: "Don't bother to get dressed. John hasn't." She stood there smiling, and I turned away, aware suddenly of how little I had on; and had to use my V-necked sweater to cover an excitement that might otherwise have been immediately apparent in the khaki shorts I was wearing—without underpants because of the heat.

As I came up the steps towards her she stood back to let me pass, and her hand, very lightly, brushed the skin between my shoulder blades.

"You're still wet," she said.

It seemed odd somehow to be sitting at the table in their elegant dining-room without a shirt; though John was doing it, and was already engaged like the children in demolishing a pile of neat little sandwiches.

I sat at the head of the table with the children noisily grabbing at my left and John on my right drinking tea and slurping it a little, while Mary plied me with raisin-bread and Old Country cookies. I felt red, swollen, confused every time she turned to me, and for some reason it was the children's presence rather than John's that embarrassed me, especially the boy's.

Almost immediately we were finished John got up.

"I'll just go," he said, "and do another twenty minutes before it's dark." It was dark already, but light enough perhaps to go on raking the grass we had cut and were carting to the incinerator. I made to follow. "It's all right," he told me. "I'll finish off. You've earned your money for today."

"Come and see our animals!" the children yelled, dragging me down the hall to their bedroom, and for ten minutes or so I sat on the floor with them, setting out farm animals and making fences, till Mary, who had been clearing the table, appeared in the doorway.

"Come on now, that's enough, it's bathtime, you kids. Off you go!"

They ran off, already half-stripped, leaving her to pick up their clothes and fold them while I continued to sit cross-legged among the toys, and her white legs, in their green sandals, moved back and forth at eye-level. When she went out I too got up, and stood watching at the bathroom door.

She was sitting on the edge of the bath, soaping the little boy's back, as I remembered my mother doing, while the children splashed and shouted. Then she dried her hands on a towel, very carefully, and I followed her into the unlighted lounge. Beyond the glass wall, in the depths of the garden, John was stooping to gather armfuls of the grass we had cut, and staggering with it to the incinerator.

She sat and patted the place beside her. I followed as in a dream. The children's voices at the end of the hallway were complaining, quarrelling, shrilling. I was sure John could see us through the glass as he came back for another load.

Nothing was said. Her hand moved over my shoulder, down my

spine, brushed very lightly, without lingering, over the place where my shorts tented; then rested easily on my thigh. When John came in he seemed unsurprised to find us sitting close in the dark. He went right past us to the drinks cabinet, which suddenly lighted up. I felt exposed and certain now that he must see where her hand was and say something.

All he said was: "Something to drink, darling?"

Without hurry she got up to help him and they passed back and forth in front of the blazing cabinet, with its mirrors and its rows of bottles and cut-crystal glasses. I was sweating worse than when I had worked in the garden, and began, self-consciously, to haul on the sweater.

I pedalled furiously away, glad to have the cooling air pour over me and to feel free again.

Back there I had been scared—but of what? Of a game in which I might, for once, be the victim—not passive, but with no power to control the moves. I slowed down and considered that, and was, without realizing it, at the edge of something. I rode on in the softening dark. It was good to have the wheels of the bike roll away under me as I rose on the pedals, to feel on my cheeks the warm scent of jasmine that was invisible all round. It was a brilliant night verging on spring. I didn't want it to be over; I wanted to slow things down. I dismounted and walked a little, leading my bike along the grassy edge in the shadow of trees, and without precisely intending it, came on foot to the entrance to the Professor's drive, and paused, looking up beyond the treetops to where he might be installed with his telescope—observing what? What events up there in the infinite sky?

I leaned far back to see. A frozen waterfall it might have been, falling slowly towards me, sending out blown spray that would take centuries, light-years, to break in thunder over my head. Time. What did one moment, one night, a lifespan mean in relation to all that?

"Hullo there!"

It was the Professor. I could see him now, in the moonlight beside the telescope, which he leaned on and which pointed not upward to the heavens but down to where I was standing. It occurred to me, as on previous occasions, that in the few moments of my standing there with my head flung back to the stars, what he might have been observing was *me*. I hesitated, made no decision. Then, out of a state of passive expectancy, willing nothing but waiting poised for my own life to occur; out of a state of being open to the spring night and to the emptiness of the hours between seven and ten when I was expected to be in, or thirteen (was it?) and whatever age I would be when man-hood finally came to me; out of my simply being there with my hand on the saddle of the machine, bare-legged, loose-sandalled, going nowhere, I turned into the drive, led my bike up to the stockade gate and waited for him to throw down the keys.

"You know which one it is," he said, letting them fall. "Just use the other to come in by the poolside."

I unlocked the gate, rested my bike against the wall of the court-yard and went round along the edge of the pool. It was clean now but heavy with shadows. I turned the key in the glass door, found my way (though this part of the house was new to me) to the stairs, and climbed to where another door opened straight on to the roof.

"Ah," he said, smiling. "So at last! You are here."

The roof was unwalled but set so deep among trees that it was as if I had stepped out of the city altogether into some earlier, more darkly-wooded era. Only lighted windows, hanging detached in the dark, showed where houses, where neighbours were.

He fixed the telescope for me and I moved into position. "There," he said, "what you can see now is Jupiter with its four moons—you see?—all in line, and with the bands across its face."

I saw. Later it was Saturn with its rings and the lower of the two pointers to the cross, Alpha Centauri, which was not one star but two. It was miraculous. From the moment below when I had looked up at a cascade of light that was still ages off, I might have been cata-pulted twenty thousand years into the nearer past, or into my own future. Solid spheres hovered above me, tiny balls of matter moving in concert like the atoms we drew in chemistry, held together by invisible lines of force; and I thought oddly that if I were to lower the telescope now to where I had been standing at the entrance to the drive I would see my own puzzled, upturned face, but as a self I had already out-grown and abandoned, not minutes but aeons back. He shifted the telescope and I caught my breath. One after another, constellations I had known since childhood as points of light to be joined up in the mind (like those picture-puzzles children make, pencilling in the scat-tered dots till Snow White and the Seven Dwarfs appear, or an old jalopy), came together now, not as an imaginary panhandle or bull's head or belt and sword, but at some depth of vision I hadn't known I possessed, as blossoming abstractions, equations luminously exploding out of their own depths, brilliantly solving themselves and playing the results in my head as a real and visible music. I felt a power in myself that might actually burst out at my ears, and at the same time saw myself, from *out there*, as just a figure with his eye to a lens. I had a clear sense of being one more hard little point in the immensity—but part of it, a source of light like all those others—and was aware for the first time of the grainy reality of my own life, and then, a fact of no large significance, of the certainty of my death; but in some dimension where those terms were too vague to be relevant. It was at the point where my self ended and the rest of it began that Time, or Space, showed its richness to me. I was overwhelmed.

Slowly, from so far out, I drew back, re-entered the present and was aware again of the close suburban dark—of its moving now in the shape of a hand. I must have known all along that it was there, working from the small of my back to my belly, up the inside of my thigh, but it was of no importance, I was too far off. Too many larger events were unfolding for me to break away and ask, as I might have, "What are you doing?"

I must have come immediately. But when the stars blurred in my eyes it was with tears, and it was the welling of this deeper salt, filling my eyes and rolling down my cheeks, that was the real overflow of the occasion. I raised my hand to brush them away and it was only then that I was aware, once again, of the Professor. I looked at him as from a distance. He was getting to his feet, and his babble of concern, alarm, self-pity, sentimental recrimination, was incomprehensible to me. I couldn't see what he meant.

"No no, it's nothing," I assured him, turning aside to button my shorts. "It was nothing. Honestly." I was unwilling to say more in case he misunderstood what I did not understand myself.

We stood on opposite sides of the occasion. Nothing of what he had done could make the slightest difference to me, I was untouched: youth is too physical to accord very much to that side of things. But what I had *seen*—what he had led me to see—my bursting into the life of things—I would look back on that as the real beginning of my existence, as the entry into a vocation, and nothing could diminish the gratitude I felt for it. I wanted, in the immense seriousness and humility of this moment, to tell him so, but I lacked the words, and silence was fraught with all the wrong ones.

"I have to go now," was what I said.

"Very well. Of course."

He looked hopeless. He might have been waiting for me to strike him a blow—not a physical one. He stood quietly at the gateway while I wheeled out the bike.

I turned then and faced him, and without speaking, offered him, very formally, my hand. He took it and we shook—as if, in the magnanimity of my youth, I had agreed to overlook his misdemeanour or forgive him. That misapprehension too was a weight I would have to bear.

Carrying it with me, a heavy counterpoise to the extraordinary lightness that was my whole life, I bounced unsteadily over the dark tufts of the driveway and out on to the road.

A Sky Full of Bright, Twinkling Stars

Pai Hsien-yung

Classical Chinese literature lacks a word for "homosexual". Instead of saying that someone "is" a homosexual, classic writers usually say what he does or enjoys, or use poetic metaphors drawn from celebrated early incidents of male intimacy. For example, to identify a man with the image of a cut sleeve was to allude to the illustrious example (taken from the historical literature of the Han dynasty) of the Emperor Ai, who awoke to find his lover stretched in mid-afternoon sleep across the imperial gown, and cut off the gown's flowing sleeve in order to rise without disturbing his beloved. Classical Chinese literature is generous in poetry, drama, and fiction depicting in positive and laudatory terms the rituals of male love.

With the arrival of Western missionaries and trade in the eighteenth century, the homosexual received a name and then was condemned for his sexuality. Since the time of the Cultural Revolution, the Party's official position has been that there are no homosexuals in China. Obviously, there are no examples of homosexual characters in contemporary Chinese fiction, except for that written in exile. The Taiwanese writer Pai Hsien-yung offers in "A Sky Full of Bright, Twinkling Stars" one of the few portrayals of the predicament of homosexuals in contemporary Chinese society. Pai's hero's stage-name, Chu Yen, is literally translated as "Crimson Flame", with all that such an image evokes, but a homonym of these Chinese characters alludes to the vermilion-painted face ("rouged cheeks") of a male warrior-actor in the traditional Chinese theatre. For the Chinese reader, Chu Yen carries within his very name the weight of both a dying acting tradition and a lost legacy of sanctioned intimacy between men.

It's always been like this. Always, he would wait until all the bright, twinkling stars in the sky slowly darkened and faded one by one before he would lean back against the stone balustrade around the lotus pond in New Park and begin to recite to us those ancient tales of his.

Maybe it's one of those stifling hot days in July or August; the ramblers in the park linger on and on, unwilling to leave, then we start to circle hurriedly around and around on the terrace surrounding the pond, treading on each other's shadows. In the thick, torrid darkness a tuft of white hair floats here, there a ravaged bald head sways, a stooped silhouette, anxiously on the prowl, beetles to and fro, until the last pair of eyes filled with desire vanishes into the murky grove; then, only then, do we start our gathering. By that time our legs are so exhausted we can hardly raise them.

We all call him "the Guru." Ah Hsiung the Primitive says that among his people, the aborigines, at the season when the first spring rain comes all the youths run naked into the rain and perform the Spring Sacrifice Dance and there will always be a white-haired, white-bearded elder presiding at the altar as the Chief Priest. Once we threw a dance party at Dark-and-Handsome's house in Wan Hua and Ah Hsiung the Primitive got drunk. He tore off all his clothes and started his tribal dance for the Spring Sacrifice. The Primitive is a strapping lad, dark and wild, with muscles bulging all over his body. He leaped around and flew through the air with abandon, his large aborigine eyes rolling like two balls of dark fire—our acting coach, Old Man Mo, says Ah Hsiung is a born martial-arts star for the movies—and the rest of us watched him, mesmerized. Then, yowling and roaring, we all ripped off our clothes and joined in the Spring Sacrifice Dance with him. We danced and danced, and suddenly Dark-and-Handsome sprang onto the table, his sinuous body undulating like crazy. In a voice piercing as a young cockerel's he declared, "We all belong to the Cult of the Spring Sacrifice!"

When you stop to think about it, who but the Guru could be our Guru? Sure, he belongs to our grandfathers' generation, yet there are plenty among those night sprites that roam the Park who outrank him in seniority. But they're a cheap lot; they haven't got the kind of style our Guru has that somehow inspires awe in people. After all, his is a unique past; in the thirties he was the biggest star under contract with the Galaxy Motion Picture Corporation in Shanghai—we have that from Dark-and-Handsome, who likes to worm his way into some of the old movie directors' homes and call their wives his godmothers.

According to Dark-and-Handsome, the Guru was a star of the first magnitude in the silent movie days; he once saw a still of the Guru in the role of T'ang Po-hu in the film classic "Three Smiles."

"You just wouldn't believe it …!" Dark-and-Handsome gasped, with his mouth popped open and his eyes rolled upwards.

But the Guru had been at the peak only a short time; once the talkies came in, he was eclipsed. He was a Southerner and couldn't speak Mandarin. At that time, Old Man Mo had told Dark-and-Handsome, everybody at the Galaxy Motion Picture Corporation poked fun at the Guru; they called him "Chu Yen, the Cardboard Lover." That night at the stone balustrade around the pond in the Park, we followed the Guru and started calling him by his professional name, Chu Yen—Crimson Flame. He turned abruptly, raised a forbidding finger and waved it at us vehemently.

"Chu Yen? Did you say Chu Yen?—He died a long time ago!"

We all began to laugh; we thought he was drunk, and indeed, the Guru had downed more than he could hold that night. His hoary mane stood out wildly, quivering in the wind; his eyebrows drew close together and made the three lines in his forehead deeper than ever. Have you ever seen furrows so deep on a person's face? It's as though they had been etched with a sharp-pointed knife, the three straight lines, right across his broad forehead, so deep that they appeared dark. He was tall and broad-shouldered; once he must have had a very impressive carriage, but now his back is bowed; he was always wrapped in an old topcoat of gray herringbone tweed; as he walked, his coat flapping in the wind gave you a sense of infinite desolation. But those strange eyes of his—what did they resemble, after all? In the dark, they were two orbs of burning emerald, they sent forth a flame that refused to die, like the eternal lamps in an ancient tomb.

"What are you laughing at?" he shouted at us. "Do you think you're going to live forever?" He walked over and jabbed a finger at Ah Hsiung the Primitive's chest. "*You* think you've got a strong body, huh?" He chucked Dark-and-Handsome under the chin. "*You* think you've got a pretty face, do you? Think you'll all live till you're forty? Fifty? Some people live long, see, like him—" He pointed at an ancient fortune-teller, a graphologist, who was dozing off at his table by the Park fence. "He can live until his beard drags along the ground, until there's nothing left of his face but a few dark holes— he'll still be alive! But Chu Yen died early—1930, 31, 32"—he laughed coldly, counting on his fingers—"Three years, he only lived three years! 'T-ang Po-hu?' All those people at the studio rushed up to call him by that name, but the moment the cameras stopped grinding on 'Loyang Bridge' they announced, 'Chu Yen is finished!' They wanted the review in *Shun Pao* to sign his death warrant: 'An actor whose artistry is dead and gone.' They not only pushed him down a well, they dumped stones in after him. Buried him alive! Didn't even give him a chance at one last breath—"

As he was saying these words, his hands suddenly closed around his own throat, his eyes bulged, he uttered stifled sounds, his face turning purple; he looked frightful, as if he was actually being strangled. We all broke out laughing, we thought he was acting. The Guru had a terrific talent all right; no matter what he played or mimicked, he made it seem real. Dark-and-Handsome said the Guru could have become a famous director, but he took to drinking; and being headstrong and full of pride, he offended all the big stars. So a first-rate film never came his way.

"Like this! It was just like this!" The Guru let go of himself. "Little brothers, you don't know what it's like to be buried alive, it's as if someone had you by the throat and you couldn't utter a sound, but you could see their faces, you could hear their voices, you could see them shooting straight at you with the camera under the klieg lights; and you? Your pulse beat slower and slower, and one by one your nerves deadened, with your own eyes you saw your limbs rot away piece by piece—And that was why I gritted my teeth and told my Prince Charming, 'Son, you must show them, for my sake!' Chiang Ch'ing was a good boy; he really didn't let me down. The day *our* 'Loyang Bridge' premiered at the Grand Theater in Shanghai, the crowd was so big it stopped the traffic on Bubbling Well Road. The minute he came galloping onto the screen in his robe of sea-green silk astride his white horse I heard myself cry out in my heart, 'Chu Yen lives again! Chu Yen lives again!' To remake 'Loyang Bridge' I staked everything I owned. Once, when I was directing him in a scene, I slapped him across the face and left five bloodred marks. But no one can ever know how much I cherished him. 'Chu Yen's Prince Charming' they all called him. He was born to be a great star; there was a spiritual quality about him—little brothers, don't think you're such charmers: not one of you has it!"

He went round the circle pointing at each of us; when he came to

Dark-and-Handsome, the boy made a face and sneered; we all roared. Dark-and-Handsome thought he was some hotshot. Some day for sure he was going to make it to Hollywood, he said. We advised him to order a pair of those Italian high-heeled boots; he was only five foot five and where was he going to find a foreign dame short enough to play opposite him?

"But why? Why?" Without warning, the Guru caught Ah Hsiung the Primitive by the arm. Ah Hsiung started; laughing, he struggled to free himself, but the Guru held him fast; he thrust his head with its mane of unruly white hair up close to Ah Hsiung's face. "Why didn't he listen to me? 'Son,' I said, 'you're a genius; whatever you do, don't ruin yourself.' The first time I laid eyes on her I knew Dandelion Chen was bad luck! Imagine, the little witch was thrown clear, not a hair on her head was injured; and later on she even became a top star at the Supreme Studios. And him? He was burned to a lump of charcoal sitting in that sports car I gave him. They wanted me to claim the body. I refused. I refused to acknowledge it. That heap of charred flesh was not my Prince Charming—" It was as if a piece of bone were stuck in the Guru's throat; he became unintelligible. "Burnt to death—we both got burnt to death—" he muttered; his burning emeralds of eyes flashed so that sparks seemed to leap from them. Ah Hsiung freed himself; panting, he ran back to us. The Guru leaned back against the stone balustrade, his head slightly bowed; a big lock of his white hair slipped forward and hung there. Behind him the enormous yellow moon was languidly sinking through the row of coconut trees on the west shore of the pond. The lotuses flowering in the pond breathed out waves of fragrance with increasing intensity. Dark-and-Handsome stood on tiptoe, stretched and yawned; we all began to feel drowsy.

There was a time several months long when you couldn't find a trace of the Guru in the Park. Within our circle there were all kinds of rumours; they all said the Guru had gotten himself arrested and put in prison by the police from the Fourth Precinct; and not only that, he had been booked on a morals charge—all this was spread around by one of those fancy boys from Sanshui Street. The way that little fancy boy told it, one night, after he left the Park as he passed through West Gate Square he saw the Guru in the China Plaza arcade. The old cuss was running after a student and trying to buttonhole him. "That schoolboy was some gorgeous bastard!" the little fairy recalled, smacking his lips. The Guru looked absolutely soused; he could hardly walk. He was swaying from side to side, trying to catch up with that student and asking him if he wanted to be a movie star. At first the student just tried to get out of his way and kept turning around and laughing; at the corner, the Guru caught up with him; he threw his arms around him and hugged him mumbling "Loyang Bridge! My Prince Charming!" and all that. The student cried out in panic, a big crowd gathered, and then the police came.

Finally one night we saw the Guru reappear in the Park. It was a most unusual summer night: for two months there hadn't been a single drop of rain in Taipei. The wind was hot; the stone balustrade in the Park was hot; the outlines of those lush tropical trees wavered in a sultry, smoky haze; the lotus flowers in the pond smelled so sweet the air tasted sticky. In the dark, thickening sky the moon—have you ever seen its like? Have you ever seen such a lewd, demonic moon before? Like an immense ball of flesh, bloodshot, floating up there, flesh-red. In the Park human shadows flickered, circling around wildly like the images on a revolving lantern. Dark-and-Handsome was sitting on the stone balustrade, decked out in a tight-fitting scarlet T-shirt, black Bermuda shorts, and sandals. Head in the air, legs swinging, he was showing off like a little peacock spreading its tail for the first time. He'd just landed a small part in "Dawn of Spring," directed by Old Man Mo. In front of the cameras for the first time in his life, he was so satisfied with himself he damn near forgot who he was. But Ah Hsiung the Primitive seemed determined to steal the scene. He showed up sporting a snug bright purple Thai silk shirt that turned the upper part of his body into an inverted triangle and white denim pants so tight they looked painted onto his bulging, sinewy legs; his steel belt-buckle was as big as a goose egg, flashing like silver. His whole body was bursting with saturated maleness, tinged with the primitive wildness of the aborigines.

When he sat next to Dark-and-Handsome, for sure they were the most eye-catching pair in the Park; but that gang of fancy boys from Sanshui Street refused to be upstaged. In groups of threes and fives, their arms around each other's shoulders, their wooden clogs clicking, they marched to and fro on the terrace as if they were demonstrating, humming amorous melodies. When a fat, bald-headed foreigner in a loud Hawaiian shirt made his way over, furtively exploring, the fancy boys brazenly hailed him with a chorus of "*Hel-lo!*"

Just when the excitement in the Park was at its height, the Guru arrived out of nowhere; his appearance was so sudden everybody was astounded, awestruck. At once they all fell silent and quietly watched the Guru's huge shadowy shape move up to the terrace. He wore a brand new sharkskin suit, pale blue and shiny. He was unusually well-groomed, which made his shock of white hair all the more striking, but he was walking with difficulty, as if he were wounded somewhere.

He'd probably gone through a lot in prison, you know; the police could be very cruel sometimes, especially to people in on morals charges. Once a little Sanshui Street fairy hooked a wrong customer and got arrested; the police really fixed him good. By the time he got out he'd been so scared he'd lost his voice; when he saw people he could only open his mouth and go *ah, ah*. People said he'd been beat up with a rubber hose. The Guru dragged his feet along heavily, with great dignity, step by step; eventually he made the stone balustrade at the end of the terrace. He stood there by himself against the balustrade, his white, unruly head lifted up high, his tall, gaunt silhouette jagged and erect, ignoring the whispers and snickers buzzing around him. In a moment excitement returned to the terrace. The night was deepening; steps grew more urgent, one by one the shadows went searching, exploring, yearning. The Guru stood there alone. Not until that flesh-ball of a red moon had languidly gone all the way down did he leave the Park. When he left he took a Sanshui Street boy along with him. The boy was called Little Jade; he was a pretty-faced little thing, but he was a cripple, so not many people paid him attention. The Guru put his arm around the boy's shoulder, and the two of them, one tall, one small, supporting each other with their incompleteness, limped together into the dark grove of Green Corals.

A Simple Enquiry

Ernest Hemingway

First the Catholic Church, then the American army, imagined a system by which a gay man or woman might be accepted as a member or a recruit and yet denied as a person. According to the Catholic dogma, homosexuals may be admitted to the Church if they don't practise; according to the army, homosexuals may fight for their country as long as they don't talk about their sexual inclinations. Church and army have created something beyond the wildest dreams of metaphysics, a being existing without deeds and without speech: the mute and invisible homosexual. This invention is, however, older than its codifiers: in the earliest days of the Catholic Church, thanks to the rhetoric of Saint Paul, homosexuals wishing to live within the community of Christ were forced to refrain from speaking out.

Indeed, the ecclesiastical and military powers are following a well-known literary device: defining something through the absence of its essential characteristics. The best examples come from the love story and the horror novel: the beauty too beautiful to describe, the horror too horrible to tell. Or, to quote from the poets:

And last of all an admiral came,
A terrible man with a terrible name.
A name that everyone knew very well
But that no one could speak and that no one could spell.

In Hemingway's "A Simple Enquiry" everything is said except the word "homosexual", and it is that very absence which gives the story its sense. Hemingway's style, which at other times became its own parody, serves here to underline the strength of what remains unsaid and to echo the untold tale. "The things which you know very well," wrote Hemingway, "you can leave out and they will be there. The things which you don't know well you will probably overdescribe."

Outside, the snow was higher than the window. The sunlight came in through the window and shone on a map on the pine-board wall of the hut. The sun was high and the light came in over the top of the snow. A trench had been cut along the open side of the hut, and each clear day the sun, shining on the wall, reflected heat against the snow and widened the trench. It was late March. The major sat at a table against the wall. His adjutant sat at another table.

Around the major's eyes were two white circles where his snow-glasses had protected his face from the sun on the snow. The rest of his face had been burned and then tanned and then burned through the tan. His nose was swollen and there were edges of loose skin where blisters had been. While he worked at the papers he put the fingers of his left hand into a saucer of oil and then spread the oil over his face, touching it very gently with the tips of his fingers. He was very careful to drain his fingers on the edge of the saucer so there was only a film of oil on them, and after he had stroked his forehead and his cheeks, he stroked his nose very delicately between his fingers. When he had finished he stood up, took the saucer of oil and went into the small room of the hut where he slept. "I'm going to take a little sleep," he said to the adjutant. In that army an adjutant is not a commissioned officer. "You'll finish up."

"Yes, Signor Maggiore," the adjutant answered. He leaned back in his chair and yawned. He took a paper-covered book out of the pocket of his coat and opened it; then laid it down on the table and lit his pipe. He leaned forward on the table to read and puffed at his pipe. Then he closed the book and put it back in his pocket. He had too much paper-work to get through. He could not enjoy reading until it was done. Outside, the sun went behind a mountain and there was no more light on the wall of the hut. A soldier came in and put some pine branches, chopped into irregular lengths, into the stove. "Be soft, Pinin," the adjutant said to him. "The major is sleeping."

Pinin was the major's orderly. He was a dark-faced boy, and he fixed the stove, putting the pine wood in carefully, shut the door, and went into the back of the hut again. The adjutant went on with his papers.

"Tonani," the major called.

"Signor Maggiore?"

"Send Pinin in to me."

"Pinin!" the adjutant shouted. Pinin came into the room. "The major wants you," the adjutant said.

Pinin walked across the main room of the hut toward the major's door. He knocked on the half-opened door. "Signor Maggiore?"

"Come in," the adjutant heard the major say, "and shut the door."

Inside the room the major lay on his bunk. Pinin stood beside the bunk. The major lay with his head on the rucksack that he had stuffed with spare clothing to make a pillow. His long, burned, oiled face looked at Pinin. His hands lay on the blankets.

"You are nineteen?" he asked.

"Yes, Signor Maggiore."

"You have ever been in love?"

"How do you mean, Signor Maggiore?"

"In love—with a girl?"

"I have been with girls."

"I did not ask that. I asked if you had been in love—with a girl."

"Yes, Signor Maggiore."

"You are in love with this girl now? You don't write her. I read all your letters."

"I am in love with her," Pinin said, "but I do not write her."

"You are sure of this?"

"I am sure."

"Tonani," the major said in the same tone of voice, "can you hear me talking?"

There was no answer from the next room.

"He cannot hear," the major said. "And you are quite sure that you love a girl?"

"I am sure."

"And," the major looked at him quickly, "that you are not corrupt?"

"I don't know what you mean, corrupt."

"All right," the major said, "you needn't be superior."

Pinin looked at the floor. The major looked at his brown face, down and up him, and at his hands. Then he went on, not smiling. "And you don't really want—" the major paused. Pinin looked at the floor. "That your great desire isn't really—" Pinin looked at the floor. The major leaned his head back on the rucksack and smiled. He was really relieved: life in the army was too complicated. "You're a good boy," he said. "You're a good boy, Pinin. But don't be superior and be careful someone else doesn't come along and take you."

Pinin stood still beside the bunk.

"Don't be afraid," the major said. His hands were folded on the blankets. "I won't touch you. You can go back to your platoon if you like. But you had better stay on as my servant. You've less chance of being killed."

"Do you want anything of me, Signor Maggiore?"

"No," the major said. "Go on and get on with whatever you were doing. Leave the door open when you go out."

Pinin went out, leaving the door open. The adjutant looked up at him as he walked awkwardly across the room and out of the door. Pinin was flushed and moved differently than he had moved when he brought in the wood for the fire. The adjutant looked after him and smiled. Pinin came in with more wood for the stove. The major, lying on his bunk, looking at his cloth-covered helmet and his snow-glasses that hung from a nail on the wall, heard him walk across the floor. The little devil, he thought, I wonder if he lied to me.

Hard Feelings

Francis King

The history of love relationships abounds in unlikely couples. The beautiful Aphrodite and the deformed Hephaestus, the reasonable Socrates and the bad-tempered Xantippe, the passionate Molly and the introspective Leopold Bloom. The links which bind them together seem unknown, perhaps unknowable. That which attracts one to the other remains mysterious to them and, to us, the outsiders, confounding. The less conventional a relationship (that is to say, the less it reflects what society sanctions), the odder those links seem to the outside world. Gay relationships, whose history has remained secret for so long, seem to the world odder still. It is as if society denied gay couples the individual unlikeliness, the private mystery, that it allows heterosexual couples.

Francis King, who so subtly depicted the stranger shades of human relationships in novels such as The Needle, Act of Darkness, The Woman Who Was God, *chooses in "Hard Feelings" a single episode in the life of an oddly assorted couple. The fact that the couple is gay signifies, in this instance, almost nothing. The characters themselves—their age, their manners, their backgrounds, their personalities—raise in the reader the question of what draws two so vastly different human beings together. Largely, their lives remain untold. The drama has begun long before the first page and hasn't come to an end by the time we reach the last line. All we are given is a fragment, one tenuous but complete encounter, through which we can suspect their entire story.*

"Has my—ahm—nephew got here before me?"

Sometimes, as now, Adrian would describe Mike as his nephew or even as his son; but more often—since he was a snob in spite of his repeated protestation "I can truthfully say that I haven't an ounce of snobbery in my make-up"—he would describe him as his secretary.

Though he was never conscious of it, his choosing of one of these des-
ignations or the other depended on whether Mike was at that moment
in favour or not. Mike was very much in favour that weekend, after a
long period of being out of it.

"Your nephew, sir? No, sir, no one has asked for you."

There had been a time when Adrian would take pains to mention
to any desk clerk that the reason why he and Mike shared a room was
that he had this dicky heart and his doctor had told him that he must
always have help within call. But in recent years he had come to realize that whether he and Mike had adjoining rooms or shared a room
was a matter of total indifference to the staffs of the anonymous London caravanserais in which on such occasions, forsaking Brown's or
Bailey's, he would always put up.

"When he arrives, send him up, would you? Say that I'm waiting
for him."

"Very good, sir." The desk clerk, who was not used to receiving
tips from customers when they checked in, or indeed at any time,
blushed as Adrian pushed a fifty-pence piece towards him. "Er—
thank you, sir."

"Is that a Rifle Brigade tie you're wearing?" There was a variation
of this worn ploy, in which Adrian asked if the tie were an Old Eton-
ian one.

"This, sir? Oh, no, sir." The young man fingered it delicately.
"Well, it may be, but if it is, I didn't know it. I bought it at Simpsons."

"It gives you a vaguely military air. Which suits you. I like to be
welcomed by a young man who's clean and well dressed and has hair
that's a reasonable length. And polite. I stopped going to the rival
establishment up the street after being cheeked by a night porter
whom one could only describe as a hippie. Perhaps he was one of
these revolting students out on strike." When Adrian laughed, the
clerk decided that he must join in too. "Well, anyone can see that
you're going to go places in this organization. I have a friend in the
hotel business—one of the biggest men—and he tells me that the right
kind of personnel are worth their weight in gold. Well, it stands to
reason. We've built all these hotels but we've done damn little about
finding the right people to staff them."

The clerk was flattered by Adrian's attention, as simple people
were usually flattered by his policy of what he called "building-up".
The opposite of building-up was, of course, pulling-down—a process

that Adrian confined only to those people not present to defend themselves against it. "Yes, I make it my policy to build up. That's the way to get the best out of others." Getting the best out of others meant getting out of them what was best for Adrian.

The diminutive page with the bags whistled in the lift and continued to whistle as he conducted Adrian down the corridor to his room. Adrian, who was unmusical, did not realize that the boy was whistling flat; but he was none the less irritated by the sound, regarding it as yet another indication of a decline in the quality of service in English hotels.

However, true to his building-up policy, he jingled the change in the pocket of his greatcoat, produced a ten-pence piece and held it out: "There you are, my lad.... And how old would you be?"

The boy had just heaved Adrian's suitcase on to the luggage rack, an exertion that had left him surprisingly breathless. "Sixteen, sir," he said, in an adenoidal voice so high-pitched that Adrian assumed it had still to break. "Thank you, sir." He palmed the coin with none of the embarrassed hesitation of the desk clerk.

Adrian noticed with distaste that the boy's shoes were scuffed and his fingernails grubby and bitten, but he resolved to persevere. "Sixteen! You're very tall for sixteen, aren't you? I should guess from your accent that you're a Geordie like myself."

"No, sir. I'm a Scouse."

There were times when Adrian, whose family had come from Northumberland, also claimed to be a Scouse, but it was too late to do so now. "And how do you like it in the south?"

"It's not so bad."

"But you don't get the same kind of folk. Not the same matiness. That's what I miss. The matiness. Give me the North Country"—he pronounced "Country" as a stage Yorkshireman would—"every time."

When the boy had gone, Adrian began to unpack the suitcase that his sister Pamela had packed for him. Though he was to be away from Tunbridge Wells only for the night, she had put in three of everything: three pairs of shoes; three of the shirts, one of them silk, that she herself washed and ironed for him, since he was adamant that they should never be sent to the laundry; three of the silk-and-wool vests and pants that he always bought from Harrods, because wool alone chafed his skin; three pairs of socks and three sets of cuff-links and three ties. The cuff-links were larger and more ornate and the ties brighter and wider than one would expect this military-looking middle-aged man, with his neat, bristling white moustache and his brogue shoes and his conservatively cut tweed suit, to wear. Drat the woman! Adrian searched everywhere but there was no sign of his Floris Malmaison toilet water. She always contrived to forget something on these trips.

Although his shirt was spotless after the journey—he had put it on for the first time that morning—he nonetheless decided to change it for another. He would wear the purple tie, he decided, with the matching purple handkerchief peeping out of the breast pocket of his jacket. Mike had given them to him, with some subtle prompting, as a birthday present only a few days before the trouble had broken. Adrian had never worn them since. But now all that was behind them at last and it was somehow symbolic of the change to have decided to take them out of the drawer again and to put them to use. Mike should be pleased.

Adrian, who was obsessive about cleanliness—in the early years it had been difficult to persuade Mike to have a bath at least once a day, to change his underclothes regularly and to wash his hands before meals—went into the bathroom in his pants and vest, to soap his neck and forearms and armpits and splash water over his face. Then he brushed his teeth vigorously and gargled with Listerine, throwing back his head and rolling his protuberant blue eyes from side to side. If only he had that toilet water! But at least he had the deodorant spray. It was the only brand of deodorant that he found he could use; every other kind brought him out into a rash.

He deliberated whether to squat on the lavatory; but he had already tried twice on the train, to no effect. It was odd how some people complained that excitement made them loose; with him it had precisely the opposite effect. He had better make sure that Pamela had remembered to pack the fruit salts.

Turning over the various medicaments in the suede leather pouch with which he always travelled, he was so absorbed that he did not hear the first knock at the door. At the second he felt a curious leap of panic, even though he had been telling himself for days how much he was looking forward to this reunion.

"Come in!"

The door opened and Mike entered, his suitcase in his hand. It was odd, Adrian had often reflected, how at these hotels there was always a page at hand to help him with his bags but Mike was usually left to lug his up himself.

"Hello, Adrian!"

"Mike! Marvellous to see you."

Adrian pulled on his blue silk dressing-gown, and then hurried over. "Let me look at you!" He gripped Mike's shoulders, holding him at arm's length. "You look wonderful, Mike. Wonderful. Not a day older. God, it's good to see you again. Here, give me that case of yours." But though he extended an arm, Adrian made no attempt to pick the case up. "No, I shouldn't put it on the bed, if I were you. There's a rack contraption for it over there. Tell me all about yourself. You got my letter saying that I thought it best if we met here? You know what it's like getting across London. Otherwise I'd have met your train at the station."

"That's OK, Adrian," Mike said in a hoarse, subdued voice that seemed to belong to someone totally different from the exuberant Mike that Adrian had once known. "I got a taxi. No time at all."

"Oh, Mike! Extravagant as ever!"

"Well, I'm just getting over this flu. Don't seem I can shake it off. I told you in my letter. I've got no energy."

Illness frightened Adrian. If he himself were ill, he rushed at once to the doctor; if others were ill, he would either rush away, ignore the fact, or say that it was "only nerves". "Well, you look in terrific health."

"I wish I felt it."

Adrian hoped that Mike was not going to be in one of his "down" moods. They could last for several days, and no exhortations to "snap out of it" or to "look on the bright side, for God's sake" were of any avail.

"Poor Mike!"

Mike was about to stretch himself out on Adrian's bed, his shoes still on; but Adrian was quick enough to stop him just in time: "Actually I thought I'd take that bed, as it's nearest to the door to the loo and you know how I often have to get up in the night. Do you mind?"

"All the same to me."

Mike stretched himself out on the other bed, putting his hands behind his head and emitting a couple of yawns so wide that Adrian could see his uvula.

"Don't tell me you're tired."

"Like I said—I'm recovering from this flu."

"Because I've planned an exciting evening for us," Adrian went on, ignoring all mention of the flu. "Two seats in the third row of the stalls for *No Sex, Please—We're British*. Pamela saw it and said that Evelyn Laye was terrific—didn't look a day over forty. And then I've booked a table—guess where?"

"Veeraswamy's?"

"You know I can't eat Indian food since I had that tummy trouble. No. I'm going to take you to Chez Pierre. Remember it?"

Mike remembered it. "Yep," he said without enthusiasm.

"You look terrific, Mike."

Adrian always imagined that if one said a thing often enough and with enough conviction, it would eventually be true. In fact, Mike looked so far from terrific that his appearance after these five years had given Adrian a disagreeable pang, instead of the uplift he had promised himself. Drink sometimes had the same kind of effect on him these days: he would sip at a glass of brandy and find that, instead of his spirits rising, all that rose was a recalcitrant heartburn.

"Well, that's nice to know."

"As handsome as ever. I bet you've been breaking hearts galore in Sheffield."

In the past Mike had liked Adrian to flatter him about the good looks and the physical strength which he had possessed so conspicuously and, even more, about the business acumen in which he had been wholly deficient. But now he merely turned his head to one side on the pillow, emitting a long sigh.

For a moment Adrian was appalled as he looked at him. God, how he had aged. His face had fallen in—could it be that he was wearing false teeth?—and instead of that marvellous ruddy colour, recalling the boyhood spent on a farm near Taunton, his complexion had a greyish sheen, as of lard. The hair had not merely thinned, retreating on either side of the widow's peak so that the forehead looked disproportionately high for the features beneath it, but it had lost all that rich, oily, blue-black vitality that Adrian had once found so exciting. Mike had always spent an inordinate amount of time caring for two things: his hands and his figure. But the hands now looked raw and rubbed, many of the fingernails broken, with a nicotine stain on the right one that made it appear as if he had spilled iodine over forefinger and middle finger; and his figure had, quite literally, gone to pot, the abdominal muscles which he used to exercise each morning with innumerable press-ups now sagging to give him a little paunch.

But he was still good-looking, Adrian hurriedly assured himself; and those violet bruise-like shadows under the brown eyes—how odd that the eyes no longer sparkled—were probably only the result of that old trouble of *overdoing things* (the euphemism that Adrian had always used). None of us got any younger; one had to remember that five years had passed and Mike was now—what was it?—well, at least thirty-one.

"It's marvellous to see you again. As though it was not five years but only five days. Yet what a lot has happened."

"It certainly has."

Adrian went over to the bed and sat down on it, one hand cupping Mike's knee, while with the other he reached for his hand. (Yes, those nails certainly were ugly; but he had probably broken them at his work.) Mike did not move, one hand still behind his head, the other limply in Adrian's, and his eyes searched the ceiling.

"I think what you've done is a marvellous thing," Adrian said. "I always knew you would. Not many people would work their way back like that. I don't mind saying that I'm proud of you, Mike. Damned proud. You're a free man again. That's how I look at it. Because all these years you were like someone in prison, weren't you?"

"I don't want to talk about it."

"No, of course, you don't. And we're not going to talk about it. But I just wanted to say how—how *proud* I am of you." Adrian squeezed the kneecap. "You realize—don't you, Mike?—that I did it all for your own good? It wasn't revenge. You realize that, don't you? But I had to make you get back your self-respect. That was the impor-tant thing. If a man loses his self-respect—well—he's done for. Fin-ished. Isn't he?"

"I don't want to talk about it, Adrian."

Adrian leapt off the bed. "Now not another word. It'll all be as if none of it had ever happened. We had such good times together before—before that nightmare. And we're going to have lots and lots of good times now. You'd better get off that bed and start getting ready, or we're going to be late."

Mike sat up, rubbing at the inflamed lids of his eyes; but he did not rise to his feet. Again he gave a huge yawn. "I'm ready," he said.

"But wouldn't you like a shower?" Adrian persisted. "Or a bath. I asked for both." He noticed that Mike's shirt was grey around the collar and hurried on: "And why don't you wear this shirt I have here?" He pulled open a drawer and held up a pale green silk shirt. "I got it in the sales—at Austin Reed—only last week. Pamela thinks it too young for me, but we know how conservative she is! You can borrow it now and, if it really suits you, perhaps I'll give it to you."

For the first time Mike showed some animation as he examined the shirt. "It's a beauty," he said. "Real silk. I thought at first it was one of those terylene jobs. You know how terylene makes me sweat. Can I really borrow it?"

"Of course. But why not have a shower first?"

"I had a bath this morning."

"After that long train journey it'll freshen you up. Go on. You'll find a cake of Chanel Gentleman's Soap in there. I brought it specially. I remembered how you like it."

"So it's the life of luxury again," Mike said, more as a question than a statement, as he stripped off first shirt and then vest. The sight, after all these years, of the dark pelt on his chest, narrowing to a line that ran down his navel and then again widened, filled Adrian with a sudden longing and sadness. Poor Mike! He was really a good boy, a very good boy! It was that Danish *au pair* slut and that whole Bayswater crowd that had really been responsible. He was weak, that was the trouble with him. A country boy, who couldn't resist the temptations that others put in his path.

"Dear Mike. Dear, *dear* Mike."

Naked, Mike came over and stood beside Adrian. Then with a nervous, tentative gesture, like someone making up his mind to stroke a dog that has the reputation of biting, he put out one of his hands and laid two fingers on the back of Adrian's neck. "I've missed you," he said.

"Have you really? Have you really, Mike?"

"Yep." He looked down at Adrian, with a small, melancholy-bitter smile that Adrian could not remember ever having seen before. "Sheffield was very different from Tunbridge Wells. And the factory was very different from the shop."

Adrian sighed. "There were often moments when I relented, Mike. I hated to think of you going through all that. But then I said to myself, 'No, it's for his own good.' And it was, Mike. Wasn't it?"

The younger man did not answer for several seconds. Then he

seemed to shake himself: "Yes, I guess it was, Adrian. Yes, I'm grateful to you."

He went into the bathroom and as Adrian continued to sit there on the bed, listening to the sounds of splashing water, there came back to him, he did not know why, Mike's voice telling him about his father: "... He was a right old bastard. Hardly a day passed when he didn't take the strap to me. But I suppose I should be grateful to him. He made me what I am. There's many a kid nowadays who needs that kind of treatment—just as I needed it—and who'll spoil for want of it." They had been lying side by side—in Amsterdam, was it?—and Mike had been a little drunk as he talked up at the ceiling with Adrian's arm across his chest, pinioning him affectionately to the vast double bed.

"Yep, this is a super shirt, Adrian."

Naked, Mike had returned to the bedroom, rubbing briskly at his hair with a towel, and peering down at the shirt.

"Oh, Mike! You silly boy! That's not the hotel towel, that's mine! Why on earth didn't you ask?" But then Adrian relented; it was a pity to spoil things at a time like this. "But it doesn't matter. Go on! Use it! Use it!"

In the darkened theatre Adrian found himself stealing surreptitious glances at the face beside him. Occasionally Mike would laugh at some joke on the stage, but for most of the time his expression remained unhappy, even despairing, the eyes dull and the corners of the mouth—there was a small cold sore on one side—turned slightly down. In the interval he did not want a drink—"No, don't let's bother," he said, shaking his head when Adrian suggested one—though in the old days he always liked his double gin and tonic and the opportunity to quiz the audience.

"Not feeling too good?"

Mike shook his head. "I'm feeling fine."

"We've so much to talk about. Over dinner, not here. I've all kinds of ideas for the future."

Mike stared emptily ahead of him, the knee that had been restless throughout the performance now once again beginning to jerk up and down.

In the restaurant Adrian said, "I know exactly what you'll like," and proceeded to order for Mike exactly what he liked himself. "This is a celebration and only the very best will do," he summed up, as he handed the menu back to the waiter. "We must fatten you up, Mike. I don't think they feed you properly in those digs of yours."

"Oh, the grub's not too bad. Plenty of it. But like I said, I've had this flu and I don't seem to be able to shake it off."

"What shall we have to drink? Champagne? Yes, it must be champagne."

After Adrian had dealt with the wine waiter at length, Mike leant forward, one large, raw hand supporting his chin, to ask, "How's Pamela?"

"Pamela?" They had not yet talked of her. "She's aged a bit, you know. But she keeps pretty fit and active. I wish *I* had her health and stamina, I can tell you that." Although Adrian's sister had undergone a hysterectomy only a few months before, it was convenient for him to maintain the fiction that her health remained far superior to his own. "She sent her love. And hopes to see you soon."

"Thanks."

Something in the intonation of the monosyllable made Adrian protest, "You mustn't think that she doesn't like you, old chap. There was a time, I know, when she was—well—jealous. And of course all that business upset her a lot, it was bound to. Especially the loss of Aunt Bea's silver. But she shares my admiration for you now. It was an extraordinary achievement, paying us back through all these years. Quite extraordinary. I can't think of many other people who would have done it."

Mike did not answer; he raised a *grissino* to his mouth and gnawed intently at the end with a dry, splintering sound, as though it were made of wood.

"I know you think that maybe I'd have been a bit more—ahm— lenient, if it hadn't been for Pam. But you're wrong, you know, I'd have behaved just the same even if she hadn't had anything to do with it. I didn't *want* to put you through it. And the money wasn't *all* that important—or the other things. I've never been one who bothered much about possessions. Now have I? But I felt that you must get your self-respect back, like I said. Otherwise—well, how could things ever be right between us?"

"Yep, Adrian. I see that, of course I see that."

Mike's tone was still apathetic and he did not look at Adrian as he spoke.

"This smoked salmon is superb, really superb. My God, they do you well here." Adrian gulped a mouthful, and then, fork and knife poised, ruminated, his eyes fixed on the third button of the shimmering, pale green shirt opposite to him.

He had first met Mike, then a marine, in one of the pubs in Portsmouth to which, telling Pamela that he was going to attend a sale in that part of the world, he would make intermittent visits in search of what he called "a teeny adventure". Adrian was experienced enough to know that Mike, like every other of his past pick-ups in that pub, was interested only in making money; but he had also sensed in the boy something unusual—a deep-seated and totally unconscious craving for affection and admiration. A visit to Tunbridge Wells, when Pamela was on a cruise, was followed by weekends in London and weekends in Paris and Amsterdam and then three weeks in Torremolinos in the house of a rich and idle homosexual who was probably Adrian's closest friend. When Mike had eventually come to the end of his term of service it had seemed natural enough to ask him if he would like to work in the antique shop which Adrian and Pamela shared. "What does he know about antiques?" Pamela had demanded, and Adrian had replied acidly, "He doesn't have to *know* about antiques. What we need is someone strong enough to do all the fetching and carrying that we can't do." But Mike, though strong, had a dislike of manual labour and the part-time helpers with whom Adrian had hoped to dispense were soon back again. What Mike, with his charm and air of openness, could do to surprising perfection was to sell.

"He's changed my whole life," Adrian would gush. "Who'd have thought that he'd make such a marvellous assistant? A totally uneducated boy like that. It's a miracle. A real miracle."

Adrian set about "civilizing" Mike—that was the word that he used to his friends and sometimes even to Mike himself—and in this mission he was generally far more successful than he had ever dared to hope. True, Mike never learned to hold a knife other than as if it were a pen and there were certain vowel sounds that no instruction could eradicate; but Adrian was soon able to boast to all and sundry, "You know, I can take him absolutely anywhere without a moment of embarrassment."

Of course Mike could be a wee bit naughty. He would drink too heavily and what he drank was often whisky for which Adrian and

Pamela had paid. Then there were the "sluts" (Adrian's word) on whom he would spend far more money than he could possibly afford and whom, when Pamela and Adrian were away, he would even bring back to the house, though emphatically and repeatedly told not to do so. "He's not really interested in girls," Adrian would say. "But he must have at least one in tow if he's to keep his self-respect." In this Adrian, so wrong about so many things that concerned Mike, probably was right.

When the netsuke disappeared—Adrian had picked it up for ten shillings in a junk shop in Battersea and, delighted with his cleverness, had assured Mike, with some exaggeration, that it was worth at least a hundred times that sum—it was natural enough to accept Mike's explanation that some customer must have pocketed it when his back was turned; after all, every dealer suffered that kind of loss from time to time. When, a few weeks later, the shop was burgled, Adrian again suspected nothing, though there were some odd features of the break-in that made one of the two detectives in charge of the case speculate that perhaps it might have been an inside job. Less than a month afterwards it was the turn of the house—among the things taken was all Aunt Bea's Georgian silver, left to Pamela alone, since the old woman had never cared for Adrian; and this time, too, the same detective talked of an inside job and questioned Adrian about everyone in his employment. Adrian admitted that he had never been entirely happy about an Irish knocker with whom he sometimes traded; and when the police revealed that this man had had a conviction for receiving stolen goods, Adrian went round saying that the police knew the identity of the culprit but just could not get enough evidence against him.

It was Pamela who finally trapped Mike. From time to time she had been complaining that small sums of money had been missing from her bag, but Adrian had pooh-poohed the idea of any theft—the trouble was, he told her, that she just splashed money around and forgot where she had done so. But Pamela, without telling Adrian, marked some five-pound notes; and one of these she found in Mike's wallet, which she searched one night while he was having a bath.

Adrian still would not have believed Mike to be dishonest—he had a rare faculty for disbelieving anything that he did not wish to believe—had it not been that Mike himself poured out his confession. Seated tearfully in nothing but a dressing-gown on the edge of his bed, with an implacable Pamela on one side of him and a horrified Adrian on the other, he admitted to everything. "Christ, I hate myself!" he kept exclaiming, between one nauseating detail and another. "You trusted me, Adrian, you did all this for me, and this is how I have to pay you back. I'm a shit, Adrian. You've got to face the fact that I'm nothing but a shit."

Eventually he broke into gulping sobs, that sounded like an effortful kind of retching, his large hands clasped between his bare knees and a thread of saliva running down his open mouth on to his chin and then to one lapel of the dressing-gown. Adrian, strangely moved as he had not been moved since the occasion, many years ago, of his mother's death, would have liked to have touched him in comfort, but he was too frightened of Pamela to do so.

"You'd better call the police," Mike said at last.

Adrian looked at Pamela. Then he said, "You know I couldn't do that."

"But Christ, you've *got* to, Adrian! I mean to say! I deserve all that's coming to me."

"I couldn't do that to an old friend like you."

What Adrian really meant was that he could not do that to himself. He had a terror of scandal.

"But look how I've treated you! The one person who ever took any real trouble with me in the whole of my life. You've got to call the police."

It was as though his desire for punishment was as intense as Pamela's desire to see punishment inflicted on him.

Adrian and Pamela stayed up late that evening discussing what course of action they must take. Meanwhile Mike lay on top of the bed in his room, still in nothing but the dressing-gown but indifferent to the cold that made his large hands grow clumsy and stiff, his teeth chatter and his body shake. Pamela had always really hated Mike, though she had pretended to like him; and like so many people who pass over the threshold of middle-age in the bitter knowledge that they have never known a reciprocated love, she regarded her possessions as extensions of her own being, so that what Mike had, in effect, done in making off with Aunt Bea's silver was to amputate a limb from her.

Eventually brother and sister managed to reach a verdict and together they went into Mike's room—it was significant that, for the first time since he had come to stay with them, neither of them knocked or asked if they might enter—and told him what it was. They would take no legal steps against him; but he would have to sign a confession of all that he had told them and over the next five years, week by week, he would have to pay back their losses.

"But you can't do that, Adrian!" Mike had cried out; and at first Adrian thought that he was protesting because the terms were too harsh. But then he went on, "You ought to hand me over to the police. That's what I deserve. I'll take my punishment."

Adrian shook his head. "Pamela and I have decided that we just couldn't bring ourselves to do that."

Mike's face was pulled out of shape, like a child's when it is about to give way to a storm of tears. Head lowered, he staggered off the bed, approached Adrian and then threw his arms around him, his head on his shoulder.

"Christ! What have I done to deserve a friend like you!"

The next day Mike went north to exile and five years of hard labour; and now the five years were over and the total restitution had been made.

Adrian raised his glass. "We must drink to the future, Mike. To our future together."

Hesitantly Mike raised his glass. "To our future together?"

"Why not? You'll come back to the shop, won't you?"

"Well. I—I don't know."

Mike put the rim of the glass to his lower lip but did not sip.

Adrian felt an upsurge of irritation that his offer should have evoked, not the expected joy, but a response so ambiguous.

"Wouldn't you *like* to come back?"

"I'd like to come back. 'Course I would, Adrian. But would it—I mean would it—would it *work*?"

"Why shouldn't it work?"

"There's Pam."

"So what?"

Mike shrugged unhappily.

"Pam and I have discussed it all." The discussions had, in fact, been prolonged and acrimonious; but as usual Adrian had finally got his way. "She's in full agreement with me. A hundred per cent. We both want you back."

"Well, I'll have to think about it, won't I, Adrian?"

"Surely you don't want to go on in those frightful digs, doing that frightful job?"

Mike shook his head, again holding the glass against his lower lip without sipping it.

"Well then?" Adrian put out a hand and covered the raw hand that was clutching the stem of the glass. "It can be as it used to be in the old days, Mike. It needn't be any different."

Mike gave a sudden, choking laugh, not of mirth but hysteria. "It's *got* to be different. You wouldn't want all that to happen again, would you?"

"It won't happen again."

In the taxi on the way back to the hotel Adrian felt tender and relaxed. He slipped an arm round Mike's shoulder: "Oh, it's good, it's damned good to have you back, Mike. All those years. I don't know how I got through them. Perhaps it was silly of me, perhaps I ought to have forgotten the whole affair and told you to return. But it wouldn't have been fair to you, would it? Would it, Mike?" Mike did not answer, his face expressionless as he stared out of the window at the lights that whisked past. "Dear Mike." Now Adrian had a hand on his knee. "You know, you're the only person I've ever loved. Yes, honestly." Adrian had said this to other people but now, in a moment of devastating clarity, he saw that it was true. He had never loved anyone else, because he had never been capable of loving; but somehow Mike had given him that capacity. Then he thought, with a piercing jab of excitement, of the hotel bedroom that awaited them.

There seemed to be an ineluctable weariness in all Mike's movements as he stripped off his clothes, dropping them unfolded, one by one, on a chair. Naked at last, he sprang into one of the beds—the one that Adrian had assigned him—and tugged sheet and blankets up to his chin. He was shivering; his jaw was trembling.

"One moment, Mike." Adrian suddenly felt that his bowels, obstinately closed all day, now wished to open. "Hang on."

His dressing-gown swished as he hurried into the bathroom. Then he came back; went awkwardly to the chair over which his jacket was draped; bent over; got something out, which he stuffed into his dressing-gown pocket; and disappeared again.

Soon he re-emerged, beaming: "There we are! Now I feel much comfier."

The dressing-gown was placed on a hanger on the door; the key was turned. Adrian was wearing only a pair of Y-fronted pants. It was his modest habit to wait to remove these until he was under the bedclothes.

"Dear Mike."

But when he put his lips to the cheek on the pillow beside him, he was astonished to taste something damp and salt.

"Mike! What's the matter?"

"What did you get from your jacket?"

"When?"

"Just now. When you went to the toilet."

"Only some Kleenex. You know how I hate tough lavatory paper."

"You took your wallet."

"What are you talking about?"

"You had all your money in your wallet. And you took it in case I should pinch it."

"Nonsense!" But there was no conviction in Adrian's voice.

"Then let me look in your dressing-gown pocket. It must be there now. Or did you hide it in the toilet?"

"Well, yes, Mike, I did take my wallet. But that was because I didn't want to put any temptation in your way. Was that so bad of me?"

"You were right not to trust me. Perhaps I would have taken it."

"Don't say such silly things. All that's behind you. We both know you've learned your lesson."

Again Adrian tried to take Mike in his arms; but the younger man remained obstinately on his back, his arms behind his head and his eyes staring upwards.

"Mike! ... You're not angry, Mike?"

A long silence.

"Mike?"

Mike then said in that hoarse, subdued voice so unlike the voice that Adrian had known, "It wouldn't do, Adrian."

"What wouldn't do? What *is* all this?"

"My coming back."

"But I *want* you back."

Mike shook his head. Then he said in the same hoarse, subdued voice: "Will I get into the other bed or will you?"

"For God's sake, Mike!"

But Mike climbed slowly, shivering, out of the bed, his arms crossed over his thin, hairy chest and his shoulders hunched, to enter the other bed with a creak and a long, trembling sigh.

"I just don't know what all the fuss is about!" Adrian raised himself on an elbow and peered at the outstretched shape in the bed beside him. "You really are incredibly touchy." When, after several seconds, Mike had still not said a word, Adrian conceded, "Oh, very well then! If that's how you want it! But I'm—ahm—I'm sorry, Mike."

Still there was no answer; and when Adrian held out a hand across the space between the two beds, Mike did not stir.

"No hard feelings?" Adrian said.

Again there was silence.

Onnagata

Yukio Mishima

Yukio Mishima's grandmother came from an aristocratic samurai family who decided that the child would live with her rather than with his less distinguished mother. Mishima spent his childhood looking after the sick old woman, staying by her side during her nervous breakdowns, dressing her sores, helping her to the lavatory, and witnessing her frequent nightmares. Later in life, he was to say that "at the age of eight, I had a sixty-year-old lover." The old woman made the child wear girls' clothes and insisted that he attend the long and complicated spectacles of Noh and Kabuki theatre. His first novel, a semi-autobiographical account of a young man's discovery of his homosexuality, was called Confessions of a Mask.

The Kabuki theatre Mishima began to attend at such an early age (and from which he later drew much of his imagery) is perhaps Japan's most popular form of entertainment. Kabuki dates from the early seventeenth century, when a former priestess, Okuni, assembled a company of women and developed a popular form of drama based on parodies of Buddhist prayers interspersed with bold and sensuous dances. The actresses were available for a fee after the performance, and the notorious disputes between suitors in the samurai audience led to the closing of the Kabuki theatres in 1629. When they reopened a few years later, the females roles were assigned to young males, but the samurai fought over them as well. Eventually, only mature men with shaved heads were permitted to perform, but even this did not eradicate Kabuki's sensuality, and the men who took on the roles of women became, under the name of onnagata, *the most revered among all actors.*

I

Masuyama had been overwhelmed by Mangiku's artistry; that was how it happened that, after getting a degree in classical Japanese literature, he had chosen to join the kabuki theatre staff. He had been entranced by seeing Mangiku Sanokawa perform.

Masuyama's addiction to kabuki began when he was a high-school student. At the time, Mangiku, still a fledgling *onnagata*, was appearing in such minor roles as the ghost butterfly in *Kagami Jishi* or, at best, the waiting maid Chidori in *The Disowning of Genta*. Mangiku's acting was unassertive and orthodox; nobody suspected he would achieve his present eminence. But even in those days Masuyama sensed the icy flames given off by this actor's aloof beauty. The general public, needless to say, noticed nothing. For that matter, none of the drama critics had ever called attention to the peculiar quality of Mangiku, like shoots of flame visible through the snow, which illuminated his performances from very early in his career. Now everyone spoke as if Mangiku had been a personal discovery.

Mangiku Sanokawa was a true *onnagata*, a species seldom encountered nowadays. Unlike most contemporary *onnagata*, he was quite incapable of performing successfully in male roles. His stage presence was colorful, but with dark overtones; his every gesture was the essence of delicacy. Mangiku never expressed anything—not even strength, authority, endurance, or courage—except through the single medium open to him, feminine expression, but through this medium he could filter every variety of human emotion. That is the way of the true *onnagata*, but in recent years this breed has become rare indeed. Their tonal coloring, produced by a particular, exquisitely refined musical instrument, cannot be achieved by playing a normal instrument in a minor key, nor, for that matter, is it produced by a mere slavish imitation of real women.

Yukihime, the Snow Princess, in *Kinkakuji* was one of Mangiku's most successful roles. Masuyama remembered having seen Mangiku perform Yukihime ten times during a single month, but no matter how often he repeated this experience, his intoxication did not diminish. Everything symbolizing Sanokawa Mangiku may be found in this play, the elements entwined, beginning with the opening words of the narrator: "The Golden Pavilion, the mountain retreat of Lord Yoshimitsu, Prime Minister and Monk of the Deer Park, stands three storeys high; its garden graced with lovely sights: the night-lodging stone, the water trickling below the rocks, the flow of the cascade heavy with spring, the willows and cherry trees planted together; the capital now is a vast, many-hued brocade." The dazzling brilliance of the set, depicting cherry trees in blossom, a waterfall, and the glittering Golden Pavilion; the drums, suggesting the dark sound of the waterfall and contributing a constant agitation to the stage; the pale, sadistic face of the lecherous Daizen Matsunaga, the rebel general; the miracle of the magic sword which shines in morning sunlight with the holy image of Fudō, but shows a dragon's form when pointed at the setting sun; the radiance of the sunset glow on the waterfall and cherry trees; the cherry blossoms scattering down petal by petal—everything in the play exists for the sake of one woman, the beautiful, aristocratic Yukihime. There is nothing unusual about Yukihime's costume, the crimson silk robe customarily worn by young princesses. But a ghostly presence of snow, befitting her name, hovers about this granddaughter of the great painter Sesshū, and the landscapes of Sesshū, permeated with snow, may be sensed across the breadth of the scene; this phantom snow gives Yukihime's crimson robe its dazzling brilliance.

Masuyama loved especially the scene where the princess, bound with ropes to a cherry tree, remembers the legend told of her grandfather, and with her toes draws in the fallen blossoms a rat, which comes to life and gnaws through the ropes binding her. It hardly needs to be said that Mangiku Sanokawa did not adopt the puppetlike movements favored by some *onnagata* in this scene. The ropes fastening him to the tree made Mangiku look lovelier than ever: all the artificial arabesques of this *onnagata*—the delicate gestures of the body, the play of the fingers, the arch of the hand—contrived though they might appear when employed for the movements of daily life, took on a strange vitality when used by Yukihime, bound to a tree. The intricate, contorted attitudes imposed by the constraint of the rope made of each instant an exquisite crisis, and the crises seemed to flow, one into the next, with the irresistible energy of successive waves.

Mangiku's performances unquestionably possessed moments of diabolic power. He used his lovely eyes so effectively that often with one flash he could create in an entire audience the illusion that the character of a scene had completely altered: when his glance embraced the stage from the *hanamichi* or the *hanamichi* from the stage, or when he darted one upward look at the bell in *Dōjōji*. In the palace scene from *Imoseyama*, Mangiku took the part of Omiwa, whose lover was stolen from her by Princess Tachibana and who has been cruelly mocked by the court ladies. At the end Omiwa rushes out onto the *hanamichi*, all but wild with jealousy and rage; just then she hears the voices of the court ladies at the back of the stage saying, "A groom without peer has been found for our princess! What joy for us all!" The narrator, seated at the side of the stage, declaims in powerful tones, "Omiwa, hearing this, at once looks back." At this moment Omiwa's character is completely transformed, and her face reveals the marks of a possessive attachment.

Masuyama felt a kind of terror every time he witnessed this moment. For an instant a diabolic shadow had swept over both the bright stage with its splendid set and beautiful costumes and over the thousands of intently watching spectators. This force clearly emanated from Mangiku's body, but at the same time transcended his flesh. Masuyama sensed in such passages something like a dark spring welling forth from this figure on the stage, this figure so imbued with softness, fragility, grace, delicacy, and feminine charms. He could not identify it, but he thought that a strange evil presence, the final residue of the actor's fascination, a seductive evil which leads men astray and makes them drown in an instant of beauty, was the true nature of the dark spring he had detected. But one explains nothing merely by giving it a name.

Omiwa shakes her head and her hair tumbles in disarray. On the stage, to which she now returns from the *hanamichi*, Funashichi's blade is waiting to kill her.

"The house is full of music, an autumn sadness in its tone," declaims the narrator.

There is something terrifying about the way Omiwa's feet hurry forward to her doom. The bare white feet, rushing ahead toward disaster and death, kicking the lines of her kimono askew, seem to know precisely when and where on the stage the violent emotions now urging her forward will end, and to be pressing toward the spot, rejoicing and triumphant even amidst the tortures of jealousy. The pain she reveals outwardly is backed with joy like her robe, on the outside dark and shot with gold thread, but bright with variegated silken strands within.

II

Masuyama's original decision to take employment at the theatre had been inspired by his absorption with kabuki, and especially with

Mangiku; he realized also he could never escape his bondage unless he became thoroughly familiar with the world behind the scenes. He knew from what others had told him of the disenchantment to be found backstage, and he wanted to plunge into that world and taste for himself genuine disillusion.

But the disenchantment he expected somehow never came. Mangiku himself made this impossible. Mangiku faithfully maintained the injunctions of the eighteenth-century *onnagata*'s manual *Ayamegusa*, "An *onnagata*, even in the dressing room, must preserve the attitudes of an *onnagata*. He should be careful when he eats to face away from other people, so that they cannot see him." Whenever Mangiku was obliged to eat in the presence of visitors, not having the time to leave his dressing room, he would turn his table with a word of apology and race through his meal, so skillfully that the visitors could not even guess from behind that he was eating.

Undoubtedly, the feminine beauty displayed by Mangiku on the stage had captivated Masuyama as a man. Strangely enough, however, this spell was not broken even by close observation of Mangiku in the dressing room. Mangiku's body, when he had removed his costume, was delicate but unmistakably a man's. Masuyama, as a matter of fact, found it rather unnerving when Mangiku, seated at his dressing table, too scantily clad to be anything but a man, directed polite, feminine greetings toward some visitor, all the while applying a heavy coating of powder to his shoulders. If even Masuyama, long a devotee of kabuki, experienced eerie sensations on his first visits to the dressing room, what would have been the reactions of people who dislike kabuki, because the *onnagata* make them uncomfortable, if shown such a sight?

Masuyama, however, felt relief rather than disenchantment when he saw Mangiku after a performance, naked except for the gauzy underclothes he wore in order to absorb perspiration. The sight in itself may have been grotesque, but the nature of Masuyama's fascination—its intrinsic quality, one might say—did not reside in any surface illusion, and there was accordingly no danger that such a revelation would destroy it. Even after Mangiku had disrobed, it was apparent that he was still wearing several layers of splendid costumes beneath his skin; his nakedness was a passing manifestation. Something which could account for his exquisite appearance on stage surely lay concealed within him.

Masuyama enjoyed seeing Mangiku when he returned to the dressing room after performing a major role. The flush of the emotions of the part he had been enacting still hovered over his entire body, like sunset glow or the moon in the sky at dawn. The grand emotions of classical tragedy—emotions quite unrelated to our mundane lives—may seem to be guided, at least nominally, by historical facts—the world of disputed successions, campaigns of pacification, civil warfare, and the like—but in reality they belong to no period. They are the emotions appropriate to a stylized, grotesquely tragic world, luridly colored in the manner of a late woodblock print. Grief that goes beyond human bounds, superhuman passions, searing love, terrifying joy, the brief cries of people trapped by circumstances too tragic for human beings to endure: such were the emotions which a moment before had lodged in Mangiku's body. It was amazing that Mangiku's slender frame could hold them and that they did not break from that delicate vessel.

Be that as it may, Mangiku a moment before had been living amidst these grandiose feelings, and he had radiated light on the stage precisely because the emotions he portrayed transcended any known to his audience. Perhaps this is true of all characters on the stage, but among present-day actors none seemed to be so honestly living stage emotions so far removed from daily life.

A passage in *Ayamegusa* states, "Charm is the essence of the *onnagata*. But even the *onnagata* who is naturally beautiful will lose his charm if he strains to impress by his movements. If he consciously attempts to appear graceful, he will seem thoroughly corrupt instead. For his reason, unless the *onnagata* lives as a woman in his daily life, he is unlikely ever to be considered an accomplished *onnagata*. When he appears on stage, the more he concentrates on performing this or that essentially feminine action, the more masculine he will seem. I am convinced that the essential thing is how the actor behaves in real life."

How the actor behaves in real life ... yes, Mangiku was utterly feminine in both the speech and bodily movements of his real life. If Mangiku had been more masculine in his daily life, those moments when the flush from the *onnagata* role he had been performing gradually dissolved like the high-water mark on a beach into the femininity of his daily life—itself an extension of the same make-believe—would have become an absolute division between sea and land, a bleak door

shut between dream and reality. The make-believe of his daily life supported the make-believe of his stage performances. This, Masuyama
was convinced, marked the true *onnagata*. An *onnagata* is the child
born of the illicit union between dream and reality.

III

Once the celebrated veteran actors of the previous generation had all
passed away, one on the heels of the other, Mangiku's authority backstage became absolute. His *onnagata* disciples waited on him like personal servants; indeed, the order of seniority they observed when
following Mangiku on stage as maids in the wake of his princess or
great lady was exactly the same they observed in the dressing room.

Anyone pushing apart the door curtains dyed with the crest of the
Sanokawa family and entering Mangiku's dressing room was certain
to be struck by a strange sensation: this charming sanctuary contained
not a single man. Even members of the same troupe felt inside this
room that they were in the presence of the opposite sex. Whenever
Masuyama went to Mangiku's dressing room on some errand, he had
only to brush apart the door curtains to feel—even before setting foot
inside—a curiously vivid, carnal sensation of being a male.

Sometimes Masuyama had gone on company business to the
dressing rooms of chorus girls backstage at revues. The rooms were
filled with an almost suffocating femininity and the rough-skinned
girls, sprawled about like animals in the zoo, threw bored glances at
him, but he never felt so distinctly alien as in Mangiku's dressing
room; nothing in these real women made Masuyama feel particularly
masculine.

The members of Mangiku's entourage exhibited no special friend-
liness toward Masuyama. On the contrary, he knew that they secretly
gossiped about him, accusing him of being disrespectful or of giving
himself airs merely because he had gone through some university. He
knew too that sometimes they professed irritation at his pedantic
insistence on historical facts. In the world of kabuki, academic learning unaccompanied by artistic talent is considered of no value.

Masuyama's work had its compensations too. It would happen
when Mangiku had a favor to ask of someone—only, of course, when
he was in a good mood—that he twisted his body diagonally from his

dressing table and gave a little nod and a smile; the indescribable charm in his eyes at such moments made Masuyama feel that he wished for nothing more than to slave like a dog for this man. Mangiku himself never forgot his dignity: he never failed to maintain a certain distance, though he obviously was aware of his charms. If he had been a real women, his whole body would have been filled with the allure in his eyes. The allure of an *onnagata* is only a momentary glimmer, but that is enough for it to exist independently and to display the eternal feminine.

Mangiku sat before the mirror after the performance of *The Castle of the Lord Protector of Hachijin*, the first item of the program. He had removed the costume and wig he wore as Lady Hinaginu, and changed to a bathrobe, not being obliged to appear in the middle work of the program. Masuyama, informed that Mangiku wanted to see him, had been waiting in the dressing room for the curtain of *Hachijin*. The mirror suddenly burst into crimson flames as Mangiku returned to the room, filling the entrance with the rustle of his robes. Three disciples and costumers joined to remove what had to be removed and store it away. Those who were to leave departed, and now no one remained except for a few disciples around the hibachi in the next room. The dressing room had all at once fallen still. From a loudspeaker in the corridor issued the sounds of stage assistants hammering as they dismantled the set for the play which had just ended. It was late November, and steam heat clouded the windowpanes, bleak as in a hospital ward. White chrysanthemums bent gracefully in a cloisonné vase placed beside Mangiku's dressing table. Mangiku, perhaps because his stage name meant literally "ten thousand chrysanthemums," was fond of this flower.

Mangiku sat on a bulky cushion of purple silk, facing his dressing table. "I wonder if you'd mind telling the gentleman from Sakuragi Street?" (Mangiku, in the old-fashioned manner, referred to his dancing and singing teachers by the names of the streets where they lived.) "It'd be hard for me to tell him." He gazed directly into the mirror as he spoke. Masuyama could see from where he sat by the wall the nape of Mangiku's neck and the reflections in the mirror of his face still made up for the part of Hinaginu. The eyes were not on Masuyama; they were squarely contemplating his own face. The flush from his exertions on the stage still glowed through the powder on his cheeks, like the morning sun through a thin sheet of ice. He was looking at Hinaginu.

Indeed, he actually saw her in the mirror—Hinaginu, whom he had just been impersonating, Hinaginu, the daughter of Mori Sanzaemon Yoshinari and the bride of the young Satō Kazuenosuke. Her marriage ties with her husband having been broken because of his feudal loyalty, Hinaginu killed herself so that she might remain faithful to a union "whose ties were so faint we never shared the same bed." Hinaginu had died on stage of a despair so extreme she could not bear to live any longer. The Hinaginu in the mirror was a ghost. Even that ghost, Mangiku knew, was at that very moment slipping from his body. His eyes pursued Hinaginu. But as the glow of the ardent passions of the role subsided, Hinaginu's face faded away. He bade it farewell. There were still seven performances before the final day. Tomorrow again Hinaginu's features would no doubt return to the pliant mold of Mangiku's face.

Masuyama, enjoying the sight of Mangiku in this abstracted state, all but smiled with affection. Mangiku suddenly turned toward him. He had been aware all along of Masuyama's gaze, but with the nonchalance of the actor accustomed to the public's stares, he continued with his business. "It's those instrumental passages. They're simply not long enough. I don't mean I can't get through the part if I hurry, but it makes everything so ugly." Mangiku was referring to the music for the new dance-play which would be presented the following month. "Mr. Masuyama, what do *you* think?"

"I quite agree. I'm sure you mean the passage after 'How slowly the day ends by the Chinese bridge at Seta.'"

"Yes, that's the place. Ho-ow slo-ow the da-ay...." Mangiku sang the passage in question, beating time with his delicate fingers.

"I'll tell him. I'm sure that the gentleman from Sakuragi Street will understand."

"Are you sure you don't mind? I feel so embarrassed about making a nuisance of myself all the time."

Mangiku was accustomed to terminate a conversation by standing, once his business had been dealt with. "I'm afraid I must bathe now," he said. Masuyama drew back from the narrow entrance to the dressing room and let Mangiku pass. Mangiku, with a slight bow of the head, went out into the corridor, accompanied by a disciple. He turned back obliquely toward Masuyama and, smiling, bowed again.

The rouge at the corners of his eyes had an indefinable charm. Masuyama sensed that Mangiku was well aware of his affection.

IV

The troupe to which Masuyama belonged was to remain at the same theatre through November, December, and January, and the program for January had already become the subject of gossip. A new work by a playwright of the modern theatre was to be staged. The man, whose sense of his own importance accorded poorly with his youth, had imposed innumerable conditions, and Masuyama was kept frantically busy with complicated negotiations intended to bring together not only the dramatist and the actors but the management of the theatre as well. Masuyama was recruited for this job because the others considered him to be an intellectual.

One of the conditions laid down by the playwright was that the direction of the play be confided to a talented young man whom he trusted. The management accepted this condition. Mangiku also agreed, but without enthusiasm. He conveyed his doubts in this manner: "I don't really know, of course, but if this young man doesn't understand kabuki very well, and makes unreasonable demands on us, it will be so hard explaining." Mangiku was hoping for an older, more mature—by which he meant a more compliant—director.

The new play was a dramatization in modern language of the twelfth-century novel *If Only I Could Change Them!* The managing director of the company, deciding not to leave the production of this new work to the regular staff, announced it would be in Masuyama's hands. Masuyama grew tense at the thought of the work ahead of him, but convinced that the play was first-rate, he felt that it would be worth the trouble.

As soon as the scripts were ready and the parts assigned, a preliminary meeting was held one mid-December morning in the reception room adjoining the office of the theatre owner. The meeting was attended by the executive in charge of production, the playwright, the director, the stage designer, the actors, and Masuyama. The room was warmly heated and sunlight poured through the windows. Masuyama always felt happiest at preliminary meetings. It was like spreading out a map and discussing a projected outing: Where do we board the bus and where do we start walking? Is there drinking water where we're going? Where are we going to eat lunch? Where is the best view? Shall we take the train back? Or would it be better to allow enough time to return by boat?

Kawasaki, the director, was late. Masuyama had never seen a play directed by Kawasaki, but he knew of him by reputation. Kawasaki had been selected, despite his youth, to direct Ibsen and modern American plays for a repertory company, and in the course of the year had done so well, with the latter especially, that he was awarded a newspaper drama prize.

The others (except for Kawasaki) had all assembled. The designer, who could never bear waiting a minute before throwing himself into his work, was already jotting down in a large notebook especially brought for the purpose suggestions made by the others, frequently tapping the end of his pencil on the blank pages, as if bursting with ideas. Eventually the executive began to gossip about the absent director. "He may be as talented as they say, but he's still young, after all. The actors will have to help him out."

At this moment there was a knock at the door and a secretary showed in Kawasaki. He entered the room with a dazed look, as if the light were too strong for him and, without uttering a word, stiffly bowed toward the others. He was rather tall, almost six feet, with deeply etched, masculine—but highly sensitive—features. It was a cold winter day, but Kawasaki wore a rumpled, thin raincoat. Underneath, as he presently disclosed, he had on a brick-colored corduroy jacket. His long, straight hair hung down so far—to the tip of his nose—that he was frequently obliged to push it back. Masuyama was rather disappointed by his first impression. He had supposed that a man who had been singled out for his abilities would have attempted to distinguish himself somehow from the stereotypes of society, but this man dressed and acted exactly in the way one would expect of the typical young man of the modern theatre.

Kawasaki took the place offered him at the head of the table. He did not make the usual polite protests against the honor. He kept his eyes on the playwright, his close friend, and when introduced to each of the actors he uttered a word of greeting, only to turn back at once to the playwright. Masuyama could remember similar experiences. It is not easy for a man trained in the modern theatre, where most of the actors are young, to establish himself on easy terms with the kabuki actors, who are likely to prove to be imposing old gentlemen when encountered off stage.

The actors assembled for this preliminary meeting managed in fact somehow to convey their contempt for Kawasaki, all with a show of the greatest politeness and without an unfriendly word. Masuyama happened to glance at Mangiku's face. He modestly kept to himself, refraining from any demonstration of self-importance; he displayed no trace of the others' contempt. Masuyama felt greater admiration and affection than ever for Mangiku.

Now that everyone was present, the author described the play in outline. Mangiku, probably for the first time in his career—leaving aside parts he took as a child—was to play a male role. The plot told of a certain Grand Minister with two children, a boy and a girl. By nature they are quite unsuited to their sexes and therefore are reared accordingly: the boy (actually the girl) eventually becomes General of the Left, and the girl (actually the boy) becomes chief lady-in-waiting in the Senyōden, the palace of the Imperial concubines. Later, when the truth is revealed, they revert to lives more appropriate to the sex of their birth: the brother marries the fourth daughter of the Minister of the Right, the sister a Middle Counselor, and all ends happily.

Mangiku's part was that of the girl who is in reality a man. Although this was a male role, Mangiku would appear as a man only in the few moments of the final scene. Up to that point, he was to act throughout as a true *onnagata* in the part of the chief lady-in-waiting at the Senyōden. The author and director were agreed in urging Mangiku not to make any special attempt even in the last scene to suggest that he was in fact a man.

An amusing aspect of the play was that it inevitably had the effect of satirizing the kabuki convention of the *onnagata*. The lady-in-waiting was actually a man; so, in precisely the same manner, was Mangiku in the role. That was not all. In order for Mangiku, at once an *onnagata* and a man, to perform this part, he would have to unfold on two levels his actions of real life, a far cry from the simple case of the actor who assumes female costume during the course of the play so as to work some deception. The complexities of the part intrigued Mangiku.

Kawasaki's first words to Mangiku were, "I would be glad if you played the part throughout as a woman. It doesn't make the least difference if you act like a woman even in the last scene." His voice had a pleasant, clear ring.

"Really? If you don't mind my acting the part that way, it'll make it ever so much easier for me."

"It won't be easy in any case. Definitely not," said Kawasaki decisively. When he spoke in this forceful manner his cheeks glowed red as if a lamp had been lit inside. The sharpness of his tone cast something of a pall over the gathering. Masuyama's eyes wandered to Mangiku. He was giggling good-naturedly, the back of his hand pressed to his mouth. The others relaxed to see Mangiku had not been offended.

"Well, then," said the author, "I shall read the book." He lowered his protruding eyes, which looked double behind his thick spectacles, and began to read the script on the table.

V

Two or three days later the rehearsal by parts began, whenever the different actors had free time. Full-scale rehearsals would only be possible during the few days in between the end of this month and the beginning of next month's program. Unless everything that needed tightening were attended to by then, there would be no time to pull the performance together.

Once the rehearsal of the parts began it became apparent to everyone that Kawasaki was like a foreigner strayed among them. He had not the smallest grasp of kabuki, and Masuyama found himself obliged to stand beside him and explain word by word the technical language of the kabuki theatre, making Kawasaki extremely dependent on him. The instant the first rehearsal was over Masuyama invited Kawasaki for a drink.

Masuyama knew that for someone in his position it was generally speaking a mistake to ally himself with the director, but he felt he could easily understand what Kawasaki must be experiencing. The young man's views were precisely defined, his mental attitudes were wholesome, and he threw himself into his work with boyish enthusiasm. Masuyama could see why Kawasaki's character should have so appealed to the playwright; he felt as if Kawasaki's genuine youthfulness were a somehow purifying element, a quality unknown in the world of kabuki. Masuyama justified his friendship with Kawasaki in terms of attempting to turn this quality to the advantage of kabuki.

Full-scale rehearsals began at last on the day after the final performances of the December program. It was two days after Christmas. The year-end excitement in the streets could be sensed even through the windows in the theatre and the dressing rooms. A battered old desk had been placed by a window in the large rehearsal room. Kawasaki and one of Masuyama's seniors on the staff—the stage manager—sat with their backs to the window. Masuyama was behind Kawasaki. The actors sat on the *tatami* along the wall. Each would go up center when his turn came to recite his lines. The stage manager supplied forgotten lines.

Sparks flew repeatedly between Kawasaki and the actors. "At this point," Kawasaki would say, "I'd like you to stand as you say, 'I wish I could go to Kawachi and have done with it.' Then you're to walk up to the pillar at stage right."

"That's one place I simply can't stand up."

"Please try doing it my way." Kawasaki forced a smile, but his face visibly paled with wounded pride.

"You can ask me to stand up from now until next Christmas, but I still can't do it. I'm supposed at this place to be mulling over something. How can I walk across stage when I'm thinking?"

Kawasaki did not answer, but he betrayed his extreme irritation at being addressed in such terms.

But things were quite different when it came Mangiku's turn. If Kawasaki said, "Sit!" Mangiku would sit, and if he said, "Stand!" Mangiku stood. He obeyed unresistingly every direction given by Kawasaki. It seemed to Masuyama that Mangiku's fondness for the part did not fully explain why he was so much more obliging than was his custom at rehearsals.

Masuyama was forced to leave this rehearsal on business just as Mangiku, having run through his scene in the first act, was returning to his seat by the wall. When Masuyama got back, he was met by the following sight: Kawasaki, all but sprawled over the desk, was intently following the rehearsal, not bothering even to push back the long hair falling over his eyes. He was leaning on his crossed arms, the shoulders beneath the corduroy jacket shaking with suppressed rage. To Masuyama's right was a white wall interrupted by a window, through which he could see a balloon swaying in the northerly wind, its streamer proclaiming an end-of-the-year sale. Hard, wintry clouds looked as if they had been blocked in with chalk against the pale blue of the sky. He noticed a shrine to Inari and a tiny vermilion torii on the roof of an old building near by. Farther to his right, by the wall, Mangiku sat erect in Japanese style on the *tatami*. The script lay open on his lap, and the lines of his greenish-gray kimono were perfectly straight. From where Masuyama stood at the door he could not see Mangiku's full face; but the eyes, seen in profile, were utterly tranquil, the gentle gaze fixed unwaveringly on Kawasaki.

Masuyama felt a momentary shudder of fear. He had set one foot inside the rehearsal room, but it was now almost impossible to go in.

VI

Later in the day Masuyama was summoned to Mangiku's dressing room. He felt an unaccustomed emotional block when he bent his head, as so often before, to pass through the door curtains. Mangiku greeted him, all smiles, from his perch on the purple cushion and offered Masuyama some cakes he had been given by a visitor.

"How do you think the rehearsal went today?"

"Pardon me?" Masuyama was startled by the question. It was not like Mangiku to ask his opinion on such matters.

"How did it seem?"

"If everything continues to go as well as it did today, I think the play'll be a hit."

"Do you really think so? I feel terribly sorry for Mr. Kawasaki. It's so hard for him. The others have been treating him in such a high-handed way that it's made me quite nervous. I'm sure you could tell from the rehearsal that I've made up my mind to play the part exactly as Mr. Kawasaki says. That's the way I'd like to play it myself anyway, and I thought it might make things easier for Mr. Kawasaki, even if nobody else helps. I can't very well tell the others, but I'm sure they'll notice if I do exactly what I'm told. They know how difficult I usually am. That's the least I can do to protect Mr. Kawasaki. It'd be a shame, when he's trying so hard, if nobody helped."

Masuyama felt no particular surge of emotion as he listened to Mangiku. Quite likely, he thought, Mangiku himself was unaware that he was in love: he was so accustomed to portraying love on a more heroic scale. Masuyama, for his part, considered that these sentiments—however they were to be termed—which had formed in

Mangiku's heart were most inappropriate. He expected of Mangiku a far more transparent, artificial, aesthetic display of emotions.

Mangiku, most unusually for him, sat rather informally, imparting a kind of languor to his delicate figure. The mirror reflected the cluster of crimson asters arranged in the cloisonné vase and the recently shaved nape of Mangiku's neck.

Kawasaki's exasperation had become pathetic by the day before stage rehearsals began. As soon as the last private rehearsal ended, he invited Masuyama for a drink, looking as if he had reached the end of his tether. Masuyama was busy at the moment, but two hours later he found Kawasaki in the bar where they had arranged to meet, still waiting for him. The bar was crowded, though it was the night before New Year's Eve, when bars are usually deserted. Kawasaki's face looked pale as he sat drinking alone. He was the kind who only gets paler the more he has had to drink. Masuyama, catching sight of Kawasaki's ashen face as soon as he entered the bar, felt that the young man had saddled him with an unfairly heavy spiritual burden. They lived in different worlds; there was no reason why courtesy should demand that Kawasaki's uncertainties and anguish should fall so squarely on his shoulders.

Kawasaki, as he rather expected, immediately engaged him with a good-natured taunt, accusing him of being a double agent. Masuyama took the charge with a smile. He was only five or six years older than Kawasaki, but he possessed the self-confidence of a man who had dwelt among people who "knew the score." At the same time, he felt a kind of envy of this man who had never known hardship, or at any rate, enough hardship. It was not exactly a lack of moral integrity which had made Masuyama indifferent to most of the backstage gossip directed against him, now that he was securely placed in the kabuki hierarchy; his indifference demonstrated that he had nothing to do with the kind of sincerity which might destroy him.

Kawasaki spoke. "I'm fed up with the whole thing. Once the curtain goes up on opening night, I'll be only too glad to disappear from the picture. Stage rehearsals beginning tomorrow! That's more than I can take, when I'm feeling so disgusted. This is the worst assignment I've ever had. I've reached my limit. Never again will I barge into a world that's not my own."

"But isn't that what you more or less expected from the outset? Kabuki's not the same as the modern theatre, after all." Masuyama's voice was cold.

Kawasaki's next words came as a surprise. "Mangiku's the hardest to take. I really dislike him. I'll never stage another play with him." Kawasaki stared at the curling wisps of smoke under the low ceiling, as if into the face of an invisible enemy.

"I wouldn't have guessed it. It seems to me he's doing his best to be co-operative."

"What makes you think so? What's so good about him? It doesn't bother me too much when the other actors don't listen to me during rehearsals or try to intimidate me, or even when they sabotage the whole works, but Mangiku's more than I can figure out. All he does is stare at me with that sneer on his face. At bottom he's absolutely uncompromising, and he treats me like an ignorant little squirt. That's why he does everything exactly as I say. He's the only one of them who obeys my directions, and that burns me up all the more. I can tell just what he's thinking: 'If that's the way you want it, that's the way I'll do it, but don't expect me to take any responsibility for what happens in the performance.' That's what he keeps flashing at me, without saying a word, and it's the worst sabotage I know. He's the nastiest of the lot."

Masuyama listened in astonishment, but he shrank from revealing the truth to Kawasaki now. He hesitated even to let Kawasaki know that Mangiku was intending to be friendly, much less the whole truth. Kawasaki was baffled as to how he should respond to the entirely unfamiliar emotions of this world into which he had suddenly plunged; if he were informed of Mangiku's feelings, he might easily suppose they represented just one more snare laid for him. His eyes were too clear: for all his grasp of the principles of theatre, he could not detect the dark, aesthetic presence lurking behind the texts.

VII

The New Year came and with it the first night of the new program.

Mangiku was in love. His sharp-eyed disciples were the first to gossip about it. Masuyama, a frequent visitor to Mangiku's dressing room, sensed it in the atmosphere almost immediately. Mangiku was wrapped in his love like a silkworm in its cocoon, soon to emerge as a butterfly. His dressing room was the cocoon of his love. Mangiku was of a retiring disposition in any case, but the contrast with the New Year's excitement elsewhere gave his dressing room a peculiarly solemn hush.

Opening night, Masuyama, noticing as he passed Mangiku's dressing room that the door was wide open, decided to take a look inside. He saw Mangiku from behind, seated before his mirror in full costume, waiting for his signal to go on. His eyes took in the pale lavender of Mangiku's robe, the gentle slope of the powdered and half-exposed shoulders, the glossy, lacquer-black wig. Mangiku at such moments in the deserted dressing room looked like a woman absorbed in her spinning; she was spinning her love, and would continue spinning forever, her mind elsewhere.

Masuyama intuitively understood that the mold for this *onnagata*'s love had been provided by the stage alone. The stage was present all day long, the stage where love was incessantly shouting, grieving, shedding blood. Music celebrating the sublime heights of love sounded perpetually in Mangiku's ears, and each exquisite gesture of his body was constantly employed on stage for the purposes of love. To the tips of his fingers, nothing about Mangiku was alien to love. His toes encased in white *tabi*, the seductive colors of his under kimono barely glimpsed through the openings in his sleeves, the long, swanlike nape of his neck were all in the service of love.

Masuyama did not doubt but that Mangiku would obtain guidance in pursuing his love from the grandiose emotions of his stage roles. The ordinary actor is apt to enrich his performances by infusing them with the emotions of his real life, but not Mangiku. The instant that Mangiku fell in love, the loves of Yukihime, Omiwa, Hinaginu, and the other tragic heroines came to his support.

The thought of Mangiku in love took Masuyama aback, however. Those tragic emotions for which he had yearned so fervently since his days as a high-school student, those sublime emotions which Mangiku always evoked through his corporeal presence on stage, encasing his sensual faculties in icy flames, Mangiku was now visibly nurturing in real life. But the object of these emotions—granted that he had some talent—was an ignoramus as far as kabuki was concerned; he was merely a young, commonplace-looking director whose only qualification as the object of Mangiku's love consisted in being a foreigner in this country, a young traveler who would soon depart the world of kabuki and never return.

VIII

If Only I Could Change Them! was well received. Kawasaki, despite his announced intention of disappearing after opening night, came to the theatre every day to complain of the performance, to rush back and forth incessantly through the subterranean passages under the stage, to finger with curiosity the mechanisms of the trap door or the *hanamichi.* Masuyama thought this man had something childish about him.

The newspaper reviews praised Mangiku. Masuyama made it a point to show them to Kawasaki, but he merely pouted, like an obstinate child, and all but spat out the words, "They're all good at acting. But there wasn't any *direction.*" Masuyama naturally did not relay to Mangiku these harsh words, and Kawasaki himself was on his best behavior when he actually met Mangiku. It nevertheless irritated Masuyama that Mangiku, who was utterly blind when it came to other people's feelings, should not have questioned that Kawasaki was aware of his good will. But Kawasaki was absolutely insensitive to what other people might feel. This was the one trait that Kawasaki and Mangiku had in common.

A week after the first performance Masuyama was summoned to Mangiku's dressing room. Mangiku displayed on his table amulets and charms from the shrine where he regularly worshipped, as well as some small New Year's cakes. The cakes would no doubt be distributed later among his disciples. Mangiku pressed some sweets on Masuyama, a sign that he was in a good mood. "Mr. Kawasaki was here a little while ago," he said.

"Yes, I saw him out front."

"I wonder if he's still in the theatre."

"I imagine he'll stay until *If Only* is over."

"Did he say anything about being busy afterward?"

"No, nothing particular."

"Then, I have a little favor I'd like to ask you."

Masuyama assumed as businesslike an expression as he could muster. "What might it be?"

"Tonight, you see, when the performance is over ... I mean, tonight...." The color had mounted in Mangiku's cheeks. His voice was clearer and higher-pitched than usual. "Tonight, when the performance is over, I thought I'd like to have dinner with him. Would you mind asking if he's free?"

"I'll ask him."

"It's dreadful of me, isn't it, to ask you such a thing."

"That's quite all right." Masuyama sensed that Mangiku's eyes at the moment had stopped roving and were trying to read his expression. He seemed to expect—and even to desire—some perturbation on Masuyama's part. "Very well," Masuyama said, rising at once, "I'll inform him."

Hardly had Masuyama gone into the lobby than he ran into Kawasaki, coming from the opposite direction; this chance meeting amidst the crowd thronging the lobby during intermission seemed like a stroke of fate. Kawasaki's manner poorly accorded with the festive air pervading the lobby. The somehow haughty airs which the young man always adopted seemed rather comic when set amidst a buzzing crowd of solid citizens dressed in holiday finery and attending the theatre merely for the pleasure of seeing a play.

Masuyama led Kawasaki to a corner of the lobby and informed him of Mangiku's request.

"I wonder want he wants with me now? Dinner together—that's funny. I have nothing else to do tonight, and there's no reason why I can't go, but I don't see why."

"I suppose there's something he wants to discuss about the play."

"The play! I've said all I want to on that subject."

At this moment a gratuitous desire to do evil, an emotion always associated on the stage with minor villains, took seed within Masuyama's heart, though he did not realize it; he was not aware that he himself was now acting like a character in a play. "Don't you see—being invited to dinner give you a marvelous opportunity to tell him everything you've got on your mind, this time without mincing words."

"All the same—"

"I don't suppose you've got the nerve to tell him."

The remark wounded the young man's pride. "All right. I'll go. I've known all along that sooner or later I'd have my chance to have it out with him in the open. Please tell him that I'm glad to accept his invitation."

Mangiku appeared in the last work of the program and was not free until the entire performance was over. Once the show ends, actors normally make a quick change of clothes and rush from the theatre, but Mangiku showed no sign of haste as he completed his dressing by putting a cape and a scarf of a muted color over his outer kimono. He waited for Kawasaki. When Kawasaki at last appeared, he curtly greeted Mangiku, not bothering to take his hands from his overcoat pockets.

The disciple who always waited on Mangiku as his "lady's maid" rushed up, as if to announce some major calamity. "It's started to snow," he reported with a bow.

"A heavy snow?" Mangiku touched his cape to his cheek.

"No, just a flurry."

"We'll need an umbrella to the car," Mangiku said. The disciple rushed off for an umbrella.

Masuyama saw them to the stage entrance. The door attendant had politely arranged Mangiku's and Kawasaki's footwear next to each other. Mangiku's disciple stood outside in the thin snow, holding an open umbrella. The snow fell so sparsely that one couldn't be sure one saw it against the dark concrete wall beyond. One or two flakes fluttered onto the doorstep at the stage entrance.

Mangiku bowed to Masuyama. "We'll be leaving now," he said. The smile on his lips could be seen indistinctly behind his scarf. He turned to the disciple, "That's all right. I'll carry the umbrella. I'd like you to go instead and tell the driver we're ready." Mangiku held the umbrella over Kawasaki's head. As Kawasaki in his overcoat and Mangiku in his cape walked off side by side under the umbrella, a few flakes suddenly flew—all but bounced—from the umbrella.

Masuyama watched them go. He felt as though a big, black, wet umbrella were being noisily opened inside his heart. He could tell that the illusion, first formed when as a boy he saw Mangiku perform, an illusion which he had preserved intact even after he joined the kabuki staff, had shattered that instant in all directions, like a delicate piece of crystal dropped from a height. At last I know what disillusion means, he thought. I might as well give up the theatre.

But Masuyama knew that along with disillusion a new sensation was assaulting him, jealousy. He dreaded where this new emotion might lead him.

May We Borrow Your Husband?

Graham Greene

In the year 8 AD, the emperor Augustus banished the poet Ovid from Rome. The reason for this harsh sentence was, perhaps, his book of poems The Art of Love, *which quickly became famous for its amorality. The book is a technical treatise instructing men on the wooing of women and women on the seduction of men. All sorts of combinations are suggested and discussed, and strategic advice is given, as if love were no different from a business or a military transaction. Similar how-to books were written in India, Egypt, the Middle East, and medieval Europe. There is a longstanding tradition of love as a game, a battle, a sleight-of-hand, a ruse.*

Graham Greene's fiction, especially the pieces he called his "entertainments", abounds in these erotic campaigns in which husbands and wives, mistresses and lovers, fulfil certain roles and undertake specific actions in the hope of winning the love that is their goal. Sometimes the enemy is formidable, as in The End of the Affair, *where the rival lover is God; other times it is a medley of opponents, as in* Travels with My Aunt. *There is something businesslike in these amorous pursuits (as in "May We Borrow Your Husband?") which recognizes the codes and conventions of our everyday life and our tactics to circumvent them. It may be, Greene seems to suggest, that these pursuits are driven by either our greed or our fear of loneliness. We are rarely rewarded. Greed is, by definition, unrewardable. And Greene recalls that in one of his dreams he came across a line in a book which stuck in his memory: "Loneliness is not shared with another—it is multiplied."*

I

I never heard her called anything else but Poopy, either by her husband or by the two men who became their friends. Perhaps I was a little in love with her (absurd though that may seem at my age) because

I found that I resented the name. It was unsuited to someone so young and so open—too open; she belonged to the age of trust just as I belonged to the age of cynicism. "Good old Poopy"—I even heard her called that by the elder of the two interior-decorators (who had known her no longer than I had): a sobriquet which might have been good enough for some vague bedraggled woman of middle age who drank a bit too much but who was useful to drag around as a kind of blind—and those two certainly needed a blind. I once asked the girl her real name, but all she said was, "Everyone calls me Poopy," as though that finished it, and I was afraid of appearing too square if I pursued the question further—too middle-aged perhaps as well, so though I hate the name whenever I write it down, Poopy she has to remain: I have no other.

I had been at Antibes working on a book of mine, a biography of the seventeenth-century poet, the Earl of Rochester, for more than a month before Poopy and her husband arrived. I had come there as soon as the full season was over, to a small ugly hotel by the sea not far from the ramparts, and I was able to watch the season depart with the leaves in the Boulevard Général Leclerc. At first, even before the trees had begun to drop, the foreign cars were on the move homeward. A few weeks earlier, I had counted fourteen nationalities, including Morocco, Turkey, Sweden and Luxembourg, between the sea and the Place de Gaulle, to which I walked every day for the English papers. Now all the foreign number-plates had gone, except for the Belgian and the German and an occasional English one, and, of course, the ubiquitous number-plates of the State of Monaco. The cold weather had come early and Antibes catches only the morning sun—good enough for breakfast on the terrace, but it was safer to lunch indoors or the shadow might overtake the coffee. A cold and solitary Algerian was always there, leaning over the ramparts, looking for something, perhaps safety.

It was the time of year I liked best, when Juan les Pins becomes as squalid as a closed fun-fair with Lunar Park boarded up and cards marked *Fermeture Annuelle* outside the Pam-Pam and Maxim's, and the Concours International Amateur de Striptease at the Vieux Colombiers is over for another season. Then Antibes comes into its own as a small country town with the Auberge de Provence full of local people and old men sit indoors drinking beer or pastis at the *glacier* in the Place de Gaulle. The small garden, which forms a roundabout on the ramparts, looks a little sad with the short stout palms bowing their brown fronds; the sun in the morning shines without any glare, and the few white sails move gently on the unblinding sea.

You can always trust the English to stay on longer than others into the autumn. We have a blind faith in the southern sun and we are taken by surprise when the wind blows icily over the Mediterranean. Then a bickering war develops with the hotel-keeper over the heating on the third floor, and the tiles strike cold underfoot. For a man who has reached the age when all he wants is some good wine and some good cheese and a little work, it is the best season of all. I know how I resented the arrival of the interior-decorators just at the moment when I had hoped to be the only foreigner left, and I prayed that they were birds of passage. They arrived before lunch in a scarlet Sprite—a car much too young for them, and they wore elegant sports clothes more suited to spring at the Cap. The elder man was nearing fifty and the grey hair that waved over his ears was too uniform to be true: the younger had passed thirty and his hair was as black as the other's was grey. I knew their names were Stephen and Tony before they even reached the reception desk, for they had clear, penetrating yet superficial voices, like their gaze, which had quickly lighted on me where I sat with a Ricard on the terrace and registered that I had nothing of interest for them, and passed on. They were not arrogant: it was simply that they were more concerned with each other, and yet perhaps, like a married couple of some years' standing, not very profoundly.

I soon knew a great deal about them. They had rooms side by side in my passage, though I doubt if both rooms were often occupied, for I used to hear voices from one room or the other most evenings when I went to bed. Do I seem too curious about other people's affairs? But in my own defence I have to say that the events of this sad little comedy were forced by all the participants on my attention. The balcony where I worked every morning on my life of Rochester overhung the terrace where the interior-decorators took their coffee, and even when they occupied a table out of sight those clear elocutionary voices mounted up to me. I didn't want to hear them; I wanted to work. Rochester's relations with the actress, Mrs. Barry, were my concern at the moment, but it is almost impossible in a foreign land not to listen to one's own tongue. French I could have accepted as a kind of background noise, but I could not fail to overhear English.

"My dear, guess who's written to me now?"

"Alec?"

"No, Mrs. Clarenty."

"What does the old hag want?"

"She objects to the mural in her bedroom."

"But, Stephen, it's divine. Alec's never done anything better. The dead faun...."

"I think she wants something more nubile and less necrophilous."

"The old lecher."

They were certainly hardy, those two. Every morning around eleven they went bathing off the little rocky peninsula opposite the hotel—they had the autumnal Mediterranean, so far as the eye could see, entirely to themselves. As they walked briskly back in their elegant bikinis, or sometimes ran a little way for warmth, I had the impression that they took their bathes less for pleasure than for exercise—to preserve the slim legs, the flat stomachs, the narrow hips for more recondite and Etruscan pastimes.

Idle they were not. They drove the Sprite to Cagnes, Vence, St. Paul, to any village where an antique store was to be rifled, and they brought back with them objects of olive wood, spurious old lanterns, painted religious figures which in the shop would have seemed to me ugly or banal, but which I suspect already fitted in their imaginations some scheme of decoration the reverse of commonplace. Not that their minds were altogether on their profession. They relaxed.

I encountered them one evening in a little sailors' bar in the old port of Nice. Curiosity this time had led me in pursuit, for I had seen the scarlet Sprite standing outside the bar. They were entertaining a boy of about eighteen who, from his clothes, I imagine worked as a hand on the boat to Corsica which was at the moment in harbour. They both looked very sharply at me when I entered, as though they were thinking, "Have we misjudged him?" I drank a glass of beer and left, and the younger said "Good evening" as I passed the table. After that we had to greet each other every day in the hotel. It was as though I had been admitted to an intimacy.

Time for a few days was hanging as heavily on my hands as on Lord Rochester's. He was staying at Mrs. Fourcard's baths in Leather Lane, receiving mercury treatment for the pox, and I was awaiting a whole section of my notes which I had inadvertently left in London. I couldn't release him till they came, and my sole distraction for a few days was those two. As they packed themselves into the Sprite of an afternoon or an evening I liked to guess from their clothes the nature of their excursion. Always elegant, they were yet successful, by the mere exchange of one *tricot* for another, in indicating their mood: they were just as well dressed in the sailors' bar, but a shade more simply; when dealing with a Lesbian antique dealer at St. Paul, there was a masculine dash about their handkerchiefs. Once they disappeared altogether for the inside of a week in what I took to be their oldest clothes, and when they returned the older man had a contusion on his right cheek. They told me they had been over to Corsica. Had they enjoyed it? I asked.

"Quite barbaric," the young man Tony said, but not, I thought, in praise.

He saw me looking at Stephen's cheek, and he added quickly, "We had an accident in the mountains."

It was two days after that, just at sunset, that Poopy arrived with her husband. I was back at work on Rochester, sitting in an overcoat on my balcony, when a taxi drove up—I recognized the driver as someone who plied regularly from Nice airport. What I noticed first, because the passengers were still hidden, was the luggage, which was bright blue and of an astonishing newness. Even the initials—rather absurdly PT—shone like newly-minted coins. There were a large suitcase and a small suitcase and a hat-box, all of the same cerulean hue, and after that a respectable old leather case totally unsuited to air travel, the kind one inherits from a father, with half a label still left from Shepheard's Hotel or the Valley of the Kings. Then the passenger emerged and I saw Poopy for the first time. Down below, the interior-decorators were watching too, and drinking Dubonnet.

She was a very tall girl, perhaps five feet nine, very slim, very young, with hair the colour of conkers, and her costume was as new as the luggage. She said, *"Finalmente,"* looking at the undistinguished façade with an air of rapture—or perhaps it was only the shape of her eyes. When I saw the young man I felt certain they were just married; it wouldn't have surprised me if confetti had fallen out from the seams of their clothes. They were like a photograph in the *Tatler*; they had camera smiles for each other and an underlying nervousness. I was sure they had come straight from the reception, and that it had been a smart one, after a proper church wedding.

They made a very handsome couple as they hesitated a moment

before going up the steps to the reception. The long beam of the Phare de la Garoupe brushed the water behind them, and the flood-lighting went suddenly on outside the hotel as if the manager had been waiting for their arrival to turn it up. The two decorators sat there without drinking, and I noticed that the elder one had covered the contusion on his cheek with a very clean white handkerchief. They were not, of course, looking at the girl but at the boy. He was over six feet tall and as slim as the girl, with a face that might have been cut on a coin, completely handsome and completely dead—but perhaps that was only an effect of his nerves. His clothes, too, I thought, had been bought for the occasion, the sports-jacket with a double slit and the grey trousers cut a little narrowly to show off the long legs. It seemed to me that they were both too young to marry—I doubt if they had accumulated forty-five years between them—and I had a wild impulse to lean over the balcony and warn them away—"Not this hotel. Any hotel but this." Perhaps I could have told them that the heating was insufficient or the hot water erratic or the food terrible, not that the English care much about food, but of course they would have paid me no attention—they were so obviously "booked", and what an ageing lunatic I should have appeared in their eyes. ("One of those eccentric English types one finds abroad"—I could imagine the letter home.) This was the first time I wanted to interfere, and I didn't know them at all. The second time it was already too late, but I think I shall always regret that I did not give way to that madness....

It had been the silence and attentiveness of those two down below which had frightened me, and the patch of white handkerchief hiding the shameful contusion. For the first time I heard the hated name: "Shall we see the room, Poopy, or have a drink first?"

They decided to see the room, and the two glasses of Dubonnet clicked again into action.

I think she had more idea of how a honeymoon should be conducted than he had, because they were not seen again that night..

II

I was late for breakfast on the terrace, but I noticed that Stephen and Tony were lingering longer than usual. Perhaps they had decided at last that it was too cold for a bathe; I had the impression, however, that they were lying in wait. They had never been so friendly to me before, and I wondered whether perhaps they regarded me as a kind of cover, with my distressingly normal appearance. My table for some reason that day had been shifted and was out of the sun, so Stephen suggested that I should join theirs: they would be off in a moment, after one more cup.... The contusion was much less noticeable today, but I think he had been applying powder.

"You staying here long?" I asked them, conscious of how clumsily I constructed a conversation compared with their easy prattle.

"We had meant to leave tomorrow," Stephen said, "but last night we changed our minds."

"Last night?"

"It was such a beautiful day, wasn't it? 'Oh,' I said to Tony, 'surely we can leave poor dreary old London a little longer?' It has an awful staying power—like a railway sandwich."

"Are your clients so patient?"

"My dear, the clients? You never in your life saw such atrocities as we get from Brompton Square. It's always the same. People who pay others to decorate for them have ghastly taste themselves."

"You do the world a service then. Think what we might suffer without you. In Brompton Square."

Tony giggled, "I don't know how we'd stand if it we had not our private jokes. For example, in Mrs. Clarenty's case, we've installed what we call the Loo of Lucullus."

"She was enchanted," Stephen said.

"The most obscene vegetable forms. It reminded me of a harvest festival."

They suddenly became very silent and attentive, watching somebody over my shoulder. I looked back. It was Poopy, all by herself. She stood there, waiting for the boy to show her which table she could take, like a new girl at school who doesn't know the rules. She even seemed to be wearing a school uniform: very tight trousers, slit at the ankle—but she hadn't realized that the summer term was over. She had dressed up like that, I felt certain, so as not to be noticed, in order to hide herself, but there were only two other women on the terrace and they were both wearing sensible tweed skirts. She looked at them nostalgically as the waiter led her past our table to one nearer the sea. Her long legs moved awkwardly in the pants as though they felt exposed.

"The young bride," Tony said.

"Deserted already," Stephen said with satisfaction.

"Her name is Poopy Travis, you know."

"It's an extraordinary name to choose. She couldn't have been *christened* that way, unless they found a very liberal vicar."

"He is called Peter. Of an undefined occupation. Not Army, I think, do you?"

"Oh no, not Army. Something to do with land perhaps—there's an agreeable *herbal* smell about him."

"You seem to know nearly all there is to know," I said.

"We looked at their police *carnet* before dinner."

"I have an idea," Tony said, "that PT hardly represents their activities last night." He looked across the tables at the girl with an expression extraordinarily like hatred.

"We were both taken," Stephen said, "by the air of innocence. One felt he was more used to horses."

"He mistook the yearnings of the rider's crotch for something quite different."

Perhaps they hoped to shock me, but I don't think it was that. I really believe they were in a state of extreme sexual excitement; they had received a *coup de foudre* last night on the terrace and were quite incapable of disguising their feelings. I was an excuse to talk, to speculate about the desired object. The sailor had been a stop-gap: this was the real thing. I was inclined to be amused, for what could this absurd pair hope to gain from a young man newly married to the girl who now sat there patiently waiting, wearing her beauty like an old sweater she had forgotten to change? But that was a bad simile to use: she would have been afraid to wear an old sweater, except secretly, by herself, in the playroom. She had no idea that she was one of those who can afford to disregard the fashion of their clothes. She caught my eye and, because I was so obviously English, I suppose, gave me half a timid smile. Perhaps I too would have received the *coup de foudre* if I had not been thirty years older and twice married.

Tony detected the smile. "A regular body-snatcher," he said. My breakfast and the young man arrived at the same moment before I had time to reply. As he passed the table I could feel the tension.

"*Cuir de Russie*," Stephen said, quivering a nostril. "A mistake of inexperience."

The youth caught the words as he went past and turned with an

astonished look to see who had spoken, and they both smiled insolently back at him as though they really believed they had the power
to take him over....

For the first time I felt disquiet.

III

Something was not going well; that was sadly obvious. The girl nearly
always came down to breakfast ahead of her husband—I have an idea
he spent a long time bathing and shaving and applying his *Cuir de
Russie*. When he joined her he would give her a courteous brotherly
kiss as though they had not spent the night together in the same bed.
She began to have those shadows under the eyes which come from
lack of sleep—for I couldn't believe that they were "the lineaments of
gratified desire". Sometimes from my balcony I saw them returning
from a walk—nothing, except perhaps a pair of horses, could have
been more handsome. His gentleness towards her might have reassured her mother, but it made a man impatient to see him squiring her
across the undangerous road, holding open doors, following a pace
behind her like the husband of a princess. I longed to see some out-
break of irritation caused by the sense of satiety, but they never
seemed to be in conversation when they returned from their walk, and
at table I caught only the kind of phrases people use who are dining
together for the sake of politeness. And yet I could swear that she
loved him, even by the way she avoided watching him. There was
nothing avid or starved about her; she stole her quick glances when
she was quite certain that his attention was absorbed elsewhere—they
were tender, anxious perhaps, quite undemanding. If one inquired
after him when he wasn't there, she glowed with the pleasure of using
his name. "Oh, Peter overslept this morning." "Peter cut himself. He's
staunching the blood now." "Peter's mislaid his tie. He thinks the
floor-waiter has purloined it." Certainly she loved him; I was far less
certain of what his feelings were.

And you must imagine how all the time those other two were closing in. It was like a medieval siege: they dug their trenches and threw
up their earthworks. The difference was that the besieged didn't
notice what they were at—at any rate, the girl didn't; I don't know
about him. I longed to warn her, but what could I have said that

wouldn't have shocked her or angered her? I believe the two would have changed their floor if that would have helped to bring them closer to the fortress; they probably discussed the move together and decided against it as too overt.

Because they knew that I could do nothing against them, they regarded me almost in the role of an ally. After all, I might be useful one day in distracting the girl's attention—and I suppose they were not quite mistaken in that; they could tell from the way I looked at her how interested I was, and they probably calculated that my interests might in the long run coincide with theirs. It didn't occur to them that, perhaps, I was a man with scruples. If one really wanted a thing scruples were obviously, in their eyes, out of place. There was a tortoiseshell star mirror at St. Paul they were plotting to obtain for half the price demanded (I think there was an old mother who looked after the shop when her daughter was away at a *boîte* for women of a certain taste); naturally, therefore, when I looked at the girl, as they saw me so often do, they considered I would be ready to join in any "reasonable" scheme.

"When I looked at the girl"—I realize that I have made no real attempt to describe her. In writing a biography one can, of course, just insert a portrait and the affair is done: I have the prints of Lady Rochester and Mrs. Barry in front of me now. But speaking as a professional novelist (for biography and reminiscence are both new forms to me), one describes a woman not so much that the reader should see her in all the cramping detail of colour and shape (how often Dickens's elaborate portraits seem like directions to the illustrator which might well have been left out of the finished book), but to convey an emotion. Let the reader make his own image of a wife, a mistress, some passer-by "sweet and kind" (the poet required no other descriptive words), if he has a fancy to. If I were to describe the girl (I can't bring myself at this moment to write her hateful name), it would be not to convey the colour of her hair, the shape of her mouth, but to express the pleasure and the pain with which I recall her—I, the writer, the observer, the subsidiary character, what you will. But if I didn't bother to convey them to her, why should I bother to convey them to you, *hypocrite lecteur?*

How quickly those two tunnelled. I don't think it was more than four mornings after the arrival that, when I came down to breakfast, I found they had moved their table next to the girl's and were entertaining her in her husband's absence. They did it very well; it was the first time I had seen her relaxed and happy—and she was happy because she was talking about Peter. Peter was agent for his father, somewhere in Hampshire—there were three thousand acres to manage. Yes, he was fond of riding and so was she. It all tumbled out—the kind of life she dreamed of having when she returned home. Stephen just dropped in a word now and then, of a rather old-fashioned courteous interest, to keep her going. Apparently he had once decorated some hall in their neighbourhood and knew the names of some people Peter knew—Winstanley, I think—and that gave her immense confidence.

"He's one of Peter's best friends," she said, and the two flickered their eyes at each other like lizards' tongues.

"Come and join us, William," Stephen said, but only when he had noticed that I was within earshot. "You know Mrs. Travis?"

How could I refuse to sit at their table? And yet in doing so I seemed to become an ally.

"Not *the* William Harris?" the girl asked. It was a phrase which I hated, and yet she transformed even that, with her air of innocence. For she had a capacity to make everything new: Antibes became a discovery and we were the first foreigners to have made it. When she said, "Of course, I'm afraid I haven't actually *read* any of your books," I heard the over-familiar remark for the first time; it even seemed to me a proof of her honesty—I nearly wrote her virginal honesty. "You must know an awful lot about people," she said, and again I read into the banality of the remark an appeal—for help against whom, those two or the husband who at that moment appeared on the terrace? He had the same nervous air as she, even the same shadows under the lids, so that they might have been taken by a stranger, as I wrote before, for brother and sister. He hesitated a moment when he saw all of us there and she called across to him, "Come and meet these nice people, darling." He didn't look any too pleased, but he sat glumly down and asked whether the coffee was still hot.

"I'll order some more, darling. They know the Winstanleys, and this is *the* William Harris."

He looked at me blankly; I think he was wondering if I had anything to do with tweeds.

"I hear you like horses," Stephen said, "and I was wondering whether you and your wife would come to lunch with us at Cagnes on Saturday. That's tomorrow, isn't it? There's a very good racecourse at Cagnes...."

"I don't know," he said dubiously, looking to his wife for a clue.

"But, darling, of course we must go. You'd love it."

His face cleared instantly. I really believe he had been troubled by a social scruple: the question whether one accepts invitations on a honeymoon. "It's very good of you," he said, "Mr...."

"Let's start as we mean to go on. I'm Stephen and this is Tony."

"I'm Peter." He added a trifle gloomily, "And this is Poopy."

"Tony, you take Poopy in the Sprite, and Peter and I will go by *autobus*." (I had the impression, and I think Tony had too, that Stephen had gained a point.)

"You'll come too, Mr. Harris?" the girl asked, using my surname as though she wished to emphasize the difference between me and them.

"I'm afraid I can't. I'm working against time."

I watched them that evening from my balcony as they returned from Cagnes and, hearing the way they all laughed together, I thought, "The enemy are within the citadel: it's only a question of time." A lot of time, because they proceeded very carefully, those two. There was no question of a quick grab which I suspect had caused the contusion in Corsica.

IV

It became a regular habit with the two of them to entertain the girl during her solitary breakfast before her husband arrived. I never sat at their table again, but scraps of the conversation would come over to me, and it seemed to me that she was never quite so cheerful again. Even the sense of novelty had gone. I heard her say once, "There's so little to do here," and it struck me as an odd observation for a honeymooner to make.

Then one evening I found her in tears outside the Musée Grimaldi. I had been fetching my papers, and, as my habit was, I made a round by the Place Nationale with the pillar erected in 1819 to celebrate—a remarkable paradox—the loyalty of Antibes to the monarchy and her resistance to *Les Troupes Etrangères*, who were seeking to re-establish the monarchy. Then, according to rule, I went on by the market and the old port and Lou-Lou's restaurant up the ramp towards the cathedral and the Musée, and there in the grey evening light, before the street-lamps came on, I found her crying under the cliff of the château.

I noticed too late what she was at or I wouldn't have said, "Good evening, Mrs. Travis." She jumped a little as she turned and dropped her handkerchief, and when I picked it up I found it soaked with tears—it was like holding a small drowned animal in my hand. I said, "I'm sorry," meaning that I was sorry to have startled her, but she took it in quite another sense. She said, "Oh, I'm being silly, that's all. It's just a mood. Everybody has moods, don't they?"

"Where's Peter?"

"He's in the museum with Stephen and Tony looking at the Picassos. I don't understand them a bit."

"That's nothing to be ashamed of. Lots of people don't."

"But Peter doesn't understand them either. I know he doesn't. He's just pretending to be interested."

"Oh well...."

"And it's not that either. I pretended for a time too, to please Stephen. But he's pretending just to get away from me."

"You are imagining things."

Punctually at five o'clock the *phare* lit up, but it was still too light to see the beam.

I said, "The museum will be closing now."

"Walk back with me to the hotel."

"Wouldn't you like to wait for Peter?"

"I don't smell, do I?" she asked miserably.

"Well, there's a trace of Arpège. I've always liked Arpège."

"How terribly experienced you sound."

"Not really. It's just that my first wife used to buy Arpège."

We began walking back, and the mistral bit our ears and gave her an excuse when the time came for the reddened eyes.

She said, "I think Antibes so sad and grey."

"I thought you enjoyed it here."

"Oh, for a day or two."

"Why not go home?"

"It would look odd, wouldn't it, returning early from a honeymoon?"

"Or go on to Rome—or somewhere. You can get a plane to most places from Nice."

"It wouldn't make any difference," she said. "It's not the place that's wrong, it's me."

"I don't understand."

"He's not happy with me. It's as simple as that."

She stopped opposite one of the little rock houses by the ramparts. Washing hung down over the street below and there was a cold-looking canary in a cage.

"You said yourself ... a mood...."

"It's not his fault," she said. "It's me. I expect it seems very stupid to you, but I never slept with anyone before I married." She gulped miserably at the canary.

"And Peter?"

"He's terribly sensitive," she said, and added quickly, "That's a good quality. I wouldn't have fallen in love with him if he hadn't been."

"If I were you, I'd take him home—as quickly as possible." I couldn't help the words sounding sinister, but she hardly heard them. She was listening to the voices that came nearer down the ramparts— to Stephen's gay laugh. "They're very sweet," she said. "I'm glad he's found friends."

How could I say that they were seducing Peter before her eyes? And in any case wasn't her mistake already irretrievable? Those were two of the questions which haunted the hours, dreary for a solitary man, of the middle afternoon when work is finished and the exhilaration of the wine at lunch, and the time for the first evening drink has not yet come and the winter heating is at its feeblest. Had she no idea of the nature of the young man she had married? Had he taken her on as a blind or as a last desperate throw for normality? I couldn't bring myself to believe that. There was a sort of innocence about the boy which seemed to justify her love, and I preferred to think that he was not yet fully formed, that he had married honestly and it was only now that he found himself on the brink of a different experience. And yet if that were the case the comedy was all the crueller. Would everything have gone normally well if some conjunction of the planets had not crossed their honeymoon with that hungry pair of hunters?

I longed to speak out, and in the end I did speak, but not, so it happened, to her. I was going to my room and the door of one of theirs was open and I heard again Stephen's laugh—a kind of laugh which is sometimes with unintentional irony called infectious; it maddened me. I knocked and went in. Tony was stretched on a double bed and Stephen was "doing" his hair, holding a brush in each hand and meticulously arranging the grey waves on either side. The dressing-table had as many pots on it as a woman's.

"You really mean he told you that?" Tony was saying. "Why, how are you, William? Come in. Our young friend has been confiding in Stephen. Such really fascinating things."

"Which of your young friends?" I asked.

"Why, Peter, of course. Who else? The secrets of married life."

"I thought it might have been your sailor."

"Naughty!" Tony said. "But *touché* too, of course."

"I wish you'd leave Peter alone."

"I don't think he'd like that," Stephen said. "You can see that he hasn't quite the right tastes for this sort of honeymoon."

"Now you happen to like women, William," Tony said. "Why not go after the girl? It's a grand opportunity. She's not getting what I believe is vulgarly called her greens." Of the two he was easily the more brutal. I wanted to hit him, but this is not the century for that kind of romantic gesture, and anyway he was stretched out flat upon the bed. I said feebly enough—I ought to have known better than to have entered into a debate with those two—"She happens to be in love with him."

"I think Tony is right and she would find more satisfaction with you, William dear," Stephen said, giving a last flick to the hair over his right ear—the contusion was quite gone now. "From what Peter has said to me, I think you'd be doing a favour to both of them."

"Tell him what Peter said, Stephen."

"He said that from the very first there was a kind of hungry femininity about her which he found frightening and repulsive. Poor boy—he was really trapped into this business of marriage. His father wanted heirs—he breeds horses too, and then her mother—there's quite a lot of lucre with that lot. I don't think he had any idea of—of the Shape of Things to Come." Stephen shuddered into the glass and then regarded himself with satisfaction.

Even today I have to believe for my own peace of mind that the young man had not really said those monstrous things. I believe, and hope, that the words were put into his mouth by that cunning drama-tizer, but there is little comfort in the thought, for Stephen's inventions were always true to character. He even saw through my apparent indifference to the girl and realized that Tony and he had gone too far; it would not suit their purpose, if I were driven to the wrong kind of action, or if, by their crudities, I lost my interest in Poopy.

'Of course,' Stephen said, 'I'm exaggerating. Undoubtedly he felt a bit amorous before it came to the point. His father would describe her, I suppose, as a fine filly."

"What do you plan to do with him?" I asked. "Do you toss up, or does one of you take the head and the other the tail?"

Tony laughed. "Good old William. What a clinical mind you have."

"And suppose," I said, "I went to her and recounted this conversation?"

"My dear, she wouldn't even understand. She's incredibly innocent."

"Isn't he?"

"I doubt it—knowing our friend Colin Winstanley. But it's still a moot point. He hasn't given himself away yet."

"We are planning to put it to the test one day soon," Stephen said.

"A drive in the country," Tony said. "The strain's telling on him, you can see that. He's even afraid to take a siesta for fear of unwanted attentions."

"Haven't you *any* mercy?" It was an absurd old-fashioned word to use to those two sophisticates. I felt more than ever square. "Doesn't it occur to you that you may ruin her life—for the sake of your little game?"

"We can depend on you, William," Tony said, "to give her creature comforts."

Stephen said, "It's no game. You should realize we are saving *him*. Think of the life that he would lead—with all those soft contours lapping him around." He added, "Women always remind me of a damp salad—you know, those faded bits of greenery positively swimming ..."

"Every man to his taste," Tony said. "But Peter's not cut out for that sort of life. He's very sensitive," he said, using the girl's own words. There wasn't any more I could think of to say.

V

You will notice that I play a very unheroic part in this comedy. I could have gone direct, I suppose, to the girl and given her a little lecture on the facts of life, beginning gently with the régime of an English public school—he had worn a scarf of old-boy colours, until Tony had said to him one day at breakfast that he thought the puce stripe was an error of judgement. Or perhaps I could have protested to the boy himself, but, if Stephen had spoken the truth and he was under a severe nervous strain, my intervention would hardly have helped to ease it. There was no move I could make. I had just to sit there and watch while they made the moves carefully and adroitly towards the climax.

It came three days later at breakfast when, as usual, she was sitting alone with them, while her husband was upstairs with his lotions. They had never been more charming or more entertaining. As I arrived at my table they were giving her a really funny description of a house in Kensington that they had decorated for a dowager duchess who was passionately interested in the Napoleonic wars. There was an ashtray, I remember, made out of a horse's hoof, guaranteed—so the dealer said—by Apsley House to have belonged to a grey ridden by Wellington at the Battle of Waterloo; there was an umbrella stand made out of a shellcase found on the field of Austerlitz; a fire-escape made of a scaling ladder from Badajoz. She had lost half that sense of strain listening to them. She had forgotten her rolls and coffee; Stephen had her complete attention. I wanted to say to her, "You little owl." I wouldn't have been insulting her—she *had* got rather large eyes.

And then Stephen produced the master-plan. I could tell it was coming by the way his hands stiffened on his coffee-cup, by the way Tony lowered his eyes and appeared to be praying over his *croissant*. "We were wondering, Poopy—may we borrow your husband?" I have never heard words spoken with more elaborate casualness.

She laughed. She hadn't noticed a thing. "Borrow my husband?"

"There's a little village in the mountains behind Monte Carlo—Peille it's called—and I've heard rumours of a devastatingly lovely old bureau there—not for sale, of course, but Tony and I, we have our winning ways."

"I've noticed that," she said, "myself."

Stephen for an instant was disconcerted, but she meant nothing by it, except perhaps a compliment.

"We were thinking of having lunch at Peille and passing the whole day on the road so as to take a look at the scenery. The only trouble is there's no room in the Sprite for more than three, but Peter was saying the other day that you wanted some time to have a hair-do, so we thought...."

I had the impression that he was talking far too much to be convincing, but there wasn't any need for him to worry: she saw nothing at all. "I think it's a marvellous idea," she said. "You know, he needs a little holiday from me. He's had hardly a moment to himself since I came up the aisle." She was magnificently sensible, and perhaps even relieved. Poor girl. She needed a little holiday, too.

"It's going to be excruciatingly uncomfortable. He'll have to sit on Tony's knee."

"I don't suppose he'll mind that."

"And, of course, we can't guarantee the quality of food en route."

For the first time I saw Stephen as a stupid man. Was there a shade of hope in that?

In the long run, of the two, notwithstanding his brutality, Tony had the better brain. Before Stephen had time to speak once more, Tony raised his eyes from the *croissant* and said decisively, "That's fine. All's settled, and we'll deliver him back in one piece by dinnertime."

He looked challengingly across at me. "Of course, we hate to leave you alone for lunch, but I am sure William will look after you."

"William?" she asked, and I hated the way she looked at me as if I didn't exist. "Oh, you mean Mr. Harris?"

I invited her to have lunch with me at Lou-Lou's in the old port—I couldn't very well do anything else—and at that moment the laggard Peter came out on to the terrace. She said quickly, "I don't want to interrupt your work...."

"I don't believe in starvation," I said. "Work has to be interrupted for meals."

Peter had cut himself again shaving and had a large blob of cotton-wool stuck on his chin: it reminded me of Stephen's contusion. I had the impression, while he stood there waiting for someone to say something to him, that he knew all about the conversation; it had been carefully rehearsed by all three, the parts allotted, the unconcerned manner practised well beforehand, even the bit about the food.... Now somebody had missed a cue, so I spoke.

"I've asked your wife to lunch at Lou-Lou's," I said. "I hope you don't mind."

I would have been amused by the expression of quick relief on all three faces if I had found it possible to be amused by anything at all in the situation.

VI

"And you didn't marry again after she left?"

"By that time I was getting too old to marry."

"Picasso does it."

"Oh, I'm not quite as old as Picasso."

The silly conversation went on against a background of fishing-nets draped over a wallpaper with a design of wine-bottles—interior decoration again. Sometimes I longed for a room which had simply grown that way like the lines on a human face. The fish soup steamed away between us, smelling of garlic. We were the only guests there. Perhaps it was the solitude, perhaps it was the directness of her question, perhaps it was only the effect of the *rosé*, but quite suddenly I had the comforting sense that we were intimate friends. "There's always work," I said, "and wine and a good cheese."

"I couldn't be that philosophical if I lost Peter."

"That's not likely to happen, is it?"

"I think I'd die," she said, "like someone in Christina Rossetti."

"I thought nobody of your generation read her."

If I had been twenty years older, perhaps, I could have explained that nothing is quite as bad as that, that at the end of what is called "the sexual life" the only love which has lasted is the love that has accepted everything, every disappointment, every failure and every betrayal, which has accepted even the sad fact that in the end there is no desire so deep as the simple desire for companionship.

She wouldn't have believed me. She said, "I used to weep like anything at that poem about 'Passing Away'. Do you write sad things?"

"The biography I am writing now is sad enough. Two people tied together by love and yet one of them incapable of fidelity. The man dead of old age, burnt-out, at less than forty, and a fashionable preacher lurking by the bedside to snatch his soul. No privacy even for a dying man: the bishop wrote a book about it."

An Englishman who kept a chandlers' shop in the old port was talking at the bar, and two old women who were part of the family knitted at the end of the room. A dog trotted in and looked at us and went away again with its tail curled.

"How long ago did all that happen?"

"Nearly three hundred years."

"It sounded quite contemporary. Only now it would be the man from the *Mirror* and not a bishop."

"That's why I wanted to write it. I'm not really interested in the past. I don't like costume-pieces."

Winning someone's confidence is rather like the way some men set about seducing a woman; they circle a long way from their true purpose, they try to interest and amuse until finally the moment comes to strike. It came, so I wrongly thought, when I was adding up the bill. She said, "I wonder where Peter is at this moment," and I was quick to reply, "What's going wrong between the two of you?"

She said, "Let's go."

"I've got to wait for my change."

It was always easier to get served at Lou-Lou's than to pay the bill. At that moment everyone always had a habit of disappearing: the old woman (her knitting abandoned on the table), the aunt who helped to serve, Lou-Lou herself, her husband in his blue sweater. If the dog hadn't gone already he would have left at that moment.

I said, "You forget—you told me that he wasn't happy."

"Please, please find someone and let's go."

So I disinterred Lou-Lou's aunt from the kitchen and paid. When we left, everyone seemed to be back again, even the dog.

Outside I asked her whether she wanted to return to the hotel.

"Not just yet—but I'm keeping you from your work."

"I never work after drinking. That's why I like to start early. It brings the first drink nearer."

She said that she had seen nothing of Antibes but the ramparts and the beach and the lighthouse, so I walked her around the small narrow backstreets where the washing hung out of the windows as in Naples and there were glimpses of small rooms overflowing with children and grandchildren; stone scrolls were carved over the ancient doorways of what had once been noblemen's houses; the pavements were blocked by barrels of wine and the streets by children playing at ball. In a low room on a ground floor a man sat painting the horrible ceramics which would later go to Vallauris to be sold to tourists in Picasso's old stamping-ground—spotted pink frogs and mauve fish and pigs with slits for coins.

She said, "Let's go back to the sea." So we returned to a patch of hot sun on the bastion, and again I was tempted to tell her what I feared, but the thought that she might watch me with the blankness of ignorance deterred me. She sat on the wall and her long legs in the tight black trousers dangled down like Christmas stockings. She said, "I'm not sorry that I married Peter," and I was reminded of a song Edith Piaf used to sing, "*Je ne regrette rien.*" It is typical of such a phrase that it is always sung or spoken with defiance.

I could only say again, "You ought to take him home," but I wondered what would have happened if I had said, "You are married to a man who only likes men and he's off now picnicking with his boy friends. I'm thirty years older than you, but at least I have always preferred women and I've fallen in love with you and we could still have a few good years together before the time comes when you want to leave me for a younger man." All I said was, "He probably misses the country—and the riding."

"I wish you were right, but it's really worse than that."

Had she, after all, realized the nature of her problem? I waited for her to explain her meaning. It was a little like a novel which hesitates on the verge between comedy and tragedy. If she recognized the situation it would be a tragedy; if she were ignorant it was a comedy, even a farce—a situation between an immature girl too innocent to understand and a man too old to have the courage to explain. I suppose I have a taste for tragedy. I hoped for that.

She said, "We didn't really know each other much before we came here. You know, weekend parties and the odd theatre—and riding, of course."

I wasn't sure where her remarks tended. I said, "These occasions are nearly always a strain. You are picked out of ordinary life and dumped together after an elaborate ceremony—almost like two animals shut in a cage who haven't seen each other before."

"And now he sees me he doesn't like me."

"You are exaggerating."

"No." She added, with anxiety, "I won't shock you, will I, if I tell you things? There's nobody else I can talk to."

"After fifty years I'm guaranteed shockproof."

"We haven't made love—properly, once, since we came here."

"What do you mean—properly?"

"He starts, but he doesn't finish; nothing happens."

I said uncomfortably, "Rochester wrote about that. A poem called 'The Imperfect Enjoyment'." I don't know why I gave her this shady piece of literary information; perhaps, like a psychoanalyst, I wanted her not to feel alone with her problem. "It can happen to anybody."

"But it's not his fault," she said. "It's mine. I know it is. He just doesn't like my body."

"Surely it's a bit late to discover that."

"He'd never seen me naked till I came here," she said with the candour of a girl to her doctor—that was all I meant to her, I felt sure.

"There are nearly always first-night nerves. And then if a man worries (you must realize how much it hurts his pride) he can get stuck in the situation for days—weeks even." I began to tell her about a mistress I once had—we stayed together a very long time and yet for two weeks at the beginning I could do nothing at all. "I was too anxious to succeed."

"That's different. You didn't hate the sight of her."

"You are making such a lot of so little."

"That's what he tries to do," she said with sudden schoolgirl coarseness and giggled miserably.

"We went away for a week and changed the scene, and everything after that was all right. For ten days it had been a flop, and for ten years afterwards we were happy. Very happy. But worry can get established in a room, in the colour of the curtains—it can hang itself up on coat-hangers; you find it smoking away in the ashtray marked Pernod, and when you look at the bed it pokes its head out from underneath like the toes of a pair of shoes." Again I repeated the only charm I could think of. "Take him home."

"It wouldn't make any difference. He's disappointed, that's all it is." She looked down at her long black legs; I followed the course of her eyes because I was finding now that I really wanted her and she said with sincere conviction, "I'm just not pretty enough when I'm undressed."

"You are talking real nonsense. You don't know what nonsense you are talking."

"Oh no, I'm not. You see—it started all right, but then he touched me"—she put her hands on her breasts—"and it all went wrong. I always knew they weren't much good. At school we used to have dormitory inspection—it was awful. Everybody could grow them big except me. I'm no Jayne Mansfield, I can tell you." She gave again that mirthless giggle. "I remember one of the girls told me to sleep with a pillow on top—they said they'd struggle for release and what they needed was exercise. But of course it didn't work. I doubt if the idea was very scientific." She added, "I remember it was awfully hot at night like that."

"Peter doesn't strike me," I said cautiously, "as a man who would want a Jayne Mansfield."

"But you understand, don't you, that, if he finds me ugly, it's all so hopeless."

I wanted to agree with her—perhaps this reason which she had thought up would be less distressing than the truth, and soon enough there would be someone to cure her distrust. I had noticed before that it is often the lovely women who have the least confidence in their looks, but all the same I couldn't pretend to her that I understood it her way. I said, "You must trust me. There's nothing at all wrong with you and that's why I'm talking to you the way I am."

"You are very sweet," she said, and her eyes passed over me rather as the beam from the lighthouse which at night went past the Musée Grimaldi and after a certain time returned and brushed all our windows indifferently on the hotel front. She continued, "He said they'd be back by cocktail-time."

"If you want a rest first"—for a little time we had been close, but now again we were getting further and further away. If I pressed her now she might in the end be happy—does conventional morality demand that a girl remains tied as she was tied? They'd been married in church; she was probably a good Christian, and I knew the ecclesiastical rules: at this moment of her life she could be free of him, the marriage could be annulled, but in a day or two it was only too probable that the same rules would say, "He's managed well enough, you are married for life."

And yet I couldn't press her. Wasn't I after all assuming far too much? Perhaps it was only a question of first-night nerves; perhaps in a little while the three of them would be back, silent, embarrassed, and Tony in his turn would have a contusion on his cheek. I would have been very glad to see it there; egotism fades a little with the passions which engender it, and I would have been content, I think, just to see her happy.

So we returned to the hotel, not saying much, and she went to her room and I to mine. It was in the end a comedy and not a tragedy, a farce even, which is why I have given this scrap of reminiscence a farcical title.

VII

I was woken from my middle-aged siesta by the telephone. For a moment, surprised by the darkness, I couldn't find the light-switch. Scrambling for it, I knocked over my bedside lamp—the telephone went on ringing, and I tried to pick up the holder and knocked over a tooth-glass in which I had given myself a whisky. The little illuminated dial of my watch gleamed up at me marking 8.30. The telephone continued to ring. I got the receiver off, but this time it was the ashtray which fell over. I couldn't get the cord to extend up to my ear, so I shouted in the direction of the telephone, "Hullo!"

A tiny sound came up from the floor which I interpreted as "Is that William?"

I shouted, "Hold on," and now that I was properly awake I realized the light-switch was just over my head (in London it was placed over the bedside table). Little petulant noises came up from the floor as I put on the light, like the creaking of crickets.

"Who's that?" I said rather angrily, and then I recognized Tony's voice.

"William, whatever's the matter?"

"Nothing's the matter. Where are you?"

"But there was quite an enormous crash. It hurt my eardrum."

"An ashtray," I said.

"Do you usually hurl ashtrays around?"

"I was asleep."

"At 8.30? William! William!"

I said, "Where are you?"

"A little bar in what Mrs. Clarenty would call Monty."

"You promised to be back by dinner," I said.

"That's why I'm telephoning you. I'm being, *responsible*, William. Do you mind telling Poopy that we'll be a little late? Give her dinner. Talk to her as only you know how. We'll be back by ten."

"Has there been an accident?"

I could hear him chuckling up the phone. "Oh, I wouldn't call it an accident."

"Why doesn't Peter call her himself?"

"He says he's not in the mood."

"But what shall I tell her?" The telephone went dead.

I got out of bed and dressed and then I called her room. She answered very quickly; I think she must have been sitting by the telephone. I relayed the message, asked her to meet me in the bar, and rang off before I had to face answering any questions.

But I found it was not so difficult as I feared to cover up; she was immensely relieved that somebody had telephoned. She had sat there in her room from half-past seven onwards thinking of all the dangerous turns and ravines on the Grande Corniche, and when I rang she was half afraid that it might be the police or a hospital. Only after she had drunk two dry Martinis and laughed quite a lot at her fears did she say, "I wonder why Tony rang you and not Peter me?"

I said (I had been working the answer out), "I gather he suddenly had an urgent appointment—in the loo."

It was as though I had said something enormously witty.

"Do you think they are a bit tight?" she asked.

"I wouldn't wonder."

"Darling Peter," she said, "he deserved the day off," and I couldn't help wondering in what direction his merit lay.

"Do you want another Martini?"

"I'd better not," she said, "you've made me tight too."

I had become tired of the thin cold *rosé* so we had a bottle of real wine at dinner and she drank her full share and talked about literature. She had, it seemed, a nostalgia for Dornford Yates, had graduated in the sixth form as far as Hugh Walpole, and now she talked respectfully about Sir Charles Snow, who she obviously thought had been knighted, like Sir Hugh, for his services to literature. I must have been very much in love or I would have found her innocence almost unbearable—or perhaps I was a little tight as well. All the same, it was to interrupt her flow of critical judgements that I asked her what her real name was and she replied, "Everyone calls me Poopy." I remembered the PT stamped on her bags, but the only real names that I could think of at the moment were Patricia and Prunella. "Then I shall simply call you You," I said.

After dinner I had brandy and she had a kümmel. It was past 10.30 and still the three had not returned, but she didn't seem to be worrying any more about them. She sat on the floor of the bar beside me and every now and then the waiter looked in to see if he could turn off the lights. She leant against me with her hand on my knee and she said such things as "It must be wonderful to be a writer", and in the glow of brandy and tenderness I didn't mind them a bit. I even began to tell her again about the Earl of Rochester. What did I care about Dornford Yates, Hugh Walpole or Sir Charles Snow? I was even in the mood to recite to her, hopelessly inapposite to the situation though the lines were:

> Then talk not of Inconstancy,
> False Hearts, and broken Vows;
> If I, by Miracle, can be
> This live-long Minute true to thee,
> 'Tis all that Heav'n allows

when the noise—what a noise!—of the Sprite approaching brought us both to our feet. It was only too true that all that heaven allowed was the time in the bar at Antibes.

Tony was singing; we heard him all the way up the Boulevard Général Leclerc; Stephen was driving with the greatest caution, most of the time in second gear, and Peter, as we saw when we came out on to the terrace, was sitting on Tony's knee—nestling would be a better description—and joining in the refrain. All I could make out was

> Round and white
> On a winter's night,
> The hope of the Queen's Navee.

If they hadn't seen us on the steps I think they would have driven past the hotel without noticing.

"You *are* tight," the girl said with pleasure. Tony put his arm round her and ran her up to the top of the steps. "Be careful," she said, "William's made me tight too."

"Good old William."

Stephen climbed carefully out of the car and sank down on the nearest chair.

"All well?" I asked, not knowing what I meant.

"The children have been very happy," he said, "and very, very relaxed."

"Got to go to the loo," Peter said (the cue was in the wrong place), and made for the stairs. The girl gave him a helping hand and I heard him say, "Wonderful day. Wonderful scenery. Wonderful...." She turned at the top of the stairs and swept us with her smile, gay, reassured, happy. As on the first night, when they had hesitated about the cocktail, they didn't come down again. There was a long silence and then Tony chuckled. "You seem to have had a wonderful day," I said.

"Dear William, we've done a very good action. You've never seen him so *détendu.*"

Stephen sat saying nothing; I had the impression that today hadn't gone quite so well for him. Can people ever hunt quite equally in couples or is there always a loser? The too-grey waves of hair were as immaculate as ever, there was no contusion on the cheek, but I had the impression that the fear of the future had cast a long shadow.

"I suppose you mean you got him drunk?"

"Not with alcohol," Tony said. "We aren't vulgar seducers, are we, Stephen?" But Stephen made no reply.

"Then what was your good action?"

"*Le pauvre petit Pierre.* He was in such a state. He had quite convinced himself—or perhaps she had convinced him—that he was *impuissant.*"

"You seem to be making a lot of progress in French."

"It sounds more delicate in French."

"And with your help he found he wasn't?"

"After a little virginal timidity. Or near virginal. School hadn't left him quite unmoved. Poor Poopy. She just hadn't known the right way to go about things. My dear, he has a superb virility. Where are you going, Stephen?"

"I'm going to bed," Stephen said flatly, and went up the steps alone. Tony looked after him, I thought with a kind of tender regret, a very light and superficial sorrow. "His rheumatism came back very badly this afternoon," he said. "Poor Stephen."

I thought it was well then to go to bed before I should become "Poor William" too. Tony's charity tonight was all-embracing.

VIII

It was the first morning for a long time that I found myself alone on the terrace for breakfast. The women in tweed skirts had been gone for some days, and I had never before known "the young men" to be absent. It was easy enough, while I waited for my coffee, to speculate

about the likely reasons. There was, for example, the rheumatism ...
though I couldn't quite picture Tony in the character of a bedside
companion. It was even remotely possible that they felt some shame
and were unwilling to be confronted by their victim. As for the victim,
I wondered sadly what painful revelation the night would certainly
have brought. I blamed myself more than ever for not speaking in
time. Surely she would have learned the truth more gently from me
than from some tipsy uncontrolled outburst of her husband. All the
same—such egoists are we in our passions—I was glad to be there in
attendance ... to staunch the tears ... to take her tenderly in my arms,
comfort her ... oh, I had quite a romantic day-dream on the terrace
before she came down the steps and I saw that she had never had less
need of a comforter.

She was just as I had seen her the first night: shy, excited, gay, with
a long and happy future established in her eyes. "William," she said,
"can I sit at your table? Do you mind?"

"Of course not."

"You've been so patient with me all the time I was in the dol-
drums. I've talked an awful lot of nonsense to you. I know you told
me it was nonsense, but I didn't believe you and you were right all the
time."

I couldn't have interrupted her even if I had tried. She was a Venus
at the prow sailing through sparkling seas. She said, "Everything's all
right. Everything. Last night—he loves me, William. He really does.
He's not a bit disappointed with me. He was just tired and strained,
that's all. He needed a day off alone—*détendu*." She was even picking
up Tony's French expressions second-hand. "I'm afraid of nothing
now, nothing at all. Isn't it strange how black life seemed only two
days ago? I really believe if it hadn't been for you I'd have thrown in
my hand. How lucky I was to meet you and the others too. They're
such wonderful friends for Peter. We are all going home next week—
and we've made a lovely plot together. Tony's going to come down
almost immediately we get back and decorate our house. Yesterday,
driving in the country, they had a wonderful discussion about it. You
won't know our house when you see it—oh, I forgot, you never *have*
seen it, have you? You must come down when it's all finished—with
Stephen."

"Isn't Stephen going to help?" I just managed to slip in.

"Oh, he's too busy at the moment, Tony says, with Mrs. Clarenty.

Do you like riding? Tony does. He adores horses, but he has so little chance in London. It will be wonderful for Peter—to have someone like that because, after all, I can't be riding with Peter all day long, there will be a lot of things to do in the house, especially now, when I'm not accustomed. It's wonderful to think that Peter won't have to be lonely. He says there are going to be Etruscan murals in the bathroom—whatever Etruscan means; the drawing-room *basically* will be eggshell green and the dining-room walls Pompeian red. They really did an awful lot of work yesterday afternoon—I mean in their heads, while we were glooming around. I said to Peter, 'As things are going now we'd better be prepared for a nursery,' but Peter said Tony was content to leave all that side to me. Then there are the stables: they were an old coach-house once, and Tony feels we could restore a lot of the ancient character and there's a lamp he bought in St. Paul which will just fit ... it's endless the things there are to be done—a good six months' work, so Tony says, but luckily he can leave Mrs. Clarenty to Stephen and concentrate on us. Peter asked him about the garden, but he's not a specialist in gardens. He said, 'Everyone to his own métier', and he's quite content if I bring in a man who knows all about roses.

"He knows Colin Winstanley too, of course, so there'll be quite a band of us. It's a pity the house won't be all ready for Christmas, but Peter says he's certain to have wonderful ideas for a really original tree. Peter thinks...."

She went on and on like that; perhaps I ought to have interrupted her even then; perhaps I should have tried to explain to her why her dream wouldn't last. Instead, I sat there silent, and presently I went to my room and packed—there was still one hotel open in the abandoned fun-fair of Juan between Maxim's and the boarded-up Striptease.

If I had stayed ... who knows whether he could have kept on pretending for a second night? But I was just as bad for her as he was. If he had the wrong hormones, I had the wrong age. I didn't see any of them again before I left. She and Peter and Tony were out somewhere in the Sprite, and Stephen—so the receptionist told me—was lying late in bed with his rheumatism.

I planned a note for her, explaining rather feebly my departure, but when I came to write it I realized I had still no other name with which to address her than Poopy.

Summer Tidings

James Purdy

"I think it undoubted," wrote Dame Edith Sitwell, *"that James Purdy will come to be recognized as one of the greatest living writers of fiction in our language."* He is an extraordinarily careful explorer of the unacknowledged, the bewildering, the unspoken. His subjects lie behind the scenes, among the details usually discarded. *"I think in a way I am dreaming all the time when I'm writing, that everything comes from the dream,"* Purdy has acknowledged. *"But the problem with my writing is to find, not the conscious story, which doesn't really interest me, but the unconscious story, which is one's own story."*

Certain places, certain names, certain objects hold in themselves the key to a story. Purdy once said that he worried for months over a newspaper photograph of an unknown man whose life he wanted to discover; another time, a pair of shoes found abandoned in a streetcar haunted him until he was able to place them in a narrative. Photographs, shoes, a yellow mackintosh (as in *"Summer Tidings"*) are the clues, but never the explanations, to stories we are made to witness, knowing however that their meaning will not be spelled out on the page. Purdy's fiction, in spite of its sometimes very explicit sexuality, is neither *"gay"* nor *"straight"*, but a complex exploration of the vital eroticism running beneath the surface of living. *"I don't think of any of my work as gay in that sense,"* Purdy explains. *"I'm just a writer. A writer is a writer, and when you say you're a 'gay writer' or a 'straight writer', you're through."*

There was a children's party in progress on the sloping wide lawn facing the estate of Mr. Teyte and easily visible therefrom despite the high hedge. A dozen school-aged children, some barely out of the care and reach of their nursemaids, attended Mrs. Aveline's birthday party for her son Rupert. The banquet or party itself was held on the site of the croquet grounds, but the croquet set had only partially been taken down, and a few wickets were left standing, a mallet or two lay about, and a red and white wood ball rested in the nasturtium bed. Mr. Teyte's Jamaican gardener, bronzed as an idol, watched the children as he watered the millionaire's grass with a great shiny black hose. The peonies had just come into full bloom. Over the greensward where the banquet was in progress one smelled in addition to the sharp odor of the nasturtiums and the marigolds, the soft perfume of June roses; the trees have their finest green at this season, and small gilt brown toads were about in the earth. The Jamaican servant hardly took his eyes off the children. Their gold heads and white summer clothing rose above the June verdure in remarkable contrast, and the brightness of so many colors made his eyes smart and caused him to pause frequently from his watering. Edna Gruber, Mrs. Aveline's secretary and companion, had promised the Jamaican a piece of the "second" birthday cake when the banquet should be over, and told him the kind thought came from Mrs. Aveline herself. He had nodded when Edna told him of his coming treat, yet it was not the anticipation of the cake which made him so absent-minded and broody as it was the unaccustomed sight of so many young children all at once. Edna could see that the party had stirred something within his mind for he spoke even less than usual to her today as she tossed one remark after another across the boundary of the privet hedge separating the two large properties.

More absent-minded than ever, he went on hosing the peony bed until a slight flood filled the earth about the blooms and squashed onto his open sandals. He moved off then and began sprinkling with tempered nozzle the quince trees. Mr. Teyte, his employer and the owner of the property which stretched far and wide before the eye with the exception of Mrs. Aveline's, had gone to a golf tournament today. Only the white maids were inside his big house, and in his absence they were sleeping most of the day, or if they were about would be indifferently spying the Jamaican's progress across the lawn, as he labored to water the already refreshed black earth and the grass as perfectly green and motionless as in a painted backdrop. Yes, his eyes, his mind were dreaming today despite the almost infernal noise of all those young throats, the guests of the birthday party. His long black lashes gave the impression of having been dampened incessantly either by the water from the hose or some long siege of tears.

Mr. Teyte, if not attentive or kind to him, was his benefactor, for somehow that word had come to be used by people who knew both the gardener and the employer from far back, and the word had come to be associated with Mr. Teyte by Galway himself, the Jamaican servant. But Mr. Teyte, if not unkind, was undemonstrative, and if not indifferent, paid low wages, and almost never spoke to him, issuing his commands, which were legion, through the kitchen and parlor maids. But once when the servant had caught pneumonia, Mr. Teyte had come unannounced to the hospital in the morning, ignoring the rules that no visits were to be allowed except in early evening, and though he had not spoken to Galway, he had stood by his bedside a few moments, gazing at the sick man as if he were inspecting one of his own ailing riding horses.

But Mrs. Aveline and Edna Gruber talked to Galway, were kind to him. Mrs. Aveline even "made" over him. She always spoke to him over the hedge every morning, and was not offended or surprised when he said almost nothing to her in exchange. She seemed to know something about him from his beginnings, at any rate she knew Jamaica, having visited there three or four times. And so the women—Edna and Mrs. Aveline—went on speaking to him over the years, inquiring of his health, and of his tasks with the yard, and so often bestowing on him delicacies from their liberal table, as one might give tidbits to a prized dog which wandered in also from the great estate.

The children's golden heads remained in his mind after they had all left the banquet table and gone into the interior of the house, and from thence their limousines had come and taken them to their own great houses. The blonde heads of hair continued to swim before his eyes like the remembered sight of fields of wild buttercups outside the great estate, stray flowers of which occasionally cropped up in his own immaculate greensward, each golden corolla as bright as the strong rays of the noon sun. And then the memory came of the glimpsed birthday cake with the yellow center. His mouth watered with painful anticipation, and his eyes again filled with tears.

The sun was setting as he turned off the hose, and wiped his fingers from the water and some rust stains, and a kind of slime which came out from the nozzle. He went into a little brick shed, and removed his shirt, wringing wet, and put on a dry one of faded pink cotton decorated with a six-petaled flower design. Ah, but the excitement of all those happy golden heads sitting at a banquet—it made one too jumpy for cake, and their voices still echoed in his ears a little like the cries of the swallows from the poplar trees.

Obedient, then, to her invitation, Galway, the Jamaican gardener, waited outside the buttery for a signal to come inside, and partake of the birthday treat. In musing, however, about the party and all the young children, the sounds of their gaiety, their enormous vitality, lung power, their great appetites, the happy other sounds of silverware and fine china being moved about, added to which had been the song of the birds now getting ready to settle down to the dark of their nests, a kind of memory, a heavy nostalgia had come over him, recollection deep and far-off weighted him down without warning like fever and profound sickness. He remembered his dead loved ones.... How long he had stood on the back steps he could not say, until Edna suddenly laughing as she opened the door on him, with flushed face, spoke: "Why, Galway, you know you should not have stood on ceremony.... Of all people, you are the last who is expected to hang back.... Your cake is waiting for you...."

He entered and sat in his accustomed place where so many times past he was treated to dainties and rewards.

"You may wonder about the delay," Edna spoke more formally today to him than usual. "Galway, we have, I fear, bad news.... A telegram has arrived.... Mrs. Aveline is afraid to open it...."

Having said this much, Edna left the room, allowing the swinging door which separated the kitchen from the rest of the house to close behind her and then continue its swing backwards and forwards like the pendulum of a clock.

Galway turned his eyes to the huge white cake with the yellow center which she had expressly cut for him. The solid silver fork in his hand was about to come down on the thick heavily frosted slice resting sumptuously on hand-painted china. Just then he heard a terrible cry rushing through the many rooms of the house and coming, so it seemed, to stop directly at him and then cease and disappear into the air and the nothingness about him. His mouth became dry, and he looked about like one who expects unknown and immediate danger. The fork fell from his brown calloused muscular hand. The cry was now repeated if anything more loudly, then there was a cavernous silence, and after some moments, steady prolonged hopeless weeping. He knew it was Mrs. Aveline. The telegram must have brought bad news. He sat on looking at the untasted cake. The yellow of its center seemed to stare at him.

Edna now came through the swinging door, her eyes red, a pocket handkerchief held tightly in her right hand, her opal necklace slightly crooked. "It was Mrs. Aveline's mother, Galway.... She is dead.... And such a short time since Mrs. Aveline's husband died too, you know...."

Galway uttered some words of regret, sympathy, which Edna did not hear, for she was still listening to any sound which might try to reach her from beyond the swinging door.

At last turning round, she spoke: "Why, you haven't so much as touched your cake...." She looked at him almost accusingly.

"She has lost her own mother...." Galway said this after some struggle with his backwardness.

But Edna was studying the cake. "We can wrap it all up, the rest of it, Galway, and you can have it to sample at home, when you will have more appetite." She spoke comfortingly to him. She was weeping so hard now she shook all over.

"These things come out of the blue," she managed to speak at last in a neutral tone as though she was reading from some typewritten sheet of instructions. "There is no warning very often as in this case. The sky itself might as well have fallen on us...."

Edna had worked for Mrs. Aveline for many years. She always wore little tea aprons. She seemed to do nothing but go from the kitchen to the front parlor or drawing room, and then return almost immediately to where she had been in the first place. She had supervised the children's party today, ceaselessly walking around, and looking down on each young head, but one wondered exactly what she was accomplishing by so much movement. Still, without her, Mrs. Aveline might not have been able to run the big house, so people said. And it was also Edna Gruber who had told Mrs. Aveline first of Galway's indispensable and sterling dependability. And it was Galway Edna always insisted on summoning when nobody else could be found to do some difficult and often unpleasant and dirty task.

"So, Galway, I will have the whole 'second' cake sent over to you just as soon as I find the right box to put it in...."

He rose as Edna said this, not having eaten so much as a crumb. He said several words which hearing them come from his own mouth startled him as much as if each word spoken had appeared before him as letters in the air.

"I am sorry ... and grieve for her grief.... A mother's death.... It is the hardest loss."

Then he heard the screen door closing behind him. The birds were still, and purple clouds rested in the west, with the evening star sailing above the darkest bank of clouds as yellow as the heads of any of the birthday children. He crossed himself.

Afterwards he stood for some time in Mr. Teyte's great green backyard, and admired the way his gardener's hands had kept the grass beautiful for the multimillionaire, and given it the endowment of both life and order. The wind stirred as the light failed, and flowers which opened at evening gave out their faint delicate first perfume, in which the four-o'clocks' fragrance was pronounced. On the ground near the umbrella tree something glistened. He stooped down. It was the sheepshears, which he employed in trimming the ragged grass about trees and bushes, great flower beds, and the hedge. Suddenly, stumbling in the growing twilight he cut his thumb terribly on the shears. He walked dragging one leg now as if it was his foot which he had slashed. The gush of blood somehow calmed him from his other sad thoughts. Before going inside Mr. Teyte's great house, he put the stained sheepshears away in the shed, and then walked quietly to the kitchen and sat down at the lengthy pine table which was his accustomed place here, got out some discarded linen napkins, and began making himself a bandage. Then he remembered he should have sterilized the wound. He looked about for some iodine, but there was none in the medicine cabinet. He washed the quivering flesh of the wound in thick yellow soap. Then he bandaged it and sat in still communion with his thoughts.

Night had come. Outside the katydids and crickets had begun an almost dizzying chorus of sound, and in the far distant darkness tree frogs and some bird with a single often repeated note gave the senses a kind of numbness.

Galway knew who would bring the cake—it would be the birthday boy himself. And the gardener would be expected to eat a piece of it while Rupert stood looking on. His mouth now went dry as sand. The bearer of the cake and messenger of Mrs. Aveline's goodness was coming up the path now, the stones of gravel rising and falling under his footsteps. Rupert liked to be near Galway whenever possible, and like his mother wanted to give the gardener gifts, sometimes coins, sometimes shirts, and now tonight food. He liked to touch Galway as he would perhaps a horse. Rupert stared sometimes at the Jamaican servant's brown thickly muscled arms with a look almost of acute disbelief.

Then came the step on the back porch, and the hesitant but loud knock.

Rupert Aveline, just today aged thirteen, stood with outstretched hands bearing the cake. The gardener accepted it immediately, his head slightly bowed, and immediately lifted it out of the cake box to expose it all entire except the one piece which Edna Gruber had cut in the house expressly for the Jamaican, and this piece rested in thick wax paper separated from the otherwise intact birthday cake. Galway fell heavily into his chair, his head still slightly bent over the offering. He felt with keen unease Rupert's own speechless wonder, the boy's eyes fixed on him rather than the cake, though in the considerable gloom of the kitchen the Jamaican servant had with his darkened complexion all but disappeared into the shadows, only his white shirt and linen trousers betokening a visible presence.

Galway lit the lamp, and immediately heard the cry of surprise and alarmed concern coming from the messenger, echoing in modulation and terror that of Mrs. Aveline as she had read the telegram.

"Oh, yes, my hand," Galway said softly, and he looked down in unison with Rupert's horrified glimpse at his bandage—the blood having come through copiously to stain the linen covering almost completely crimson.

"Shouldn't it be shown to the doctor, Galway?" the boy inquired, and suddenly faint, he rested his hand on the servant's good arm for support. He had gone very white. Galway quickly rose and helped the boy to a chair. He hurried to the sink and fetched him a glass of cold water, but Rupert refused this, continuing to touch the gardener's arm.

"It is your grandmother's death, Rupert, which has made you upset...."

Rupert looked away out the window through which he could see his own house in the shimmery distance; a few lamps had been lighted over there, and the white exterior of his home looked like a ship in the shadows, seeming to move languidly in the summer night.

In order to have something to do and because he knew Rupert

wished him to eat part of the cake, Galway removed now all the remaining carefully wrapped thick cloth about the birthday cake and allowed it to emerge yellow and white, frosted and regal. They did everything so well in Mrs. Aveline's house.

"You are ... a kind ... good boy," Galway began with the strange musical accent which never failed to delight Rupert's ear. "And now you are on your way to being a man," he finished.

Rupert's face clouded over at this last statement, but the music of the gardener's voice finally made him smile and nod, then his eyes narrowed as they rested on the bloodstained bandage.

"Edna said you had not tasted one single bite, Galway," the boy managed to speak after a struggle to keep his own voice steady and firm.

The gardener, as always, remained impassive, looking at the almost untouched great cake, the frosting in the shape of flowers and leaves and images of little men and words concerning love, a birthday, and the year 1902.

Galway rose hurriedly and got two plates.

"You must share a piece of your own birthday cake, Rupert ... I must not eat alone."

The boy nodded energetically.

The Jamaican cut two pieces of cake, placed them on large heavy dinner plates, all he could find at the moment, and produced thick solid silver forks. But then as he handed the piece of cake to Rupert, in the exertion of his extending his arm, drops of blood fell upon the pine table.

At that moment, without warning, the whole backyard was illuminated by unusual irregular flashing lights and red glares. Both Rupert and Galway rushed at the same moment to the window, and stared into the night. Their surprise was, if anything, augmented by what they now saw. A kind of torchlight parade was coming up the far greensward, in the midst of which procession was Mr. Teyte himself, a bullnecked short man of middle years. Surrounded by other men, his well-wishers, all gave out shouts of congratulation in drunken proclamation of the news that the owner of the estate had won the golf tournament. Suddenly his pals raised Mr. Teyte to their shoulders, and shouted in unison over the victory.

Listening to the cries growing in volume, in almost menacing nearness as they approached closer to the gardener and Rupert, who stood like persons besieged, the birthday boy cautiously put his hand in that of Galway.

Presently, however, they heard the procession moving off beyond their sequestered place, the torchlights dimmed and disappeared from outside the windows, as the celebrators marched toward the great front entrance of the mansion, a distance of almost a block away, and there, separated by thick masonry, they were lost to sound.

Almost at that same moment, as if at some signal from the disappearing procession itself, there was a deafening peal of thunder, followed by forks of cerise lightning flashes, and the air so still before rushed and rose in furious elemental wind. Then they heard the angry whipping of the rain against the countless panes of glass.

"Come, come, Rupert," Galway admonished, "your mother will be sick with worry." He pulled from a hook an enormous mackintosh, and threw it about the boy. "Quick, now, Rupert, your birthday is over...."

They fled across the greensward where only a moment before the golf tournament victory procession with its torches had walked in dry clear summer weather. Galway who wore no covering was immediately soaked to the skin.

Edna was waiting at the door, as constant in attendance as if she were a caryatid now come briefly to life to receive the charge of the birthday boy from the gardener, and in quick movement of her hand like that of a magician she stripped from Rupert and surrendered back to Galway his mackintosh, and then closed the door against him and the storm.

The Jamaican waited afterwards for a time under a great elm tree, whose leaves and branches almost completely protected him from the full fury of the sudden violent thundershower, now abating.

From the mackintosh, however, he fancied there came the perfume of the boy's head of blonde hair, shampooed only a few hours earlier for his party. The odor came now swiftly in great waves to the gardener's dilating nostrils, an odor almost indistinguishable from the blossoms of honeysuckle. He held the mackintosh tightly in his hand for a moment, then drawing it closer to his mouth and pressing it hard against his nostrils, he kissed it once fervently as he imagined he saw once again the golden heads of the birthday party children assembled at the banquet table.

On Certainty

Stan Persky

When Dante, in the Divine Comedy, *comes to the third ring of the seventh circle of Hell, he meets his old teacher Brunetto Latini, condemned to that place for lusting after young boys. Latini's punishment is that he must run perpetually through the sand without ever finding the object of his desire. The body that lusts for the body is never satisfied, or only for an instant.*

In Paradise, Dante had been led by Beatrice Portinari, whom he had seen once, as an eight-year-old girl on a bridge in Florence, and who had become in his dreams the object of his absolute love. The story is told that, returning to Florence after his Comedy *had been written, Dante was surprised to find that no one had heard of his unforgettable Beatrice. The soul that longs for the soul prolongs the moment of that love—incomprehensible to other mortals such as Dante's fellow Florentines—throughout eternity. In this way did the thirteenth century distinguish between love of the spirit and love of the flesh.*

Stan Persky, whose personal erotic experiences serve as fictional points of departure for reflections on art, society, and politics, rediscovers Dante's dichotomy in the contemporary setting of Germany after the fall of Communism. His object of desire is what Nabokov called a "faunlet", the male equivalent of Lolita, the "nymphet"; his Beatrice is Wittgenstein, the Austrian philosopher who disarmingly reflected on the relationships between knowledge and language; and Persky himself becomes the fictional narrator of his own memoir since, as he says, "memory without fiction is incoherent".

Between the anticipations of the evening and the loss of the day's memory (… and more, no doubt), we occupy the present tremulous moment. While Manuel sprawled in sleep above the gathering traffic hum of Hamburg's Reeperbahn boulevard in that interlude dividing the end of the afternoon from the early evening, I, having woken from our nap before him, sat reading at a small dressing table at the foot of the bed, pausing occasionally to glance up at the blond boy's tousled hair.

I'd first happened upon Ludwig Wittgenstein's *On Certainty* (*Über Gewissheit*) while reading Ray Monk's biography of the Austrian-born philosopher. It was, like almost everything Wittgenstein wrote, unsystematic, fragmentary, and unfinished. It was also the last thing he wrote, working on this topic right up until two days before his death in April 1951. My admiration was roused by the fact that Wittgenstein simply kept on, scribbling thoughts into his notebook, to the very end: "I do philosophy now like an old woman who is always mislaying something and having to look for it again: now her glasses, now her keys". There's really nothing else to do. Impending death ought not be treated as something out of the ordinary, the dying Wittgenstein seemed to imply.

On Certainty was, as well, exactly the subject that was most on my mind. I was indifferent to the current decline of Wittgenstein's reputation. Instead, I was immured in the mixture of my body's certainty of desire for Manuel, and my puzzlement over almost everything else, from the identity of the other to that of the new societies emerging from the wreckage of the Communist states. Why hadn't the East German Communist Party simply ordered its forces to shoot? In fact, there was a confused story that such an order had been given; the opening of the Berlin Wall appeared to be a sort of mistake that, once made, could not be retracted from history's claws. Wittgenstein seemed to offer, at least, another way of asking about what we knew.

In addition to Manuel, there was another person in my life, Alexander Goertz. He's the one with whom I began reading *On Certainty*. Goertz (everybody called him by his surname) was a rosy-cheeked, blond-haired musicology student, in his early twenties, of Hungarian-Germanic parentage, whom I met indirectly through my friend Michael Morris, perhaps a week or two after I'd met Manuel. It had been intimated to me that Goertz might, in some fashion, become my young intellectual companion in Berlin and, immediately seeing the need for such a person in my life, I took him as such.

Goertz's interests in music ranged from the medieval composer-nun Hildegaard of Bingen, to the obscure American musical inventor of the 1940s, Harry Parch; he was in his period of walking down stairs backwards; he was a vegetarian (so we regularly went for lunch at a cheap Indian restaurant on Grohlmanstrasse); he was one of the few people who could recount a dream in such a way that I wasn't bored by it; he invented devices to purify the sound of electric guitars, etc. Though some regarded him as merely quirky, I had no difficulty in recognizing his genius. More important, when I mentioned Wittgenstein's name (I'd just read the biography), Goertz at once declared his interest. Thus we began reading *On Certainty* in Berlin— sitting in the room where I was staying at Michael's place, the one I called the Boyopolis Chamber, in which Vincent Trasov's painting of the word *Knabe* ("boy") hung on the wall before us—puzzling out its fragments rather randomly, since the form of its composition seemed to lend itself to such a reading.

The problem Wittgenstein set himself was roughly as follows. In 1939, the English philosopher G.E. Moore published an article, "Proof of the External World", in which he claimed to *know* a number of common-sense propositions, such as "Here is one hand and here is another." In an earlier paper, "A Defence of Common Sense", he made similar claims, e.g., "The earth existed for a long time before my birth," and "I have never been far from the earth's surface." Thus, Moore attempted to defeat philosophical skepticism about objective reality by a number of "obvious" assertions.

Upon becoming reinterested in Moore's remarks about certainty, Wittgenstein replied (in his notebook), "If you do know that *here is one hand*, we'll grant you all the rest." The sweep of that opening gesture delighted me. The question he posed was "Now, can one enumerate what one knows (like Moore)? Straight off like that, I believe not—for otherwise the expression 'I know' gets misused," adding, "We just do not see how very specialized the use of 'I know' is."

Instead, Wittgenstein turned the problem of knowing around: "What we can ask is whether it can make sense to doubt it." He meant that quite literally. "Do I, in the course of my life, make sure that I know that here is a hand—my own hand, that is?" Wittgenstein asked, and then tried to explain why such an announcement would be most odd, or to think of conversational examples where such a claim might make sense.

Now, pondering *On Certainty* in the Florida Hotel in Hamburg, I wondered if its author might be amused to know that he was being read in a brothel (for it was slowly dawning on me that that's what the Florida indeed was). Or perhaps it was simply me who was pleased that philosophy could be at home here, too.

That evening, behind the Exquisit bar in the hotel, Manuel's best friend, Detlef, was the host of his own birthday party, pouring drinks for the men and boys who filled the bar stools, while deftly accepting little gifts from new arrivals—they were buzzed in to the second-floor establishment through the locked metal door—as well as taking phone calls offering best wishes on his thirtieth birthday.

I was introduced to Detlef, shook hands with him, and he poured Manuel and me glasses of imitation champagne, with which we toasted him. He was a solidly built, dark-haired man in a denim shirt and jeans, the edge of his butt perched on a tall stool, legs confidently sprawled. You could see what he must have looked like at eighteen. Had some of the middle-aged men who now crowded the bar once slept with him? He was taciturn, cool. His style was more *noblesse* than *oblige*. Manuel's enthusiastic greeting was returned rather indifferently, I thought. When Manuel asked if he should take up my invitation to visit me in Canada, Detlef dismissively replied, "Sure. Why not?", as though he had left the invitations of men far behind him, as though he knew exactly what they were worth. Detlef soon turned his attention elsewhere. I wondered if their friendship was as close as Manuel supposed.

The bar was at the far end of the room, most of which was filled with arrangements of horsehair couches, armchairs, and low rectangular tables upon which to set drinks. By the entranceway were a couple of blinking video games, a telephone, doors to the toilet, and another door leading down a corridor of hotel rooms. The main room gave off onto another smaller one, up one step, which was apparently used for breakfast. That night a buffet had been laid out on a long table for the guests. We filled our plates with cold cuts and potato salad, and found a free sofa.

After a while, Manuel suggested that we visit the other gay bars of Hamburg. Outside, in the cold drizzle, we hailed a taxi that took us to the St. George district on the far side of the train station. We aimlessly traipsed from one bar to the other—the Universum, the Club König— each slightly differing in decor and demeanour, but all of them strangely empty. Back at the Exquisit, Detlef's party went on. We had a nightcap before going upstairs at midnight. In bed, I touched the blond boy and he quickly grew hard.

When we went downstairs for breakfast in the morning, we discovered that the entire bar had been ripped apart and was in the process of a weekend renovation. Wiring dangled from the ceiling. The furniture had been piled up against the walls. To Manuel's annoyance, the breakfast room was temporarily housed in a suite off the corridor; the coffee was cold, the bread stale. We escaped the wreckage, taking a cab across town where we found a basement bar that was just opening. There was hot coffee, and a pinball machine to amuse my guide in this labyrinth.

Oversized windshield wipers swept away the rain pelting the smoky-grey windows of the tour bus. When Manuel had asked, "What do you want to do?", I had said, "Let's see Hamburg." It was one of those standard city sightseeing tours for visiting strangers, probably boring for Manuel, who knew Hamburg, but I liked it; i.e., I liked being inside out of the rain, being with Manuel, liked not having to do anything, while the city—narrow, villa-lined streets, a fountain in a lake—floated by us in a wet haze.

At the harbour, where there was a shopping stop as the tour more or less ended, we got off the bus, hunched under a small umbrella. It was too cold to imagine I was looking for Herbert List or Herbert Tobias, the ghosts who had brought me to Hamburg. I had been looking at their pictures all that spring, and I wanted to see the places where those photographers had made their daily rounds. I could barely see the harbour cranes and anchored ships through the grey mist and slanting rain. Certain jumbled streets that angled toward the slate-coloured water tempted me (was I looking for some long-gone bar of the 1920s—The Parrot's Perch?—where List had gone?), but I saw that the shivering waif at my side had had enough.

On the Reeperbahn we searched for an open restaurant—not easy to locate on a street that only awoke with dark—until, just as we were about to give it up, we stumbled upon a place that served a traditional plate of *Eisbein* (hamhocks on a bed of spicy sauerkraut). A television mounted high up behind me was showing a Chinese comedy film. Manuel watched it with pleasure, while I enjoyed looking at his beauty, his grey-blue eyes following the slapstick on the screen. We had no idea in the world where we could go from here; he'd already seen so much of the realm of men and our unreliable promises.

At the Florida—after a trip to a local department store to buy jeans and black bikini underwear for Manuel—we glanced into the breakfast room, where in the late afternoon gloom the men and boys, slouched in the postures of people who had accustomed themselves to purgatory, gossiped over the debris of food and construction equipment. Upstairs, as the grey afternoon darkened further, there was nothing to do except languidly cuddle in bed.

Though the surfaces of the city were cold and wet, inhospitable even, I was nonetheless deep inside it looking out, rather than the other way around. Manuel was attentive to my desire; his manners charmed me. I could never have found my own way into and through that garish maze; if I had entered the Exquisit myself (utilizing one of those gay guides that offered the symbol "R" for "rent"), I would have been faced with the opaque backs of the men and young men at the bar, or Detlef's cool demeanour; instead, I had been led by the hand. But to where? In one sense, to no more than a slightly shabby waterfront sex hotel. But in another, was it not into the heart-of-the-heart of the body's, or the city's, secrets? We lay in the tangle of white sheets in a brothel sanctum.

Manuel liked me to impale myself astride his condom-covered erection; he said he got hot seeing me jack off onto his belly as he came inside me. It amused him to watch me cry out as I reached back to place my hand on his bare thigh, feeling the convulsion of its muscle as his groin bucked up into me. Afterwards, he napped.

I sat naked in a chair by the little table, once more looking out over the wet Reeperbahn as I returned from the animal world to the uniquely human one that Wittgenstein wrote about. At that moment my body involuntarily quivered, still shaken by its recent fucking, so that it took an effort of will to keep my hand steady enough to read the page it held.

At first, when I was reading *On Certainty* with Goertz, we dipped into its passages playfully, in no fixed order. "Suppose some adult had told a child that he had been on the moon," Wittgenstein speculated, thinking of what sense might be made of Moore's claim that he knew he had never been far from the earth's surface. "The child tells me the story, and I say it was only a joke, the man hadn't been on the moon; no one has ever been on the moon; the moon is a long way off and it is impossible to climb up there or fly there.—If now the child insists, saying perhaps there is a way of getting there which I don't know, etc., what reply could I make to him?" he wondered.

We liked the unintended irony of those passages about the moon. A decade after Wittgenstein's death, the impossibility of one's having been on it had itself been dissolved. That season, coincidentally, they were playing a song in the bars which included, amid the blur of techno-sound and the interstellar static, the voice of the astronaut Neil Armstrong, who had first stepped onto the moon, proclaiming in slightly botched grammar, "One small step for [a] man, one giant leap for mankind."

I had been reading *On Certainty* as though I were seeking the answer to a Zen riddle, and in that hotel room—my body, the ground of first knowledge, still alive to the place where it had been so recently penetrated, and the boy who had done so now innocently asleep, looking like boys I had seen in the photographs of List and Tobias—I came as close to understanding Wittgenstein as I would.

Since Wittgenstein saw the human as residing in language—the rest an unspeakable mystery—doubting and certainty were simply possibilities in the practices of language. "A doubt about existence only works in a language-game," he proposed. "We should first have to ask: what would such a doubt be like?" Certainty, Wittgenstein says, is, "*as it were*, a tone of voice in which one declares how things are...." Later, he adds, "Do I want to say, then, that certainty resides in the nature of the language-game?"

That is, "it's not a matter of *Moore's* knowing that there's a hand there, but rather we should not understand him if he were to say, 'Of course I may be wrong about this.' We should ask, 'What is it like to make such a mistake as that?'" Because "the *questions* that we raise and our *doubts* depend on the fact that some propositions are exempt from doubt...certain things are *in deed* not doubted." In the end, "If you tried to doubt everything you would not get as far as doubting anything. The game of doubting itself presupposes certainty."

It was not that I knew something with certainty, but that my doubts depended on my not doubting certain things, which is different from knowing certainly. I thought I had been looking for certainty (of a Cartesian kind); what Wittgenstein wanted to show me was that there was no separating certainty from doubts. What was of interest, he suggested, were the doubts, and the set of undoubted propositions—the language-games or, simply, the "background"—necessary to sustain them.

If I had transformed my desire for Manuel into the equation "Desire is the body's first epistemology," Wittgenstein solved at least half the riddle. I had still to discover the other half of the maxim that I sensed might complete my declaration about what the body knew, or where its knowledge led.

One day in early April, 1951, Wittgenstein picked up his notebook and sighed into it, "It is so difficult to find the *beginning*. Or better: it is difficult to begin at the beginning. And not try to go further back."

The bars were again a failure. At midnight on a Friday, they yawned in emptiness. I was uncertain if the explanation—which various bartenders offered their version of—was to be found in a seasonal economic downturn, the lateness or earliness of the hour, or was simply an unaccountable mystery. In a narrow, sparsely populated room, a singer on a makeshift stage held a microphone and sang or lip-synched an unmemorable tune.

We sat up in bed till three or four in the morning, gossiping through the baffle of language. Those leisurely conversations—in the middle of the night, or dawdling long after breakfast—were what took the relationship from urgent desire to a more diffused enamourment. Manuel claimed to make a good living from hustling, and held up Detlef as a role-model, as a possibility of how one could make the successful transition to a later stage in life. Detlef was how he imagined himself ten years down the road. But since I didn't seem to fit the picture of one of those lavish-spending gentlemen from whom he drew sustenance, what was he doing with me?

"Because I said I would go to Hamburg with you," Manuel replied. I asked him if he had any regrets. "Not at all," he said. "You like doing sex?" I asked. "Yes," he answered, "like you love writing books." (Did he really say that, or had I misunderstood, mistranslated?) Sometime in the middle of the night, I was swallowing the length of his hard cock; soon, he had covered himself in his jism. When he asked, just before we fell asleep, "What do you like best about Hamburg?", I of course answered, "Making love in Hamburg with you."

Back in Berlin, we parted on the platform of the Zoo train station after four days together, I to catch the S-Bahn to the apartment I was temporarily house-sitting in the streets of the theologians in the Moabit district, Manuel to re-enter the traffic of the city that would lead to his place (I'd never seen it) on Martin-Luther-Strasse, not far from the bars near Nollendorf Platz where we had first met.

There were images and sounds from the last days—a renovator's drill gouging the ceiling below that woke us on Saturday morning, art museums, bubblebaths, chill rain, a pool hall that rescued us from boredom while waiting for the Hamburg–Berlin train. A blond-haired boy in black bikini underwear sits on the edge of a hotel bed, takes off his white socks and quickly sniffs them to make sure they can be worn again later.

For a few days, I became a fanatical philosophical dualist. When I woke in my familiar bed on a cool, cloudy Berlin morning, feeling the little aches and pains of middle age (a slightly twisted ankle, stiffness in my right shoulder), it was a reminder that Manuel was twenty. The thought of him bore with it reflections on the transience of our intimacies. About twenty-four hours before I'd been fucked, and yet now it was utterly forgotten by my body, while *I*, on the other hand, remembered that he had taken my pen, written my name on the bottom of his big toe, then his own on the bottom of the other one, and brought his feet together, pressing our written-on-flesh names against each other, making me laugh. But what was this "body" I separated myself from; who was this "I" that I thought about apart from the body's sensations?

Meanwhile, life went on; we obeyed the orders-of-the-day. I had dinner with Michael and Vincent; we argued about the difference between "pornography" and the "erotic"; Michael showed me new photos of young men. Goertz turned up for lunch; again, we attempted to untangle a passage of Wittgenstein. I visited a publisher in the Kreuzberg district of the city; i.e., I made the rounds.

One night, as I walked home from the bar to catch the S-Bahn at the Zoo station, I turned into the Ku'damm and found the great boulevard jammed with honking cars and crowds several deep on the sidewalk gazing up at the huge electronic news screen on the corner as it announced the narrow vote by which the German parliament had chosen Berlin to once again be unified Germany's capital. I rode the S-Bahn to the old soot-layered brick station at Bellevue, clambered down the station steps into the night, and up another flight onto the footbridge that crossed the flowing Spree, and turned the corner into Calvinstrasse.

Manuel and I appeared in each other's lives casually. In the middle of the afternoon, standing on a busy streetcorner across from the Zoo station, dithering in my mind over something trivial, he materializes out of the blue—actually, out of the Presse Café, one of his favourite hangouts, which is right next door to the international press shop where I'd just bought a newspaper. "Are you free?" I ask him. He laughs. "You're simply impossible," he says, a phrase I particularly like because it's the same one he admonishingly addresses to his erect cock, shaking a finger at it, as though his body too were distinct from himself. And in minutes, we're on the S-Bahn riding home.

After we play for a while, he asks for a rubber. Then he's inside me. I reach behind, cupping his ass in my hand, to press him deeper into my body. Later, lying on my back, his teeth nip at my groin as I come. Then, even later, after he's gone—to meet his jolly aunt from Florida? to hustle in the Zoo station?—my body doesn't remember. As was my habit, I sought an aphorism to encapsulate that peculiar dualism I experienced: *the body fucks and forgets; I remember and write.* I'm left with inconsequential details of our couplings—the disposal of a used condom, the sight of cloud formations when I open the curtains again—whose only possible use, if any, is to enter the narrative.

But what does it mean to say that the body forgets? It experiences the pleasure of Manuel's body (or the aches and pains of its own), but shortly afterwards, as the sensation dissolves (or the stomach cramps at night go away in the morning), it's almost as if it never happened. I, having an identity, remember what happened to me—even if memory is unreliable, and cuts out at odd moments like a power disruption in a large city—but the body is indifferent to identity. It's solely concerned with sensation, is *sense-full*, and thus "senseless". It doesn't contemplate death; I do.

My dualism, I noticed, seemed to divide in a rather different way from the standard philosophical terms of "body/mind" (or "mind/brain", as it became in contemporary debates). For me the set was "body/me", where "me" is a language-rooted (Wittgensteinian?) conception. "I" or "me" is not mind, not brain, but that which is associated with the words identifying myself. In a way, my dualism skirted the question of whether mind could be reduced to the material(ism) of the brain; instead, "me" was rather more like a fictional character.

And indeed, that was how *fictional dualism* seemed to work. I could use the body's memories for only a very short time, and then I had to "make up" what it felt like to be in the bubblebath with Manuel in Hamburg. Memory without fiction was incoherent.

For the moment, I saw dualism everywhere. I had begun to learn reflexive verbs in German, which makes considerably more use of that grammatical device than in other languages I knew. E.g., when I wanted to say, "I remember," in German, it went *ich erinnere mich*— literally, "I remind me," thus implying, at least in terms of syntactic logic, that there was a "me" for "I" to remind.

But if I had a use, as a writer, for what I remembered, then what did other people do with the bits and pieces left over from the experiences that the body, perforce, forgets? While we (artists) made art of it, for others it went into gossip, anecdotes, ways of presenting themselves, for summing themselves up, for reminiscing; in short, for pretty much what the rest of us (artists included) did with it. Was the difference between us—i.e., we artists make art, non-artists don't— merely tautological rather than significant?

Of course, one couldn't go on believing "fictional dualism" forever. But I could go on, for as long as it might last, seeing Manuel, reading philosophy, watching the sky over Berlin, meeting Goertz for lunch.

One afternoon, some weeks later, Goertz came by with his guitar. The windows and balcony door were open onto the courtyard and the thick foliage of the chestnut tree. By then I was again staying at Michael's, in the Boyopolis room; it was warm and muggy though the sky was thick with rainclouds. Goertz played some pieces by Leo Brouwer, a Cuban whose name I'd heard and had mentioned to him. I thought about the obvious fact that I liked Goertz so much more than Manuel, notwithstanding the fate imposed by desire. Listening to the sounds, watching Goertz's fingers on the strings, I was astonished that someone could do that, that it could be done at all—the skills involved seemed so difficult compared to what I did in making sentences or doing philosophy puzzles.

"I'd better play some Bach," Goertz joked after playing one of Brouwer's works, "just to make sure I'm not frightening the neighbours." As he played, it began to rain. In the middle of the afternoon, the storm gathered in a fury I'd never seen or heard before. The noise of the deluge, pelting the chestnut tree, echoing in the courtyard, drowned out the music. We sat and listened to its consuming roar.

Manuel phoned one night, late, from the bar. I was sitting at the black-topped desk, looking into the night sky, which was filled with the whop-whopping sound of unseen helicopter blades. There'd been choppers over Berlin all day, occasioned by the arrival of a flock of visiting foreign dignitaries from NATO. Perhaps he was bored at the bar (I could hear its disco-rhythm in the background); he said he'd come over in half an hour and spend the night (I didn't ask why he couldn't sleep at his own place). When he hadn't shown up an hour later, I fell asleep in familiar puzzlement. I'd never understand his appearances, his no-shows. He'd been agitatedly distracted of late; things were going badly, I assumed; landlords, creditors, bureaucrats were all demanding payment.

At a quarter to three he woke me. I didn't understand all the details of a tale about getting stopped for riding the S-Bahn without a ticket; I was tired. He crawled into bed with me, and quickly dropped off into exhausted slumber. A great deal of the pleasure I took with Manuel, it occurred to me, consisted in simply looking at him while he slept; it was a pleasure I connected with that of looking at the moving clouds. He slept with his mouth slightly open, or with a childish thumb between his lips; he threw the comforter off, and I was filled with a certain wonder to see his naked body.

Manuel slept until noon the next day. I gave him some money to go to the bakery for breakfast pastries while I laid out the plates, put on the coffee. From the kitchen window, I watched him come back up the street, recognizing even from a distance the bakery's familiar tan wrapping paper, a package of strawberry cakes balanced in his hand.

After breakfast, he asked, "Do you want to go swimming?"

"I don't swim," I said, puzzled.

"In the bath," he laughed.

Then in the warm, soap-bubble froth of bathwater, we slid across each other's bodies again. I put my finger up to the knuckle into his asshole, and he turned his haunch in such a way as to permit me to go in deeper. His cum landed on his belly, as the bath water lapped about us. We towelled off, went back to bed for more.

I'd said earlier, over breakfast, that I wanted to go to the Zoo station to pick up a newspaper and smokes. He proposed that he sleep a bit more, that I wake him when I came back, and we'd have coffee and the rest of the strawberry cake before he went off to "work". Maybe I could get him a copy of *B.Z.* (the local screaming tabloid), he suggested. There was a parting sentence, as he lay in the comforter, but I missed the verb. He may have asked if I trusted him enough to leave him alone in the apartment. The thought had crossed my mind.

The errands took a half-hour. When I came into the house, I noticed from the corner of my eye, passing through my work-room into the room where we slept, something amiss on my desk. Something white on its black surface, something red out of place. The bed with its tangled comforter was otherwise empty. The place where I kept cash, tickets, passport, and traveller's cheques had been disturbed. There was an instant of bodily thrill, a rush of adrenalin, at taking in so instantaneously what had happened.

Yet, I felt strangely cool about the theft, unlike the first time he had stolen money from my pocket. Then, when it was far too early for a real narrative to have formed, I'd simply experienced the emotions of someone who had been robbed, but now I also saw it as a final turn (or "plot twist") in the story. My mind breathed easily as I methodically began to assess the damage, going first to the maroon-coloured gym bag where I stored my money and documents, but eidetically remembering the disarrangement on the desk, of white, of red.

The cash (again, a relatively small sum) was, of course, gone. But what about the traveller's cheques? Some were there, even scattered about, as he'd hastily rifled the bag. If he'd taken any of them, that meant a dreary sorting out at American Express. I took the handful of cheques with me into my work-room to match the numbers against those I'd written down in the back pages of my red notebook. Only the cash was missing, I ascertained.

The white object left on the desk was a note. As I was about to glance at it, I realized that my red notebook, in which I had just checked the serial numbers of my traveller's cheques, had also been left on the desk, out of its usual place amid the stack of books that was my current reading. Though I was relieved that the notebook was still there, its placement meant that Manuel, for some reason, had been in it.

I went through its pages until I found what was missing. The strip of photobooth pictures of him that had been shot in the train station just before we left for Hamburg and which I had pasted into the back cover of the book had been removed. Was he concerned to make it harder for the police, in the unlikely event I should call them, to find him?

I turned to his note, written in capital letters.

DEAR STAN,
    I'M SORRY I HAVE TO DO THIS. I'M REALLY STUPID.
I'M NOT DOING IT BECAUSE I WANT TO, BUT BECAUSE
I'VE GOT NO OTHER CHOICE. WE'LL NEVER SEE EACH
OTHER AGAIN.
    TSCHÜSS,
    MANUEL

At last, certainty filled me. Something had happened, and while
there were perhaps doubts about Manuel's conflicting motives (at
least, I hoped there were conflicting motives), there was no doubt
about the event. At that moment, sometime in the late afternoon, a
new batch of clouds rolled in, the sky darkened again.

The certainty (and doubts) before me seemed curiously distant
from the things Moore claimed to know and which Wittgenstein pondered as possible doubts. The material damage was relatively minimal. I still had my documents, my traveller's cheques, and my
irreplaceable notebook. His arithmetic was odd, though, since he
would've made more money by sticking around.

Did I doubt that this was my hand and that was my other one? It
was possible that he had enjoyed the sex *and* nonetheless decided to
steal from me. It was even possible that he liked me, though that was
certainly in the realm of uncertainty. He had given me a surfeit of
bodily pleasure. What sort of thief was it who left you sexually content and apologized for stealing from you? A damn elegant one, I
thought to myself.

Had I been to the moon? I was charmed that our encounter had
begun and ended with writing. All that summer, I had been deluged
with visual images—the photographs of List and Tobias; Michael's
drawings; snapshots, porn, ads—even as I insisted on words. I'd
feared I would forget what Manuel looked like, and now that he had
taken the only pictures of him that I had (although, oddly, they had
not helped me remember what he looked like when I had them), all I
had, by way of remembrance, were words. On the first night we met,
he had written out the bibliographic details of *Hustlers' Lives,* the
book in which he was interviewed; on the last occasion, he had
penned a note of apology for stealing from me. What I had left of

him, apart from my memory, were those two pieces of his writing.

Had the earth existed for a long time before I was born? It was possible that I might run into him again, but it felt like a natural end to the narrative. But what was the nature of that narrative that I'd sought to fulfil by choice and interpretation of accident? Certainly, there was no pre-ordained "narrative" that "wanted" "you" to do "x", or go to Hamburg, or fall in love with a blond-haired boy—no other, greater source which overrode the secondariness of one's personal life compared to the primacy of the world. Nor was there a "narrative" independent of us discerning some shape to seemingly contingent events, but our seeing a narrative made life something it wasn't heretofore.

If desire is the body's first epistemology, the knowledge toward which I aspire at last is the story.

I loved the wildly romantic boyish despair of that last line, "We'll never see each other again."

Well, of course we would. Or at least hear each other again. A few days later, Manuel called from Cologne (or that's where he said he was; I was only certain that it was him). The rest was lost in the blur of language. "Why did you steal from me?" I managed. "I don't know," he said. He was going off with the alleged jealous suitor to Mexico. He'd call me again.

That night, I was drinking sweet vermouth and soda in Tabasco's. Henk, the bartender, was listening to one of the customers at the bar tell his tale of woe. A dark-haired boy with a faint downy moustache wandered into the bar and ordered a beer in heavily accented English. I had been vaguely expecting to see a certain blond boy I'd noticed in Tabasco's once or twice before.

When whoever it is (invariably unexpected) begins the conversation—he's Portuguese, his name is José, he's travelling in Europe, wants to know if I'm looking for a good time—all that matters is to recognize: This is what I requested from the world. Many miss it altogether, deny they've asked for anything, mistakenly decide that this is not exactly what they asked for, etc.

He sits naked astride my thighs, his medium-sized hard dick nestled under my balls, the light from the nighttime street outside glowing on his smooth torso. My cock slides up and down in the grip of his fist, he tips his head forward and aims a stream of saliva he's built up in his mouth (he comes from a culture where expensive lubricants are not available) so that it lands where his hand provides a spit-slickened groove for my dick.

When I walked José to the neighbourhood main drag so that he could get a cab back to the bar, there was a low-key, full moon over Paulstrasse.

Torridge

William Trevor

Curiously, we hardly ever expect to be the object of revenge. Agamemnon, returning victorious from Troy, doesn't anticipate the fury of Clytemnestra; Fortunato, about to be walled up alive, is blind to the narrator's deadly grievance in Poe's "The Cask of Amontillado". We believe that we can carry on our harassing and hounding for ever, without fear of retaliation. From totalitarian governments to schoolyard bullies, victimizers seem to lack the imagination to foresee retribution. Cornered by one of his victims' relatives on his way home from a torture session in the Chile of General Pinochet, an officer was stabbed several times in the chest. As he fell, he looked up at his assailant and managed to breathe out one last question: "Why are you doing this to me?"

One of the prerequisites of revenge is patience. Those who wait are rewarded, as the Good Book has it, with the destruction of their enemies. Sometimes, as in the case of the Count of Monte Cristo, revenge must wait many years; sometimes, as with the genie in the bottle on the third Arabian night, several centuries. Yet, on a few occasions revenge can be almost immediate, as in the case recounted by Margaret Atwood of the jilted woman who had all her ex-lover's mail forwarded to an address in Equatorial Guinea. Revenge in all its shades and colours is one of William Trevor's recurrent themes.

According to Trevor, "all fiction has its autobiographical roots in the sense that as a person you are your characters' litmus paper, their single link with reality. They taste as you taste, they hear as you hear. The blue they see is your blue, the pain they experience is your pain." The reader might ask what remote act in Trevor's past lent Torridge inspiration for his revenge.

Perhaps nobody ever did wonder what Torridge would be like as a man—or what Wiltshire or Mace-Hamilton or Arrowsmith would be like, come to that. Torridge at thirteen had a face with a pudding look, matching the sound of his name. He had small eyes and short hair like a mouse's. Within the collar of his grey regulation shirt the knot of his House tie was formed with care, a maroon triangle of just the right shape and bulk. His black shoes were always shiny.

Torridge was unique in some way: perhaps only because he was beyond the pale and appeared, irritatingly, to be unaware of it. He wasn't good at games and had difficulty in understanding what was being explained in the classroom. He would sit there frowning, half smiling, his head a little to one side. Occasionally he would ask some question that caused an outburst of groaning. His smile would increase then. He would glance around the classroom, not flustered or embarrassed in the least, seeming to be pleased that he had caused such a response. He was naive to the point where it was hard to believe he wasn't pretending, but his naïveté was real and was in time universally recognised as such. A master called Buller Yeats reserved his cruellest shafts of scorn for it, sighing whenever his eyes chanced to fall on Torridge, pretending to believe his name was Porridge.

Of the same age as Torridge, but similar in no other way, were Wiltshire, Mace-Hamilton and Arrowsmith. All three of them were blond-haired and thin, with a common sharpness about their features. They wore, untidily, the same clothes as Torridge, their House ties knotted any old how, the laces in their scuffed shoes often tied in several places. They excelled at different games and were quick to sense what was what. Attractive boys, adults had more than once called them.

The friendship among the three of them developed because, in a way, Torridge was what he was. From the first time they were aware of him—on the first night of their first term—he appeared to be special. In the darkness after lights-out someone was trying not to sob and Torridge's voice was piping away, not homesick in the least. His father had a button business was what he was saying: he'd probably be going into the button business himself. In the morning he was identified, a boy in red and blue striped pyjamas, still chattering in the washroom. "What's your father do, Torridge?" Arrowsmith asked at breakfast, and that was the beginning. "Dad's in the button business," Torridge beamingly replied. "Torridge's, you know." But no one did know.

He didn't, as other new boys, make a particular friend. For a while he attached himself to a small gang of homesick boys who had only their malady in common, but after a time this gang broke up and Torridge found himself on his own, though it seemed quite happily so. He was often to be found in the room of the kindly housemaster of Junior House, an ageing white-haired figure called Old Frosty, who listened sympathetically to complaints of injustice at the hands of other masters, always ready to agree that the world was a hard place. "You should hear Buller Yeats on Torridge, sir," Wiltshire used to say in Torridge's presence. "You'd think Torridge had no feelings, sir." Old Frosty would reply that Buller Yeats was a frightful man. "Take no notice, Torridge," he'd add in his kindly voice, and Torridge would smile, making it clear that he didn't mind in the least what Buller Yeats said. "Torridge knows true happiness," a new young master, known as Mad Wallace, said in an unguarded moment one day, a remark which caused immediate uproar in a Geography class. It was afterwards much repeated, like "Dad's in the button business" and "Torridge's, you know." The true happiness of Torridge became a joke, the particular property of Wiltshire and Mace-Hamilton and Arrowsmith. Furthering the joke, they claimed that knowing Torridge was a rare experience, that the private realm of his innocence and his happiness was even exotic. Wiltshire insisted that one day the school would be proud of him. The joke was worked to death.

At the school it was the habit of certain senior boys to "take an interest in" juniors. This varied from glances and smiles across the dining hall to written invitations to meet in some secluded spot at a stated time. Friendships, taking a variety of forms, were then initiated. It was flattering, and very often a temporary antidote for homesickness, when a new boy received the agreeable but bewildering attentions of an important fifth-former. A meeting behind Chapel led to the negotiating of a barbed-wire fence on a slope of gorse bushes, the older boy solicitous and knowledgeable. There were well-trodden paths and nooks among the gorse where smoking could take place with comparative safety. Further afield, in the hills, there were crude shelters composed of stones and corrugated iron. Here, too, the emphasis was on smoking and romance.

New boys very soon became aware of the nature of older boys' interest in them. The flattery changed its shape, an adjustment was made—or the new boys retreated in panic from this area of school life. Andrews and Butler, Webb and Mace-Hamilton, Dillon and Pratt, Tothill and Goldfish Stewart, Good and Wiltshire, Sainsbury

Major and Arrowsmith, Brewitt and King: the liaisons were renowned, the combinations of names sometimes seeming like a music hall turn, a soft-shoe shuffle of entangled hearts. There was faithlessness, too: the Honourable Anthony Swain made the rounds of the senior boys, a fickle and tartish *bijou*, desired and yet despised.

Torridge's puddingy appearance did not suggest that he had *bijou* qualities, and glances did not readily come his way in the dining-hall. This was often the fate, or good fortune, of new boys and was not regarded as a sign of qualities lacking. Yet quite regularly an ill-endowed child would mysteriously become the object of fifth- and sixth-form desire. This remained a puzzle to the juniors until they themselves became fifth- or sixth-formers and desire was seen to have to do with something deeper than superficial good looks.

It was the apparent evidence of this truth that caused Torridge, first of all, to be aware of the world of *bijou* and protector. He received a note from a boy in the Upper Fifth who had previously eschewed the sexual life offered by the school. He was a big, black-haired youth with glasses and a protruding forehead, called Fisher.

"Hey, what's this mean?" Torridge enquired, finding the note under his pillow, tucked into his pyjamas. "Here's a bloke wants to go for a walk."

He read the invitation out: "*If you would like to come for a walk meet me by the electricity plant behind Chapel. Half-past four Tuesday afternoon. R.A.J. Fisher.*"

"Jesus Christ!" said Armstrong.

"You've got an admirer, Porridge," Mace-Hamilton said.

"Admirer?"

"He wants you to be his *bijou*," Wiltshire explained.

"What's it mean, *bijou*?"

"Tart it means, Porridge."

"Tart?"

"Friend. He wants to be your protector."

"What's it mean, protector?"

"He loves you, Porridge."

"I don't even know the bloke."

"He's the one with the big forehead. He's a half-wit actually."

"Half-wit?"

"His mother let him drop on his head. Like yours did, Porridge."

"My mum never."

Everyone was crowding around Torridge's bed. The note was passed from hand to hand. "What's your dad do, Porridge?" Wiltshire suddenly asked, and Torridge automatically replied that he was in the button business.

"You've got to write a note back to Fisher, you know," Mace-Hamilton point out.

"Dear Fisher," Wiltshire prompted, "I love you."

"But I don't even—"

"It doesn't matter not knowing him. You've got to write a letter and put it in his pyjamas."

Torridge didn't say anything. He placed the note in the top pocket of his jacket and slowly began to undress. The other boys drifted back to their own beds, still amused by the development. In the washroom the next morning Torridge said:

"I think he's quite nice, that Fisher."

"Had a dream about him, did you, Porridge?" Mace-Hamilton enquired. "Got up to tricks, did he?"

"No harm in going for a walk."

"No harm at all, Porridge."

In fact, a mistake had been made. Fisher, in his haste or his excitement, had placed the note under the wrong pillow. It was Arrowsmith, still allied with Sainsbury Major, whom he wished to attract.

That this error had occurred was borne in on Torridge when he turned up at the electricity plant on the following Tuesday. He had not considered it necessary to reply to Fisher's note, but he had, across the dining-hall, essayed a smile or two in the older boy's direction: it had surprised him to meet with no response. It surprised him rather more to meet with no response by the electricity plant. Fisher just looked at him and then turned his back, pretending to whistle.

"Hullo, Fisher," Torridge said.

"Hop it, look. I'm waiting for someone."

"I'm Torridge, Fisher."

"I don't care who you are."

"You wrote me that letter." Torridge was still smiling. "About a walk, Fisher."

"Walk? What walk?"

"You put the letter under my pillow, Fisher."

"Jesus!" said Fisher.

The encounter was observed by Arrowsmith, Mace-Hamilton and

Wiltshire, who had earlier taken up crouched positions behind one of the chapel buttresses. Torridge heard the familiar hoots of laughter, and because it was his way he joined in. Fisher, white-faced, strode away.

"Poor old Porridge," Arrowsmith commiserated, gasping and pretending to be contorted with mirth. Mace-Hamilton and Wiltshire were leaning against the buttress, issuing shrill noises.

"God," Torridge said, "*I* don't care."

He went away, still laughing a bit, and there the matter of Fisher's attempt at communication might have ended. In fact it didn't, because Fisher wrote a second time and this time he made certain that the right boy received his missive. But Arrowsmith, still firmly the property of Sainsbury Major, wished to have nothing to do with R.A.J. Fisher.

When he was told the details of Fisher's error, Torridge said he'd guessed it had been something like that. But Wiltshire, Mace-Hamilton and Arrowsmith claimed that a new sadness had overcome Torridge. Something beautiful had been going to happen to him, Wiltshire said: just as the petals of friendship were opening the flower had been crudely snatched away. Arrowsmith said Torridge reminded him of one of Picasso's sorrowful harlequins. One way or the other, it was agreed that the experience would be beneficial to Torridge's sensitivity. It was seen as his reason for turning to religion, which recently he had done, joining a band of similarly inclined boys who were inspired by the word of the chaplain, a figure known as God Harvey. God Harvey was ascetic, seemingly dangerously thin, his face all edge and as pale as paper, his cassock odorous with incense. He conducted readings in his room, offering coffee and biscuits afterwards, though not himself partaking of these refreshments. "God Harvey's linnets" his acolytes were called, for often a hymn was sung to round things off. Welcomed into this fold, Torridge regained his happiness.

R.A.J. Fisher, on the other hand, sank into greater gloom. Arrowsmith remained elusive, mockingly faithful to Sainsbury Major, haughty when Fisher glanced pleadingly, ignoring all his letters. Fisher developed a look of introspective misery. The notes that Arrowsmith delightedly showed around were full of longing, increasingly tinged with desperation. The following term, unexpectedly, Fisher did not return to the school.

There was a famous Assembly at the beginning of that term, with much speculation beforehand as to the trouble in the air. Rumour had it that once and for all an attempt was to be made to stamp out the smiles and the glances in the dining-hall, the whole business of *bijoux* and protectors, even the faithless behaviour of the Honourable Anthony Swain. The school waited and then the gowned staff arrived in the Assembly Hall and waited also, in grim anticipation on a raised dais. Public beatings for past offenders were scheduled, it was whispered: the Sergeant-major—the school's boxing instructor, who had himself told tales of public beatings in the past—would inflict the punishment at the headmaster's bidding. But that did not happen. Small and bald and red-skinned, the headmaster marched to the dais unaccompanied by the Sergeant-major. Twitching with anger that many afterwards declared had been simulated, he spoke at great length of the school's traditions. He stated that for fourteen years he had been proud to be its headmaster. He spoke of decency, and then of his own dismay. The school had been dishonoured; he would wish certain practices to cease. "I stand before you ashamed," he added, and paused for a moment. "Let all this cease," he commanded. He marched away, tugging at his gown in a familiar manner.

No one understood why the Assembly had taken place at that particular time, on the first day of a summer term. Only the masters looked knowing, as though labouring beneath some secret, but pressed and pleaded with they refused to reveal anything. Even Old Frosty, usually a most reliable source on such occasions, remained awesomely tight-lipped.

But the pronounced dismay and shame of the headmaster changed nothing. That term progressed and the world of *bijoux* and their protectors continued as before, the glances, the meetings, cigarettes and romance in the hillside huts. R.A. J. Fisher was soon forgotten, having never made much of a mark. But the story of his error in placing a note under Torridge's pillow passed into legend, as did the encounter by the electricity plant and Torridge's deprivation of a relationship. The story was repeated as further terms passed by; new boys heard it and viewed Torridge with greater interest, imagining what R.A.J. Fisher had been like. The liaisons of Wiltshire with Good, Mace-Hamilton with Webb, and Arrowsmith with Sainsbury Major continued until the three senior boys left the school. Wiltshire, Mace-Hamilton and Arrowsmith found fresh protectors then, and later these new liaisons came to an end in a similar manner. Later still, Wiltshire, Mace-Hamilton and

Arrowsmith ceased to be *bijoux* and became protectors themselves.

Torridge pursued the religious side of things. He continued to be a frequent partaker of God Harvey's biscuits and spiritual uplift, and a useful presence among the chapel pews, where he voluntarily dusted, cleaned brass, and kept the hymn-books in a state of repair with Sellotape. Wiltshire, Mace-Hamilton and Arrowsmith continued to circulate stories about him which were not true: that he was the product of virgin birth, that he possessed the gift of tongues but did not care to employ it, that he had three kidneys. In the end there emanated from them the claim that a liaison existed between Torridge and God Harvey. "Love and the holy spirit," Wiltshire pronounced, suggesting an ambience of chapel fustiness and God Harvey's grey boniness. The swish of his cassock took on a new significance, as did his thin, dry fingers. In a holy way the fingers pressed themselves on to Torridge, and then their holiness became a passion that could not be imagined. It was all a joke because Torridge was Torridge, but the laughter it caused wasn't malicious because no one hated him. He was a figure of fun; no one sought his downfall because there was no downfall to seek.

The friendship between Wiltshire, Mace-Hamilton and Arrowsmith continued after they left the school, after all three had married and had families. Once a year they received the Old Boys' magazine, which told of the achievements of themselves and the more successful of their school-fellows. There were Old Boys' cocktail parties and Old Boys' Day at the school every June and the Old Boys' cricket match. Some of these occasions, from time to time, they attended. Every so often they received the latest rebuilding programme, with the suggestion that they might like to contribute to the rebuilding fund. Occasionally they did.

As middle age closed in, the three friends met less often. Arrowsmith was an executive with Shell and stationed for longish periods in different countries abroad. Once every two years he brought his family back to England, which provided an opportunity for the three friends to meet. The wives met on these occasions also, and over the years the children. Often the men's distant schooldays were referred to, Buller Yeats and Old Frosty and the Sergeant-major, the little red-skinned headmaster, and above all Torridge. Within the three families, in fact, Torridge had become a myth. The joke that had begun when they were all new boys together continued, as if driven by its own impetus. In the minds of the wives and children the innocence of Torridge, his true happiness in the face of mockery and his fondness for the religious side of life, all lived on. With some exactitude a physical image of the boy he'd been took root; his neatly knotted maroon House tie, his polished shoes, the hair that resembled a mouse's fur, the pudding face with two small eyes in it. "My dad's in the button business," Arrowsmith had only to say to cause instant laughter. "Torridge's, you know." The way Torridge ate, the way he ran, the way he smiled back at Buller Yeats, the rumour that he'd been dropped on his head as a baby, that he had three kidneys, all this was considerably appreciated, because Wiltshire and Mace-Hamilton and Arrowsmith related it well.

What was not related was R.A.J. Fisher's error in placing a note beneath Torridge's pillow, or the story that had laughingly been spread about concerning Torridge's relationship with God Harvey. This would have meant revelations that weren't seemly in family circles, the explanation of the world of *bijou* and protector, the romance and cigarettes in the hill-side huts, the entangling of hearts. The subject had been touched upon among the three husband and their wives in the normal course of private conversation, although not everything had been quite recalled. Listening, the wives had formed the impression that the relationships between older and younger boys at their husband's school were similar to the platonic admiration a junior girl had so often harboured for a senior girl at their own schools. And so the subject had been left.

One evening in June, 1976, Wiltshire and Mace-Hamilton met in a bar called the Vine, in Piccadilly Place. They hadn't seen one another since the summer of 1974, the last time Arrowsmith and his family had been in England. Tonight they were to meet the Arrowsmiths again, for a family dinner in the Woodlands Hotel, Richmond. On the last occasion the three families had celebrated their reunion at the Wiltshires' house in Cobham and the time before with the Mace-Hamiltons in Ealing. Arrowsmith insisted that it was a question of turn and turn about and every third time he arranged for the family dinner to be held at his expense at the Woodlands. It was convenient because, although the Arrowsmiths spent the greater part of each biennial leave with Mrs. Arrowsmith's parents in Somerset, they always stayed for a week at the Woodlands in order to see a bit of London life.

In the Vine in Piccadilly Place Wiltshire and Mace-Hamilton hurried over their second drinks. As always, they were pleased to see one another, and both were excited at the prospect of seeing Arrowsmith and his family again. They still looked faintly alike. Both had balded and run to fat. They wore inconspicuous blue suits with a discreet chalk stripe, Wiltshire's a little smarter than Mace-Hamilton's.

"We'll be late," Wiltshire said, having just related how he'd made a small killing since the last time they'd met. Wiltshire operated in the import-export world; Mace-Hamilton was a chartered accountant.

They finished their drinks. "Cheerio," the barman called out to them as they slipped away. His voice was deferentially low, matching the softly-lit surroundings. "Cheerio, Gerry," Wiltshire said.

They drove in Wiltshire's car to Hammersmith, over the bridge and on to Barnes and Richmond. It was a Friday evening; the traffic was heavy.

"He had a bit of trouble, you know," Mace-Hamilton said.

"Arrows?"

"She took a shine to some guy in Mombasa."

Wiltshire nodded, poking the car between a cyclist and a taxi. He wasn't surprised. One night six years ago Arrowsmith's wife and he had committed adultery together at her suggestion. A messy business it had been, and afterwards he'd felt terrible.

In the Woodlands Hotel Arrowsmith, in a grey flannel suit, was not entirely sober. He, too, had run a bit of fat although, unlike Wiltshire and Mace-Hamilton, he hadn't lost any of his hair. Instead, it had dramatically changed colour: what Old Frosty had once called "Arrows' blond thatch" was grey now. Beneath it his face was pinker than it had been and he had taken to wearing spectacles, heavy and black-rimmed, making him look even more different from the boy he'd been.

In the bar of the Woodlands he drank whisky on his own, smiling occasionally to himself because tonight he had a surprise for everybody. After five weeks of being cooped up with his in-laws in Somerset he was feeling good. "Have one yourself, dear," he invited the barmaid, a girl with an excess of lipstick on a podgy mouth. He pushed his own glass towards her while she was saying she didn't mind if she did.

His wife and his three adolescent children, two boys and a girl, entered the bar with Mrs. Mace-Hamilton. "Hi, hi, hi," Arrowsmith called out to them in a jocular manner, causing his wife and Mrs. Mace-Hamilton to note that he was drunk again. They sat down while he quickly finished the whisky that had just been poured for him. "Put another in that for a start," he ordered the barmaid, and crossed the floor of the bar to find out what everyone else wanted.

Mrs. Wiltshire and her twins, girls of twelve, arrived while drinks were being decided about. Arrowsmith kissed her, as he had kissed Mrs. Mace-Hamilton. The barmaid, deciding that the accurate conveying of such a large order was going to be beyond him, came and stood by the two tables that the party now occupied. The order was given; an animated conversation began.

The three women were different in appearance and in manner. Mrs. Arrowsmith was thin as a knife, fashionably dressed in a shade of ash-grey that reflected her ash-grey hair. She smoked perpetually, unable to abandon the habit. Mrs. Wiltshire was small. Shyness caused her to coil herself up in the presence of other people so that she often resembled a ball. Tonight she was in pink, a faded shade. Mrs. Mace-Hamilton was carelessly plump, a large woman attired in a carelessly chosen dress that had begonias on it. She rather frightened Mrs. Wiltshire. Mrs. Arrowsmith found her trying.

"Oh, heavenly little drink!" Mrs. Arrowsmith said, briefly drooping her blue-tinged eyelids as she sipped her gin and tonic.

"It *is* good to see you," Mrs. Mace-Hamilton gushed, beaming at everyone and vaguely raising her glass. "And how they've all grown!" Mrs. Mace-Hamilton had not had children herself.

"Their boobs have grown, by God," the older Arrowsmith boy murmured to his brother, a reference to the Wiltshire twins. Neither of the two Arrowsmith boys went to their father's school: one was at a preparatory school in Oxford, the other at Charterhouse. Being of an age to do so, they both drank sherry and intended to drink as much of it as they possibly could. They found these family occasions tedious. Their sister, about to go to university, had determined neither to speak nor to smile for the entire evening. The Wiltshire twins were quite looking forward to the food.

Arrowsmith sat beside Mrs. Wiltshire. He didn't say anything but after a moment he stretched a hand over her two knees and squeezed them in what he intended to be a brotherly way. He said without conviction that it was great to see her. He didn't look at her while he spoke. He didn't much care for hanging about with the women and children.

In turn Mrs. Wiltshire didn't much care for his hand on her knees and was relieved when he drew it away. "Hi, hi, hi," he suddenly called out, causing her to jump. Wiltshire and Mace-Hamilton had appeared.

The physical similarity that had been so pronounced when the three men were boys and had been only faintly noticeable between Wiltshire and Mace-Hamilton in the Vine was clearly there again, as if the addition of Arrowsmith had supplied missing reflections. The men had thickened in the same way; the pinkness of Arrowsmith's countenance was a pinkness that tinged the other faces too. Only Arrowsmith's grey thatch of hair seemed out of place, all wrong beside the baldness of the other two: in their presence it might have been a wig, an impression it did not otherwise give. His grey flannel suit, beside their pinstripes, looked like something put on by mistake. "Hi, hi, hi," he shouted, thumping their shoulders.

Further rounds of drinks were bought and consumed. The Arrow-smith boys declared to each other that they were drunk and made further *sotto voce* observations about the forming bodies of the Wiltshire twins. Mrs. Wiltshire felt the occasion becoming easier as Cinzano Bianco coursed through her bloodstream. Mrs. Arrowsmith was aware of a certain familiar edginess within her body, a desire to be elsewhere, alone with a man she did not know. Mrs. Mace-Hamilton spoke loudly of her garden.

In time the party moved from the bar to the dining-room. "Bring us another round at the table," Arrowsmith commanded the lip-sticked barmaid. "Quick as you can, dear."

In the large dim dining-room waiters settled them around a table with little vases of carnations on it, a long table beneath the chande-lier in the centre of the room. Celery soup arrived at the table, and smoked salmon and pâté, and the extra rounds of drinks Arrowsmith had ordered, and bottles of Nuits St. Georges, and bottles of Vouvray and Anjou Rosé, and sirloin of beef, chicken à la king and veal esca-lope. The Arrowsmith boys laughed shrilly, openly staring at the tops of the Wiltshire twins' bodies. Potatoes, peas, spinach and carrots were served. Mrs. Arrowsmith waved the vegetable away and smoked between courses. It was after this dinner six years ago that she had made her suggestion to Wiltshire, both of them being the worse for wear and it seeming not to matter because of that. "Oh, *isn't* this jolly?" the voice of Mrs. Mace-Hamilton boomed above the general hubbub.

Over Chantilly trifle and Orange Surprise the name of Torridge was heard. The name was always mentioned just about now, though sometimes sooner. "Poor old bean," Wiltshire said, and everybody laughed because it was the one subject they all shared. No one really wanted to hear about the Mace-Hamiltons' garden; the comments of the Arrowsmith boys were only for each other; Mrs. Arrowsmith's needs could naturally not be voiced; the shyness of Mrs. Wiltshire was private too. But Torridge was different. Torridge in a way was like an old friend now, existing in everyone's mind, a family subject. The Wiltshire twins were quite amused to hear of some freshly remembered evidence of Torridge's naïveté; for the Arrowsmith girl it was better at least than being questioned by Mrs. Mace-Hamilton; for her brothers it was an excuse to bellow with simulated mirth. Mrs. Mace-Hamilton considered that the boy sounded frightful, Mrs. Arrowsmith couldn't have cared less. Only Mrs. Wiltshire had doubts: she thought the three men were hard on the memory of the boy, but of course had not ever said so. Tonight, after Wiltshire had recalled the time when Torridge had been convinced by Arrowsmith that Buller Yeats had dropped dead in his bath, the younger Arrowsmith boy told of a boy at his own school who'd been convinced that his sister's dog had died.

"Listen," Arrowsmith suddenly shouted out. "He's going to join us. Old Torridge."

There was laughter, no one believing that Torridge was going to arrive, Mrs. Arrowsmith saying to herself that her husband was pitiful when he became as drunk as this.

"I thought it would be a gesture," Arrowsmith said. "Honestly. He's looking in for coffee."

"You bloody devil, Arrows," Wiltshire said, smacking the table with the palm of his hand.

"He's in the button business," Arrowsmith shouted. "Torridge's, you know."

As far as Wiltshire and Mace-Hamilton could remember, Torridge had never featured in an Old Boys' magazine. No news of his career had been printed, and certainly no obituary. It was typical, somehow, of Arrowsmith to have winkled him out. It was part and parcel of him to want to add another dimension to the joke, to recharge its batteries. For the sight of Torridge in middle age would surely make funnier the reported anecdotes.

"After all, what's wrong," demanded Arrowsmith noisily, "with old school pals all meeting up? The more the merrier."

He was a bully, Mrs. Wiltshire thought: all three of them were bullies.

Torridge arrived at half-past nine. The hair that had been like a mouse's fur was still like that. It hadn't greyed any more; the scalp hadn't balded. He hadn't run to fat; in middle age he'd thinned down a bit. There was even a lankiness about him now, which was reflected in his movements. At school he had moved slowly, as though with caution. Jauntily attired in a pale linen suit, he crossed the dining room of the Woodlands Hotel with a step as nimble as a tap dancer's.

No one recognized him. To the three men who'd been at school with him the man who approached their dinner table was a different person, quite unlike the figure that existed in the minds of the wives and children.

"My dear Arrows," he said, smiling at Arrowsmith. The smile was different too, a brittle snap of a smile that came and went in a matter-of-fact way. The eyes that had been small didn't seem so in his thinner face. They flashed with a gleam of some kind, matching the snap of his smile.

"Good God, it's never old Porridge!" Arrowsmith's voice was slurred. His face had acquired the beginnings of an alcoholic crimson, sweat glistened on his forehead.

"Yes, it's old Porridge," Torridge said quietly. He held his hand out towards Arrowsmith and then shook hands with Wiltshire and Mace-Hamilton. He was introduced to their wives, with whom he shook hands also. He was introduced to the children, which involved further hand-shaking. His hand was cool and rather bony: they felt it should have been damp.

"You're nicely in time for coffee, Mr. Torridge," Mrs. Mace-Hamilton said.

"Brandy more like," Arrowsmith suggested. "Brandy, old chap?"

"Well, that's awfully kind of you, Arrows. Chartreuse I'd prefer, really."

A waiter drew up a chair. Room was made for Torridge between

Mrs. Mace-Hamilton and the Arrowsmith boys. It was a frightful mistake, Wiltshire was thinking. It was mad of Arrowsmith.

Mace-Hamilton examined Torridge across the dinner table. The old Torridge would have said he'd rather not have anything alcoholic, that a cup of tea and a biscuit were more his line in the evenings. It was impossible to imagine this man saying his dad had a button business. There was a suavity about him that made Mace-Hamilton uneasy. Because of what had been related to his wife and the other wives and their children he felt he'd been caught out in a lie, yet in fact that wasn't the case.

The children stole glances at Torridge, trying to see him as the boy who'd been described to them, and failing to. Mrs. Arrowsmith said to herself that all this stuff they'd been told over the years had clearly been rubbish. Mrs. Mace-Hamilton was bewildered. Mrs. Wiltshire was pleased.

"No one ever guessed," Torridge said, "what became of R.A.J. Fisher." He raised the subject suddenly, without introduction.

"Oh God, Fisher," Mace-Hamilton said.

"Who's Fisher?" the younger of the Arrowsmith boys enquired.

Torridge turned to flash his quick smile at the boy. "He left," he said. "In unfortunate circumstances."

"You've changed a lot, you know," Arrowsmith said. "Don't you think he's changed?" he asked Wiltshire and Mace-Hamilton.

"Out of recognition," Wiltshire said.

Torridge laughed easily. "I've become adventurous. I'm a late developer, I suppose."

"What kind of unfortunate circumstances?" the younger Arrowsmith boy asked. "Was Fisher expelled?"

"Oh no, not at all," Mace-Hamilton said hurriedly.

"Actually," Torridge said, "Fisher's trouble all began with the writing of a note. Don't you remember? He put it in my pyjamas. But it wasn't for me at all."

He smiled again. He turned to Mrs. Wiltshire in a way that seemed polite, drawing her into the conversation. "I was an innocent at school. But innocence eventually slips away. I found my way about eventually."

"Yes, of course," she murmured. She didn't like him, even though she was glad he wasn't as he might have been. There was malevolence in him, a ruthlessness that seemed like a work of art. He seemed like a work of art himself, as though in losing the innocence he spoke of he had recreated himself.

"I often wonder about Fisher," he remarked.

The Wiltshire twins giggled. "What's so great about this bloody Fisher?" the older Arrowsmith boy murmured, nudging his brother with an elbow.

"What're you doing these days?" Wiltshire asked, interrupting Mace-Hamilton, who had begun to say something.

"I make buttons," Torridge replied. "You may recall my father made buttons."

"Ah, here're the drinks," Arrowsmith rowdily observed.

"I don't much keep up with the school," Torridge said as the waiter placed a glass of Chartreuse in front of him. "I don't so much as think about it except for wondering about poor old Fisher. Our headmaster was a cretin," he informed Mrs. Wiltshire.

Again the Wiltshire twins giggled. The Arrowsmith girl yawned and her brothers giggled also, amused that the name of Fisher had come up again.

"You will have coffee, Mr. Torridge?" Mrs. Mace-Hamilton offered, for the waiter had brought a fresh pot to the table. She held it poised about a cup. Torridge smiled at her and nodded. She said:

"Pearl buttons d'you make?"

"No, not pearl."

"Remember those awful packet peas we used to have?" Arrowsmith enquired. Wiltshire said:

"Use plastics at all? In your buttons, Porridge?"

"No, we don't use plastics. Leathers, various leathers. And horn. We specialise."

"How every interesting!" Mrs. Mace-Hamilton exclaimed.

"No, no. It's rather ordinary really." He paused, and then added, "Someone once told me that Fisher went into a timber business. But of course that was far from true."

"A chap was expelled a year ago," the younger Arrowsmith boy said, contributing this in order to cover up a fresh outburst of sniggering. "For stealing a transistor."

Torridge nodded, appearing to be interested. He asked the Arrowsmith boys where they were at school. The older one said Charterhouse and his brother gave the name of his preparatory school. Torridge nodded again and asked their sister and she said she was waiting to go to university. He had quite a chat with the Wiltshire twins about their school. They considered it pleasant the way he bothered, seeming genuinely to want to know. The giggling died away.

"I imagined Fisher wanted me for his *bijou*," he said when all that was over, still addressing the children. "Our place was riddled with fancy larks like that. Remember?" he added, turning to Mace-Hamilton.

"Bijou?" one of the twins asked before Mace-Hamilton could reply.

"A male tart," Torridge explained.

The Arrowsmith boys gaped at him, the older one with his mouth actually open. The Wiltshire twins began to giggle again. The Arrowsmith girl frowned, unable to hide her interest.

"The Honourable Anthony Swain," Torridge said, "was no better than a whore."

Mrs. Arrowsmith, who for some minutes had been engaged with her own thoughts, was suddenly aware that the man who was in the button business was talking about sex. She gazed diagonally across the table at him, astonished that he should be talking in this way.

"Look here, Torridge," Wiltshire said, frowning at him and shaking his head. With an almost imperceptible motion he gestured towards the wives and children.

"Andrew and Butler. Dillon and Pratt. Tothill and Goldfish Stewart. Your dad," Torridge said to the Arrowsmith girls, "was always very keen. Sainsbury Major in particular."

"Now look here," Arrowsmith shouted, beginning to get to his feet and then changing his mind.

"My gosh, how they broke chaps' hearts, those three!"

"Please don't talk like this." It was Mrs. Wiltshire who protested, to everyone's surprise, most of all her own. "The children are quite young, Mr. Torridge."

Her voice had become a whisper. She could feel herself reddening with embarrassment, and a little twirl of sickness occurred in her stomach. Deferentially, as though appreciating the effort she had made, Torridge apologised.

"I think you'd better go," Arrowsmith said.

"You were right about God Harvey, Arrows. Gay as a grip he was, beneath that cassock. So was Old Frosty, as a matter of fact."

"Really!" Mrs. Mace-Hamilton cried, her bewilderment turning into outrage. She glared at her husband, demanding with her eyes that instantly something should be done. But her husband and his two friends were briefly stunned by what Torridge had claimed for God Harvey. Their schooldays leapt back at them, possessing them for a vivid moment: the dormitory, the dining-hall, the glances and the invitations, the meetings behind Chapel. It was somehow in keeping with the school's hypocrisy that God Harvey had had inclinations himself, that a rumour begun as an outrageous joke should have contained the truth.

"As a matter of fact," Torridge went on, "I wouldn't be what I am if it hadn't been for God Harvey. I'm what they call queer," he explained to the children. "I perform sexual acts with men."

"For God's sake, Torridge," Arrowsmith shouted, on his feet, his face the colour of ripe strawberry, his watery eyes quivering with rage.

"It was nice of you to invite me tonight, Arrows. Our alma mater can't be too proud of chaps like me."

People spoke at once, Mrs. Mace-Hamilton and Mrs. Wiltshire, all three men. Mrs. Arrowsmith sat still. What she was thinking was that she had become quietly drunk while her husband had more boisterously reached the same condition. She was thinking, as well, that by the sound of things he'd possessed as a boy a sexual urge that was a lot livelier than the one he'd once exposed her to and now hardly ever did. With boys who had grown to be men he had had a whale of a time. Old Frosty had been a kind of Mr. Chips, she'd been told. She'd never heard of Sainsbury Major or God Harvey.

"It's quite disgusting," Mrs. Mace-Hamilton's voice cried out above the other voices. She said the police should be called. It was scandalous to have to listen to unpleasant conversation like this. She began to say the children should be leaving the dining room, but changed her mind because it appeared that Torridge himself was about to go. "You're a most horrible man," she cried.

Confusion gathered, like a fog around the table. Mrs. Wiltshire, who knew that her husband had committed adultery with Mrs. Arrowsmith, felt another bout of nerves in her stomach. "Because she was starved, that's why," her husband had almost violently confessed when she'd discovered. "I was putting her out of her misery." She had wept then and he had comforted her as best he could. She had not told him that he had never succeeded in arousing in her the desire to make love: she had always assumed that to be a failing in herself, but now for some reason she was not so sure. Nothing had been directly said that might have caused this doubt, but an instinct informed Mrs. Wiltshire that the doubt should be there. The man beside her smiled his brittle, malevolent smile at her, as if in sympathy.

With his head bent over the table and his hands half hiding his face, the younger Arrowsmith boy examined his father by glancing through his fingers. There were men whom his parents warned him against, men who would sit beside you in buses or try to give you a lift in a car. This man who had come tonight, who had been such a joke up till now, was apparently one of these, not a joke at all. And the confusion was greater: at one time, it seemed, his father had been like that too.

The Arrowsmith girl considered her father also. Once she had walked into a room in Lagos to find her mother in the arms of an African clerk. Ever since she had felt sorry for her father. There'd been an unpleasant scene at the time, she'd screamed at her mother and later in a fury had told her father what she'd seen. He'd nodded, wearily seeming not to be surprised, while her mother had miserably wept. She'd put her arms around her father, comforting him; she'd felt no mercy for her mother, no sympathy or understanding. The scene formed vividly in her mind as she sat at the dinner table: it appeared to be relevant in the confusion and yet not clearly so. Her parents' marriage was messy, messier than it looked. Across the table her mother grimly smoked, focussing her eyes with difficulty. She smiled at her daughter, a soft, inebriated smile.

The older Arrowsmith boy was also aware of the confusion. Being at a school where the practice which had been spoken of was common enough, he could easily believe the facts that had been thrown about. Against his will, he was forced to imagine what he had never imagined before: his father and his friends as schoolboys, engaged in passion with other boys. He might have been cynical about this image but he could not. Instead it made him want to gasp. It knocked away the smile that had been on his face all evening.

The Wiltshire twins unhappily stared at the white tablecloth, here and there stained with wine or gravy. They, too, found they'd lost the urge to smile and instead shakily blinked back tears.

"Yes, perhaps I'd better go," Torridge said.

With impatience Mrs. Mace-Hamilton looked at her husband, as if expecting him to hurry Torridge off or at least to say something. But Mace-Hamilton remained silent. Mrs. Mace-Hamilton licked her lips, preparing to speak herself. She changed her mind.

"Fisher didn't go into a timber business," Torridge said, "because poor old Fisher was dead as a doornail. Which is why our cretin of a headmaster, Mrs. Mace-Hamilton, had that Assembly."

"Assembly?" she said. Her voice was weak, although she'd meant it to sound matter-of-fact and angry.

"There was an Assembly that no one understood. Poor old Fisher had strung himself up in a barn on his father's farm. I discovered that," Torridge said, turning to Arrowsmith, "years later: from God Harvey actually. The poor chap left a note but the parents didn't care to pass it on. I mean it was for you, Arrows."

Arrowsmith was standing, hanging over the table. "Note?" he said. "For me?"

"Another note. Why d'you think he did himself in, Arrows?"

Torridge smiled, at Arrowsmith and then round the table.

"None of that's true," Wiltshire said.

"As a matter of fact it is."

He went, and nobody spoke at the dinner table. A body of a schoolboy hung from a beam in a barn, a note on the straw below his dangling feet. It hung in the confusion that had been caused, increasing the confusion. Two waiters hovered by a sideboard, one passing the time by arranging sauce bottles, the other folding napkins into cone shapes. Slowly Arrowsmith sat down again. The silence continued as the conversation of Torridge continued to haunt the dinner table. He haunted it himself, with his brittle smile and his tap dancer's elegance, still faithful to the past in which he had so signally failed, triumphant in his middle age.

Then Mrs. Arrowsmith quite suddenly wept and the Wiltshire twins wept and Mrs. Wiltshire comforted them. The Arrowsmith girl got up and walked away, and Mrs. Mace-Hamilton turned to the three men and said they should be ashamed of themselves, allowing all this to happen.

On Ruegen Island

Christopher Isherwood

When the young Christopher Isherwood heard from his uncle, who had just returned from Germany, that Berlin was a modern Babylon of unspeakable vices, his immediate thought was that this was a city he must visit. In 1929 Isherwood moved to Berlin, where, according to Stephen Spender, he was "more than a young rebel passing through a phase of revolt against parents, conventional morality, and orthodox religion." What Spender most admired was the anger with which Isherwood railed against the institutions of "heterosexual dictatorship" that "came between people and their direct unprejudiced approach to one another". But Isherwood's Berlin stories are anything but angry. Instead, the narrator identifies himself by the famous words, "I am a camera with its shutter open, quite passive, recording, not thinking."

It is likely that a writer such as Virginia Woolf would have understood the contradiction between Isherwood's civil wrath and his artistic detachment (indeed, the Woolfs' Hogarth Press was the first to publish selections from the Berlin diaries). "It is fatal for anyone who writes to think of their sex," she observed in A Room of One's Own, *"for anything written with that conscious bias is doomed to death."*

SUMMER 1931

I wake early and go out to sit on the veranda in my pyjamas. The wood casts long shadows over the fields. Birds call with sudden uncanny violence, like alarm-clocks going off. The birch-trees hang down laden over the rutted, sandy earth of the country road. A soft bar of cloud is moving up from the line of trees along the lake. A man with a bicycle is watching his horse graze on a patch of grass by the path; he wants to disentangle the horse's hoof from its tether-rope. He pushes the horse with both hands, but it won't budge. And now an old woman in a shawl comes walking with a little boy. The boy wears a dark sailor suit; he is very pale and his neck is bandaged. They soon turn back. A man passes on a bicycle and shouts something to the man with the horse. His voice rings out, quite clear yet unintelligible, in the morning stillness. A cock crows. The creak of the bicycle going past. The dew on the white table and chairs in the garden arbour, and dripping from the heavy lilac. Another cock crows, much louder and nearer. And I think I can hear the sea, or very distant bells.

The village is hidden in the wood, away up to the left. It consists almost entirely of boarding-houses, in various styles of seaside architecture—sham Moorish, old Bavarian, Taj Mahal, and the rococo doll's house, with white fretwork balconies. Behind the woods is the sea. You can reach it without going through the village, by a zig-zag path, which brings you out abruptly to the edge of some sandy cliffs, with the beach below you, and the tepid shallow Baltic lying almost at your feet. This end of the bay is quite deserted; the official bathing-beach is round the corner of the headland. The white onion-domes of the Strand Restaurant at Baabe wobble in the distance, behind fluid waves of heat, a kilometre away.

In the wood are rabbits and adders and deer. Yesterday morning I saw a roe being chased by a Borzoi dog, right across the fields and in amongst the trees. The dog couldn't catch the roe, although it seemed to be going much the faster of the two, moving in long graceful bounds, while the roe went bucketing over the earth with wild rigid jerks, like a grand piano bewitched.

There are two people staying in this house, besides myself. One of them is an Englishman, named Peter Wilkinson, about my own age. The other is a German working-class boy from Berlin, named Otto Nowak. He is sixteen or seventeen years old.

Peter—as I already call him; we got rather tight the first evening, and quickly made friends—is thin and dark and nervous. He wears horn-rimmed glasses. When he gets excited, he digs his hands down between his knees and clenches them together. Thick veins stand out at the sides of his temples. He trembles all over with suppressed, nervous laughter, until Otto, rather irritated, exclaims: *"Mensch, reg' Dich bloss nicht so auf!"*

Otto has a face like a very ripe peach. His hair is fair and thick, growing low on his forehead. He has small sparkling eyes, full of naughtiness, and a wide, disarming grin, which is much too innocent to be true. When he grins, two large dimples appear in his peach-bloom cheeks. At present, he makes up to me assiduously, flattering me, laughing at my jokes, never missing an opportunity of giving me a crafty, understanding wink. I think he looks upon me as a potential ally in his dealings with Peter.

This morning we all bathed together. Peter and Otto are busy building a large sand fort. I lay and watched Peter as he worked furiously, enjoying the glare, digging away savagely with his child's spade, like a chain-gang convict under the eyes of an armed warder. Throughout the long, hot morning, he never sat still for a moment. He and Otto swam, dug, wrestled, ran races or played with a rubber football, up and down the sands. Peter is skinny but wiry. In his games with Otto, he holds his own, it seems, only by an immense, furious effort of will. It is Peter's will against Otto's body. Otto is his whole body; Peter is only his head. Otto moves fluidly, effortlessly; his gestures have the savage, unconscious grace of a cruel, elegant animal. Peter drives himself about, lashing his stiff, ungraceful body with the whip of his merciless will.

Otto is outrageously conceited. Peter has bought him a chest-expander, and, with this, he exercises solemnly at all hours of the day. Coming into their bedroom, after lunch, to look for Peter, I found Otto wrestling with the expander like Laocoön, in front of the looking-glass, all alone: "Look, Christoph!" he gasped. "You see, I can do it! All five strands!" Otto certainly has a superb pair of shoulders and chest for a boy of his age—but his body is nevertheless somehow slightly ridiculous. The beautiful ripe lines of the torso taper away too suddenly to his rather absurd little buttocks and spindly, immature legs. And these struggles with the chest-expander are daily making him more and more top-heavy.

This evening Otto had a touch of sunstroke, and went to bed early, with a headache. Peter and I walked up to the village, alone. In the Bavarian café, where the band makes a noise like Hell unchained, Peter bawled into my ear the story of his life.

Peter is the youngest of a family of four. He has two sisters, both married. One of the sisters lives in the country and hunts. The other is what the newspapers call "a popular society hostess". Peter's elder brother is a scientist and explorer. He has been on expeditions to the Congo, the New Hebrides, and the Great Barrier Reef. He plays chess, speaks with the voice of a man of sixty, and has never, to the best of Peter's belief, performed the sexual act. The only member of the family with whom Peter is at present on speaking terms is his hunting sister, but they seldom meet, because Peter hates his brother-in-law.

Peter was delicate, as a boy. He did not go to a preparatory school but, when he was thirteen, his father sent him to a public school. His father and mother had a row about this which lasted until Peter, with his mother's encouragement, developed heart trouble and had to be removed at the end of his second term. Once escaped, Peter began to hate his mother for having petted and coddled him into a funk. She saw that he could not forgive her and so, as Peter was the only one of her children whom she cared for, she got ill herself and soon afterwards died.

It was too late to send Peter back to school again, so Mr. Wilkinson engaged a tutor. The tutor was a very high-church young man who intended to become a priest. He took cold baths in winter and had crimpy hair and a Grecian jaw. Mr. Wilkinson disliked him from the first, and the elder brother made satirical remarks, so Peter threw himself passionately on to the tutor's side. The two of them went for walking-tours in the Lake District and discussed the meaning of the Sacrament amidst austere moorland scenery. This kind of talk got them, inevitably, into a complicated emotional tangle which was abruptly unravelled, one evening, during a fearful row in a barn. Next morning, the tutor left, leaving a ten-page letter behind him. Peter meditated suicide. He heard later indirectly that the tutor had grown a moustache and gone out to Australia. So Peter got another tutor, and finally went up to Oxford.

Hating his father's business and his brother's science, he made music and literature into a religious cult. For the first year, he liked Oxford very much indeed. He went out to tea-parties and ventured to talk. To his pleasure and surprise, people appeared to be listening to what he said. It wasn't until he had done this often that he began to notice their air of slight embarrassment. "Somehow or other," said Peter, "I always struck the wrong note."

Meanwhile, at home, in the big Mayfair house, with its four bathrooms and garage for three cars, where there was always too much to eat, the Wilkinson family was slowly falling to pieces, like something gone rotten. Mr. Wilkinson with his diseased kidneys, his whisky, and his knowledge of "handling men", was angry and confused and a bit pathetic. He snapped and growled at his children when they passed near him, like a surly old dog. At meals nobody ever spoke. They avoided each other's eyes, and hurried upstairs afterwards to write letters, full of hatred and satire, to their intimate friends. Only Peter had no friend to write to. He shut himself up in his tasteless, expensive bedroom and read and read.

And now it was the same at Oxford. Peter no longer went to tea-parties. He worked all day, and, just before the examinations, he had a nervous breakdown. The doctor advised a complete change of scene, other interests. Peter's father let him play at farming for six months in Devonshire, then he began to talk of the business. Mr. Wilkinson had been unable to persuade any of his other children to take even a polite interest in the source of their incomes. They were all unassailable in their different worlds. One of his daughters was about to marry into the peerage, the other frequently hunted with the Prince of Wales. His elder son read papers to the Royal Geographical Society. Only Peter hadn't any justification for his existence. The other children behaved selfishly, but knew what they wanted. Peter also behaved selfishly, and didn't know.

However, at the critical moment, Peter's uncle, his mother's brother, died. This uncle lived in Canada. He had seen Peter once as a child and had taken a fancy to him, so he left him all his money, not very much, but enough to live on, comfortably.

Peter went to Paris and began studying music. His teacher told him that he would never be more than a good second-rate amateur, but he only worked all the harder. He worked merely to avoid thinking, and had another nervous breakdown, less serious than at first. At this time, he was convinced that he would soon go mad. He paid a visit to London and found only his father at home. They had a furious quarrel on the first evening; thereafter, they hardly exchanged a word. After a week of silence and huge meals, Peter had a mild attack of homicidal mania. All through breakfast, he couldn't take his eyes off a pimple on his father's throat. He was fingering the bread-knife. Suddenly the left side of his face began to twitch. It twitched and twitched, so that he had to cover his cheek with his hand. He felt certain that his father had noticed this, and was intentionally refusing to remark on it—was, in fact, deliberately torturing him. At last, Peter could stand it no longer. He jumped up and rushed out of the room,

412   Christopher Isherwood

out of the house, into the garden, where he flung himself face down-
wards on the wet lawn. There he lay, too frightened to move. After a
quarter of an hour, the twitching stopped.

That evening Peter walked along Regent Street and picked up a
whore. They went back together to the girl's room, and talked for
hours. He told her the whole story of his life at home, gave her ten
pounds and left her without even kissing her. Next morning a mysterious rash appeared on his left thigh. The doctor seemed at a loss to
explain its origin, but prescribed some ointment. The rash became
fainter, but did not altogether disappear until last month. Soon after
the Regent Street episode, Peter also began to have trouble with his
left eye.

For some time already, he had played with the idea of consulting a
psycho-analyst. His final choice was an orthodox Freudian with a
sleepy, ill-tempered voice and very large feet. Peter took an immediate
dislike to him, and told him so. The Freudian made notes on a piece
of paper, but did not seem offended. Peter later discovered that he was
quite uninterested in anything except Chinese art. They met three
times a week, and each visit cost two guineas.

After six months Peter abandoned the Freudian, and started going
to a new analyst, a Finnish lady with white hair and a bright conversational manner. Peter found her easy to talk to. He told her, to the best
of his ability, everything he had ever done, ever said, ever thought, or
ever dreamed. Sometimes, in moments of discouragement, he told her
stories which were absolutely untrue, or anecdotes collected from
case-books. Afterwards, he would confess to these lies, and they
would discuss his motives for telling them, and agree that they were
very interesting. On red-letter nights Peter would have a dream, and
this gave them a topic of conversation for the next few weeks. The
analysis lasted nearly two years, and was never completed.

This year Peter got bored with the Finnish lady. He heard of a
good man in Berlin. Well, why not? At any rate, it would be a change.
It was also an economy. The Berlin man only cost fifteen marks a
visit.

"And you're still going to him?" I asked.

"No...." Peter smiled. "I can't afford to, you see."

Last month, a day or two after his arrival, Peter went out to
Wannsee, to bathe. The water was still chilly, and there were not many
people about. Peter had noticed a boy who was turning somersaults

by himself, on the sand. Later the boy came up and asked him for a match. They got into conversation. It was Otto Nowak.

"Otto was quite horrified when I told him about the analyst. 'What!' he said, 'you give that man fifteen marks a day just for letting you talk to him! You give me ten marks and I'll talk to you all day, and all night as well!'" Peter began to shake all over with laughter, flushing scarlet and wringing his hands.

Curiously enough, Otto wasn't being altogether preposterous when he offered to take the analyst's place. Like many very animal people, he has considerable instinctive powers of healing—when he chooses to use them. At such times, his treatment of Peter is unerringly correct. Peter will be sitting at the table, hunched up, his downward-curving mouth lined with childhood fears: a perfect case-picture of his twisted, expensive upbringing. Then in comes Otto, grins, dimples, knocks over a chair, slaps Peter on the back, rubs his hands and exclaims fatuously: *"Ja, ja ... so ist die Sache!"* And, in a moment, Peter is transformed. He relaxes, begins to hold himself naturally; the tightness disappears from his mouth, his eyes lose their hunted look. As long as the spell lasts, he is just like an ordinary person.

Peter tells me that, before he met Otto, he was so terrified of infection that he would wash his hands with carbolic after picking up a cat. Nowadays, he often drinks out of the same glass as Otto, uses his sponge, and will share the same plate.

Dancing has begun at the Kurhaus and the café on the lake. We saw the announcements of the first dance two days ago, while we were taking our evening walk up the main street of the village. I noticed that Otto glanced at the poster wistfully, and that Peter had seen him do this. Neither of them, however, made any comment.

Yesterday was chilly and wet. Otto suggested that we should hire a boat and go fishing on the lake: Peter was pleased with this plan, and agreed at once. But when we had waited three quarters of an hour in the drizzle for a catch, he began to get irritable. On the way back to the shore, Otto kept splashing with his oars—at first because he couldn't row properly, later merely to annoy Peter. Peter got very angry indeed, and swore at Otto, who sulked.

After supper, Otto announced that he was going to dance at the Kurhaus. Peter took this without a word, in ominous silence, the corners of his mouth beginning to drop; and Otto, either genuinely unconscious of his disapproval or deliberately overlooking it, assumed that the matter was settled.

After he had gone out, Peter and I sat upstairs in my cold room, listening to the pattering of the rain on the window.

"I thought it couldn't last," said Peter gloomily. "This is the beginning. You'll see."

"Nonsense, Peter. The beginning of what? It's quite natural that Otto should want to dance sometimes. You mustn't be so possessive."

"Oh, I know, I know. As usual, I'm being utterly unreasonable.... All the same, this is the beginning...."

Rather to my own surprise the event proved me right. Otto arrived back from the Kurhaus before ten o'clock. He had been disappointed. There had been very few people there, and the band was poor.

"I'll never go again," he added, with a languishing smile at me. "From now on I'll stay every evening with you and Christoph. It's much more fun when we're all three together, isn't it?"

Yesterday morning, while we were lying in our fort on the beach, a little fair-haired man with ferrety blue eyes and a small moustache came up to us and asked us to join in a game with him. Otto, always over-enthusiastic about strangers, accepted at once, so that Peter and I had either to be rude or follow his example.

The little man, after introducing himself as a surgeon from a Berlin hospital, at once took command, assigning to us the places where we were to stand. He was very firm about this—instantly ordering me back when I attempted to edge a little nearer, so as not to have such a long distance to throw. Then it appeared that Peter was throwing in quite the wrong way: the little doctor stopped the game in order to demonstrate this. Peter was amused at first, and then rather annoyed. He retorted with considerable rudeness, but the doctor's skin wasn't pierced. "You hold yourself so stiff," he explained, smiling. "That is an error. You try again, and I will keep my hand on your shoulder-blade to see whether you really relax.... No. Again you do not!"

He seemed delighted, as if this failure of Peter's were a special triumph for his own methods of teaching. His eye met Otto's. Otto grinned understandingly.

Our meeting with the doctor put Peter in a bad temper for the rest of the day. In order to tease him, Otto pretended to like the doctor very much: "That's the sort of chap I'd like to have for a friend," he said with a spiteful smile. "A real sportsman! You ought to take up sport, Peter! Then you'd have a figure like he has!"

Had Peter been in another mood, this remark would probably have made him smile. As it was, he got very angry: "You'd better go off with your doctor now, if you like him so much!"

Otto grinned teasingly. "He hasn't asked me to—yet!"

Yesterday evening, Otto went out to dance at the Kurhaus and didn't return till late.

* * *

There are now a good many summer visitors to the village. The bathing-beach by the pier, with its array of banners, begins to look like a medieval camp. Each family has its own enormous hooded wicker beach-chair, and each chair flies a little flag. There are the German city flags—Hamburg, Hanover, Dresden, Rostock and Berlin, as well as the National, Republic and Nazi colours. Each chair is encircled by a low sand bulwark upon which the occupants have set inscriptions in fir-cones: *Waldesruh. Familie Walter. Stahlhelm. Heil Hitler!* Many of the forts are also decorated with the Nazi swastika. The other morning I saw a child of about five years old, stark naked, marching along all by himself with a swastika flag over his shoulder and singing *"Deutschland über alles"*.

The little doctor fairly revels in this atmosphere. Nearly every morning he arrives, on a missionary visit, to our fort. "You really ought to come round to the other beach," he tells us. "It's much more amusing there. I'd introduce you to some nice girls. The young people here are a magnificent lot! I, as a doctor, know how to appreciate them. The other day I was over at Hiddensee. Nothing but Jews! It's a pleasure to get back here and see real Nordic types!"

"Let's go to the other beach," urged Otto. "It's so dull here. There's hardly anyone about."

"You can go if you like," Peter retorted with angry sarcasm: "I'm afraid I should be rather out of place. I had a grandmother who was partly Spanish."

But the little doctor won't let us alone. Our opposition and more or less openly expressed dislike seem actually to fascinate him. Otto is always betraying us into his hands. One day, when the doctor was speaking enthusiastically about Hitler, Otto said, "It's no good your talking like that to Christoph, Herr Doktor. He's a communist!"

This seemed positively to delight the doctor. His ferrety blue eyes gleamed with triumph. He laid his hand affectionately on my shoulder.

"But you *can't* be a communist! You *can't!*"

"Why can't I?" I asked coldly, moving away. I hate him to touch me.

"Because there isn't any such thing as communism. It's just an hallucination. A mental disease. People only imagine that they're communists. They aren't really."

"What are they, then?"

But he wasn't listening. He fixed me with his triumphant, ferrety smile.

"Five years ago I used to think as you do. But my work at the clinic has convinced me that communism is a mere hallucination. What people need is discipline, self-control. I can tell you this as a doctor. I know it from my own experience."

This morning we were all together in my room, ready to start out to bathe. The atmosphere was electric, because Peter and Otto were still carrying on an obscure quarrel which they had begun before breakfast, in their own bedroom. I was turning over the pages of a book, not paying much attention to them. Suddenly Peter slapped Otto hard on both cheeks. They closed immediately and staggered grappling about the room, knocking over the chairs. I looked on, getting out of their way as well as I could. It was funny, and, at the same time, unpleasant, because rage made their faces strange and ugly. Presently Otto got Peter down on the ground and began twisting his arm: "Have you had enough?" he kept asking. He grinned: at that moment he was really hideous, positively deformed with malice. I knew that Otto was glad to have me there, because my presence was an extra humiliation for Peter. So I laughed, as though the whole thing were a joke, and went out of the room. I walked through the woods to Baabe, and bathed from the beach beyond. I felt I didn't want to see either of them again for several hours.

If Otto wishes to humiliate Peter, Peter in his different way also wishes to humiliate Otto. He wants to force Otto into making a certain kind of submission to his will, and this submission Otto refuses instinctively to make. Otto is naturally and healthily selfish, like an animal. If there are two chairs in a room, he will take the more comfortable one without hesitation, because it never even occurs to him to consider Peter's comfort. Peter's selfishness is much less honest, more civilized, more perverse. Appealed to in the right way, he will make any sacrifice, however unreasonable and unnecessary. But when Otto takes the better chair as if by right, then Peter immediately sees a challenge which he dare not refuse to accept. I suppose that—given their two natures—there is no possible escape from this situation. Peter is bound to go on fighting to win Otto's submission. When, at last, he ceases to do so, it will merely mean that he has lost interest in Otto altogether.

The really destructive feature of their relationship is its inherent quality of boredom. It is quite natural for Peter often to feel bored with Otto—they have scarcely a single interest in common—but Peter, for sentimental reasons, will never admit that this is so. When Otto, who has no such motives for pretending, says, "It's so dull here!" I invariably see Peter wince and look pained. Yet Otto is actually far less often bored than Peter himself; he finds Peter's company genuinely amusing, and is quite glad to be with him most of the day. Often, when Otto has been chattering rubbish for an hour without stopping, I can see that Peter really longs for him to be quiet and go away. But to admit this would be, in Peter's eyes, a total defeat, so he only laughs and rubs his hands, tacitly appealing to me to support him in his pretence of finding Otto inexhaustibly delightful and funny.

On our way back through the woods, after my bathe, I saw the ferrety little blond doctor advancing to meet me. It was too late to turn back. I said "Good morning" as politely and coldly as possible. The doctor was dressed in running-shorts and a sweater; he explained that he had been taking a "*Waldlauf*". "But I think I shall turn back now," he added. "Wouldn't you like to run with me a little?"

"I'm afraid I can't," I said rashly. "You see, I twisted my ankle a bit yesterday."

I could have bitten my tongue out as I saw the gleam of triumph in his eyes. "Ah, you've sprained your ankle? Please let me look at it!" Squirming with dislike, I had to submit to his prodding fingers. "But it is nothing, I assure you. You have no cause for alarm."

As we walked the doctor began to question me about Peter and Otto, twisting his head to look up at me, as he delivered each sharp, inquisitive little thrust. He was fairly consumed with curiosity.

"My work in the clinic has taught me that it is no use trying to help this type of boy. Your friend is very generous and very well meaning, but he makes a great mistake. This type of boy always reverts. From a scientific point of view, I find him exceedingly interesting."

As though he were about to say something specially momentous, the doctor suddenly stood still in the middle of the path, paused a moment to engage my attention, and smilingly announced:

"He has a criminal head!"

"And you think that people with criminal heads should be left to become criminals?"

"Certainly not. I believe in discipline. These boys ought to be put into labour-camps."

"And what are you going to do with them when you've got them there? You say that they can't be altered, anyhow, so I suppose you'd keep them locked up for the rest of their lives?"

The doctor laughed delightedly, as though this were a joke against himself which he could, nevertheless, appreciate. He laid a caressing hand on my arm:

"You are an idealist! Do not imagine that I don't understand your point of view. But it is unscientific, quite unscientific. You and your friend do not understand such boys as Otto. I understand them. Every week, one or two such boys come to my clinic, and I must operate on them for adenoids, or mastoid, or poisoned tonsils. So, you see, I know them through and through!"

"I should have thought it would be more accurate to say you knew their throats and ears."

Perhaps my German wasn't quite equal to rendering the sense of this last remark. At all events, the doctor ignored it completely. "I know this type of boy very well," he repeated. "It is a bad degenerate type. You cannot make anything out of these boys. Their tonsils are almost invariably diseased."

* * *

There are perpetual little rows going on between Peter and Otto, yet I cannot say that I find living with them actually unpleasant. Just now, I am very much taken up with my new novel. Thinking about it, I often go out for long walks, alone. Indeed, I find myself making more and more frequent excuses to leave them to themselves; and this is selfish, because, when I am with them, I can often choke off the beginnings of a quarrel by changing the subject or making a joke. Peter, I know, resents my desertions. "You're quite an ascetic," he said maliciously the other day, "always withdrawing for your contemplations." Once, when I was sitting in a café near the pier, listening to the band, Peter and Otto came past. "So this is where you've been hiding!" Peter exclaimed. I saw that, for the moment, he really disliked me.

One evening, we were all walking up the main street, which was crowded with summer visitors. Otto said to Peter, with his most spiteful grin: "Why must you always look in the same direction as I do?" This was surprisingly acute, for, whenever Otto turned his head to stare at a girl, Peter's eyes mechanically followed his glance with instinctive jealousy. We passed the photographer's window, in which, every day, the latest groups snapped by the beach cameramen are displayed. Otto paused to examine one of the new pictures with great attention, as though its subject were particularly attractive. I saw Peter's lips contract. He was struggling with himself, but he couldn't resist his own jealous curiosity—he stopped too. The photograph was of a fat old man with a long beard, waving a Berlin flag. Otto, seeing that his trap had been successful, laughed maliciously.

Invariably, after supper, Otto goes dancing at the Kurhaus or the café by the lake. He no longer bothers to ask Peter's permission to do this; he has established the right to have his evenings to himself. Peter and I generally go out too, into the village. We lean over the rail of the pier for a long time without speaking, staring down at the cheap jewellery of the Kurhaus lights reflected in the black water, each busy with his own thoughts. Sometimes we go into the Bavarian café and Peter gets steadily drunk—his stern, Puritan mouth contracting slightly with distaste as he raises the glass to his lips. I say nothing. There is too much to say. Peter, I know, wants me to make some provocative remark about Otto which will give him the exquisite relief of losing his temper. I don't, and we drink—keeping up a desultory conversation about books and concerts and plays. Later, when we are returning home, Peter's footsteps will gradually quicken until, as we enter the house, he leaves me and runs upstairs to his bedroom. Often we don't get back till half past twelve or a quarter to one, but it is very seldom that we find Otto already there.

Down by the railway station, there is a holiday home for children from the Hamburg slums. Otto has got to know one of the teachers from this home, and they go out dancing together nearly every evening. Sometimes the girl, with her little troop of children, comes marching past the house. The children glance up at the windows and, if Otto happens to be looking out, indulge in precocious jokes. They nudge and pluck at their young teacher's arm to persuade her to look up, too.

On these occasions, the girl smiles coyly and shoots one glance at Otto from under her eyelashes, while Peter, watching behind the curtains, mutters through clenched teeth: "Bitch ... bitch ... bitch...." This persecution annoys him more than the actual friendship itself. We always seem to be running across the children when we are out walking in the woods. The children sing as they march—patriotic songs about the Homeland—in voices as shrill as birds. From far off, we hear them approaching, and have to turn hastily in the opposite direction. It is, as Peter says, like Captain Hook and the Crocodile.

Peter has made a scene, and Otto has told his friend that she mustn't bring her troop past the house any more. But now they have begun bathing on our beach, not very far from the fort. The first morning this happened, Otto's glance kept turning in their direction. Peter was aware of this, of course, and remained plunged in gloomy silence.

"What's the matter with you to-day, Peter?" said Otto. "Why are you so horrid to me?"

"Horrid to *you?*" Peter laughed savagely.

"Oh, very well then." Otto jumped up. "I see you don't want me here." And, bounding over the rampart of our fort, he began to run along the beach towards the teacher and her children, very gracefully, displaying his figure to the best possible advantage.

Yesterday evening there was a gala dance at the Kurhaus. In a mood of unusual generosity, Otto had promised Peter not to be later than a quarter to one, so Peter sat up with a book to wait for him. I didn't feel tired, and wanted to finish a chapter, so suggested that he should come into my room and wait there.

I worked. Peter read. The hours went slowly by. Suddenly I looked at my watch and saw that it was a quarter past two. Peter had dozed off in his chair. Just as I was wondering whether I should wake him, I heard Otto coming up the stairs. His footsteps sounded drunk.

Finding no one in his room, he banged open my door. Peter sat up with a start.

Otto lolled grinning against the doorpost. He made me a half-tipsy salute. "Have you been reading all this time?" he asked Peter.

"Yes," said Peter, very self-controlled.

"Why?" Otto smiled fatuously.

"Because I couldn't sleep."

"Why couldn't you sleep?"

"You know quite well," said Peter between his teeth.

Otto yawned in his most offensive manner. "I don't know and I don't care.... Don't make such a fuss."

Peter rose to his feet. "God, you little swine!" he said, smacking Otto's face hard with the flat of his hand. Otto didn't attempt to defend himself. He gave Peter an extraordinarily vindictive look out of his bright little eyes. "Good!" He spoke rather thickly. "Tomorrow I shall go back to Berlin." He turned unsteadily on his heel.

"Otto, come here," said Peter. I saw that, in another moment, he would burst into tears of rage. He followed Otto out on to the landing. "Come here," he said again, in a sharp tone of command.

"Oh, leave me alone," said Otto, "I'm sick of you. I want to sleep now. Tomorrow I'm going back to Berlin."

This morning, however, peace has been restored—at a price. Otto's repentance has taken the form of a sentimental outburst over his family: "Here I've been enjoying myself and never thinking of them.... Poor mother has to work like a dog, and her lungs are so bad.... Let's send her some money, shall we, Peter? Let's send her fifty marks...." Otto's generosity reminded him of his own needs. In addition to the money for Frau Nowak, Peter has been talked into ordering Otto a new suit, which will cost a hundred and eighty, as well as a pair of shoes, a dressing-gown, and a hat.

In return for this outlay, Otto has volunteered to break off his relations with the teacher. (We now discover that, in any case, she is leaving the island tomorrow.) After supper, she appeared, walking up and down outside the house.

"Just let her wait till she's tired," said Otto. "I'm not going down to her."

Presently the girl, made bold by impatience, began to whistle. This sent Otto into a frenzy of glee. Throwing open the window, he danced up and down, waving his arms and making hideous faces at the teacher who, for her part, seemed struck dumb with amazement at this extraordinary exhibition.

"Get away from here!" Otto yelled. "Get out!"

The girl turned, and walked slowly away, a rather pathetic figure, into the gathering darkness.

"I think you might have said goodbye to her," said Peter, who could afford to be magnanimous, now that he saw his enemy routed.

But Otto wouldn't hear of it.

"What's the use of all those rotten girls, anyhow? Every night they came pestering me to dance with them.... And you know how I am, Peter—I'm so easily persuaded.... Of course, it was horrid of me to leave you alone, but what could I do? It was all their fault, really...."

Our life has now entered upon a new phase. Otto's resolutions were short-lived. Peter and I are alone together most of the day. The teacher has left, and with her, Otto's last inducement to bathe with us from the fort. He now goes off, every morning, to the bathing-beach by the pier, to flirt and play ball with his dancing-partners of the evening. The little doctor has also disappeared, and Peter and I are free to bathe and loll in the sun as unathletically as we wish.

After supper, the ritual of Otto's preparations for the dance begins. Sitting in my bedroom, I hear Peter's footsteps cross the landing, light and springy with relief—for now comes the only time of the day when Peter feels himself altogether excused from taking any interest in Otto's activities. When he taps on my door, I shut my book at once. I have been out already to the village to buy half-a-pound of peppermint creams. Peter says goodbye to Otto, with a vain lingering hope that, perhaps to-night, he will, after all, be punctual: "Till half past twelve, then...."

"Till one," Otto bargains.

"All right," Peter concedes. "Till one. But don't be late."

"No, Peter, I won't be late."

As we open the garden gate and cross the road into the wood, Otto waves to us from the balcony. I have to be careful to hide the peppermint creams under my coat, in case he should see them. Laughing guiltily, munching the peppermints, we take the woodland path to Baabe. We always spend our evenings in Baabe, nowadays. We like it better than our own village. Its single sandy street of low-roofed houses among the pine-trees has a romantic, colonial air; it is like a ramshackle, lost settlement somewhere in the backwoods, where people come to look for a non-existent gold mine and remain, stranded, for the rest of their lives.

In the little restaurant, we eat strawberries and cream, and talk to the young waiter. The waiter hates Germany and longs to go to America. *"Hier ist nichts los."* During the season, he is allowed no free time at all, and in the winter he earns nothing. Most of the Baabe boys are Nazis. Two of them come into the restaurant sometimes and engage us in good-humoured political arguments. They tell us about their field-exercises and military games.

"You're preparing for war," says Peter indignantly. On these occasions—although he has really not the slightest interest in politics—he gets quite heated.

"Excuse me," one of the boys contradicts, "that's quite wrong. The Führer does not want war. Our program stands for peace, with honour. All the same ..." he adds wistfully, his face lighting up, "war can be fine, you know! Think of the ancient Greeks!"

"The ancient Greeks," I object, "didn't use poison gas."

The boys are rather scornful at this quibble. One of them answers loftily, "That's a purely technical question."

At half past ten we go down, with most of the other inhabitants, to the railway station, to watch the arrival of the last train. It is generally empty. It goes clanging away through the dark woods, sounding its harsh bell. At last it is late enough to start home; this time, we take the road. Across the meadows, you can see the illuminated entrance of the café by the lake, where Otto goes to dance.

"The lights of Hell are shining brightly this evening," Peter is fond of remarking.

Peter's jealousy has turned into insomnia. He has begun taking sleeping-tablets, but admits that they seldom have any effect. They merely make him feel drowsy next morning, after breakfast. He often goes to sleep for an hour or two in our fort, on the shore.

This morning the weather was cool and dull, the sea oyster-grey. Peter and I hired a boat, rowed out beyond the pier, then let ourselves drift, gently, away from the land. Peter lit a cigarette. He said abruptly:

"I wonder how much longer this will go on...."

"As long as you let it, I suppose."

"Yes.... We seem to have got into a pretty static condition, don't we? I suppose there's no particular reason why Otto and I should ever stop behaving to each other as we do at present...." He paused, added: "Unless, of course, I stop giving him money."

"What do you think would happen then?"

Peter paddled idly in the water with his fingers. "He'd leave me."

The boat drifted on for several minutes. I asked: "You don't think he cares for you, at all?"

"At the beginning he did, perhaps.... Not now. There's nothing between us now but my cash."

"Do you still care for him?"

"No ... I don't know. Perhaps.... I still hate him, sometimes—if that's a sign of caring."

"It might be."

There was a long pause. Peter dried his fingers on his handkerchief. His mouth twitched nervously.

"Well," he said at last, "what do you advise me to do?"

"What do you want to do?"

Peter's mouth gave another twitch.

"I suppose, really, I want to leave him."

"Then you'd better leave him."

"At once?"

"The sooner the better. Give him a nice present and send him back to Berlin this afternoon."

Peter shook his head, smiled sadly:

"I can't."

There was another long pause. Then Peter said: "I'm sorry, Christopher.... You're absolutely right, I know. If I were in your place, I'd say the same thing.... But I can't. Things have got to go on as they are—until something happens. They can't last much longer, anyhow.... Oh, I know I'm very weak...."

"You needn't apologize to me," I smiled, to conceal a slight feeling of irritation: "I'm not one of your analysts!"

I picked up the oars and began to row back towards the shore. As we reached the pier, Peter said:

"It seems funny to think of now—when I first met Otto, I thought we should live together for the rest of our lives."

"Oh, my God!" The vision of a life with Otto opened before me, like a comic inferno. I laughed out loud. Peter laughed, too, wedging his locked hands between his knees. His face turned from pink to red, from red to purple. His veins bulged. We were still laughing when we got out of the boat.

In the garden the landlord was waiting for us. "What a pity!" he exclaimed. "The gentlemen are too late!" He pointed over the meadows, in the direction of the lake. We could see the smoke rising above the line of poplars, as the little train drew out of the station: "Your friend was obliged to leave for Berlin, suddenly, on urgent business. I hoped the gentlemen might have been in time to see him off. What a pity!"

This time, both Peter and I ran upstairs. Peter's bedroom was in a terrible mess—all the drawers and cupboards were open. Propped up on the middle of the table was a note, in Otto's cramped, scrawling hand:

Dear Peter. Please forgive me I couldn't stand it any longer here so I am going home.
Love from Otto.
Don't be angry.

(Otto had written it, I noticed, on a fly-leaf torn out of one of Peter's psychology books: *Beyond the Pleasure-Principle*.)

"Well...!" Peter's mouth began to twitch. I glanced at him nervously, expecting a violent outburst, but he seemed fairly calm. After a moment, he walked over to the cupboards and began looking through the drawers. "He hasn't taken much," he announced, at the end of his search. "Only a couple of my ties, three shirts—lucky my shoes don't fit him!—and, let's see ... about two hundred marks...." Peter started to laugh, rather hysterically: "Very moderate, on the whole!"

"Do you think he decided to leave quite suddenly?" I asked, for the sake of saying something.

"Probably he did. That would be just like him.... Now I come to think of it, I told him we were going out in that boat, this morning—and he asked me if we should be away for long...."

"I see...."

I sat down on Peter's bed—thinking, oddly enough, that Otto has at last done something which I rather respect.

Peter's hysterical high spirits kept him going for the rest of the morning; at lunch he turned gloomy, and wouldn't say a word.

"Now I must go and pack," he told me when we had finished.

"You're off, too?"

"Of course."

"To Berlin?"

Peter smiled. "No, Christopher. Don't be alarmed! Only to England...."

"Oh...."

"There's a train which'll get me to Hamburg late to-night. I shall probably go straight on ... I feel I've got to keep travelling until I'm clear of this bloody country...."

There was nothing to say. I helped him pack, in silence. As Peter put his shaving-mirror into the bag, he asked: "Do you remember how Otto broke this, standing on his head?"

"Yes, I remember."

When we had finished, Peter went out on to the balcony of his room: "There'll be plenty of whistling outside here, to-night," he said.

I smiled: "I shall have to go down and console them."

Peter laughed: "Yes. You will!"

I went with him to the station. Luckily, the engine-driver was in a hurry. The train only waited a couple of minutes.

"What shall you do when you get to London?" I asked.

Peter's mouth curved down at the corners; he gave me a kind of inverted grin: "Look round for another analyst, I suppose."

"Well, mind you beat down his prices a bit!"

"I will."

As the train moved out, he waved his hand: "Well, goodbye, Christopher. Thank you for all your moral support!"

Peter never suggested that I should write to him, or visit him at home. I suppose he wants to forget this place, and everybody concerned with it. I can hardly blame him.

It was only this evening, turning over the pages of a book I have been reading, that I found another note from Otto, slipped between the leaves.

Please dear Christopher don't you be angry with me too because you aren't an idiot like Peter. When you are back in Berlin I shall come and see you because I know where you live;

I saw the address on one of your letters and we can have a nice talk.

Your loving friend,
Otto.

I thought, somehow, that he wouldn't be got rid of quite so easily.

Actually, I am leaving for Berlin in a day or two, now. I thought I should stay on till the end of August, and perhaps finish my novel, but suddenly, the place seems so lonely. I miss Peter and Otto, and their daily quarrels, far more than I should have expected. And now even Otto's dancing-partners have stopped lingering sadly in the twilight, under my window.

Pigs Can't Fly

Shyam Selvadurai

According to Shyam Selvadurai, "Pigs Can't Fly" started off as a one-page writing exercise. "I was trying, for a lark, to imitate Faulkner's style in the first section of The Sound and the Fury. *Instead of a mentally handicapped person, I chose to write from the perspective of a very young boy watching his mother get dressed." The boy observing his mother draping the sari and putting on her makeup and jewelry awakened in Selvadurai a certain memory: he remembered not only how he would watch his mother get dressed but also how he would dress himself in his mother's saris and jewels. "I recall how sensuous the material of the sari felt around my body, and how the moment I had that sari on, I was transfigured: became another, greater self."*

Moments of joy such as this one, present or remembered, enlarge the self. In that miraculous instant, we grow in the world and long to touch those around us with the same magic. If we succeed, our growth is no longer illusory. We are that colossus, that giant Alice in Wonderland shooting up to the ceiling after downing the bottle labeled "Drink Me". If we don't, if we are, as Selvadurai says he was, "ridiculed by other adults and my peers", the magic vanishes, the joy evaporates, and, like Alice shrinking to the point where she falls in her own pool of tears, we are reduced to something even smaller than we were in the pale beginning.

Spend-the-day days, besides Christmas and other festive occasions, were the days most looked forward to by all of us cousins, aunts and uncles.

For the adults it was the one day of the month they were free of their progeny. The eagerness with which they looked forward to this occasion was seen in the way our Amma woke us extra early on those days and hurried us through our morning preparations. Then, after a quick breakfast, we would be driven to the house of our grandparents for a spend-the-day.

The first thing that met our eyes on entering our grandparents' house was the dark corridor running the length of the house, on one side of which were the bedrooms and on the other the living and dining rooms. This corridor, with its old photographs on both walls and its roof so high that our footsteps echoed, scared me a little. The living room, into which we would be ushered—after carefully wiping our feet on the doormat—to pay our respects to our grandparents was also dark and smelt like old clothes that had been locked away in a suitcase for a long time. There Ammachi and Appachi sat, enthroned in big reclining chairs. Appachi usually looked up from his paper and said vaguely, "Ah hello, hello," before going back behind it, but Ammachi always called us towards her with the beckoning of her middle and index fingers. Our legs trembling slightly, we would go to her, the thought of the big canes she kept behind her almariah strongly imprinted on our minds. She would grip each face in her plump hands, kiss us wetly on both cheeks and say, "God has blessed me with fifteen grandchildren who will look after me in my old age."

She smelt of stale coconut oil and the diamond mukkuchi in her nose always pressed painfully against my cheek.

When the aunts and uncles eventually drove away, waving gaily at us from car windows, we waved back at the retreating cars with not even a pretence of sorrow. For one glorious day of the month we were free of parental control and the ever watchful eyes and always talebearing tongues of the house servants.

We were not, alas, completely abandoned, as we would have so liked to have been. Ammachi and Janaki were supposedly in charge. Janaki, cursed with the task of having to cook for twenty-four extra people, had little time for supervision and preferred actually to have nothing at all to do with us. If called upon to come and settle a dispute she would rush out, her hands red from grinding curry paste, and box the ears of the first person who happened to be in her path. We had learned that Janaki was to be appealed to only in the most dire emergencies. The one we knew, by tacit agreement, never to appeal to was Ammachi. Like the earth goddess in the folk tales, she was not to be disturbed from her tranquillity, because to do so would be to cause a catastrophic earthquake.

In order to minimize interference by either Ammachi or Janaki, we had developed and refined a system to handle conflict and settle disputes ourselves. Two features formed the framework of this system: territoriality and leadership.

In terms of territoriality, the area of my grandparents' compound was divided into two. The front garden, the road and the field that lay in front of the house belonged to "the boys" although included in this term was also my female cousin Mina. In this territory, two factions reigned in conflict, one led by Mina, the other by my brother Varuna, who, because of a prevailing habit, had been renamed Diggy-Nose and then simply Diggy.

The second territory was named "the girls," included in which, however, was I, a boy. It was to this territory of "the girls," confined to the back garden and the kitchen porch, that I seemed to have gravitated naturally, my earliest memories of those spend-the-days always belonging in the back garden of my grandparents' home. The joy of standing for hours on a cricket field under the sweltering sun, watching the ball roll from crease to crease, with the occasional variation of a sixer or a four, was as incomprehensible to me as the purely transcendent Christian God must have been to my Hindu ancestors.

The primary attraction of the girls' territory for me was its potential for the imagination and fantasy. Whatever the game, be it the imitation of adult domestic functions or the enactment of some well-loved fairy story, I would discover some new way to enliven the game, some new twist to add to the plot of a familiar tale. Under my leadership my girl cousins would conduct a raid on my grandparents' dirty-clothes basket, discovering in this odorous treasure trove saris, blouses, sheets, curtains with which we conceived costumes to complement our voyages of imagination.

The reward for my leadership was to always play the leading part in the fantasy. If it was cooking-cooking we were playing I was the chef; if it was Cinderella or Thumbelina, I was the much beleaguered heroine of these tales.

From amongst all these varied and fascinating games, bride-bride was my favourite. In it, I was able to combine many of the elements of the other games I loved and with time, bride-bride, which had taken a few hours to play initially, became an event that spread out over the whole day, planned for weeks in advance.

For me the culmination of this game and my ultimate flight of fantasy was the moment when I put on the clothes of the bride. In the late afternoon, usually after tea, I and the older cousins would enter Janaki's room. From my sling bag I would bring out my most prized possession, an old white sari, slightly yellow with age, its border torn and missing most of its sequins. Then the dressing of the bride would begin, and there, by the transfiguration I saw taking place in Janaki's cracked, full-length mirror, by the sari being wrapped around my body, the veil attached to my head, the rouge to my cheeks, lipstick to my lips, kohl to my eyes, I was able, as it were, to leave the constraints of my self and ascend into another more brilliant, more beautiful self, a self to whom this day was consecrated, and around whom the world, represented by my cousins pinning my veil, draping my sari, putting flowers in my hair, seemed to revolve. It was a self, magnified like the "goddesses" of the Sinhala and Tamil screen, larger than life; and like them, like the Malini Fonsekas and the Geetha Kumarasinghes, I was an icon, a graceful, benevolent, perfect being on whom the adoring eyes of the world rested.

Those spend-the-day days, the remembered innocence of childhood, are now coloured, especially for the other cousins, by the hues of the twilight sky. It is a portrait made even more sentimental by all of us having to leave Sri Lanka because of the current civil war and forge a new home in Canada.

For myself, however, those spend-the-days bring back the memory of a time that marked the beginning of my exile from the world I loved. Like the beam of a lighthouse on a moonless night that spreads a path across the black waters of the sea towards the harbour, that time pointed me away from the vast expanse of all that seemed possible as a child, towards the narrow harbour of adulthood.

Those spend-the-day days began to change with the return of Kanthi Aunty and Cyril Uncle from abroad with their daughter Tanuja, who was quickly renamed "Her Fatness," in that cruelly insightful way children have.

At first we had no difficulty with the newcomer in our midst. In fact we found her quite willing to accept that, by reason of her recent arrival, she would necessarily begin at the bottom.

In the hierarchy of bride-bride, the person with the least importance, less than even the priest and the page boys, was the groom. It was a role we considered stiff and boring, that held no attraction for any of us. Indeed, if we could have dispensed with that role altogether we would have, but alas it was an unfortunate adjunct to the ceremony of marriage. My sister Sonali, with her patient good-naturedness, but also sensing that I might have a mutiny on my hands if I asked anyone else to play that role, always donned the long pants and tattered jacket, borrowed from my grandfather's clothes chest. It was now deemed fitting that Her Fatness should take over the role and thus leave Sonali free to wrap a bed sheet around her body, in the manner of a sari, and wear araliyas in her hair like the other bridesmaids.

The first two spend-the-days Her Fatness accepted her role without a murmur and played it with all the skilled unobtrusiveness of a bit player. The third spend-the-day however, all that changed.

That spend-the-day turned out to be my grandmother's sixtieth birthday. Instead of dropping us off and driving away as usual, the aunts and uncles stayed on for lunch, a slight note of peevish displeasure in their voices. We were late because etiquette (or rather my father) demanded that my Amma wear a sari for the grand occasion. My Amma's tardiness and her insistence on getting her palu to fall to exactly above her knees, drove us all to distraction (especially Diggy, who quite rightly feared that, in his absence, Mina would try to persuade the better members of his team to defect to her side). Even I, who usually loved the ritual of watching my Amma get dressed, stood in her doorway with the others and fretfully demanded if she was ever going to be ready.

When we finally did arrive at Ramanaygam Road, everyone had been there almost an hour. We were ushered inside to kiss my grandparents and present Ammachi with her gift, the three of us clutching different ends of the present. All the uncles and aunts were seated in the living room. Her Fatness stood in between Kanthi Aunty's knees, next to Ammachi. When she saw me, Her Fatness gave me an accusing, hostile look and pressed further between her mother's knees. Kanthi Aunty turned away from her discussion with Mala Aunty and, seeing me, smiled and said in a tone that was as heavily sweetened as undiluted rose syrup, "So what is this I hear, aah? Nobody will play with my little daughter."

I looked at her and then glanced at Her Fatness, shocked by the lie. All my faculties stiffened into alertness like those of a deer that had just caught the scent of a stalking leopard.

Kanthi Aunty wagged her finger at me and said in a playful, chiding tone, "Now, now. You must be nice to my little daughter.

After all she's just come from abroad and everything."

Fortunately I was prevented from having to answer. It was my turn to present my cheek to Ammachi and for the first time I did so willingly, preferring the prick of the diamond mukuchi to Kanthi Aunty's honeyed admonition.

Kanthi Aunty, in spite of the fact that she hardly spoke to any of us and would pat our heads affectionately whenever we walked past or greeted her, always made us feel deeply uneasy. We sensed that beneath her benevolence lurked a seething anger, tempered by guile, that would have deadly consequences if unleashed in our direction. I had heard my Amma say to her sister Aunty Neliya that "Poor Kanthi was embittered by the humiliations she had suffered abroad. After all darling, what a thing, her, forced to work as a servant in a whitey's house to make ends meet."

Once Ammachi had opened the present and thanked us for it (and insisted on kissing us once again), we were finally allowed to leave. Her Fatness had already disappeared. I hurried out of the front door and made my way along the edge of the open drain that ran around the side of the house.

When I reached the back garden I found all the cousins squatted on the porch in a circle. They were so absorbed in what was happening in the centre that none of them even heard my greeting. Lakshmi finally became aware of my presence and beckoned me over excitedly. I reached the circle and the cause of her excitement became clear. In the middle sat a long-legged doll with shiny gold hair. Her dress was like that of a fairy queen, the gauze skirt sprinkled with tiny silver stars. Next to her sat her male counterpart, dressed in a pale blue suit. I stared in wonder at the marvellous toys. For us cousins, who had grown up under a government that strictly limited all foreign imports, such toys were unimaginable. Her Fatness turned to the other cousins and asked them if they wanted to hold the dolls for a moment. They nodded eagerly and the dolls passed from hand to hand. I moved closer to get a better look and my gaze involuntarily rested on Her Fatness. She gave me a smug look. I looked at the toys again and immediately Her Fatness's scheme became evident to me. It was with these dolls that she had hoped to seduce the cousins away from me.

Unfortunately for her, Her Fatness had underestimated the power of bride-bride. When the cousins had passed the dolls around, they bestirred themselves and without so much as a backward glance hurried down the steps to prepare for bride-bride. As I followed them, I glanced back triumphantly at Her Fatness who sat on the porch clasping her dolls.

When lunch was over my grandparents retired to their room for a nap. The adults settled on the verandah to read the newspaper or doze off in the huge armchairs. We, the bride-to-be and the bridesmaids retired into Janaki's room for the long-awaited ritual of dressing the bride.

The ritual was soon disturbed, however, by the sound of booming laughter. At first we ignored it, but when it persisted, getting louder and more drawn out, Sonali went to the door and looked out. Her slight gasp brought us all to the door.

On the porch the groom strutted up and down, his head thrown back, his stomach stuck out. He sported a huge bristly moustache (torn out of the broom) and a cigarette (rolled paper and talcum powder) which he held between his fingers and puffed on vigorously. The younger cousins, instead of getting dressed and putting the final touches to the altar, sat along the edge of the porch and watched with great amusement.

"Aha me hearties!" the groom cried on seeing us and opened his hands expansively, "Bring me my fair maiden, for I must be off to my castle before the sun setest."

We looked at the groom, aghast by the change in his behaviour. The groom sauntered towards us. He stopped in front of me, winked expansively and with his hand under my chin, tilted my head back.

"Ahh!" he cried, "A bonny lass, a bonny lass indeed."

"Stop it!" I cried and slapped his hand. "The groom is not supposed to make a noise."

"Why not?" Her Fatness cried back, dropping her hearty voice and accent. "Why can't the groom make a noise?"

"Because."

"Because of what?"

"Because the game is called bride-bride, not groom-groom."

Her Fatness seized her moustache and flung it to the ground dramatically.

"Well I don't want to be the groom any more. I want to be the bride."

We stared at her in disbelief, amazed by her impudent challenge to my position.

"You can't," I finally said.

"Why not?" Her Fatness demanded. "Why should you always be the bride? Why can't someone else have a chance too?"

"Because ..." Sonali said, joining in, "because he is the bestest bride of all."

"But he's not even a girl," Her Fatness said, closing in on the lameness of Sonali's defence. "A bride is a girl, not a boy."

She looked around at the other cousins and then her gaze rested on me.

"A boy cannot be the bride," she said with deep conviction. "A girl must be the bride."

I stared at her, defenceless in the face of her logic. Fortunately Sonali, loyal to me as always, came to my rescue. She stepped in between us and said fiercely to Her Fatness, "If you can't play properly, go away. We don't need you."

"Yes!" Lakshmi, another of my supporters, cried. The other cousins, emboldened by Sonali's fierceness, murmured in agreement.

Her Fatness looked at all of us for a moment and then her gaze rested on me.

"You're a pansy," she said, her lips curling in disgust.

We looked at her blankly.

"A faggot," she said, her voice rising against our uncomprehending stares.

"A sissy!" she cried in desperation.

Though we still didn't understand her, it was clear now that this was an insult.

"Give me that coat," Sonali said. She stepped up to Her Fatness and began to pull at the coat. "We don't like you any more."

"Yes!" Lakshmi cried, "go away you fatty-boom-boom!"

That was an insult we all understood and we burst out laughing. Someone even began to sing, "Hey fatty-boom-boom, sweet sugar dumpling. Hey fatty-boom-boom let me tell you something."

Her Fatness pulled off her coat and trousers. "I hate you all," she cried, "I wish you were all dead."

She flung the groom's clothes on the ground, stalked out of the backyard and around the side of the house. We went back to our preparations chuckling to ourselves over the new nickname we had found for her.

When the bride was dressed, Lakshmi, the maid of honour, went out of Janaki's room to make sure that everything was in place. She gave the signal and the priest and choir boys began to sing with a certain want of harmony and proper lyrics, "The voice that breathed oh eeeden, the first and glorious day—"

Solemnly, I made my way down the steps towards the altar that had been placed at one end of the back-garden. When I reached the altar, however, I heard the kitchen door open and I turned to see Her Fatness with Kanthi Aunty. The discordant singing died out.

Kanthi Aunty's benevolent smile and honeyed tone had completely disappeared, and her eyes were narrowed with anger.

"Who's calling my daughter fatty?" Kanthi Aunty cried. She came to the edge of the porch.

We stared at her, not daring to own up.

Her gaze fell on me and her eyes widened for a moment. Then a smile spread across her face.

"What's this?" she said, the honey seeping back into her voice. She came down a few steps and crooked her finger at me. I looked down at my feet and refused to go to her.

"Come here, come here," she said.

Unable to disobey her command any more, I went to her reluctantly. She looked me up and down for a moment and then gingerly, as if she was examining raw meat at the market, turned me around.

"What's this you're playing?" she asked.

"It's bride-bride, Aunty," Sonali said.

"Bride-bride," she murmured.

Her hand closed on my arm in a tight grip.

"Come with me," she said.

I resisted, but her grip tightened, her nails digging into my elbow. She pulled me towards the back door.

"No," I cried, suddenly afraid. "No, I don't want to."

I was so scared that I even hit out at her.

She kept her grip firmly on my arm and dragged me through the kitchen, past Janaki, who looked up curiously, into the hallway and towards the living room. I felt a heaviness begin to build in my stomach. I didn't know what I was afraid of, but instinctively I knew that Kanthi Aunty had something terrible in mind.

As we entered the living room, Kanthi Aunty cried out, her voice brimming over with laughter, "See what I found!"

The other aunts and uncles looked up from their papers or

bestirred themselves from their sleep. They gazed at me in amazement as if I had suddenly made myself visible, like a spirit. I glanced at them and my eyes came to rest on my Amma's face. Seeing her expression, I felt my dread deepen. I lowered my eyes. The sari suddenly felt suffocating around my body and the hairpins which held the veil in place pricked at my scalp.

Then the silence was broken by the booming laugh of Cyril Uncle, Kanthi Aunty's husband. As if she had been hit, my Amma swung around in his direction. The other aunts and uncles began to laugh too and I watched as my Amma looked from one to the other like a trapped animal. Her gaze finally came to rest on my father and for the first time I noticed that he was the only one not laughing. Seeing the expression on his face, the way he kept his eyes lowered to his paper, I felt the heaviness in my stomach begin to push its way up my throat.

"Ey Chelva," Cyril Uncle cried out jovially to my father, "looks like you have a funny one here."

My father pretended he had not heard and with an inclination of his head, indicated to my Amma to get rid of me.

She waved her hand in my direction. I picked up the edges of my veil and fled to the back.

On the way home, that evening, both my parents kept their eyes averted from me. My Amma glanced at my father occasionally, but he refused to meet her gaze. Sonali, as if sensing my unease held my hand tightly in hers.

Later, through the connecting bathroom between my parents' room and ours, I heard my parents fighting.

"How long has this been going on?" my father demanded.

"I don't know," my Amma cried defensively, "it was as new to me as it was to you."

"You should have known, you should have kept an eye on him."

"What should I have done? Stood over him while he was playing?"

"If he turns out funny like that Rankotwera boy, if he turns out to be the laughing stock of Colombo, it'll be all your fault," my father said in a tone of finality. "You always spoil him and encourage all his nonsense."

"What do I encourage?" Amma demanded fiercely.

"You are the one who allows him to come in here while you're dressing and play with your jewellery."

My Amma was silent in the face of the truth.

Of all the children, I alone was allowed to enter my mother's bedroom and watch her get dressed for special occasions. It was an experience I considered almost religious, for even though I adored the female stars of the local screen my mother was the final statement in female beauty for me.

When I knew my mother was getting dressed for a special occasion, I always positioned myself outside her door. Once she had put on her underskirt and blouse, she would ring for Nandini to bring her sari and then, while taking it from her, hold the door open to me as well. To enter that room was, to me, a greater boon than that granted by any god to a mortal. There were two reasons for this. The first was the jewellery box which lay open on the dressing table. With a joy akin to ecstasy, I would lean over and gaze at the jewels, the faint smell of perfume rising out of the box each time I picked up a piece of jewellery and held it against my nose or ears or throat. The second was the various pleasure of watching my Amma drape her sari; watching her shake open the yards of material, which, like a Chinese banner caught by the wind, would linger in the air for a moment before drifting gently to the floor; watching her pick up one end of the sari, tuck it into the waistband of her skirt, make the pleats and then with a flick of her wrists invert the pleats and tuck them into her waistband: and finally watching her drape the palu across her breasts and pin it into place with a brooch.

When Amma was finished, she would check to make sure that the back of the sari had not risen up with the pinning of the palu then move back and look at herself in the mirror. Standing next to her or seated on the edge of the bed, I too would look at her reflection in the mirror and, with the sigh of contentment of an artist who has finally captured the exact effect he wants, I would say, "You should have been a film star, Amma."

"A film star?" she would say and lightly smack the side of my head. "What kind of a low-class-type person do you think I am?"

In spite of the smack, I could tell that Amma was never angered by my comment.

A week after that spend-the-day I positioned myself outside my parents' door. When Nandini arrived with the sari my Amma took it and quickly shut the door. I waited patiently, thinking my Amma had not put on her blouse and skirt as yet, but the door never opened. Finally, perplexed that my Amma had forgotten, I knocked timidly on the door. I received no answer but I could hear her moving around inside. I knocked a little louder and called out "Amma," through the keyhole. Again I received no answer and was about to call out again, when she replied gruffly, "Go away. Can't you see I am busy?"

I stared disbelievingly at the door for a moment. Inside I could hear the rustling of the sari as it brushed along the floor. I lifted my hand to knock again when suddenly the full implication of her words came to me, set in the context of the quarrel I had heard the last spend-the-day. My hand fell loosely by my side.

I crept away quietly to my bedroom without any further resistance, sat down on the edge of my bed and looked at my feet for a long time. It was clear to me that I had done something wrong but what it was I couldn't comprehend. I thought of what my father had said about turning out "funny." The word "funny" as I understood it meant one of two things. The first was humorous and the second strange and puzzling as in the expression, "that's funny." Neither of these, I felt, fitted the sense in which my father had used that word. There had been a sense of disgust in his intonation.

Later, Amma came out of her room and called the servants to give them their instructions for the evening. As I listened to the sound of her voice, I realized that something had changed forever between us.

A little while after they had left for their dinner party, Sonali came looking for me, and though unaware of what had passed she slipped her hand in mine. I pushed her hand roughly away, afraid that if I let her squeeze my hand I would start crying.

The next morning my mother and I were like two people who had had a terrible fight the night before. I found it hard to look her in the eye and she was in an unusually gay mood.

When Amma came to awaken us the following spend-the-day, I was already up and in the middle of folding my sari. Something in her expression, however, made me hurriedly return the sari to the bag.

"What's that?"

She came towards me, her hand outstretched. After a moment I gave her the bag. She glanced at its contents briefly.

"Get up it's spend-the-day," she said. Then with the bag in her hand, she went to the window and looked out into the back garden. The seriousness of her expression, as if I had done something so terrible that even the usual punishment of a caning would not suffice, frightened me.

I was brushing my teeth after breakfast when Nandini came to the bathroom door, peered inside and said with a sort of grim pleasure, "Missie wants to talk to you in her room." Seeing the alarm in my face, she nodded and said sagely, "Up to some kind of mischief as usual. Good-for-nothing child."

Diggy was standing in the doorway to Amma's room, one foot scratching impatiently against the other. Amma was putting on her lipstick. She looked up from the mirror, saw me and indicated with her lipstick for both of us to come inside and sit down on the edge of the bed. Diggy gave me a baleful look as if it was my fault that Amma was taking such a long time to get ready. He followed me into the room, his slippers dragging along the ground.

Finally Amma closed the lid of her lipstick, pressed her lips together to even out the colour and then turned to us.

"Okay, mister," she said to Diggy, "I am going to tell you something and this is an order."

We watched her carefully.

"I want you to include your brother in your cricket team."

We looked at her in shocked silence.

Then Diggy cried, "Ah! Come on, Amma!" and, simultaneously, I too cried out, "I don't want to play with them. I hate cricket!"

"I don't care what you want," Amma said, "it's good for you."

"He's useless," Diggy cried, "we'll never win if he's in our team."

Amma held up her hand to silence us. "That is an order," she said with a tone of finality.

"Why?" I asked, ignoring her gesture. "Why do I have to play with the boys?"

"Why?" Amma said. "Because the sky is so high and pigs can't fly, that's why."

"Please, Amma! Please!"

I held out my arms to her.

Amma turned away quickly, picked up her handbag from the toilet table and said, almost to herself, "If the child turns out funny, it's the mother they always blame, never the father."

She clicked her handbag shut.

I put my head in my hands and began to cry. "Please, Amma, please," I said through my sobs.

She continued to face the window.

I flung myself on the bed with a wail of anguish. I waited for her to come to me as she always did when I cried, waited for her to take me in her arms, rest my head against her breasts and say in her special voice, "What's this now, who's the little man who's crying."

She didn't heed my weeping any more than she had heeded my cries the last time I had knocked on her door.

Finally I stopped crying and rolled over on my back. Diggy had left. Amma turned to me now that I had become quiet and said cheerfully, "You'll have a good time, just wait and see."

"Why can't I play with the girls?" I replied.

"You can't, that's all."

"Why?"

She shifted uneasily.

"You're a big boy now. And big boys must play with other boys."

"That's stupid."

"It doesn't matter," she said finally. "Life is full of stupid things and sometimes we just have to do them."

"I won't," I said with defiance, "I won't play with the boys."

Her face suffused with anger, she reached down, caught me by the shoulders, shook me hard and then dropped me back on the bed. She turned away and ran her hand through her hair. I watched with gloating triumph. Inadvertently, I had broken her cheerful façade, forced her to show how much it pained her to do what she was doing, how little she actually believed in the justness of her actions.

After a moment she turned to me and said in almost a pleading tone, "You'll have a good time."

I looked at her and said with contemptuous disbelief, "No I won't."

Her back straightened. She crossed to the door and stopped. Without turning around she said, stiffly, "The car leaves in five minutes. If you're not in there by then, watch out."

I lay back on the bed and gazed at the mosquito net swinging gently in a breeze. In my mind's eye, I saw the day that lay ahead of me. The thought of having to waste the most precious day of the month in that field in front of my grandparents' house, the hot sun beating down on my head, the perspiration running down the side of my face, made a sense of frustration begin to build inside of me. The picture of what would take place in the back garden came into focus. I saw Her Fatness seizing my place as leader of the girls, claiming for herself the rituals I had so carefully invented and planned. I saw Her Fatness standing in front of Janaki's mirror as the girls dressed her hair, pinned her veil and draped her sari. The thought was so insupportable that it made me sit up in bed. Something had to be done! I could not give up that easily, could not let Her Fatness, whose sneaking to Kanthi Aunty had forced me into the position I was in now, so easily usurp my place! But what could I do?

As if in answer an object which rested just at the periphery of my vision claimed my attention. I turned my head slightly and saw my sling bag. Like the sight of the relief regiment to the besieged inhabitant of a fort, that sling bag was the most beautiful thing I had ever seen. I reached out, picked up the bag and hugged it close to my chest. This was my answer! Without the sari in that sling bag, it was impossible for the girls to play bride-bride. I thought of Her Fatness with triumph. What would she drape around her body? A bedsheet like the bridesmaids? No! Without the sari she would not be able to play bride-bride properly!

I opened the bag and gazed at the sari. This would ensure reentry into the girls' world. Her Fatness would need some convincing before she accepted me back into that world. But I felt confident that when I offered to let her wear the sari I would be allowed in.

There was, however, another obstacle. I would have to get out of playing cricket. Amma had laid down an order, and I knew Diggy well enough to know that in spite of all his seeming boldness he would never dare to disobey an order from Amma.

While I was pondering the obstacle, I heard the car start up and its sound reminded me of another problem that I hadn't considered. How was I going to smuggle the sari into the car? Amma would be waiting in the car for me and if I arrived with the sling bag, she would make me take it back. There was no way to slip it in without her noticing. I sat still listening to the whir of the car motor counterpointed with the clatter of Nandini clearing the breakfast table. Gradually a plan revealed itself to me.

I took the sari out of the bag and folded the bag so that it looked like there was something in it. Taking the sari with me, I went to the bedroom door and looked out. The hallway was empty. I went into my room, which was next to my parents', and crouched down on one side of the doorway. I took off my slippers and held them with the sari in the crook of my arms. The curtain in the doorway of my room blew slightly in the breeze and I moved a little further away from it so that I would not be seen. After what seemed like an interminable amount of time, I heard Amma coming down the hallway to fetch me from her room. I crouched down even lower as the sound of her foosteps got closer. From underneath the edge of the curtain, I saw her slippered feet pass by. As she entered her room I stood up, pushed aside the curtain and darted down the hallway. She came out of her room quickly and called to me, but I didn't stop.

Thankfully someone had kept the back door of the car open. I jumped in and quickly, before either Diggy or Sonali or the driver could react, I stuffed the sari into Sonali's sling bag. When I was sure that it was well hidden, I lay back against the car seat, panting.

Soon Amma came out and got into the car. She glared at me and I returned her look innocently. I turned and smiled at Sonali secretively. Sonali, my strongest ally, was doing her best to keep the surprise out of her face. By way of explanation, I said, with pretended gloominess, "I can't play with you today. Amma says that I must play with the boys."

Sonali looked at me in amazement and then turned to Amma.

"Why can't he play with the girls?" she said.

"Why?" Amma said, "Because the sky is so high and pigs can't fly."

Amma sounded less sure of herself this time and a little weary. I squeezed Sonali's hand in reassurance and glanced at her quickly. Looking in front, I saw that Diggy had turned in his seat and was regarding me morosely. I was quickly reminded that the sari in the bag was worth nothing if I couldn't get out of the long day of cricket that lay ahead of me.

All the way to my grandparents' house, I gazed at the back of Diggy's head as if hoping inspiration would come from it. The sound of his feet kicking against the bottom part of the car seat made it clear to me that, however bad the consequences, he had decided to follow Amma's orders. The sound of that ill-natured kicking made me search all the more desperately for an escape.

When the car turned down Ramanaygam Road, I still had not thought of something and my bright flame of hope began to flicker.

Mina was standing on top of the wall waiting for us, her legs apart, her hands on her hips, her panties already brown underneath her short dress. The other male cousins were also on the wall on either side of her. I looked at their stern faces and aggressive stance. Diggy saw them and pushed behind me, impatient to get out.

As we walked up the path to pay our respects to Ammachi and Appachi, I whispered to Sonali to keep the sari hidden and to tell no one about it. When we went into the living room, Her Fatness, who was between Kanthi Aunty's knees, gave me a triumphant look. I smiled back sweetly and was rewarded with a scowl.

I went through the ritual of presenting my cheek to my grandparents, my mind working furiously on a means of escape from the cricket game. No scheme presented itself. Finally, when it was time for the adults to leave, my flame of hope had been reduced to a few faintly glowing embers.

"Now you children be good," Amma said and looked pointedly at me.

"I don't want to hear that you've given Ammachi and Appachi any trouble."

I watched the departing cars with a sense of sorrow, as if with them went my hope. Diggy came down to the gate, where I was standing, and grabbed my arm impatiently. I followed reluctantly as he hurried across the road, clutching my arm, as if afraid I would run away.

The wickets had already been set up in the field in front of my grandparents' house and the other cousins were seated under the guava tree. When they saw us come towards them, they stopped their talking and stared at us.

Muruges, who was on Diggy's team, stood up.

"What's he doing here?" he demanded, waving his half-eaten guava at me.

"He's going to play."

"What?" the others cried in amazement.

They looked at Diggy as if he had lost his mind.

"He's quite good," Diggy answered half-heartedly.

"If he's going to be on our team, I'm changing sides," Muruges declared and some of the others murmured in agreement.

"Come on guys," Diggy said desperately, but they remained obstinate.

Diggy turned to Mina. "I'll trade you Arjie for Sanjay."

Mina spat out the seeds of the guava she was eating.

"Do you think I'm mad or something?"

"Ah, come on," Diggy said in a wheedling tone, "he's good. We've been practising the whole week."

"If he's so good, why don't you keep him yourself? Maybe with him on your team, you might finally win."

"Yeah," Sanjay cried, insulted that I was considered an equal trade for him. "Why don't you keep the girlie-boy?"

At the new nickname "girlie-boy," everyone roared with laughter and even Diggy grinned.

I should have felt humiliated and dejected that nobody wanted me on their team. Instead, I felt the joy of relief begin to dance inside of me. The escape I had searched for now presented itself without any effort on my part. If Diggy's best team members were threatening to abandon him he would have no alternative but to let me go. I looked at my feet, so that nobody would see the hope rekindled in my eyes.

Unfortunately, the nickname "girlie-boy" had an effect for which I hadn't bargained. The joke at my expense seemed to clear the air. After laughing heartily for a long time, Muruges withdrew his threat.

"What the hell," he said, benevolently, "it can't hurt to have another fielder. But," he said as a warning to Diggy, "he cannot bat."

Diggy nodded as if he had never even considered letting me bat. Since each side had only 50 overs, it was vital to send the best batsmen in first. Often the younger cousins never got a chance.

I glared at Muruges, and he, thinking that my look was a reaction to the new nickname, said, "Girlie-boy" again.

Diggy now laughed uproariously, but in his laugh I detected a slight note of servility while at the same time relief that the catastrophe of losing his team had been averted. I saw that the balance he was trying to maintain between following Amma's orders and keeping his team members happy was extremely precarious. All was not lost. Such a fragile balance would be easy to unsettle.

The opportunity to do this presented itself almost immediately.

Our team was to go first. In deciding the batting order, there was a certain system that the boys always followed. The captain would mark numerals in the sand with hyphens next to each numeral and then cover the numerals with the bat. The players, who had been asked to turn their backs, would then come over and choose a hyphen. What was strange to me about this exercise was its redundancy, for, when the numbers were uncovered, no matter what the batting order, the older and better players always went first, the younger cousins assenting without a murmur.

When Diggy uncovered the numbers, I was first in the batting order and Diggy was second. Muruges had picked one of the highest numbers and would hence bat towards the end, if at all.

"Well," Muruges said to Diggy in a tone that spoke of promises already made. "I'll take Arjie's place."

Diggy nodded vigorously, as if Muruges had read his very thoughts. Unfortunately for him, I had other plans.

"I want to go first," I said firmly and waited for my request to produce the necessary consequences. Surely now Diggy would have to get rid of me. My audacity in daring to suggest that Muruges wait his turn would almost certainly tip the scales and force Diggy to let me go.

Diggy too seemed to wait as if watching to see in which direction the scales would tip. Mina, unexpectedly, came to my defence. "He is the first!" she cried. "Fair is fair!"

In a game of only 50 overs, a weak opening bat would be ideal from the point of view of her team.

Muruges, who was crouched down fixing his leg pads, straightened up slowly. The slowness of his action conveyed, profoundly, his anger at my daring to make such a suggestion and at the same time sent out a challenge to Diggy, daring him to change the batting order.

"Fair is fair," I echoed Mina, "I picked first place and I should be allowed to play!"

"You can't," Diggy said desperately, "Muruges always goes first."

I let out a cry of protest. "But I got first place, that's not fair."

"Yes," Mina cried, "it's not fair."

Mina's team, encouraged by her, also began to cry out, "Fair is fair."

Diggy quickly crossed over to Muruges, put his arm around his shoulder, turned him away from the others and talked earnestly to him. But Muruges shook his head, unconvinced with whatever Diggy was saying. Finally Diggy dropped his hand from Muruges's shoulder and cried out in exasperation at him, "Come on, man!"

In response, Muruges began to unbuckle his leg pads. Diggy put his hand on his shoulder conciliatorily but he shrugged it off. Diggy, seeing that Muruges was determined, turned to me.

"Come on, Arjie," he said pleadingly. "You can go later in the game."

"No," I said stubbornly and just to show how determined I was, I picked up the bat.

Muruges, seeing my action, threw the leg pads at my feet.

"I'm in your team now," he announced to Mina.

"Ah no! Come on man!" Diggy howled in protest.

To rub salt in Diggy's wounds I cried out at Muruges, "Go! We don't need you!"

My impudent words had the effect I desired. Muruges began to cross over to where Mina's team was.

Diggy turned towards me and grabbed the bat.

"*You* go!" he cried, "We don't need *you.*"

Just to make sure he would keep his threat, I held onto the bat and cried out, "You're a cheater! I chose to bat first!"

Diggy pulled at the bat even harder and finally got it out of my grip. He started to walk with it towards Muruges.

"I hate you! I hate you all!" I yelled, savouring the drama of the moment, now that my success was guaranteed.

I went too far, however, for Diggy turned and looked at me for a moment. Then he howled as he realized how he had been tricked. Instead of giving Muruges the bat, he lifted it above his head and ran towards me. I turned and fled across the field towards my grandparents' gate. When I reached it, I quickly opened the latch, went in and then put the latch back into place. Diggy stopped when he reached the gate. Safe on my side, I made a holmang face at him through the slats in the gates. He came close and I retreated a little. Putting his head through the slats he hissed at me, "If you ever come near the field again, you'll be sorry."

"Don't worry," I replied tartly, "I never will."

With that rejoinder, I forever closed any possibility of entering the boys' world again. But I didn't care, and just to show how much I didn't care I turned my back on Diggy and skipped up the path singing, "Who's afraid of the big bad wolf, fa-la-la-la-la."

When I reached the end of the path I paused to consider my strategy in getting myself accepted into the girls' world again. Now that all obstacles had been cleared out of my path, I realized that I had not thought of how exactly I would begin my overtures towards Her Fatness. Her scowl in my grandparents' living room had made clear her continued animosity towards me. I would have to find a way to make her lower her defences enough to allow me into the girls' world. The sari would certainly be a good incentive for her but, I realized with distaste, I would also need to do a lot of grovelling and pleading. I began to make my way along the open drain that ran parallel to the side of the house.

As I got closer to the backyard I could hear their voices and especially Her Fatness ordering everyone around. When I came around the corner of the house I paused and watched the girls preparing for bride-bride. I saw that the wedding cake had been made in exactly the same way I had always made it and that Her Fatness had taken upon herself the sole honour of decorating it.

Sonali was the first to become aware of my presence. Then one by one the other cousins stopped their work and stared at me. Her Fatness rose to her feet.

"What do you want?" she said.

I came forward a bit and she immediately stepped towards me, like a female mongoose defending her young against a cobra.

"Go away!" she cried, holding up her hand. "Boys are not allowed here."

I didn't heed her command.

"Go away," she cried again. "Otherwise I'm going to tell Ammachi!"

I looked at her for a moment, but fearing that she would see the hatred in my eyes, I lowered my gaze to the ground.

"I want to play bride-bride, please," I said, trying to sound as pathetic and inoffensive as possible.

"Bride-bride," Her Fatness repeated mockingly.

"Yes," I said, in a shy whisper.

Sonali stood up. "Can't he play?" she said to Her Fatness. "He'll be very good."

The other cousins murmured in agreement.

Her Fatness considered their requests.

"I have something that you don't have," I said quickly, hoping to sway her decision.

"What?"

"The sari!"

"The sari?" she echoed. A look of malicious slyness flickered across her face.

"Yes," I said. "Without the sari you can't play bride-bride."

"Why not?" Her Fatness said with mocking indifference.

Her lack of concern about the sari puzzled me. Fearing that the sari might not have the same importance for her as it did for me I cried out, "Why not?" and pretended to be amazed that she would ask such a question. "What is the bride going to wear? A bedsheet?"

Her Fatness pushed the neckline of her dress back onto her shoulder.

"Where is the sari?" she said very casually.

"It's a secret," I said. I was not going to give it to her until I was firmly entrenched in the girls' world again. "If you let me play, I will give it to you when it's time for the bride to get ready."

A slight smile crossed her face.

"The thing is, Arjie," she said in a very reasonable tone, "we've already decided what everyone is going to be for bride-bride and we don't need anyone else."

"But there must be some parts you need people for," I said and then added, "I'll play any part."

"Any part," Her Fatness repeated. Her eyes narrowed and she looked at me appraisingly.

"Let him play," Sonali and the other cousins said to Her Fatness.

"I'll play *any* part," I reiterated.

"You know what?" Her Fatness said suddenly, as if the idea had just dawned on her, "We don't have a groom."

All the cousins watched us closely.

The bitter pill of humiliation Her Fatness wanted me to swallow was clear, but so great was my longing to be part of the girls' world again that I swallowed it.

"I'll take it," I said.

"Okay," Her Fatness said as if it mattered little to her whether I did or not.

The other cousins cried out in delight and I smiled, happy that my goal had been at least partially achieved. Sonali beckoned to me to come and help them. I went towards where the preparations were being made for the wedding feast but Her Fatness quickly stepped in front of me.

"The groom cannot help with the cooking."

"Why not?" I protested.

"Because grooms don't do that."

"They do."

"Have you ever heard of a groom doing that?"

I hadn't, so I demanded half angrily, half sarcastically, "What do grooms do then?"

"They go to office."

"Office?" I said.

Her Fatness nodded and pointed to the table on the back porch. The look on her face told me she wouldn't tolerate any argument.

"I can't go to office," I said quickly. "It's Sunday."

"We're pretending it's Monday," Her Fatness said glibly.

I glared at her. Not satisfied with the humiliation she had forced me to accept, she was determined to keep my participation in bride-bride to a minimum. For an instant, I thought to refuse her, but seeing the warning look in her eyes, I finally acquiesced and went up the porch steps.

From the porch, I watched the other cousins busily preparing for bride-bride. Using a stone as a stamp, I began to bang it on the table as if stamping papers. I noted with pleasure that the sound irritated Her Fatness. I pressed an imaginary buzzer loudly. Getting no response from anyone, I pressed it even louder. Finally the other cousins looked up. "Boy," I called out imperiously to Sonali. "Come here, boy."

Sonali left her cooking and came up the steps with the cringing attitude of the office peons at my father's bank.

"Yes sir, yes sir," she said breathlessly. Her performance was so accurate that the other cousins stopped to observe her.

"Take this to the bank manager in Bambalapitiya," I said.

Bowing again she took the imaginary letter and hurried down the steps. I pressed my buzzer again. "Miss," I called to Lakshmi.

"Yes, sir, coming sir," Lakshmi said, fluttering her eyelashes with the exaggerated coyness we had seen in Sinhala comedies. She came up the steps shaking her hips exaggeratedly for the amusement of the other cousins.

When she had finished the dictation and gone down the steps, the other cousins cried out "Me! Me!" and clamoured to be the one I would call next. Before I could choose one of them Her Fatness stormed up the steps.

"Stop that!" she cried at me, "You're disturbing us."

"No!" I cried back, now that I had the support of the other cousins.

"If you can't behave, go away."

"If I go away, you won't get the sari."

Her Fatness looked at me a long moment and then smiled.

"What sari," she said. "I bet you don't even have the sari."

"Yes, I do," I cried earnestly.

"Where?"

"It's a secret."

"You are lying. I know you don't have it."

"I do! I do!"

"Show me."

"No."

"You don't have it and I'm going to tell Janaki you're disturbing us."

I didn't move, wanting to see if she would carry out her threat. She crossed behind the table and walked towards the kitchen door. When she got to the door I was sure she was serious, I quickly jumped up.

"Where is it?" I said urgently to Sonali.

She pointed to Janaki's room.

I quickly opened Janaki's door and ran inside. Sonali's bag was lying on the bed and I picked it up and rushed out. Her Fatness had come away from the kitchen door.

"Here!" I cried.

Her Fatness folded her arms. "Where?" she said sarcastically.

I opened the bag, put my hand inside and felt around for the sari. I touched a piece of clothing and drew it out. It was only Sonali's change of clothes. I put my hand inside again and this time brought out an Enid Blyton book. There was nothing else in the bag.

"Where is the sari?" Her Fatness demanded sarcastically.

I glanced at Sonali and she gave me an equally puzzled look.

"Liar, Liar on the wall, who's the liarest one of all!" Her Fatness cried.

I turned towards Janaki's door wondering if the sari had fallen out by mistake. Then I saw a slight smirk on Her Fatness's face and the truth came to me. She knew where the sari was! She must have discovered it earlier on and hidden it! With a sudden rush of rage I realized how badly I had been duped by her. She had known all along about the sari and had just strung me along, humiliated me for nothing. Her

Fatness saw the comprehension in my eyes and her arms dropped by her side as if in readiness. She inched back towards the kitchen door for safety. But I wasn't interested in her for the moment. What I wanted was the sari. I rushed into Janaki's room.

"I'm going to tell Janaki you're in her room!" Her Fatness cried.

"Tell and catch my long fat tail!" I cried back.

I looked around Janaki's room. Her Fatness must have hid it here. There was no other place. I lifted Janaki's mattress. There was nothing under it, save for a few Sinhala love comics. I crossed over to Janaki's suitcase and began to go through the clothes she kept neatly folded in there. As silent as a shadow, Her Fatness slipped into the room. Becoming aware of her presence, I turned towards her, but too late. She took the sari from the shelf where she had hidden it and ran out of the door. Leaving the suitcase still open, I ran after her. The sari clutched to her chest, she rushed for the kitchen door. Luckily Sonali and Lakshmi were blocking her way. Seeing me coming at her, she jumped off the porch and began to run towards the corner of the house. I leapt off the porch and chased after her. If she got to the front of the house, she would go straight to Ammachi.

Just as she reached the open drain, I managed to grab onto her arm. She turned desperately and struck out at me. Ducking her blow, I grabbed at the sari and managed to get some of it in my hand. She tried to take the sari back from me, but I held on tightly. Crying out, she jerked away from me with her whole body, hoping to wrest the sari from my grip. With a rasping sound, the sari began to tear. I yelled at her to stop pulling the sari, but she jerked away again, and the sari tore all the way down, each end falling away from the other. There was a moment of stunned silence. I gazed at the half of the sari in my hand, at the jagged end and long threads that hung from it. Then, with a wail of anguish, I rushed at Her Fatness and grabbed her hair. She screamed and flailed at me, but I got a clump of her hair in my hand. I pulled her head so far to one side, that it almost touched her shoulder. She let out a guttural sound, dropped then struck out desperately at me. Her fist caught me in the stomach and she managed to loosen my grip. Leaving a tuft of hair in my hand, she began to run towards the porch steps, crying out, "Janakiii! Ammachiii! Janakiii!"

I ran after her and grabbed hold of the sleeve of her dress before she went up the porch steps. She struggled against my grip and the seam of the sleeve ripped open and hung down her arm like a broken limb. Free once again, she stumbled up the steps towards the kitchen door shouting at the top of her voice, "Janakiii! Ammachiii! Janakiii! Amachiii!"

Janaki rushed out of the kitchen. She raised her hand and looked around for the first person to wallop but when she saw Her Fatness with her torn dress, she held her raised hand to her cheek and cried out in consternation, "Buddu Ammo!"

Now Her Fatness began to cry out only for Ammachi.

Janaki came hurriedly towards her. "Shhh! Shhhh!" she said urgently but Her Fatness only increased the volume of her cries.

"What's wrong? What's wrong?" Janaki cried impatiently.

Her Fatness pointed towards me.

"Janakiii!" she cried. "See what that boy did."

"I didn't do anything," I yelled back, enraged that she was trying to push the blame onto me. "You're the one who tore my sari."

I ran back to where the sari lay on the ground, picked it up and held it out to Janaki.

"You did it!" Her Fatness cried out through her tears, "You did it and now you're blaming me!"

"Liar, Liar," I yelled back.

"Yes!" Sonali cried, coming to my defence. "She did it and now she's blaming him."

"It's her fault!" Lakshmi cried, also taking my side.

Now all the voices of the girl cousins rose in a babble protesting my case and accusing Her Fatness.

"Quiet!" Janaki cried in desperation, "Quiet!"

But nobody heeded her. We all crowded around her so determined to give our version of the story, that it was a while before we became aware of Ammachi's presence in the kitchen doorway. Gradually, like the hush that descends on a garrison town at the sound of the enemy guns, we all became quiet. Even Her Fatness stopped her wailing.

Ammachi looked at all of us and then her gaze came to rest on Janaki.

"How many times have I told you to keep these children quiet," she said, her tone awful.

Janaki, always so full of anger, now wrung her hands like a child in fear of punishment.

"I told them,..." she started to say querulously, but Ammachi raised her hand for silence.

Her Fatness began to cry again, more out of fear than anything else. Ammachi glared at her, and, as if to deflect her look, Her Fatness held up her arm with the ripped sleeve.

"Who did that?" Ammachi said after a moment.

Her Fatness pointed at me and her crying got even louder. Ammachi looked at me sternly and then beckoned me with her index finger.

"Look!" I cried and held out the sari as if in supplication, "Look at what she did!"

But Ammachi was unmoved by the sight of the sari and continued to beckon me.

As I looked at her, I could almost hear the singing of the cane as it came down through the air and then the sharp crack followed by the searing pain. The time Diggy had been caned for climbing the roof came back to me, his cries for mercy, his shouts of agony and loud sobs.

Suddenly I felt my rage, which had temporarily disappeared, return. Why was it that I was going to get that dreaded caning? It was Her Fatness who had torn the sari. The image of my Amma locking me out of her room and of her prohibiting me to play with the girls flashed through my mind and I saw the unjustness of everything I had been forced to endure. Before I could stop myself, I cried out angrily at Ammachi, "It's not fair! Why should I be punished, when she's the one who tore the sari?"

Ammachi continued to beckon to me. "Come here," she said.

"No," I cried. "I won't."

Ammachi came to the edge of the porch, but rather than backing away I stood my ground.

"Come here, you vamban," she said to me sharply.

"No," I cried back, "I hate you you old fatty."

The other cousins and even Janaki gasped at my audacity. Ammachi began to come down the steps. I stood my ground for a few moments, but then my courage gave out. I turned and, with the sari still in my hands, fled.

I ran around the side of the house, along the walkway leading to the gate and out of the gate. Across the street the boys were at their cricket game. I looked back and heard footsteps coming around the side of the house. Not wishing to linger by the gate any longer I ran down the road towards the sea. At the railway lines I paused briefly, then ran across and scrambled over the rocks to the beach. When I reached the beach my legs were trembling so much that I hurriedly sat down on a rock. "I hate them, I hate them all," I whispered to myself. I put my head in my lap and felt the first tears begin to wet my knees.

"I wish I was dead, I wish I was dead."

I beat my fists against the rock until my knuckles were sore and scratched.

When my tears were spent I lay still listening to the sound of the waves. Their regular rhythm had a calming effect on me. I sat up and leaned against the rock behind me, watching the waves come in and go out. After a while, however, the heat of the rocks became unbearable and I stood up, removed my slippers and went down the beach to the edge of the sea.

As I looked out at the sea it came to me that I had never seen the sea this colour before. Our visits to the beach were usually in the early evening when the sea was a turquoise blue. Now, under the midday sun, the ocean had become a hard silver, so bright that it hurt my eyes.

The sand burnt against my ankles and I moved closer to the waves to cool my feet. I looked down the deserted beach, whose white sand almost matched the colour of the sea, and saw the tall buildings of the Fort area shimmering in the distance like a mirage. This beach seemed so foreign from the beach of the early evening which was always crowded with strollers and joggers and vendors. I looked back at the sea and it seemed to me that both the beach and the sea, once so familiar, were like an unknown country into which I had journeyed by hazard.

I felt instinctively that something had permanently changed, that everything that had happened today had pushed me into a territory unfamiliar to me. What exactly the change was I lacked the sophistication to say.

I looked at the sari in my arms and its torn and soiled state was a sad reminder of how the enchantment of spend-the-days had ended for me. I held the sari close to my chest. No, I would never enter the girls' world again. Never stand in front of Janaki's mirror as I watched the transformation take place before my eyes, the girl cousins draping my sari, pinning my veil, arranging my bouquet, applying kohl to my eyes, rouge to my cheek, lipstick to my lips. No more would I step out of that room and make my way down the porch steps to the altar, a creature beautiful and adored, the personification of all that was good and perfect in the world. That creature was gone forever, as lifeless as the torn sari that lay in my arms.

I looked out again at that vast expanse of ocean. The large waves, impersonal to my despair, threw themselves against the beach, their tips frothing and hissing angrily. Their uncaring power reminded me of what the unfamiliar territory of the future held for me. Soon I would have to turn around and go back to my grandparents' house where Ammachi awaited me with her thinnest cane, the one that left deep impressions on the back of our thighs, so deep that sometimes they had to be treated with Gentian Violet. The thought of that cane as it cut through the air, humming like a mosquito, made me wince, even now, so far away from it.

After that there was the loneliness. The future spend-the-days that stretched before me no longer to be enjoyed, no longer looked forward to. I would be caught between the boys' and the girls' world, not belonging or wanted in either. I would be forced to think of things with which to amuse myself, find ways to endure the lunches and teas listening to the cousins discuss what they had done and what they planned to do for the rest of the day.

The bells of St. Fatima's Church rang out the angelus and their melancholy peals seemed like a summon to the fate that awaited me. It was noon and hence lunchtime. Time to return to my grandparents' house. My absence at the lunch table would be construed as another act of defiance and eventually Janaki would be sent to fetch me. Then the punishment I received would be even more severe.

I turned away from the sea, with a heavy heart, and slowly went back up the beach, not caring that the sand burnt the soles of my feet. My slippers were by the rocks and I put them on. At the railway lines I paused and looked back at the sea one last time. Then I turned, crossed the railway lines and began my walk up Ramanaygam Road to the future that awaited me.

The Reservoir

Evgeny Popov

"It would not be overly daring to assert that our culture suffers from something like a chronic ailment which might be defined as 'hostility toward differentness'. [We aim to give] a vivid, though not exhaustive, indication of what the homeless stratum of literature in our country is like." With this introductory note, twenty-three Soviet writers submitted a folio-sized collection of their work entitled Metropol *to the official Writers' Union in January 1979 and, in a public confrontation, demanded publication without censorship as guaranteed by the 1977 Brezhnev Constitution. The union suppressed the anthology, provoking a major intellectual and political* cause célèbre. *Copies were circulated secretly within the Soviet Union, and a complete English translation was eventually published in the West. The consequences for the writers themselves varied: one writer's citizenship was revoked, and several were expelled from the Writers' Union. Others had difficulty publishing subsequent work.*

A young man named Evgeny Popov, who was listed in Metropol *as both a contributing writer and an editor, found himself at the centre of the political furor. His application for entry into the Writers' Union— with its assurance of professional status—was suspended, prompting six important associates to pledge publicly to resign. In the end, despite further protests on his behalf by American writers such as Edward Albee, Arthur Miller, William Styron, John Updike, and Kurt Vonnegut, his membership was indefinitely denied. Evgeny Popov's contribution to* Metropol *was the short story "The Reservoir", in the black satirical tradition of Bulgakov and Gogol.*

At first even Bublik seemed to us a decent sort. He paid good money for a two-story house, with cultivated lot, to the grass widow of Vasil-Vasilka. Vasil, an embezzler of the people's wealth, was sent up for selling things on the side—roofing tin, ceramic floor tile, and steam radiators—which he also offered us in his "good neighborly" way, and we heard him out, heard what he had to say, but we didn't get involved, preferring to walk the straight and narrow. Because we're old-time residents of Siberia. Besides, do you think in my own town I couldn't get hold of some damn ceramic crap? What a joke that would be. Besides, that would partly go against the policy of raising living standards and the principles of harnessing the outlying regions of our vast Motherland. Now we're not any of your kulaks, you know; it's just that these days everybody lives well this way, and they're a whole lot better off than your former kulak fools, who tried to get ahead when the time wasn't ripe, tried to leap over the backs of others and not bring anyone along with them. For which they were very severely but justly punished.

But Lord, Lord. God in heaven above. What for, really? How much effort they put in. Used to deliver bottled gas on Saturdays. That was Kosorezov, a wise and clever man. Went to a lot of trouble, thank you very much—could put a machine or a man on a job when he had to…. Bushes and bushes of raspberries, beds and beds of strawberries. It was an elegant and heady sight to see, easy on the eyes and comforting to the soul … a beautiful, elegant, heady sight to see.

But best of all was our reservoir. Lord in heaven, what a reservoir! Constantly fed by crystalline, subterranean waters. Truly, it sweetened our lives on our stifling summer days. In its tender waters our mischievous lads would splash, a merry flock. And our girls, our maidens, like Youth itself, would lie stretched out, like kittens, on the crunchy quartz sand. Studying for their exams or just surrendering themselves to the usual girlish dreams—the life of proud labor before them, a family, marriage, raising children, proper relations between the sexes.

And round about them us—the parents. The women knitting something out of mohair or talking about who was vacationing where in the south or who had bought what new acquisitions for the household. Under the willow trees Colonel Zhestakanov and Professor Burevich would do battle in a game of checkers. Mitva-the-Bark-Beetle would argue with the physicist Lysukhin about whether the numbers for different grades of Czech beer corresponded to their actual alcoholic content. Some people worked on crossword puzzles, others on production problems they had encountered on their jobs. And me? I would look at all this and, honest to God, my heart would rejoice, but it would also roll over. The years of hunger during the war, when I was left in the reserves, would come back to me, and I'd remember the time when me and my spouse were number 261, standing in line for corn flour in the black morning blizzard next to the movie theater Rote Front. My leg had gone numb from cold; I couldn't feel my foot in its thick felt boot, couldn't feel it at all. Afterward they rubbed it with goose grease. When I remember that, honest to God, I'd like to personally strangle all these loudmouths and troublemakers with my own two hands. They badmouth everything but they guzzle their fill of shashlik and Pepsi Cola. I wish all those stinking bastards had been in my place, standing in line in 1947. I'd like to see what kind of tune they'd sing then, the sniveling rats.

As for those two young men, who had the look of artists about them—I won't start trying to hide or justify our blunders—at first we actually took a liking to them.

It was theater director Bublik who brought them here, to our town, along with his good-looking wife, the singer. The only good thing about Bublik, the scum, was that during his time as director he often cheered us up by having various celebrities visit Pustaya Chush ("Empty Nonsense", that's the name of our workingman's town). One time you'd see the singer M, parading around, dangling a handkerchief and bellowing "Live in fame and glory"; another time the magician T would amuse everyone by making Zhestakanov's pocket watch disappear and turn up in Mitya-the-Bark-Beetle's boot. Then another time our celebrated portraitist Spozhnikov would be sitting up on the heights, painting a portrait of our reservoir against the background of its natural surroundings. Strange that those intelligent people didn't detect the rotten inner core of this Bublik before we did. Very strange.

Now, at first glance those two were the simplest, most ordinary long-haired kids. But it's not by chance, you know, that we have the old folk saying: some simplicity is worse than thievery. Although it's also true that modesty is a virtue. Well, one of them was kind of tall, a blue-eyed athlete type. The other was more of a weakling, on the dark side, and a little brighter than the first one. Our gals, our young maidens, crowded around in droves when they saw how skillful these fellows were at table tennis. And these boys, no way would they say any low words to the girls or make any vulgar or suggestive gestures. Oh no. They were all modest and above board, you see, those bastards whacking away at their little white ball. Until it happened.

But once it happened, everyone started yelling that we had made it up. What was there for us to "make up"? We didn't have the slightest inkling of anything until all of a sudden the most honest-to-God, out-and-out swinish scandal erupted, the consequences of which are ineradicable, sad, and shameful. Even the dachas are being boarded up tight, the second-hand dealers are scurrying about, rustling through the autumn leaves, the fruit trees are being dug up and carted off for transplanting, and there's no joy in anybody's face, just depression and weariness, disillusionment and fear.

Although with only half a brain we could have guessed right away. They even went around holding hands, not to mention the fact that they obviously, *obviously,* avoided our gals.

And the gals, the little pranksters, were glad to have a laugh. They put the smaller one's hair into little braids, like the Uzbek women do. They smeared some bright lipstick on his mouth. Then they went and looped a spare, empty brassiere over his fairly hefty chest, which was more than standard size. And laugh! My how they laughed.

And all of us, at the time—we laughed too—in our ignorance, and had a good time, while also being aware of a certain vulgarity in this relatively pointed joke. We laughed and had a good time—until it happened.

Lord in heaven! I'll remember it for the rest of my life. You see, the disposition of forces was like this. The pond. Those two on a raft near the shore. The gals right there with them. All of us sitting under the trees. Bublik the director and his wife the singer nowhere to be seen.

The girls had no sooner fastened this harmless female ornament over the younger one's chest than the older one jumped up, turning pale, with his blue eyes getting all dark, and he gives poor Nastya a trained boxer's jab right in the solar plexus from which the poor child, without a murmur, not even an "Ow," falls over on the sand.

We all stood there with our mouths hanging open. But he didn't waste a second. He cut loose the raft and in the wink of an eye the pair of them were out in the middle of the reservoir, where they started cursing in the foulest and dirtiest way. The tall one was all in a fury. The short one would only mutter in reply, but using filthy language. Also he stuck his tongue out at the tall one. At which the first one, twitching and jerking in the strangest way, shouted: "Ah, you whore!" And smacked the shorter one in the face. Then that one goes crashing to his knees and starts kissing his comrade's bare and dirty feet, half covered by the waves washing over them.

And Lord, Lord. God in heaven above! The tall one kicked him with all his might and with a piercing scream, the first one landed in the water. But this threw the raft off balance, and one end shot up, throwing the second one in the water too. The two of them, without a gurgle, began to disappear beneath the waves. Then they surfaced for a moment, apparently not knowing how to swim—after which, again without a gurgle, they sank to the bottom for good.

A terrible silence fell.

We all stood there, thunderstruck. Our gals hovered around like so many frightened little animals as Nastya came to. The nurses woke up. Infants began to cry. Dogs began to howl.

Colonel Zhestakanov was the first to gather his wits together. With a shout, "I'll save those fairies—so they can answer to a people's comradely court," this superb swimmer, who had won more than a few swimming championships in his youth, plunged into the water and disappeared for a long time. Coming back up, he floated on his back for a while, after which, without wasting words, he dove again.

But neither Colonel Zhestakanov's second, nor his subsequent soundings of the reservoir bottom produced any favorable results. The Colonel muttered, "How can it be?" But they had disappeared.

We figured out that we had better hurry over to Bublik's, since he was to blame, so to speak, for this "triumph." But he had disappeared, too, along with his good-looking wife the singer. The wind from the pine forest was blowing freely through their empty dacha, ruffling the tulle curtains. A coffee cup rolled on its side on the rug, having dumped its contents on an issue of some glossy magazine that was obviously not one of our Soviet magazines. Bright orange flowers languished like abandoned waifs in their pretty ceramic vases. Bublik and his good-looking wife the singer had vanished.

And when, a few days later, we sent a delegation of our people to the musical comedy theater, the administration there, staring at the floor, informed us that Bublik had already made a clean escape and had taken off for parts unknown. And it was only afterwards that we understood the embarrassed look on these honest people's faces, when it finally came out exactly what unknown parts director Bublik had taken off for. Turned out it was the United States of America, and the two of them had brazenly emigrated right under everybody's nose—him and his good-looking wife the singer. Well, what the hell, it's not all that surprising that they went to the U.S.A. Seems it'll be easier for them there to engage in degeneracy, which in our country is barred by good, hard roadblocks. So it's not surprising.

What's surprising is something else. What's surprising is that when the militia arrived at the lake and the scuba divers got there too, they didn't find anyone either. We begged the scuba divers to keep at it, and they really tried to cover every square centimeter of the bottom, but it was all in vain. The two "artists" were gone.

You know, later on we discussed another idea—maybe we should go to the necessary expense and drain the pond, find out what was going on, and get to the bottom of everything, so that there wouldn't be this leftover smell of the devil's work or papistry, so that there wouldn't be this weariness and depression, disillusionment and fear— what the hell, we had enough money. But we missed our chance, and now we're really paying for our foolish gullibility, negligence, and dizzy-headedness.

Because literally on the very next day, after everything seemed to have quieted down, the town was suddenly treated to the terrible screams of someone being killed. It turned out to be Comrade Zhestakanov, who loved night swimming. The poor soul could barely get his breath, his eyes were popping out of his head, and all he could do was point at the watery traces of moonlight, repeating: "It's them! It's them. There. There."

After being revived with a glass of vodka, he got hold of himself. But he still insisted he had swum out to the raft at twelve midnight, the raft out in the middle of the reservoir, and on this raft there suddenly appeared two skeletons sadly embracing and singing a song ever so softly, "No need for sorrow, all of life lies ahead." How do you like that?

And even though Zhestakanov was soon being treated by the psychiatrist Tsarkov-Kolomensky, it didn't help anyone. The skeletons were also seen and heard by Professor Burevich, Comrade K., Mitya-the-Bark-Beetle (and Mitya's mother-in-law), the metalworker Yeprev and his buddy Shenopin, Angelina Stepanovna, Edward Ivanovich, Yuri Aleksandrovich, Emma Nikolaevna, me, and even the physicist Lysukhin, who as a man of science was so shaken by this spectacle that he began to drink dangerously.

People tried to scare them off by shouting "Scat" and firing a double-barreled shotgun, but none of it helped. The skeletons weren't always visible, it's true. But the damn raft moved around literally on its own, and you could hear yelling, singing, lamentations, hoarse curses, smacking kisses, and prayers at night *all the time!*

I'm not one of your Zhestakanovs, I grant you. I never was at the front. And I'm not your physicist Lysukhin. Never had higher education. I'm just a normal average person, and not an especially big vodka drinker either. *But I personally swear to you myself that I heard this with my own ears:* "My darling, my darling," and then a wheezing sound, but such a sound it made my hair stand on end.

And after we tried everything over and over again, guns and stones and chlorophosphate, the end came—the end for us, the end for our town, the end for the reservoir. The dachas are being boarded up tight, and the second-hand dealers are scurrying about everywhere, rustling through the autumn leaves, the fruit trees are being dug up and carted off for transplanting , and there's no joy in anybody's face, just depression and weariness, disillusionment and fear.

So what would you have us do? We're none of us mystics or priests. But also we're not fools enough to live in a place like this where some degenerate corpses with their lustful skeletons gleaming in the moonlight try to lure people or get close to them and scare them and drive people straight into the psychiatric hospitals, leaving the women without any courage and the men without good sense and the children without their happy childhood or a clear vision of their perspectives in life and of working for the good of our vast Motherland. O Lord, O Lord. God in heaven above.

The World Well Lost

Theodore Sturgeon

Theodore Sturgeon was a science-fiction writer who revolutionized the genre. "I have my own definition of science, which derives from scientia, which is the Latin word that means knowledge," he explained. "To me, science fiction is knowledge fiction, and it's knowledge not only of physical and chemical laws but also the quasi- and soft sciences, and also matters of the human heart and mind. This is all knowledge, and so to me it's all legitimate science fiction." One subject that Sturgeon legitimized for science fiction was sex, in all its astounding diversity. There now exist entire anthologies that attest to the freedom Sturgeon found in science fiction to depict and explore alternative sexualities. But in the 1940s, his early stories were often considered too erotically daring for publication in science-fiction magazines. "The World Well Lost" was ground-breaking when it was published in 1953—the first science-fiction story to sympathetically portray homosexuality.

According to the "Prime Directive" which Sturgeon later created for the Star Trek *television series, the overriding law of the United Federation of Planets—the governing body of the known universe—"prohibits Federation interference with the normal development of alien life and societies." In his fiction, Sturgeon gleefully challenges our reading of this directive again and again by asking: in any society, what does the notion of "normal development" signify? And under whose social code—in "The World Well Lost" there is more than one—is any of us allowed the fulfilment of personal freedom?*

All the world knew them as loverbirds, though they were certainly not birds, but humans. Well, say humanoids. Featherless bipeds. Their stay on earth was brief, a nine-day wonder. Any wonder that lasts nine days on an earth of orgasmic trideo shows; time-freezing pills; synapse-inverter fields which make it possible for a man to turn a sunset to perfumes, a masochist to a fur-feeler; and a thousand other euphorics—why, on such an earth, a nine-day wonder is a wonder indeed.

Like a sudden bloom across the face of the world came the peculiar magic of the loverbirds. There were loverbird songs and loverbird trinkets, loverbird hats and pins, bangles and baubles, coins and quaffs and tidbits. For there was that about the loverbirds which made a deep enchantment. No one can be told about a loverbird and feel this curious delight. Many are immune even to a solidograph. But watch loverbirds, only for a moment, and see what happens. It's the feeling you had when you were twelve, and summer-drenched, and you kissed a girl for the very first time and knew a breathlessness you were sure could never happen again. And indeed it never could—unless you watched loverbirds. Then you are spellbound for four quiet seconds, and suddenly your very heart twists, and incredulous tears sting and stay; and the very first move you make afterward, you make on tiptoe, and your first word is a whisper.

This magic came over very well on trideo, and everyone had trideo; so for a brief while the earth was enchanted.

There were only two loverbirds. They came down out of the sky in a single brassy flash, and stepped out of their ship, hand in hand. Their eyes were full of wonder, each at the other, and together at the world. They seemed frozen in a full-to-bursting moment of discovery; they made way for one another gravely and with courtesy, they looked about them and in the very looking gave each other gifts—the color of the sky, the taste of the air, the pressures of things growing and meeting and changing. They never spoke. They simply *were* together. To watch them was to know of their awestruck mounting of staircases of bird notes, of how each knew the warmth of the other as their flesh supped silently on sunlight.

They stepped from their ship, and the tall one threw a yellow powder back to it. The ship fell in upon itself and became a pile of rubble, which collapsed into a pile of gleaming sand, which slumped compactly down to dust and then to an airblown emulsion so fine that Brownian movement itself hammered it up and out and away. Anyone could see that they intended to stay. Anyone could know by simply watching them that next to their wondrous delight in each other came their delighted wonder at earth itself, everything and everybody about it.

Now, if terrestrial culture were a pyramid, at the apex (where the power is) would sit a blind man, for so constituted are we that only by blinding ourselves, bit by bit, may we rise above our fellows. The man at the apex has an immense preoccupation with the welfare of the whole, because he regards it as the source and structure of his elevation, which it is, and as an extension of himself, which it is not. It was such a man who, in the face of immeasurable evidence, chose to find a defense against loverbirds, and fed the matrices and coordinates of the loverbird image into the most marvelous calculator that had ever been built.

The machine sucked in symbols and raced them about, compared and waited and matched and sat still while its bulging memory, cell by cell, was silent, was silent—and suddenly, in a far corner, resonated. It grasped this resonance in forceps made of mathematics, snatched it out (translating furiously as it snatched) and put out a fevered tongue of paper on which was typed:

DIRBANU

Now this utterly changed the complexion of things. For earth ships had ranged the cosmos far and wide, with few hindrances. Of these hindrances, all could be understood but one, and that one was Dirbanu, a transpalactic planet which shrouded itself in impenetrable fields of force whenever an earth ship approached. There were other worlds which could do this, but in each case the crews knew why it was done. Dirbanu, upon discovery, had prohibited landings from the very first until an ambassador could be sent to Terra. In due time one did arrive (so reported the calculator, which was the only entity that remembered the episode) and it was obvious that Earth and Dirbanu had much in common. The ambassador, however, showed a most uncommon disdain of Earth and all its work, curled his lip and went wordlessly home, and ever since then Dirbanu had locked itself tight away from the questing Terrans.

Dirbanu thereby became of value, and fair game, but we could do nothing to ripple the bland face of her defenses. As this impregnability repeatedly proved itself, Dirbanu evolved in our group mind through the usual stages of being: the Curiosity, the Mystery, the Challenge, the Enemy, the Enemy, the Enemy, the Mystery, the Curiosity, and finally That-which-is-too-far-away-to-bother-with, or the Forgotten.

And suddenly, after all this time, Earth had two genuine natives of

Dirbanu aboard, entrancing the populace and giving no information. This intolerable circumstance began to make itself felt throughout the world—but slowly, for this time the blind men's din was cushioned and soaked by the magic of the loverbirds. It might have taken a very long time to convince the people of the menace in their midst had there not been a truly startling development:

A direct message was received from Dirbanu.

The collective impact of loverbird material emanating from transmitters on Earth had attracted the attention of Dirbanu, which promptly informed us that the loverbirds were indeed their nationals, that in addition they were fugitives, that Dirbanu would take it ill if Earth should regard itself as a sanctuary for the criminals of Dirbanu but would, on the other hand, find it in its heart to be very pleased if Earth saw fit to return them.

So from the depths of its enchantment, Terra was able to calculate a course of action. Here at last was an opportunity to consort with Dirbanu on a friendly basis—great Dirbanu which, since it had force fields which Earth could not duplicate, must of necessity have many other things Earth could use; mighty Dirbanu before whom we could kneel in supplication (with purely-for-defense bombs hidden in our pockets) with lowered heads (making invisible the knife in our teeth) and ask for crumbs from their table (in order to extrapolate the location of their kitchens).

Thus the loverbird episode became another item in the weary procession of proofs that Terra's most reasonable intolerance can conquer practically anything, even magic.

Especially magic.

So it was that the loverbirds were arrested, that the *Starmite* 439 was fitted out as a prison ship, that a most carefully screened crew was chosen for her, and that she struck starward with the cargo that would gain us a world.

Two men were the crew—a colorful little rooster of a man and a great dun bull of a man. They were, respectively, Rootes, who was Captain and staff, and Grunty, who was midship and inboard corps. Rootes was cocky, springy, white and crisp. His hair was auburn and so were his eyes, and the eyes were hard. Grunty was a shambler with big gentle hands and heavy shoulders half as wide as Rootes was high. He should have worn a cowl and rope-belted habit. He should, perhaps, have worn a burnoose. He did neither, but the effect was there. Known only to him was the fact that words and pictures, concepts and comparisons were an endless swirling blizzard inside him. Known only to him and Rootes was the fact that he had books, and books, and books, and Rootes did not care if he had or not. Grunty he had been called since he first learned to talk, and Grunty was name enough for him. For the words in his head would not leave him except one or two at a time, with long moments between. So he had learned to condense his verbal messages to breathy grunts, and when they wouldn't condense, he said nothing.

They were primitives, both of them, which is to say that they were doers, while Modern Man is a thinker and/or a feeler. The thinkers compose new variations and permutations of euphoria, and the feelers repay the thinkers by responding to their inventions. The ships had no place for Modern Man, and Modern Man had only the most casual use for the ships.

Doers can co-operate like cam and pushrod, like ratchet and pawl, and such linkage creates a powerful bond. But Rootes and Grunty were unique among crews in that these machine parts were not interchangeable. Any good captain can command any good crew, surroundings being equivalent. But Rootes would not and could not ship out with anyone but Grunty, and Grunty was just that dependent. Grunty understood this bond, and the fact that the only way it could conceivably be broken would be to explain it to Rootes. Rootes did not understood it because it never occurred to him to try, and had he tried, he would have failed, since he was inherently non-equipped for the task. Grunty knew that their unique bond was for him, a survival matter. Rootes did not know this, and would have rejected the idea with violence.

So Rootes regarded Grunty with tolerance and a modified amusement. The modification was an inarticulate realization of Grunty's complete dependability. Grunty regarded Rootes with ... well, with the ceaseless, silent flurry of words in his mind.

There was, besides the harmony of functions and the other link, understood only by Grunty, a third adjunct to their phenomenal efficiency as a crew. It was organic, and it had to do with the stellar drive.

Reaction engines were long forgotten. The so-called "warp" drive was used only experimentally and on certain crash-priority war-craft where operating costs were not a factor. The *Starmite* 439 was, like most interstellar craft, powered by an RS plant. Like the transistor, the Referential Stasis generator is extremely simple to construct and very difficult indeed to explain. Its mathematics approaches mysticism and its theory contains certain impossibilities which are ignored in practice. Its effect is to shift the area of stasis of the ship and everything in it from one point of reference to another. For example, the ship at rest on the Earth's surface is in stasis in reference to the ground on which it rests. Throwing the ship into stasis in reference to the centre of the earth gives it instantly an effective speed equal to the surface velocity of the planet around its core—some one thousand miles per hour. Stasis referential to the sun moves the Earth out from under the ship at the Earth's orbital velocity. GH stasis "moves" the ship at the angular velocity of the sun about the Galactic Hub. The galactic drift can be used, as can any simple or complex mass center in this expanding universe. There are resultants and there are multipliers, and effective velocities can be enormous. Yet the ship is constantly in stasis, so that there is never an inertia factor.

The one inconvenience of the RS drive is that shifts from one referent to another invariably black the crew out, for psychoneural reasons. The blackout period varies slightly between individuals from one to two and a half hours. But some anomaly in Grunty's gigantic frame kept his blackout periods down to thirty or forty minutes, while Rootes was always out for two hours or more. There was that about Grunty which made moments of isolation a vital necessity, for a man must occasionally be himself, which in anyone's company Grunty was not. But after stasis shifts Grunty had an hour or so to himself while his commander lay numbly spread-eagled on the blackout couch, and he spent these in communions of his own devising. Sometimes this meant only a good book.

This, then, was the crew picked to man the prison ship. It had been together longer than any other crew in the Space Service. Its record showed a metrical efficiency and a resistance to physical and psychic debilitations previously unheard of in a trade where close confinement on long voyages had come to be regarded as hazards. In space, shift followed shift uneventfully, and planetfall was made on schedule and without incident. In port Rootes would roar off to the fleshpots, in which he would wallow noisily until an hour before takeoff, while Grunty found, first, the business office, and next, a bookstore.

They were pleased to be chosen for the Dirbanu trip. Rootes felt no remorse at taking away Earth's new delight, since he was one of the very few who was immune to it. ("Pretty," he said at his first encounter.) Grunty simply grunted, but then, so did everyone else. Rootes did not notice, and Grunty did not remark upon the obvious fact that though the loverbirds' expression of awestruck wonderment in each other's presence had, if anything, intensified, their extreme pleasure in Earth and the things of Earth had vanished. They were locked, securely but comfortably, in the after cabin behind a new transparent door, so that their every move could be watched from the main cabin and control console. They sat close, with their arms about one another, and though their radiant joy in the contact never lessened, it was a shadowed pleasure, a lachrymose beauty like the wrenching music of the wailing wall.

The RS drive laid its hand on the moon and they vaulted away. Grunty came up from blackout to find it very quiet. The loverbirds lay still in each other's arms, looking very human except for the high joining of their closed eyelids, which nictated upward rather than downward like a Terran's. Rootes sprawled limply on the other couch, and Grunty nodded at the sight. He deeply appreciated the silence, since Rootes had filled the small cabin with earthy chatter about his conquests in port, detail by hairy detail, for two solid hours preceding their departure. It was a routine which Grunty found particularly wearing, partly for its content, which interested him not at all, but mostly for its inevitability. Grunty had long ago noted that these recitations, for all their detail, carried the tones of thirst rather than of satiety. He had his own conclusions about it, and, characteristically, kept them to himself. But inside, his spinning gusts of words could shape themselves well to it, and they did. "And man, she moaned!" Rootes would chant. "And take money? She *gave* me money. And what did I do with it? Why, I bought up some more of the same." *And what you could buy with a shekel's worth of tenderness, my prince!* his silent words sang. "... across the floor and around the rug until, by damn, I thought we're about to climb the wall. Loaded, Grunty-boy, I tell you, I was loaded!" *Poor little one* ran the hushed susurrus, *thy poverty is as great as thy joy and a tenth as great as thine empty noise.* One of Grunty's greatest pleasures was taken in the fact that this kind of chuntering was limited to the first day out, with barely another word on the varied theme until the next departure, no matter how many months away that might be. *Squeak to me of love, dear mouse*, his words would chuckle. *Stand up on your cheese and nibble away at your dream.* Then, wearily, *But oh, this treasure I carry is too heavy a burden, in all its fullness, to be so tugged at by your clattering vacuum!*

Grunty left the couch and went to the controls. The preset courses checked against the indicators. He logged them and fixed the finder control to locate a certain mass-nexus in the Crab Nebula. It would chime when it was ready. He set the switch for final closing by the push-button beside his couch, and went aft to wait.

He stood watching the loverbirds because there was nothing else for him to do.

They lay quite still, but love so permeated them that their very poses expressed it. Their lax bodies yearned each to each, and the tall one's hand seemed to stream toward the fingers of his beloved, and then back again, like the riven tatters of a torn fabric straining toward oneness again. And as their mood was a sadness too, so their pose, each and both, together and singly expressed it, and singly each through the other silently spoke of the loss they had suffered, and how it ensured greater losses to come. Slowly the picture suffused Grunty's thinking, and his words picked and pierced and smoothed it down, and murmured finally, *Brush away the dusting of sadness from the future, bright ones. You've sadness enough for now. Grief should live only after it is truly born, and not before.*

His words sang,

> *Come fill the cup and in the fire of spring*
> *Your winter garment of repentance fling.*
> *The bird of time has but a little way*
> *To flutter—and the bird is on the wing.*

and added *Omar Khayyam, born circa 1073*, for this, too, was one of the words' functions.

And then he stiffened in horror; his great hands came up convulsively and clawed the imprisoning glass....

They were smiling at him.

They were smiling, and on their faces and on and about their bodies there was no sadness.

They had *heard* him!

He glanced convulsively around at the Captain's unconscious form, then back to the loverbirds.

That they should recover so swiftly from blackout was, to say the least, an intrusion; for his moments of aloneness were precious and more than precious to Grunty, and would be useless to him under the scrutiny of those jewelled eyes. But that was a minor matter compared to this other thing, this terrible fact that they *heard*.

Telepathic races were not common, but they did exist. And what he was now experiencing was what invariably happened when humans encountered one. He could only send; the loverbirds could only receive. And they *must not* receive him! No one must. No one must know what he was, what he thought. If anyone did, it would be a disaster beyond bearing. It would mean no more flights with Rootes. Which, of course, meant no flights with anyone. And how could he live—where could he go?

He turned back to the loverbirds. His lips were white and drawn back in a snarl of panic and fury. For a blood-thick moment he held their eyes. They drew closer to one another, and together sent him a radiant, anxious, friendly look that made him grind his teeth.

Then, at the console, the finder chimed.

Grunty turned slowly from the transparent door and went to his couch. He lay down and poised his thumb over the push-button.

He *hated* the loverbirds, and there was no joy in him. He pressed the button, the ship slid into a new stasis, and he blacked out.

The time passed.

"Grunty!"

"?"

"You feed them this shift?"

"Nuh."

"Last shift?"

"Nuh."

"What the hell's matter with you, y'big dumb bastich? What you expect them to live on?"

Grunty sent a look of roiling hatred aft. "Love," he said.

"Feed 'em," snapped Rootes.

Wordlessly Grunty went about preparing a meal for the prisoners. Rootes stood in the middle of the cabin, his hard small fists on his hips, his gleaming auburn head tilted to one side, and watched every move. "I didn't used to have to tell you anything," he growled, half pugnaciously, half worriedly. "You sick?"

Grunty shook his head. He twisted the tops of two cans and set them aside to heat themselves, and took down the water suckers.

"You got it in for those honeymooners or something?"

Grunty averted his face.

"We get them to Dirbanu alive and healthy, hear me? They get sick, you get sick, by God. I'll see to that. Don't give me trouble, Grunty. I'll take it out on you. I never whipped you yet, but I will."

Grunty carried the tray aft. "You hear me?" Rootes yelled.

Grunty nodded without looking at him. He touched the control and a small communication window slid open in the glass wall. He slid the tray through. The taller loverbird stepped forward and took it eagerly, gracefully, and gave him a dazzling smile of thanks. Grunty growled low in his throat like a carnivore. The loverbird carried the food back to the couch and they began to eat, feeding each other little morsels.

A new stasis, and Grunty came fighting up out of blackness. He sat up abruptly, glanced around the ship. The Captain was sprawled out across the cushions, his compact body and outflung arm forming the poured-out, spring-steel laxness usually seen only in sleeping cats. The loverbirds, even in deep unconsciousness, lay like hardly separate parts of something whole, the small one on the couch, the tall one on the deck, prone, reaching, supplicating.

Grunty snorted and hove to his feet. He crossed the cabin and stood looking down on Rootes.

The hummingbird is a yellowjacket, said his words, *Buzz and dart, hiss and flash away. Swift and hurtful, hurtful....*

He stood for a moment, his great shoulder muscles working one against the other, and his mouth trembled.

He looked at the loverbirds, who were still motionless. His eyes slowly narrowed.

His words tumbled and climbed, and ordered themselves:

I through love have learned three things,
Sorrow, sin and death it brings.
Yet day by day my heart within
Dares shame and sorrow, death and sin....

And dutifully he added *Samuel Ferguson, born 1810*. He glared at the loverbirds and brought his fist into his palm with a sound like a club on an anthill. They had heard him again, and this time they did not smile, but looked into each other's eyes and then turned together to regard him, nodding gravely.

Rootes went through Grunty's books, leafing and casting aside. He had never touched them before. "Buncha crap," he jeered. "Garden of the Plynck. Wind in the Willows. Worm Ouroborous. Kid stuff."

Grunty lumbered across and patiently gathered up the books the Captain had flung aside, putting them one by one back into their places, stroking them as if they had been bruised.

"Isn't there nothing in here with pictures?"

Grunty regarded him silently for a moment and then took down a tall volume. The Captain snatched it, leafed through it. "Mountains," he growled. "Old houses." He leafed. "Damn boats." He smashed the book to the deck. "Haven't you got *any* of what I want?"

Grunty waited attentively.

"Do I have to draw a diagram?" the Captain roared. "Got that ol' itch, Grunty. You wouldn't know. I feel like looking at pictures, get what I mean?"

Grunty stared at him, utterly without expression, but deep within him a panic squirmed. The Captain never, *never* behaved like this in mid-voyage. It was going to get worse, he realized. Much worse. And quickly.

He shot the loverbirds a vicious, hate-filled glance. If they weren't aboard....

There could be no waiting. Not now. Something had to be done. Something....

"Come on, come on," said Rootes. "Goddlemighty Godfrey, even a deadbutt like you must have *something* for kicks."

Grunty turned away from him, squeezed his eyes closed for a tortured second, then pulled himself together. He ran his hand over the books, hesitated, and finally brought out a large, heavy one. He handed it to the Captain and went forward to the console. He slumped down there over the file of computer tapes, pretending to be busy.

The Captain sprawled onto Grunty's couch and opened the book. "Michelangelo, what the hell," he growled. He grunted, almost like his shipmate. "Statues," he half-whispered, in withering scorn. But he ogled and leafed at last, and was quiet.

The loverbirds looked at him with a sad tenderness, and then together sent beseeching glances at Grunty's angry back.

The matrix-pattern for Terra slipped through Grunty's fingers, and he suddenly tore the tape across, and across again. A filthy place, Terra. *There is nothing,* he thought, *like the conservatism of license.* Given a culture of sybaritics, with an endless choice of mechanical titillations, and you have a people of unbreakable and hidebound formality, a people with few but massive taboos, a shockable, narrow, prissy people obeying the rules—even the rules of their calculated depravities—and protecting their treasured, specialized pruderies. In such a group there are words one may not use for fear of their fanged laughter, colors one may not wear, gestures and intonations one must forego, on pain of being torn to pieces. The rules are complex and absolute, and in such a place one's heart may not sing lest, through its warm free joyousness, it betray one.

And if you must have joy of such a nature, if you must be free to be your pressured self, then off to space ... off to the glittering black loneliness. And let the days go by, and let the time pass, and huddle beneath your impenetrable integument, and wait, and wait, and every once in a long while you will have that moment of lonely consciousness when there is no one around to see; and then it may burst from you and you may dance, or cry, or twist the hair on your head till your eyeballs blaze, or do any of the other things your so unfashionable nature thirstily demands.

It took Grunty half a lifetime to find this freedom: No price would be too great to keep it. Not lives, nor interplanetary diplomacy, nor Earth itself were worth such a frightful loss.

He would lose it if anyone knew, and the loverbirds knew.

He pressed his heavy hands together until the knuckles crackled. Dirbanu, reading it all from the ardent minds of the loverbirds; Dirbanu flashing the news across the stars; the roar of reaction, and then Rootes, Rootes, when the huge and ugly impact washed over him....

So let Dirbanu be offended. Let Terra accuse this ship of fumbling, even of treachery—anything but the withering news the loverbirds had stolen.

Another new stasis, and Grunty's first thought as he came alive in the silent ship was *It has to be soon.*

He rolled off the couch and glared at the unconscious loverbirds. The helpless loverbirds.

Smash their heads in.

Then Rootes ... what to tell Rootes?

The loverbirds attacked him, tried to seize the ship?

He shook his head like a bear in a beehive. Rootes would never believe that. Even if the loverbirds could open the door, which they could not, it was more than ridiculous to imagine those two bright and slender things attacking anyone—especially so rugged and massive an opponent.

Poison? No—there was nothing in the efficient, unfailingly beneficial food stores that might help.

His glance strayed to the Captain, and he stopped breathing.

Of course!

He ran to the Captain's personal lockers. He should have known that such a cocky little hound as Rootes could not live, could not strut and prance as he did unless he had a weapon. And if it was the kind of weapon that such a man would characteristically choose—

A movement caught his eye as he searched.

The loverbirds were awake.

That wouldn't matter.

He laughed at them, a flashing, ugly laugh. They cowered close together and their eyes grew very bright.

They knew.

He was aware that they were suddenly very busy, as busy as he. And then he found the gun.

It was a snug little thing, smooth and intimate in his hand. It was exactly what he had guessed, what he had hoped for—just what he needed. It was silent. It would leave no mark. It need not even be aimed carefully. Just a touch of its feral radiation and throughout the body the axones suddenly refuse to propagate nerve impulses. No thought leaves the brain, no slightest contraction of heart or lung occurs again, ever. And afterward, no sign remains that a weapon has been used.

He went to the serving window with the gun in his hand. *When he wakes, you will be dead,* he thought. *Couldn't recover from stasis blackout. Too bad. But no one's to blame, hm? We never had Dirbanu passengers before. So how could we know?*

The loverbirds, instead of flinching, were crowding close to the window, their faces beseeching, their delicate hands signing and signalling, frantically trying to convey something.

He touched the control, and the panel slid back.

The taller loverbird held up something as if it would shield him. The other pointed at it, nodded urgently, and gave him one of those accursed, hauntingly sweet smiles.

Grunty put up his hand to sweep the thing aside, and then checked himself.

It was only a piece of paper.

All of the cruelty of humanity rose up in Grunty. *A species that can't protect itself doesn't deserve to live.* He raised the gun.

And then he saw the pictures.

Economical and accurate, and for all their subject, done with the ineffable grace of the loverbirds themselves, the pictures showed three figures:

Grunty himself, hulking, impassive, the eyes glowing, the tree-trunk legs and hunched shoulders.

Rootes, in a pose so characteristic and so cleverly done that Grunty gasped. Crisp and clean, Rootes' image had one foot up on a chair, both elbows on the high knee, the head half turned. The eyes fairly sparkled from the paper.

And a girl.

She was beautiful. She stood with her arms behind her, her feet slightly apart, her face down a little. She was deep-eyed, pensive, and to see her was to be silent, to wait for those downcast lids to lift and break the spell.

Grunty frowned and faltered. He lifted a puzzled gaze from these exquisite renderings to the loverbirds, and met the appeal, the earnest, eager, hopeful faces.

The loverbird put a second paper against the glass.

There were the same three figures, identical in every respect to the previous ones, except for one detail: they were all naked.

He wondered how they knew human anatomy so meticulously.

Before he could react, still another sheet went up.

The loverbirds, this time—the tall one, the shorter one, hand in hand. And next to them a third figure, somewhat similar, but tiny, very round, and with grotesquely short arms.

Grunty stared at the three sheets, one after the other. There was something ... something....

And then the loverbird put up the fourth sketch, and slowly, slowly, Grunty began to understand. In the last picture, the loverbirds were shown exactly as before, except that they were naked, and so was the small creature beside them. He had never seen loverbirds naked before. Possibly no one had.

Slowly he lowered the gun. He began to laugh. He reached through the window and took both the loverbirds' hands in one of his, and they laughed with him.

Rootes stretched easily with his eyes closed, pressed his face down into the couch, and rolled over. He dropped his feet to the deck, held his head in his hands and yawned. Only then did he realize Grunty was standing just before him.

"What's the matter with you?"

He followed Grunty's grim gaze.

The glass door stood open.

Rootes bounced to his feet as if the couch had turned white-hot. "Where—what—"

Grunty's crag of a face was turned to the starboard bulkhead. Rootes spun to it, balanced on the balls of his feet as if he were boxing. His smooth face gleamed in the red glow of the light over the airlock.

"The lifeboat ... you mean they took the lifeboat? They got away?"

Grunty nodded.

Rootes held his head. "Oh, fine," he moaned. He whipped around to Grunty. "And where the hell were you when this happened?"

"Here."

"Well, what in God's name happened?" Rootes was on the trembling edge of foaming hysteria.

Grunty thumped his chest.

"You're not trying to tell me you let them go?"

Grunty nodded, and waited—not for very long.

"I'm going to burn you down," Rootes raged. "I'm going to break you so low you'll have to climb for twelve years before you get a barracks to sweep. And after I get done with you I'll turn you over to the Service. What do you think they'll do to you? What do you think they're going to do to *me*?"

He leapt at Grunty and struck him a hard, cutting blow to the cheek. Grunty kept his hands down and made no attempt to avoid the fist. He stood immovable, and waited.

"Maybe those were criminals, but they were Dirbanu nationals," Rootes roared when he could get his breath. "How are we going to explain this to Dirbanu? Do you realize this could mean war?"

Grunty shook his head.

"What do you mean? You know something. You better talk while you can. Come on, bright boy—what are we going to tell Dirbanu?"

Grunty pointed at the empty cell. "Dead," he said.

"What good will it do us to say they're dead? They're not. They'll show up again some day, and—"

Grunty shook his head. He pointed to the star chart. Dirbanu showed as the nearest body. There was no livable planet within thousands of parsecs.

"They didn't go to Dirbanu!"

"Nuh."

"Damn it, it's like pulling rivets to get anything out of you. In that lifeboat they go to Dirbanu—which they won't—or they head out, maybe for years, to the Rim stars. That's all they can do!"

Grunty nodded.

"And you think Dirbanu won't track them, won't bring 'em down?"

"No ships."

"They have ships!"

"Nuh."

"The loverbirds told you?"

Grunty agreed.

"You mean their own ship that they destroyed, and the one the ambassador used were all they had?"

"Yuh."

Rootes strode up and back. "I don't get it. I don't begin to get it. What did you do it for, Grunty?"

Grunty stood for a moment, watching Rootes' face. Then he went to the computing desk. Rootes had no choice but to follow. Grunty spread out the four drawings.

"What's this? Who drew these? *Them?* What do you know. *Damn!* Who is the chick?"

Grunty patiently indicated all of the pictures in one sweep. Rootes looked at him, puzzled, looked at one of Grunty's eyes, then the other, shook his head, and applied himself to the pictures again. "This is more like it," he murmured. "Wish I'd 'a known they could draw like this." Again Grunty drew his attention to all the pictures and away from the single drawing that fascinated him.

"There's you, there's me. Right? Then this chick. Now, here we are again, all buff naked. Damn, what a carcass. All right, all right, I'm going on. Now, this is the prisoners, right? And who's the little fat one?"

Grunty pushed the fourth sheet over. "Oh," said Rootes. "Here everybody's naked too. Hm."

He yelped suddenly and bent close. Then he rapidly eyed all four sheets in sequence. His face began to get red. He gave the fourth picture a long, close scrutiny. Finally he put his finger on the sketch of the round little alien. "This is ... a ... a Dirbanu—"

Grunty nodded. "Female."

"Then those two—they were—"

Grunty nodded.

"So that's it!" Rootes fairly shrieked with fury. "You mean we been shipped out all this time with a coupla God damned *fairies*? Why, if I'd a' known that I'd a' killed 'em!"

"Yuh."

Rootes looked up at him with a growing respect and considerable amusement. "So you got rid of 'em so's I wouldn't kill 'em and mess everything up?" He scratched his head. "Well, I'll be billy-be-damned. You got a think-tank on you after all. Anything I can't stand, it's a fruit."

Grunty nodded.

"God," said Rootes, "it figures. It really figures. Their females don't look anything like the males. Compared with them, our females are practically identical to us. So the ambassador comes, and sees what looks like a planet full of queers. He knows better but he can't stand the sight. So back he goes to Dirbanu, and Earth gets brushed off."

Grunty nodded.

"Then these pansies here run off to Earth, figuring they'll be at home. They damn near made it, too. But Dirbanu calls 'em back, not wanting the likes of them representing their planet. I don't blame 'em a bit. How would you feel if the only Terran on Dirbanu was a fluff? Wouldn't you want him out of there, but quick?"

Grunty said nothing.

"And now," said Rootes, "we better give Dirbanu the good news."

He went forward to the communicator.

It took a surprisingly short time to contact the shrouded planet. Dirbanu acknowledged and coded out a greeting. The decoder over the console printed the message for them:

GREETINGS STARMITE 439. ESTABLISH ORBIT. CAN YOU DROP PRISONERS TO DIRBANU? NEVER MIND PARACHUTE.

"Whew," said Rootes. "Nice people. Hey, you notice they don't say come on in. They never expected to let us land. Well, what'll we tell 'em about their lavender lads?"

"Dead," said Grunty.

"Yeah," said Rootes. "That's what they want anyway." He sent rapidly.

In a few minutes the response clattered out of the decoder.

STAND BY FOR TELEPATH SWEEP. WE MUST CHECK PRISONERS. MAY BE PRETENDING DEATH.

"Oh-oh," said the Captain. "This is where the bottom drops out."

"Nuh," said Grunty, calmly.

"But their detector will locate—oh—I see what you're driving at. No life, no signal. Same as if they weren't here at all."

"Yuh."

The decoder clattered.

DIRBANU GRATEFUL. CONSIDER MISSION COMPLETE. DO NOT WANT BODIES. YOU MAY EAT THEM.

Rootes retched. Grunty said, "Custom."

The decoder kept clattering.

NOW READY FOR RECIPROCAL AGREEMENT WITH TERRA.

"We go home in a blaze of glory," Rootes exulted. He sent, TERRA ALSO READY. WHAT DO YOU SUGGEST?

The decoder paused, then:

TERRA STAY AWAY FROM DIRBANU AND DIRBANU WILL STAY AWAY FROM TERRA. THIS IS NOT A SUGGESTION. TAKES EFFECT IMMEDIATELY.

"Why that bunch of bastards!"

Rootes pounded his codewriter, and although they circled the planet at a respectful distance for nearly four days, they received no further response.

The last thing Rootes had said before they established the first stasis on the way home was: "Well, anyway—it does me good to think of those two queens crawling away in that lifeboat. Why, they can't even starve to death. They'll be cooped up there for *years* before they get anywhere they can sit down."

It still rang in Grunty's mind as he shook off the blackout. He glanced aft to the glass partition and smiled reminiscently. "For years," he murmured. His words curled up and spun, and said,

> *... Yes; love requires the focal space*
> *Of recollection or of hope,*
> *Ere it can measure its own scope.*
> *Too soon, too soon comes death to show*
> *We love more deeply than we know!*

Dutifully, then, came the words: *Coventry Patmore, born 1823.*

He rose slowly and stretched, revelling in his precious privacy. He crossed to the other couch and sat down on the edge of it.

For a time he watched the Captain's unconscious face, reading it with great tenderness and utmost attention, like a mother with an infant.

His words said, *Why must we love where the lightning strikes, and not where we choose?*

And they said, *But I'm glad it's you, little prince. I'm glad it's you.*

He put out his huge hand, and with a feather touch, stroked the sleeping lips.

Bragg and Minna

Timothy Findley

The most vicious campaign regarding homosexuality and creativity was led by Edmund Bergler, the best-known analytic theorist of homosexuality in the 1950s: "If a homosexual is a great artist, this is so despite, and not because of his homosexuality. In the great artist who is a homosexual, a small autarchic corner has been rescued from the holocaust of illness." Much the same argument was held by the Nazis regarding the genius of Jews and of blacks.

Typologies, whether they classify races, temperaments, sexes, or astrological signs, suggest patterns of behaviour along which certain characters must tread. Typologies demand hierarchies and rules of normality. Anything or anyone that doesn't fit one of a number of set categories is therefore sick or abnormal. The remarkable characteristic of typologies is that, ultimately, even the exceptions must be classified.

In some societies, however, those sufficiently unique—the lunatics, the malformed, the strange in mind or body—are not despised but held as holy. It is thought that their uniqueness is a blessing from the gods, whose touch has spared them the disgrace of the common human lot. All of Timothy Findley's protagonists (Hooker Winslow in The Last of the Crazy People, *Robert Ross in* The Wars, *Hugh Selwyn Mauberley in* Famous Last Words, *Lilah Kemp in* Headhunter) *are exceptions in the society that exiles them. Like the child in "Bragg and Minna", they fit no categories. Their qualities, their defects, surface and vanish and surface again in the narration of their lives, which become, in the eyes of the reader, quietly heroic.*

This is what Minna had written before she died:
Bragg always said we shouldn't have the baby and everything was done a man can do to prevent it. Still, I wanted her and she was born and now I realize I've given birth to all of Bragg's worst fears.

Bragg could see himself walking with the others up the hill—whatever the hill was called—the hill that led to Ku-Ring-Gai. He could see the three men walking upwards and the other two, the man and the woman, waiting on the level where the car was parked. He could see all this with perfect recall—staring down from the Plexiglas window, riding in the 747 high above the Pacific Ocean. All he had to do in order to regain the scene on the hill—or any scene—was turn the memory projector on in his mind and run the film: three men walking up the hill to Ku-Ring-Gai—himself; his lover, Col; and Nob, the sad, mad poet from Sydney who was their guide that afternoon.

The day he was scanning—which was yesterday—had been humid, hot and dusty and the air had been thick with the sound of feeding insects. For whatever reason, the insects themselves could not be seen and Bragg—so appallingly tense to begin with—had begun to extract from their invisibility the sort of menace endured by the blind. He kept on trying to brush the sound of them away from his eyes and he dared not speak for fear he would swallow something deadly.

Everything had gone awry....

(Now, that's a nice old-fashioned phrase, my dear; he thought—in Minna's voice:

There I was, so hot and dry
and everything had gone awry....)

Still, it was true. All or any hope that some happy trace of Minna would emerge from his search had faded completely. What he had wanted was a sign—a signal that he could lay her ghost to rest at Ku-Ring-Gai without a sense of despair. But no such signs or signals had been forthcoming. On the other hand, his search for *Minna memori* had not been without its clues that she had definitely passed that way before him. The signs of her passage had been unmistakable: the red wine spilled on all the rugs, the dirty jokes repeated with all their Minna-twists-and-turns, the dark brown trail of cigarette butts and burns as plain as the bread crumbs scattered by Hansel and Gretel when they entered the deadly wood. So Bragg could say: "I certainly know she's been here"—but all he got in reply was a nod without elaboration. The trouble was that everyone Bragg had interviewed had wanted to protect him from the truth—they didn't want to be the first to spill the beans: as if he didn't know the beans were in the pot.

All this, of course, was part of the usual Minna Joyce conspiracy; the network of spies and allies set up everywhere she went. Long ago Bragg had said that if Minna had chosen to go down into the Antarctic, she could have established a successful branch of the Minna Joyce conspiracy amongst the King penguins. Such was the power of her belief in who she was and in everything she did, no matter the consequence.

Damn the consequence! That was her motto. And damn the mayhem she brought wherever she went and damn the anguish she left behind whenever she went away.

So, now he was carrying Minna's ashes up the hill to Ku-Ring-Gai....

He was watching Nob, "the sad, mad poet from Sydney" (that was a quote from one of Minna's letters), struggling up the path before him, bleeding his gin-soaked perspiration into his dark green shirt. He wondered what it was that Stanley Nob—so undeniably sad, but maybe not so mad—had known about Minna? What had they shared that Nob was refusing to share with Bragg? Had they slept so happily together...? Did he sleep with everyone he met, the way that Minna had? Bragg could so easily make the picture of it: Nob was so damned good looking ... Bragg had wanted him himself. But the picture of himself with Nob was not the picture Bragg was making climbing up the hill. The picture he was making had to do with desperation: maybe the very picture of desperation itself. It was of Nob and Minna sweating—bathed in their mutual sorrow—struggling the way she had struggled with him, with Bragg, against his refusal to give her a child: struggling in behalf of her own determination that he would. *Come on and fuck, you bastard!* she had told him—yelling at him. *Don't you understand? If we don't fuck, we die.*

If we don't fuck, we die.

Another nice old-fashioned phrase, my dear.

Had she known, even then, that she was dying—or was it just the babble of someone driving someone else to climax?

On the hill, Bragg shut his eyes because he didn't want to look any more at Nob's sweating back. It told him the one sure thing he didn't want to know: that Minna had escaped him utterly.

On the plane—which was taking them to San Francisco—there was a washed-out, brazen girl who looked like Janis Joplin. She was wandering up and down the aisles, claiming she was alone but treating all the passengers as if they were her relatives and friends. Bragg could see she was almost totally gone on something—more than likely cocaine—and she kept augmenting whatever it was with swigs of whisky from a so-called can of beer.

Bragg had seen her fill the beer can earlier from a bottle of Chivas Regal she kept amongst some clothing in her bag. The bag was one of those shapeless, woven things they sell in every market-place from Marrakesh to Lima—its colours bleached and blotched from infusions of too much sun and too much dye. When the girl sat down beside him, shaking out her brown frizzy hair, Bragg could smell a whole biography of odours rising from the lumpy shape in her lap: of suntan lotion, hash oil, bourbon and expensive perfume. He noticed the girl held onto the bag as if it were alive and he also noticed that her fingernails were chewed.

"Hey," she said—lifting her black-rimmed Foster Grants high enough for Bragg to see her eyes—"am I sitting here?" She squinted at him, smiling and ingratiating—wincing at the light. Her eyes were like two cracked marbles that might have been green.

"You may be sitting here now," Bragg said, "but not when my friend comes back."

"Oh," the girl said. "You're not alone. Dammit." She seemed to be genuinely disappointed.

"That's right," Bragg told her. "My friend has gone to the washroom."

"You mean he's gone to the head," she said. "On a plane they call it the head. The same as on a ship...."

"I always call it the washroom."

"Oh, the *wash* room," the girl said—making fun of him. "Oh, the *wash* room!" she said. "I have to go to the *wash* room!" She laughed and took another swig from her beer can.

Bragg looked away from her and sat still. He hoped that Col would come back soon and make the girl move on. It wasn't just that she was becoming obnoxious. Bragg could deal with that; he'd certainly had the requisite training. But the girl was beginning to remind him of Minna—the husky voice that wandered up and down the scale—the smell of her perfume, which he knew by now was Opium—and the stench of alcohol. It was unbearable.

Then the girl said: "You know what, mister? You look awful sad. Like someone died."

Bragg didn't utter.

"Me, I'm not allowed to look sad," the girl informed him, trying not to smile. "I'm not allowed to look sad, cause I'm going home now, to be married. In San Francisco." She was silent for a moment and Bragg turned to look at her and then she said: "Is this a smoking section we're sitting in?"

He held up his cigarette so the Janis Joplin girl could see it burning. *Now she's going to ask me for one;* he thought—*and then she'll come back and back and back and ask me over and over for more cigarettes—all the way to San Francisco. That's how she'll trap me. That's how she'll bond me to her: just the way Minna did. And next thing I know, I'll be lifting her luggage off the carousel—arranging for her cab and making sure she gets to her hotel.*

"You got a cigarette?" she asked.

"No," said Bragg. "I haven't. I'm smoking my very last one."

"Oh," the girl said, and she laughed out loud. "You expecting a firing squad or something?" She got up slowly then and went away from him down the aisle.

There was a great solid plain of clouds below them now above the sea, and Bragg could not imagine where they were. The Janis Joplin girl had wandered off in search of another vacant seat—and Bragg had watched her pausing here and there to stare down into someone's face and asking them: "should I be sitting here?"—then moving on. Squinting, he could turn her all too easily into Minna and he could all too easily imagine Minna doing the same thing, re-arranging the passengers to suit herself—except that Minna would have phrased her injunction differently. Minna would have said: "I can't imagine how this has happened ..." smiling, charming, poised for the punch line: "but you're sitting in my seat ..." blowing smoke in her victim's face—"and you'll have to move your ass."

Or, if she was working in her lady-mode: "I wonder if you'd mind...?" And then: "of course, I can have you forcibly removed...."

And she would have had the baby with her; carrying the child for all the world to see on her hip. Minna with Stella, running all the way to Australia, just to escape from Bragg and die in peace.

Or, so he believed.

Colin Marsh and Stuart Bragg had met in Toronto before Bragg's marriage to Minna went on the rocks. But Colin had nothing to do with driving them apart; that was all internal, deep inside the marriage itself and, indeed, so deep that even Bragg and Minna, with all the help of all the psychoanalysts in the world would not have known where to look for the fissures. Some people seek each other out—Col remembered being told—in order to complete a circle. But what we have not been told is that, sometimes the circle being completed is a kind of death trap. We have not been told some people seek each other out in order to be destroyed.

Now, when Col came back they ordered drinks but were otherwise silent. Col was good at feeling out a silence. He could tell, before he put his hands out, where the snakes were going to be.

We are told, Col thought, as he looked at his friend beside him, an awful pack of lies about love. Some big cheese in everyone's life is always handing down some line about people being made for each other, as if the violins would always play: as if Anne Murray would always sing at all the anniversaries. The truth was, no one sang. The only example Col had ever had of anyone getting all the way through to the end intact had been his parents—and they had so many secrets from one another, it had only been their lies that kept them together.

Col looked away and began to scan the covers of the books being read around him. He wondered if any of the books were Bragg's—or Minna's. It was always the strangest feeling when that happened; when he saw, with a start, the cover of one of Bragg's or Minna's books. Strangers, it seemed, were invading his private world—the world at home where the books were written and Bragg leaned over his pages, looking like a giant bug—a beetle by lamplight.

Bragg's room was upstairs—his cabinet, as he liked to call it—though it hadn't any door, but only a curtain. Col used to go up late at night to see if Bragg was ready to go to bed—but the back beneath the lamplight and the cigarette smoke that curled up past the green glass shade were all the signal he needed to go away. Col slept halfway down the hall in a room between Bragg's cabinet and Minna's bedroom. Bragg slept sometimes with one and sometimes the other. Sometimes, he slept in the sunroom—bunched on the wicker couch with Ben, his dog. This was in the house on Collier Street—not the one they lived in now, on Binscarth up in north Rosedale. Minna had refused to live in Rosedale. "Them as live in Rosedale," Minna had said to Col, in her tea-time imitation of Eliza Doolittle, "are them as keep their shit in jars."

My dear.

Col smiled even now, as he thought of Minna's hatred for what she called *ladyhood*. She saw it as the enemy of everything she wanted women to be. It had almost destroyed her—or so she claimed— brought up the way she was, with "a silver spoon in every orifice...." Not that getting rid of them was easy. Minna's life, until she met Bragg and married him, had been a life of inherited privilege mixed with deliberate squalor. She'd gone to live in Parkdale, "my dear— with all its resident rubbies and gentle crazies, dressed in all weathers in their summer coats and woollen mittens and all their hair cut straight across in bangs and all with their tam-o'-shanters pulled down over their ears and their eyes as crafty and innocent all at once as the eyes of bears...." She used to talk like that to Col, when they sat together over her bottles of Côtes-du-Rhône in the kitchen late at night. And she would wave her cigarette as she talked, weaving her images out of smoke, and her voice was hoarse, and Col had defi- nitely fallen in love with her, thought not the way Bragg had fallen in love—not fiercely, as if to be in love was to call up all your anger—but in love the way all men were in love with the made-up women in their minds: those women who never get a chance to come down into the streets and walk around real because once they were real, like Minna, they threw you off balance and blew you away. A boy like Col could be in love with such a woman because he never had to contend with her needs. He only had to watch and listen and pay attention and pour the wine. And Col could do this by the hour.

She told him—more or less in the voice with which she wrote—of how she had moved into Parkdale out of Rosedale after her mother and father had been divorced and each one wanted her to live with them "and do good works." Like marry Harry Connacher and raise two dozen kids—(her mother's version of a good work)—or "use that brain of yours to conquer the real-estate world"—(her father's ver- sion). Minna's version of a good work had been to go and live among the poor—"not only the poor in pocket, but the poor who were in pain and maddened by the same confusion that tampered with me. And you know"—and here, she had burst out laughing—"you know what I discovered? Half the people I was consorting with on Queen Street were *artists*! Artists and actors and poets and playwrights! Novelists, like Bragg. And, oh my God, it suddenly occurred to me that—looking out from the very same pain and madness—the only difference between the schizoids and the artists was articulation. And when I realized that what I had was articulation, I started to write like someone possessed—because I saw so clearly that I had found—*don't laugh*—but I had found, at last, a true good work that I could do with all my heart." Here, Minna sat back and drank a great, long draft of Côtes-du-Rhône and made a kind of doodle on the oilcloth with her fingernail. And when she spoke again, she spoke almost shyly:

"I figure that's the one and maybe the only thing my mom and dad were right about, Col. The doing of good works. It only depends on what a good work is. For me, it's putting an end to all the silence out on Queen Street. It's putting words where no words are and giving articulation to all that noise behind those eyes I'd been watching, innocent and crafty as a bear's...." Then she had looked up and said: "you understand what I'm saying, here?"

Col had said "yes"—that he understood. And, of course, that was precisely what Minna had done with her books: she had given articulation to "all that noise."

Minna's office on Collier Street had been the dining-room and it had french doors with dozens of panes of glass she had painted over with white enamel. No one was allowed inside and she had kept it locked whenever she was working. Given her love of wine and people, Minna had almost phenomenal discipline and she produced much more than Bragg. Bragg was a slow and careful writer, and his books, which some considered to be very, very fine, were rather like etchings on brass over which he laboured long and achingly and hard. One of his favourite quotations came from Flaubert, who said: *I spent the morning putting in a comma—and the afternoon taking it out.* Bragg really did do that. He could spend the whole day writing a single sentence and tear it up before he went to bed. He produced his books at three-year intervals—all of them short and terse—and there were five of them, going on six—the sixth being written, but not to be published until the coming fall. Minna had written eleven books before she died—and there were four in bureau drawers. Not that she'd written with any less care than Bragg, but she'd had a good deal more to tell—and she'd told it with less ambiguity. And this was very much the way she had lived.

Bragg saw that Col had fallen asleep and after he'd ordered a second drink, he tried to sit back and relax. But he couldn't make himself comfortable. The seats had not been made for human beings.

His mind flew around the plane like a bird not knowing where to land. As always, it wanted to avoid the subject of Minna but no matter where it perched, she turned up—somehow—under its claws.

The baby. That was the final bone of contention and the birth of the child had driven them apart.

Bragg had never wanted children. He didn't trust his genes. He even had a theory that "maybe I'm a genetic homosexual." This theory was that, since there had been genetic defects in other generations of his family—clubbed feet—cleft palates—mongoloid children—mental illness—maybe his genes were calling a halt. Maybe his genes were saying: *no more babies.*

Ergo: "what better way than to create a homosexual?"

Minna had stared at him—at first in amusement, then in horror.

"You know who you sound like, don't you? I mean—I trust you know exactly who this sounds like, standing here talking in our living-room on Collier Street?"

Bragg gave two or three blinks—his way of trying to call up words when the words wouldn't come.

"No," he said. "I don't know who it sounds like."

"Hitler," said Minna. "Adolf Fucking Hitler!"

She took an explosive drag on her cigarette and almost drowned herself in wine by drinking it too quickly.

Bragg was amazed and confused all at once.

"I don't think I quite understand," he said. "You mean that because I think I may be a genetic homosexual, that makes me like Adolf Hitler?"

"Yes!" she shouted.

Bragg sat down.

"You'll have to explain," he said. "I'm not quite up to this."

"You've heard, I trust, of the Master Race?"

"Of course I have."

"Well—think about it! Think what Hitler was willing to do in order to achieve it. Think what he *did*! My dear, he would have loved it if you'd come along and spouted your genetic homosexual nonsense." She looked at him and leaned down into his face before she spoke again. "You're playing right into his hands, Bragg! You're playing right into the hands of every goddamned maniac who thinks he can line up the human race and cull it by its genes. Blue eyes here and brown eyes over there!"

"It was only a theory, Minna. You don't have to get so excited."

"YOU ARE NOT A GENETIC HOMOSEXUAL, GOD DAMN IT! THERE IS NO SUCH THING AS A GENETIC HOMOSEXUAL!"

She stood in the middle of the room and virtually screamed this at him.

It frightened him.

Didn't she understand? He was trying to save her from giving birth to monsters.

"MAYBE WHAT I WANT IS MONSTERS!" she yelled.

Bragg could believe this.

Then she said—very quietly—folding her hands before her: "at least the monsters would be ours." And when she lifted her head, she was crying.

Bragg stood up and put his arms around her and took her back to the sofa where he poured her another glass of wine and held out her box of cigarettes and sat down beside her.

"I'm frightened," he said. "I can't have children."

Minna sniffed and blew her nose half-heartedly on a wad of yellow Facelle she'd found behind the pillows.

"I'll kick Col out of the house," she told him. "I'll kick Col out of the house and I'll cut your balls off...."

Good. She was laughing.

But she wasn't laughing. She was crying again and trying to speak:

"I'm thirty-eight years old," she said. "In another year it will be too late. I love you, Bragg, and you love me. The only thing that matters, having children, is that those who have them love one another...."

"Oh, come off it," Bragg said. "Don't pull that one on me. Adolf Hitler's parents loved one another."

"But I want a baby."

"Have one. Be my guest."

"You bastard! How dare you say that? I don't want anyone's baby. I want yours. I want yours. I want it to be ours."

"I'm sorry," said Bragg. "I really am sorry. The answer is no."

They sat there—holding one another's hands—sipping their wine and smoking their cigarettes, each one plotting through the twilight how they would thwart the other.

In the long run, Minna won.

Stella was born on a rainy day in autumn.

Bragg took Minna down to the Wellesley Hospital and he and Col sat out in the waiting room. Col read magazines. Bragg went mad.

Minna was in labour twenty-two hours. At one point, the doctor came and asked Bragg's permission to administer an anaesthetic. Minna had refused it—but the pain was terrible.

Bragg said: no—that if Minna wanted the anaesthetic she would ask for it. She knew what she was doing and she hadn't wanted drugs and she hadn't wanted Bragg to be in the delivery room. Everything was being done the way she wanted it and Bragg was not going to interfere.

"I'm sorry," said the doctor. "She's really in very bad and quite unnecessary pain." And then he went away.

Two hours later, he came back into the room.

Bragg didn't have to ask. He was sure that Minna was dead. Either Minna was dead or the child was dead; or both. The doctor's face was full of all this possible information.

"Your wife will be fine," the doctor said. "She had a very bad time, but she'll be fine. She's a strong, resilient woman."

Suddenly, the doctor sat down in one of the leather chairs. He pushed back his surgeon's cap and did the unthinkable: he lighted a cigarette. He noticed both Col and Bragg had watched him do this in disbelief. He smiled and waved the cigarette in the air and said to them brightly: "I also drink and drive."

Bragg, who had been standing, sat down. Colin went over to the window and watched the rain.

"I'm waiting for the bad news, doctor," said Bragg. "It's obvious you've come to tell me something has gone wrong. The child," he said, "is the child alive?"

"Yes," said the doctor. "The child is alive. You have a girl—and your wife has already said she wants to call her Stella."

"That means star," said Col.

"Indeed, sir. Yes—it does. Stella means star."

The doctor sat far back in his chair and put both his hands on its arms. He began to pick obsessively at the leather under his right thumb.

"Well?" said Bragg.

The doctor took a drag on his cigarette and regarded what his thumb nail had accomplished in terms of wrecking the arm of the chair. "Your daughter...." he began. "Stella...."

"Yes?"

"She has six fingers on each hand. She has six toes on each foot."

Bragg lay back against the sofa—stared at the ceiling and put his hand across his mouth. He didn't utter a word.

After a moment, the doctor stood up and crushed his cigarette underfoot. Then he said: "I'm afraid that isn't all."

Bragg crouched and waited.

Col was wishing that he hadn't come.

"There's brain damage, too. Not anyone's fault. Just one of those things a person can't foresee. I warned your wife...."

"I warned her, too," said Bragg.

But the doctor didn't seem to hear him. He went right on talking. "There's always a danger with the mother past the age of thirty-five. I told her that—warned her. But—" He threw up his empty hands. "—who listens any longer?" Then he said: "I repeat. She's a strong, resilient woman and she will recover."

"What about the baby?" Bragg asked. "Will the baby recover?"

"Stella," the doctor informed him, "will not recover. Of course she will not recover. No one with half a brain can recover, Mister Bragg. Your daughter, I'm afraid, is doomed. I'm sorry."

Before he left, the doctor turned at the door and said: "You can come and see me any time you want—but not today. I've just spent thirty-six hours on my feet and I'm going home, now, to die."

He was gone.

Col said: "what can I do for you?"

Bragg said: "you can take me home and let me screw you to the wall."

Later on, Bragg went into the ravine along Rosedale Valley Road and he walked in the mud. Coming to an open space, he found a fallen tree and he sat in the rain and let the weather have its way.

Six months later, Minna discovered she had inoperable cancer of the lung.

She hung around the house for several days and played with Stella. Bragg said nothing. He'd hardly said a word since Stella was born. All he did was pretend to write.

Finally, Minna came up the stairs one day—it was early summer now—and she was carrying Stella the way she always did, against her hip.

"I'm going to leave you, Bragg," she said.

Bragg set down his pen and put one hand against his temple to support his head. With the other hand, he turned out the lamp.

He sat on the bed and watched her for what seemed hours while she packed. He memorized her face and the way she moved and he memorized her smell.

"Where in Australia?" he asked her.

"I don't know. I've never been there. Probably Sydney. They say it's quite civilized."

"Go where the doctors are good—that's all that matters," he said. "Just be sure you end up somewhere where the doctors are good."

"Soon as I know where we're going to be, I'll write."

"What about Stella—after you ...?"

"Die? Not to worry. I'm determined I'm going to find her somebody desperate as me to love her and I'll leave her there."

Bragg could only think that Minna was crazy: mad. How could a sane person speak so blithely of "finding somebody desperate as me" to take in a child who was doomed to be a baby all her life? He wanted to yell at her; forbid her to go. He wanted to turn the police and the courts and ten thousand social workers onto her case and have her restrained. But how could a man do that to someone like Minna? All Minna wanted was to do good works in love.

In the long run—judging from the myriad of sources stamped on all her cards and letters—Minna had taken the whole of Australia to be her safe, good place: *almost as rewarding,* as she wrote to Col, *as taking up residence in Parkdale.*

She was a faithful, if somewhat spotty correspondent. Weeks could go by without a word. She was in Brisbane; she was in Cairns; she was in Adelaide; she was in Perth. At the end, she was in Sydney. And in all these places, she walked with Stella on her hip and in all these places she made what she herself called a raft of friends, though none—as she confessed to Bragg—as desperate as she for Stella's love. Still, this did not deter her. Right until the very last month, she was on her feet and walking.

One time, she wrote to Bragg and said: *I wonder if I ever told you why I called her Stella. Not for the sky-stars, my dear, but for the stars she holds in her fists: the six-pointed stars of Stella's hands.*

Another time, she wrote and said: *six fingers bad—five fingers good. That ring a bell? Get out your* Animal Farm *and read. We've been bamboozled far too long into accepting there can be no acceptance for those of us with four legs.*

Finally, she wrote and said: *I may have them here in Sydney. Childless as you and me for all those years—and they love her, Bragg. Their names are Viv and Charlie Roeback—comfortable as two old shoes. Charlie looks like Sidney Greenstreet playing Doctor Johnson. Viv looks like a mountain moved by faith. And they love her, Bragg. They love her....*

Thank God, however, they did not—apparently—love her desperately. So, at least, they appeared to be realists.

It was only in the last of all the letters, written just before the cancer and its necessary regimen of heavy, incapacitating drugs finally forced her to lay down her pen, that Minna mentioned Nob—*the sad, mad poet of Sydney*—with whom she had shared a house before she went into the hospital to die. *He's a great, tall, crazy man who spent some time in an asylum for depression,* she wrote. *Just my type. Tell Col he writes about the noises in behind the eyes of bears; he'll understand. I'll always love you, Bragg—but I love this man a little, too. I'm even going to be cruel enough to say—because I have to, don't I, tell the truth? Crazy Stan Nob would have given me a dozen babies— drop of a hat, Bragg. Drop of a hat. Farewell.*

And that was all.

The next letter came from Viv and Charlie Roeback, saying that Minna was dead and they had Stella, safe and sound.

When they got to Sydney, it was Charlie Roeback who met them. Bragg had never seen a man so large. It required, in the restaurant, two chairs side by side to hold him.

Bragg and Col had come down slowly from Cairns to Brisbane to Sydney, taking their time to seek out all those others Minna had cultivated: the Minna Joyce Conspiracy. They also took the time to stare at the hordes of rosella birds and cockatoos and cockatiels and the wading ibis and the jabirus and the tiny, crazy peaceful doves, no longer than a box of cigarettes. In a zoo, when they saw a duck-billed platypus, Col remained silent. All he could think of was Minna, shouting at Bragg in the living-room below him: MAYBE I WANT TO GIVE BIRTH TO MONSTERS!

And now they were in Sydney, where they had come to say good-bye to Stella and to scatter Minna's ashes on the heights at Ku-Ring-Gai.

Bragg, in the aeroplane above the Pacific, approaching San Francisco, turned on the memory projector again in his mind and rolled the film.

Three men walking up the hill, and down at the bottom Viv and Charlie Roeback waiting by the car with Stella lying in the shade.

Stanley Nob's sweating green back had reached the top and he was turning this way and that with shaded eyes to see where they must go.

Bragg, arriving out of breath, could hardly stand up straight he was so out of shape. He clutched the box of Minna's ashes to his breast and patted it reassuringly several times. "It's all right, now," he said. "We're here."

Stretching out before them and receding through the shimmering dust and heat, a great plateau of rock surrounded them on every side. Stone waves rolled beneath them, dizzy-making if you looked too far afield.

"I think," said Nob, "it's over that way where she wants to be scattered." And he began to walk away from them, making for a place unseen beyond the low-lying scrub that was everywhere in evidence.

Bragg and Col set out to follow him, but almost at once, Col stopped in his tracks and pointed down at the rocks.

"Look," he said. "Petroglyphs."

And, indeed, there were. Rock carvings—deep incisions—God knew how old, of beasts and fish and birds.

And men.

"What are these, Nob?" Col asked.

Nob called back: "the Aborigines put them there. We don't really know just when—but long before the white men came."

The patterns were all quite similar. As Bragg and Col went forward over the rock face in Nob's direction, they encountered, over and over, the shapes of turtles, birds and sometimes snakes. The "beasts" turned out to be giant platypus. And everywhere, in a context with the animals—or totems—there were etchings of stick men and women—the sexes plainly and even grotesquely limned with oversize phalluses and breasts.

One feature ran consistently with the rest. There was always a moon—though never full. This moon was always in its quarter phase and it always shone in the sky directly above the figures of the men and women.

"Over here!" Nob cried. "I've found it."

What Nob had found was a curious variation on all the other petroglyphs.

For sure, the snakes and the birds and the turtles and the platypus were all in evidence—just as the moon and two stick figures, male and female were equally in evidence. But here, there was also another figure—of a kind that had not appeared before. It was a human figure— of a kind that had not appeared before. It was a human figure— yes—but not at all the same as the others near which it had been carved.

This human figure had long flowing hair—and the way it had been carved, with multiple streaks and lines, the hair appeared to be white and possibly the hair of an albino. One arm was stretched out sideways, one arm was held down flat against the figure's side. One leg was longer than the other—and the shorter leg was resting on a sort of triangular shoe, or little box.

"What does it mean?" Bragg asked—expecting Nob to answer with assurance.

But—"nobody knows," said Nob. "There's been all kinds and every sort of conjecture. Most archaeologists think it's a shaman figure—maybe a witch. It's female, at any rate."

Bragg looked down at the magical figure cut at his feet and a curious, worrying noise set up in his mind: a kind of racket, like a buzzsaw carving trees.

Nob said: "this is where she wanted to be scattered. Just here over these figures and in the sky."

He turned away—and so did Col as Bragg undid the hook that held the lid in place. Before he opened the lid, he kissed the box and then he withdrew Minna's ashes handful by handful and threw them like an offering upon the stones.

The plane was now approaching San Francisco and Bragg could see the Janis Joplin girl going into one of the washrooms or—as she would say—the head. The sight of her, so Minna-like, was jarring since he'd just finished scattering Minna's ashes in his mind.

Col said: "twenty minutes and we're there."

Bragg wasn't sure he wanted that.

He could see the great grey fog that lay above the city and he thought of all the men and women living in its shadow. Here was a city, he thought, that once was the symbol of all the bright hope in the Western world. And now it was a city gripped by terror, numbed with the shock of AIDS.

We have probably come to the end, for all we know—Bragg thought—of human congress. Certainly, it marked the end of human passion as it affected homosexuals—and, more and more, it affected everyone.

All his life, he'd been taught that he was an outcast—part of a scourge upon mankind. All the offshoots of this thinking had always seemed, to Bragg, to be so ridiculous and paranoid, he'd never paid attention. Now, there were people down in that city who were dying because of sex.

He tried not to dwell on this and he put it aside.

The Janis Joplin girl came out of the head and she was barely recognizable. Somehow, she had managed a magical transformation and the cotton shirt and the frizzy hair had been replaced with a neat, black dress and a chignon. She was, in fact, quite beautiful and appeared to be serene about the prospect before her. "I'm going home, now, to be married," she had said. "And I'm not allowed to be sad...."

All at once, Bragg went racing back in his mind to the very first day he'd realized he was in love with Minna Joyce. She, too, had worn a neat, black dress and had put her air up thus. How long ago this was, it hardly mattered. Ten years: twelve. How wonderful she was—had been—would always be, stepping forward into their lives together with so much confidence and joy.

Dear God, he thought. I know now why she wanted her ashes scattered there at Ku-Ring-Gai. It was the joy and the liveliness—the sense of endless celebration that clung to all the figures in the rock. And the figures where the shaman stood—the very place where Minna's ashes fell....

It was not a shaman at all.

He knew it, now, as surely as Minna must have known it the minute she encountered the crazy figure cut in the rock so utterly and absolutely unlike all the others.

It was a child. A child. The child of the two stick figures rejoicing by its side beneath the moon. And the child had long, albino hair and one six-fingered hand stretched out for all the world to see forever— and it stood on one good leg and one short leg, for which her parents had made a loving box. Forever. And forever visible.

A shiver went down his back. And he knew right then, as he waited to debark the plane, that he would return to Ku-Ring-Gai with Stella on his shoulder. Or his hip.

La Chance Existe

Helen Garner

*Gay fiction abounds with personal narratives of "coming out".
Rivalled in popularity only by tales of sexual initiation, these stories
define a crucial moment in gay life when a character identifies himself
as a political being by declaring a sexual preference outside the norm
defined by prejudice. Perhaps, for the typical straight character, experiencing sexual initiation and claiming a sexual identity are so concurrent
that they can be contained in one single story. For the gay protagonist—
like the narrator in Helen Garner's story—the deliberation and the
mustering of courage necessitate a second, distinct chapter of chroni-
cling as the character prepares to embrace the identity of a political
minority.*

*But fictional characters, like the rest of us, embody a mixture of
inclinations, and sexual preference is far more fluid than the catego-
rizers allow. In fiction, at least, a handful are permitted the freedom of
Virgina Woolf's Orlando, drifting from one sex to the other across the
ages. Certain characters are able to experience a simultaneous multiplicity of pleasures, such as the fortunate inhabitants of Ursula K. Le
Guin's* The Left Hand of Darkness. *The protagonist of André Pieyre de
Mandiargues' "The Astragalus" falls, during an erotic encounter, into a
reverie in which she is not only a woman and a man, but also the
animals of the forest, the trees, the stones, and ultimately the sky itself.
To this list, Helen Garner, one of Australia's finest explorers of the
complexities of human intimacy, adds the gentle narrator in "La
Chance Existe", tentatively moving along the shifting terrain of an all-
embracing erotic experience.*

I am the kind of person who always gets stopped at Customs. Julie
says it's because I can't keep my eyes still. "You look as if you're constantly checking the whereabouts of the exits," she said. She'll never

really trust me again, I suppose. It shits me but I can't blame her. I love her, that's all, and I feel like serving her.

When we got to Boulogne we had to hang around for three hours waiting for the ferry because of a strike on the other side. I would have sat in a café and read *Le Monde*, but Julie wanted to walk round and look at things, seeing she'd only been in France a couple of days. Her French was hopeless and she was too proud to try. When I met her plane at Orly she was already agitated about not being able to understand. We went straight to a bar in the airport and she insisted on ordering. The waiter, tricked by her good accent, made a friendly remark which seemed to require an answer: her face went rigid with panic and she turned away. The waiter shrugged and went back behind the counter. She hit the table with her fist and groaned between clenched teeth. "It's pathetic! I should be able to! I'm not stupid!"

"For Christ's sake, woman," I said. "You've only been in the country fifteen minutes. What do you *want* from yourself?"

Boulogne was dismal, as I had predicted. I kept telling her we should go south, down to Italy where she'd never been, but she had to go to London, she said, to meet this bloke she'd fallen in love with just before she left Australia. He was coming after her, she was dying to see him again. She fell in love with this guy, who was a musician, because at a gig she found him between sets sitting by himself in a sort of booth thing reading a book called *The Meaning of Meaning*. She told me he was extremely thin. It sounded like a disaster to me. Love will not survive a channel crossing, I pointed out, let alone the thirty-six hours from Melbourne to London. But I was so glad to be with her again, and she wasn't listening.

We walked, in our Paris boulevard shoes, over the lumpy cobbles of Boulogne. We found a huge archway which led on to a beaten dirt track that curved round the outside of the old city, at the foot of its high walls. Julie was excited. "It's old! It must have been trying to be impregnable!" The track was narrow. "Single file, Indian style," she chanted, charging ahead of me.

It was eleven o'clock on a weekday morning in July, and there was no-one about. A nippy breeze came up off the channel. The water was grey and disturbed, a sea of shivers.

We tramped along merrily for twenty minutes, round the shoulder of the hill the old city stood on, turning back now and then to look at the view. The track became narrower.

"Let's go back," I said. "You can't see the sea round this side. It stinks."

"Not yet. Look. What are those caravans down there?"

"I dunno. Gypsies or something. Come on, Julie."

She pressed on. The track was hardly a track at all: it was brambly, and was obviously about to run out against a wing of a castle about a hundred yards ahead. I was ten steps behind her when she gave a sharp cry of disgust and stopped dead. I caught up with her. There was a terrible smell, of shit and things rotting. At her feet was the mangled corpse of a large bird: it looked as if it had been torn to bits. Its head was a yard away from its neck, half its beak had been wrenched off, and there were dirty feathers everywhere, stuck in the spiky bushes, fluttering in the seawind. The shit was human. Its shapes were man-made; it was meat-eater's shit, foul.

We looked at each other. The murder was fresh. In the crisp breeze the feathers on the creature's breast riffled and subsided like an expensive haircut. It was very quiet up there.

"Someone's looking at us from one of those caravans," said Julie without moving her lips. "This is their shitting place. It's their fucking dunny. They must be laughing at us." She gave a high-pitched giggle, pushed past me, and ploughed away through the prickly bushes, back the way we'd come.

Back amongst houses, we stood at the top of an alley in the depths of which two little boys were engaged in a complicated, urgent game with a ball and a piece of rope. One dropped his end in annoyance and walked away. The other, who had glasses and a fringe and a white face, sang out after him, in a voice clear enough for even Julie to understand.

"La chance exis—te!"

"What a sophisticated remark," said Julie.

On the boat, when it finally turned up, we didn't even have the money for a drink. The sky and the sea were grey. The line between them tilted this way and that.

"Will it be rough?" said Julie. "What if I spew?"

"You won't spew. We'll walk around and talk to each other. I'll keep your mind off your stomach."

My glasses are the kind that are supposed to adapt automatically to the intensity of the light, but they failed to go clear again when we went down into the inside part of the ship. Cheap rubbish. The downstairs part was badly lit. I hate going back to England. I hate being able to understand everything that's going on around me. I miss that feeling of your senses having to strain an inch beyond your skin that you get in places where people aren't speaking your language.

Julie darted down the stairs and grabbed a couple of seats. We got out books and kicked our bags under the little table. On the wall near us was the multi-lingual sign warning passengers about the danger of rabies and the fines you get. Julie knelt up on her seat and read it with interest.

"Rabies. What's that in French. *La rage.* Ha. You don't have to be a dog to die of *that.*"

Julie is suspicious, and full of disgust. When she laughs you see that one of her back teeth is missing on the left side. If she chooses you she loves you fiercely, lashes you if you fail yourself. A faint air of contempt hangs about her even when she's in good spirits. She says she's never going home. Everyone always says that when they first get here.

She flung herself round into the seat. "I saw Lou just before I left Melbourne," she said. "I told him I'd be seeing you. He laughed. He said, '*That* fuckin' little poofter!'" She glanced sideways.

"News travels fast." I knew that's what Lou would have said. It made me tired. He could do the dope and the bum cheques on his own now. I took a breath and went in at the deep end.

"When I first got here," I said, "I knew I was going to have to do something. That's what I came for. I used to walk around Paris all night, looking for men and running away from them. For example. One night I was in the metro. It was packed and I was standing up holding on to one of those vertical chrome poles. A boy got on at Clignancourt. He squeezed through the crowd to the pole.

"He wasn't looking at me, but I could feel him—I might've been imagining it, but warmth passed between us. I was burning all down one side. My heart was thumping. His hand on the pole was so close to my mouth I could have kissed it. The train was swaying, all the people were swaying, and I edged my hand up the pole till it was almost touching his. I felt sick, I wanted to touch him so much. I could smell his skin. I thought I was going to pass out. Then at the next stop he calmly let go of the pole and pushed through the crowd and got off."

Julie put her feet up on the low table between us and folded her arms round her legs and laid her head sideways on her knees. She was having trouble controlling her mouth. "What's your favourite name of a metro station?" she said.

"What? I don't know. Trocadéro."

"Mine's Château d'Eau."

"Ever been up on top of that station? You'd hate it. It's not safe for women."

"Remember that time you shat on my green Lois Lane jacket?"

"It was an accident! I had diarrhoea!"

"You were so busy looking at yourself in the mirror you didn't know you were standing on my clothes."

"The dry cleaner got it off! Why do you have to remind me?"

"'It's dog mess,' you said to the lady at the dry cleaner. Dog *mess*." She gave a snort of laughter.

"It came off, anyway." I opened the newspaper and rattled it.

"Being homosexual must mean something," she said. "What happens? Is everything possible?"

"How do you mean?" Was she going to ask me what we did? I'd tell her. I'd tell her anything.

"I mean, if both of you have the same equipment does that mean it's more equal? Do people fall into habits of fucking or being fucked? Or does everyone do everything?"

"It's not really all that different," I said, feeling shy but trying to be helpful. "Not when you're in a relationship, anyway."

"Oh." She looked disappointed, and stared out the porthole at the grey sky and the grey water. Her cardigan sleeves were pushed up to her elbows and I could see the mist of blond hairs that fogged her skin. Her legs were downy like that, too. We can wear each other's clothes. She's the same height as me, with slightly more cowboy-like hips: light passes between the tops of her thighs.

"I never want to fuck with anyone unless it puts me in danger," she said suddenly. "I don't mean physical. I mean unless there's a chance they'll make me sad."

"Break your heart."

"I'll never get married. Or even live with anyone again, probably."

"What about shithead? The bass player? Isn't that why we're making this fucking trip?"

"Are you afraid of getting old?" she said in a peculiar voice.

"My hair's starting to recede." I pulled it back off my forehead to show her.

"Oh, bullshit. What are you, twenty-five? Look at your little round forehead. A pretty little globe."

"And I'm getting hairs on my back," I said, "like my father." I didn't mention that I twist round in front of the bathroom mirror with the tweezers in my hand.

"Can't we afford one drink and share it?" she said.

"No. We have to get the bus to Rowena's."

"Last week," she said, her head still on her knees, "I was in the Louvre. I was upstairs, heading along one of the main galleries. I saw this young bloke sitting on a bench with a little pack on his back. He was about your age, English I'd say. He looked tired, and lonely, and he gave me a look. I wanted to go and sit next to him and say, 'Will we go and have a cup of coffee? Or talk to each other?' But I was too ... I kept walking and went down the steps to the room where all those Rubens paintings are, of Louis Whichever-it-was and Marie de Medici. I stayed in there for ten minutes walking round, and I hated the paintings, they made me feel like spewing—all those pursed-up little mouths smirking. I went back up the steps and the boy was gone."

The boat heaved on towards Folkestone.

"Why is it so hard to talk about sex?" she said, almost in tears. "Every time you think you're close to saying what you mean, your mind just veers away from it, and you say something that's not quite the point."

What would they know here about summer? The wind was sharp. People in the queue had blue lips. I was stopped before we got anywhere near Customs, this time by a smart bastard in plain clothes who was cruising up and down the bedraggled line of tourists with passports in their hands.

"His *jacket*," muttered Julie. It was orange and black houndstooth. "My God. What's happened to this country?"

"Don't get me started on that subject." I stood still and proffered my bag. Some look must appear on my face in their presence, or maybe it's the smell of fear they say dogs can pick up. He was nasty in that bored way; idle malice. No point getting hot under the collar. While he rooted through our bags, and Julie stood with her arms folded and her chin up and her eyes far away over his garish shoulder, he asked her an impertinent question.

"How long've you known this feller?"

"I beg your pardon?"

"I said, how long've you known this feller you're travelling with?"

You can't take that tone to a woman these days. "What's that got to do with you?" said Julie.

He stopped rummaging and looked up at her, with one of her shirts in his hand. God, she still had that old pink thing with the mended collar. He narrowed his eyes and let his slot of a mouth drop open half an inch. Here's a go, he was thinking. I kicked her ankle. She reached out, took the pink shirt and said, folding it as skilfully as a salesgirl in Georges, "Six years or so. Nice jacket. Is that Harris?"

He wasn't quite stupid enough to answer. He shoved the pink shirt back in among the other garments and walked away. Our bags stood unzipped, sprouting private objects.

On the train to London I read and she stared at people. At Leicester Square we ran down the stairs into the tube. I caught the eye of a good-looking boy who was coming up. I turned to look back at him as he passed and she slashed me across the face with her raincoat. The zip got me near the eye.

"What did you—" I yelled.

She was laughing furiously. "You should have seen the look on your face."

"What look?"

"Like *this*." She pulled a face: mouth half-open, eyes rolling up and to one side, like a dim-witted whore.

In the basement room we were supposed to keep the wooden shutters closed because Rowena said there was a prowler who stood up on the windowsill. But the room was dim and stuffy. I took off my clothes, then slid the window up and shoved open the top half of the slatted shutter. Julie whipped off her dress and stared at me.

"You still look like a little goat," she said. "Pan, up on his hind legs."

I got under the sheet. "Come on. Let's go to sleep."

"I'm all speeded up. I'm looking for something to read."

"Well, don't rustle the pages all night." I turned on my side and closed my eyes. When she got into the bed she hardly weighed it down at all.

"Talk to me," she said behind me.

I flipped over on to my back and saw she was lying there with her hands under her head. "What'll I say?"

"Do you get just as miserable as you used to when you were straight?"

"Are you kidding?"

She shifted so that the sides of our legs touched lightly, all the way down. "Come on. Talk."

"Maybe more miserable," I said. "It's all real now. Before, I was in a dream for years, even when I was with you. Everything was blurred and messy. Now I know exactly what I want, and I also know I'll never get it."

"Oh hell."

"What?"

"What *do* you want?"

"Everything. I want to love some man forever and at the same time I want to fuck everyone I see. Some days I could fuck trees. Lamp posts! Dogs! The air!"

She whistled a little tune, and laughed.

"In the Tuileries," I said, "there is a powdery white dust."

"What else?"

"It's a cruising place at night. Not that part with the rows of trees, they lock that. The part between the gates and the Maillol statues. I love it."

"Why?"

"It's like a dance. It's mysterious. People move together and apart, no-one speaks, everyone's faceless. It's terrifically exciting, and grace-ful. The point of it is nothing to do with who."

Her face was quite calm, her eyes raised to the ceiling. Turning my head I could see pale freckles, a gold sleeper, a series of tiny parallel cracks in her lower lip. The skin of her leg felt very much alive to me, almost humming with life.

"Once," she said, "I was coming down that narrow winding stair-case in one of the towers of Notre Dame. Two American blokes were coming down behind me, and I heard one of them say, 'Hey! This is *steep*! My depth perception is shot already!'"

We rolled towards each other and into each other's arms. I pushed myself against her belly, pushed my face into her neck and she took me in her arms, in her legs. I cooled myself on her. Her limbs were as strong as mine. Her face hung over me and blurred in the dim room. I could smell her open flesh, she smelled like metal, salty. I swam into her and we fucked, so slow I could have fainted. She turned over and lay on her back on me; I was in her from behind and had my hand on her cunt from above as if it were my own, my arm holding her.

And then under the hum and murmur of breathing I heard the soft thump of the man's foot against the closed lower half of the shutter. Fingers gripped the edge and a head floated in silhouette, fuzzy against the glimmer of the garden. My skin opened to welcome him.

Divorce in Naples

William Faulkner

In his Nobel Prize acceptance speech, William Faulkner defined as ephemeral and doomed any story that did not partake of the "old verities" of the heart: "love and honor and pity and pride and compassion and sacrifice." And he explored these universal truths best through the social relationships within the families of his imaginary Yoknapatawpha County, Mississippi. Each of these families is a society in embryo, each is a kind of native soil in which the old verities are either nurtured or twisted by parental affections and blood ties. For Faulkner, these contorted families define laws that operate within their households, and then apply these laws to the world outside. Hatred between father and son is carried on into larger forms of disloyalty; opposition between brothers and sisters becomes exploitation of peers and rivalry between friends. The heart of these trusts and betrayals lies in the relationship between husband and wife.

In "Divorce in Naples", Faulkner takes his explorations outside the family traditions of Yoknapatawpha County, to the closed world of a ship and its clan of sailors. In this very different place, the relationship is never specifically identified, as if its protagonists lack the words to define it. What matters, Faulkner seems to say, is not the specific sexual nature of these bonds, but the fact that here, too, the same old verities must find expression.

I

We were sitting at a table inside: Monckton and the bosun and Carl and George and me and the women, the three women of that abject glittering kind that seamen know or that know seamen. We were talking English and they were not talking at all. By that means they could speak constantly to us above and below the sound of our voices in a tongue older than recorded speech and time too. Older than the thirty-four days of sea time which we had but completed, anyway. Now and then they spoke to one another in Italian. The women in Italian, the men in English, as if language might be the sex difference, the functioning of the vocal cords the inner biding until the dark pairing time. The men in English, the women in Italian: a decorum as of two parallel streams separated by a levee for a little while.

We were talking about Carl, to George.

"Why did you bring him here, then?" the bosun said.

"Yes," Monckton said. "I sure wouldn't bring my wife to a place like this."

George cursed Monckton: not with a word or even a sentence; a paragraph. He was a Greek, big and black, a full head taller than Carl; his eyebrows looked like two crows in overlapping flight. He cursed us all with immediate thoroughness and in well-nigh faultless classic Anglo-Saxon, who at other times functioned in the vocabulary of an eight-year-old by-blow of a vaudeville comedian and a horse, say.

"Yes, sir," the bosun said. He was smoking an Italian cigar and drinking ginger beer; the same tumbler of which, incidentally, he had been engaged with for about two hours and which now must have been about the temperature of a ship's showerbath. "I sure wouldn't bring my girl to a dive like this, even if he did wear pants."

Carl meanwhile had not stirred. He sat serene among us, with his round yellow head and his round eyes, looking like a sophisticated baby against the noise and the glitter, with his glass of thin Italian beer and the women murmuring to one another and watching us and then Carl with that biding and inscrutable foreknowledge which they do not appear to know that they possess. "*Èinnocente*," one said; again they murmured, contemplating Carl with musing, secret looks. "He may have fooled you already," the bosun said. "He may have slipped through a porthole on you any time these three years."

George glared at the bosun, his mouth open for cursing. But he didn't curse. Instead he looked at Carl, his mouth still open. His mouth closed slowly. We all looked at Carl. Beneath our eyes he raised his glass and drank with contained deliberation.

"Are you still pure?" George said. "I mean, sho enough."

Beneath our fourteen eyes Carl emptied the glass of thin, bitter, three per cent beer. "I been to sea three years," he said. "All over Europe."

George glared at him, his face baffled and outraged. He had just shaved; his close blue jowls lay flat and hard as a prizefighter's or a pirate's, up to the black explosion of his hair. He was our second cook. "You damn lying little bastard," he said.

The bosun raised his glass of ginger beer with an exact replica of Carl's drinking. Steadily and deliberately, his body thrown a little back and his head tilted, he poured the ginger beer over his right shoulder at the exact speed of swallowing, still with that air of Carl's, that grave and cosmopolitan swagger. He set the glass down, and rose. "Come on," he said to Monckton and me, "let's go. Might as well be board ship if we're going to spend the evening in one place."

Monckton and I rose. He was smoking a short pipe. One of the women was his, another the bosun's. The third one had a lot of gold teeth. She could have been thirty, but maybe she wasn't. We left her with George and Carl. When I looked back from the door, the waiter was just fetching them some more beer.

II

They came into the ship together at Galveston, George carrying a portable victrola and a small parcel wrapped in paper bearing the imprint of a well-known ten-cent store, and Carl carrying two bulging imitation leather bags that looked like they might weigh forty pounds apiece. George appropriated two berths, one above the other like a Pullman section, cursing Carl in a harsh, concatenant voice a little overburred with *v*'s and *r*'s and ordering him about like a nigger, while Carl stowed their effects away with the meticulousness of an old maid, producing from one of the bags a stack of freshly laundered drill serving jackets that must have numbered a dozen. For the next thirty-four days (he was the messboy) he wore a fresh one for each meal in the saloon, and there were always two or three recently washed ones drying under the poop awning. And for thirty-four evenings, after the galley was closed, we watched the two of them in pants and undershirts, dancing to the victrola on the after well deck above a hold full of Texas cotton and Georgia resin. They had only one record for the machine and it had a crack in it, and each time the needle clucked George would stamp on the deck. I don't think that either one of them was aware that he did it.

It was George who told us about Carl. Carl was eighteen, from Philadelphia. They both called it Philly; George in a proprietorial tone, as if he had created Philadelphia in order to produce Carl, though it later appeared that George had not discovered Carl until Carl had been to sea for a year already. And Carl himself told some of it: a fourth or fifth child of a first generation of Scandinavian-American shipwrights, brought up in one of an identical series of small frame houses a good trolley ride from salt water, by a mother or an older sister: this whom, at the age of fifteen and weighing perhaps a little less than a hundred pounds, some ancestor long knocking his quiet bones together at the bottom of the sea (or perhaps havened by accident in dry earth and become restive with ease and quiet) had sent back to the old dream and the old unrest three or maybe four generations late.

"I was a kid, then," Carl told us, who had yet to experience or need a shave. "I thought about everything but going to sea. I thought once I'd be a ballplayer or maybe a prize fighter. They had pictures of them on the walls, see, when Sis would send me down to the corner after the old man on a Saturday night. Jeez, I'd stand outside on the street and watch them go in, and I could see their legs under the door and hear them and smell the sawdust and see the pictures of them on the walls through the smoke. I was a kid then, see. I hadn't been nowheres then."

We asked George how he had ever got a berth, even as a messman, standing even now about four inches over five feet and with yet a face that should have followed monstrances up church aisles, if not looked down from one of the colored windows themselves.

"Why shouldn't he have come to sea?" George said. "Ain't this a free country? Even if he ain't nothing but a damn mess." He looked at us, black, serious. "He's a virgin, see? Do you know what that means?" He told us what it meant. Someone had evidently told him what it meant not so long ago, told him what he used to be himself, if he could remember that far back, and he thought that perhaps we didn't know the man, or maybe he thought it was a new word they had just invented. So he told us what it meant. It was in the first night watch and we were on the poop after supper, two days out of Gibraltar, listening to Monckton talking about cauliflower. Carl was taking a shower (he always took a bath after he had cleared the saloon after supper. George, who only cooked, never bathed until we were in port and the petite cleared) and George told us what it meant.

Then he began to curse. He cursed for a long time.

"Well, George," the bosun said, "Suppose you were one, then? What would you do?"

"What would I do?" George said. "What wouldn't I do?" He cursed for some time, steadily. "It's like the first cigarette in the morning," he said. "By noon, when you remember how it tasted, how you felt when you was waiting for the match to get to the end of it, and when that first drag—" He cursed, long, impersonal, like a chant.

Monckton watched him: not listened: watched, nursing his pipe. "Why, George," he said, "you're by way of being almost a poet."

There was a swipe, some West India Docks crum; I forget his name. "Call that lobbying the tongue?" he said. "You should hear a Lymus mate laying into a fo'c'sle of bloody Portygee ginneys."

"Monckton wasn't talking about the language," the bosun said. "Any man can swear." He looked at George. "You're not the first man that ever wished that, George. That's something that has to be *was* because you don't know you are when you are." Then he paraphrased unwitting and with unprintable aptness Byron's epigram about women's mouths. "But what are you saving him for? What good will it do you when he stops being?"

George cursed, looking from face to face, baffled and outraged.

"Maybe Carl will let George hold his hand at the time," Monckton said. He reached a match from his pocket. "Now, you take Brussels sprouts—"

"You might get the Old Man to quarantine him when we reach Naples," the bosun said.

George cursed.

"Now, you take Brussels sprouts," Monckton said.

III

It took us some time that night, to get either started or settled down. We—Monckton and the bosun and the two women and I—visited four more cafés, each like the other one and like the one where we had left George and Carl—same people, same music, same thin, colored drinks. The two women accompanied us, with us but not of us, biding and acquiescent, saying constantly and patiently and without words that it was time to go to bed. So after a while I left them and went back to the ship. George and Carl were not aboard.

The next morning they were not there either, though Monckton and the bosun were, and the cook and the steward swearing up and down the galley; it seemed that the cook was planning to spend the day ashore himself. So they had to stay aboard all day. Along toward midafternoon there came aboard a smallish man in a soiled suit who looked like one of those Columbia day students that go up each morning on the East Side subway from around Chatham Square. He was hatless, with an oiled pompadour. He had not shaved recently, and he spoke no English in a pleasant, deprecatory way that was all teeth. But he had found the right ship and he had a note from George, written on the edge of a dirty scrap of newspaper, and we found where George was. He was in jail.

The steward hadn't stopped cursing all day, anyhow. He didn't stop now, either. He and the messenger went off to the consul's. The steward returned a little after six o'clock, with George. George didn't look so much like he had been drunk; he looked dazed, quiet, with his wild hair and a blue stubble on his jaw. He went straight to Carl's bunk and he began to turn Carl's meticulous covers back one by one like a traveler examining the bed in a third-class European hotel, as if he expected to find Carl hidden among them. "You mean," he said, "he ain't been back? He ain't been back a-*tall?*"

"We haven't seen him," we told George. "The steward hasn't seen him either. We thought he was in jail with you."

He began to replace the covers; that is, he made an attempt to draw them one by one up the bed again in a kind of detached way, as if he were not conscious, sentient. "They run," he said in a dull tone. "They ducked out on me. I never thought he'd a done it. I never thought he'd a done me this way. It was her. She was the one made him done it. She knew what he was, and how I...." Then he began to cry, quietly, in that dull, detached way. "He must have been sitting there with his hand in her lap all the time. And I never suspicioned. She kept on moving her chair closer and closer to his. But I trusted him. I never suspicioned nothing. I thought he wouldn't a done nothing serious without asking me first, let alone ... I trusted him."

It appeared that the bottom of George's glass had distorted their shapes enough to create in George the illusion that Carl and the woman were drinking as he drank, in a serious but celibate way. He left them at the table and went back to the lavatory; or rather, he said that he realized suddenly that he was in the lavatory and that he had better be getting back, concerned not over what might transpire while he was away, but over the lapse, over his failure to be present at his own doings which the getting to the lavatory inferred. So he returned to the table, not yet alarmed; merely concerned and amused. He said he was having a fine time.

So at first he believed that he was still having such a good time that he could not find his own table. He found the one which he believed should be his, but it was vacant save for three stacks of saucers, so he made one round of the room, still amused, still enjoying himself; he was still enjoying himself when he repaired to the center of the dance floor where, a head above the dancers, he began to shout "Porteus ahoy!" in a loud voice, and continued to do so until a waiter who spoke English came and removed him and led him back to that same vacant table bearing the three stacks of saucers and the three glasses, one of which he now recognized as his own.

But he was still enjoying himself, though not so much now, believing himself to be the victim of a practical joke, first on the part of the management, and it appeared that he must have created some little disturbance, enjoying himself less and less all the while, the center of an augmenting clump of waiters and patrons.

When at last he did realize, accept the fact, that they were gone, it must have been pretty bad for him: the outrage, the despair, the sense of elapsed time, an unfamiliar city at night in which Carl must be found, and that quickly if it was to do any good. He tried to leave, to break through the crowd, without paying the score. Not that he would have beaten the bill; he just didn't have time. If he could have found Carl within the next ten minutes, he would have returned and paid the score twice over: I am sure of that.

And so they held him, the wild American, a cordon of waiters and clients—women and men both—and he dragging a handful of coins from his pockets ringing onto the tile floor. Then he said it was like having your legs swarmed by a pack of dogs: waiters, clients, men and women, on hands and knees on the floor, scrabbling after the rolling coins, and George slapping about with his big feet, trying to stamp the hands away.

Then he was standing in the center of an abrupt wide circle, breathing a little hard, with the two Napoleons in their swords and pallbearer gloves and Knights of Pythias bonnets on either side of him. He did not know what he had done; he only knew that he was under arrest. It was not until they reached the Prefecture, where there was an interpreter, that he learned that he was a political prisoner, having insulted the king's majesty by placing foot on the king's effigy on a coin. They put him in a forty-foot dungeon, with seven other political prisoners, one of whom was the messenger.

"They taken my belt and my necktie and the strings out of my shoes," he told us dully. "There wasn't nothing in the room but a barrel fastened in the middle of the floor and a wooden bench running all the way round the walls. I knew what the barrel was for right off, because they had already been using it for that for some time. You was expected to sleep on the bench when you couldn't stay on your feet no longer. When I stooped over and looked at it close, it was like looking down at Forty-second Street from a airplane. They looked just like Yellow cabs. Then I went and used the barrel. But I used it with the end of me it wasn't intended to be used with."

Then he told about the messenger. Truly, Despair, like Poverty, looks after its own. There they were: the Italian who spoke no English, and George who scarcely spoke any language at all; certainly not Italian. That was about four o'clock in the morning. Yet by daylight George had found the one man out of the seven who could have served him or probably would have.

"He told me he was going to get out at noon, and I told him I would give him ten lire as soon as I got out, and he got me the scrap of paper and the pencil (this, in a bare dungeon, from among men stripped to the skin of everything save the simplest residue of clothing necessary for warmth: of money, knives, shoelaces, even pins and loose buttons) and I wrote the note and he hid it and they let him out and after about four hours they come and got me and there was the steward."

"How did you talk to him, George?" the bosun said. "Even the steward couldn't find out anything until they got to the consul's."

"I don't know," George said. "We just talked. That was the only way I could tell anybody where I was at."

We tried to get him to go to bed, but he wouldn't do it. He didn't even shave. He got something to eat in the galley and went ashore. We watched him go down the side.

"Poor bastard," Monckton said.

"Why?" the bosun said. "What did he take Carl there for? They could have gone to the movies."

"I wasn't thinking about George," Monckton said.

"Oh," the bosun said. "Well, a man can't keep on going ashore anywhere, let alone Europe, all his life without getting ravaged now and then."

"Good God," Monckton said. "I should hope not."

George returned at six o'clock the next morning. He still looked dazed, though still quite sober, quite calm. Overnight his beard had grown another quarter inch. "I couldn't find them," he said quietly. "I couldn't find them nowheres." He had to act as messman now, taking Carl's place at the officers' table, but as soon as breakfast was done, he disappeared; we heard the steward cursing him up and down the ship until noon, trying to find him. Just before noon he returned, got through dinner, departed again. He came back just before dark.

"Found him yet?" I said. He didn't answer. He stared at me for a while with that blank look. Then he went to their bunks and hauled one of the imitation leather bags down and tumbled all of Carl's things into it and crushed down the lid upon the dangling sleeves and socks and hurled the bag out onto the well deck, where it tumbled once and burst open, vomiting the white jackets and the mute socks and the underclothes. Then he went to bed, fully dressed, and slept fourteen hours. The cook tried to get him up for breakfast, but it was like trying to rouse up a dead man.

When he waked he looked better. He borrowed a cigarette of me and went and shaved and came back and borrowed another cigarette. "Hell with him," he said. "Leave the bastard go. I don't give a damn."

That afternoon he put Carl's things back into his bunk. Not carefully and not uncarefully: he just gathered them up and dumped them into the berth and paused for a moment to see if any of them were going to fall out, before turning away.

IV

It was just before daylight. When I returned to the ship about midnight, the quarters were empty. When I waked just before daylight, all the bunks save my own were still vacant. I was lying in a halfdoze, when I heard Carl in the passage. He was coming quietly; I had scarcely heard him before he appeared in the door. He stood there for a while, looking no larger than an adolescent boy in the halflight, before he entered. I closed my eyes quickly. I heard him, still on tiptoe, come to my bunk and stand above me for a while. Then I heard him turn away. I opened my eyes just enough to watch him.

He undressed swiftly, ripping his clothes off, ripping off a button that struck the bulkhead with a faint click. Naked, in the wan light, he looked smaller and frailer than ever as he dug a towel from his bunk where George had tumbled his things, flinging the other garments aside with a kind of dreadful haste. Then he went out, his bare feet whispering in the passage.

I could hear the shower beyond the bulkhead running for a long time; it would be cold now, too. But it ran for a long time, then it ceased and I closed my eyes again until he had entered. Then I watched him lift from the floor the undergarment which he had removed and thrust it through a porthole quickly, with something of the air of a recovered drunkard putting out of sight an empty bottle. He dressed and put on a fresh white jacket and combed his hair, leaning to the small mirror, looking at his face for a long time.

And then he went to work. He worked about the bridge deck all day long; what he could have found to do there we could not imagine. But the crew's quarters never saw him until after dark. All day long we watched the white jacket flitting back and forth beyond the open doors or kneeling as he polished the brightwork about the companions. He seemed to work with a kind of fury. And when he was forced by his duties to come topside during the day, we noticed that it was always on the port side, and we lay with our starboard to the dock. And about the galley or the after deck George worked a little and loafed a good deal, not looking toward the bridge at all.

"That's the reason he stays up there, polishing that brightwork all day long," the bosun said. "He knows George can't come up there."

"It don't look to me like George wants to," I said.

"That's right," Monckton said. "For a dollar George would go up to the binnacle and ask the Old Man for a cigarette."

"But not for curiosity," the bosun said.

"You think that's all it is?" Monckton said. "Just curiosity?"

"Sure," the bosun said. "Why not?"

"Monckton's right," I said. "This is the most difficult moment in marriage: the day after your wife has stayed out all night."

"You mean the easiest," the bosun said. "George can quit him now."

"Do you think so?" Monckton said.

We lay there five days. Carl was still polishing the brightwork in the bridge-deck companions. The steward would send him out on deck, and go away; he would return and find Carl still working on the port side and he would make him go to starboard, above the dock and the Italian boys in bright, soiled jerseys and the venders of pornographic postcards. But it didn't take him long there, and then we would see him below again, sitting quietly in his white jacket in the stale gloom, waiting for suppertime. Usually he would be darning socks.

George had not yet said one word to him; Carl might not have been aboard at all, the very displacement of space which was his body, impedeless and breathable air. It was now George's turn to stay away from the ship most of the day and all of the night, returning a little drunk at three and four o'clock, to waken everyone by hand, save Carl, and talk in gross and loud recapitulation of recent and always different women before climbing into his bunk. As far as we knew, they did not even look at one another until we were well on our way to Gibraltar.

Then Carl's fury of work slacked somewhat. Yet he worked steadily all day, then, bathed, his blond hair wet and smooth, his slight body in a cotton singlet, we would see him leaning alone in the long twilight upon the rail midships or forward. But never about the poop where we smoked and talked and where George had begun again to play the single record on the victrola, committing, unrequested and anathemaed, cold-blooded encore after encore.

Then one night we saw them together. They were leaning side by side on the poop rail. That was the first time Carl had looked astern, looked toward Naples since that morning when he returned to the ship, and even now it was the evening on which the Gates of Hercules had sunk into the waxing twilight and the River Ocean began to flow down into the darkling sea and overhead the crosstrees swayed in measured and slow recover against the tall night and the low new moon.

"He's all right now," Monckton said. "The dog's gone back to his vomit."

"I said he was all right all the time," the bosun said. "George didn't give a damn."

"I wasn't talking about George," Monckton said. "George hasn't made the grade yet."

V

George told us. "He'd keep on moping and mooning, see, and I'd keep on trying to talk to him, to tell him I wasn't mad no more. Jeez, it had to come some day; a man can't be an angel all your life. But he wouldn't even look back that way. Until all of a sudden he says one night:

"'What do you do to them?' I looked at him. "'How does a man treat them?'

"'You mean to tell me,' I says, 'that you spent three days with her and she ain't showed you that?'

"'I mean, give them,' he says. 'Don't men give—'

"'Jeez Christ,' I says, 'you done already give her something they would have paid you money for it in Siam. Would have made you the prince or the prime minister at the least. What do you mean?'

"'I don't mean money,' he says. 'I mean....'

"'Well,' I says, 'if you was going to see her again, if she was going to be your girl, you'd give her something. Bring it back to her. Like something to wear or something: they don't care much what, them foreign women, hustling them wops all their life that wouldn't give them a full breath if they was a toy balloon; they don't care much what it is. But you ain't going to see her again, are you?'

"'No,' he says. 'No,' he says. 'No.' And he looked like he was fixing to jump off the boat and swim on ahead and wait for us at Hatteras.

"'So you don't want to worry about that,' I says. Then I went up and played the vic again, thinking that might cheer him up, because he ain't the first, for Christ's sake; he never invented it. But it was the next night; we was at the poop rail then—the first time he had looked back—watching the phosrus along the logline, when he says:

"'Maybe I got her into trouble.'

"'Doing what?' I says. 'With what? With the police? Didn't you make her show you her petite?' Like she would have needed a ticket, with that face full of gold; Jeez, she could have rode the train on her face alone; maybe that was her savings bank instead of using her stocking.

"'What ticket?' he says. So I told him. For a minute I thought he was crying, then I seen that he was just trying to not puke. So I knew what the trouble was, what had been worrying him. I remember the first time it come as a surprise to me. 'Oh,' I says, 'the smell. It don't mean nothing,' I says; 'you don't want to let that worry you. It ain't that they smell bad,' I says, 'that's just the Italian national air.'"

And then we thought that at last he really was sick. He worked all day long, coming to bed only after the rest of us were asleep and snoring, and I saw him in the night get up and go topside again, and I followed and saw him sitting on a windlass. He looked like a little boy, still, small, motionless in his underclothes. But he was young, and even an old man can't be sick very long with nothing but work to do and salt air to breathe; and so two weeks later we were watching him and George dancing again in their undershirts after supper on the after well deck while the victrola lifted its fatuous and reiterant ego against the waxing moon and the ship snored and hissed through the long seas off Hatteras. They didn't talk; they just danced, gravely and tirelessly as the nightly moon stood higher and higher up the sky. Then we turned south, and the Gulf Stream ran like blue ink alongside, bubbled with fire by night in the softening latitudes, and one night off Tortugas the ship began to tread the moon's silver train like an awkward and eager courtier, and Carl spoke for the first time after almost twenty days.

"George," he said, "do me a favor, will you?"

"Sure, bud," George said, stamping on the deck each time the needle clucked, his black head shoulders above Carl's sleek pale one, the two of them in decorous embrace, their canvas shoes hissing in unison: "Sure," George said. "Spit it out."

"When we get to Galveston, I want you to buy me a suit of these pink silk teddybears that ladies use. A little bigger than I'd wear, see?"

Minor Heroism

Allan Gurganus

The father of the British writer J.R. Ackerley was a successful importer of tropical fruit who became known as "The Banana King". He was also notoriously unflappable. When Ackerley was only ten, his father had told him that "in the matter of sex there was nothing he had not done, no experience he had not tasted, no scrape he had not got into and out of." One evening, years later, Ackerley decided to bring up the subject of a male lover before his father at dinner. Nonplussed by the son's confession, his father looked calmly across the table and said, "It's all right, old boy. I prefer not to know. So long as you enjoyed yourself, that's the main thing." Only after the old man's death, when Ackerley reconstructed his father's sexual history (including a possible homosexual relationship and a complete second family existing intact in another city) in My Father and Myself, did the truth behind his father's attitude become apparent.

We don't expect parents to have histories. At times, the discovery of one's parents' past can become an intimidating threat, a vicarious nightmare, an accusation we'll never live down, an expectation we'll never live up to. And yet, it is that past that we inherit, with its guilty deeds and its unanswered questions: we are all meant to continue the stories our parents left unfinished. Like Ackerley, Allan Gurganus is not interested in indictment or dismissal of the father's story. Instead, with both affection and irony, "Minor Heroism" explores those ancestral continuities, borne through time in various guises which the protagonists fail to see.

I.   AT WAR, AT HOME

Imagine him in his prime. A fairly rich and large-eared farm boy newly cured of being a farm boy by what he called Th' War, meaning the second one. He'd signed up in Charlottesville when most of his fraternity had done it as a group, and up till then he had been somewhat humorlessly typical. He had been hung up with the rest of them in the fraternity of the university that Jefferson designed, and he was as lean and carefully prepared as all the very best Virginia hams. And it would seem to follow that, in 1942, my father began being made more valuable by several years of smoke. But his smoke was not the curative Virginia kind; it was the high-flying smoke of German cities burning. My father was a bombardier. He became a minor hero in the Second World War and a major hero in Virginia/Carolina. He was photographed as Betty Grable stood on tiptoe to kiss him. He was tall. He still is. But his height meant most when he was dressed as an officer in our Army Air Corps. Today, in civvies, he is just another mildly handsome businessman. It was in uniform that Father looked most like himself.

Heroes should have looks. His were better than most, better than wholesome. It was one of those faces that fit handsomely into photographs and under a brimmed cap. It seemed to know in every pose that captions would be under it eventually. His profile, nearly as good as a Barrymore's, was better for being blunted slightly by boarding-school boxing. With very combed blond hair waving back in the way hair did then, his was a face that even from the front told much about itself in silhouette. Many of the photos still exist.

When I was a child in the years just after that war, people cornered me with accounts of my father's valor. They told me in front of other children how, though everybody's father had certainly helped with it, mine had done more than most to insure that the Nazi plot to rule the world—to rule the very ground on which this birthday party was now taking place—had been crushed by the Americans. They mentioned the Freedoms, four in all, and promised that the whole white world was now capable of worshiping in whichever ways it chose. They said to me, "Do you know what your father did?" I was told how people had printed "Welcome Richard!" on broad banners made of sheets that stretched all the way across Main Street.

But before the war was won and he came home, there was the business about what they made my grandmother do. Though bossy when alone with family, she was a remarkably shy woman, even for then. In North Carolina, in 1942, shyness was less unusual than it is today. Both her parents' families had been equally distinguished and austere, and, as if to commemorate this, she parted her hair impartially down the middle and most always wore the same rare brooch at the exact center of her collar and throat. I once saw her hiding in the dark back hallway of her house; eyes opened very wide, she stood against a wall, as unwanted guests on the front porch repeatedly rang the door chimes.

She had been reared at home with her three sisters, on a Raleigh side street in a house cool most of the year with the amount of marble in it: veined tabletops, hearths arched and white as tombs, classical statuary, athletic and luminous in dark corners. The marble hearths and statues floated upright in the house's murk. Tabletops rode the gloom like oval rafts. It seemed the marble objects were the rooms' true residents, directing every household current into eddies split around themselves and cooling off whatever drifted past them.

But Grandmother's wish for the stillness of 1909 was inappropriate in 1942. There was a war going on and her son, they told her, was crucial to the local view of it. They put much unnecessary pressure on a lady so easily swayed. All it took was one unscrupulous question about how much patriotism she really felt as, after all, a longtime member of the DAR. At this, she said that yes, yes, she would do it, but only if they did not ask her to speak. Of course, those present assured her, she wouldn't have to utter one syllable she didn't rightly feel she could or should utter. But no one believed she would stay silent once she got up there and got the feel of it from all the bunting hung around. They forced her, in this way, to sit on public platforms. When the speaker selling war bonds acknowledged her, seated there as formal as her central brooch, she winced in recognition of her name and nodded back to him and tried to smile out at the audience like a mother, but she looked like a potentially bereaved one.

Mrs. Roosevelt herself came through on a decorated train and got off and walked over to the platform they'd set up outside the station, and not even then would my grandmother speak a public sentence to those gathered on the street and hanging out the windows of the Bank and those who dangled legs like extra letters over the sign usually spelling Ekstein's Finer Men's Apparel. Suspended from four lampposts were giant photos of my father in uniform, in profile. When Mrs. Roosevelt came over as the ceremony ended and said how handsome my father must be, to judge from his pictures over there, my grandmother finally spoke. She was nodding and thanking Eleanor Roosevelt as an equal when she noticed that Mrs. Roosevelt wore no hat, which seemed odd in one of her station. What she was wearing, its weight tugging at the fabric of one shoulder, was a huge pale, wide-mouthed orchid which, some suggested afterwards, had looked much like her.

But Mrs. Roosevelt had won them over nonetheless, and it was lucky that others overheard what she said to Grandmother about my father's good looks. Grandmother would never have repeated it to anyone. Though she acknowledged things graciously, she never started them. In this way, she had become an adult and then a wife and, quite soon after that, a mother. Some were annoyed by this belief of hers that silence was always in good taste, but most people felt it was probably fine the way she was; that somehow it was more patriotic for a wife and mother not to say too much—except, of course, for Mrs. Roosevelt, and some people even felt that way about Mrs. Roosevelt.

The photograph of Betty Grable kissing my father's flat cheek seemed to hold the house up. I was born in 1947 and, as far as I knew, it had always been there. People who did not come often to the house would sometimes ask to see it. They were led back to the den, where it was hung with the medals. Smiling, they stooped to get the picture window's reflection off of it, and they'd shake their heads and nod appreciatively. I remember someone's saying that when you were young during a war it is hard to know later if you liked being young during a war or liked just being young or maybe even the war itself, who knows?

In the picture, he does not return her kiss but stands there; a statuesque soldier, newly decorated for minor heroism, accepts the homage of a distant voluptuous country. He is enjoying it probably, but he does not smile, for at that moment the fate of the Western world as we now know it still hung in the balance. But Betty Grable could smile. It was all right if she did, and the official Army photographer, whose job it was to photograph the wake of morale she left behind, snapped an Army camera, and there it was—on most front pages in either Carolina and with practically the whole page to itself in our local *Falls Herald Traveler*. And though manliness and the national moment forbade he show it, yes, certainly my father was enjoying the kiss synchronized with flashbulbs, just as local boys too young to go themselves were not too young to go at themselves several times a day upon finding this hometown representative in a favorite national fantasy with a Grable whose legs were here not even photographed to advantage, though the boys knew them well enough from other pictures. The local boys looked over at the grainy photograph they'd cut out and pinned up to the wallpaper beside their beds, and for a while there, several times a day, any number of them were replacing my father in his uniform, with Grable breathing right there beside them in her WAC's outfit shortened way beyond regulations. And after the ceremony, as the dots of flashbulbs were still dying out of their vision, there the boys were, there he was, the local high-school valedictorian, in the south of England, wearing my father's uniform and medals and walking across a muddy camp with Grable on his arm. He was looking down at her little WAC's cap pinned to the blond hair swept up on top. Pulling back the tent flap, she goes in first; he waits, takes a few more drags from the Camel he is smoking, then flips it smoothly into a nearby puddle and goes in himself. She is right there, patriotically spread-eagled on the tent floor, waiting for more minor heroism. In the flexed nostrils of the class valedictorian, the stink of weatherproofed canvas combines with the scent of Betty Grable's own perfume, a perfume that all the factories at home are working overtime to make available for her to bolster soldiers' morale, perfume that all the smokestacks smoke for hours to make one ounce of, perfume that all the factory girls at home helped make with skilled fingers, factory girls waiting up in their little rooms for men, disheveled healthy girls with their own skilled factory hands working up themselves with thoughts of soldierhood and regulation bayoneting and, oh, how crucial my own father was to local high-school boys behind closed doors in the early spring of 1945.

But when I was eight years old, some adult would take me aside and say, "Bryan, do you know what your father did before you were even born? Has he told you about what he did?" I said I didn't know for sure but that they used to paint little German planes on their bombers every time they shot a real one down, and my daddy's score was very high. They said no, not that. Not exactly. It was Dresden, the terrible and decisive firebombing of Dresden, that had been his real moment.

I nodded and always imagined a city of plate and saucer monuments and crockery apartments and wartime's smoking smokestacks made of stacked white bottomless coffee cups. And in the center of the shining city was an oil depot, looking very like a soup tureen of

Mother's—a white one too large for just us to use but brought out for dinner parties and reunions and once, I remembered, filled with vegetable alphabet soup. I'd stood, amazed to see the very spindly alphabet I was then learning to draw between blue lines fattened up and floating on the top of something I and all my family, even my illiterate younger brother, could drink down like reading. But the tureen I imagined there in Dresden was a million gallons high and filled to the top with the crudest, blackest German oil that fueled the deadly U-boats. A remarkable target for my father in his clear air over the heart of gleaming Dresden. In my conception, the black bomb wobbles toward the very shadow of it growing on the glossy upper disc of all those gallons. The life-sized shadow meets the real bomb falling in and going off down at the very bottom. Such beautiful war-movie slow motion now allows a perfect view of all the damage as the tank pops jaggedly open and out the gallons rush into the tranquil city. Black oil gluts the sewers of the sanitation system. The overflow is fingering up and out into the gutters and makes a black street map of the white municipality. Borne along in the dark gloss are clusters of diced carrots and chopped celery from my mother's kitchen, and there come the fat paste letters of the alphabet, movable type sucked down with the black into the gasping manholes. The level rises—filling, incidentally, the holes, which are the handles of the chaste white coffee cups. Darkness crawls about and then above the town and finally defines a surface that a cup or saucer may float along on briefly, till tilting, then filling viscously, they sink in, one by one, until they are underneath. Now everything is underneath. All the quaintness of Germany, all the cuckoo clocks are under, all the perfect German sheet music played by countless amateurs on Sundays, and, worst for me, all the inedible lost letters of my mother's English alphabet have become one glossy black deluge which now shows just the tiny moving shadow of my father's bomber, speeding back to England, back to the USO show, which will not begin till he is there in a seat being saved for him.

The photographers are smoking at the airport now; they are awaiting him. They are men also in the Army. Their job is to photograph the bombardiers like my handsome father, crawling from the cockpit, less exerted than excited by the damage he has done, looking clean and highly combed as when he left some hours ago.

But by the time I was imagining the bombing of Dresden, my father was done with all that. The war had been won. Dresden's place setting was being sorted out. With Germany having an Occupation forced upon it, it was time my father settled into a job himself. His fading local glamor at least proved useful in helping him choose a career. Cashing in on people's memories of him, he became an insurance salesman. It was not hard, selling insurance, and with his law degree, with the certificates Grandfather had given him, with the smattering of rents collected from the colored-tenant houses—the only remnants of Grandmother's "fortune"—Father felt he could more than make do. He married a clever girl he'd met at a deb party before the war. He brought her south from Richmond and carried her into a thirty-thousand-dollar house already paid for in advance by his cashing in certificates in companies making aluminum and small-screened televisions—all companies on the brink of booming when he sold their stocks. But though he was without much business sense, still there was the thirty-thousand-dollar house, much larger than what one could buy oneself today for that amount of money. So my father and my mother moved into a house that echoed slightly because it had more rooms than furniture. Sometimes the guest room was occupied by a recurrent itinerant aunt; but when she was gone the doors were closed, the heating ducts turned off, and three bedrooms, now accommodating only boxes full of unused wedding gifts, again stood very vacant.

My father still wrote to war buddies. They often passed through town en route to Florida, howling in through the front door to hug him. A lot of them were dark men, hairy in a way my father and his fair Carolina friends were not. It seemed that all New Yorkers were brown-eyed and sooty from the city; they looked odd here in the clear to amber light of our Tidewater. Mentioning their wives waiting in the car, they lifted eyebrows suggestively, as in the old days—as if that were some notorious and easy girl out there. Mother never liked their wives much, and when they'd left, Father told her she was a snob. "War buddies' wives are not necessarily war buddies themselves," she quipped. Once, when he insisted, after hanging up the phone, that they drive two hundred miles to a motel where someone from his squadron was staying on the way to Miami, Mother mentioned a bridge tournament; she said, "Show him my picture," and settled luxuriously back onto the couch with the latest novel by Daphne du Maurier. "He already saw your picture and he's heard more about

you than you'd ever guess!" my father shouted as he stormed out with
the car keys and an unopened bottle of Jack Daniel's and, slamming
the door, rattled the china cabinet. Very early the next morning, he
came in drunk and in a loud voice over the telephone canceled an
afternoon appointment to sell Group Life. My mother wandered
down to breakfast in her quilted yellow housecoat, and noticed a broken headlight on the Packard parked at the wrong angle outside.
When they'd settled at the table, coffee poured, she offered him the
usual tirade about his egotism, her suffering, and their marriage,
which she liked to say was "crumbling, Richard, crumbling!" I sat
eating scrambled eggs with a big round training spoon, and my
younger brother dropped his baby bottle on the floor, then looked
down at it till I picked it up. "Oh yeah?" my father said. And then she
said, "Don't you use that trashy New York slang around your children." "Oh yeah?" he said.

But when you are definitely home from the European Theater, which
is dead now, and war buddies you'd have given your life for now
phone less and less, are more and more just Christmas cards with
photos of new children, cards signed in a woman's hand, when insurance (fire, burglary, auto, and life) is now what people think of when
they think of you, when Marilyn Monroe is filling the shoes of Betty
Grable, who's retired, what do you do then?

You find that the headaches are because you suddenly need reading
glasses. You resign yourself to buying bourbon by the case because it is
cheaper and you now have room to store that much, and you have no
doubt that it will somehow get drunk up. You call your two sons soldiers when they submit stiff-faced, thin-armed, to Jonas Salk's discovery. You pay someone to keep the yard worthy of your wartime
aerial-photo vision of its symmetry and shape from overhead. You
take your wife to the occasions you count on the country club to
invent, and there, with friends who have become clients and friends
who have not become clients and with clients who want to become
your friends, the two of you get more than genteelly drunk, even by
Eastern Carolina's lubricated standards, And afterward, after the
baby-sitter has been overpaid to cover your tardiness and the fact that
the front of your jacket is dark from some accidental spillage and to
cover the expense of the cab that must be called to get her home, in the
silence after that, of the house becoming increasingly more valuable as

the boxwoods expand themselves outside, with the hint of dawn coming on, you both manage to know what a prime moment in the history of your physiques this is.

Otherwise, you learn to make do, and when some threat arises you are soldierly in disposing of it. Almost, there are not enough threats anymore. Here you are, among the most successful of the bombardiers, now grounded, in the awful safety of this decade, in its suburbs. You do what you can around the house and grounds to re-create some of that drama you remember from the forties. All the events that made one's life eventful: The Axis. Roosevelt Dead. Hiroshima.

The furnace explodes early one morning. You carry Helen outside, dump her onto a lawn chair, rush back for the sleeping boys, dash across the street and pull the fire alarm. Later the fire chief emerges from the basement of the house and ambles around the engine and out toward your family group, huddled in pajamas among the neighbors, who have brought blankets, coffee, garden hoses. "Nothing serious," he says. "The furnace sort of exploded. A little soot, but nothing serious."

"What do you mean, 'nothing serious'? You should have heard it. I thought we were being attacked or something."

"Noisy," the fire chief admits, scratching his head, trying to be both tactful and professional, "but nothing serious."

The next day, you order a fire-alarm system for the house. While the children grumble, while a siren howls and neighbors watch over fences, you stage your first weekly fire drill. After two of these, the drills are discontinued.

It is a personal affront when tent caterpillars invade four of the yard's eleven trees. A neighbor says you'll have to burn them out; only thing they understand. The yardman prepares to do it, till you curtly give him the day off. This job, worthy of you, will require a little strategy. There are moments when a father and his boys must work together. Standing in the back door, you shout, "Now is the time for all good boys to come to the aid of their father and their yard!" "*What?*" Helen asks.

You put a torch together—a broom handle, rags, some kerosene. You ignite it with your wartime Zippo. Up into the infested tree nearest the house you crawl. This is a mission; for once, in peacetime, you know exactly what you're going to do. The boys watch idly from the ground as you sear the first lumps of worms out of the plum tree.

Smoke suddenly everywhere and such a smell. "You two down there, don't just stand around. Stomp on the ones getting away." Clusters of black caterpillars, pounds of them, are toppling from their webs, falling to the ground and steaming.

Making girlish noises, your sons start hopping on the smoldering worms. Bradley jogs about, eyes straight ahead; he lifts his knees and make a calisthenic game of it. Feeling dizzy, Bryan shuts his eyes, holds out his arms for balance, and earnestly pretends he's dancing, though his tennis shoes keep slipping out from under him.

In the tree, you find you've started muttering almost forgotten, complicated curses from the war as, one by one, you solemnly eradicate these black colonies of pests. Your sons' whimpering infuriates you suddenly. "Shut up down there, you two. You'll do your job and keep your mouths closed. These things are going to get to other trees. They'll get over into the Bennetts' yard if we don't kill them now. This is no game here, this is an emergency, so quit squealing like sissies and stomp on them. That clear?"

Your two children look up at the orange glow inside the tree, at a single wing-tip shoe visible among the leaves. In unison, they say, "Yes sir."

II.   MY ELDER SON

I'm not as young as I used to be and it follows that my sons aren't either. Bradley, our baby, is twenty-five now and makes a hundred and twenty thousand dollars a year. He graduated third in his class from the law school of the University of Virginia. He's now with a fine corporation-law firm working out of Georgetown. Brad married Elaine last May at a garden wedding that was rained out but that was nice anyway. The bridesmaids' dresses were made of some thin material that got transparent when wet. Elaine is from a fine old Maryland family. Her father served as attorney general of the state a few administrations back. Now Brad and Elaine are renovating a town house in Washington, doing most of the work themselves. What with Elaine's small private income and her looks and taste, and with Brad's salary, my wife and I feel good about their progress in life. Elaine always remembers us with little cards and gifts on birthdays and anniversaries. It's a comfort.

Bryan is our elder son. He's twenty-seven and a mystery to me. Two years ago he gave up a fairly good job as a designer of furniture. He decided to become a writer. When he was home last Christmas, we heard him typing a few times, but he never offered to show us anything he'd written. I have no doubt that it's good. He has always had a real flair for the arts. But if you've never read a word your son has written and if you understand the kind of money a writer can expect to make, it's hard to work up any real enthusiasm for this occupation.

To support himself, Bryan does articles for a magazine called *Dance World*. When people ask me what he's doing, I tell them he writes for a magazine in New York. If they ask me which one, then I'm forced to level with them. I'd have to be a writer myself to describe the sinking feeling I get when I tell this about my elder son. Helen says that my attitude in the matter is unreasonable. All I know is, the first year he worked for the magazine he sent us a free subscription, and it got so I couldn't even stand to see copies on the coffee table. I could hardly believe some of the pictures of the men. Looking at them, you didn't know whether to laugh or cry or get angry or what.

My wife also informs me that there are two kinds of dance, ballet and modern, and that Bryan's specialty is modern. Helen says, with lots of enthusiasm, that modern is less costumed but just as athletic as ballet. Somehow, knowing this doesn't help.

You might say Bryan and I have never really seen eye to eye. He has always had certain mannerisms and his talents are unlike my own. When he was younger he stayed pale from spending too much time indoors. I kept telling Helen that one day he'd discover the world outside. I said, "Now he keeps a diary, he paints still lifes, he reads French like a Frenchman, but believe you me, one day he'll come around. You watch."

I see I might have been wrong. He's twenty-seven years old and I think the only women he ever talks to are waitresses. He lives with some actor-model roommate. We had lunch with them in New York. The roommate met us at the restaurant. I was expecting somebody thin who looked pretty much like Bryan. In walks this big, broad-shouldered kid, taller than me and with a suntan and a jaw like a lifeguard's. For a second, I was ashamed of myself for having jumped to certain conclusions. Then the first thing I noticed was his handshake. One of those dead fish. Second thing I noticed was, he'd smashed his thumbnail in something; it was black. Third thing was that all his fingernails were black. Nail polish. I could hardly understand what this meant. I thought it must be for medicinal purposes, because how could anybody do that for decoration? Helen was staring so hard I had to nudge her under the table. Usually she's the one nudging me. Afterwards she said she wouldn't have been so startled if it had been red polish, but black?

Now that we've met Jacques, he seems to be everywhere we look. Helen never forgets a face, and she keeps finding his picture in magazine ads—mostly for whiskey and shirts, once for soap. In these ads his nails are never black. I won't get over that. The kid looked like he should be on the U.S. Olympic team carrying a torch—and then the handshake, the nails, and his trying to talk all during lunch about the music of the forties. He kept asking Helen and me about Kay Kayser and his Kollege of Musical Knowledge, and about the Andrew Sisters. Helen surprised me by remembering the name of each Andrews Sister and knowing the order in which some'd died. She entered right into the discussion. He asked her how it felt to have heard "Tangerine" when it was new, and Helen was sitting right there telling him. Jacques kept saying over and over again, "What a period, what a period!" For a person like myself, who loved the forties, the silliness of this kind of conversation made me sick. As if anybody like that could ever understand what it meant to be alive then.

You send your sons to the best schools possible, and you hope that their friends will be bright kids from similar backgrounds. Sometimes I wonder what my son and this type of person have in common. Then I take a guess, and right away I'm wishing I could forget my own conclusions.

I was not going to mention it, but as long as I've built up this much steam I might as well. Last spring, Bryan came down to his brother's wedding in Baltimore. We were glad he came. It was right that he should be there, but I won't even begin to describe the person, the creature, he brought along with him. Everyone who saw this particular person immediately got very disturbed. This particular person somehow managed to get into and spoil about half of Bradley and Elaine's wedding pictures. Elaine's parents were obliged to find a place for Bryan and his guest to stay during the weekend of the wedding. They were certainly very gracious about it and never said one word about this person's appearance. But Helen was so upset and embarrassed she cried most of the nights we were there. Because of the strain, she looked terrible at the wedding.

Of course, it was Helen who was always telling Bryan he was gifted. She was enrolling him in adult art classes with nude models when he was twelve damn years old, buying him thirty-dollar picture books full of abstract paintings, driving him fifteen miles to the next town because our local barbers couldn't "cut with the curl." I told her she was spoiling him, but beyond that what could I do? I'd always said that the boys should have nothing but the best. No, I'm definitely not blaming Helen. After all, that's one reason you make your money, so you can spoil your kids in ways you weren't.

You start off with a child, a son, and for the first six years he's on your side. It's clear there's nothing wrong with him. He's healthy, and you're relieved. He's pretty much like all the others. Not quite as noisy, maybe not quite as tough, but that might be a good sign, too. Then things somehow get off the track. He's coming in with a bloodied nose once a week, and you know damned well that nothing happened to the kid that did it. He's inside listening to records when he ought to be outside playing with the others. His face starts looking unlike yours and hers. You come home from a hard day's work and find him sitting in a high-backed chair cutting shapes out of colored paper and spreading them on the rug. You wonder for a moment if this white-skinned kid can be fourteen years old; can he be half your responsibility, half your fault? Of course, there are times when everything seems well enough. He takes out girls. He learns to drive. His tenor comes and goes, then comes to stay. One day you see he's nicked himself while shaving, and all the time you feel you should be grooming an heir he grows paler, taller, and more peculiar. He locks doors behind himself and startles you in the dark hallways of your own house. You're afraid of his next phase—afraid how the finished product will compare with the block's other boys, with his own kid brother who plays on the junior varsity and mows other people's lawns for money.

At the PTA open house a teacher pulls you aside and tells you, all excited, "Bryan can do anything he likes in the world. How few of us can do absolutely anything we like. He's among the chosen few, and I thought you both should know." His mother beams all evening, but afterwards you find him in the kitchen, at the table, dripping candle wax on black paper. "An experiment," he mumbles as you walk into the room toward the refrigerator. You feel clumsy and you try with your expression to apologize for having barged in like this through the swinging door. But, after all, you tell yourself, it *is* your kitchen and your table, that is your son. The "anything" his sad teacher promised gives you more distress than comfort.

He drops calling you just Dad and changes you to Father. One night you turn on the television and hear him say, "Television is for fools," and dash out of the room, offended by your need to see the news. You expect more from him as he gets older, but the distance grows. He reminds you of a thin, peculiar fellow you knew slightly in the Army, a bookworm nobody spoke to.

Till last New Year's Eve, I felt I'd had a pretty good track record as a father. I mean, I knew I'd made some mistakes, but somehow, over the years, you forget specifically what they've been. Bryan had come south for Christmas for the first time in two years. Helen and I got home from a party at the Club. We were slightly drunk. Bryan was sitting up reading when we got in. He was curled on the living-room couch in a floor-length maroon bathrobe he'd worn most of his visit. He was reading something he'd brought down from New York. He laughs at our books and magazines, picks up Helen's novels and giggles at them and puts them down again.

Charlie Fentress had announced his daughter's engagement at the New Year's Eve party. The band played a few bars of the Wedding March. Bradley and Elaine weren't married yet and Brad had decided to spend Christmas with his college roommate on St. Thomas. Only Bryan was home. Edward and Mildred Fox took Helen and me aside at the party to say they just wanted to let us know they were going to be grandparents. They were hugging each other and they both had tears in their eyes. The band played "Auld Lang Syne." It seemed everyone was being honored and rewarded by their children but us. Bryan had laughed at our suggestion that he come to the party and see his old friends. "What would I talk to them about?" he asked. "The pill, kindergarten car pools?" His quickness with words has made him all the more upsetting. But we got home and there was our son on the couch. There he was. His hair cut in a shaggy expensive way, and wearing a silk bathrobe. He looked over his shoulder at us as we stood in the foyer taking off our coats and rubbers with a little drunken difficulty.

"How was the prom, kids?" he asked and turned back to his

book. I walked into the living room. On the coffee table before the couch I saw a bottle of cognac I'd paid forty bucks for, three years earlier. A snifter was beside it and a lot of wet rings, some of the cognac spilled on the tabletop.

"Who told you you could open that bottle?" I asked him.

"Father, it's New Year's Eve. Let up a little." The back of his head was still toward me.

"Look what you've done to that table. Your mother breaks her back keeping this place decent and you act like you're at the goddamned Holiday Inn."

It's easy enough now to say I shouldn't have cuffed him. But I felt like doing it, and I was just drunk enough to do what I felt like doing. He hadn't even bothered to turn around while I was talking. I took a backswing while he was reading. Helen said, "Richard!" in a warning tone of voice, but like me, she really didn't think I'd do it. I smacked him with my best golfer's swing right across his fashionable haircut, and knocked him off the couch onto the floor. It scared me as much as it seemed to scare him. For a minute he lay blinking up at me, mouth open, on the carpet. We were like that for a second. His mouth open, mine open, and Helen with both hands pressed over hers. Then she was all over me, trying to hold my arms like I was going to kill him. He got up, straightened his robe, and marched upstairs. The whole thing was so sloppy it made me sick. Even with all I'd drunk I couldn't sleep.

The next morning there was to be a New Year's Day church service at Trinity Episcopal. Helen had asked Bryan to come with us, but we didn't think he'd get up, since it was before his usual rising time, which was anywhere from noon till three. Helen and I were eating breakfast. We were dressed for church, eating without talking, trying not to think about the night before, but thinking about it anyway.

We were both staring at our eggs and coffee when Bryan came downstairs, all dressed for church. His head was bound up in a professional-looking gauze-and-tape bandage that covered most of his hair and forehead. The tanned ears stuck up over the white cap. He looked like someone recovering from brain surgery. Helen was drinking her coffee as he came in. In the middle of swallowing, she went into a genteel coughing fit. Bryan poured himself a cup. As he was adding cream and sugar, he said cheerfully, "Father, when people at church ask what happened to me—and inevitably they will ask—I intend to tell them exactly who's responsible for this."

I sat staring down the table at him. We were squared off, me at my usual place, he at his. I started chewing on my back molars in a way I hadn't done since the War. He went on drinking his coffee. Once in a while, he'd glance up at me over his cup. He seemed pleased with himself. Helen was staring at him with her mouth half open. She would look from him to me, her face all strained, as if she wanted me to explain him to her. So this is it, I thought. That one over there with the bandages, that's my elder son and heir. I had to decide then whether I would really break his head or if I'd let things go. At some point, you have to decide with children whether you're going to kill them or let them go.

I thought of those foreign-exchange students we sometimes had to dinner when they passed through our town. Odd-looking kids with funny-shaped glasses, sometimes bad teeth, and accents half the time Helen and I couldn't understand. But we always pretended we did. You could tell when they had asked a question, and even though you hadn't really caught it, you still nodded and said, "Yes." And when it turned out that the question couldn't be answered with a simple Yes, when they stared at us, at least we'd shown that we had wanted to agree. In the long run, that was all Helen and myself could do for International Good Will.

So at this breakfast I decided to give Bryan the benefit of the doubt. I told myself I'd treat him at least as well as we treated these nonwhite foreign students who come to dinner for just one night. You didn't even expect thank-you notes from them. These kids' customs were so different, their homes so far from us here. But we were always kind to them, thinking of American kids who'd be in their country someday. So I told myself there at the table, if not as a father then at least as a host and an American, I should treat Bryan at least as well as one of them. After all, a foreigner is mostly what he's been to us.

Helen didn't want him to go out bandaged like that, but you have to take your own kid to church. Besides, if we hadn't taken him he'd have called a cab and how would that have looked? I'm sure he told whoever asked about his head whatever it was he'd decided to tell.

He left for New York that very afternoon, still wrapped up like somebody with amnesia. Except for Bradley's wedding, we haven't seem him since. I suspect that he's in secret correspondence with his mother, and that's fine and natural, I suppose. Some days she's more tearful than others. In the middle of a meal, she'll fold her napkin, place it on the table, leave the room.

Someday he'll probably publish a story or a whole book about what a tyrant I've been. I can imagine a chapter listing all the times I ever raised my voice or hit him. Of course, people always believe what's down in black and white before they'll listen to just one man's word about what happened. I have made some mistakes, I know. But I won't accept his verdict of me. I'm not a villain. If anything, I've wanted too much for him, and, considering all the ways you can go wrong with a son, it seems the one he would be quickest to forgive.

III.   ADDENDUM

In this drawing I am doing, a tall red man holds the hand of a small white boy. The man wears a decorative uniform: policeman, soldier, milkman. He is much taller than the child, but his right arm has been conveniently elongated, elasticized like a sling or bandage so it easily supports the boy's white hand.

My art teacher called me out into the hallway on the last day of school and whispered, "You mustn't tell the other children, but you're the best drawer I have ever taught in eighteen years. The most imaginative. Of your age group, I mean." Now, deciding to place the man and boy before a doorway just like that one there, with a similar selection of Mother's houseplants sprouting all around them, I recall Miss Whipple's compliment. I feel fully capable of adding exactly what I intend. When I'm done, people will say, "Look. He's drawn a man, a boy, a doorway, and some plants in pots." There is a comfort in knowing you can make things recognizable.

I have lots of room on this table we inherited early from my former grandfather and his shy-in-public wife. It was built to seat a family of ten, plus guests. I am alone here at my usual end. Mother, Daddy, Bradley, and I each have a whole side to ourselves and must speak up to be heard by everyone. Venetian blinds cross the dining-room window, and sunshine throws a laddered shadow straight across the walnut surface of the table. The round-ended bars of light rest there in a row, like giant versions of my own crayons.

My brother and his friends are playing baseball in the front yard. They chant their jeers to various Episcopalian cadences. A few minutes back, a foul ball rattled off the roof. The grandfather clock in the foyer musically commemorates each and every fifteen minutes, however uneventful, and my crayon seems responsible for every drowsy sound.

The surface of the table gives a sudden jerk, and the crayoned frond of the potted palm I'm drawing takes an unexpected twist. I look up and watch my handsome father seat himself at the far end of the table and spread his mail like a game of solitaire. Crosshatched with sunlight, his white shirt is dazzling and reflected in the tabletop. From his favorite coffee cup, steam climbs. It twists and plaits itself up through the alternating stripes of sun and slatted shadow. He holds an envelope to the light and rips into it with one finger. With that same hand, he slapped me two days ago. It burned across my face and swiveled my whole head in that direction. I go back to my control of crayons. Maybe he'll take his bills into the study and leave me here to excel privately at drawing.

His voice startles me. "Why don't you go outside and play with the others? It would do you some good." I continue drawing. Indoor clouds rain blue and purple pellets on the houseplants. "Did you hear me down there?" "Yes sir." "What don't you like about baseball? Are you afraid you'll get hurt or what?" I know I must say something. "I like drawing." A pause. Still watching me, he drinks from his coffee cup. "But it's summer, Bryan. It's a beautiful summer morning and you're seven years old and when—" "Eight," I say, not looking up. "What?" "Eight years old." "All right, then, eight, all the more reason. If you've got to draw on a day like this, what's in here that you can't draw just as well outside?" All the floating clumps of leaves have sprouted pots. "I asked you a question. What do you find to draw, sitting in here like this?" A challenge. He thinks I don't know. Most Imaginative of My Age, and he thinks I don't even know what I'm drawing. Tell him an airplane, tell him an airplane. "You," I say, despite myself. "Drawing me?" Why did I tell? Now he'll want to see it. Casually, he glances again through his mail. "So, you're drawing your dad, huh? Well, let's have a look." I note that he's forgotten all about the baseball game. After slapping me two times in one week, he's crazy if he thinks I'll spend all morning drawing him and then get up and walk to the far end of the table and deliver it. He only notices my drawing when he wants to show that it's a waste of time. I won't let him see this. Absolutely not. Unless it's that or getting slapped again.

"It's really not any good," I assure him.

"Let me see it."

"You won't think it's any good. You'll get mad 'cause it's not the way you really look."

"Bring it here."

"Well, I drew in the door and plants behind you, and I think you really have to see it from down here at this end, because this is where I drew it from."

"I can turn around and see those," he says, peeved at conceding this. "Bring it here, Bryan."

I concentrate on the black crayon in my damp right fist. I study the picture itself. "Daddy," I begin, definite. "I just don't feel like you would ... I don't want you ... to see it ... yet. I'll show you later, in a minute, later on."

"This is getting ridiculous, young man. I'm asking you to bring that to me. Are you going to bring it or aren't you? It's that simple."

I have included him here, but that makes the drawing even more mine, less his. It's the one thing in this house of his that's really mine right now. The man's mouth is a single horizontal line. The boy's a silly U-shape. "It's mine," I say quietly.

"You said it was a picture of me."

"It is, but I'm the one that did it. Please Daddy, don't make me this time."

A long silence from the far end of the table. "I'm waiting, Bryan. Bring that down here right this second."

Almost before I think of it, the crayon is scribbling. In tight black loops it traps and eclipses half the page. I choose one figure. The face and hands are lost forever underneath an oily whorl. There is the chanting from the front yard, the scratchy circling of my crayon, less loud as black wax accumulates. My exertion delicately clinks his coffee cup against its saucer. As I scrawl, feeling sick and elated at this solution, I grind my teeth and stare straight at my enormous father, smaller than usual at the far end of the table. He seems to be sitting for a portrait as I furiously describe a neat black cyclone on the page. His jaw is set. I can hear his breathing. I know the signs. Any second he will lunge down here, grab me by the shirt, lift and shake me, slap me once with a hand the full size of my head; he'll shove me, stumbling, toward my room, shrieking in my own defense. Now, just as he places both palms on the table to come for me, I stand. I lift the drawing by its upper corners and carry the page as if wet.

I move toward his chair, the only chair with arms. He is waiting there to punish me for drawing during the summer, for drawing anything but him all day, for then un-drawing him without permission. I stare between his eyes at the faint inch making two eyebrows one grim horizontal line.

I warily approach him in my acolyte's gait. I hold up the drawing, a white flag, between his body and mine. I am now beside his chair. Seated, he is just as tall as I am standing. On his forehead there are rows of pores, and over that the teeth marks where the comb passed through his hair. His back is pressed straight against the chair, hands still tense on the table's edge. Over his business mail I place my artwork. One flimsy piece of white paper with some colored markings on it. His eyes move from my face down to my drawing. He sees the figure there. I hear him quietly exhale. His solid hands reach out and pick the paper up. I am very conscious of the hands. There I am, that's me, I feel him thinking. He has recognized himself. I release my breath and gratefully inhale some of Miss Whipple's wonder at my own imagination. Good for something, it has just spared me a whipping. I've sketched an image of him for himself, while I am permanently off the page, and saved. He is not asking why the uniformed gentleman's longer arm is weighed with this bristling black cancellation. He is now responding to the easy magic of a drawing of a uniform on a tall figure, the horizontal mouth, the buttons and braid.

"So, there I am ...," he says, relaxing. "Why'd you do this crossing out? What was that under there?"

I have lost interest in the drawing. I stare out the window at the summer lawn where my brother and six neighbor kids are climbing a young evergreen, tilting it almost to the ground. "Nothing," I say.

"So, there I am. Those are sure some ears you gave me. What are these round things here on front? Are those medals? Medals for what? He hesitates to risk a guess. I look back from the venetian blinds and stare at him. He sits studying the drawing, his face rosy, jovial now. More than anything, I want suddenly to hug him, to move forward and throw my arms around his neck. I want to cry and have him hold me. Lift me off the floor and up into the air and hold me. Instead, there seems to be a layer of electricity around him. I know I will be shocked for touching him with no reason. Somewhere in the house an alarm will sound, the grandfather clock will gong all out of sequence, the door chimes will go wild, sirens will howl out of the heating ducts, and foul balls will crash through every window in the place. I look at him and, in answer to his question, shrug.

He holds the drawing out for me to take. He's done with it. Slipping past his chair, I saunter to the back door and, on my way outside, turn around. I see him seated in stripes of light at the vacant family table. Sad, he holds my own drawing out to me as if offering a gift or an apology or some artwork of his own. Something changes in me, seeing him like this, but as I pass into the sunlight I fight to keep my voice quite cool and formal and call back, "I"m finished, Daddy. You may keep it now. It's yours."

Jeopardy

Michael Dorris

Strange lands and separation are the travelling salesman's lot. He has no fixed place: no office, desk space, nameplate, none of the physical symbols of status awarded by the hierarchy of business. His home is on the road. He is a solitary creature. In popular jokes, he is driven as much by his need for sex as by the requirement to make a sale. On the American stage, he is either the Dionysian huckster of The Music Man *and* The Rainmaker, *or the tragic Everyman of Arthur Miller's* Death of a Salesman, *victimized by his own false values and by those of his society. His prototype is the rag-and-bone man who travels from town to town in the early days of Europe; perhaps he is also distantly related to the Pied Piper of Hamelin and the Wandering Jew.*

Such professional wanderers, like the protagonist of Michael Dorris' "Jeopardy", live precarious lives. They cannot afford to be gruff or aloof. Those who seek a friendly reception through flattery, joking, or bombast often meet with contempt. Always on the move, they lack the assurance of a circle of friends. The classic Chinese book of wisdom I Ching represents them as fire in the grass on a mountain, which cannot linger in one spot, but must travel on to new fuel: a bright light of short duration with no dwelling place.

The backseat and floor of my blue '89 Buick LeSabre are awash in industry pamphlets and reprints, the mess a result of my stopping too quickly at too many red lights. Next to me on the passenger side slumps a trash bag full of empty Hardee's and Burger King wrappings, their contents consumed on the fly. I have this idea to recycle— inspired by a panicky talk show I tuned in on the long drive from Billings to Bozeman—but all that happens is greater accumulation. That's the sum of good intentions.

On this Friday morning at the end of a long work week my schedule puts me into Kalispell, a spic-and-span town at the northwest tip of Nowhere, Montana, beautiful to look at but cold, and I don't mean only climate-cold, either. All the docs are clustered in two or three professional buildings, cement-block forts with Muzak and back issues of *People* in waiting rooms guarded by blond, Charlie's Angels–haired women. I check my list: my first stop is Dee Dee, about whom I have noted in the margin: "Kid with allergy. Likes Dairy Queen blizzard (tropical?). 6."

The "6" refers to the minutes of chitchat it usually takes to admit me to the inner sanctum. I get paid by the number of scrips—physician signatures acknowledging our conversations—that I collect, not by time spent or volume of orders. It all boils down to human contact, though the verbal conversation is pretty much one way, me to her, with her replies made in eyebrows, sighs, shrugs, and head movements.

"Lots of pollen around, huh? Hey, maybe your little boy.... That's not him in the frame on your desk? I can't believe how he's grown. No.... Maybe he could try this new inhaler. It's a miracle worker. Just remember, you don't know where you got it, right, because I could get in major trouble and it's just because we're friends, you know, and I had allergies myself as a kid. Sure I do. Three puffs a day this time of year, and not a wheeze. Don't mention it, I just hope it helps him, because that's what counts, that's why I'm in this business, to help people. And if you could just get me in to see the physician for five minutes, max, I want to tell him about this product, not yet commercially available—amazing stuff, really, the cutting edge. I'm positive he'd want to know about it direct, not hear it from his competition or from a patient who had read about it in *Time* or somewhere. Well, not yet, but they've assigned a science reporter. I'll just sit over here and straighten out my schedule—I've got more appointments than I can handle and I just wish all of them were.... No, whenever, no problem, no hurry. Forget I'm here, but if he has three minutes, I'll be quick. Cross my heart. So ... hey, are you still using that old pen from my last visit? That's kind of sentimental. I'm touched. But let me give you a new one. Take one for your son, too. Good, two. Kids lose things. Tell me about it."

I check my watch. Six minutes flat.

And then I sit, not watching Dee Dee not watch me, and read an article about John Travolta's happy marriage. Every once in a while I make a point of catching Dee Dee's eye, and salute. Meanwhile she waves in a procession of strep throats and backaches, varicose veins and odd pains in the chest. I make a game of guessing the ailment as well as the amount of consult time by focusing on the mouths: indignant-grim versus scared-grim, ready-to-be-mad versus ready-to-cry. I'm the only cheerful presence—besides Dee Dee's hair—in the room, the only healthy delegate in a convention of germs. Still, inside an hour, I'm out the front door with three signatures.

Next on the list comes Lisa, the mother type. She presides over a whole clinic of potential scrip-signers, all stacked neatly behind a single swinging half-door. Ducks in a row, fish in a barrel. Those docs are so overworked with Medicaids that they're glad for the diversion, actually ask questions about the product to keep me talking. They see my face and head for Mr. Coffee like kids who'd rather play at cleaning their rooms than do their homework, or people so bored that they sit around their houses waiting for Jehovah's Witnesses to drop by. The answer to a rep's prayer. With them it isn't getting your toe in the door, it's escaping before dark, not a dilemma I often encounter and not one I'm complaining about either.

Sympathy's the key to Lisa's lock, as it is with a lot of them. You open your heart wide enough, she presses the buzzer under her desk and it's Hello Sesame. The challenge is keeping the story straight. What sad tale did I use last time? Which detail made her pupils tighten, her neck muscles tense to attention? With the pity freaks my life has to be soap opera, and believe me, these women have a memory. Lisa almost trips me up halfway through today's installment of My Unfair Divorce.

"I thought you said you'd been happily married for four years before you got the boot," she challenges, her face balled up into a loose fist. "Now, suddenly, it's three."

Call her Perry Mason.

"Well, it's both, I guess." I'm thinking fast. "See, I don't like to admit it but we lived together for year before we actually tied the knot." This is a calculation on my part, a hope that Lisa, the romantic, will forgive shacking up more than she will gross exaggeration.

She shakes her head in a disapproval that's more interested than serious. "They do that now."

I nod, sharing her despair at the decline of morals. "*Her* idea," I confess, seizing sudden inspiration and running with it. "I'm the old-fashioned type."

I hold up my left hand to show I still wear a ring, even separated. I let that band of gold speak volumes about the kind of guy I am.

Lisa's eyes approve, though I notice that her ring finger's bare. In unrequited love with one of the docs is my bet, one of those men whose wives don't understand the pressures of the medical profession, Lisa's specialty.

"What did you say her name was?"

Great. A test. I flip through my mental Rolodex. Betsy? Maria? Luanne? How did I read Lisa the first time? Not ethnic, certainly, so Maria's out, but am I married up or down? Am I left for a rich boy or for a bum?

"Betsy?" I venture. Betsy the bitch whose father had opposed our marriage because I wasn't good enough for her. Betsy, who even now, while I'm out trying to make an honest dollar, is probably sipping a gin and tonic at the country club with the pro after her tennis lesson.

"That's right," Lisa recalls. Bingo. "Well, you hang in there, honey. One of these days you're going to meet a girl who'll appreciate you. I promise."

Right, I think, and then what? How many visits of happily ever after before you get bored? No way. So I sigh, sorry for myself but brave, uncomplaining.

"I'm staying with my dad now," I add for good measure. You can't beat the truth for authentic details. "He's been kind of low since he was laid off his job. Watches 'Jeopardy' three times a day on the satellite dish, even tapes it."

Lisa nods. I'm a good son, too. There's no end to my virtue.

"I know they're looking forward to seeing you." She gestures toward the examining rooms with her chin, trying to cheer me up. "It won't be long. I'll arrange it so they're all free at the same time. Why should *you* have to wait?"

The end of the day I reserve for Patt. She's not bad-looking in a kind of white starched way. I could imagine her taking off her glasses, shaking out her hair, unlacing her shoes. We have this flirt thing going, the game being that I'm chasing and she's holding me at bay, just barely. One of these days, if I don't watch out, she'll decide to take me up on dinner, whatever.

"So, is the divorce final?" she wants to know first thing, giving me a wink. "No more Maria?" Her fingers caress the sample box of lavender bath beads, the exact size and shape of Som-U-Rest, the sleeping pill I represent on the side.

"Maria who?" With Patt I sort of sit on the edge of her desk, my thigh brushing the telephone so she has to consciously avoid touching me if a call comes in.

"Then why still the ring? You carrying a torch?"

I look at my finger. Damn. "Can I be honest?"

That snags her. It's almost too easy.

"See, in my profession I meet a lot of women, some of them lonely."

Patt could imagine.

"Well, you understand, a man on the road. Some might think I'm looking for a one-night stand, which I'm not, but all those jokes about traveling salesmen? It's a, you know, occupational stereotype."

Patt snorts, warning me I am pushing this maybe too far.

"I can read your mind," I inform her. "You think because I kid around with you I do it with everybody, right? That I come on to all the women I meet?"

"Well ...?" Patt sees the trap, but plows ahead anyway.

I close my eyes, open them, then speak slowly, as though revealing something that isn't easy to admit. "Truth, okay? The ring's protection. It says, 'Sorry, taken,' which avoids misunderstanding. Hey, listen to me. Now you'll think I spill my life story to everybody. It isn't even that interesting."

"No," Patt automatically objects. "No, it is, really."

"Don't be nice, all right? It's just with you I feel I can be ... what? Myself?"

She doesn't move, expecting me to go on. Instead I let the silence grown, wait her out. Finally she reaches over, touches my hand where it rests on my leg.

"I told you, don't be nice."

"I'm not being nice," Patt says. "I hear you, is all."

A woman and her little boy come through the door from the examining rooms. Patt and I both sit up straighter, as though caught in the act.

"He says to squeeze us in next Tuesday," the woman tells Patt, who searches the book for a free fifteen minutes.

"Tuesday he's solid."

"He *said*," the woman insists.

"I'll have to do some shuffling." Patt's not a bit pleased with the physician's disregard for her careful appointment keeping. She looks up at me, Mr. Reasonable, not asking for a thing of her that's hard. "Why don't you run in while I make a couple of calls," she suggests, and glances at the clock. "Maybe we can continue this conversation later. If you're free."

I give her a look like, are you kidding?

Of course by the time I come out, my samples bag a little lighter, Patt has remembered an engagement she can't get out of. I grab my shirt, try to hold my breaking heart in one piece, but the fact is I'm relieved at the prospect of a quiet night at the Outlaw Inn, writing up my report, filing my receipts. After a day of smiling, being whoever people need me to be, I'm ready to grab a bite, call Dad, do some work, then crash in front of the in-room HBO.

The outlaw is big, two indoor pools big, with an instant-cash machine in the lobby, the accommodations of choice for Salt Lake City–based Delta crews on a layover and for businessmen like myself, even though it does come on a bit strong. Each building has a theme—the roundup, Indians, bank robberies, what have you—that leaks from the halls into the individual guest rooms, and the restaurant menu features "a taste of Montana," which means huckleberries dumped into everything from breast of chicken to Irish coffee.

First thing after check-in, I try Dad to see how he's making out. He and I have become one of those can't live with him/can't live without him relationships after batching it together for a year. I let the phone go five rings before I bag it and head for the lounge. Probably he stayed late at the library, boning up for the next "Jeopardy" open-call contestants' competition. I figure a couple or three B&B's have my name on them after the day I've put in.

The Branding Iron is Friday-full. I stand in the entrance and let my eyes adjust to the smoky light while I check for a familiar face. You do this job long enough and you meet people, on the road like yourself. Sure enough, sitting alone in a booth there's Jim Dohene, a rep for a medical supplies concern out of Denver.

As I head across the room, I inventory what facts I've stored about his life: married, no kids; about thirty-five thousand dollars a year; drives an Olds; not too bad in the sack.

The last time I saw him was Spokane a year ago. We both had a few drinks and started trading war stories, tales only a fellow rep would understand the full significance of, and over the course of an hour or two, each of us taking turns standing another round, we built what I can only call a sense of trust between us. Then, one thing led to another, as it sometimes will do.

On the road, trust makes or breaks you. You have to know the odds when you hear a lead about a doc or a secretary, because it can backfire in a major way. Somebody might say: "Take the aggressive tack with that one. She folds like an accordion." Or, "Be sure to call him by his first name. He hates that formal crap." If the advice is accurate, it's time-saving, important to know. It could be three, four personal visits before you psyched it out for yourself. But if it's a curve ball, if she says, "Fuck you, buddy" when you get pushy, or he goes, "I spent eight years and a hundred thousand bucks to be addressed as *doctor* except by my closest friends," it's damage that can't easily be repaired.

Jim, I recall as I squeeze his shoulder, waking him up from wherever his mind has wandered, is okay. He clued me that Kathi in Missoula was a sucker for chocolate, and my next swing through Montana I scored three scrips in thirty minutes.

"What's happening, stranger?" I say in greeting. "Still raking it in with that new line of double-carbon prescription forms?"

"God, the word gets out." Jim pats my hand, good sign number one. "Such as you left a trail of artificially mellow desk clerks in Great Falls last time you passed through. What do you use, a stun gun?"

"That isn't what she called it this afternoon." I make a face, thinking of Patt. "But what can I say? Some products sell themselves." I drop into the seat opposite and blow a kiss to the waitress to get her attention.

"I guess that's why you're here alone."

"Doesn't mean I have to leave that way." I raise my shoulders, hold up my palms, and provide him an easy out if he wants it. "And anyway, they never stay the night. I guess the husband would catch on."

"In your dreams. What's that new pill you're dealing got in it, anyway?"

We small talk like that back and forth, ironing out the kinks, giving us each time. Jim gets to the tape before me.

"So," he asks, pairing up two significant facts of my life at the same moment. "You still unattached, and how's your dad doing?"

I give him credit. No wonder he pulls in the bucks.

"Sorry to say, and okay, considering," I answer.

Jim shakes his head, understanding.

"I just tried to call him, but no answer," I continue, deciding to tackle the second point first. This early in the evening there's no need to rush if we both want to go there. "Probably out on the town."

"Party animal." Jim nods, raises his margarita. "Must run in the family."

Number two. I take his meaning, clink glasses. "So, been through Spokane lately?"

Jim pauses his drink in midair, cocks his head as if searching his memory banks, then puts his glass to his lips and takes a deep swallow.

"Spokane, Spokane, Spokane?" He gives his I've-just-made-a-sale smile. "I can't remember the last good night's sleep I had in that town."

"You can't, huh?"

"Let's see. Wait a minute, wait a minute, it's coming back to me, kind of in a hangover haze. The Sheraton, right?"

Beneath the table our knees bump. I signal the waitress. "Mine," I tell Jim. "I've got some catch-up to play."

He settles back into his seat. Now that we both know where we're headed, we can relax.

"So, your dad...."

"I'm not going to kid you. He's obsessed. I tried to get him on Prozac, but no. He'd rather follow his dream to land a spot on a quiz program, to show the world how smart he is."

"He needs to get out, meet people," Jim says. "Have some fun."

"Life's too short not to," I agree, and lay a ten down on the table to wait for our drinks. "You grab the opportunity when it presents itself or it passes you standing still."

Jim nods. He buys that theory one hundred percent and is ready and able to prove it.

"Which building they put you in?" I ask. "You a cowboy tonight?"

"Everybody's a cowboy in Montana after the sun goes down. It's a state of mind. You eat yet or what?"

I glance at my watch and see it's only eight-thirty. Too early to head upstairs, and we're both still way too sober anyhow. "Well, I had this hot date," I say. "But we must have got our signals crossed."

Jim pushes the menu in my direction. "I'd recommend the trout. It was fresh ... once. So who did you see today?"

"I started with Dee Dee."

"Her kid's nose still a faucet?"

Later in the dark, kept awake by Jim's snores, I punch in Dad's number by touch, counting each of the little buttons and hoping I don't make a mistake and wake up a stranger in the middle of the night. I don't plan to talk when he answers, just hear his "Hello" to make sure he made it home all right, and then hang up. I let the damn thing ring a long time. Maybe he unplugged the phone, got absent-minded, and left it that way. Maybe he covered it with a pillow and is sleeping too soundly. Maybe he stashed it in the refrigerator again.

Dad lets the details slide. An idea man, he calls himself, always one step ahead, but in fact he usually has too many plans going at once.

"I should have been an architect," he informs me the night before I left. We're sitting on the couch, naturally watching his "Jeopardy," his steady beat since he was force-retired from the TV station.

"You don't have the patience," I tell him. The woman in the middle is beating the two-time champ. She's on a roll, marching down World Geography toward the $1,000 square. Alex Trebek smiles as she buzzes in again.

"I love that blueprint paper," Dad says. His eyes stay fixed on the screen, ready. "All you need is a ruler and the right kind of eraser. Supplies you can carry in your back pocket, stuff you can work with out of your own home."

The Daily Double is under the $600 and the woman goes for broke, her whole stash of $3,100. She's nervous and eager, like a person high above a pool on a springboard, thinking out a half-gainer. The answer box swings around: "Belgian Congo."

"What is Zaire?" Dad shouts.

The woman licks her upper lip, juggling countries. The other two contestants are rooting against her.

"You just have to learn the symbols," Dad continues on his other track. "Windows, closets. The doors are drawn half-open to show the direction of their swing. You can mock in the landscaping, everything. You're your own boss. All that matters is your imagination, and that gets better and better with experience."

"Zaire," the woman announces at last, pleased with her memory. When there's no applause from the studio audience she looks unsure. "It *is* Zaire," she insists hopelessly. Alex shakes his head. He's sorry.

"In Double Jeopardy the answer has to be in the form of a question," he reminds her. The woman's money screen blips. Wipeout.

"A pool is nothing," Dad says. "Four lines at right angles."

"Who's this house for, anyway?" I ask him.

"Not my grandchildren, that's for damn sure."

I tense up, ready to go another round, but this time he only winks at me, nods toward the hallway. "Thirsty?"

"I could."

"Get me one too, while you're up." He's tricky.

I push myself out of my chair, go to the kitchen, open the refrigerator. Meanwhile I hear Dad switch channels to the station, Channel 7, that let him go. He does that from time to time, hoping to see snow, but when I come back into the living room empty-handed, everything on-screen appears normal, except there's no sound, thanks to the mute button. Ed Finley, about whom Dad has some strong negative emotions, is standing in front of a weather map pointing to a red lightning bolt in the vicinity of Ohio and working his mouth, talking and smiling, his little pig eyes as desperate as ever.

"We're all out of beer but the phone was in there."

"They could get a trained seal to do that." Dad points his thumb toward Ed. "Hold a stick in its mouth, clap with its flippers. Did I tell you how much take-home he gets?"

Ed Finley was not in Dad's corner when it counted, despite their long professional association on opposite sides of the #2 camera. Now, as I watch, the weatherman opens a large umbrella decorated with happy faces, meaning rain tomorrow.

"The telephone?" I ask.

Dad sighs, switches back to "Jeopardy," now in the last write-down question phase.

"It got on my nerves," Dad says, irritated. "I let it cool off."

The topic is the U.S. Presidency and the answer is Harry Truman's vice president. The three contestants screw up their faces, chew on their magic pencils, wait for inspiration. Finally, as the theme music winds down, they each scribble on the pads in front of them, but without conviction. You can tell the Zaire woman has done it again, bet over her head.

"Who is Alben W. Barkley?" Dad yells at the TV. "I win."

One after another the contestants come up with zero, except for the woman. She learned her lesson after all and has held back a dollar, and that gets her a ticket to tomorrow's show. The way she crows you'd think she's won the Publishers Clearing House sweepstakes instead of guessing Al Smith and losing $1,600.

I wake up alone in my bed still wearing my half-buttoned shirt. The TV is on, sun is pouring through the space where the blinds don't quite meet, and a line of light shows under the bathroom door. I listen for the sound of the shower.

"You in there?" I call. No answer. The room feels empty, though I have no recollection of Jim leaving. I have some difficulty even remembering what we got into last night.

I roll onto my stomach, reach for the phone, and dial Dad. The digital clock reads seven-twelve. After ten rings I give up and stare at the receiver as if it can tell me where the fuck he is. "I should call somebody." I must say this aloud, because I hear my own advice. I try to think of logical explanations: the lines are down, he's brushing his teeth, I forgot to use the correct area code. I dial his number again, listen to the ring while I get out of bed, dig my address book out of my case, and look up Dad's neighbor, Mrs. Kelsey.

"I'm overreacting," I explain when I tell her why I'm calling, "but if you could just check?"

"The newspaper was on his porch last night," she whispers, ominously proven right in her suspicions. "Still folded."

"I'll hang on," I tell her. "I'll wait while you go knock."

It's almost ten o'clock by the time I get done talking with the ambulance and the coroner and a funeral home whose name popped into my head. There's nothing left for me to do before I head back to Tacoma except report in to the district manager and have her cancel the rest of my appointments.

When I've finished all the business, I suddenly can't catch my breath. A panic rises in me, steady as water running into a tub, and I think I'm going to pass out. Somehow this is a familiar feeling— asthma, my chest squeezing shut. It comes back to me: I'd wake up like this and Dad would appear next to my bed with a brown grocery bag. He'd bunch it around a small opening and make me breathe into it while he counted. One, two three, four, four and a half, five. By the time I got to ten I was back in control.

I look around the room and all I can find is a plastic laundry sack in a bureau drawer. It will have to do. I gather the opening into a tunnel, blow inside until my lungs are empty, hold them that way, then draw in slowly. Again. I see the sides of the bag move, expand and contract with the force of my oxygen. I don't know how many times I do this, but when I stop I don't need the bag anymore, and I have an idea.

I ask the motel operator for Jim's room.

"I'm sorry, sir. Mr. Dohene checked out a little over two hours ago."

I imagine Jim all brushed and neat. He's nobody I think of from one month to the next, so why can't I let it go? If we run into each other again and we're both free and in the mood, fine. If not, no biggie. Still, I call his company in Denver, pretend I'm a relative who needs to know his schedule.

"Is this a medical emergency or a personal matter?" the receptionist inquires, following procedure before releasing information. She might have to explain her reasons to Jim or to her boss and is covering her ass.

"A death," I say. For some reason I use my salesman's voice, the one that gets me through the door to the inner offices, the one they can't resist.

"Just one moment, please."

She smells a practical joke or worse, another rep trying to beat her guy to an appointment. She'll bump the call up the line to someone used to saying "no." I can tell the truth, some part of it. Jim and I are old friends who had dinner, a few drinks. Fast-forward through the part about wearing each other out all night and get to the punch line: I just heard that my dad passed away six hundred miles from here and I don't want to be alone, okay?

While I wait, listening to the piped music playing over the receiver in between recorded commercials for the company's products, mentally rehearsing my story, I glance around the room. Towels everywhere, my shorts still where Jim tossed them behind the chair, the ice bucket full of water, my sample case open on the floor.

"Screw it," I say into the phone. If I need comfort, I'll prescribe it for myself. I reach for my appointment book and dial Patt's office before I remember that today's Saturday. What's her last name?

Higgins? No, that's Lisa. Jones, Smith, Robinson, Peters! Double T double P is how I've stored it my memory. I locate the Kalispell directory and scroll down the possibilities. No Patt or P, but wait, there is: Bob and Patt, on Seventh Street South. Bob?

I recognize her voice right off when she finally answers.

"Guess who?" I say, "Just wondering if your previous engagement is out of the way."

There's a long pause and for a minute I think she doesn't place me. "It's Don," I remind her. "From yesterday."

"Hi, *Sally,*" Patt answers, bearing down on the name. "Hey, I can't talk now. Bob and I are in the middle of something, if you know what I mean."

"How about later? Just to, you know, talk?"

"Mmmm. That's too bad. Can I call you back, like on *Monday* or something?"

"I'm only in town today, but I could wait around for you."

"Great. Talk to you after the weekend."

"You don't even know where I'm staying. I'm—"

"Sally, I've really got to run. Say hello to Rick."

Dial tone. Okay. I turn to Higgins, and there she is, Lisa. No disguise. I imagine her reaction to my news, all sympathy and concern. She'll want me to come to dinner, probably, and maybe I'll take her up on it. I don't have to be in Tacoma until tomorrow.

"Lisa, it's Don Banta," I identify myself right off.

"Who?"

"Don. We talked at your office? I used to be married to Betsy?" I'm proud of myself for recalling this detail with no prompting.

"Who?"

"I'm a drug rep."

"Oh. Right, right. The one who lives with his father. I'm sorry. At the end of the week I leave the office at the office. What can I do for you?"

"Well, I was hoping you were free. For lunch? There's something I want your advice about."

"My advice?"

"I don't want to go into it over the phone."

"That sounds mysterious, but it won't work out for today. I'm running my kids to ten things at once: piano, gymnastics, skating, a birthday party."

Kids. "I assumed you were single."

"Only in my prayers. But really, if you want to tell me what you need, maybe there's something—*Teresa, give that to her!* This place is a zoo."

"No, that's great. You're busy. I'll catch you the next time through."

"Okay, if you're sure. Bye-bye."

That leaves only Dee Dee, and her line's busy. While I wait to try again I can't keep my mind off Dad. He drives me nuts. He gets these projects started and then drops them when he loses interest. Sometimes I don't even know until afterwards, and then by accident, like when I was walking down a side street downtown one early evening on my way to scope out a new bar, Aunt Fred's, and what do I see in a storefront window? A polished headstone, a life-size example of what can be ordered from a mason, according to the sign, for under a thousand dollars. It rests on a nest of black velvet, and is elevated so that the inscription catches the eye.

Charles William Banta
At Rest
1919–1986

"Can I help you?" the clerk asks when I walk through the door. He's no more than twenty-five, Italian good-looking, dark eyes, and far enough away from death to sell it with a clear conscience. I circle the slab of granite.

"A fine piece of work," he encourages. His voice is deeper than you'd expect.

Either the name or the dates alone could be a coincidence, but both?

"Johnny," the young man identifies himself and holds out his hand for me to shake.

"Johnny," I say. "Charlie Banta is my dad."

Johnny, still grinning, tries to place the name. I nod toward the stone and watch him read.

"Oh, shit."

"Johnny, I've got to ask you: what's going on?"

He looks around for another customer, glances over at the phone to make sure it isn't ringing.

"I didn't do the sale," he says at last. "It happened before I started working here."

"But you know the story."

"I heard about it. This older guy—I mean, your father—comes in one day and orders a stone, for himself he claims. Wants top of the line, the best engraving. Makes a down payment of two hundred dollars, so the owner—Curtis?—goes ahead and places the order. It comes back a month later, we call the ... your dad ... and he says he's changed his mind. Curtis was totally pissed. Talked about small-claims court but it was too much of a hassle. So for revenge he sends the rock back to have the year of death carved in, then sticks it in the window. Sick, huh?"

It was Dad all over.

"Do you, does he, live in the neighborhood? I guess he'd be pretty upset to see it, but it's been here all this time, at least a year, and—"

"He hasn't seen it, and if he did, he'd laugh or want a commission for the use of his name," I say. Johnny in his embarrassment has developed a great blush, which makes him look even better. "And me, I'm on my way over to a place I heard about. Aunt Fred's?"

Johnny gives a half-smile, relieved and something more.

"I guess it's cool if you're still into disco."

"Not necessarily."

Dee Dee must have just gotten off the phone because she's there on the first ring.

"Doctor Anderson?"

"It's Don Banta," I tell her. "I represent Allied Pharmaceuticals."

"You're the one who gave me that sample for Jeremy."

I figure Jeremy must be the kid in the photo on her desk.

"The same."

"Amazing."

"What is amazing?"

"Mr. Banta, you may very well have saved my son's life this morning."

I had been leaning back against the pillows, but sit up straight at this announcement.

"He had an attack about four, the worst one ever. I used his old prescription, I patted his chest, but nothing helped. Finally I called 911 but while I was waiting for the ambulance his lips started to go blue and suddenly I remembered that inhaler and what you called it: a miracle worker. I needed a miracle. It was still in my purse."

"What happened?"

"What happened is it calmed him down." Dee Dee's voice is strained with exhaustion. "I can't believe you're calling me. It's like you knew."

"He's all right now?"

"Mr. Banta, my family owes you a big one. If ever—*if ever*— there's anything...."

I close my eyes and I feel the chain of things: Dad to me, me to Dee Dee, Dee Dee to her kid. There's purposes we don't suspect, side paths we don't venture but a few steps down, and yet there's a give-and-take that leads forward, a surprise when we don't even know we need it. For the first time in a while I remember I'm a part of the flow, more than I admit, a river that can best be witnessed from very far away. "It's like you knew all along," Dee Dee repeats for the lack of anything else to add.

"I ..." I begin, but then the words stick. My fingers curl tight around the receiver and I stare at my packed suitcase where it waits by the door.

"Are you there?" Dee Dee wants to know. "Hello? Mr. Banta?"

I don't answer, I don't have one thing to say, and after a moment, the line goes dead.

Rupert and Gerald

D.H. Lawrence

"The creative, spontaneous soul sends forth its promptings of desire and aspiration in us," wrote D.H. Lawrence in 1920. "These promptings are our true fate, which is our business to fulfil. A fate dictated from outside, from theory or from circumstance, is a false fate." One of Lawrence's finest stories, "The Prussian Officer", portrays the bitter consequence of gay passion lived falsely. But in "Rupert and Gerald", probably written around 1916, Lawrence attempted the harder task of depicting a passionate, tormented, positive struggle to be conscious of and truthful to one's fate. He must have known that Rupert Birkin—who prefers the physique of the soldier to that of any woman—would provoke the indignation of British society. That same year, Lawrence's novel The Rainbow, *because of its graphic sexuality written in a style which he defended as a "pulsing, frictional to and fro which works up to culmination", had been seized and destroyed in its entire first edition. He never published Rupert's story, and he removed some references to Rupert's love for Gerald from his next novel,* Women in Love, *for which it might have functioned as a prologue. Nevertheless, in spite of Lawrence's cuts, when the novel was published the periodical* John Bull *warned its readers that Lawrence's description of Rupert and Gerald's relationship was "sheer filth from beginning to end.... This is the sort of book," thundered the reviewer, "which in the hands of a boy in his teens might pave the way to unspeakable moral disaster."*

The acquaintance between the two men was slight and insignificant. Yet there was a subtle bond that connected them.

They had met four years ago, brought together by a common friend, Hosken, a naval man. The three, Rupert Birkin, William Hosken, and Gerald Crich had then spent a week in the Tyrol together, mountain-climbing.

Birkin and Gerald Crich felt take place between them, the moment they saw each other, that sudden connection which sometimes springs up between men who are very different in temper. There had been a subterranean kindling in each man. Each looked towards the other, and knew the trembling nearness.

Yet they had maintained complete reserve, their relations had been, to all knowledge, entirely casual and trivial. Because of the inward kindled connection, they were even more distant and slight than men usually are, one towards the other.

There was, however, a certain tenderness in their politeness, an almost uncomfortable understanding lurked under their formal, reserved behaviour. They were vividly aware of each other's presence, and each was just as vividly aware of himself, in presence of the other.

The week of mountain-climbing passed like an intense brief lifetime. The three men were very close together, and lifted into an abstract isolation, among the upper rocks and the snow. The world that lay below, the whole field of human activity, was sunk and subordinated, they had trespassed into the upper silence and loneliness. The three of them had reached another state of being, they were enkindled in the upper silences into a rare, unspoken intimacy, an intimacy that took no expression, but which was between them like a transfiguration. As if thrown into the strange fire of abstraction, up in the mountains, they knew and were known to each other. It was another world, another life, transfigured, and yet most vividly corporeal, the senses all raised till each felt his own body, and the presence of his companions, like an essential flame, they radiated to one enkindled, transcendent fire, in the upper world.

Then had come the sudden falling down to earth, the sudden extinction. At Innsbruck they had parted, Birkin to go to Munich, Gerald Crich and Hosken to take the train for Paris and London. On the station they shook hands, and went asunder, having spoken no word and given no sign of the transcendent intimacy which had roused them beyond the everyday life. They shook hands and took leave casually, as mere acquaintances going their separate ways. Yet there remained always, for Birkin and for Gerald Crich, the absolute recognition that had passed between them then, the knowledge that was in their eyes as they met at the moment of parting. They knew they loved each other, that each would die for the other.

Yet all this knowledge was kept submerged in the soul of the two men. Outwardly they would have none of it. Outwardly they only stiffened themselves away from it. They took leave from each other even more coldly and casually than is usual.

And for a year they had seen nothing of each other, neither had they exchanged any word. They passed away from each other, and, superficially, forgot.

But when they met again, in a country house in Derbyshire, the enkindled sensitiveness sprang up again like a strange, embarrassing fire. They scarcely knew each other, yet here was this strange, unacknowledged, inflammable intimacy between them. It made them uneasy.

Rupert Birkin, however, strongly centred in himself, never gave way in his soul, to anyone. He remained in the last issue detached, self-responsible, having no communion with any other soul. Therefore Gerald Crich remained intact in his own form.

The two men were very different. Gerald Crich was the fair, keen-eyed Englishman of medium stature, hard in his muscles and full of energy as a machine. He was a hunter, a traveller, a soldier, always active, always moving vigorously, and giving orders to some subordinate.

Birkin on the other hand was quiet and unobtrusive. In stature he was long and very thin, and yet not bony, close-knit, flexible, and full of repose, like a steel wire. His energy was not evident, he seemed almost weak, passive, insignificant. He was delicate in health. His face was pale and rather ugly, his hair dun-coloured, his eyes were of a yellowish-grey, full of life and warmth. They were the only noticeable thing about him, to the ordinary observer, being very warm and sudden and attractive, alive like fires. But this chief attraction of Birkin's was a false one. Those that knew him best knew that his lovable eyes were, in the last issue, estranged and unsoftening like the eyes of a wolf. In the last issue he was callous, and without feeling, confident, just as Gerald Crich in the last issue was wavering and lost.

The two men were staying in the house of Sir Charles Roddice, Gerald Crich as friend of the host, Rupert Birkin as friend of his host's daughter, Hermione Roddice. Sir Charles would have been glad for Gerald Crich to marry the daughter of the house, because this young man was a well-set young Englishman of strong conservative temperament, and heir to considerable wealth. But Gerald Crich did not care for Hermione Roddice, and Hermione Roddice disliked Gerald Crich.

She was a rather beautiful woman of twenty-five, fair, tall, slender, graceful, and of some learning. She had known Rupert Birkin in Oxford. He was a year her senior. He was a fellow of Magdalen College, and had been, at twenty-one, one of the young lights of the place, a coming somebody. His essays on Education were brilliant, and he became an inspector of schools.

Hermione Roddice loved him. When she had listened to his passionate declamations, in his rooms in the Blackhorse Road, and when she had heard the respect with which he was spoken of, five years ago, she being a girl of twenty, reading political economy, and he a youth of twenty-one, holding forth against Nietzsche, then she devoted herself to his name and fame. She added herself to his mental and spiritual flame.

Sir Charles thought they would marry. He considered that Birkin, hanging on year after year, was spoiling all his daughter's chances, and without pledging himself in the least. It irked the soldierly knight considerably. But he was somewhat afraid of the quiet, always-civil Birkin. And Hermione, when Sir Charles mentioned that he thought of speaking to the young man, in order to know his intentions, fell into such a white and overweening, contemptuous passion, that her father was nonplussed and reduced to irritated silence.

"How vulgar you are!" cried the young woman. "You are not to dare to say a word to him. It is a friendship, and it is not to be broken-in upon in this fashion. Why should you want to rush me into marriage? I am more than happy as I am."

Her liquid grey eyes swam dark with fury and pain and resentment, her beautiful face was convulsed. She seemed like a prophetess violated. Her father withdrew, cold and huffed.

So the relationship between the young woman and Birkin continued. He was an inspector of schools, she studied Education. He wrote also harsh, jarring poetry, very real and painful, under which she suffered; and sometimes, shallower, gentle lyrics, which she treasured as drops of manna. Like a priestess she kept his records and his oracles, he was like a god who would be nothing if his worship were neglected.

Hermione could not understand the affection between the two men. They would sit together in the hall, at evening, and talk without any depth. What did Rupert find to take him up, in Gerald Crich's conversation? She, Hermione, was only rather bored, and puzzled.

Yet the two men seemed happy, holding their commonplace discussion. Hermione was impatient. She knew that Birkin was, as usual, belittling his own mind and talent, for the sake of something that she felt unworthy. Some common correspondence which she knew demeaned and belied him. Why would he always come down so eagerly to the level of common people, why was he always so anxious to vulgarize and betray himself? She bit her lip in torment. It was as if he were anxious to deny all that was fine and rare in himself.

Birkin knew what she was feeling and thinking. Yet he continued almost spitefully against her. He *did* want to betray the heights and depths of nearly religious intercourse which he had with her. He, the God, turned round upon his priestess, and became the common vulgar man who turned her to scorn. He performed some strange metamorphosis of soul, and from being a pure, incandescent spirit burning intense with the presence of God, he became a lustful, shallow, insignificant fellow running in all the common ruts. Even there was some vindictiveness in him now, something jeering and spiteful and low, unendurable. It drove her mad. She had given him all her trembling, naked soul, and now he turned mongrel, and triumphed in his own degeneration. It was his deep desire, to be common, vulgar, a little gross. She could not bear the look of almost sordid jeering with which he turned on her, when she reached out her hand, imploring. It was as if some rat bit her, she felt she was going insane. And he jeered at her, at the spiritual woman who waited at the tomb, in her sandals and her mourning robes. He jeered at her horribly, knowing her secrets. And she was insane, she knew she was going mad.

But he plunged on triumphant into intimacy with Gerald Crich, excluding the woman, tormenting her. He knew how to pitch himself into tune with another person. He could adjust his mind, his consciousness, almost perfectly to that of Gerald Crich, lighting up the edge of the other man's limitation with a glimmering light that was the essence of exquisite adventure and liberation to the confined intelligence. The two men talked together for hours, Birkin watching the hard limbs and the rather stiff face of the traveller in unknown countries, Gerald Crich catching the pale, luminous face opposite him, lit up over the edge of the unknown regions of the soul, trembling into new being, quivering with new intelligence.

To Hermione, it was insupportable degradation that Rupert Birkin should maintain this correspondence, prostituting his mind and his understanding to the coarser stupidity of the other man. She felt confusion gathering upon her, she was unanchored on the edge of madness. Why did he do it? Why was he, whom she knew as her leader, star-like and pure, why was he the lowest betrayer and the ugliest of blasphemers? She held her temples, feeling herself reel towards the bottomless pit.

For Birkin did get a greater satisfaction, at least for the time being, from his intercourse with the other man, than from his spiritual relation with her. It satisfied him to have to do with Gerald Crich, it fulfilled him to have this other man, this hard-limbed traveller and sportsman, following implicitly, held as it were consummated within the spell of a more powerful understanding. Birkin felt a passion of desire for Gerald Crich, for the clumsier, cruder intelligence and the limited soul, and for the striving, unlightened body of his friend. And Gerald Crich, not understanding, was transfused with pleasure. He did not even know he loved Birkin. He thought him marvellous in understanding, almost unnatural, and on the other hand pitiful and delicate in body. He felt a great tenderness towards him, of superior physical strength, and at the same time some reverence for his delicacy and fineness of being.

All the same, there was no profession of friendship, no open mark of intimacy. They remained to all intents and purposes distant, mere acquaintances. It was in the other world of the subconsciousness that the interplay took place, the interchange of spiritual and physical richness, the relieving of physical and spiritual poverty, without any intrinsic change of state in either man.

Hermione could not understand it at all. She was mortified and in despair. In his lapses, she despised and revolted from Birkin. Her mistrust of him pierced to the quick of her soul. If his intense and pure flame of spirituality only sank to this guttering prostration, a low, degraded heat, servile to a clumsy Gerald Crich, fawning on a coarse, unsusceptible being, such as was Gerald Crich and all the multitudes of Gerald Criches of this world, then nothing was anything. The transcendent star of one evening was the putrescent phosphorescence of the next, and glory and corruptibility were interchangeable. Her soul was convulsed with cynicism. She despised her God and her angel. Yet she could not do without him. She believed in herself as a priestess, and that was all. Though there were no God to serve, still she was a priestess. Yet having no altar to kindle, no sacrifice to burn, she would be barren and useless. So she adhered to her God in him, which she claimed almost violently, whilst her soul turned in bitter cynicism from the prostitute man in him. She did not believe in him, she only believed in that which she could gather from him, as one gathers silk from the corrupt worm. She was the maker of gods.

So, after a few days, Gerald Crich went away and Birkin was left to Hermione Roddice. It is true, Crich said to Birkin: "Come and see us, if ever you are near enough, will you?", and Birkin had said yes. But for some reason, it was concluded beforehand that this visit would never be made, deliberately.

Sick, helpless, Birkin swung back to Hermione. In the garden, at evening, looking over the silvery hills, he sat near to her, or lay with his head on her bosom, while the moonlight came gently upon the trees, and they talked, quietly, gently as dew distilling, their two disembodied voices distilled in the silvery air, two voices moving and ceasing like ghosts, like spirits. And they talked of life, and of death, but chiefly of death, his words turning strange and phosphorescent, like dark water suddenly shaken alight, whilst she held his head against her breast, infinitely satisfied and completed by its weight upon her, and her hand travelled gently, finely, oh, with such exquisite quivering adjustment, over his hair. The pain of tenderness he felt for her was almost unendurable, as her hand fluttered and came near, scarcely touching him, so light and sensitive it was, as it passed over his hair, rhythmically. And still his voice moved and thrilled through her like the keenest pangs of embrace, she remained possessed by him, possessed by the spirit. And the sense of beauty and perfect, blade-keen ecstasy was balanced to perfection, she passed away, was transported.

After these nights of superfine ecstasy of beauty, after all was consumed in the silver fire of moonlight, all the soul caught up in the universal chill-blazing bonfire of the moonlit night, there came the morning, and the ash, when his body was grey and consumed, and his soul ill. Why should the sun shine, and hot gay flowers come out, when the kingdom of reality was the silver-cold night of death, lovely and perfect.

She, like a priestess, was fulfilled and rich. But he became more hollow and ghastly to look at. There was no escape, they penetrated further and further into the regions of death, and soon the connection with life would be broken.

Then came his revulsion against her. After he loved her with a tenderness that was anguish, a love that was all pain, or else transcendent white ecstasy, he turned upon her savagely, like a maddened dog. And like a priestess who is rended for sacrifice, she submitted and endured. She would serve the God she possessed, even though he should turn periodically into a fierce dog, to rend her.

So he went away, to his duties, and his work. He had made a passionate study of education, only to come, gradually, to the knowledge that education is nothing but the process of building up, gradually, a complete unit of consciousness. And each unit of consciousness is the living unit of that great social, religious, philosophic idea towards which mankind, like an organism seeking its final form, is laboriously growing. But if there *be* no great philosophic idea, if, for the time being, mankind, instead of going through a period of growth, is going through a corresponding process of decay and decomposition from some old, fulfilled, obsolete idea, then what is the good of educating? Decay and decomposition will take their own way. It is impossible to educate for this end, impossible to teach the world how to die away from its achieved, nullified form. The autumn must take place in every individual soul, as well as in all the people, all must die, individually and socially. But education is a process of striving to a new, unanimous being, a whole organic form. But when winter has set in, when the frosts are strangling the leaves off the trees and the birds are silent knots of darkness, how can there be a unanimous movement towards a whole summer of florescence? There can be none of this, only submission to the death of this nature, in the winter that has come upon mankind, and a cherishing of the unknown that is unknown for many a day yet, buds that may not open till a far off season comes, when the season of death has passed away.

And Birkin was just coming to a knowledge of the essential futility of all attempt at social unanimity in constructiveness. In the winter, there can only be unanimity of disintegration, the leaves fall unanimously, the plants die down, each creature is a soft-slumbering grave, as the adder and the dormouse in winter are the soft tombs of the adder and the dormouse, which slip about like rays of brindled darkness, in summer.

How to get away from this process of reduction, how escape this phosphorescent passage into the tomb, which was universal though unacknowledged, this was the unconscious problem which tortured

Birkin day and night. He came to Hermione, and found with her the pure, translucent regions of death itself, of ecstasy. In the world the autumn was setting in. What should a man add himself on to?—to science, to social reform, to aestheticism, to sensationalism? The whole world's constructive activity was a fiction, a lie, to hide the great process of decomposition, which had set in. What then to adhere to?

He ran about from death to death. Work was terrible, horrible because he did not believe in it. It was almost a horror to him, to think of going from school to school, making reports and giving suggestions, when the whole process to his soul was pure futility, a process of mechanical activity entirely purposeless, sham growth which was entirely rootless. Nowhere more than in education did a man feel the horror of false, rootless, spasmodic activity more acutely. The whole business was like dementia. It created in him a feeling of nausea and horror. He recoiled from it. And yet, where should a man repair, what should he do?

In his private life the same horror of futility and wrongness dogged him. Leaving alone all ideas, religious or philosophic, all of which are mere sounds, old repetitions, or else novel, dexterous, sham permutations and combinations of old repetitions, leaving alone all the things of the mind and the consciousness, what remained in a man's life? There is his emotional and his sensuous activity, is not this enough?

Birkin started with madness from this question, for it touched the quick of torture. There was his love for Hermione, a love based entirely on ecstasy and on pain, and ultimate death. He *knew* he did not love her with any living, creative love. He did not even desire her: he had no passion for her, there was no hot impulse of growth between them, only this terrible reducing activity of phosphorescent consciousness, the consciousness ever liberated more and more into the void, at the expense of the flesh, which was burnt down like dead grey ash.

He did not call this love. Yet he was bound to her, and it was agony to leave her. And he did not love anyone else. He did not love any woman. He *wanted* to love. But between wanting to love, and loving, is the whole difference between life and death.

The incapacity to love, the incapacity to desire any woman, positively, with body and soul, this was a real torture, a deep torture indeed. Never to be able to love spontaneously, never to be moved by a power greater than oneself, but always to be within one's own control, deliberate, having the choice, this was horrifying, more deadly than death. Yet how was one to escape? How could a man escape from being deliberate and unloving, except a greater power, an impersonal, imperative love should take hold of him? And if the greater power should not take hold of him, what could he do but continue in his deliberateness, without any fundamental spontaneity?

He did not love Hermione, he did not desire her. But he wanted to force himself to love her and to desire her. He was consumed by sexual desire, and he wanted to be fulfilled. Yet he did not desire Hermione. She repelled him rather. Yet he *would* have this physical fulfilment, he would have the sexual activity. So he forced himself towards her.

She was hopeless from the start. Yet she resigned herself to him. In her soul, she knew this was not the way. And yet even she was ashamed, as of some physical deficiency. She did not want him either. But with all her soul, she *wanted* to want him. She would do anything to give him what he wanted, that which he was raging for, this physical fulfilment he insisted on. She was wise; she thought for the best. She prepared herself like a perfect sacrifice to him. She offered herself gladly to him, gave herself into his will.

And oh, it was all such a cruel failure, just a failure. This last act of love which he had demanded of her was the keenest grief of all, it was so insignificant, so null. He had no pleasure of her, only some mortification. And her heart almost broke with grief.

She wanted him to take her. She wanted him to take her, to break her with his passion, to destroy her with his desire, so long as he got satisfaction. She looked forward, tremulous, to a kind of death at his hands, she gave herself up. She would be broken and dying, destroyed, if only he would rise fulfilled.

But he was not capable of it, he failed. He could not take her and destroy her. He could not forget her. They had too rare a spiritual intimacy, he could not now tear himself away from all this, and come like a brute to take its satisfaction. He was too much aware of her, and of her fear, and of her writhing torment, as she lay in sacrifice. He had too much deference for her feeling. He could not, as she madly wanted, destroy her, trample her, and crush a satisfaction from her. He was not experienced enough, not hardened enough. He was always aware of *her* feelings, so that he had none of his own. Which made this last love-making between them an ignominious failure, very, very cruel to bear.

And it was this failure which broke the love between them. He hated her, for her incapacity in love, for her lack of desire for him, her complete and almost perfect lack of any physical desire towards him. Her desire was all spiritual, all in the consciousness. She wanted him all, all through the consciousness, never through the senses.

And she hated him, and despised him, for his incapacity to wreak his desire upon her, his lack of strength to crush his satisfaction from her. If only he could have taken her, destroyed her, used her all up, and been satisfied, she would be at last free. She might be killed, but it would be the death which gave her consummation.

It was a failure, a bitter, final failure. He could not take from her what he wanted, because he could not, bare-handed, destroy her. And she despised him that he could not destroy her.

Still, though they had failed, finally, they did not go apart. Their relation was too deep-established. He was by this time twenty-eight years old, and she twenty-seven. Still, for his spiritual delight, for a companion in his conscious life, for someone to share and heighten his joy in thinking, or in reading, or in feeling beautiful things, or in knowing landscape intimately and poignantly, he turned to her. For all these things, she was still with him, she made up the greater part of his life. And he, she knew to her anguish and mortification, he was still the master-key to almost all life, for her. She wanted it not to be so, she wanted to be free of him, of the strange, terrible bondage of his domination. But as yet, she could not free herself from him.

He went to other women, to women of purely sensual, sensational attraction, he prostituted his spirit with them. And he got *some* satisfaction. She watched him go, sadly, and yet not without a measure of relief. For he would torment her less, now.

She knew he would come back to her. She knew, inevitably as the dawn would rise, he would come back to her, half-exultant and triumphant over her, half-bitter against her for letting him go and wanting her now, wanting the communion with her. It was as if he went to the other, the dark, sensual, almost bestial woman thoroughly and fully to degrade himself. He despised himself, essentially, in his attempts at sensuality, she knew that. So she let him be. It was only his rather vulgar arrogance of a sinner that she found hard to bear. For before her, he wore his sins with braggadocio, flaunted them a little in front of her. And this alone drove her to exasperation to the point of uttering her contempt for his childishness and his instability.

But as yet, she forbore, because of the deference he still felt towards her. Intrinsically, in his spirit, he still served her. And this service she cherished.

But he was becoming gnawed and bitter, a little mad. His whole system was inflamed to a pitch of mad irritability, he became blind, unconscious to the greater half of life, only a few things he saw with feverish acuteness. And she, she kept the key to him, all the while.

The only thing she dreaded was his making up his mind. She dreaded his way of seeing some particular things vividly and feverishly, and of his acting upon this special sight. For once he decided a thing, it became a reigning universal truth to him, and he was completely inhuman.

He was, in his own way, quite honest with himself. But every man has his own truths, and is honest with himself according to them. The terrible thing about Birkin, for Hermione, was that when once he decided upon a truth, he acted upon it, cost what it might. If he decided that his eye did really offend him, he would in truth pluck it out. And this seemed to her so inhuman, so abstract, that it chilled her to the depths of her soul, and made him seem to her inhuman, something between a monster and a complete fool. For might not she herself easily be found to be this eye which must needs be plucked out?

He had stuck fast over this question of love and of physical fulfilment in love, till it had become like a monomania. All his thought turned upon it. For he wanted to keep his integrity of being, he would not consent to sacrifice one half of himself to the other. He would not sacrifice the sensual to the spiritual half of himself, and he could not sacrifice the spiritual to the sensual half. Neither could he obtain fulfilment in both, the two halves always reacted from each other. To be spiritual, he must have a Hermione, completely without desire: to be sensual, he must have a slightly bestial woman, the very scent of whose skin soon disgusted him, whose manners nauseated him beyond bearing, so that Hermione, always chaste and always stretching out her hands for beauty, seemed to him the purest and most desirable thing on earth.

He knew he obtained no real fulfilment in sensuality, he became disgusted and despised the whole process as if it were dirty. And he knew that he had no real fulfilment in his spiritual and aesthetic intercourse with Hermione. That process he also despised, with considerable cynicism.

And he recognized that he was on the point either of breaking, becoming a thing, losing his integral being, or else of becoming insane. He was now nothing but a series of reactions from dark to light, from light to dark, almost mechanical, without unity or meaning.

This was the most insufferable bondage, the most tormenting affliction, that he could not save himself from these extreme reactions, the vibration between two poles, one of which was Hermione, the centre of social virtue, the other of which was a prostitute, antisocial, almost criminal. He knew that in the end, subject to this extreme vibration, he would be shattered, would die, or else, worse still, would become a mere disordered set of processes, without purpose or integral being. He knew this, and dreaded it. Yet he could not save himself.

To save himself, he must unite the two halves of himself, spiritual and sensual. And this is what no man can do at once, deliberately. It must happen to him. Birkin willed to be sensual, as well as spiritual, with Hermione. He might will it, he might act according to his will, but he did not bring to pass that which he willed. A man cannot create desire in himself, nor cease at will from desiring. Desire, in any shape or form, is primal, whereas the will is secondary, derived. The will can destroy, but it cannot create.

So the more he tried with his will, to force his senses towards Hermione, the greater misery he produced. On the other hand his pride never ceased to contemn his profligate intercourse elsewhere. After all, it was *not* that which he wanted. He did not want libertine pleasures, not fundamentally. His fundamental desire was, to be able to love completely, in one and the same act: both body and soul at once, struck into a complete oneness in contact with a complete woman.

And he failed in this desire. It was always a case of one or the other, of spirit or of senses, and each, alone, was deadly. All history, almost all art, seemed the story of this deadly half-love: either passion, like Cleopatra, or else spirit, like Mary of Bethany or Vittoria Colonna.

He pondered on the subject endlessly, and knew himself in his reactions. But self-knowledge is not everything. No man, by taking thought, can add one cubit to his stature. He can but know his own height and limitation.

He knew that he loved no woman, that in nothing was he really complete, really himself. In his most passionate moments of spiritual enlightenment, when like a saviour of mankind he would pour out his soul for the world, there was in him a capacity to jeer at all his own righteousness and spirituality, justly and sincerely to make a mock of it all. And the mockery was so true, it bit to the very core of his right-eousness, and showed it rotten, shining with phosphorescence. But at the same time, whilst quivering in the climax-thrill of sensual pangs, some cold voice could say in him: "You are not really moved; you could rise up and go away from this pleasure quite coldly and calmly; it is not radical, your enjoyment."

The knew he had not loved, could not love. The only thing then was to make the best of it, have the two things separate, and over them all, a calm detached mind. But to this he would not acquiesce. "I should be like a Neckan," he said to himself, "like a sea-water being, I should have no soul." And he pondered the stories of the wistful, limpid creatures who watched ceaselessly, hoping to gain a soul.

So the trouble went on, he became more hollow and deathly, more like a spectre with hollow bones. He knew that he was not very far from dissolution.

All the time, he recognized that, although he was always drawn to women, feeling more at home with a woman than with a man, yet it was for men that he felt the hot, flushing, roused attraction which a man is supposed to feel for the other sex. Although nearly all his liv-ing interchange went on with one woman or another, although he was always terribly intimate with at least one woman, and practically never intimate with a man, yet the male physique had a fascination for him, and for the female physique he felt only a fondness, a sort of sacred love, as for a sister.

In the street, it was the men who roused him by their flesh and their manly, vigorous movement, quite apart from all the individual character, whilst he studied the women as sisters, knowing their meaning and their intents. It was the men's physique which held the passion and the mystery to him. The women he seemed to be kin to, he looked for the soul in them. The soul of a woman and the physique of a man, these were the two things he watched for, in the street.

And this was a new torture to him. Why did not the face of a woman move him in the same manner, with the same sense of hand-some desirability, as the face of a man? Why was a man's beauty, the beauté mâle, so vivid and intoxicating a thing to him, whilst female beauty was something quite unsubstantial, consisting all of look and gesture and revelation of intuitive intelligence? He thought women beautiful purely because of their expression. But it was plastic form that fascinated him in men, the contour and movement of the flesh itself.

He wanted all the time to love women. He wanted all the while to feel this kindled, loving attraction towards a beautiful woman, that he would often feel towards a handsome man. But he could not. Whenever it was a case of a woman, there entered in too much spiritual, sisterly love; or else, in reaction, there was only a brutal, callous sort of lust.

This was an entanglement from which there seemed no escape. How can a man *create* his own feelings? He cannot. It is only in his power to suppress them, to bind them in the chain of the will. And what is suppression but a mere negation of life, and of living.

He had several friendships wherein this passion entered, friendships with men of no very great intelligence, but of pleasant appearance: ruddy, well-nourished fellows, good-natured and easy, who protected him in his delicate health more gently than a woman would protect him. He loved his friend, the beauty of whose manly limbs made him tremble with pleasure. He wanted to caress him.

But reserve, which was as strong as a chain of iron in him, kept him from any demonstration. And if he were away for any length of time from the man he loved so hotly, then he forgot him, the flame which invested the beloved like a transfiguration passed away, and Birkin remembered his friend as tedious. He could not go back to him, to talk as tediously as he would have to talk, to take such a level of intelligence as he would have to take. He forgot his men friends completely, as one forgets the candle one has blown out. They remained as quite extraneous and uninteresting persons living their life in their own sphere, and having not the slightest relation to himself, even though they themselves maintained a real warmth of affection, almost of love for him. He paid not the slightest heed to this love which was constant to him, he felt it sincerely to be just nothing, valueless.

So he left his old friends completely, even those to whom he had been attached passionately, like David to Jonathan. Men whose presence he had waited for cravingly, the touch of whose shoulder suffused him with a vibration of physical love, became to him mere figures, as nonexistent as is the waiter who sets the table in a restaurant.

He wondered very slightly at this, but dismissed it with hardly a thought. Yet, every now and again, would come over him the same passionate desire to have near him some man he saw, to exchange intimacy, to unburden himself of love of this new beloved.

It might be any man, a policeman who suddenly looked up at him, as he inquired the way, or a soldier who sat next to him in a railway carriage. How vividly, months afterwards, he would recall the soldier who had sat pressed up close to him on a journey from Charing Cross to Westerham; the shapely, motionless body, the large, dumb, coarsely-beautiful hands that rested helpless upon the strong knees, the dark brown eyes, vulnerable in the erect body. Or a young man in flannels on the sands at Margate, flaxen and ruddy, like a Viking of twenty-three, with clean, rounded contours, pure as the contours of snow, playing with some young children, building a castle in sand, intent and abstract, like a seagull or a keen white bear.

In his mind was a small gallery of such men: men whom he had never spoken to, but who had flashed themselves upon his senses unforgettably, men whom he apprehended intoxicatingly in his blood. They divided themselves roughly into two classes: these white-skinned, keen-limbed men with eyes like blue-flashing ice and hair like crystals of winter sunshine, the northmen, inhuman as sharp-crying gulls, distinct like splinters of ice, like crystals, isolated, individual; and then the men with dark eyes that one can enter and plunge into, bathe in, as in a liquid darkness, dark-skinned, supple, night-smelling men, who are the living substance of the viscous, universal heavy darkness.

His senses surged towards these men, towards the perfect and beautiful representatives of these two halves. And he knew them, by seeing them and by apprehending them sensuously, he knew their very blood, its weight and savour; the blood of the northmen sharp and red and light, tending to be keenly acrid, like cranberries, the blood of the dark-limbed men heavy and luscious, and in the end nauseating, revolting.

He asked himself, often, as he grew older, and more unearthly, when he was twenty-eight and twenty-nine years old, would he ever be appeased, would he ever cease to desire these two sorts of men. And a wan kind of hopelessness would come over him, as if he would never escape from this attraction, which was a bondage.

For he would never acquiesce to it. He could never acquiesce to his own feelings, to his own passion. He could never grant that it should be so, that it was well for him to feel this keen desire to have and to possess the bodies of such men, the passion to bathe in the very substance of such men, the substance of living, eternal light, like eternal snow, and the flux of heavy, rank-smelling darkness.

He wanted to cast out these desires, he wanted not to know them. Yet a man can no more slay a living desire in him, than he can prevent his body from feeling heat and cold. He can put himself into bondage, to prevent the fulfilment of the desire, that is all. But the desire is there, as the travelling of the blood itself is there, until it is fulfilled or until the body is dead.

So he went on, month after month, year after year, divided against himself, striving for the day when the beauty of men should not be so acutely attractive to him, when the beauty of woman should move him instead.

But that day came no nearer, rather it went further away. His deep dread was that it would always be so, that he would never be free. His life would have been one long torture of struggle against his own innate desire, his own innate being. But to be so divided against oneself, this is terrible, a nullification of all being.

He went into violent excess with a mistress whom, in a rather antisocial, ashamed spirit, he loved. And so for a long time he forgot about this attraction that men had for him. He forgot about it entirely. And then he grew stronger, surer.

But then, inevitably, it would recur again. There would come into a restaurant a strange Cornish type of man, with dark eyes like holes in his head, or like the eyes of a rat, and with dark, fine, rather stiff hair, and full, heavy, softly-strong limbs. Then again Birkin would feel the desire spring up in him, the desire to know this man, to have him, as it were to eat him, to take the very substance of him. And watching the strange, rather furtive, rabbit-like way in which the strong, softly-built man ate, Birkin would feel the rousedness burning in his own breast, as if this were what he wanted, as if the satisfaction of his desire lay in the body of the young, strong man opposite.

And then in his soul would succeed a sort of despair, because this passion for a man had recurred in him. It was a deep misery to him. And it would seem as if he had always loved men, always and only loved men. And this was the greatest suffering to him.

But it was not so, that he always loved men. For weeks it would be all gone from him, this passionate admiration of the rich body of a man. For weeks he was free, active, and living. But he had such a dread of his own feelings and desires, that when they recurred again, the interval vanished, and it seemed the bondage and the torment had been continuous.

This was the one and only secret he kept to himself, this secret of his passionate and sudden, spasmodic affinity for men he saw. He kept this secret even from himself. He knew what he felt, but he always kept the knowledge at bay. His a priori were: "I *should not* feel like this," and "It is the ultimate mark of my own deficiency, that I feel like this." Therefore, though he admitted everything, he never really faced the question. He never accepted the desire, and received it as part of himself. He always tried to keep it expelled from him.

Gerald Crich was the one towards whom Birkin felt most strongly that immediate, roused attraction which transfigured the person of the attracter with such a glow and such a desirable beauty. The two men had met once or twice, and then Gerald Crich went abroad, to South America. Birkin forgot him, all connection died down. But it was not finally dead. In both men were the seeds of a strong, inflammable affinity.

Therefore, when Birkin found himself pledged to act as best man at the wedding of Hosken, the friend of the mountain-climbing holiday, and of Laura Crich, sister of Gerald, the old affection sprang awake in a moment. He wondered what Gerald would be like now.

Hermione, knowing of Hosken's request to Birkin, at once secured for herself the position of bridesmaid to Laura Crich. It was inevitable. She and Rupert Birkin were running to the end of their friendship. He was now thirty years of age, and she twenty-nine. His feeling of hostility towards Hermione had grown now to an almost constant dislike. Still she held him in her power. But the hold became weaker and weaker. "If he breaks loose," she said, "he will fall into the abyss."

Nevertheless he was bound to break loose, because his reaction against Hermione was the strongest movement in his life, now. He was thrusting her off, fighting her off all the while, thrusting himself clear, although he had no other foothold, although he was breaking away from her, his one rock, to fall into a bottomless sea.

Mr. Wilde's Second Chance

Joanna Russ

In 1892, Francis Dufresne imagined a world in which Napoleon hadn't lost the war. The French invaded England, took over Spain and Russia, and settled over Europe a glorious empire in which all civilization was French. Nothing is memorable about this novel except its rewriting of history and the inspired detail of Manchester becoming the centre of world cuisine. To change the past is an eternally impossible and danger-ous wish. At its best, it frees the imagination from the constricts of fact and produces little masterpieces such as Adolfo Bioy Casares's The Celestial Plot, in which Rome has been defeated by Carthage, or Philippe Jullian's The Flight to Egypt, in which the Grand Duchess Olga, eldest daughter of the last Czar of Russia, escapes the Bolshevik Revolution, helps Nasser arm Egypt, and founds her own African king-dom, called Ici. At its worst, it feeds the rage of those who deny the Holocaust and other abominations.

"Do you know the great drama of my life?" confided Oscar Wilde to André Gide. "It's that I have put my genius into my life; all I've put into my works is my talent." Gide did not record the tone of voice in which these words were pronounced. We don't know if the witticism was a regret or a boast. Wilde's talent was recognized and admired; his genius punished with prison and a miserable, inglorious death. He had, more than most people, a solid sense of reality and few illusions about just rewards. "The good ended happily, and the bad unhappily. That is what Fiction means," says one of his cynical characters in The Impor-tance of Being Earnest. With these elements, Joanna Russ, the remark-able science-fiction writer, has constructed a small fable that is both poignant and cautionary.

This is a tale told to me by a friend after the Cointreau and the music as we sat in the dusk waiting for the night to come.

When Oscar Wilde (he said) died, his soul was found too sad for heaven and too happy for hell. A tattered spirit with the look of a debased street imp led him through miles of limbo into a large, foggy room, very like (for what he could see of it) a certain club in London. His small, grimy scud of a guide went up to a stand something like that used by ladies for embroidery or old men for chess, and there it stopped, spinning like a top.

"Yours!" it squeaked.

"Mine?"

But it was gone. On the stand was a board like the kind used for children's games, and nearby a dark lady in wine-colored silk moved pieces over a board of her own. The celebrated writer bent to watch her—she chanced to look up—it was Ada R—, the victim of the most celebrated scandal of the last decade. She had died of pneumonia or a broken heart in Paris; no one knew which. She gave him, out of her black eyes, a look so tragic, so shrinking, so haunted, that the poet (the most courteous of men, even when dead) bowed and turned away. The board before him was a maze of colored squares and meandering lines, and on top was written "O. O'F. Wilde" in coronet script, for this was his life's pattern and each man or woman in the room labored over a board on which was figured the events of his life. Each was trying to rearrange his life into a beautiful and ordered picture, and when he had done that he would be free to live again. As you can imagine, it was both exciting and horribly anxious, this reliving, this being down on the board and at the same time a dead—if not damned—soul in a room the size of all Aetna, but queerly like a London club when it has just got dark and they have lit the lamps. The lady next to Wilde was pale as glass. She was almost finished. She raised one arm—her dark sleeve swept across the board—and in an instant her design was in ruins. Mr. Wilde picked up several of the pieces that had fallen and handed them to the lady.

"If you please," she said. "You are still holding my birthday and my visits to my children."

The poet returned them.

"You are generous," said she. "But then everyone here is generous. They provide everything. They provide all of one's life."

The poet bowed.

"Of course, it is not easy," said the lady. "I try very hard. But I cannot seem to finish anything. I am not sure if it is the necessary organizing ability that I lack or perhaps the aesthetic sense; something ugly always seems to intrude...." She raised her colored counters in both hands, with the grace that had once made her a favorite of society.

"I have tried several times before," she said.

It was at this point that the poet turned and attempted to walk away from his second chance, but wherever he went the board preceded him. It interposed itself between him and old gentlemen in velvet vests; it hovered in front of ladies; it even blossomed briefly at the elbow of a child. Then the poet seemed to regain his composure; he began to work at the game; he sorted and matched and disposed, although with what public in view it was not possible to tell. The board—which had been heavily overlaid in black and purple (like a drawing by one of Mr. Wilde's contemporaries)—began to take on the most delicate stipple of color. It breathed wind and shadow like the closes of a park in June. It spread itself like a fan.

O. O'F. Wilde, the successful man of letters, was strolling with his wife in Hyde Park in the year nineteen-twenty-five. He was sixty-nine years old. He had written twenty books where Oscar Wilde had written one, fifteen plays where the degenerate and debauché had written five, innumerable essays, seven historical romances, three volumes of collected verse, had given many public addresses (though not in the last few years), and had received a citation (this was long in the past) from Queen Victoria herself. The tulips of Hyde Park shone upon the Wildes with a mild and equable light. O. O'F. Wilde, who had written twenty books, and—needless to say—left his two sons a unimpeachable reputation, started, clutched at his heart, and died.

"That is beautiful, sir, beautiful," said a voice in the poet's ear. A gentleman—who was not a *gentleman*—stood at his elbow. "Seldom," said the voice, "have we had one of our visitors, as you might say, complete a work in such a short time, and such a beautiful work, too. And such industry, sir!" The gentleman was beside himself. "Such enthusiasm! Such agreeable docility! You know, of course, that few of our guests display such an excellent attitude. Most of our guests—"

"Do you think so?" said Mr. Wilde curiously.

"Lovely, sir! Such agreeable color. Such delicacy."

"I see," said Mr. Wilde.

"I'm so glad you do, sir. Most of our guests don't. Most of our guests, if you'll permit me the liberty of saying so, are not genteel. Not genteel at all. But you, sir—"

Oscar Wilde, poet, dead at forty-four, took his second chance from the table before him and broke the board across his knee. He was a tall, strong man for all his weight, nearly six feet tall.

"And then?" I said.

"And then," said my friend, "I do not know what happened."

"Perhaps," said I, "they gave him his second chance, after all. Perhaps they had to."

"Perhaps," said my friend, "they did nothing of the kind....

"I wish I knew," he added. "I only wish I knew!"

And there we left it.

The Siege

Sergio Ramírez

By the 1980s, the enthusiasm sparked by the promise of popular governments in much of Latin America during the sixties had been all but snuffed out. In Central America the guerrilla wars in El Salvador and Guatemala continued unresolved, and in Nicaragua the revolution that in 1979 had succeeded in toppling the dictatorship of Anastasio Somoza found itself dogged by economic difficulties, political scandals, and the American-supported Contra forces. In 1985, Sergio Ramírez, Nicaragua's vice-president and one of the foremost fiction writers of Central America, put an end to his literary silence of almost ten years and published several new stories in the acerbic style for which he had become known.

Before the Sandinista Revolution, Ramírez had written novels and short stories in the realistic tradition of the so-called "indigenist" writers such as José Arguedas and Romulo Gallegos. These narratives chronicle the fate of the Latin American underdogs—the Indians, the peasants—and give them a new kind of heroic stature. Absent from this literature for the longest time, however, was the man persecuted not because (or not only because) of his low position in society and the blood of his ancestors, but because of his sexuality. In "The Siege", written in 1967, Ramírez traces revealing connections between these two apparent threats to absolute power.

It was dusk when Septimio woke, and the rays of the setting sun were sparkling in the depths of the chiffonier's oval mirror like precious embers. The pages of a fashion magazine were stuck to his stomach with sweat. Naked beneath his silk kimono, he could feel the perspiration trickling down between his shoulder blades. As he stood up, he stumbled over the china tureen he had left on the floor. It shattered, and cold soup splashed his feet.

"Avelino," he whispered surreptitiously. "Avelino!" he called a second time, looking around for him in the gloom that neither of them could get accustomed to. They were always blundering into flower vases and chairs. They knocked over the plaster statues, then had to grope to replace them on their tables, or push the pieces against the skirting until they could sweep them up along with all the rubbish thrown at them, by the feeble glow of the altar light in the bedroom or the angel's torch if they had lit it.

"Avelino," he called out once more, his voice by now almost a whimper. Night was falling rapidly outside; the six o'clock train whistled in the distance.

They must be coming by now, if they hadn't already surrounded the house, crawling their way through the coffee bushes and snipping the wire fences. They would be hidden behind the tree trunks or would be up in the branches, silently, ruthlessly demolishing the garden.

"Open the door," he heard.

"Who is it?" he asked.

"It's me—quick."

"Is that you, Avelino?"

Septimio crawled over to the door. Outside, the stairs ended in a small landing. He was nerving himself to turn the white egg of the doorknob, slippery from his moist palm, when he caught the sound of stifled laughter on the other side.

"Who's there?" he shouted in terror.

"It's me, Avelino, open up."

"Is that really you, Avelino?"

"Yes of course, dearie," came the sniggering reply.

"Go to hell," he screamed, though he was unsure whether his words were audible or merely came out as a choked sob.

Bewildered, he retreated to the living room and propped himself against his mother's piano, where a family of mice was nesting. The previous night's siege had left him and Avelino broken in spirit and in body after they had put out the blaze in the kitchen, and then had to abandon the orchard to their attackers. They had ducked under the four-poster bed and sheltered there until daybreak from the stones that rained in through the shattered windows. At first light they had crept out bleary-eyed through the glass door to the balcony and wearily began to sweep up all the stones and unripe fruit that littered the parquet floor. The mist had lifted and the palm trees were swaying in the morning breeze. From the balcony they could see the railway siding, where a handful of men trudged along the tracks to work.

He was still cowering by the piano when the walls of the house started to shake to an unbearable rhythm. Then stones began to land on the roof tiles, which broke and crashed down onto the ceiling above him. Outside, people were tearing at the branches of the fruit trees, uprooting the fences. He crawled through the doorway and locked himself in the bedroom.

"Too bad for Avelino," he whined. "Nobody told him to go out." Now, for the first time he had to face the attacks alone, and suddenly as he edged under the bed for shelter he was hit by the smell of stale urine, spit, and foul shoes from the floor. The rough boards scratched at the flaccid skin of his naked torso, and the medallion he always wore around his neck jabbed into him. Apart from the house and grounds, it was all he had inherited from his mother, a lock of whose hair he kept in it. Avelino's only legacy from his mother had been the angel.

They had been forced to abandon the ground floor, which they had previously used to store coffee beans and gardening tools. Once Avelino had gone down there barefoot to the bathroom beyond the kitchen; he had found the hand-basin full of dead mice floating among the magnolia and jasmine petals they put in the water every afternoon to perfume it. Disgusted, Avelino picked them up one by one by their tails and threw them out into the yard. He spent the whole morning being sick, and refused to eat lunch. It was then they decided never again to venture down to the bathroom or toilet, and instead relied on the rose-patterned chamber pots they kept in the bedroom.

He heard stones pattering on the roof again. This time they sounded like an endless rainstorm, and he couldn't help wondering where Avelino was: what can they be doing to you all alone out there in the dark, poor captive Avelino? The stones thundered down like the day of the last judgement.

In one corner of the room stood the angel Avelino had inherited. It was a life-sized plaster figure, with real herons' feathers for wings. Once a month they removed the purple tunic with its gold embroidery to clean it, and then the angel was left completely naked. Before they became victims of the siege, they would light the angel's torch as they went to bed, and lie there in its flickering light making believe they had been locked in a church somewhere.

Now he could make out clearly the sound of footsteps on the roof, and plaster from the ceiling mouldings showered the furniture. He hid his head in his hands, as if the pieces could hit him even under the bed. Suddenly, an image of his mother came into his mind.

"It hurts here," she had said, pointing to her chest as she was feeding bananas to the green parrots in their cages, and then slid to the ground and lay in a heap next to the sink. Her tiny purple mouth kissed the air as though she were thanking the audience at the end of one of her operatic recitals, but her face was pallid, with none of the paint she used to wear to make herself look rosy-cheeked in the footlights (the same she used to retouch her saints' faces) but which made her cheeks so taut she could never smile to acknowledge the applause. She lay there, tiny and fragile in her green velvet dress, a paper rose at the neck, on her feet the suede slippers battered out of shape by sun and rain. He had run over from pruning the rose bushes and knelt beside her as she breathed her last, on that golden afternoon, miles from the nearest town.

So he was left in charge of the garden, with its *araucarias*, hedgerows, and the cypresses beyond the house that made the far side as gloomy as a cemetery. He had to look after the cages, an ant-eaten dovecote high in a *chilamate* tree, rose bushes and begonias, and the two-story house as well, its balconies floating in the dawn mists. And he was all alone to tend the coffee plantation shaded by banana trees, and the orchard full of oranges, limes, medlars, sweet lemons and guavas. Until one day Avelino, who had also lost his mother, arrived from another village. Septimio took him in, and from that moment the two lived in the house together, getting by on what they could sell of flowers and fruit. A week after Avelino moved in, his angel was brought to the station by train, then carted up to the house.

"Couldn't we give it to the church?" Septimio had suggested when he saw how big it was. But Avelino got so upset, because it was all he had to remember his mother by, that Septimio hadn't insisted.

"You'll destroy the house," he shouted from under the bed. By now they were scampering all over the roof. "Come down from there, dammit," he shrieked, but this only made things worse, and tiles began to cascade down into the yard. He guessed they must want to get in via the roof. Then they would rip up the boards on the ceiling.

And all they had to do to reach the balcony was to sling ropes around the pillars then swarm up. Or they could jump down out of the trees onto the landing; the glass door was only bolted, and if they smashed the glass they could easily get in. Perhaps they didn't know that.

Fewer tiles seemed to be crashing down now.

"Get off there, will you?" he begged them.

"This isn't something I like doing, but it's my duty," the inspector had said. "We've received complaints that you two are cohabiting immorally."

"Who says so?" Septimio had asked, deeply offended.

"It doesn't matter who, but word has it that you two have set up house together, that you never leave the place, that you don't behave like men. I'm only here to warn you. I won't have any indecency in this town, so be careful."

"Captain," Septimio put in, "you know it's only malicious gossip...."

"That may be: how on earth should I know? But just watch how you behave. Why don't you act your age, Septimio, you're old enough to be my father."

A crowd was waiting for them as they left the police station, and a gang of children ran after them to the edge of the village, shouting abuse. That was the night the siege began.

Septimio had no idea what time it might be; he had a bitter taste in his mouth and a terrible thirst. He couldn't remember how long he'd been in that same position. It must have been hours. The noises on the roof ceased and he could hear voices fading in the distance. That's the way it always is, you think they're leaving then all of a sudden they come back again. What can they have done to Avelino? He's not as strong as he looks; he can't take much because of his asthma. He dozed off with the stench from the floor in his nostrils, watched over by all the angels of the house. He had only come to love them once Avelino's life-sized heavyweight had been coaxed into the bedroom to take its place alongside the heavenly hosts his mother had strewn everywhere. Cherubim topped the bedposts; two angels entwined in a passionate embrace round the frame of the huge mirror in the living room; entire armies of angels riding their clouds careered across wardrobe doors and the walls.

He could hear the voices near the house again. He knew what they were doing: they were relieving themselves in the begonias—the

rivulets streamed across the garden. He thought of Avelino defenceless out there in the hands of those brutes who were pissing in the
flower tubs; Avelino, delicate as a flower; taking turns to piss,
Avelino. He was only half-awake; his hands were numb and covered
in saliva from gagging himself with them in an attempt to choke back
the suffering. Suddenly he heard Avelino's voice calling him. He
hadn't the faintest idea how much later this was.

"It's me, Avelino—open up." The sound only just reached him
from somewhere down on the ground.

"Who's that out there?" he asked.

"It's me, open the door."

"Is this another trick?"

"No. Open the door so I can come up."

Septimio crawled over to the glass door and cautiously pushed it
open. He saw day was dawning.

"Avelino, where are you?"

"I'm down here in the garden, can't you see me?"

Septimio got to his knees and peered over the balustrade.

"Open up, for God's sake."

"Have they gone?"

"Yes, they're far away by now."

Scarcely able to stand, Septimio crossed the bedroom, staggered
through the living room, and opened the door at the top of the stairs.
Avelino stood there exhausted, his forehead streaming blood, his
body lost inside a huge pair of trousers. Septimio led him over to the
rocking chair to examine the wound over his eyebrow.

"What made you go out?"

"I was hungry and went to get something to eat."

"You went into town?"

"I ran into them on the way back. They dragged me here."

Septimio settled him gently into the chair, then went to fetch some
alcohol from a drawer in the chiffonier. He also brought a sheet,
which he tore into strips to make a bandage, and a washbowl.

"You shouldn't have gone out, Avelino."

"I was starving, and I thought I'd be back before nightfall."

Septimio wiped his bloodstained face.

"Are you sure they won't return?"

"No, not now. They pissed on the flowers; they let me go, then
they left."

"Sit still, you've got a bad cut. Sometimes when you think they've gone for good, they sneak back."

"No, not this time, it's already daylight."

Septimio moved the bowl away from the rocking chair, and folded up the piece of the sheet he didn't need. He put on his glasses to inspect the wound before bandaging it.

"Does it hurt?"

"Like hell."

"What did they do to you?" he asked as he wrapped the cloth around.

"Nothing. They just tried to scare me."

Septimio didn't say a word. Avelino fumbled with the buttons of his shirt, and his paunch flopped over the waistband of his trousers.

"They threw stones at me," he sobbed. His gold teeth glinted.

"D'you see why you ought never to go out?"

"But I was really hungry. I bought some crackers and a tin of sardines."

Septimio finished the bandage, then steered Avelino into the bedroom and helped him lie on the bed. Avelino touched his wound, and called out: "Septimio!"

"What is it?"

"They took me off into the bushes."

The angel stood naked in its corner.

"Tomorrow we must remember to dress the angel," Septimio said, stretching out beside him.

"Yes, tomorrow." Avelino's head was throbbing so much he kept his eyes closed tight as he spoke. "They told me: keep your mouth shut or we'll do you in."

"What are they like, Avelino?"

"Filthy, cruel," he answered softly.

Mist swirled into the room. In the bed, Septimio was almost bald; it looked as though someone had anointed Avelino's head with ashes.

Ganymede

Daphne du Maurier

Ganymede, son of the king who gave his name to Troy, was chosen for his beauty to be cupbearer to the gods. Zeus, falling in love with the handsome youth, disguised himself in eagle's feathers and abducted him from the Trojan plain. In the high Middle Ages, Ganymede became a synonym for "gay". In the twelfth century, a dialogue between Ganymede and Helen, using both characters as emblematic of their sexualities, discussed the relative merits of boys and women as lovers. A couple of centuries later, Shakespeare's Rosalind, banished to the forests of Arden and disguising herself as a "moonish youth", called herself Ganymede and concluded the play's litany of love vows with the declaration "And so am I for no woman." In the eighteenth century, the pictorial representations of Zeus and Ganymede reduced the youth to a baby, thereby discreetly censoring the myth's sexuality. In our time, the story of Zeus and Ganymede rarely has a happy ending. Zeus can no longer bring Ganymede to Olympus. He must be satisfied with simply knowing that Ganymede is there, in a place in which he himself is a stranger. The young boy possesses everything the older man cannot attain: not only youth, but youth's setting.

Italy is an Arcadia to which northern inhabitants can lay no claim except in the imagination. For writers from Byron to Henry James, from Forster and Lawrence to Tennessee Williams and Ian McEwan, Italy is the land where the senses run unrestricted, uninhibited by the rules and conventions established for countries in winter. Venice above all, built impossibly on water, beautiful in the sun, is desire's equivocal realm from which Zeus will never steal—as Daphne du Maurier, echoing Thomas Mann's Death in Venice, *concludes in "Ganymede".*

I

They call it Little Venice. That was what drew me here in the first place. And you have to admit that there is a curious resemblance—at least for people like myself, with imagination. There is a corner, for instance, where the canal takes a bend, fronted by a row of terraced houses, and the water itself has a particular stillness, especially at night, and the glaring discordancies that are noticeable during the day, like the noise of the shunting from Paddington Station, the rattle of the trains, the ugliness, all that seems to vanish. Instead ... the yellow light from the street lamps might be the mysterious glow you get from those old lanterns set in brackets on the corner of some crumbling palazzo, whose shuttered windows look blindly down upon the stagnant sweetness of a side-canal.

It is, and I must repeat this, essential to have imagination, and the house-agents are clever—they frame their advertisements to catch the eye of waverers like myself. "Two-roomed flat, with balcony, overlooking canal, in the quiet backwater known as Little Venice," and instantly, to the famished mind, the aching heart, comes a vision of another two-roomed flat, another balcony, where, at the hour of waking the sun makes patterns on a flaking ceiling, water patterns, and the sour Venetian smell comes through the window with the murmur of Venetian voices, the poignant "Ohé!" as the gondola rounds the bend and disappears.

In Little Venice we have traffic too. Not sharp-nosed gondolas, of course, gently rocking from side to side, but barges pass my window carrying bricks, and sometimes coal—the coal-dust dirties the balcony; and if I shut my eyes, surprised by the sudden hooting, and listen to the rapid chug-chug of the barge's engine, I can fancy myself, with my same shut eyes, waiting for a *vaporetto* at one of the landing-stages. I stand on the wooden planking, hemmed in by a chattering crowd, and there is a great surge and throbbing as the vessel goes hard astern. Then the *vaporetto* is alongside, and I, with my chattering crowd, have gone on board and we are off again, churning the water into wavelets with our wash, and I am trying to make up my mind whether to go direct to San Marco, and so to the piazza and my usual table, or to leave the *vaporetto* higher up the Grand Canal and thus prolong exquisite anticipation.

The hooting stops. Then barge passes. I cannot tell you where they go. There is a junction, close to Paddington, where the canal splits. This does not interest me; all that interests me is the barge's hooter, the echo of the engine, and—if I am walking—the barge's wake in the canal water, so that, glancing down the bank, I can see a film of oil amongst the bubbles, and then the oil disperses, and the bubbles too, and the water becomes still.

Come with me, and I'll show you something. You see the street across the canal, that one there, with the shops, going toward Paddington Station; and you see the bus stop, halfway down, and the board with blue letters on it. Your eyes won't be able to pick it up at this distance, but I can tell you that it reads M A R I O, and it's the name of a small restaurant, an Italian restaurant, hardly more than a bar. They know me there. I go there every day. You see, the lad there—he's training to be a waiter—reminds me of Ganymede....

II

I am a classical scholar. I suppose that was really the trouble. Had my interests been scientific, or geographical, or even historical—though history has associations enough, heaven knows—then I don't believe anything would have happened. I could have gone to Venice, and enjoyed my holiday, and come away again, without losing myself to such an extent that.... Well, what occurred there meant a total break with everything that had gone before.

You see, I've given up my job. My superior was exceedingly nice about it all, most sympathetic in fact, but, as he said, they really couldn't afford to take risks, they couldn't permit one of their employees—and, naturally, that applied to me—to continue working for them if he had been connected ... that was the word he used, not mixed-up but connected ... with what he called unsavoury practices.

Unsavoury is a hideous word. It's the most hideous word in the dictionary. It conjures up, to my mind, all that is ugly in life, yes, and in death too. The savoury is the joy, the élan, the zest that goes with mind and body working in unison; the unsavoury is the maladorous decay of vegetation, the rotted flesh, the mud beneath the water of the canal. And another thing. The word unsavoury suggests a lack of personal cleanliness: unchanged linen, bed-sheets hanging to dry, the fluff off combs, torn packets in waste-paper baskets. None of this can I abide. I am fastidious. Above all things I am fastidious. So that when my superior mentioned the word unsavoury I knew I had to go. I knew I could never allow him, or anyone, so to misinterpret my actions that they could consider what had taken place as, to put it bluntly, nauseous. So, I resigned. Yes, I resigned. There was nothing else for it. I just cut myself loose. And I saw the advertisement in the house-agent's column, and here I am in Little Venice....

I took my holiday late that year because my sister, who lives in Devon, and with whom I usually spend three weeks in August, suddenly had domestic trouble. A favourite cook left after a lifetime of devotion, and the household was disorganized. My nieces wanted to hire a caravan, my sister wrote me: they were all determined to go camping in Wales, and although I would be welcome she was sure it was not the sort of break that would appeal to me. She was right. The idea of hammering tent-pegs into the ground in a tearing wind, or sitting humped four abreast in a tiny space while my sister and her daughters produced luncheon out of a tin, filled me with misgiving. I cursed the cook whose departure had put an end to the pleasurable series of long, lazy days to which I had been accustomed, when, relaxing in a chaise-longue, favourite book in hand, and most delightfully fed, I had idled away my Augusts for many years.

When I protested over a series of trunk calls that I had nowhere to go, my sister said, or rather shouted over the muffled line, "Get abroad for a change. It would do you a world of good to break routine. Try France, or Italy." She even suggested a cruise, which frightened me even more than a caravan.

"Very well," I told her coldly, for in a sense I blamed her for the cook's departure and the cessation of my comfort, "I will go to Venice," thinking that, if I was obliged to get myself out of the rut, then I would at least be obvious. I would go, guidebook in hand, to a tourist's paradise. But not in August. Definitely not in August. I would wait until my compatriots and my friends across the Atlantic had been and gone again. Only then would I venture forth, when the heat of the day was done, and some measure of peace had returned to the place I believed was beautiful.

I arrived the first week in October.... You know how sometimes a holiday, even a brief one, a visit to friends for the week-end, can go wrong from the start. One departs in rain, or misses a connexion, or wakes with a chill, and the thread of ill-luck laced with irritation continues to mar every hour. Not so with Venice. The very fact that I had left it late, that the month was October, that the people I knew were now back again at office desks, made me more aware of my own good fortune.

I reached my destination just before dusk. Nothing had gone amiss. I had slept in my sleeper. I had not been annoyed by my fellow travellers. I had digested my dinner of the preceding night and my luncheon of the day. I had not been obliged to over-tip. Venice with all its glories lay before me. I collected my baggage and stepped out of the train, and there was the Grand Canal at my feet, the thronging gondolas, the lapping water, the golden *palazzi*, the dappled sky.

A fat porter from my hotel who had come to meet the train, so like a deceased member of the royal family that I dubbed him Prince Hal on the spot, seized my trappings from me. I was wafted, as so many travellers have been wafted before me, through the years and centuries, from the prosaic rattle of the tourist train to an instant dream world of romance.

To be met by boat; to travel by water; to loll upon cushions, swaying from side to side, even with a Prince Hal shouting the sights in one's ear in appalling English—all this makes for a loosening of restraint. I eased my collar. I threw off my hat. I averted my eyes from my walking-stick and my umbrella and my burberry tucked in the hold-all—I invariably travel with a hold-all. Lighting a cigarette, I was aware, surely for the first time in my life, of a sense of abandon, of belonging—certainly not to the present, nor to the future, nor even to the past, but to a period of time that was changeless and was Venetian time, that was outside the rest of Europe and even the world, and existed, magically, for myself alone.

Mark you, I realized there must be others. In that dark gondola floating by, at that wide window, even on the bridge from which, as we passed underneath, a figure peering down suddenly withdrew, I knew there must be others who, like myself, found themselves suddenly enchanted, not by the Venice they perceived, but by the Venice they felt within themselves. That uncelestial city from which no traveller returns....

What am I saying, though? I anticipate thoughts and events which no doubt I could not have had during that first half-hour from station to hotel. It is only now, in retrospect, that I realize there must be others like myself who, with the first glimpse, become enchanted, damned. Oh yes, indeed, we know all about the rest, the obvious rest. The people clicking cameras, the hubbub of nationalities, the students, the schoolmistresses, the artists. And the Venetians themselves—the Prince Hal porter, for instance, and the fellow who steered the gondola and was thinking of his pasta supper and his wife and children and the lire I would give him, and all those homeward bounders in the *vaporetti* no different from other homeward bounders at home who go by bus or tube—those people are part of the Venice of today, just as their forebears were part of the Venice that is past: dukes and merchants, and lovers, and ravished maidens. No, we have a different key. A different secret. It is what I said before, the Venice within ourselves.

"To ze right," shouted Prince Hal, "famous palazzo now belonging to American gentleman." Foolish and useless as his information was, it did at least suggest that some tycoon, weary of making money, had created an illusion, and, stepping into the speed-boat I saw tethered at the steps, believed himself immortal.

That was what I felt like, you see. I had the sense of immortality, the knowledge, instantaneous as I left the station and heard the lapping water, that time contained me. I was not imprisoned. I was held. And then we left the Grand Canal and were in the backwaters, and Prince Hal fell silent, and there was no sound except the stroke of the long oar as we were propelled along the narrow stream. I remember thinking—curious, wasn't it?—of the waters that usher us into this life at birth, of the waters that contain us in the womb. Somehow they must have the same stillness, the same force.

We came out of darkness into light, we shot under a bridge—it was only later that I realized it was the Bridge of Sighs—and there was the lagoon in front of us, and a hundred stabbing, flickering lights, and a great jostle of figures, of people walking up and down. I had to cope at once with my unaccustomed lire, with the gondolier, with Prince Hal, before being swallowed up in the hotel and the paraphernalia of desk-clerk, keys, and page showing me to my room. Mine was one of the smaller hotels, basking in the proximity of the more famous, yet comfortable enough at first glance, though a little stuffy perhaps—odd how they keep a room tight closed before a guest arrives. As I threw open the shutters the warm damp air from the lagoon infiltrated slowly, and the laughter and footsteps of the promenaders floated upwards while I unpacked. I changed and descended, but one glance at the half-empty dining-room decided me against dining there, although my pension terms permitted it, and I went out and joined the promenaders by the lagoon.

The sensation I had was strange, and never experienced before.

Not the usual anticipation of the traveller on the first evening of his holiday, who looks forward to his dinner and the pleasure of new surroundings. After all, in spite of my sister's mockery I was no John Bull. I used to know Paris quite well. I had been to Germany. I had toured the Scandinavian countries before the war. I had spent an Easter in Rome. It was only that I had been idle of late years, without initiative, and to take my annual holiday in Devon saved planning and, incidentally, my purse.

No, the sensation I had now, as inevitably I walked past the Doge's palace—which I recognized from postcards—and into the Piazza San Marco, was one of ... I hardly know how to describe it ... recognition. I don't mean the feeling "I have been here before". I don't mean the romantic dream "This is re-incarnation". Neither of those things. It was as though, intuitively, I had become, at last, myself. I had arrived. This particular moment in time had been waiting for me, and I for it. Curiously, it was like the first flavour of intoxication, but more heightened, more acute. And deeply secret. It is important to remember that; deeply secret. This sensation was somehow palpable, invading the whole of me, the palms of my hands, my scalp. My throat was dry. Physically, I felt I was infused with electricity, that I had become some sort of power-house radiating, into the damp atmosphere of this Venice I had never seen, currents which, becoming charged with other currents, returned to me again. The excitement was intense, almost unbearable. And, to look at me, nobody would guess anything. I was just another Englishman at the fag-end of the tourist season, strolling, walking-stick in hand, on his first night in Venice.

Although it was nearly nine o'clock the crowd was still dense on the piazza. I wondered how many amongst them felt the same current, the same intuition. Nevertheless, I must dine, and to escape the crowd I chose a turning to the right halfway down the piazza which brought me to one of the side-canals, very dark and still, and as luck had it to a restaurant nearby. I dined well, with excellent wine, at far less expense than I had feared, and lighting a cigar—one of my small extravagances, a really good cigar—I strolled back again to the piazza, that same electric current with me still.

The crowd had thinned, and instead of strolling had concentrated into two marked groups before two separate orchestras. These orchestras—rivals, so it appeared—had their stance in front of a couple of cafés, also rivals. Separated by perhaps some seventy yards, they played against one another with gay indifference. Tables and chairs were set out about the orchestras, and the café clientèle drank and gossiped and listened to the music in a semi-circle, backs turned to the rival orchestra whose beat and rhythm made discord to the ear. I happened to be close to the orchestra in mid-piazza. I found an empty table and sat down. A burst of applause from the second audience nearer the church gave warning that the rival orchestra had come to a breathing-space in its repertoire. This was the signal for ours to play louder still. It was Puccini, of course. As the evening progressed there came the songs of the day, the hit tunes of the moment, but as I sat down and looked about for a waiter to bring me a liqueur, and accepted—at a price—the rose offered to me by an ancient crone in a black shawl, the orchestra was playing Madame Butterfly. I felt relaxed, amused. And then I saw him.

I told you I was a classical scholar. Therefore you will understand—you should understand—that what happened in that second was transformation. The electricity that had charged me all evening focused on a single point in my brain to the exclusion of all else; the rest of me was jelly. I could sense the man at my table raise his hand and summon the lad in the white coat carrying a tray, but I myself was above him, did not exist in his time; and this self who was nonexistent knew with every nerve fibre, every brain-cell, every blood corpuscle that he was indeed Zeus, the giver of life and death, the immortal one, the lover; and that the boy who came towards him was his own beloved, his cup-bearer, his slave, his Ganymede. I was poised, not in the body, not in the world, and I summoned him. He knew me, and he came.

Then it was all over. The tears were pouring down my face and I heard a voice saying, "Is anything wrong, *signore?*"

The lad was watching me with some concern. Nobody had noticed anything; they were all intent upon their drinks, or their friends, or the orchestra, and I fumbled for my handkerchief and blew my nose and said, "Bring me a curaçao."

III

I remember sitting staring at the table in front of me, still smoking my cigar, not daring to raise my head, and I heard his quick footstep beside me. He put down the drink and went away again, and the question uppermost in my mind was, "Does he know?"

You see, the flash of recognition was so swift, so overwhelming, that it was like being jerked into consciousness from a lifetime of sleep. The absolute certainty of who I was and where I was, and the bond between us, possessed me just as Paul was possessed on the Damascus road. Thank heaven I was not blinded by my visions; no one would have to lead me back to the hotel. No, I was just another tourist come to Venice, listening to a little string band and smoking a cigar.

I let five minutes or so go by, and then I lifted my head and casually, very casually, looked over the heads of the people towards the café. He was standing alone, his hands behind his back, watching the orchestra. He seemed to me about fifteen, not more, and he was small for his age, and slight, and his white mess jacket and dark trousers reminded me of an officer's kit in Her Majesty's Mediterranean fleet. He did not look Italian. His forehead was high, and he wore his light brown hair *en brosse*. His eyes were not brown but blue, and his complexion was fair, not olive.

There were two other waiters hovering between the tables, one of them about eighteen or nineteen and both of them obvious Italians, the eighteen-year-old swarthy and fat. You could tell at a glance they were born to be waiters, they would never rise to anything else, but my boy, my Ganymede, the very set of his proud head, the expression on his face, the air of grave tolerance with which he regarded the orchestra, showed him to be of a different stamp ... my stamp, the stamp of the immortals.

I watched him covertly, the small clasped hands, the small foot in its black shoe tapping time to the music. If he recognized me, I said to myself, he will look at me. This evasion, this play of watching the orchestra, is only a pretext, because what we have felt together, in that moment out of time, has been too strong for both of us. Suddenly—and with an exquisite feeling of delight and apprehension in one—I knew what was going to happen. He made a decision. He looked away from the orchestra and directly across to my table, and still grave, still thoughtful, walked up to me and said,

"Do you wish for anything more, *signore?*"

It was foolish of me, but, do you know, I could not speak. I could only shake my head. Then he took away the ash-tray and put a clean one in its place. The very gesture was somehow thoughtful, loving, and my throat tightened and I was reminded of a biblical expression surely used by Joseph about Benjamin. I forget the context, but it says somewhere in the Old Testament "for his bowels did yearn upon his brother". I felt that, exactly.

I went on sitting there until midnight, when the great bells sounded and filled the air, and the orchestras—both of them—put away their instruments, and the straggling listeners melted away. I looked down at the scrap of paper, the bill, which he had brought me and put beside the ash-tray, and, as I glanced at the scribbled figures and paid, it seemed to me that the smile he gave me, and the little bow of deference, were the answer I had been seeking. He knew. Ganymede knew.

I went off alone across the now deserted piazza, and passed under the colonnade by the Doge's place where an old hunched man was sleeping. The lights were no longer bright but dim, the damp wind troubled the water and rocked the row of gondolas on the black lagoon, but my boy's spirit was with me, and his shadow too.

I awoke to brilliance. The long day to be filled, and what a day! So much to experience and to see, from the obvious interiors of San Marco and the Doge's palace to a visit to the Accademia and an excursion up and down the Grand Canal. I did everything the tourist does except feed the pigeons; too fat, too sleek as they were, I picked my way amongst them with distaste. I had an ice at Florians. I bought picture postcards for my nieces. I leant over the Rialto bridge. And the happy day, of which I enjoyed every moment, was only a preliminary to the evening. Deliberately I had avoided the café on the right-hand side of the piazza. I had walked only on the opposite side.

I remember I got back to my hotel about six, and lay down on my bed and read Chaucer for an hour—The Canterbury Tales in a Penguin edition. Then I had a bath and changed. I went to the same restaurant to dine where I had dined the night before. The dinner was equally good and equally cheap. I lit my cigar and strolled to the piazza. The orchestras were playing. I chose a table on the fringe of the crowd, and as I put down my cigar for a moment I noticed that my hand was trembling. The excitement, the suspense, was unbearable. It seemed to me impossible that the family group at the table beside me should not perceive my emotion. Luckily I had an evening paper with me. I opened it and pretended to read. Someone flicked a cloth on my table, and it was the swarthy waiter, the ungainly youth, asking for my order. I motioned him away. "Presently," I said, and went on reading, or rather going through the motions of reading. The orchestra began to play a little jigging tune, and looking up I saw that Ganymede was watching me. He was standing by the orchestra, his hands clasped behind his back. I did nothing. I did not even move my head, but in a moment he was at my side.

"A curaçao, *signore?*" he said

Tonight recognition went beyond the first instantaneous flash. I could feel the chair of gold, and the clouds above my head, and the boy was kneeling beside me, and the cup he offered me was gold as well. His humility was not the shamed humility of a slave, but the reverence of a loved one to his master, to his god. Then the flash was gone and, thank heaven, I was in control of emotion. I nodded my head and said, "Yes, please," and ordered half a bottle of Evian water to be brought to me with the curaçao.

As I watched him slip past the tables towards the café, I saw a large man in a white raincoat, and a broad-brimmed trilby hat step out from the shadows beneath the colonnade and tap him on the shoulder. My boy raised his head and smiled. In that brief moment I experienced evil. A premonition of disaster. The man, like a great white slug, smiled back at Ganymede and gave him an order. The boy smiled again, and disappeared.

The orchestra swung out of the jigging tune and ceased, with a flourish, to a burst of applause. The violinist wiped the perspiration from his forehead and laughed at the pianist. The swarthy waiter brought them drinks. The old woman in the shawl came to my table as she had done the night before and offered me a rose. This time I was wiser: I refused. And I became aware that the man in the white mackintosh was watching me from behind a column....

Do you know anything of Greek mythology? I only mention the fact because Poseidon, the brother of Zeus, was also his rival. He was especially associated with the horse; and a horse—unless it is winged—symbolizes corruption. The man in the white mackintosh was corrupt. I knew it instinctively. Intuition bade me beware. When Ganymede returned with my curaçao and my Evian I did not even look up, but continued reading the newspaper. The orchestra, refreshed, took the air once more. The strains of "Softly Awakes my Heart" strove for supremacy with the "Colonel Bogey" march from its rival near the church. The woman with the shawl, her roses all unsold, came back to my table in desperation. Brutally I shook my head, and in doing so saw that the man in the white mackintosh and the trilby hat had moved from the column and was now standing beside my chair.

The aroma of evil is a deadly thing. It penetrates, and stifles, and somehow challenges at the same time. I was afraid. Most definitely I was afraid, but determined to give battle, to prove that I was the stronger. I relaxed in my chair, and, inhaling the last breath of my cigar before laying it in the ashtray, puffed the smoke full in his face. An extraordinary thing happened. I don't know whether the final inhalation turned me giddy, but for an instant my head swam, and the smoke made rings before my eyes, and I saw his hideous, grinning face subside into what seemed to be a trough of sea and foam. I could even feel the spray. When I had recovered from the attack of coughing brought on by my cigar the air cleared: the man in the white mackintosh had disappeared, and I found that I had knocked over and smashed my half-bottle of Evian water. It was Ganymede himself who picked up the broken pieces, it was Ganymede who wiped the table with his cloth, it was Ganymede who suggested, without my ordering it, a fresh half-bottle.

"The *signore* has not cut himself?" he said.

"No."

"The *signore* will have another curaçao. There may be some pieces of glass in this. There will be no extra charge."

He spoke with authority, with quiet confidence, this child of fifteen who had the grace of a prince, and then, with exquisite hauteur, he turned to the swarthy youth who was his companion-at-arms, and handed him my debris with a flow of Italian. Then he brought me the second half-bottle of Evian, and the second glass of curaçao.

"*Un sedativo*," he said, and smiled.

He was not cocky. He was not familiar. He knew, because he had always known, that my hands were trembling and my heart was beating, and I wanted to be calm, to be still.

"*Piove*," he said, lifting his face and holding up his hand, and indeed it was beginning to rain, suddenly, for no reason, out of a star-studded sky. But a black straggling cloud like a gigantic hand blotted out the stars as he spoke, and down came the rain on to the piazza. Umbrellas went up like mushrooms, and those without them spread across the piazza and away home like beetles to their lair.

Desolation was instant. The tables were bare, the chairs upturned against them. The piano was covered with a tarpaulin, the music-stands were folded, the lights inside the café became dim. Everyone melted away. It was as though there had never been an orchestra, never been an audience of clapping people. The whole thing was a dream.

I was not dreaming, though. I had come out, like a fool, without my umbrella. I waited under the colonnade beside the now deserted café, with the rain from a nearby spout spattering the ground in front of me. I could hardly believe it possible that five minutes ago all had been gay and crowded, and now this wintered gloom.

I turned up the collar of my coat, trying to make up my mind whether to venture forth across the streaming piazza, and then I heard a quick brisk footstep leave the café and trot away under the colonnade. It was Ganymede, his small upright figure still clad in his white mess jacket, his large umbrella above him like a pennant.

My way was to the left, towards the church. He was walking to the right. In a moment or two he might turn away altogether, and disappear. It was a moment of decision. You will say I made the wrong one. I turned to the right, I followed him.

It was a strange and mad pursuit. I had never done such a thing in my life before. I could not help myself. He trotted ahead, his footsteps loud and clear, along the tortuous narrow passages winding in and out beside silent, dark canals, and there was no other sound at all except his footsteps and the rain, and he never once looked back to see who followed him. Once or twice I slipped: he must have heard me. On, on he went, over bridges, into the shadows, his umbrella bobbing up and down above his head, and a glimpse of his white mess jacket showing now and then as he lifted the umbrella higher. And the rain still sluiced from the roofs of the silent houses, down to the cobbles and the pavings below, down to the styx-like canals.

Then I missed him. He had turned a corner sharply. I began to run. I ran into a narrow passage, where the tall houses almost touched their neighbours opposite, and he was standing in front of a great door with an iron grille before it, pulling a bell. The door opened, he folded his umbrella and went inside. The door clanged behind him. He must have heard me running, he must have seen me brought up short when I turned the corner into the passage. I stood for a moment staring at the iron grille above the heavy oak door. I looked at my watch: it wanted five minutes to midnight. The folly of my pursuit struck me in all its force. Nothing had been achieved but to get very wet, to have caught a chill in all probability, and to have lost my way.

I turned to go, and a figure stepped out of a doorway opposite the house with the grille and came towards me. It was the man in the white mackintosh and the broad-brimmed trilby hat.

He said, with a bastard American accent, "Are you looking for somebody, *signore?*"

IV

I ask you, what would you have done in my position? I was a stranger in Venice, a tourist. The alleyway was deserted. One had read stories of Italians and vendettas, of knives, of stabs in the back. One false move, and this might happen to me.

"I was taking a walk," I replied, "but I seem to have missed my way."

He was standing very close to me, much too close for comfort. "Ah! you missa your way," he repeated, the American accent blending with music-hall Italian. "In Venice, that happens all the time. I see you home."

The lantern light above his head turned his face yellow under the broad-brimmed hat. He smiled as he spoke, showing teeth full of gold stoppings. The smile was sinister.

"Thank you," I said, "but I can manage very well."

I turned and began to walk back to the corner. He fell into step beside me.

"No trouble," he said, "no trouble at all-a."

He kept his hands in the pockets of his white mackintosh, and his shoulder brushed mine as we walked side by side. We moved out of the alleyway into the narrow street by the side-canal. It was dark. Drips of water fell from the roof-gutters into the canal.

"You like Venice?" he asked.

"Very much," I answered; and then—foolishly, perhaps—"It's my first visit."

I felt like a prisoner under escort. The tramp-tramp of our feet echoed in hollow fashion. And there was no one to hear us. The whole of Venice slept. He gave a grunt of satisfaction.

"Venice very dear," he said. "In the hotels, they robba you always. Where are you staying?"

I hesitated. I did not want to give my address, but if he insisted on coming with me what could I do?

"The Hotel Byron," I said.

He laughed in scorn. "They putta twenty per cent on the bill," he said. "You ask for a cup of coffee, twenty per cent. It's always the same. They robba the tourist."

"My terms are reasonable," I said. "I can't complain."

"Whatta you pay them?" he asked.

The cheek of the man staggered me. But the path by the canal was very narrow, and his shoulder still touched mine as we walked. I told him the price of my room at the hotel, and the pension terms. He whistled.

"They take the skin off your back," he said. "Tomorrow you senda them to hell. I find you little apartment. Very cheap, very O.K."

I did not want a little apartment. All I wanted was to be rid of the man, and back in the comparative civilization of the Piazza San Marco. "Thank you," I replied, "but I'm quite comfortable at the Hotel Byron."

He edged even closer to me, and I found myself nearer still to the black waters of the canal. "In little apartment," he said, "you do as you like-a. You see your friends. Nobody worry you."

"I'm not worried at the Hotel Byron," I said.

I began to walk faster, but he kept pace with me, and suddenly he withdrew his right hand from his pocket and my heart missed a beat. I thought he had a knife. But it was to offer me a tattered packet of Lucky Strikes. I shook my head. He lit one for himself.

"I finda you little apartment," he persisted.

We passed over a bridge and plunged into yet another street, silent, ill-lit, and as we walked he told me the names of people for whom he had found apartments.

"You English?" he asked. "I thought-a so. I found apartment last year for Sir Johnson. You know Sir Johnson? Very nice man, very discreet. I find apartment too for film-star Bertie Poole. You know Bertie Poole? I save him five hundred thousand lire."

I had never heard of Sir Johnson or Bertie Poole. I became more and more angry, but there was nothing I could do. We crossed a second bridge, and to my relief I recognized the corner near the restaurant where I had dined. The canal here formed, as it were, a bay, and there were gondolas moored side by side.

"Don't bother to come any further," I said. "I know my way now."

The unbelievable happened. We had turned the corner together, marching as one man, and then, because the narrow path could not hold us two abreast, he dropped a pace behind, and, in doing so, slipped. I heard him gasp, and a second later he was in the canal, the white mackintosh splaying about him like a canopy, the splash of his great body rocking the gondolas. I stared for a moment, too surprised to take action. And then I did a terrible thing. I ran away. I ran into the passage that I knew would lead me finally into the Piazza San Marco, and, when I came to it, walked across it briskly, and so past the Doge's palace and back to my hotel. I encountered no one. As I said before, the whole of Venice slept. At the Hotel Byron, Prince Hal was yawning behind the desk. Rubbing the sleep from his eyes, he took me up in the lift. As soon as I entered my room I went straight to the wash-basin and took the small bottle of medicinal brandy with which I invariably travelled. I swallowed the contents at a single draught.

V

I slept badly and had appalling dreams, which did not surprise me. I saw Poseidon, the god Poseidon, rising from an angry sea, and he shook his trident at me, and the sea became the canal, and then Poseidon himself mounted a bronze horse, the bronze horse of Colleoni, and rode away, with the limp body of Ganymede on the saddle before him.

I swallowed a couple of aspirin with my coffee, and rose late. I don't know what I expected to see when I went out. Knots of people reading newspapers, or the police—some intimation of what had happened. Instead, it was a bright October day, and the life of Venice continued.

I took a steamer to the Lido and lunched there. I deliberately idled away the day at the Lido in case of trouble. What was worrying me was that, should the man in the white mackintosh have survived his ducking of the night before and bear malice towards me for leaving him to his plight, he might have informed the police—perhaps hinting, even, that I had pushed him in. And the police would be waiting for me at the hotel when I returned.

I gave myself until six o'clock. Then, a little before sunset, I took the steamer back. No cloudbursts tonight. The sky was a gentle gold, and Venice basked in the soft light, painfully beautiful.

I entered the hotel and asked for my key. It was handed to me by the clerk with a cheerful, "*Buona sera, signore*," together with a letter from my sister. Nobody had inquired for me. I went upstairs and changed, came down again, and had dinner in the hotel restaurant. The dinner was not in the same class as the dinner in the restaurant the two proceeding nights, but I did not mind. I was not very hungry. Nor did I fancy my usual cigar. I lit a cigarette instead. I stood for about ten minutes outside the hotel, smoking and watching the lights on the lagoon. The night was balmy. I wondered if the orchestra was playing in the piazza, and if Ganymede was serving drinks. The thought of him worried me. If he was in any way connected to the man in the white mackintosh, he might suffer for what had happened. The dream could have been a warning—I was a great believer in dreams. Poseidon carrying Ganymede astride his horse.... I began to walk towards the Piazza San Marco. I told myself I would just stand near the church and see if both orchestras were playing.

When I came to the piazza I saw that all was as usual. There were the same crowds, the same rival orchestras, the same repertoires played against each other. I moved slowly across the piazza towards the second orchestra, and I put on my dark glasses as a form of protection. Yes, there he was. There was Ganymede. I spotted his brush of light hair and his white mess jacket almost immediately. He and his swarthy companion were very busy. The crowd around the orchestra was thicker than usual because of the warm night. I scanned the audience, and the shadows behind the colonnade. There was no sign of the man in the white mackintosh. The wisest thing, I knew, was to leave, return to the hotel, go to bed, and read my Chaucer. Yet I lingered. The old woman selling roses was making her rounds. I drew nearer. The orchestra was playing a theme-song from a Chaplin film. Was it *Limelight*? I did not remember. But the song was haunting, and the violinist drew every ounce of sentiment from it. I decided to wait until the end of the song and then return to the hotel.

Someone snapped his fingers to give an order, and Ganymede turned to take it. As he did so he looked over the heads of the seated crowd straight at me. I was wearing the dark glasses, and I had a hat. Yet he knew me. He gave me a radiant smile of welcome, and ignoring the client's order darted forward, seized a chair, and placed it beside an empty table.

"No rain tonight," he said. "Tonight everybody is happy. A curaçao, *signore?*"

How could I refuse him, the smile, the almost pleading gesture? If anything had been wrong, if he had been anxious about the man in the white mackintosh, surely, I thought, there would have been some sort of hint, some warning glance? I sat down. A moment later he was back again with my curaçao.

Perhaps it was more potent than the night before, or perhaps, in my disturbed mood, it had a greater effect on me. Whatever it was, the curaçao went to my head. My nervousness vanished. The man in the white mackintosh and his evil influence no longer troubled me. Perhaps he was dead. What of it? Ganymede remained unharmed. And to show his favour he stood only a few feet away from my table, hands clasped behind his back, on the alert to serve my instant whim.

"Do you never get tired?" I said boldly.

He whisked away my ash-tray and flicked the table.

"No, *signore*," he answered, "for my work is a pleasure. This sort of work." He gave me a little bow.

"Don't you go to school?"

"School?" He jerked his thumb in a gesture of dismissal. "*Finito*, school. I am a man. I work for my living. To keep my mother and my sister."

I was touched. He believed himself a man. And I had an instant vision of his mother, a sad, complaining woman, and of a little sister. They all of them lived behind the door with the grille.

"Do they pay you well here in the café?" I asked.

He shrugged his shoulders.

"In the season, not so bad," he said, "but the season is over. Two more weeks, and it is finished. Everyone goes away."

"What will you do?"

He shrugged again.

"I have to find work somewhere else," he said. "Perhaps I go to Rome. I have friends in Rome."

I did not like to think of him in Rome—such a child in such a city. Besides, who were his friends?

"What would you like to do?" I inquired.

He bit his lips. For a moment he looked sad. "I should like to go to London," he said. "I should like to go to one of your big hotels. But that is impossible I have no friends in London."

I thought of my own immediate superior, who happened to be a director, amongst his other activities, of the Majestic in Park Lane.

"It might be arranged," I said, "with a little pulling of strings."

He smiled, and made an amusing gesture of manipulating with both hands. "It is easy, if you know how," he said, "but if you don't know how, better to …" and he smacked his lips and raised his eyes. The expression implied defeat. Forget about it.

"We'll see," I said. "I have influential friends."

He made no attempt to seize advantage.

"You are kind to me, *signore*," he murmured, "very kind indeed."

At that moment the orchestra stopped, and as the crowd applauded he clapped with them, his condescension perfect.

"Bravo … bravo …" he said. I almost wept.

When later I paid my bill, I hesitated to over-tip in case he was offended. Besides, I did not want him to look upon me merely as a tourist client. Our relationship went deeper.

"For your mother and your little sister," I said, pressing five hundred lire into his hand, seeing, in my mind's eye, the three of them tiptoeing to Mass in St. Mark's, the mother voluminous, Ganymede in his Sunday black, and the little sister veiled for her first Communion.

"Thank you, thank you, *signore*," he said, and added, "*A domani.*"

"*A domani*," I echoed, touched that he should already be looking forward to our next encounter. As for the wretch in the white mackintosh, he was already feeding the fishes in the Adriatic.

The following morning I had a shock. The reception clerk telephoned my room to ask whether I would mind leaving it vacant by midday. I did not know what he meant. The room had been booked for a fortnight. He was full of excuses. There had been a misunderstanding, he said; this particular room had been engaged for many weeks, he thought the travel agent had explained the fact. Very well, I said, huffed, put me somewhere else. He expressed a thousand regrets. The hotel was full. But he could recommend a very comfortable little flat that the management used from time to time as an annexe. And there would be no extra charge. My breakfast would be brought to me just the same, and I should even have a private bath.

"It's very upsetting," I fumed. "I have all my things unpacked."

Again a thousand regrets. The porter would move my luggage. He would even pack for me. I need not stir hand or foot myself. Finally I consented to the new arrangement, though I certainly would not permit anyone but myself to touch my things. Then I went downstairs and found Prince Hal, with a barrow for my luggage, awaiting me below. I was in a bad humour, with my arrangements upset, and quite determined to refuse the room in the annexe on sight, and demand another.

We skirted the lagoon, Prince Hal trundling the baggage, and I felt something of a fool stalking along behind him, bumping into the promenaders, and cursed the travel agent who had presumably made the muddle about the room in the hotel.

When we arrived at our destination, though, I was obliged to change my tune. Prince Hal entered a house with a fine, even beautiful façade, whose spacious staircase was spotlessly clean. There was no lift, and he carried my luggage on his shoulder. He stopped on the first floor, took out a key, fitted it to the left-hand door, and threw it open. "Please to enter," he said.

It was a charming apartment, and must have been at some time or other the salon of a private *palazzo*. The windows, instead of being closed and shuttered like the windows in the Hotel Byron, were wide open to a balcony, and to my delight the balcony looked out upon the Grand Canal. I could not be better placed.

"Are you sure," I inquired, "that this room is the same price as the room in the hotel?"

Prince Hal stared. He obviously did not understand my question. "Please?" he said.

I left it. After all, the reception clerk had said so. I looked about me. A bathroom led out of the apartment. There were even flowers by the bed.

"What do I do about breakfast?" I asked.

Prince Hal pointed to the telephone. "You ring," he said, "they answer below. They bring it." Then he handed over the key.

When he had gone I went once more to the balcony and looked out. The canal was full of bustle and life. All Venice was below me.

The speed-boats and the *vaporetti* did not worry me, the changing animated scene was one of which I felt I could never grow tired. Here I could sit and laze all day if I so desired. My luck was incredible. Instead of cursing the travel agent I blessed him. I unpacked my things for the second time in three days, but this time, instead of being a number on the third floor of the Hotel Byron, I was lord and master of my own minute *palazzo*. I felt like a king. The great Campanile bell sounded midday and, since I had breakfasted early, I was in the mood for more coffee. I lifted the telephone. I heard a buzz in answer, and then a click. A voice said, "Yes?"

"*Café complet,*" I ordered.

"At once," replied the voice. Was it ... could it be ... that too-familiar American accent?

I went into the bathroom to wash my hands, and when I returned there was a knock at the door. I called out, "*Avanti!*" The man who bore in the tray was not wearing a white mackintosh or a trilby hat. The light-grey suit was carefully pressed. The terrible suède shoes were yellow. And he had a piece of sticking plaster on his forehead. "What did I tell you?" he said. "I arrange-a everything. Very nice. Very O.K."

VI

He put the tray down on the table near the window and waved his hand at the balcony and the sounds from the Grand Canal.

"Sir Johnson spend-a the day here," he said. "All the day he lie on his balcony with his, how-do-you-call-them?"

He raised his hands in the gesture of field-glasses, and swerved from side to side. His gold-filled teeth showed as he smiled.

"Mr. Bertie Poole, different altogether," he added. "A speed-boat to the Lido, and back here after dark. Little dinners, little parties, with his friends. He made-a de whoopee."

The knowing wink filled me with disgust. Officiously he began to pour out the coffee for me. It was too much.

"Look here," I said. "I don't know your name, and I don't know how this business has come about. If you have come to an under-standing with the clerk at the Hotel Byron it's nothing to do with me."

He opened his eyes in astonishment.

"You don't like-a the apartment?" he said.

"Of course I like it," I replied. "That's not the point. The point is, I made my own arrangements and now...."

But he cut me short. "Don't wory, don't worry," he said, waving his hand. "You pay here less than you pay at Hotel Byron. I see to it. And nobody come to disturb you. Nobody at all-a." He winked again, and moved heavily towards the door. "If there is anything you want," he said, "just ring-a the bell. O.K.?"

He left the room. I poured the coffee into the Grand Canal. For all I knew it might be poisoned. Then I sat down to think out the situation.

I had been in Venice for three days. I had booked, as I thought, my room at the Hotel Byron for a fortnight. I had, therefore, ten days left of my holiday. Was I prepared to spend the ten days in this delicious apartment, at what I had been assured was no extra expense, under the aegis of this tout? He apparently bore no malice towards me for his tumble in the canal. The sticking plaster bore evidence to his fall, but the subject had not been mentioned. He looked less sinister in his light-grey suit than he had done in the white mackintosh. Perhaps I had let my imagination run away with me. And yet.... I dipped my finger in the coffee-pot, and raised it to my lips. It tasted all right. I glanced at the telephone. If I lifted it his odious American voice would answer. I had better telephone the Hotel Byron from outside, or better still, make my inquiry in person.

I locked the cupboards and the chest-of-drawers, and my suitcases too, and pocketed the keys. I left the room, locking the door of the apartment. No doubt he would have a pass-key, but it could not be helped. Then I went downstairs, walking-stick at the ready in case of attack, and so out into the street. No sign of the enemy anywhere below. The building appeared uninhabited. I went back to the Hotel Byron and tried to get some information from the staff, but my luck was out. The clerk at the reception desk was not the one who had telephoned me in the morning about the change of room. Some new arrival was waiting to check in, and the clerk was impatient. Because I was no longer under the roof I did not interest him. "Yes, yes," he said, "it's all right, when we are full here we make arrangements to board our guests outside. We have had no complaints." The couple waiting to check in sighed heavily. I was holding them up.

Frustrated, I left the desk and walked away. There seemed nothing to be done. The sun was shining, a light breeze rippled the water of the lagoon, and the promenaders, without coats and hats, strolled peacefully, taking the air. I supposed I could do the same. After all, nothing very grave had happened. I was the temporary owner of an apartment overlooking the Grand Canal, a matter to strike envy into the breasts of all these tourists. Why should I worry? I boarded a *vaporetto*, and went and sat in the church by the Accademia to gaze at the Bellini Madonna and Child. It calmed my nerves.

I spent the afternoon sleeping and reading upon my balcony without benefit of field-glasses—unlike Sir Johnson, whoever he might be—and nobody came near me. As far as I could see none of my things had been touched. The little trap I had set—a hundred lire note between two ties—was still in place. I breathed a sigh of relief. Possibly, after all, things would work out well.

Before going out to dinner I wrote a letter to my superior. He was always inclined to patronize me, and it was something of a coup to tell him that I had found myself a delightful apartment with quite the finest view in Venice. "By the way," I said, "what chance is there at the Majestic for young waiters to train? There is a very good lad here, of excellent appearance and manners, just the right type for the Majestic. Can I give him any hope? He is the sole support of a widowed mother and orphan sister."

I dined in my favourite restaurant—I was *persona grata* by now, in spite of the lapse of the night before—and strolled on to the Piazza San Marco without a qualm. The tout might appear, white mackintosh and all, but I had dined too well to care. The orchestra was surrounded by sailors from a destroyer which had anchored in the lagoon. There was much changing of hats, and laughter, and demanding of popular tunes, and the audience entered into the fun, clapping the sailor who pretended to seize the fiddle. I laughed uproariously with the rest of them, Ganymede by my side. How right my sister had been to encourage me to go to Venice instead of to Devon. How I blessed the vagaries of her cook!

It was in mid-laughter that I was carried out of myself. There were clouds above my head and below me, and my right arm, outstretched on the empty chair before me, was a wing. Both arms were wings, and I was soaring above the earth. Yet I had claws too. The claws held the lifeless body of the boy. His eyes were closed. The wind currents bore me upward through the clouds, and my triumph was such that the still body of the boy only seemed to me more precious and more mine. Then I heard the sound of the orchestra again, and with it laughter and clapping, and I saw that I had put out my hand and gripped Ganymede's, and he had not withdrawn it, but had let it remain there.

I was filled with embarrassment. I snatched mine away and joined in the applause. Then I picked up my glass of curaçao.

"Fortune," I said, raising my glass to the crowd, to the orchestra, to the world at large. It would not do to single out the child.

Ganymede smiled. "The *signore* enjoys himself," he said.

Just that, and no more. But I felt he shared my mood. An impulse made me lean forward. "I have written to a friend in London," I said, "a friend who is a director of a big hotel. I hope to have an answer from him in a few days' time."

He showed no surprise. He bowed, then clasped his hands behind his back and looked over the heads of the crowd.

"It is very kind of the *signore*," he said.

I wondered how much faith he had in me, and whether it exceeded that which he put in his friends in Rome.

"You will have to give me your name and all particulars," I told him, "and I suppose a reference from the proprietor here."

A brief nod of the head showed that he understood. "I have my papers," he said proudly, and I could not help smiling, thinking of the dossier that probably contained a report from his school and a recommendation to whoever might employ him. "My uncle too will speak for me," he added. "The *signore* has only to ask my uncle."

"And who is your uncle?" I inquired.

He turned to me, looking for the first time a little modest, a little shy. "The *signore* has moved to his apartment in the Via Goldoni, I believe," he said. "My uncle is a great man of business in Venice."

His uncle ... the appalling tout was his uncle. All was explained. It was a family relationship. I need never have worried. Instantly I placed the man as the brother of the nagging mother, both of them, no doubt, playing on the feelings of my Ganymede, who wished to show his independence and get away from them. Still, it had been a narrow escape. I might have offended the man mortally when he took his tumble into the canal.

"Of course, of course," I said, pretending I had known all the time, for he seemed to take it for granted that this was the case and I had no desire to seem a fool. Then I went on. "A very comfortable apartment. Do you know it?"

"Naturally I know it, *signore*," he said, smiling. "It is I who will bring you your breakfast every morning."

I nearly fainted. Ganymede bring my breakfast.... It was too much to absorb in one moment. I concealed my emotion by ordering another curaçao, and he darted off to obey me. I was, as the French say, *bouleversé*. To be tenant of the delicious apartment was one thing—and at no extra cost—but to have Ganymede thrown in, as it were, with my breakfast was almost more than flesh and blood could stand. I made an effort to compose myself before he returned, but his announcement had thrown me into such a flutter that I could hardly sit in my seat. He was back, with the glass of curaçao.

"Pleasant dreams, *signore*," he said.

Pleasant dreams, indeed.... I had not the courage to look at him. And when I had swallowed my curaçao I took advantage of his temporary summons by another client to slip away, although it was long before midnight. I got back to the apartment by instinct rather than by conscious thought—I had not seen where I was going—and then noticed, on the table, the still unposted letter to London. I could have sworn I had taken it with me when I went out to dinner. However, the morning would do. I was too agitated to go out again tonight.

I stood on the balcony and smoked another cigar, an unheard-of excess, and then went through my small store of books with the idea of presenting one to Ganymede when he brought me my breakfast. His English was so good that it needed a tribute, and the idea of a tip was somehow distasteful. Trollope was not right for him, nor Chaucer either. And the volume of Edwardian memoirs would be quite beyond his understanding. Could I bear to part with my well-worn Shakespeare Sonnets? Impossible to come to a decision. I would sleep on it—if I could sleep, which seemed very doubtful. I took two soneryl tablets, and passed out.

When I awoke it was past nine o'clock. The traffic on the Canal might have indicated high noon. The day was brilliantly fine. I rushed from my bed to the bathroom and shaved, a thing I usually did after breakfast, and then, putting on my dressing-gown and slippers, moved the table and the chair on to the balcony. Then, in trepidation, I went to the telephone and lifted the receiver. There came the buzz and the click, and with a rush of blood to the heart I recognized his voice.

"*Buon giorno, signore.* You slept well?"

"Very well," I answered. "Will you bring me a *café complet?*"

"*Café complet,*" he repeated.

I hung up and went and sat on the balcony. Then I remembered I had not unlocked the door. I did this, and returned to the balcony. My excitement was intense, and irrational. I even felt a trifle sick. Then, after five minutes that seemed eternity, came the knock on the door. He entered, tray poised high at shoulder level, and his bearing was so regal, his carriage so proud that he might have been bringing me ambrosia or a swan instead of coffee and a roll and butter. He was wearing a morning coat with thin black stripes, the type of jacket worn by valets at a club.

"A good appetite, *signore,*" he said.

"Thank you," I replied.

I had my small present ready on my knee. The Shakespeare Sonnets must be sacrificed. They were irreplaceable in that particular edition, but no matter. Nothing else would do. First, though, before the presentation, I would sound him.

"I want to make you a little present," I told him.

He bowed in courtesy. "The *signore* is too good," he murmured.

"You speak English so well," I continued, "that you need to hear only the best. Now, tell me, who do you think has been the greatest Englishman?"

He considered the matter gravely. And he stood, as he did on the Piazza San Marco, with his hands clasped behind his back.

"Winston Churchill," he said.

I might have known it. Naturally the boy lived in the present, or it would be more correct to say, in this instance, the immediate past.

"A good answer," I said, smiling, "but I want you to think again. No, I'll put my question another way. If you had some money to spend, and you could spend it on anything you wanted connected with the English language, what would be the first thing you would buy?"

This time there was no hesitation. "I would buy a long-playing gramophone record," he said, "a long-playing gramophone record of Elvis Presley or Johnnie Ray."

I was disappointed. It was not the answer I had hoped for. Who were these creatures? Crooners? Ganymede must be educated to better things. On second thought, I would not part with the Sonnets.

"Very well," I said, hoping I did not sound offhand, and I put my hand in my pocket and took out a thousand-lire note, "but I suggest you buy Mozart instead."

The note disappeared, crumpled out of sight in his hand. It was discreetly done, and I wondered if he had been able to glimpse the figure. After all, a thousand lire is a thousand lire. I asked him how he managed to evade his duties at the café to bring me my breakfast, and he explained that his work did not begin there until just before midday. And, anyway, there was an understanding between the proprietor of the café and his uncle.

"Your uncle," I said, "seems to have an understanding with many people." I was thinking of the reception clerk at the Hotel Byron.

Ganymede smiled. "In Venice," he said, "everybody knows everybody."

I noticed that he glanced with admiration at my dressing-gown, which, when I had bought it for travelling, I had thought a shade too bright. Remembering the gramophone records, I reminded myself that he was, after all, nothing but a child, and one should not expect too much.

"Do you ever have a day off?" I asked him.

"On Sundays," he said. "I take it in turn with Beppo."

Beppo must be the unsuitable name of the swarthy youth at the café.

"And what do you do on your day off?" I inquired.

"I go out with my friends," he replied.

I poured myself more coffee, and I wondered if I dared. A rebuff would be so hurtful.

"If you have nothing better to do," I said, "and should be free next Sunday, I will take you for a trip to the Lido." I felt myself blush, and bent over the coffee-pot to hide it.

"In a speed-boat?" he asked quickly.

I was rather nonplussed. I had visualized the usual *vaporetto*. A speed-boat would be very expensive.

"That would depend," I hedged. "Surely on a Sunday they would all be booked?"

He shook his head firmly. "My uncle knows a man who has speed-boats for hire," he said. "They can be hired for the whole day."

Heavens above, it would cost a fortune! It would not do to commit myself. "We'll see," I said. "It would depend on the weather."

"The weather will be fine," he said, smiling. "It will stay fine now for the rest of the week."

His enthusiasm was infectious. Poor child, he must have few treats. On his feet all day and half the night serving tourists. A breath of air in a speed-boat would seem like paradise.

"Very well, then," I said. "If it's fine, we'll go."

I stood up, brushing the crumbs off my dressing-gown. He took my gesture as one of dismissal, and seized the tray.

"Can I do anything else for the *signore?*" he asked.

"You can post my letter," I said. "It's the one I told you about, to the friend who is a director of a hotel."

He lowered his eyes modestly, and waited for me to hand him the letter.

"Shall I see you this evening?" I asked.

"Of course, *signore,*" he said. "I will keep a table for you, at the usual time."

I let him go and went to run my bath, and it was only when I lay soaking in hot water that an unpleasant thought occurred to me. Was it possible that Ganymede had also brought breakfast for Sir Johnson, and had gone to the Lido in a speed-boat with Bertie Poole? I dismissed the thought. It was far too offensive....

The week remained fine, as he had foretold, and each day I became more entranced with my surroundings. No sign of anyone in the apartment. My bed was made as if by magic. The uncle remained *perdu.* And in the morning, as soon as I touched the telephone, Ganymede replied, and brought my breakfast. Every evening the table at the café awaited me, the chair upturned, the glass of curaçao and the half-bottle of Evian water in their place. If I had no more strange visions, and no more dreams, at least I found myself in a happy holiday mood, without a care in the world, and with what I can only call a telepathic understanding, an extraordinary sympathy, between Ganymede and myself. No other client existed but me. He did his duty, but remained at my beck and call. And the morning breakfasts on the balcony were the high peak of the day.

Sunday dawned fine. The high wind that might have meant a *vaporetto* was not forthcoming, and when he bore in my coffee and roll the smile on his face betrayed his excitement.

"The *signore* will come to the Lido?" he asked.

I waved my hand. "Of course," I said. "I never break a promise."

"I will make arrangements," he said, "if the *signore* will be at the first landing-stage to the apartment by half-past eleven."

And for the first time since bringing my breakfast he vanished without further conversation, such was his haste. It was a little alarming. I had not even inquired about the price.

I attended Mass in St. Mark's, a moving experience, and one that put me in a lofty mood. The setting was magnificent, and the singing could not have been bettered. I looked around for Ganymede, half expecting to see him enter leading a little sister by the hand, but there was no sign of him in the vast crowd. Oh well, the excitement of the speed-boat had proven too much for him.

I came out of the church into the dazzling sunshine, and put on my dark glasses. There was scarcely a ripple on the lagoon. I wished he had chosen a gondola. In a gondola I could have lain full-length, stretched at my ease, and we could have gone to Torcello. I might even have brought the Shakespeare Sonnets with me, and read one or two of them aloud to him. Instead, I must indulge his youthful whim and enter the age of speed. Blow the expense! It would never happen again.

I saw him standing by the water's edge, changed into brief shorts and a blue shirt. He looked very much younger, a complete child. I waved my walking-stick and smiled.

"All aboard?" I called gaily.

"All aboard, *signore*," he replied.

I made for the landing-stage and saw, drawn up to it, a magnificent varnished speed-boat complete with cabin, a small pennant at the prow, a large ensign at the stern. And standing by the controls, in a flaming orange shirt open at the neck, betraying his hairy chest, was a great ungainly figure I recognized with dismay. At sight of me he touched the klaxon, and revved up the engine so that it roared.

"We go places," he said, with a revolting smile. "We hit-a the headlines. We have fun."

VII

I stepped aboard, my heart like lead, and was instantly thrown off balance as our horrible mechanic thrust the engine into gear. I clutched at his ape-like arm, to save myself from falling, and he steadied me into the seat beside him, at the same time opening the throttle to such an extent that I feared for my eardrums. We bounced across the lagoon at a fearful speed, hitting the surface every moment with a crash that nearly split the craft in two, and nothing could be seen of the grace and colour of Venice because of the wall of water that rose on either side of us.

"Must we go so fast?" I screamed, endeavouring to make myself heard above the deafening roar of the engine. The tout grinned at me, showing his gold-filled teeth, and shouted back, "We break-a the records. This most powerful boat in Venice."

I resigned myself to doom. I was not only ill-prepared for the ordeal, but ill-dressed. My dark blue coat was already spattered with salt-water, and there was a smear of oil on my trouser leg. The hat I had brought to protect me against the sun was useless. I needed a flying helmet and a pair of goggles. To leave my exposed seat and crawl to the cabin would be risking certain injury to my limbs. Besides, I should get claustrophobia, and the noise inside a confined space would be even worse. On, on we sped, rocking every craft in sight, heading for the Adriatic, and to show off his skill as a helmsman the monster beside me began to perform acrobatics, making great circles and heading into our own wash.

"You watch-a her rise," he bellowed in my ear, and rise we did, to such an extent that my stomach turned over with the inevitable thud of our descent, and the spray that we had not left behind us trickled over my collar and down my back. Standing in the prow, revelling in every moment, his light hair tossed about in the breeze we were making, stood Ganymede, a sea-sprite, joyous and free. He was my only consolation, and the sight of him there, turning now and again to smile, prevented me from ordering an instant return to Venice.

When we reached the Lido, a pleasant enough trip by *vaporetto*, I was not only wet but deaf into the bargain, the spray and the roar of the engine combined having successfully blocked my right ear. I stepped ashore shaken and silent, and it was odious when the tout took my arm and shepherded me into a waiting taxi, while Ganymede leapt in front beside the driver. Where to now, I asked myself? How fatal to make a picture of one's day in fantasy. In the church, during the singing of Mass, I had seen myself landing with Ganymede from some smooth craft piloted by a discreet non-entity, and then the two of us strolling to a little restaurant I had marked down on my previous visit. How delightful, I had thought, to sit at a corner table with

618 Daphne du Maurier

him, choosing the menu, watching his happy face, seeing it colour, perhaps, with the wine, and getting him to talk about himself, about his life, about the complaining mother and little sister. Then, with the liqueurs, we would make plans for the future, should my letter to my London superior prove successful.

None of this happened. The taxi drew up with a swerve before a modern hotel facing the Lido bathing-beach. The place was crammed, despite the lateness of the season, and the tout, known apparently to the maître d'hôtel, thrust his way through the chattering crowd into the airless restaurant. To follow in his wake was bad enough, the flaming orange shirt making him conspicuous, but worse was to come. The table in the centre was already filled with hilarious Italians talking at the tops of their voices, who at sight of us rose in unison, pushing back their chairs to make room. A dyed blonde with enormous ear-rings and reeking of scent swooped upon me with a flow of Italian.

"My sister, *signore*," said the tout, "she make-a you welcome. She no speak-a the English."

Was this Ganymede's mother? And the full-bosomed young woman beside her with scarlet fingernails and jangling bangles, was this the little sister? My head whirled.

"It is a great honour, *signore*," Ganymede murmured, "that you invite my family to lunch."

I saw down, defeated. I had invited nobody. But the matter was out of my hands. The uncle—if uncle indeed he was, the monster, the tout—was handing round to everyone menus the size of placards. The maître d'hôtel was bending himself in two in an effort to please. And Ganymede ... Ganymede was smiling into the eyes of some loathsome cousin who, with clipped moustache and crew-cut, was making the motions of a speed-boat going through the water with a pudgy, olive hand.

I turned to the tout in desperation. "I had not expected a party," I said. "I am afraid I may not have brought enough money."

He broke off his discussion with the maître d'hôtel.

"Don't worry ... don't worry ..." he said, waving the air. "You leave-a the bill to me. We settle later."

Settle later.... It was all very well. By the time the day was over I should not be in a position to settle anything. An enormous plate of noodles was set before me, topped with a rich meat sauce, and I saw that my glass was being filled with a particular barolo that, taken in the middle of the day, means certain death.

"You 'avin' fun?" said Ganymede's sister, pressing my foot with hers.

Hours later I found myself on the beach, still seated between her and her mother, both of them changed into bikinis, lying on either side of me like porpoises, while the cousins, the uncles, the aunts splashed into the sea and back again, shrieking and laughing, and Ganymede, beautiful as an angel from heaven, presided at the gramophone that had suddenly materialized from outer space, repeating again and again the long-playing record that he had bought with my thousand lire.

"My mother wants so much to thank you," said Ganymede, "for writing to London. If I go, she will come too, and my sister."

"We all go," said his uncle. "We make one big party. We all go to London and set-a the Thames on fire."

It was over at last. The final splashing in the sea, the final poke from the scarlet toe of the sister, the final bottle of wine. I had a splitting head, and my inside had turned on me. One by one the relations came to shake me by the hand. The mother, voluble with thanks, embraced me. That none of them were to accompany us back to Venice in the speed-boat and continue the party there was the one measure of solace left to me at the end of the disastrous day.

We climbed aboard. The engine started. We were away. And this should have been the return journey I had already made in fantasy—the smooth, rather idling return over limpid water, Ganymede at my side, a new intimacy having grown up between us because of the hours spent in each other's company, the sun, low on the horizon, turning the island that was Venice into a rose façade.

Half-way across, I saw that Ganymede was struggling with a rope that lay coiled across the stern of our craft, and the uncle, easing the throttle so that our progress was suddenly slowed, left the controls to help him. We began to rock from side to side in a sickly fashion.

"What is going to happen now?" I called.

Ganymede shook the hair our of his eyes and smiled. "I water-ski," he said. "I follow you home to Venice on my skis."

He dived into the cabin and came out again with the skis. Together the uncle and nephew fixed the rope and the skis, and then Ganymede flung off his shirt and his shorts and stood upright, a small bronzed figure in a bathing slip.

The uncle beckoned me. "You sit-a here," he said. "You pay out the rope so."

He secured the rope to a bollard in the stern and put the end into my hands, then rushed forward to the driving seat and started to roar the engine.

"What do you mean?" I cried. "What do I have to do?"

Ganymede was already over the side and in the water, fixing his bare feet into the slots of the skis, and then, unbelievably, pulling himself up into a standing position while the craft began to race ahead. The uncle sounded the klaxon with an ear-splitting screech, and the craft, gathering momentum, sped over the water at top speed. The rope, made fast to the bollard, held, though I still clung to the end, while on our wake, steady as a rock on his dancing skis, the small figure of Ganymede was silhouetted against the already vanishing Lido.

I seated myself in the stern of the boat and watched him. He might have been a charioteer, and the two skis his racing steeds. His hands were stretched before him, holding the guide-rope as a charioteer would gather his reins, and as we circled once, twice, and he swung out in an arc on his corresponding course, he raised his hand to me in salutation, a smile of triumph on his face.

The sea was the sky, the ripple on the water wisps of cloud, and heaven knows what meteors we drove and scattered, the boy and I, soaring towards the sun. I know that at times I bore him on my shoulders, and at others he slipped away, and once it was as though both of us plunged headlong into a molten mist which was neither star nor sky, but the luminous rings encircling a star.

As the craft swung into the straight again and bounced away on its course, he signalled to me with one hand, pointing to the rope on the bollard. I did not know whether he meant me to loosen it or make it more secure, and I did the wrong thing, jerked it, for he over-balanced instantly and was flung into the water. He must have hurt himself, for I saw that he made no attempt to swim.

Flustered, I shouted to the uncle, "Stop the engine! Go astern!"

Surely the right thing to do was to bring the boat to a standstill? The uncle, startled, seeing nothing but my agitated face, put the engine hard into reverse. His action threw me off my feet, and by the time I had scrambled up again we were almost on top of the boy. There was a mess of churning water, of tangled rope, of sudden, splintering wood, and leaning over the side of the boat I saw the slim body of Ganymede drawn into the suction of the propeller, his legs enmeshed, and I bent down to lift him clear. I put out my hands to grip his shoulders.

"Watch the rope," yelled the uncle. "Pull it clear."

But he did not know that the boy was beside us, was beneath us, and that already he had slipped from my hands which struggled to hold him, to bear him aloft, that already ... God, already ... the water was beginning to colour crimson with his blood.

VIII

Yes, yes, I told the uncle. Yes, I would pay compensation, I would pay anything they asked. It had been my fault, an error of judgement. I had not understood. Yes, I would pay any and every item he liked to put down on his list. I would telegraph to my bank in London, and perhaps the British Consul would help me, would give advice. If I could not raise the money immediately I would pay so much a week, so much a month, so much a year. Indeed, the rest of my life I would continue to pay, I would continue to support the bereaved, because it was my fault, I agreed that it was all my fault.

An error of judgement on my part had been the cause of the accident. The British Consul sat by my side, and he listened to the explanations of the uncle, who produced his notebook and his sheaf of bills.

"This gentleman take-a my apartment for two weeks, and my nephew he bring-a him his breakfast every day. He bring-a flowers. He bring-a coffee and rolls. He insists my nephew look after him and no one else. This gentleman take great fancy to the boy."

"Is that true?"

"Yes, it's true."

The lighting of the apartment was extra, it seemed. And the heating for the bath. The bath had to be heated from below in a special way. There was a man's time for coming in to repair a shutter. The boy's time, he told the Consul, for bringing my breakfast, for not going to the café before midday. And the time for taking a Sunday off that was not the regular Sunday. He did not know if the gentleman was prepared to pay for these items.

"I have already said that I will pay for everything."

The notebook was consulted again, and there was the damage to the engines of the speed-boat, the cost of the water-skis that were smashed beyond repair, the charge for the craft that had been hailed to tow us back to Venice, to tow the speed-boat back to Venice with Ganymede unconscious in my arms, and the telephone call from the quayside for the ambulance. One by one he read out the items from the notebook. The hospital charges, the doctor's fees, the surgeon's fees.

"This gentleman, he insist he pay for everything."

"Is that true?"

"Yes, it's true."

The yellow face against the dark suit seemed fatter than before, and the eyes, puffy with weeping, looked sideways at the Consul.

"This gentleman, he write to his friend in London about my nephew. Perhaps already there is a job waiting for the boy, a job he can no longer take. I have a son, Beppo, my son also a very good boy, known to the gentleman here. Beppo and my nephew they both work at the café every night, and serve the gentleman. The gentleman so fond of these boys, he follow them home. Yes, I see it with my own eyes, he follow them home. Beppo would like to go to London in place of his poor cousin. This gentleman arrange it, perhaps? He write again to his friend in London?"

The Consul coughed discreetly. "Is this true? Did you follow them home?"

"Yes, it's true."

The uncle took out a large handkerchief and blew his nose.

"My nephew very well brought-up boy. My son the same. Never give any trouble. All the money they earn they give to their family. My nephew he had very great trust in this gentleman, and he tell me, he tell all the family, his mother, his sister, that this gentleman will take him back to London. His mother, she buy a new dress, and his sister too, she buy new clothes for the boy to go to London. Now, she ask-a herself, what happens to the clothes, they cannot be worn, they are no use."

I said to the Consul that I would pay for everything.

"His poor mother, she break-a her heart," the voice continued, "and his sister too, she lose-a all interest in her work, she become nervous, ill. Who is to pay for the funeral of my nephew? Then this gentleman, he kindly say, no expense to be spared."

No expense to be spared, and let that go too for the mourning, and the veils, and the wreaths, and the music, and the weeping, and the procession, the endless long procession. And I would pay, too, for the touists clicking cameras and feeding pigeons who knew nothing of what had happened, and for those lovers lying in each other's arms in gondolas, and for the echo of the Angelus sounding from the Campanile, and the lapping water from the lagoon, and the chug-chug of the *vaporetto* leaving the landing-stage which turns into the chug-chug of a coal barge in the Paddington canal.

It passes, of course—not the coal barge over there, I mean, but the horror. The horror of accident, of sudden death. You see, as I told myself afterwards, if it had not been an accident it would have been a war. Or he would have come to London and grown up, grown fat, turned into a tout like the uncle, grown ugly, old. I don't want to make excuses for anything. I don't want to make excuses for anything at all. But—because of what hapened—my life has become rather different. As I said before, I've moved my quarters in London to this district. I've given up my job, I've dropped my friends, in a word ... I've changed. I still see my sister and my nieces from time to time. No, I don't possess any other family. There was a younger brother who died when I was five, but I don't remember him at all: I've never given him a thought. My sister has been my only living relative for years.

Now, if you will excuse me, I see by my watch it is nearly seven o'clock. The restaurant down the road will be open. And I like to be there on time. The fact is, the boy who is training there as a waiter celebrates his fifteenth birthday this evening, and I have a little present for him. Nothing very much, you understand—I don't believe in spoiling these lads—but it seems there is a singer called Perry Como much in favour amongst the young. I have the latest record here. He likes bright colours, too—I rather thought this blue and gold carat might catch his eye....

Old Boys

Patrick Gale

The Greeks confined the public expression of exclusively male passion to some rigorously formalized rituals. In Athens, the setting was the gymnasium, where those possessed by love would come in the morning to observe the young students until midday, when the odour of sweat, oil, and earth was sure to provoke amorous advances. For the Athenians, according to Roberto Calasso, the beloved was never to reciprocate in the pleasure but was supposed to "contemplate in a state of sobriety the enticement of the other drunken with Aphrodite". He was supposed to await the time when he too, as a mature lover, would be possessed by the goddess and seek out the boys at the gym.

Contemporary stories of schoolboy love have often gained acceptance with the common reader. Classic accounts of English school life such as Stalky & Co., Tom Brown's Schooldays, *and* The History of Sandford and Merton *are full of homoerotic connotations. The accepted notion seems to be that boys will be boys, and that this adolescent phase will come to an end on the last day of class. Patrick Gale refuses to embrace this dictum and, as so often in his fiction, he turns upside down the comfortable stories which society invents to explain its own ghosts. In "Old Boys", the scent of young men permeates more than the school playing-field, and Gale has some hilariously disarming questions to ask about the rites of reciprocity.*

The last verse of the school hymn was stirring stuff about strapping on breastplates, guarding imperilled shores and standing shoulder to shoulder against some unidentified foe. Foreigners presumably, or Sin. Boys in the gallery, spared the embarrassment of sitting with family, bellowed the familiar words with the clannish fervour of a rugby crowd. Below them, the fourteen diminutive choristers piped a descant, barely audible above the efforts of the heartier element. Wives, fragrant and carefully dressed for a long summer day, faces raised over hymnals, delighted in the relative fragility of their own voices.

"But of course it's sexy. It's *desperately* sexy," Elsa had insisted as they were dressing that morning. "You can't imagine. Standing there surrounded by all that young masculinity. The odour of testosterone is quite overpowering. I'd *love* to be a headmaster's wife. I'd be a tremendous tease, wearing lots of scent and rustly silk things."

The chaplain commanded them to prayer and the chapel filled briefly with the sounds of thumping knees, dropped hymn books and skittering leather cushions. Colin glanced across at Elsa, lovely face partly shaded by a hat brim, subtly painted lips barely parted, eyes obediently closed. He could imagine her here, as a master's wife, jet black hair shaken out over a tumbled silk headscarf, hugging herself against the cold on a playing-field touchline, calling out,

"Come on House!"

with a fine show of loyalty, then catching the eye of a nearby prefect and making him blush. She would be bewitching and shameless and boys would jostle to sit by her at lunch so as to admire her cleavage. On the whole, he decided, she was safer cloistered in her cubbyhole at the World Service; left too long in an environment like this one, she would become more than ever like the young Elizabeth Taylor and prove the catalyst for some drama of horrific erotic violence.

Between them Harry clasped his hands tightly together and repeated the Lord's Prayer slightly too loud. He had a summer cold and had just started confirmation classes. Elsa looked first at him then at Colin, smiling mischievously over their son's head.

This, of course, had been her idea. She had often said that she thought Harry should follow in his father's footsteps, and he had only recently seen that she meant it seriously. He had promised himself that no child of his would be sent away to boarding school, but already Elsa had persuaded him to parcel Harry off to an eminently respectable prep school in the South Downs where, apparently, the small boy thrived on pre-breakfast Latin. Enjoying lazy Saturday mornings in bed at an age when most of his contemporaries were woken at nine o'clock sharp and dragged off to fly kites and throw rugger balls, Colin was coming to understand the terms of the similar betrayal his parents had practised on him at the same age. Public school, however, was different. He had always sworn he would draw the line there, that Harry would attend an excellent day school, with girls in every year, not just the sixth form. Somewhere he could drop Latin for Spanish or Italian. And yet here he was, attending an Old Boy's Day for the first time since leaving the place eighteen years ago, with a view to "casing the joint", as Elsa put it, for Harry.

"If he doesn't like it, mind you," he had stipulated, "if he has the slightest reservation—"

"Then he doesn't have to go," Elsa broke in, assuring him with a soft touch on the back on his fist.

And Harry adored her. Colin remembered loathing his mother at that age, never forgiving her for sending him away. Yet Harry still seemed to drink Elsa in with his eyes. She handled him so well, Colin reflected. She knew when to be sweet, when to be boyishly joshing, when to be sexy. And she *was* sexy with him. Colin had watched the care with which she chose clothes for the boy's Sundays out of school. She tended to wear firmer bras for him and clinging cashmere.

"Little boys like tits, silly," she explained. "Haven't you noticed? All the popular boys have mums who are a bit, well ..." and she smoothed down her jersey in explanation, smiling to herself.

"Well?" she asked as they left the chapel and headed out into a flag-stoned quadrangle where swallows swooped through the sunshine in search of flies. "Are the happy memories flooding back?"

"Not really," he said. "Thank God most of my teachers seem to have left."

"Probably dead," Harry piped up.

"Thank you, Harry," Colin told him.

"What about friends? Surely you recognize somebody?"

"No," Colin said, faintly relieved. "Not yet. Let's go and find some lunch."

"Sherry with the housemaster first," she reminded him.

"Oh Fuck."

"Harry!" Elsa seemed genuinely surprised, but couldn't help smile at the evident pride on Harry's face at having produced an adult expletive in adult company. "Darling!" she added and chuckled, patting his shoulder.

They drifted with the noisy crowd out of the quadrangle and Harry expressed a wish to piss.

"I'll wait here," Elsa said, arranging herself on a bench below a towering horse chestnut. "Don't be long. I'm thirsty." Following a line of instinctive memory, Colin led his son along a corridor, across another quadrangle and into a dingy, green-tiled lavatory where they peed side by side at a urinal and then, only because each had the other with him, laboriously washed their hands.

The old swaths of graffiti had been painted over and the roller-towels had been replaced with hot-air hand driers, but the room retained an inexpungeable dankness and a threatening quality. For the first time that day, Colin was assailed by memories, none of them sunny ones. He flinched instinctively when three tall boys burst nois-ily in through the swing door. He panicked that Harry was taking so long over drying his hands, then remembered that he was thirty-five and these hulking bullies had become children. The boys fell respect-fully silent and went seriously about their business as he shepherded Harry back into the sunlight.

"How do people know if it's a Ladies or a Gents?" Harry asked. "There's no sign on the door."

"There aren't any ladies," Colin told him. "And when there are I suppose they just hold on until they find somewhere safe."

Elsa came smiling from beneath the tree to meet them.

"I just met Keith Bedford," she said.

"Who?"

"He's a newscaster," Harry explained patiently.

"You never told me he was here with you," she went on.

"He wasn't."

"Well he said he was."

"Must be younger than me, then. You never remember the younger ones because they were so unimportant. They didn't count."

"You boys are so hard and peculiar."

Elsa took his arm as they cut back across the first quadrangle and headed out onto a broad stone path that lay along one side of a huge lawn studded with old plane trees and bounded by a high flint wall. Colin was surprised that Harry forsook his habitual place on Elsa's other side and came to walk beside his father, touched perhaps by the exclusive maleness of the place. Again she caught Colin's eye and gave him a discreet smile. At such times, when some parents would be sad-dened at their impotence in the face of nature, she seemed soothed, taking little reminders of biological determination as signs of a covenant that, having produced a perfectly adjusted male, she could soon relinquish all responsibility for him. Colin sighed.

"What is it?" she asked.

"I'd forgotten it was so beautiful. It's idyllic, really. Do you like it, Harry?"

"It's okay," said Harry. "It's very big. Isn't there a playground?"

"All this," Colin said, gesturing at the trees tall as cathedrals, the old wrought-iron benches, the distant cloisters, "this is the playground."

With perfect timing, a troop of boys in military uniform jogged out from behind the rifle range and went puffing pinkly by, in tight formation. Harry turned to stare openly.

"Would I have to do that?" he asked.

"Only if you like it. Well actually, everyone has to do it for a year, then you can give it up and do social work instead if you prefer."

"Social work?"

"Doing gardening for old ladies, clearing weeds from the river, helping out at a school for the handicapped, that sort of thing. There was even a group that helped build houses on a sort of estate for the unfortunate somewhere."

"You're joking," Elsa said.

"God's own truth."

They walked on past the art gallery, the theatre workshop, the music school, the serried tablets to the loyal fallen in the War Cloisters and the house famous for having produced a prominent Fascist, two trade union leaders and at least three Russian spies among its boys.

"Those were just the ones that got caught," chuckled Elsa. "Perhaps Harry could be a spy? His languages are getting so good."

"There it is," said Colin and pointed.

They were out on a public street now, but every plot of land and building in sight was still school property. Up ahead loomed Colin's old house. It was a towering red brick affair with turrets, curious flint "teeth" around each window and such a mess of fire escapes and extensions added on that it was hard to tell which was the front and which the back. A bevy of well-upholstered female servants, fraudulently got up in black and white for the occasion instead of their usual nylon housecoats, were variously directing guests to the cloakrooms, handing them sherry or waving them on out to join the crowd in the garden where their sisters circulated with trays of canapés.

"Look, darling. That was Daddy's house. You could go there."

"Why?" said Harry, singularly unimpressed.

"It's no beauty," Colin confessed. "If you want to live in the really old bit by the chapel as well as having your lessons there, you'll have to go in for the scholarship exam."

"You must be joking," said Harry and Colin abandoned the briefly dangled possibility of annual holidays somewhere hot which a scholarship would have afforded them. Elsa demonstrated her frightening ability to read his mind.

"We can start borrowing Mummy's cottage in Devon," she said with a quick smile into the air before her. "Oh look, Harry, they've put out a trampoline in the garden. Do you want to have a go?"

At last, just when he was congratulating himself on their absence, Colin began to meet contemporaries from his days at the school. They were none of them friends—sex, geography, money and, in one case, death had dismantled all his schoolboy friendships—the thickening silhouettes before him were merely those of old acquaintance. In every case he found himself remembering not only a name but a nickname and at least one cruel fact to which they would be vulnerable: an armoury of psychological stings—flat feet, ginger pubic hair, a tendency to stutter, dead fathers, alcoholic mothers—which he reached for out of a long-dormant instinct to wound or be wounded. They stood around on the lawn holding their careers against each other's to compare them for size, inspecting one another's wives and mustering a chortling bonhomie which in seven out of eight cases Colin estimated to be entirely phoney. Acute embarrassment drove them all to assume the speech patterns of men twenty years their senior, of their fathers, in fact.

"You called that man 'old chap'," Elsa said, faintly appalled, as they were herded in through an entrance hall drab as Colin remembered it, to the sludge-green dining room where a "fork luncheon" awaited them. "You never talk like that."

"I know," he said, "I'm sorry. It just slipped out. I think it's infectious."

"The housemaster's a darling."

"Really? We haven't spoken."

"Oh really, Colin, that's what we're here for. Go and introduce yourself. He's the one by the fireplace with the toddler on his hip and the smile."

"But he looks about twenty-five."

"He is. Much healthier than the crusty types you had in your day and the wife's no battleaxe either."

Colin did as he was told and spoke with the housemaster, who was, indeed, a darling. There was something of Peter Pan about him and Colin realized that this was why he was good at his job. A part of his development seemed to have been arrested. He had failed to acquire the callused outer layer that marked every other man in the room. He spoke to boys with the authority of a gentle older brother and to fathers with the cheerful respectfulness of their ideal son. He was enthusiastic about everything from crab *vol au vents* to the school viol consort. His irony was confected from natural wit rather than harsh experience. He was entirely unsuited to life in an adult community. Colin was surprised, after introducing Harry, then having a chat that seemed to be about nothing of any consequence, to hear the man say,

"Well, we'd be delighted to have him in the house, provided he passes the exams, of course...."

"Oh," Colin said. "Well then. Thanks very much. I'll tell Elsa the good news."

They shook hands and Harry's small fate was sealed. Colin glanced out of the window and saw his son sitting on a low wall, crumbily munching a meringue and watching some comparatively huge boys kick a football about a caged-in yard. He was disturbed at how the boy was finding his place as swiftly and naturally as a newly weaned addition to some fiercely hierarchical animal society.

Elsa was one of those rare women with a genuine interest in cricket. She came from a long line of cricketers and, being an only child, had received the full benefit of her father's instruction. She liked knowledge, particularly when it had so little practical application. It pleased Colin to watch her sweep aside the patronage of cricketing men with the breadth of her understanding, not least because he had not a sporting bone in his body. When he took her a cup of coffee, he found her arguing a fine point of test-match history with a tall, mop-headed youth who wore the kind of cricketing jersey only permitted to members of the school team; a deity, in schoolboy terms, yet she was winning the argument.

"But then," she sighed, gently tapping the youth's broad chest with one long finger, having pressed home her triumphant point, "I can see you're an expert. What do *I* know? I've never even played the game." The youth flushed as Elsa turned to Colin.

"Coffee. How lovely. Darling, this is Hargreaves."

Hargreaves offered Colin a hand.

"How do you do, sir."

"Marvellous to be called sir," Elsa said. "Madam always sounds supercilious and shopkeepery."

"They've offered Harry a place," Colin told her. "Subject to exams, of course."

"But of course they did."

"I thought I'd take a look round. See how things have changed. Want to come?"

Elsa wrinkled her nose.

"Changing rooms and things? Do we have to? I was going to catch the start of the match. Hargreaves can show me the way."

"Of course I can," said Hargreaves.

Glad to have a chance to explore on his own, Colin took a second coffee and wandered off. The house was on its best behaviour, the presence of parents neutering its habitual rowdiness, but here and there its true nature pierced the skin of decorum with a reassuringly rude noise. Colin inspected the changing room, rank with sweat and sweet shampoo, the pitifully stocked library, the day room, and a new study block, where, from the momentarily hostile glances, he sensed he had interrupted something and retreated. Here and there, boys unhampered by family were engaged in small acts of vandalism or self-improvement. One little older than Harry pored over a surprisingly undistinguished newspaper, frowning at a pouting model's breasts as though checking through a page of algebraic calculations. Uncertain of what he was looking for—some confirmation perhaps that these familiar scenes were not so irrelevant as they now felt—Colin walked back to the staircase and made for the dormitories. Here, too, little had changed. There were still no radiators or curtains, but the old thin mattresses which dipped in the middle had been replaced. He sat on a bed and was happy to find that it still betrayed the slightest movement with a creak. He walked to one of the big windows, merciless in cold weather, and saw a crowd of visitors trailing over the athletics track below towards the cricket fields nearer the river. A woman turned and called out. It was Elsa. He saw Harry sprinting to catch up with her. The boy looked up to chatter to her as they walked. If he liked the place, did Colin have the right to deprive him of the experience?

Thinking he should join them, he left his coffee cup on a chest of drawers and started back along the dormitory corridor. He passed an open door and looked in just long enough to recognize the face of a large man peering up at the beams. He moved swiftly on, halted when he heard people on the stairs and doubled back to dart into the linen room. He sat on a bench where he would not be visible from the door. He needed to recover. His heart pounded as though he had just run up the stairs. Sweat beaded on his forehead and he swept it away with a handkerchief. It was him, unmistakably him. The black hair had grown grizzled, the rangy frame become slightly leaner, but the thick eyebrows and large, once-broken nose had been instantly recognizable. Colin touched the handkerchief to his upper lip, recalling how the man's eyes dropped to meet his for a fraction of a second before Colin hurried on.

The day room was where all but the eldest boys spent their free time and evenings. It was high-ceilinged and L-shaped. Around the walls huddled wooden cubicles. Each boy had a cubicle. It had a desk, a cupboard, a bench and an electric light, all of them ancient. This cramped space—sizes varied and the less cramped ones were highly sought-after—was the only space in the entire school wherein one could be moderately private. The new boy had to make a mental adjustment in which the cluster of rooms, garden, pets and family he called home were compressed into a space a Victorian street urchin would have scorned. Here his individuality could be expressed in postcards, ornaments, toys, a choice of curtain and cushion cover, a store of food and even a corrugated plastic roof. Here, too, he would learn his first brutal lessons in the danger of expressing individuality of the wrong sort.

Colin and, crucially, Colin's mother, had been drilled in these matters by an older cousin. The cousin was still at the school but would be prevented, on his honour, from coming to Colin's assistance or in any way singling him out, once Colin joined him there. Colin had been scrupulous. His curtain and cushion were of a wholly unremarkable green fabric. He had no photographs of his parents but, at his sudden insistence, had brought along one of his older sister looking sulky in a bathing costume. This he pinned up alongside a calendar with a different dog breed pictured every month. He brought no toys, nothing whatever of especial monetary or sentimental value beyond a tinny transistor radio. Yet somehow, obscurely, he was found wanting.

At first insignificant violence was offered him, daring him to react and so give an excuse for fiercer reprisals. Boys would trip him from behind—"ankle-walking" it was called—as he walked along the corridor from the dining room. He was flicked with wet towel-corners when queueing for a wash-basin. They made small verbal attacks, too, mocking, relying on the support of those around them.

"Hey!" they would call. "Hey, you!"

"Yes?" he would ask, turning.

"Nothing," came the smirking reply, "nothing."

And by common consent, Nothing, then Nuts, became his nickname, until long after anyone could remember the reason why.

"Above all you must learn not to react," his cousin had insisted. Everyone, it seemed, went through a period of being picked upon, but the brief initiation period could be prolonged into indefinite persecution if the would-be initiate gave the wrong sort of encouragement. So Colin met whips, trippings and mockery with polite equanimity, if not quite gratitude.

He wrote home saying how much he was enjoying himself, and there *were* things to enjoy. He enjoyed singing, with no great finesse, in the school choral society. He took up pottery and made an ashtray for his father. He won a small measure of popularity among his immediate peers as cox of the first-year rowing team—even if this did mean being tossed into freezing river water whenever they lost a race. But as well as being designed to transfer all one's respect from the adults—who vanished from view and consequently power soon after six o'clock—to the prefects, the school's social system induced a tantalizing sense that there were unspeakably grown-up pleasures to be tasted, if only one could chance on some secret password.

He was kept from despair by the salutary spectacle of other boys, often well into their second year, who had been cast forever beyond acceptance and were fair game even for "new bugs" like himself to tease. There was one with grotesquely protuberant ears who appeared to have given up washing, one who could easily be provoked to spectacular tantrums in which he actually stamped his feet and cried, and a third, called Bollocks because his balls had still not dropped, who babbled in a high-pitched voice about the consolations of Christianity even as one tore his essays and scattered his textbooks into muddy puddles. The one with the ears and sour smell was later diagnosed as a schizophrenic, but only once exposed to a society with marginally less appetite for aberration, in his first year at Exeter.

Colin's initiation came six weeks into his first term, on a Sunday night. Sundays were always a dangerous time. Envy was in the air, because some boys had been whisked out to lunch by their parents, and a bogus holiday mood tended to curdle without warning. A few boys were still trying to finish their Saturday night essays but most were idle, bored and fractious, their dissatisfaction fuelled by a thorough perusal of that other world of luxuries and freedom paraded so unfeelingly through the Sunday colour supplements. It was the housemaster's night off, which meant he was more thoroughly absent than usual, being interruptable only *in extremis*. A boy had once been blinded with a fencing foil on a Sunday night. Only last Sunday evening, the day room had taken on a nightmarish air when someone produced a set of darts stolen from the pub and began throwing them at people's ankles for a laugh. Colin's cousin had warned him about Sunday nights. Colin was duly lying low in his cubicle, behind his irreproachable curtain, reading Balzac and trying not to be noticed. A fight with cartons of gone-off milk had flared and died. A game of table tennis was threatening to turn nasty. Someone was playing *Dark Side of the Moon* yet again, with the usual cluster of boys gathered religiously to mouth the lyrics and strum imaginary guitars. Any minute the youngest "new bug" would be called on to ring the bell for evening prayers. Only minutes lay between Balzac and the relative safety of a frosty bed.

It was a rogue attack, begun by Bollocks in an extravagant bid for acceptance by the crowd. Colin was startled as he whisked back the curtain and yelped,

"Do you accept Jesus as your personal saviour?"

A few boys jeered out of habit, mocking the squeaky voice and stutter, but others simply gathered to watch.

"I'm not sure," Colin admitted.

"Do you accept Jesus as your personal saviour?" Bollocks repeated and Colin decided to gamble on his superior status, as would-be initiate over pariah.

"Why should I?" he jeered. "Sp-Sp-Spastic-Features!"

For a moment it was uncertain which way the scene would turn, as Bollocks groped in his sports jacket for something; then he produced a can of lighter fuel, liberally anointed the curtain and pronounced,

"Then, heretic, you fry."

And he struck a match. Colin swore and shrank back into his cubicle as the air filled with smoke and the irreproachable green was engulfed in flames. Then one of the third-years, secure in his status as a useful football player and twenty-a-day smoker, decided that Bollocks was going too far. To loud cheers, he set off a fire extinguisher, dousing the flames, then turning the jet on the pariah. Seizing the moment, Colin dashed out to land a vigorous kick on Bollocks's backside, but he had misjudged the feelings of the crowd.

He was grabbed. His trousers and underpants were gleefully tugged down around his ankles and he was bent over the ping-pong table while his arse was given a stinging "douche" from what remained in the fire extinguisher. When that was no longer deemed amusing, hot, bony hands hoisted him into one of the large plastic dustbins and a saucer of meatily rancid butter was pressed down on his hair. When he tried to clear it off it was followed by a faceful of long-forgotten milk and something wet and nameless down the back of his shirt. Blinded and fighting back the urge to retch, Colin flailed out wildly in his effort to keep his balance as his tormentors lifted the dustbin into the air. Once his eyes were sufficiently clear to see where they were carrying him, he froze and swore again. The walls above the cubicles were clad in handsome wooden panelling which reached twelve feet or more. The panelling was very thick—built like that, perhaps, to disguise pipework—and it was possible to clamber around the room on the top of it. Colin and his dustbin were hoisted overhead and, with much cheering, balanced precariously where two sections of the panel pathway formed a corner. Then the bell rang for evening prayers and the room emptied as everyone raced up the corridor to kneel at their chairs in the dining room. Apathetic sixth-formers drifted through from their studies to follow them. Most ignored him. One blew a gobbet of chewing gum at him and another shouted some witticism in German which raised a knowing laugh.

Then he was alone. Gingerly he tried to stand but the dustbin rocked sickeningly and he dropped back to crouching in the garbage. If he fell he had no doubt he would break his neck, or at best crack his skull on the grimy parquet floor. He pictured his funeral. There would be white lilies and the headmaster would speak damningly and at length, summoning his murderers by name and making them pray around the coffin. There would be mass expulsions, reported in the national press and a new, fiercely disciplinarian regime would be instituted. First-years would keep Colin's name alive with tears of gratitude.

For the first time since his father had left him sitting on a trunk in Waterloo Station six weeks before, Colin lowered his guard and allowed himself the luxury of homesick tears.

"Oh for Fuck's sake!"

He blinked and looked over the rim of the dustbin. It was Hardy, one of the prefects and a senior officer in the school army corps. Tall, dark, terrifying, Hardy rarely spoke to his juniors, keeping discipline by the sheer authority of his presence. When he did speak it tended to be with withering sarcasm.

"Sorry, Hardy," Colin stammered, expecting to be punished for the wrongs done to him, which was the usual way.

"Can't you get down?"

"I ... I don't think so."

"Well in Christ's name stay still then."

Hardy tossed the novel he had been carrying onto the ping-pong table, then clambered over the cubicles below Colin and steadied the dustbin for him.

"Go on. Get out."

Hastily tugging up his underwear and trousers, Colin clambered out onto the ledge. Hardy dropped the dustbin to the floor, magnificently impervious to the mess he created. He jumped down after it. Colin followed more carefully. Hardy looked at him and wrinkled his nose.

"You stink. Christ!"

"Sorry Hardy."

"Not your fault. What's your name?"

"Cowper."

"Well take a shower, Cowper. Now."

"But what about evening prayers?"

"Oh sod those. Come on."

Hardy led the way to the changing room and through it to the showers, where the air was still ripe with cigarette smoke. While Colin hastily undressed, Hardy set a shower running. As Colin slipped in past him, he shut the door behind them, then he leant against the wall casually smoking while Colin washed himself in the blast of hot water. Rubbing his pale skin with soap, he became aware of bits of him that had been scraped or bruised in the attack. He looked around for a bottle of shampoo and began to wash the butter out of his hair.

"It'll need more than that," Hardy told him, tossing his cigarette stub into a puddle where it fizzled. "Here. Let me." He came to stand so close that the shower splashed onto his jeans and linen jacket, leaving dark stains. Colin wondered if he was drunk. "Give," Hardy said and Colin passed him the shampoo. Hardy filled his palm with the dark green liquid and began to rub it into Colin's scalp, brow furrowed with concentration.

At prep school, the assistant matrons—bored daughters of good families, marking time—used to let themselves into the bathrooms to wash one's hair. They were breezily teasing about his coyness and it was all acutely embarrassing. This was quite different. Hardy had been at the pub and his breath was sour-sweet with beer and tobacco. Their hands had scratched busily at his scalp as though conquering an itch but Hardy's hands moved slowly. His touch was no less firm but he used his fingertips instead of his nails. He reached round to the back of Colin's head, while working fiercely at his temples with his thumbs. He was getting soaked. Colin felt wet denim against one of his thighs. He felt an overwhelming urge to pee and found, to his horror, that he was getting an erection. Desperate that Hardy shouldn't see it, he tried his usual technique of taking deep breaths and imagining his hand being cut off with a breadknife.

Outside the bell rang again, calling first-years to bed. There was a stampede of boys out in the corridor. Any minute someone might come in for a smoke. Smiling faintly, as at some private joke, Hardy pushed Colin's head back into the water and began to comb away the lather with his fingers. Nothing would get rid of the erection. Panic seemed to be making things worse. Colin felt his cock actually brush against Hardy's jeans. Hardy spotted it and chuckled.

"What's this? Eh?"

He tapped at it experimentally with a huge wet hand. Colin was mortified. He shut his eyes.

"I … I'm sorry, Hardy."

He tried to turn away but the older boy still had a hand on the back of his neck. Pummelling his back, the water seemed to be getting hotter.

"For fuck's sake, stop apologizing," Hardy told him. "Look at me."

Colin opened his eyes just in time to find Hardy bending down to kiss him. He gave a little yelp, then was silenced by a rough mouth against his and the extraordinary sensation of a tongue plunging between his lips to seek out his own. The hand that was on the back of his neck slipped down until an arm grasped him across the shoulder blades while another hand slipped between his legs and began to wank him, vigorously.

Colin had only learnt to toss himself off a few weeks before. The age at which such knowledge is acquired depends entirely on the company into which chance throws a boy. He had risen swiftly through his prep school hierarchy and so found himself, at the age when he might have learned, captain of a comparatively prepubescent dormitory and thus deprived of exemplary demonstrations. He was haunted by painful erections, and the occasional wet dream, and forced to join in the smutty bragging of his peers in the hope that many were as ignorant as he. It was inconceivable that one might ask even a close friend how to masturbate, so he suffered in silence. On graduating to public school, he was placed at last in a mixed-age dormitory and had to wait only weeks before being made a party to a guffawing discussion of comparative techniques. Left hand, right hand, underwater, upside down against a sheet—suddenly he had not only knowledge but choice. His experience of induced orgasm was still novel, so experiencing it at the hands of another was, literally, staggering. After freezing with his hands at his sides for a few seconds, he found his knees buckling and flung his arms around Hardy as though teetering on a cliff edge. He wanted to piss. He wanted to come. He wanted to cry out, and he wasn't entirely sure he hadn't done all three by the time Hardy had done with him. Hardy took one last, long kiss, then turned off the shower and held Colin's sobbing face to his chest.

"Well!" he said softly, as though the whole thing had surprised him too. "Well well."

There were footsteps and chatter suddenly in the changing room and the door to the showers was flung open. Two fifth-formers stood in the doorway, the laughter dying in their throats. They stared for a moment. Colin tried to pull away but Hardy held him close.

"Fuck off," he told them.

"Sorry, Hardy," one of them said. "The lights were off and we didn't—"

"Just fuck off."

"Sorry, Hardy."

They turned to go. Hardy called after them.

"Gilks?"

"Yes?"

One turned.

"Leave your cigarettes on the step and we'll say no more about it."

"Of course. Sorry, Hardy."

Gilks left his cigarettes and closed the door quietly behind him.

"Ignorant, nouveau-riche wankers," Hardy muttered and started to chuckle. Colin looked up at him uncertainly as his chuckle turned to full-chested laughter. How could he take this crisis so lightly? Surely they were doomed now? Hardy ruffled his hair.

"What did you say your name was?" he asked.

"Cowper, Hardy."

"This isn't quite a death camp. I meant your Christian name."

He lent a sour emphasis to the epithet, as to an obscenity.

"Oh. Sorry. It's Colin."

"Colin," Hardy murmured to himself as though trying the name out. He tugged someone's towel down off the hot pipes. "Colin Cowper." He wrapped it around Colin's shoulders. "Well mine's Lucas." He held out a hand and Colin obediently shook it. In the gloom he saw Hardy smile.

"Um. Hello," Colin said.

"Know how to cook scrambled eggs?"

"Yes."

"Good. You can make me some tomorrow."

So saying, Hardy sloped out of the shower room, his soaked clothes leaving a trail of water. He tugged another towel down in passing and walked out rubbing roughly at his hair.

The next day there was no scandal. Although Gilks and his friend would certainly have told everyone about what they had seen, there was no allusion either to the dustbin episode or to Colin's having been found in Hardy's embrace. Far from finding his initiation into house society compromised, Colin found himself suddenly cosily in the ranks of the accepted. He was never teased or bullied again and, if any outsider threatened him, his elders in the house drew ranks to protect him. An intellectual as well as a sportsman, extravagantly hip yet not so rebellious as to damage the system he knocked, Hardy was a house hero. As his implicitly acknowledged "little man", Colin attained an unofficial official position overnight, not unlike the pretty convict singled out as his cell-mate by a respected criminal. Awed, Bollocks paid for a new cubicle curtain in suitably pagan red velvet.

Hardy called Colin regularly to his bedsit in the prefect's wing, where, behind a locked door, their gasps and cries smothered by the guitars and serious lyrics of the latest concept album, they had sex. Perhaps, even, made love. In retrospect, their bedplay was unadvanced, innocent even, consisting of no more than hour upon cheek-pinking hour of kissing culminating occasionally in rushed mutual masturbation. As the weeks progressed, however, the crude lovemaking was punctuated by moments of unbridled romance which, for Colin at least, would never be matched. Hardy acquired someone's car for the evening and drove him to London for dinner. He borrowed a punt and took him for picnics on the river. He summoned him to deliciously transgressive moonlit trysts in the cricket pavilion (during one of which they took great pleasure in defiling the sacred grass of the cricket square). He introduced him to port, read him Cavafy, and once, when they were both drunk with regret at it being the last night of term, stole a key and led Colin up a spiral staircase to the roof of the chapel tower where they lay shivering, gazing up at the stars. Looking back from the years when he began a painful education in the difficult wooing of women, Colin realized that similar scenes could never be re-enacted with as much pleasure, however delicious his female partner, because with Lucas he had played the part of a girl: an old-fashioned, politically incorrect, all-demanding girl. Within the ritualized, hermetic environment of the school, Lucas, too, had been able to play a role—that of the all-powerful hero—which would be ridiculously unsustainable in the world beyond the institution's venerable confines.

As it was, the relationship had no reality beyond the school terms. In the holidays each returned to his family, which, in Lucas's case, meant Iran, where his father worked for an oil company. Neither would have dreamed of corresponding. They saw each other for the last time a little over a year since their first encounter. Lucas won a scholarship to Cambridge and vanished into the glamour of a year off, honouring Colin with a brief succession of postcards from the Mediterranean, which petered out somewhere in the Peloponnese. After that, Colin's only sexual experiences at school were with his fist. He snubbed all approaches that were made. Lucas had lent him stature, protected him from the system. He had worried that with Lucas gone he would be vulnerable again but his fears were groundless; he remained safe, coloured by boys' respect for the one who had gone, protected in absentia.

* * *

"Colin? It is Colin, isn't it?"

He had found him. Oh God he had found him! Colin stood, hurriedly, brushing his palms on his trousers before shaking hands.

"Lucas!"

He felt fourteen again. Lucas still towered over him. His grip was firm as ever. His forearms were now wreathed in black hairs. He wore a chunky gold watch. He smelled of money.

"What were you doing in *here?*"

"I was just, er—"

Lucas grinned.

"You were hiding. That's okay. I was hiding too."

They laughed. Lucas slapped him on the shoulder and held open the door to the corridor. His accent had acquired a touch of American, like a sun-tan. It suited him.

"The old boys are a pretty grim bunch, huh?"

"Yes," Colin agreed as, by unspoken assent, they headed for the stairs and the sunlight. "Ghastly."

"So what are you doing here?"

"Casing the joint for Harry. My son. He's nearly thirteen. I wasn't sure, I'm still not, but Elsa's been on at me. My wife."

Grinning, Lucas nodded, showing a wing of fine lines around each eye.

"I know."

"You met her?"

"No. I mean I knew you'd got married. I saw it in the papers."

"Ah."

Lucas held open the door to the yard and Colin could not help but notice that he too wore a plain gold band.

"You're settled too?" he asked, unsure how he felt about this.

"And how. Ten years now. Funnily enough, we're sniffing around for a place to send Willy."

"Could do worse."

"Could do better. Christ, this place still has tin baths! I know America's spoiled me but even by English standards the plumbing here is medieval."

"Ah but the academic standards...."

"Yes. I know I know. I've heard it. It's always the ones who didn't come to these places who fight to perpetuate the whole thing. Left to us it would turn coed and be handed over to the state, right? I tell you, Colin, night after night I've had nothing but 'academic excellence', 'valuable networking', 'cultural heritage'. I had to agree to come just to get some peace. Where's—Elsa, did you say her name was?"

"Watching cricket. She's a fanatic."

"That's where I left my lot too. We brought a picnic. Seeing the alma mater was one thing, but I balked at sherry with the housemaster. So. It's been a long time."

"It certainly has."

Again Colin felt Lucas's great hand on his back, only this time it moved up to his shoulder and rested there. What the hell? No one was staring. They were two married men now. Two very obviously married men. He fought back a disturbing desire to kiss him full on the lips then and there and forced himself to talk personal history. By the time the cricket match was in sight, and its dense band of brightly coloured spectators gathered around the drinks marquee, he had told Lucas everything. The year off teaching in the Sudan. Oxford. Law school. The Bar. His mother's death. Elsa. Harry.

"There they are," he said, raising a manly hand in reply to Elsa's languorous wave from a deck chair. "But what about you? You've been in America?"

"Ever since Cambridge. I studied film at UCLA and wasted some time directing budgetless art, then I got into scripts and hit it lucky. Sucked into Hollywood. A living hell but obscenely well paid. But that's where Fran came along so it was worth every minute."

"Your wife."

"My man, Colin, my man." Lucas laughed, giving Colin a playful punch in the ribs. "Jesus. There he is now, the impossibly cute one chatting up your wife. He was married, of course, but she's a wild thing and very understanding, so she let us have custody of the kid. Fran had always spent more time with him in any case. Anyway, I've gotten into production now and Fran's company are transferring him to London so—" he shrugged and gestured around them with his spare hand, "here we are sorting out Willy's future. Christ but I hope he can pass the exam. American schools are so *backward*, you have no idea."

"Darling!"

Elsa raised a hand which she clearly intended Colin to kiss. He merely clutched it, masking his panic with a sort of benevolent leer. She was drinking Pimm's. The questionably blond American at her side stood to introduce her.

"Elsa, this is Lucas."

"How do you do."

"Hello."

They shook hands.

"And this is *my* one!" Elsa laughed. "Darling, meet Fran. It's such fun. They're moving to England and I've promised to help them find a lovely house. I've been telling them about that nice one for sale near us. You know? With the pretty old conservatory? Lucas do sit here. I don't think those old trouts will dare come back. Darling? Can you see if the boys are all right? I gave Harry his pocket money and I think he might be trying to buy Pimm's."

Colin walked into the mouth of the tent. The air inside was baking, heavy with alcohol, flowers and the smell of hot, damp grass. He spotted Harry buying innocuous enough ice creams for himself and a boy with snowy blond hair, jeans and a baseball cap. In his suit and tie, Harry looked like a bank manager beside him. Suddenly thirsty, Colin turned back to ask the others what they wanted. Mid-anecdote, Elsa was tapping a hand on one of Lucas's knees as he sprawled in his deck-chair. His—Colin sought a usable word—friend, was laughing uproariously. Contenting himself with a more elegant chuckle, Lucas flicked a glance over Elsa's head to meet Colin's gaze and Colin felt a huge, threatening alteration in the scene, as though the ground had changed its angle or all the trees had suddenly grown another yard. Perhaps it was just the heat.

A Diamond Guitar

Truman Capote

Truman Streckfus Persons (who chose to be known by the less memorable name of Truman Capote) found in prisons the obvious climax for what he claimed was a new genre: the nonfiction novel, the story of actual people and events told with the devices of fiction. His classic In Cold Blood *set the trend for hundreds of such accounts, from the pulp true-crime thriller to Norman Mailer's* The Executioner's Song.

One likely place for readers to find homosexual characters has been in prison: consider Jean Genet's The Miracle of the Rose, *Manuel Puig's* Kiss of the Spider Woman, *Reinaldo Arenas's* The Brightest Star, *John Herbert's play* Fortune and Men's Eyes, *and Oscar Wilde's* De Profundis. *As settings for gay fiction, prisons are ambiguous places. In Arenas and in Puig, for instance, forced confinement keeps the homosexual away from "decent" society but also gives the inmates licence (to say nothing of the need) to seek the erotic in the new, "criminal" society into which they have been forced. In John Herbert, in Genet, in stories such as Capote's "A Diamond Guitar", prisons are not only stages for the playing out of sexual desires, but also places that bring the fantasies of desire to an overbearing close.*

The nearest town to the prison farm is twenty miles away. Many forests of pine trees stand between the farm and the town, and it is in these forests that the convicts work; they tap for turpentine. The prison itself is in a forest. You will find it there at the end of a red rutted road, barbed wire sprawling like a vine over its walls. Inside, there live one hundred and nine white men, ninety-seven Negroes and one Chinese. There are two sleep houses—great green wooden buildings with tar-paper roofs. The white men occupy one, the Negroes and the Chinese the other. In each sleep house there is one large potbellied stove, but the winters are cold here, and at night with the pines waving frostily and a freezing light falling from the moon, the men, stretched on their iron cots, lie awake with the fire colors of the stove playing in their eyes.

The men whose cots are nearest the stove are the important men—those who are looked up to or feared. Mr. Schaeffer is one of these. Mr. Schaeffer—for that is what he is called, a mark of special respect—is a lanky, pulled-out man. He has reddish, silvering hair, and his face is attenuated, religious; there is no flesh to him; you can see the workings of his bones, and his eyes are a poor, dull color. He can read and he can write, he can add a column of figures. When another man receives a letter, he brings it to Mr. Schaeffer. Most of these letters are sad and complaining; very often Mr. Schaeffer improvises more cheerful messages and does not read what is written on the page. In the sleep house there are two other men who can read. Even so, one of them brings his letters to Mr. Schaeffer, who obliges by never reading the truth. Mr. Schaeffer himself does not receive mail, not even at Christmas; he seems to have no friends beyond the prison, and actually he has none there—that is, no particular friend. This was not always true.

One winter Sunday some winters ago Mr. Schaeffer was sitting on the steps of the sleep house carving a doll. He is quite talented at this. His dolls are carved in separate sections, then put together with bits of spring wire; the arms and legs move, the head rolls. When he has finished a dozen or so of these dolls, the Captain of the farm takes them into town, and there they are sold in a general store. In this way Mr. Schaeffer earns money for candy and tobacco.

That Sunday, as he sat cutting out the fingers for a little hand, a truck pulled into the prison yard. A young boy, handcuffed to the Captain of the farm, climbed out of the truck and stood blinking at the ghostly winter sun. Mr. Schaeffer only glanced at him. He was then a man of fifty, and seventeen of those years he'd lived at the farm. The arrival of a new prisoner could not arouse him. Sunday is a free day at the farm, and other men who were moping around the yard crowded down to the truck. Afterward, Pick Axe and Goober stopped by to speak with Mr. Schaeffer.

Pick Axe said, "He's a foreigner, the new one is. From Cuba. But with yellow hair."

"A knifer, Cap'n says," said Goober, who was a knifer himself. "Cut up a sailor in Mobile."

"Two sailors," said Pick Axe. "But just a café fight. He didn't hurt them boys none."

"To cut off a man's ear? You call that not hurtin' him? They give him two years, Cap'n says."

Pick Axe said, "He's got a guitar with jewels all over it."

It was getting too dark to work. Mr. Schaeffer fitted the pieces of his doll together and, holding its little hands, set it on his knee. He rolled a cigarette; the pines were blue in the sundown light, and the smoke from his cigarette lingered in the cold, darkening air. He could see the Captain coming across the yard. The new prisoner, a blond young boy, lagged a pace behind. He was carrying a guitar studded with glass diamonds that cast a starry twinkle, and his new uniform was too big for him; it looked like a Halloween suit.

"Somebody for you, Schaeffer," said the Captain, pausing on the steps of the sleep house. The Captain was not a hard man; occasionally he invited Mr. Schaeffer into his office, and they would talk together about things they had read in the newspaper. "Tico Feo," he said as though it were a name of a bird or a song, "this is Mr. Schaeffer. Do like him, and you'll do right."

Mr. Schaeffer glanced up at the boy and smiled. He smiled at him longer than he meant to, for the boy had eyes like strips of sky—blue as the winter evening—and his hair was as gold as the Captain's teeth. He had a fun-loving face, nimble, clever; and, looking at him, Mr. Schaeffer thought of holidays and good times.

"Is like my baby sister," said Tico Feo, touching Mr. Schaeffer's doll. His voice with its Cuban accent was soft and sweet as a banana. "She sit on my knee also."

Mr. Schaeffer was suddenly shy. Bowing to the Captain, he walked off into the shadows of the yard. He stood there whispering the names of the evening stars as they opened in flower above him. The stars were his pleasure, but tonight they did not comfort him; they did not make him remember that what happens to us on earth is lost in the endless shine of eternity. Gazing at them—the stars—he thought of the jeweled guitar and its worldly glitter.

It could be said of Mr. Schaeffer that in his life he'd done only one really bad thing: he'd killed a man. The circumstances of that deed are unimportant, except to say that the man deserved to die and that for it Mr. Schaeffer was sentenced to ninety-nine years and a day. For a long while—for many years, in fact—he had not thought of how it was before he came to the farm. His memory of those times was like a house where no one lives and where the furniture has rotted away. But tonight it was as if lamps had been lighted through all the gloomy dead rooms. It had begun to happen when he saw Tico Feo coming through the dusk with his splendid guitar. Until that moment he had not been lonesome. Now, recognizing his loneliness, he felt alive. He had not wanted to be alive. To be alive was to remember brown rivers where the fish run, and sunlight on a lady's hair.

Mr. Schaeffer hung his head. The glare of the stars had made his eyes water.

The sleep house usually is a glum place, stale with the smell of men and stark in the light of two unshaded electric bulbs. But with the advent of Tico Feo it was as though a tropic occurrence had happened in the cold room, for when Mr. Schaeffer returned from his observance of the stars, he came upon a savage and garish scene. Sitting cross-legged on a cot, Tico Feo was picking at his guitar with long swaying fingers and singing a song that sounded as jolly as jingling coins. Though the song was in Spanish, some of the men tried to sing it with him, and Pick Axe and Goober were dancing together. Charlie and Wink were dancing too, but separately. It was nice to hear the men laughing, and when Tico Feo finally put aside his guitar, Mr. Schaeffer was among those who congratulated him.

"You deserve such a fine guitar," he said.

"Is diamond guitar," said Tico Feo, drawing his hand over its vaudeville dazzle. "Once I have a one with rubies. But that one is stole. In Havana my sister work in a, how you say, where make guitar; is how I have this one."

Mr. Schaeffer asked him if he had many sisters, and Tico Feo, grinning, held up four fingers. Then, his blue eyes narrowing greedily, he said, "Please, mister, you give me doll for my two little sister?"

The next evening Mr. Schaeffer brought him the dolls. After that he was Tico Feo's best friend and they were always together. At all times they considered each other.

Tico Feo was eighteen years old and for two years had worked on a freighter in the Caribbean. As a child, he'd gone to school with nuns, and he wore a gold crucifix around his neck. He had a rosary too. The rosary he kept wrapped in a green silk scarf that also held three other treasures: a bottle of Evening in Paris cologne, a pocket mirror and a Rand McNally map of the world. These and the guitar were his only possessions, and he would not allow anyone to touch them. Perhaps he prized his map the most. At night, before the lights were turned off, he would shake out his map and show Mr. Schaeffer the places he'd been—Galveston, Miami, New Orleans, Mobile, Cuba, Haiti, Jamaica, Puerto Rico, the Virgin Islands—and the places he wanted to go to. He wanted to go almost everywhere, especially Madrid, especially the North Pole. This both charmed and frightened Mr. Schaeffer. It hurt him to think of Tico Feo on the seas and in far places. He sometimes looked defensively at his friend and thought, "You are just a lazy dreamer."

It is true that Tico Feo was a lazy fellow. After that first evening he had to be urged even to play his guitar. At daybreak when the guard came to rouse the men, which he did by banging a hammer on the stove, Tico Feo would whimper like a child. Sometimes he pretended to be ill, moaned and rubbed his stomach; but he never got away with this, for the Captain would send him out to work with the rest of the men. He and Mr. Schaeffer were put together on a highway gang. It was hard work, digging at frozen clay and carrying croker sacks filled with broken stone. The guard had always to be shouting at Tico Feo, for he spent most of the time trying to lean on things.

Each noon, when the dinner buckets were passed around, the two friends sat together. There were some good things in Mr. Schaeffer's bucket, as he could afford apples and candy bars from the town. He liked giving these things to his friend, for his friend enjoyed them so much, and he thought, "You are growing; it will be a long time until you are a grown man."

Not all the men liked Tico Feo. Because they were jealous, or for more subtle reasons, some of them told ugly stories about him. Tico Feo himself seemed unaware of this. When the men gathered around him, and he played his guitar and sang his songs, you could see that he felt he was loved. Most of the men did feel a love for him; they waited for and depended upon the hour between supper and lights out. "Tico, play your box," they would say. They did not notice that afterward there was a deeper sadness than there had ever been. Sleep jumped beyond them like a jack rabbit, and their eyes lingered ponderingly on the firelight that creaked behind the grating of the stove. Mr. Schaeffer was the only one who understood their troubled feeling, for he felt it too. It was that his friend had revived the brown rivers where the fish run, and ladies with sunlight in their hair.

Soon Tico Feo was allowed the honor of having a bed near the stove and next to Mr. Schaeffer. Mr. Schaeffer had always known that his friend was a terrible liar. He did not listen for the truth in Tico Feo's tales of adventure, of conquests and encounters with famous people. Rather, he took pleasure in them as plain stories, such as you would read in a magazine, and it warmed him to hear his friend's tropic voice whispering in the dark.

Except that they did not combine their bodies or think to do so, though such things were not unknown at the farm, they were as lovers. Of the seasons, spring is the most shattering: stalks thrusting through the earth's winter-stiffened crust, young leaves cracking out on old left-to-die branches, the falling-asleep wind cruising through all the newborn green. And with Mr. Schaeffer it was the same, a breaking up, a flexing of muscles that hardened.

It was late January. The friends were sitting on the steps of the sleep house, each with a cigarette in this hand. A moon thin and yellow as a piece of lemon rind curved above them, and under its light, threads of ground frost glistened like silver snail trails. For many days Tico Feo had been drawn into himself—silent as a robber waiting in the shadows. It was no good to say to him, "Tico, play your box." He would only look at you with smooth, under-ether eyes.

"Tell a story," said Mr. Schaeffer, who felt nervous and helpless when he could not reach his friend. "Tell about when you went to the racetrack in Miami."

"I not ever go to no racetrack," said Tico Feo, thereby admitting to his wildest lie, one involving hundreds of dollars and a meeting with Bing Crosby.. He did not seem to care. He produced a comb and pulled it sulkily through his hair. A few days before, this comb had been the cause of a fierce quarrel. One of the men, Wink, claimed that Tico Feo had stolen the comb from him, to which the accused replied by spitting in his face. They had wrestled around until Mr. Schaeffer and another man got them separated. "Is my comb. You tell him!" Tico Feo had demanded of Mr. Schaeffer. But Mr. Schaeffer with quiet firmness had said no, it was not his friend's comb—an answer that seemed to defeat all concerned. "Aw," said Wink, "if he wants it so much, Christ's sake, let the sonofabitch keep it." And later, in a puzzled uncertain voice, Tico Feo had said, "I thought you was my friend." "I am," Mr. Schaeffer had thought, though he said nothing.

"I not go to no racetrack, and what I said about the widow

woman, that is not true also." He puffed up his cigarette to a furious glow and looked at Mr. Schaeffer with a speculating expression. "Say, you have money, mister?"

"Maybe twenty dollars," said Mr. Schaeffer hesitantly, afraid of where this was leading.

"Not so good, twenty dollar," Tico said, but without disappointment. "No important, we work our way. In Mobile I have my friend Frederico. He will put us on a boat. There will not be trouble," and it was as though he were saying that the weather had turned colder.

There was a squeezing in Mr. Schaeffer's heart; he could not speak.

"Nobody here can run to catch Tico. He run the fastest."

"Shotguns run faster," said Mr. Schaeffer in a voice hardly alive. "I'm too old," he said, with the knowledge of age churning like nausea inside him.

Tico Feo was not listening. "Then, the world. The world, *el mundo*, my friend." Standing up, he quivered like a young horse; everything seemed to draw close to him—the moon, the callings of screech owls. His breath came quickly and turned to smoke in the air. "Should we go to Madrid? Maybe someone teach me to bullfight. You think so, mister?"

Mr. Schaeffer was not listening either. "I'm too old," he said. "I'm too damned old."

For the next several weeks Tico Feo kept after him—the world, *el mundo*, my friend; and he wanted to hide. He would shut himself in the toilet and hold his head. Nevertheless, he was excited, tantalized. What if it could come true, the race with Tico across the forests and to the sea? And he imagined himself on a boat, he who had never seen the sea, whose whole life had been land-rooted. During this time one of the convicts died, and in the yard you could hear the coffin being made. As each nail thudded into place, Mr. Schaeffer thought, "This is for me, it is mine."

Tico Feo himself was never in better spirits; he sauntered about with a dancer's snappy, gigolo grace, and had a joke for everyone. In the sleep house after supper his fingers popped at the guitar like firecrackers. He taught the men to cry *olé,* and some of them sailed their caps through the air.

When work on the road was finished, Mr. Schaeffer and Tico Feo were moved back into the forests. On Valentine's Day they ate their lunch under a pine tree. Mr. Schaeffer had ordered a dozen oranges from the town and he peeled them slowly, the skins unraveling in a spiral; the juicier slices he gave to his friend, who was proud of how far he could spit the seeds—a good ten feet.

It was a cold beautiful day, scraps of sunlight blew about them like butterflies, and Mr. Schaeffer, who liked working with the trees, felt dim and happy. Then Tico Feo said, "That one, he no could catch a fly in his mouth." He meant Armstrong, a hog-jowled man sitting with a shotgun propped between his legs. He was the youngest of the guards and new at the farm.

"I don't know," said Mr. Schaeffer. He'd watched Armstrong and noticed that, like many people who are both heavy and vain, the new guard moved with a skimming lightness. "He might could fool you."

"I fool him, maybe," said Tico Feo, and spit an orange seed in Armstrong's direction. The guard scowled at him, then blew a whistle. It was the signal for work to begin.

Sometime during the afternoon the two friends came together again; that is, they were nailing turpentine buckets onto trees that stood next to each other. At a distance below them a shallow bouncing creek branched through the woods. "In water no smell," said Tico Feo meticulously, as though remembering something he'd heard. "We run in the water; until dark we climb a tree. Yes, mister?"

Mr. Schaeffer went on hammering, but his hand was shaking, and the hammer came down on his thumb. He looked around dazedly at his friend. His face showed no reflection of pain, and he did not put the thumb in his mouth, the way a man ordinarily might.

Tico Feo's blue eyes seemed to swell like bubbles, and when in a voice quieter than the wind sounds in the pinetops he said, "Tomorrow," these eyes were all that Mr. Schaeffer could see.

"Tomorrow, mister?"

"Tomorrow," said Mr. Schaeffer.

The first colors of morning fell upon the walls of the sleep house, and Mr. Schaeffer, who had rested little, knew that Tico Feo was awake too. With the weary eyes of a crocodile he observed the movements of his friend in the next cot. Tico Feo was unknotting the scarf that contained his treasures. First he took the pocket mirror. Its jellyfish light trembled on his face. For a while he admired himself with serious delight, and combed and slicked his hair as though he were preparing to step out to a party. Then he hung the rosary about his neck. The cologne he never opened, nor the map. The last thing he did was to tune his guitar. While the other men were dressing, he sat on the edge of his cot and tuned the guitar. It was strange, for he must have known he would never play it again.

Bird shrills followed the men through the smoky morning woods. They walked single file, fifteen men to a group, and a guard bringing up the rear of each line. Mr. Schaeffer was sweating as though it were a hot day, and he could not keep in marching step with his friend, who walked ahead, snapping his fingers and whistling at the birds.

A signal had been set. Tico Feo was to call, "Time out," and pretend to go behind a tree. But Mr. Schaeffer did not know when it would happen.

The guard named Armstrong blew a whistle, and his men dropped from the line and separated to their various stations. Mr. Schaeffer, though going about his work as best he could, took care always to be in a position where he could keep an eye on both Tico Feo and the guard. Armstrong sat on a stump, a chew of tobacco lopsiding his face, and his gun pointing into the sun. He had the tricky eyes of a cardsharp; you could not really tell where he was looking.

Once another man gave the signal. Although Mr. Schaeffer had known at once that it was not the voice of his friend, panic had pulled at his throat like a rope. As the morning wore on there was such a drumming in his ears he was afraid he would not hear the signal when it came.

The sun climbed to the center of the sky. "He is just a lazy dreamer. It will never happen," thought Mr. Schaeffer, daring for a moment to believe this. "But first we eat, " said Tico Feo with a practical air as they set their dinner pails on the bank above the creek. They ate in silence, almost as though each bore the other a grudge, but at the end of it Mr. Schaeffer felt his friend's hand close over his own and hold it with a tender pressure.

"Mister Armstrong, time out...."

Near the creek Mr. Schaeffer had seen a sweet gum tree, and he was thinking it would soon be spring and the sweet gum ready to chew. A razory stone ripped open the palm of his hand as he slid off the slippery embankment into the water. He straightened up and began to run; his legs were long, he kept almost abreast of Tico Feo, and icy geysers sprayed around them. Back and forth through the woods the shouts of men boomed hollowly like voices in a cavern, and there were three shots, all highflying, as though the guard were shooting at a cloud of geese.

Mr. Schaeffer did not see the log that lay across the creek. He thought he was still running, and his legs thrashed about him; it was as though he were a turtle stranded on its back.

While he struggled there, it seemed to him that the face of his friend, suspended above him, was part of the white winter sky—it was so distant, judging. It hung there but an instant, like a hummingbird, yet in that time he'd seen that Tico Feo had not wanted him to make it, had never thought he would, and he remembered once thinking that it would be a long time before his friend was a grown man. When they found him, he was still lying in the ankle-deep water as though it were a summer afternoon and he were idly floating on the stream.

Since then three winters have gone by, and each has been said to be the coldest, the longest. Two recent months of rain washed deeper ruts in the clay road leading to the farm, and it is harder than ever to get there, harder to leave. A pair of searchlights has been added to the walls, and they burn there through the night like the eyes of a giant owl. Otherwise, there have not been many changes. Mr. Schaeffer, for instance, looks much the same, except that there is a thicker frost of white in his hair, and as a result of a broken ankle he walks with a limp. It was the Captain himself who said that Mr. Schaeffer had broken his ankle attempting to capture Tico Feo. There was even a picture of Mr. Schaeffer in the newspaper, and under it this caption: "Tried to Prevent Escape." At the time he was deeply mortified, not because he knew the other men were laughing, but because he thought of Tico Feo seeing it. But he cut it out of the paper anyway, and keeps it in an envelope along with several clippings pertaining to his friend: a spinster woman told the authorities he'd entered her home and kissed her, twice he was reported seen in the Mobile vicinity, finally it was believed that he had left the country.

No one has ever disputed Mr. Schaeffer's claim to the guitar. Several months ago a new prisoner was moved into the sleep house. He was said to be a fine player, and Mr. Schaeffer was persuaded to lend him the guitar. But all the man's tunes came out sour, for it was as though Tico Feo, tuning his guitar that last morning, had put a curse upon it. Now it lies under Mr. Schaeffer's cot, where its glass diamonds are turning yellow; in the night his hand sometimes searches it out, and his fingers drift across the strings: then, the world.

Two

Isaac Bashevis Singer

Like most of Isaac Bashevis Singer's work, "Two" was originally writ-
ten in Yiddish and translated by his nephew, Joseph. Accepting the
Nobel Prize for Literature in 1978, Singer explained why he did his
writing in Yiddish. According to him, this almost forgotten language
was "a language of exile, without a land, without frontiers, not sup-
ported by any government, a language which possesses no words for
weapons, ammunition, military exercises, war tactics; a language that
was despised by both gentiles and emancipated Jews." And he con-
cluded: "In a figurative way, Yiddish is the wise and humble language
of us all, the idiom of the frightened and hopeful humanity."

"I was born with the feeling that I am part of an unlikely adventure,
something that couldn't have happened, but happened just the same,"
Singer once remarked. Such an observation, with its mixed tone of
delight and fatalism, could just as easily have been voiced by either
Ezriel Dvorahs or Zissel Yomtov, the most improbable pair of star-
crossed lovers in Singer's canon. In Jewish tradition, homosexuality is
condemned. The Old Testament explicitly forbids the sexual inter-
course of male with male—"Thou shalt not lie with mankind, as with
womankind: it is abomination" (Leviticus, 18:22)—and homosexual
males are not allowed to take part in orthodox religious ceremonies.
Singer's wonderment at the variety of the human experience overrides
this indictment and joyfully portrays two who, through sheer love, find
a way to live together in a world that would otherwise reject them.

For almost ten years after the wedding Reb Yomtov's wife, Menuha,
did not bear a child. Already it was rumored in Frampol that she was
barren and a divorce was imminent. But she became pregnant and
both Yomtov and Menuha referred to the coming child as "she."

The father wanted a girl because the Gemara says, "A daughter first is a good omen for the children to come." The mother wanted a daughter because she had it in mind to name her after her dead mother. When she entered her late months, her belly didn't become high and pointy but round and broad—a sign that she was carrying a female child. Accordingly, she prepared a layette of little shirts and jackets festooned with lacework and embroidery, and a pillow with ribbons. The father put aside in a box the first gulden toward a dowry.

Actually, Reb Yomtov had other reasons for wanting a daughter. He, a Talmudic scholar entrusted with removing the impure fat and veins from kosher meat, had the soul of a female. When he prayed, he didn't appeal so much to the Almighty as to the Shechinah, the female counterpart of God. According to the cabala, the virtues of men bring about the union of God and the Shechinah as well as the copulations of angels, cherubim, seraphim, and sacred souls in Heaven. Full union on high will take place only after the redemption, the coming of the Messiah. In the midst of the Eighteen Benedictions Yomtov would exclaim, "Oh, Mama!" When he was still a boy studying the Pentateuch in cheder, he was drawn more to the matriarchs than to the patriarchs. He preferred to glance into such volumes as the *Ze'enah u-Re'enah* and *The Lamp of Light* rather than the Gemara, the commentaries, and the Response. Yomtov was small and stout, with a sparse beard and small hands and feet. At home he wore silk dressing gowns and slippers with pom-poms. He curled his earlocks, primped before the mirror, and carried all kinds of trinkets—a carved snuffbox, a pearl-handled penknife, and a little ivory hand, a charm, left him by a grandmother. On Simchas Torah or during banquets he didn't drink strong spirits but demanded sweet brandy. The people made fun of him. "You're a softy, Yomtov! Worse than a woman."

Well, for all that Menuha and Yomtov expected a girl, the powers that decide such things saw to it that they had a boy. True, the midwife made a mistake and announced to the mother that the baby was a girl, but she soon acknowledged her mistake. Menuha grew terribly upset that between a yes and a no a daughter had turned into a son. Yomtov couldn't bring himself to believe it and demanded to be shown. Just the same, people were invited to the pre-circumcision party and cheder boys came to recite the Shema. Zissel being a name for both a man and a woman, the boy was named that after a great-aunt. Since his gowns, jackets, and bonnets had already been prepared, the infant was dressed in them, and when the mother carried Zissel in the street, strangers assumed he was a girl.

It is the custom that when a boy turns three his hair is cut, he is wrapped in a prayer shawl and carried to cheder. But Zissel had such elegant curls that his mother refused to trim them. The parents carried their precious offspring to cheder, but when the child spied the old teacher with his white beard, the whipping bench and the whip he began to howl. His slate with the alphabet printed for him to read was strewn with candy, raisins, and nuts he was told had been left there by an angel from Heaven, but the child would not be appeased. The next morning he was brought again to cheder and given a honey cake. This time Zissel carried on so that he suffered a convulsion and turned blue. Thereupon the parents decided to keep him at home until the following term. A rebbetzin who tutored girls at home taught him his alphabet. Zissel studied with her willingly. The rest of the time he played with other children. Since his hair was long and he didn't go to cheder, boys his age avoided him. He spent most of his time with girls and enjoyed their ways and their games. The boys played with sticks, barrel hoops, and rusty nails. They fought, got dirty, and tore their clothes, but the girls picked flowers in the orchards, sang songs, danced in circles, rocked their dolls, and their dresses and aprons stayed clean.

"Why can't I be a girl?" he asked his mother.

"You were supposed to be a girl," his mother replied. She kissed and fondled him and wove his hair into a braid for a joke, and added, "What a shame, you would have made such a lovely girl."

Time, which often is the implement of destiny, did its work. Zissel grew up and against his will began attending cheder. He was stripped of his dresses and made to put on a gaberdine, pants, a ritual garment, and a skullcap. He was taught reading—the Pentateuch, Rashi's commentaries, and the Gemara. The matchmakers early began to plan matches for him. But Zissel remained a girlish boy. He couldn't stand the brawls and recklessness of the daredevil boys, and he couldn't climb trees, whistle, tease dogs, or chase the community billy goat. When the cheder boys quarreled with him, they called him "girl" and tried to lift the skirts of his gaberdine as if he were really female. The teacher and his assistant refrained from whipping him because the few times they did he promptly burst into tears. Also, his skin was delicate. They overlooked it when he came late or left before the others. On Fridays, the boys accompanied their fathers to the steam bath.

In the summer, they bathed in the river and learned to swim. But Zissel was bashful and never undressed before strangers. The truth was that he suffered anxiety and all kinds of doubts. He already was convinced that to be a male was unworthy and that the signs of manhood were a disgrace.

When no one was home, Zissel put on his mother's dress, her high-heeled shoes, camisole, and bonnet, and admired his reflection in the mirror. On Sabbaths in the house of prayer, he gazed up at the section where the women sat and he envied them looking on from behind the grate, all dressed up in their furs and jackets, jewels, colored ribbons, tassels, and frills. He liked their pierced earlobes and tried to pierce his own with a needle. His parents grasped that something was not right about their Zissel. They took to punishing him and calling him a dunce. This only made things worse for him. He often locked himself in his room, cried, and said a prayer in Yiddish from his mother's prayer book with its gold-embossed covers and copper clasp. His tears burned, and he dabbed his eyes with the edge of a kerchief, as women do.

When Zissel turned fifteen, matches were proposed for him in earnest. A quiet, handsome boy and an only son besides, he was offered girls from wealthy homes. His mother occasionally went to look over the proposed brides and she later described to Zissel their conduct and appearance. One was tall and thin with a deep voice and a wart on her upper lip; another was short and stout with big breasts and almost no neck; a third was red-haired, marked with freckles, and had the green eyes of a cat. Each time, Zissel found some pretext not to become engaged. He was afraid to marry, sure that a wife would forsake him the first day after the wedding. Suddenly he began to find virtues in his own sex. He saw the rascals of his childhood grown into respectable youths who recited the Gemara and the commentaries in a chant, discussed serious things among themselves, paced to and fro across the study house in deep deliberation. The girls on the other hand had become frivolous. Their laughter was loud; they flirted, danced wantonly, and it seemed to Zissel that they were mocking him.

Of all the youths, Zissel liked best one called Ezriel Dvorahs. Ezriel came from Lublin and behaved in big-city fashion. He was tall, slim, and dark, with earlocks tucked behind his ears and black eyes with brows that grew together over his nose. His gaberdine was always spotless, and he polished his kid boots daily. Although he wasn't engaged yet, he already wore a silver watch in his vest pocket. The marriage brokers assailed him with prospective matches, and the other students competed to be his study partner. When Ezriel spoke, everyone stopped reading the text to listen. When it was time to take a walk along Synagogue Street, several boys were always ready to accompany him. When he strolled past the marketplace, girls rushed to the windows and stared at him from behind drawn curtains as if he had just arrived from Lublin.

It happened that Ezriel, who was two years older than Zissel, chose him to be his study partner. Zissel accepted it as an honor. On Sabbaths he wished it were the weekday again so that he might study together with Ezriel. When it occurred some morning that Ezriel didn't show up at the study house, Zissel walked around steeped in longing. At times, Ezriel took Zissel with him to the baker's, where they ate prune rolls for their second breakfast. Ezriel confided in Zissel about the matches he was being offered and told him stories of Lublin. But sometimes Ezriel acted friendly toward the other boys and then Zissel felt a pang of resentment—he wanted Ezriel to think better of him than of anyone else.

After a while, Ezriel chose another partner. Out of distress, to show Ezriel that he could get along without him, Zissel agreed to become engaged. The bride-to-be was a beauty from Tomaszów, slender and fair, with blue eyes and a braid hanging to her waist. Zissel's mother couldn't stop praising her good looks. The articles of betrothal were signed in Tomaszów, and his prospective father-in-law, a timber merchant, gave Zissel a gold watch as an engagement present.

When Zissel came home after the betrothal, the youths at the study house gave him a friendly reception. He treated them to cake and brandy, as was the custom, and they offered him congratulations and questioned him discreetly about the bride. They had heard of her loveliness and envied Zissel his good luck. Ezriel joined in wishing him mazel tov, but he didn't ask for details. He didn't even ask Zissel to show him the gold watch with the engraved inscription on the back.

Ezriel was on the verge of being engaged himself, and shortly this was arranged. The prospective bride, a local girl, was homely. Her father was fairly well off and had promised a handsome dowry; still, the people of Frampol wondered why a gifted youth like Ezriel should settle for such a match. Apparently Ezriel regretted his decision, too, since he didn't show up at the study house for a few days and even failed to treat his fellow students to the customary brandy and cake. From the day of Zissel's engagement, Ezriel had grown cool toward him and avoided him.

Zissel wanted to delay his marriage a year or two; making Ezriel jealous was sweeter to him than becoming the husband of the Tomaszów belle. But the bride's parents were in a hurry for the wedding, since the bride had already turned eighteen. Zissel was taken to Tomaszów and the wedding was held. During the Virtue Dance when first the bride, then the groom was led to the wedding chamber, Zissel was overcome by trembling. With hesitation he went to his bride lying in the bed, but he could not do what he knew he was supposed to. In the morning the women came to examine the sheet and perform the Kosher Dance of Consummation; they did not find what they were looking for.

The following night, attendants again escorted the couple to their wedding bed, accompanied by musicians and the wedding jester, and this was repeated on each of the Seven Days of the Benedictions. Since both sets of parents felt that a spell had been cast over the couple, the groom's mother went to the rabbi, who gave her an amulet, an amber over which an incantation had been said, and a list of suggestions. The bride's mother secretly consulted a witch, who supplied her own devices. In fact, the cures recommended by both the rabbi and the witch were the same.

Within a few weeks Ezriel married, but his match, too, was unsuccessful. Soon after the wedding he and his bride began to quarrel, and within a few months Ezriel went back to his mother. One day Zissel, who was boarding at his father-in-law's in Tomaszów, received a letter from Ezriel in Frampol, and as he read it he marveled. In an elaborate handwriting and a Hebrew full of flowery phrases Ezriel described his anguish; he called Zissel "my beloved and the desire of my soul," he reminded him of how pleasant it had been in the old days, when they had studied the Gemara, strolled down Synagogue Street together, eaten prune rolls at the baker's, and confided to each other the secrets of their hearts. If he had the fare, he would come to Tomaszów as swiftly as an arrow shot from a bow.

When Zissel finished reading, he was overcome with joy and he forgave Ezriel all his past neglect. He answered in a long letter full of words of affection, confessed that his wedding had caused him heartache and shame, and so that Ezriel could come to visit him he enclosed a banknote he took from his dowry without telling his father-in-law.

Without business in Tomaszów, Ezriel had no excuse to go there, but letters between the friends went back and forth frequently. Ezriel was an ardent correspondent. His words often rhymed and were full of insinuations and puns. Zissel answered in the same vein. Both quoted passages from the Song of Songs. They compared their love to that between Jacob and Joseph or David and Jonathan. The fact was, they yearned one for the other. Ezriel began to call Zissel Zissa.

This correspondence continued until they decided to meet at an inn lying between Tomaszów and Frampol. Ezriel told his mother that he was going to inquire about a teaching position. He took along his prayer shawl and phylacteries and a satchel. It was hard for Zissel to find an excuse for leaving, and he therefore decided on a trick. In the morning, after his father-in-law had gone to his business, his mother-in-law had gone to the drygoods store, and his dainty wife had gone to the butcher shop, Zissel opened the wardrobe, put on a pair of women's drawers, a camisole, a dress, and shoes with high heels. He draped a shawl over his shoulders and covered his head with a kerchief. His beard had not yet grown. When he caught a glimpse of himself in the mirror, he hardly knew his own face and he was certain that no one would recognize him. The Spirit of Perversity had whispered in his ear that he shouldn't be a fool—to take from his father-in-law and mother-in-law whatever was handy. After a brief deliberation, he obeyed. He took the dowry from its place of safekeeping, along with his wife's jewelry, and hid them in a hand basket, which he covered with a cloth. Then he went outside. When the women in the street saw him, they assumed that a strange woman had come to town on a visit.

Thus, Zissel walked past the market and saw from afar his wife pushing her way toward the butcher's block. He pitied her, but he had already broken the commandments that forbid a man to dress in women's clothes and to steal, and he hurried along.

On Church Street, Zissel found a peasant cart heading for Frampol and for a trifle the peasant let him ride as far as the inn. There Zissel got off and asked for Ezriel. He said that he was Ezriel's wife and the proprietor exclaimed, "He just told me he was about to meet his partner!"

"A wife is the best partner," Zissel replied, and the innkeeper pointed to Ezriel's room.

Ezriel was pacing back and forth as is the way of the impatient. When Zissel came in, Ezriel looked with bewilderment at the young woman who was smiling at him so coquettishly. "Who are you?" he asked, and Zissel answered, "You don't know? I'm Zissa!"

They fell into each other's arms, kissed, and laughed in rapture. They vowed never to part again. After a while Ezriel said, "It wouldn't be safe to stay around here too long. When your in-laws find out what you've done they'll send police after you and we would both fall into the net."

So next morning they bade farewell to the innkeeper, telling him they were going back to Frampol. Instead, they turned off into a side road and hired a wagon to take them to Kraśnik, and from Kraśnik they went on to Lublin.

Since they had money, and jewelry besides, they quickly rented an apartment in Lublin, bought furniture and everything needed to maintain a household. Lublin is a big city and no one asked the couple who they were or checked whether Ezriel's wife went to the ritual bath. Thus the pair lived for several years together, indulging themselves to their hearts' desire. In Frampol and Tomaszów, the two missing husbands were sought for a time, but since they couldn't be found, it was assumed that they had gone off somewhere to the other side of the ocean. Both wives were adjudged deserted.

Zissel, known as Zissa, made friends with matrons and even maidens. They gave him advice on cooking, baking, sewing, darning, and embroidering. They also confided their womanly secrets to him. Zissel's beard had begun to sprout by now, but it was merely a fuzz. He plucked some of it, singed the rest, and from time to time committed the transgression of shaving. In order that the women shouldn't become suspicious, Zissel told them that he had stopped menstruating early, which was the reason he couldn't become pregnant. They comforted their poor sister, shed a tear over her fate, and kissed her. Zissel became so involved with his female cronies he often forgot what he was. He turned into an expert cook and prepared broths and groats for Ezriel and baked him delicious pastries. Each Friday he made the challah offering, said the benediction over the candles, went on the

Sabbath to the women's section of the synagogue, as women must, and read the Pentateuch in Yiddish.

The money Zissel had stolen from his father-in-law was finally exhausted. Ezriel opened a store and at first it appeared that he might prosper, but he sat for days behind the counter and not a customer showed up. When one did come in, it was to demand goods at less than cost. No matter how Ezriel strained, he couldn't eke out a living. He developed wrinkles in his forehead and sprouted gray threads in his beard. He fell into debt. Things went so badly it came to pass that Zissel didn't have enough to celebrate the Sabbath properly, and he was forced to make Sabbath dinner without meat or pudding. On Fridays, he left pots of water boiling on the stove so that the neighbors would think that Sabbath dishes were cooking. Tears ran down his face. Following the Friday-night services, Ezriel came home from the synagogue in a patched gaberdine and a ratty fur hat. In a sorrowful voice he began to chant the hymn of greeting the angels and recite the "Woman of Virtue." Zissel had lit the candles and covered the table. He wore a Sabbath dress adorned with arabesques, slippers, white stockings, and a silk head kerchief. He gazed into a Yiddish prayer book. It was true that the two had broken the law, but they hadn't abandoned their faith in God and the Torah.

When the women who were fond of Zissa learned that Ezriel was on the verge of bankruptcy and that Zissa's pantry was empty, they began to seek means of helping the couple. They collected money and tried to give it to Ezriel, but he refused to accept it, as is the habit of the proud, who would rather suffer than hold out a hand for assistance. Zissel would have accepted the money, but Ezriel sternly forbade him to do so. When her friends saw that Zissa couldn't be helped with generosity, they offered suggestions—that Zissa peddle goods door to door; that, since she was so versed in studies, she become a rebbetzin who teaches girls to write a letter in Yiddish; that, being such a marvelous cook, she open a soup kitchen. It just so happened that the attendant at the local ritual bath died at this time, which seemed to Zissa's chums an omen that she had been fated to take the other's place. They went to the community leaders with this request, and when women persist they manage to get their own way. At first Zissa refused to take the job, but Ezriel had to have someone support him. Zissa became the bath attendant.

In a ritual bathhouse, the attendant's work is to shave the women's heads, to trim their fingernails and toenails, to scrub and clean them before they immerse themselves. The attendant is also responsible for seeing to it that her charges immerse themselves completely, so that no part, even the shaved scalp, sticks out. The attendant also lets blood, applies leeches and cupping glasses. Because the women are on such intimate terms with the attendant, they reveal to her the most private matters about themselves, their husbands, and their families. It is therefore important that she be a person who can keep her lips sealed. She needs to be particularly skilled with brides, who are usually bashful and often frightened.

Well, it turned out that Zissa became the most adroit bath attendant in Lublin. The women loved it when she attended them and they gossiped with her. Zissa was especially gentle with brides. This was soon known, and they came from all over the city. Besides her wages Zissa received tips, and sometimes when the pair was rich a small percentage of the dowry. Ezriel could now sit around in idleness. He tried to pass time playing cards but this wasn't in his nature. Gradually, he turned into a glutton and a slugabed. He would wake in the middle of the night to eat a second supper. During the day he took naps under the feather bed. He became so lazy he even stopped going to services. He was not yet forty, but he had fallen into melancholy.

When Zissel came home from the ritual bath late at night, he tried to cheer Ezriel up with kind words and tales about the women, but instead of cheering him up he only depressed him further. Ezriel accused Zissel of having accepted his masculinity, of committing treacherous offenses against him. Sometimes the two wrangled all night and at times came to blows. The words they uttered during their outbursts and while making up astounded them.

One time an important wedding was held in Lublin. The bride was a ravishing virgin of seventeen, the daughter of a rich and distinguished family. The groom was a wealthy youth from Zamośé. It was said that the groom would receive as a wedding present a silver Hanukkah lamp with stairs to climb for lighting the candles, it was so tall. Well, but the girl was shy and it came hard for her mother and sisters-in-law to introduce her into the ways of womanhood. Zissa was called in to study "The Pure Well" with the bride, and patiently to instruct her in her wifely duties. The bride quickly grew so attached to Zissa that she clung to her as to a sister. On the night before the wedding she came to immerse herself in the ritual bath where Zissa was the attendant. Zissa saw to it that the old habitués of the bath didn't tease the young bride or mock her, as they often did newcomers. It was the custom for musicians to escort the prospective bride to the ritual bath and to play for her on that special night.

When the bride—Reizl was her name—undressed and Zissel saw her dazzling flesh, what Ezriel most feared came to be. For the first time in his life Zissel felt desire for a woman. Soon desire turned to passion. He tried to conceal this from Ezriel but Ezriel was aware that a change had come over Zissel. Zissel now counted the days until Reizl would come to the bath again, and he fretted lest she promptly become pregnant and he would not see her until after the birth. When Reizl was there, Zissel devoted so much time to her that it aroused resentment among the other matrons. Reizl herself was perplexed by the bath attendant's attentiveness and suddenly she grew ashamed before her. As the Gemara says, "The person sees not, but his star sees," and so it was with Reizl.

One winter day a blizzard struck Lublin the like of which its oldest residents could not remember. Wind swept the snow from the gutters, heaped it in piles on roofs, pounded it against windows, howled around corners as if a thousand witches had hanged themselves. Chimneys collapsed, shutters were torn off, windowpanes were blown from their frames. Although ovens were heated and no wood was spared, the houses were almost as cold inside as outside. Women due to cleanse themselves after menstruation put off their visit to the ritual bath until the following day. Ezriel warned Zissel not to leave the house since demons were afoot outside, but Zissel replied that the bath attendant could not neglect her duties. One newly wed woman might want to use the bath. In fact, Zissel knew that Reizl was scheduled to come to the bath that evening.

Zissel wrapped himself up, took a stick in hand, and went outside, putting himself at God's mercy. The wind pushed and drove him along. Finally it lifted him and tossed him into a pile of snow. As he lay there, a sleigh drawn by a team of horses came by. Inside were Reizl and her husband, both wrapped in furs and covered with blankets. Reizl saw the plight of the bath attendant and called to the coachman to stop. In short, they rescued Zissel and revived him with spirits, and all three rode on to the bathhouse. Reizl's mother had begged her daughter not to risk her life by going out, but Reizl and her husband didn't want to lose a night. Her husband and the coachman went to the study house nearby to wait, and Reizl was turned over to Zissel's care.

That evening Reizl was the only woman in the bathhouse, and she was afraid of the dismal powers that hold sway over such places, but gradually Zissa calmed her, soaping and washing her gently and longer than was usual. From time to time the bath attendant kissed Reizl and addressed her in terms of endearment.

After Reizl had immersed herself and climbed the steps, ready for the bath attendant to wrap her in a towel sheet and dry her, Satan's voice rang in Zissel's ears: "Seize the while! Assail and defile!" The words had all the force bestowed upon the Tempter, and Zissel hurled himself at Reizl. For a moment Reizl was stricken dumb with terror. Then she erupted in violent screams, but there was no one to hear and come to her rescue. As they struggled they fell down the slippery steps into the water. Zissel tried to break loose from Reizl, but in their frenzy Reizl would not let go. Their heads soon sank to the bottom of the bath; only their feet showed on the surface of the water.

The coachman kept going from the study house to the sleigh to check on the horses, which stood covered with hides, and see if Reizl had come from the bath. The wind had stopped and the moon had emerged, pale as the face of a corpse after ablution, its light congealed upon the shrouds of the night.

According to the coachman's calculations, it was past time for Reizl to have come out, and he went to discuss her absence with her husband. After some deliberation, the men decided to go into the bath and see if anything could be wrong. They walked through the ante-room, calling Reizl's name. The echoes of their voices sounded as hollow as if they came from a ruin. They went on into the room where the ritual bath was located. Except for a single candle flickering in an earthen holder and reflected in the puddles on the stone floor, the place was empty. Suddenly the husband glanced down into the water and screamed. The coachman cried out in a terrible shout. They pulled the bodies from the water; Reizl and Zissel were both dead. The coachman rushed to alarm the people, and the neighborhood filled with commotion and turmoil. It happened that two members of the Burial Society were warming themselves in the study house. When they removed Zissa's body, a fresh tumult erupted. The secret was out that the bath attendant was male.

When the ruffians in a tavern close by realized the shameless farce Zissel had been playing, they seized whatever weapon they could find and ran to beat Ezriel. Ezriel was sitting wrapped in his caftan, searching his soul. It was cold in the house and the flame of the candle casts ominous shadows. Although he did not foresee that his end was at hand, he was consumed by gloom. Suddenly he heard violent voices, heavy steps on the stairs, the crashing in of his door. Before he could stand up, the crowd fell upon him. One man tore out half his beard, another snatched off his ritual garment, a third beat him with a cudgel. Soon his limp body fell forward upon his attackers.

Reizl had a funeral such as Lublin had never seen. Ezriel and Zissel were quickly put to rights and buried behind the fence late at night without anyone to follow their hearses or to say Kaddish. Only the gravedigger recited the passages which are said while the corpse is covered with earth. Oddly enough, like every housewife Zissel had put aside a little nest egg, which the members of the Burial Society found among the Passover dishes and used as payment for the cleansing and the plot.

The mound under which Ezriel and Zissel lay was soon overgrown with weeds. But one morning the cemetery watchman saw a board there with an inscription from the Second Book of Samuel: "Lovely and pleasant in their lives and in their deaths they were not divided." Who put the board up was never discovered. If the rains haven't washed it away, mold hasn't rotted it, wind hasn't broken it, and zealots haven't torn it out, it still stands there to this day.

Notes on the Authors

Sherwood Anderson was born in Ohio in 1876. His novels include *Many Marriages* (1923), *Dark Laughter* (1925), *Beyond Desire* (1932), and *Kit Brandon* (1936). His best work is thought to be in his short-story collections, *Winesburg, Ohio* (1919), *The Triumph of the Egg* (1921), *Horses and Men* (1923), and *Death in the Woods* (1933). His nonfiction includes the critical work *Perhaps Women* (1931), a collection of essays, *Home Town* (1940), and his *Memoirs*, published posthumously in 1942. He died in 1941.

James Baldwin was born in New York in 1924. His novels include *Go Tell It on the Mountain* (1953), *Giovanni's Room* (1956), *Another Country* (1962), *Tell Me How Long the Train's Been Gone* (1968), *If Beale Street Could Talk* (1974), and *Just Above My Head* (1979). Baldwin published plays including *Blues for Mister Charlie* (1964) and *The Amen Corner* (1968), and a collection of short stories, *Going to Meet the Man* (1965). His equally important nonfiction works, such as *Notes of a Native Son* (1955) and *The Fire Next Time* (1963), were collected in a single volume entitled *The Price of the Ticket* (1985). He died in 1987 in France, where he had lived as an expatriate for many years.

Ann Beattie was born in Washington, D.C. in 1947. She has published four short-story collections, *Distortions* (1976), *Secrets and Surprises* (1978), *The Burning House* (1982), and *Where You'll Find Me and Other Stories* (1986). Beattie's novels include *Chilly Scenes of Winter* (1976), *Falling into Place* (1980), *Love Always* (1985), and *Picturing Will* (1989).

Marie-Claire Blais was born in 1939 in Quebec City. Her novels in English translation include *Mad Shadows* (1960), *Tête Blanche* (1961), *A Season in the Life of Emmanuel* (1966), the two novellas *The*

Day Is Dark and *Three Travelers* (1967), *The Manuscripts of Pauline Archange* (1969), *David Sterne* (1973), *The Wolf* (1974), *Dürer's Angel* (1976), *The Fugitive* (1978), *Nights of the Underground* (1979), and *Deaf to the City* (1981). She has also published plays and poetry.

Ray (Douglas) Bradbury was born in Waukegan, Illinois in 1920. His fiction includes *The Martian Chronicles* (1950), *The Illustrated Man* (1951), *The Golden Apples of the Sun* (1953), *Fahrenheit 451* (1953), *Dandelion Wine* (1957), *A Medicine for Melancholy* (1959), *Something Wicked This Way Comes* (1963), *I Sing the Body Electric* (1969), and *Long after Midnight* (1976). He also wrote plays and motion-picture scripts, including the screenplay for John Huston's film of Melville's *Moby-Dick* (1956).

Truman Capote (Truman Streckfus Persons) was born in New Orleans in 1924. His novels include *Other Voices, Other Rooms* (1948), *The Grass Harp* (1951), *Breakfast at Tiffany's* (1958), and *In Cold Blood* (1966). He also wrote screenplays, including an adaptation of Henry James's *Turn of The Screw*, retitled *The Innocents* (1961). Important shorter works were collected in *A Tree of Night* (1949) and *Music for Chameleons* (1980). He died in 1984.

John Cheever was born in Quincy, Massachusetts in 1912. His novels include *The Wapshot Chronicle* (1957), *The Wapshot Scandal* (1964), *Falconer* (1977), and the novella *Oh What a Paradise It Seems* (1982). Sixty-one of his best short stories were republished in a critically acclaimed volume, *The Stories of John Cheever* (1978). Cheever died in 1982.

Marco Denevi was born in 1922 in Argentina. His work in English translation includes *Rose at Ten* (1955), the short story *Secret Ceremony* (1960), and *The Redemption of the Cannibal Woman* (1993). He is the author of several plays—*Los expedientes* (*The Files*, 1957), *El Emperador de la China* (*The Emperor of China*, 1959) and *El cuarto de la noche* (*The Chamber of Night*, 1962)—three short novels and various collections of stories, including *Falsificaciones* (*Fakes*, 1966), a book of apocryphal texts.

Michael Dorris was born in Dayton, Washington in 1945. His fiction includes *A Yellow Raft in Blue Water* (1987), *The Crown of Columbus* (written with his wife, novelist Louise Erdrich, 1991) and a collection of short stories, *Working Men* (1993). *The Broken Cord*, an award-winning nonfiction account of his adopted son's struggles with fetal alcohol syndrome, was published in 1987.

Daphne du Maurier was born in London in 1907. Her works include *Jamaica Inn* (1936), *Rebecca* (1938), *My Cousin Rachel* (1951), and several collections of short stories and volumes of memoirs. She died in 1989.

William Faulkner was born in New Albany, Mississippi in 1897. His novels include *Sartoris* (1929), *The Sound and the Fury* (1929), *As I Lay Dying* (1930), *Sanctuary* (1931), *Light in August* (1932), *Absalom, Absalom!* (1936), *The Hamlet* (1940), *Requiem for a Nun* (1951), and *A Fable* (1954). He also published four volumes of short stories, later republished as *Collected Stories* (1950), and two volumes of poems. He was awarded the Nobel Prize for Literature in 1950. He died in 1962.

Timothy Findley was born in Toronto in 1930. His novels include *The Last of the Crazy People* (1967), *The Butterfly Plague* (1969), *The Wars* (1977), *Famous Last Words* (1981), *Not Wanted on the Voyage* (1984), *The Telling of Lies* (1986), and *Headhunter* (1993). He has also published two short-story collections, *Dinner Along the Amazon* (1984) and *Stones* (1989).

E. (Edward) M. (Morgan) Forster was born in London in 1879. He was educated at Cambridge, where he returned in 1927 to deliver the Clark Lectures, published as *Aspects of the Novel*. His novels include *The Longest Journey* (1907), *A Room with a View* (1908), *Howard's End* (1910), and *A Passage to India* (1924). Forster wrote the libretto for Benjamin Britten's opera *Billy Budd* (1951), and published essays, criticism, and travel-writing until his death in 1970. A novel about homosexuality, *Maurice*, was circulated privately as early as 1913 but was not published until 1971. Several explicitly gay short stories were also published posthumously in *The Life to Come and Other Stories* (1972).

Patrick Gale was born in 1962 in Newport, Isle of Wight. His novels include *The Aerodynamics of Pork* (1985), *Ease* (1985), *Kansas in August* (1987), *Facing the Tank* (1987), *Little Bits of Baby* (1989), and *The Cat Sanctuary* (1990).

Helen Garner was born in Geelong, Victoria, Australia in 1942. Her novels include *Monkey Grip* (1977), *Honour* and *Other People's Children* (two novellas, 1980), and *The Children's Bach* (1984). She has published one volume of short stories, *Postcards from Surfers* (1985).

Graham Greene was born in Berkhamsted, England in 1904. His novels include *The Power and the Glory* (1940), *The End of the Affair* (1951), *The Quiet American* (1955), *A Burnt-Out Case* (1961), *Travels with my Aunt* (1969), *The Honorary Consul* (1973), *The Human Factor* (1978), and *Monsignor Quixote* (1982). He also wrote several volumes of short stories, republished as *The Collected Stories* (1972), as well as essays and literary criticism. His last published book was a dream diary entitled *A World of My Own* (posthumous, 1992). He died in Switzerland in 1991.

Allan Gurganus was born in Rocky Mount, North Carolina in 1947. He has published a novel, *Oldest Living Confederate Widow Tells All* (1989), and a collection of novellas and short stories, *White People* (1990).

Ernest Hemingway was born in Oak Park, Illinois in 1899. His novels include *The Sun Also Rises* (1926), *A Farewell to Arms* (1929), *For Whom the Bell Tolls* (1940), and *The Old Man and the Sea* (1952). His short-story collections include *In Our Time* (1925), *Men Without Women* (1927), and *Winner Takes Nothing* (1933), later republished with a play as *The Fifth Column and the First Forty-Nine Stories* (1938). He was awarded the Nobel Prize for Literature in 1954. He committed suicide in 1961.

Desmond Hogan was born in Ballinasloe, Ireland in 1950. His novels include *The Ikon Maker* (1976) and *The Leaves on Grey* (1980). He has published three collections of short fiction, *The Diamonds at the Bottom of the Sea* (1979), *Children of Lir* (1981), and *Lebanon Lodge* (1988), and two plays, *A Short Walk to the Sea* (1975) and *Sanctified Distances* (1976).

Christopher Isherwood was born in Cheshire, England in 1904. His novels include *Mr. Norris Changes Trains* (1935), *Goodbye to Berlin* (1939), *A Single Man* (1964), and *A Meeting by the River* (1967). He collaborated with W.H. Auden on three plays, *On The Frontier*, *The Ascent of F6*, and *The Dog Beneath the Skin*, and on a travel book about China, *Journey to a War*. He also published four autobiographical volumes, *Down There on a Visit* (1962), *Kathleen and Frank* (1971), *Christopher and His Kind* (1976), and *My Guru and his Disciple* (1980). He died in California in 1986.

Francis King was born in Adelboden, Switzerland in 1923, raised in India, and schooled at Oxford. His novels include *To the Dark Tower* (1946), *The Dividing Stream* (1951), *The Widow* (1957), *The Custom House* (1961), *Flights* (1973), *The Action* (1979), and *Act of Darkness* (1983). He has published five short-story collections, including *The Brighton Belle* (1968), *Hard Feelings* (1976), and *Indirect Method* (1980). He has also written travel books and a study of E.M. Forster.

W. (William) P. (Patrick) Kinsella was born in Edmonton, Alberta in 1935. His short-fiction collections include *Dance Me Outside* (1977), *Scars* (1978), *The Moccasin Telegraph* (1983), *The Thrill of the Grass* (1984), *The Alligator Report* (1985), and *The Fencepost Chronicles* (1986). Equally well known are his novels, *Shoeless Joe* (1982) and *The Iowa Baseball Confederacy* (1986).

D. (David) H. (Herbert) Lawrence was born in 1885 in Eastwood, Nottinghamshire. His novels include *The White Peacock* (1911), *Sons and Lovers* (1913), *The Rainbow* (1915), *Women in Love* (1920), *The Plumed Serpent* (1926), and *Lady Chatterley's Lover*, which was not legally published in England until 1960. His short stories, poems, travel writings, literary criticism, essays, and posthumous writings have all been collected. Unexpurgated editions of his novels are in the process of being published. He died in New Mexico in 1930.

John Lonie was born in Melbourne, Australia in 1946. His scriptwriting credits include two mini-series, *The Paper Man* (1990) and *Frankie's House* (1992). His fiction includes a collection of three novellas entitled *Love, Sex and Memory* (1994).

Bernard MacLaverty was born in Belfast in 1942. His novels include *Lamb* (1980) and *Cal* (1983). He has published three short-story collections, *Secrets* (1977), *A Time to Dance* (1982) and *The Great Profundo* (1987).

David Malouf was born in Brisbane, Australia in 1934. His novels include *Johnno* (1975), *An Imaginary Life* (1978), *Harland's Half Acre* (1984), *The Great World* (1990), and *Remembering Babylon* (1993). He has published one collection of short stories, *Antipodes* (1985), an opera libretto, *Baa Baa Black Sheep* (1993), an autobiography, *12 Edmonstone Street* (1985), and five volumes of poetry.

Yukio Mishima (Hiraoka Kimitake) was born in Tokyo in 1925. His books in English translation include *The Temple of the Golden Pavilion* (1958), *Confessions of a Mask* (1960), *Death in Midsummer and Other Stories* (1966), *Thirst for Love* (1969), and *Sun and Steel* (1970). He also published *Five Modern Noh Plays* (1957). He delivered to his publisher the final volume of his tetralogy, *The Sea of Fertility*, on the morning of his ritual suicide in 1970.

Alice Munro was born in Wingham, Ontario in 1931. Her short-story collections include *Dance of the Happy Shades* (1968), *Lives of Girls and Women* (1971), *Something I've Been Meaning To Tell You* (1974), *Who Do You Think You Are?* (1978), *The Moons of Jupiter* (1982), *The Progress of Love* (1986), and *Friend of my Youth* (1990).

John O'Hara was born in Pottsville, Pennsylvania in 1905. His novels include *Appointment in Samarra* (1934), *Butterfield 8* (1935), *A Rage to Live* (1949), *Ten North Frederick* (1955), *From the Terrace* (1958), and *The Lockwood Concern* (1965). He also published the libretto for *Pal Joey* (1952), based on his 1940 novel, four collections of short stories, and a volume of literary columns. He died in 1970.

Pai Hsien-yung was born in Kwangsi Province, China in 1937 and emigrated to Taiwan in 1951. His collection of short stories, *Taipei jen* (1971), was translated into English as *Wandering in the Garden, Waking from a Dream* (1982). He now lives in the United States.

Stan Persky was born in Chicago in 1941 and settled in Canada in

1965. His books include *Wrestling the Angel* (1977), *Son of Socred* (1979), *The House That Jack Built* (1980), *At the Lenin Shipyard* (1981), *America, The Last Domino* (1984), *Buddy's* (1989), and *Mixed Media, Mixed Messages* (1992).

Evgeny Popov was born in 1946 in Siberia. He made his literary debut in 1976 with two stories published in the magazine *Novy mir*. He contributed both as a writer and editor to *Metropol*, an almanac of Soviet literature which was banned by the Writers' Union in 1979. Between 1981 and 1987 he was unable to publish in Russia. Since glasnost, two novels and a collection of short stories have appeared. His first novel to be published in English is *The Soul of a Patriot* (1993).

James Purdy was born in Ohio in 1923. His novels include *63: Dream Palace* (1956), *Malcolm* (1959), *The Nephew* (1960), *Cabot Wright Begins* (1964), *Eustace Chisholm* (1967), *In a Shallow Grave* (1976), *Narrow Rooms* (1978), *In the Hollow of his Hand* (1986), *Candles of Your Eyes* (1986), and *Out with the Stars* (1992). His collections of short stories include *Color of Darkness* (1957) and *Children Is All* (1962). He has also published several volumes of plays and poems; his *Collected Poems* was published in 1990.

Sergio Ramírez was born in Nicaragua in 1942. His novel, *To Bury Our Fathers*, and his short-fiction collection, *Stories*, were published in English translation in 1984 and 1986 respectively.

Joanna Russ was born in 1937 in New York. Her novels include *And Chaos Died* (1970), *The Female Man* (1975), *We Who Are About to* (1977), *The Two of Them* (1978), and *The Zanzibar Cat* (1983). Her short fiction includes *Extra(Ordinary) People* (1984) and *The Hidden Side of the Moon* (1987).

Françoise Sagan (Françoise Quoiriz) was born in Cajarc, France in 1935. At the age of seventeen she wrote her first novel, *Bonjour Tristesse*, published in 1954 to international acclaim. Since then she has written numerous novels, short stories and plays, many of them translated into English, including *A Certain Smile* (1956), *Wonderful Clouds* (1961), *Scars on the Soul* (1974), and *The Unmade Bed* (1978). She has also written three volumes of autobiography.

Shyam Selvadurai was born in Sri Lanka in 1965 and emigrated to Canada in 1984. His stories have been published in *The Toronto South Asian Review* and *Montreal Serai*. His 1990 docu-drama, "What's in a Name?", was developed for TV Ontario. His first book is titled *Funny Boy* (1994).

Isaac Bashevis Singer was born in Radzymin, Poland in 1904. His work in English translation includes *The Family Moskat* (1950), *Satan in Goray* (1955), *The Magician of Lublin* (1960), *The Slave* (1967), *Enemies, a Love Story* (1972), and *Shosha* (1978). A memoir entitled *In My Father's Court* was translated in 1967. He was awarded the Nobel Prize for Literature in 1978. A selection of his short fiction, *The Collected Stories*, was published by the author in 1982. He died in 1991.

Theodore (Hamilton) Sturgeon was born in St. George, Staten Island, New York in 1918. His novels include *More Than Human* (1953), *Venus Plus X* (1960), *The Rare Breed* (1966), *Amok Time* (based on his *Star Trek* television script, 1978), and *Godbody* (1987). He published twenty-four short-story collections, including *E Pluribus Unicorn* (1953), *A Touch of Strange* (1958), *The Golden Helix* (1979), and *A Touch of Sturgeon* (posthumous, 1988). He died in 1985.

Rose Tremain was born in 1943. Her novels include *Sadler's Birthday* (1976), *The Cupboard* (1981), *Letter to Sister Benedicta* (1978), *The Swimming Pool Season* (1985), *Restoration* (1989) and *Sacred Country* (1992). She has also published a volume of short stories entitled *The Colonel's Daughter* (1984), a biography of Stalin, a history of suffragettes, and several dramas for radio and television.

William Trevor was born in Mitchelstown, County Cork, Ireland in 1928. His novels include *The Old Boys* (1964), *Mrs. Eckdorf in O'Neill's Hotel* (1969), *The Children of Dynmouth* (1976), and *Fools of Fortune* (1983). His short-fiction collections include *Angels at the Ritz* (1975), *Lovers of Their Time and Other Stories* (1978), *Beyond the Pale* (1981), and *Two Lives* (1991). *The Collected Stories of William Trevor* was published in 1992 and his autobiographical essays, *Excursions in the Real World* in 1993.

(Maurice) Denton Welch was born in Shanghai in 1915 but lived most of his life in England. He wrote an autobiographical volume, *Maiden Voyage* (1943), the novel *In Youth Is Pleasure* (1944), and a collection of short stories, *Brave and Cruel* (1946). He died in 1948. Welch's other works have been published posthumously: *A Voice Through a Cloud* (1950), *Journals* (1952, 1984), and *The Stories of Denton Welch* (1985).

Peter Wells was born in New Zealand and is best known as an independent film-maker. His film *A Death in the Family* (1986) won the Best Drama Prize at the American Film Festival, New York. His short-story collection, *Dangerous Desires* (1991), won the Reed Fiction Prize.

Edmund White was born in Cincinnati in 1940. He is the author of five novels, including *A Boy's Own Story* (1982), *Caracole* (1985), and *The Beautiful Room Is Empty* (1988), as well as two collections of short stories, *Aphrodisiac* (1982) and *The Darker Proof* (with Adam Mars-Jones, 1988). His non-fiction includes *States of Desire: Travels in Gay America* (1980) and *Genet: A Biography* (1993). He edited *The Faber Book of Gay Short Fiction* (1991).

Tennessee (Thomas Lanier) Williams was born in Mississippi in 1911. His plays include *The Glass Menagerie* (1945), *A Streetcar Named Desire* (1947), *Cat on a Hot Tin Roof* (1955), *Suddenly Last Summer* (1958), *Sweet Bird of Youth* (1959), and *The Night of the Iguana* (1961). He published two novels, two volumes of short stories, *One Arm* (1948) and *Hard Candy* (1954), a volume of poetry entitled *In The Winter of Cities* (1956), and his *Memoirs* (1975). He died in 1983.

Sources

1955 by Ernest Hemingway. Reprinted by permission of Charles Scribner's Sons, an imprint of Macmillan Publishing Company, and Vedder, Price, Kaufman, and Kammholz.

Hogan, Desmond, "Ties," from *Lebanon Lodge* by Desmond Hogan, copyright © 1988 by Desmond Hogan. Reprinted by permission of Rogers, Coleridge & White Ltd.

Isherwood, Christopher, "On Ruegan Island," from *Calamus: Male Homosexuality in 20th Century Literature* edited by David Galloway and Christian Sabisch, copyright © 1982 by Christopher Isherwood. Reprinted by permission of Donadio & Ashworth, Inc.

King, Francis, "Hard Feelings," from *One Is a Wanderer* by Francis King, copyright © 1985 by Francis King. Published in the U.K. by Century Hutchinson/Random Century Group. Reprinted by permission of A.M. Heath and Company Limited.

Kinsella, W.P., "Punchlines," from *The Further Adventures of Slugger McBatt* by W.P. Kinsella, copyright © 1988 by W.P. Kinsella. Published in Canada by Collins Publishers and in the United States by Houghton Mifflin. Reprinted by permission of HarperCollins Publishers Ltd.

Lonie, John, "Contact," from *Travelling on Love in a Time of Uncertainty* by John Lonie, copyright © 1989 by John Lonie. Originally published by *Outrage Magazine*, Melbourne. Reprinted by permission of the author.

MacLaverty, Bernard, "The Drapery Man," from *The Great Profundo and Other Stories* by Bernard MacLaverty, copyright © 1987 by Bernard MacLaverty. Reprinted by permission of Jonathan Cape Ltd./Random Century Group.

Malouf, David, "Southern Skies," from *Antipodes* by David Malouf, copyright © 1985 by David Malouf. Reprinted by permission of Chatto & Windus/Random Century Group and Rogers, Coleridge & White Ltd.

Mishima, Yukio, "Onnagata," from *Death in Midsummer and Other Stories* by Yukio Mishima, copyright © 1966 by New Directions Publishing Corp. Reprinted by permission of New Directions Publishing Corp. Translated by Donald Keene.

Munro, Alice, "The Turkey Season," from *The Moons of Jupiter* by Alice Munro, copyright © 1982 by Alice Munro. Reprinted by permission of the Virginia Barber Literary Agency, Inc.

O'Hara, John, "The Sharks," from *The Selected Short Stories of John O'Hara* by John O'Hara, copyright © 1960, 1961, 1962 by John O'Hara. Reprinted by permission of Random House, New York and the United States Trust Company of New York.

Pai, Hsien-yung, "A Sky Full of Bright, Twinkling Stars" from *Wandering in the Garden, Waking from a Dream* by Pai Hsien-yung, copyright © 1982 by Pai Hsien-yung. Reprinted by permission of Indiana University Press. Translated by the author and Patia Yacin.

Persky, Stan, "On Certainty," copyright © 1994 by Stan Persky. Reprinted by permission of the author.

Popov, Evgeny, "The Reservoir," translated by George Saunders, from *Metropol Literary Almanac*, edited by Vasily Aksyonov, Viktor Yerefeyev, Fazil Iskander, Andrei Bitov, and Evgeny Popov, copyright © 1979 by Metropol, 1982 by Ardis/Rlt. Reprinted by permission of W.W. Norton & Company, Inc.

Purdy, James, "Summer Tidings," from *A Day After the Fair* by James Purdy, copyright © 1977 by James Purdy. Reprinted by permission of the author.

Ramírez, Sergio, "The Siege," from *Stories* by Sergio Ramírez, English translation copyright © 1986 by Readers International. Translated by Nick Caistor. Reprinted by permission of Readers International.

Russ, Joanna, "Mr.Wilde's Second Chance," from *The Hidden Side of the Moon* by Joanna Russ, copyright © 1981, 1988 by Joanna Russ. Reprinted by permission of St. Martin's Press, Inc., New York and the author.

Sagan, Françoise, "The Unknown Visitor," from *Silken Eyes* by Françoise Sagan, copyright © 1977 by André Deutsch Ltd. and Dell Publishing Ltd. Reprinted by permission of Georges Borchardt, Inc. Translated by Joanna Kilmartin.

Selvadurai, Shyam, "Pigs Can't Fly," copyright © 1992 by Shyam Selvadurai. Originally published in the *Toronto South Asian Review*, Spring 1992. Reprinted by permission of the author.

Singer, Isaac Bashevis, "Two," from *Old Love* by Isaac Bashevis Singer, copyright © 1976, 1979 by Isaac Bashevis Singer. Published in the U.K. by Jonathan Cape Ltd. Reprinted by permission of Farrar, Straus & Giroux, Inc. and A. M. Heath and Company Ltd.

Sturgeon, Theodore, "The World Well Lost," from *E Pluribus Unicorn* by Theodore Sturgeon, copyright © 1953 by Theodore Sturgeon. Reprinted by